PROJECT NOUGHT

BY CHELSEY FUREDI

CLARION BOOKS

Imprints of HarperCollinsPublishers

HARPER
alley

Clarion Books is an imprint of HarperCollins Publishers.
HarperAlley is an imprint of HarperCollins Publishers.
Project Nought
Copyright © 2023 by Chelsey Furedi
All rights reserved. Manufactured in Bosnia and Herzegovina.
No part of this book may be used or reproduced
in any manner whatsoever without written permission except
in the case of brief quotations embodied in critical articles and reviews.
For information address HarperCollins Children's Books,
a division of HarperCollins Publishers, 195 Broadway, New York, NY 10007.
www.harperalley.com

ISBN 978-0-35-838168-6 – ISBN 978- 0-35-838169-3 (pbk.)

Typography by Andrea Miller
23 24 25 26 27 GPS 10 9 8 7 6 5 4 3 2 1

First Edition

FOR MY COMIC READERS WHO HAVE GONE
THREE YEARS WITHOUT A NEW CHAPTER.
I KNOW THIS WAS QUITE THE WAIT!
—C.F.

CHAPTER ONE

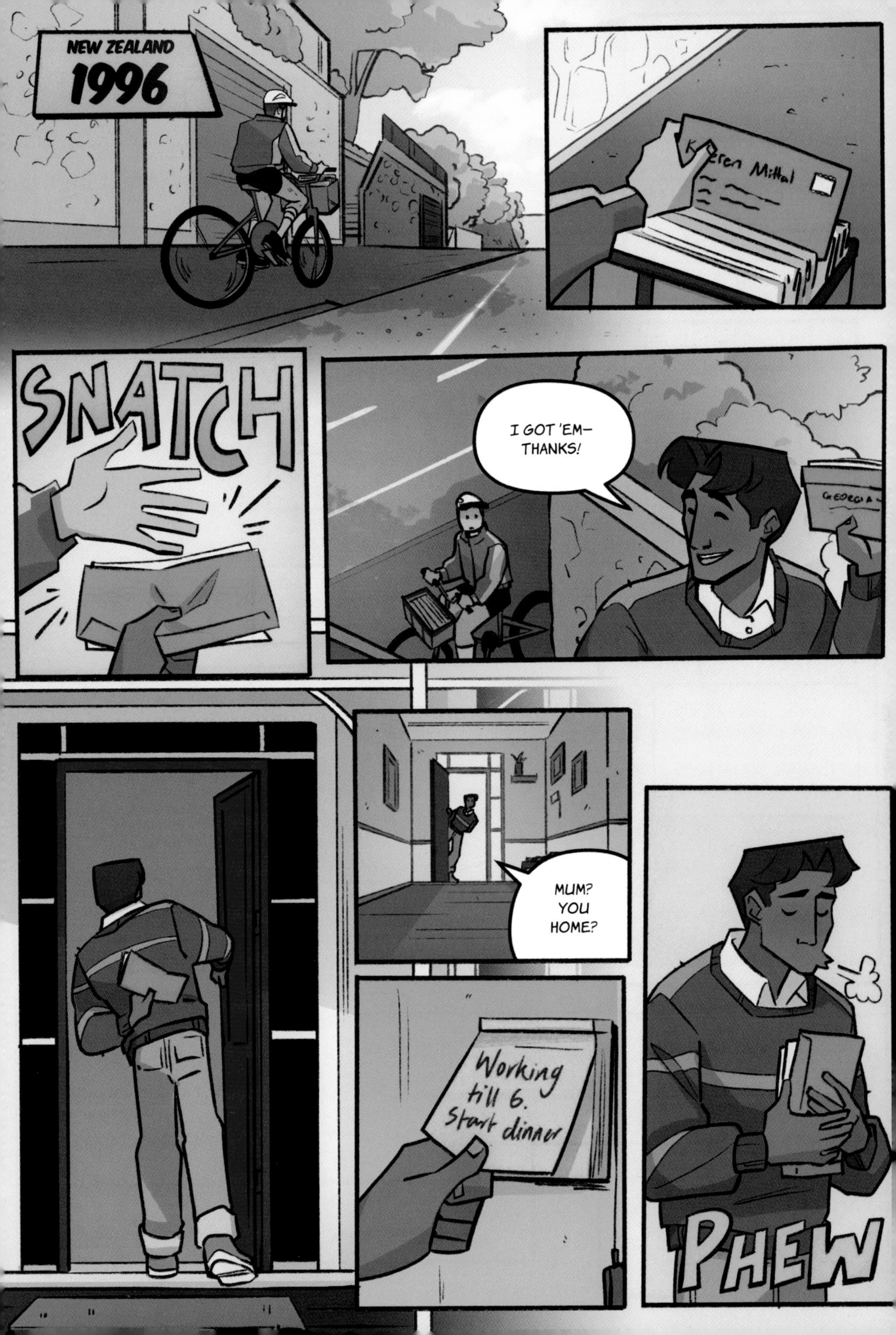
NEW ZEALAND
1996
SNATCH
I GOT 'EM—
THANKS!
MUM?
YOU
HOME?
Working
till 6.
Start dinner
PHEW

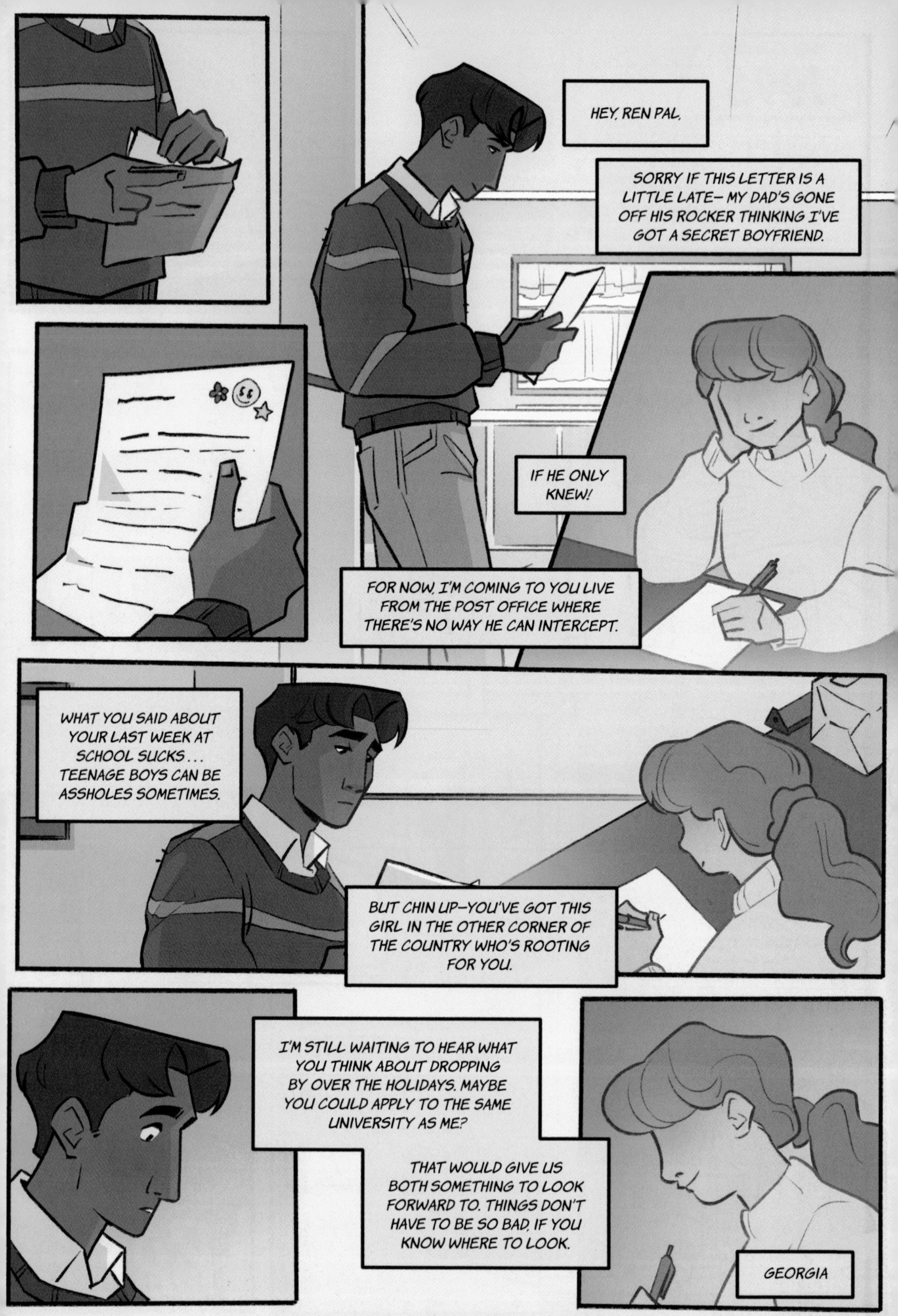
HEY, REN PAL,
SORRY IF THIS LETTER IS A LITTLE LATE— MY DAD'S GONE OFF HIS ROCKER THINKING I'VE GOT A SECRET BOYFRIEND.
IF HE ONLY KNEW!
FOR NOW, I'M COMING TO YOU LIVE FROM THE POST OFFICE WHERE THERE'S NO WAY HE CAN INTERCEPT.
WHAT YOU SAID ABOUT YOUR LAST WEEK AT SCHOOL SUCKS . . . TEENAGE BOYS CAN BE ASSHOLES SOMETIMES.
BUT CHIN UP—YOU'VE GOT THIS GIRL IN THE OTHER CORNER OF THE COUNTRY WHO'S ROOTING FOR YOU.
I'M STILL WAITING TO HEAR WHAT YOU THINK ABOUT DROPPING BY OVER THE HOLIDAYS. MAYBE YOU COULD APPLY TO THE SAME UNIVERSITY AS ME?
THAT WOULD GIVE US BOTH SOMETHING TO LOOK FORWARD TO. THINGS DON'T HAVE TO BE SO BAD, IF YOU KNOW WHERE TO LOOK.
GEORGIA

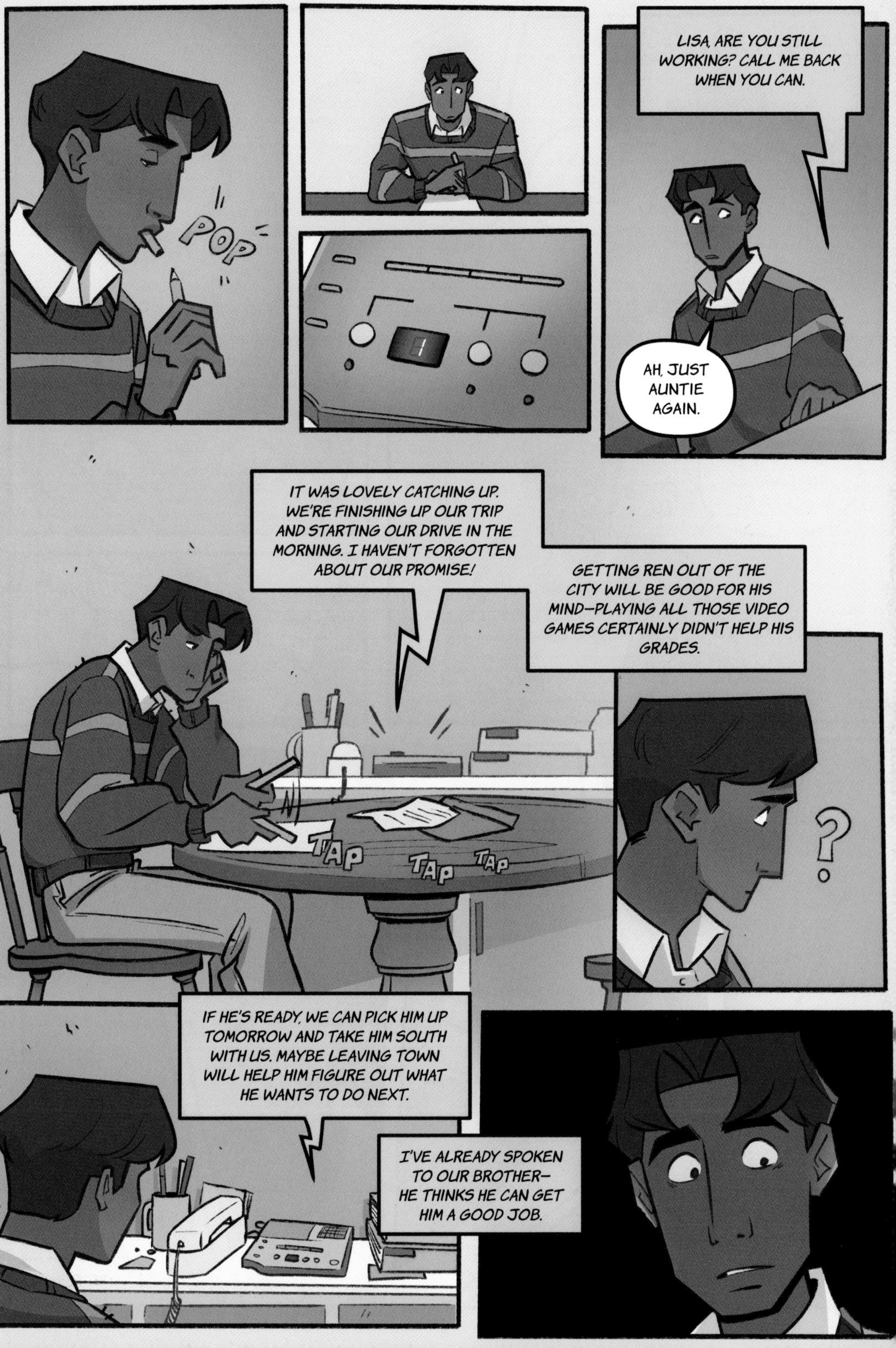
POP
LISA, ARE YOU STILL WORKING? CALL ME BACK WHEN YOU CAN.
AH, JUST AUNTIE AGAIN.
IT WAS LOVELY CATCHING UP. WE'RE FINISHING UP OUR TRIP AND STARTING OUR DRIVE IN THE MORNING. I HAVEN'T FORGOTTEN ABOUT OUR PROMISE!
GETTING REN OUT OF THE CITY WILL BE GOOD FOR HIS MIND—PLAYING ALL THOSE VIDEO GAMES CERTAINLY DIDN'T HELP HIS GRADES.
TAP
TAP
TAP
?
IF HE'S READY, WE CAN PICK HIM UP TOMORROW AND TAKE HIM SOUTH WITH US. MAYBE LEAVING TOWN WILL HELP HIM FIGURE OUT WHAT HE WANTS TO DO NEXT.
I'VE ALREADY SPOKEN TO OUR BROTHER—HE THINKS HE CAN GET HIM A GOOD JOB.

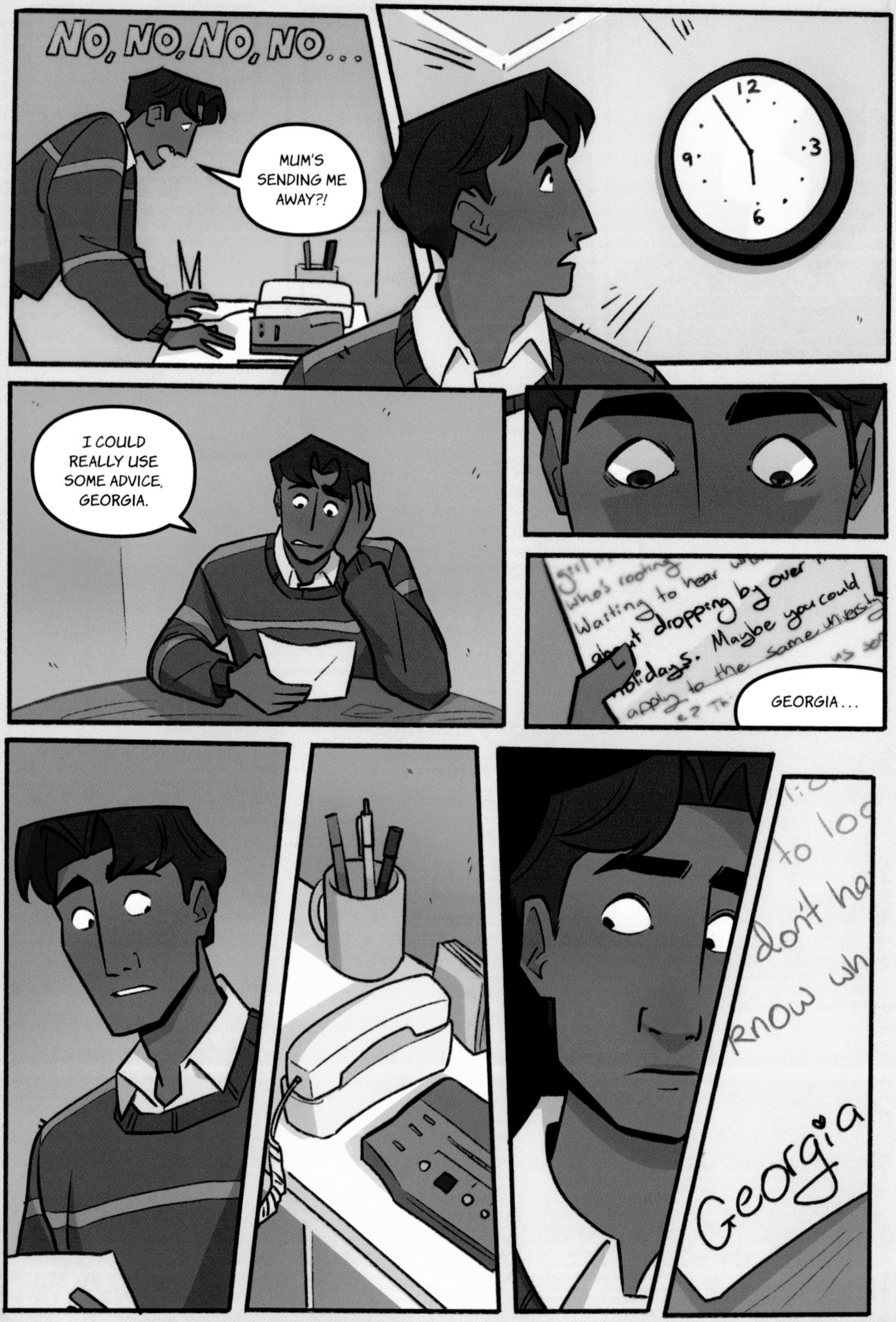
NO, NO, NO, NO . . .
MUM'S SENDING ME AWAY?!
I COULD REALLY USE SOME ADVICE, GEORGIA.
GEORGIA . . .
Georgia

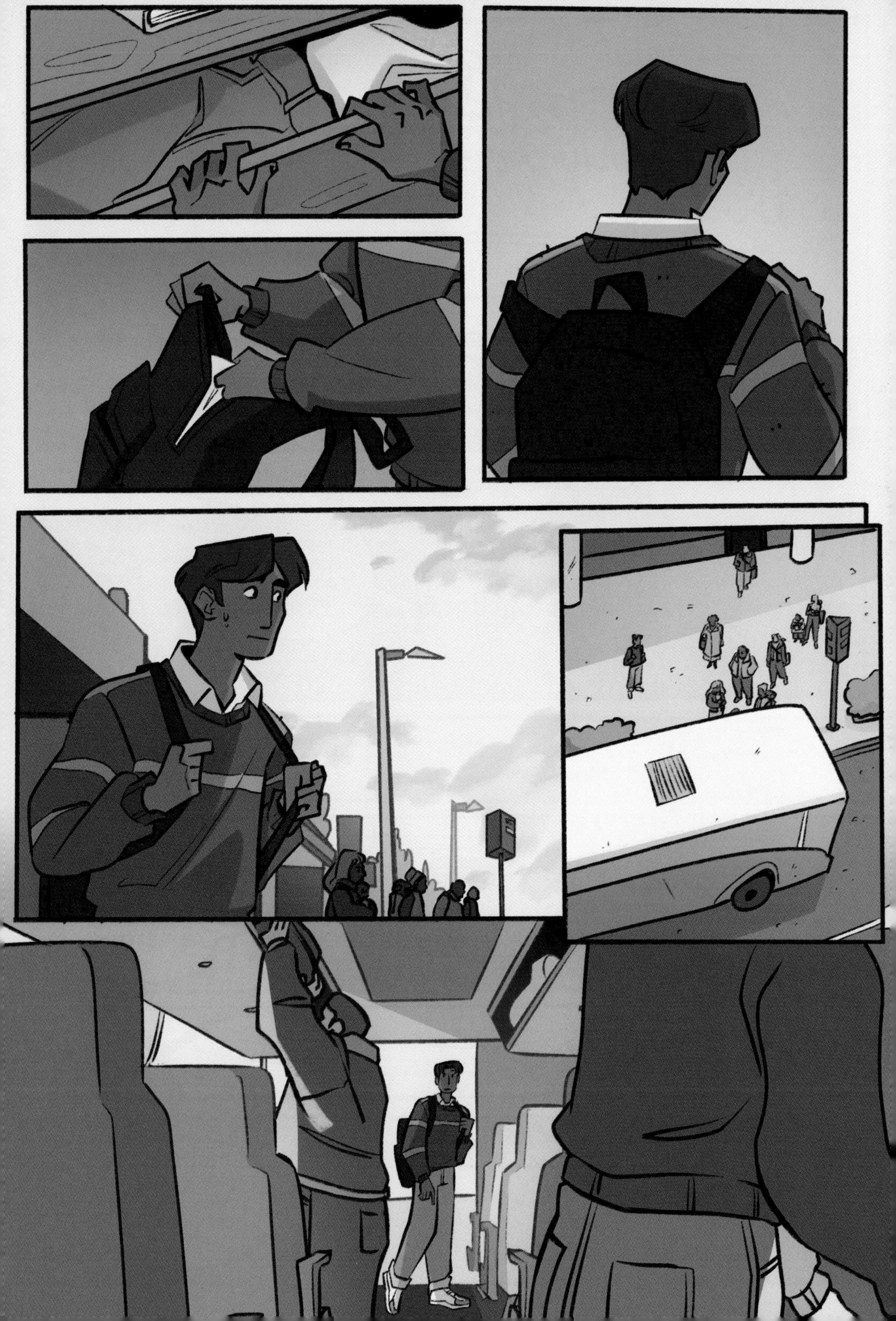

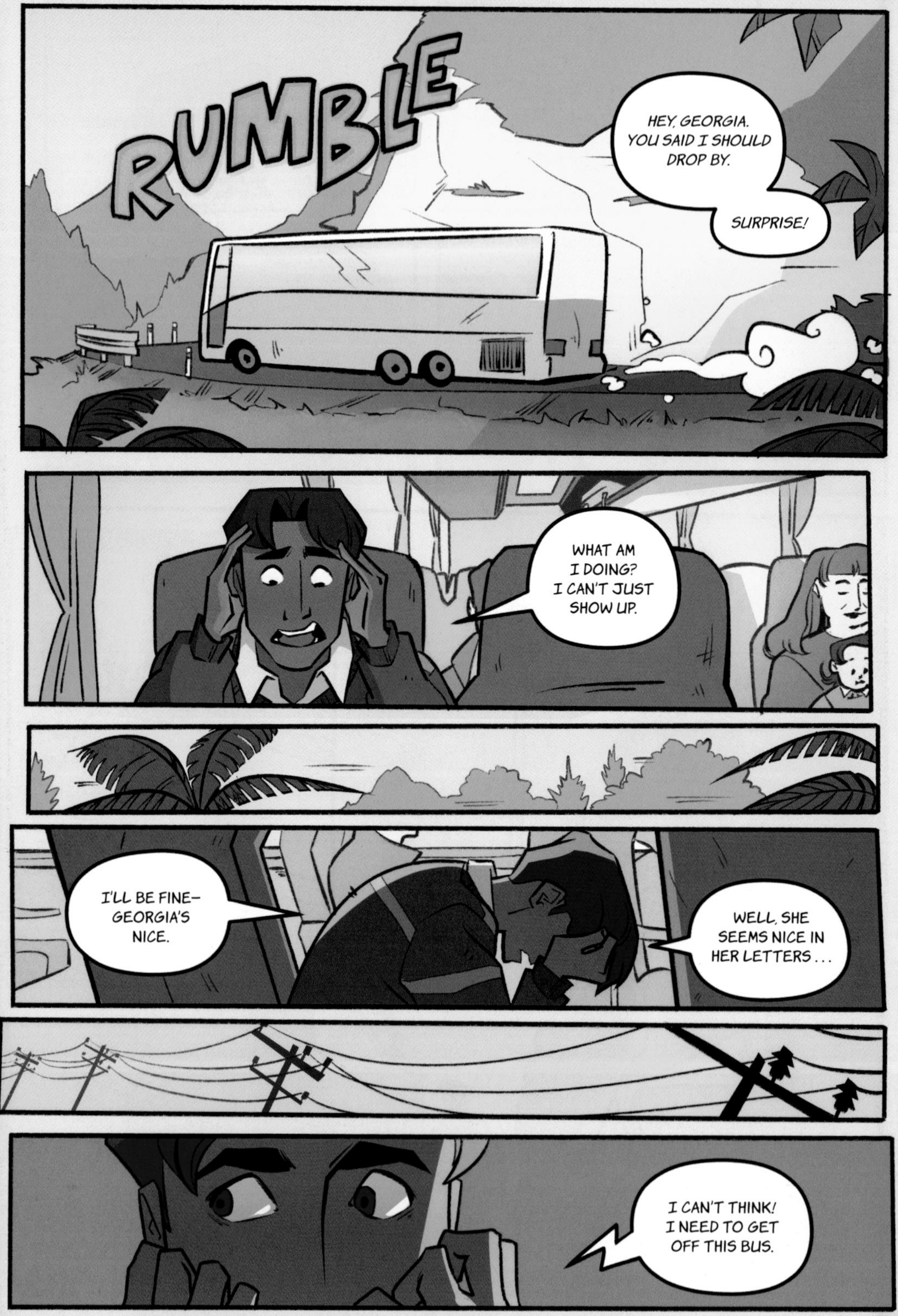
RUMBLE
HEY, GEORGIA. YOU SAID I SHOULD DROP BY.
SURPRISE!
WHAT AM I DOING? I CAN'T JUST SHOW UP.
I'LL BE FINE–GEORGIA'S NICE.
WELL, SHE SEEMS NICE IN HER LETTERS . . .
I CAN'T THINK! I NEED TO GET OFF THIS BUS.

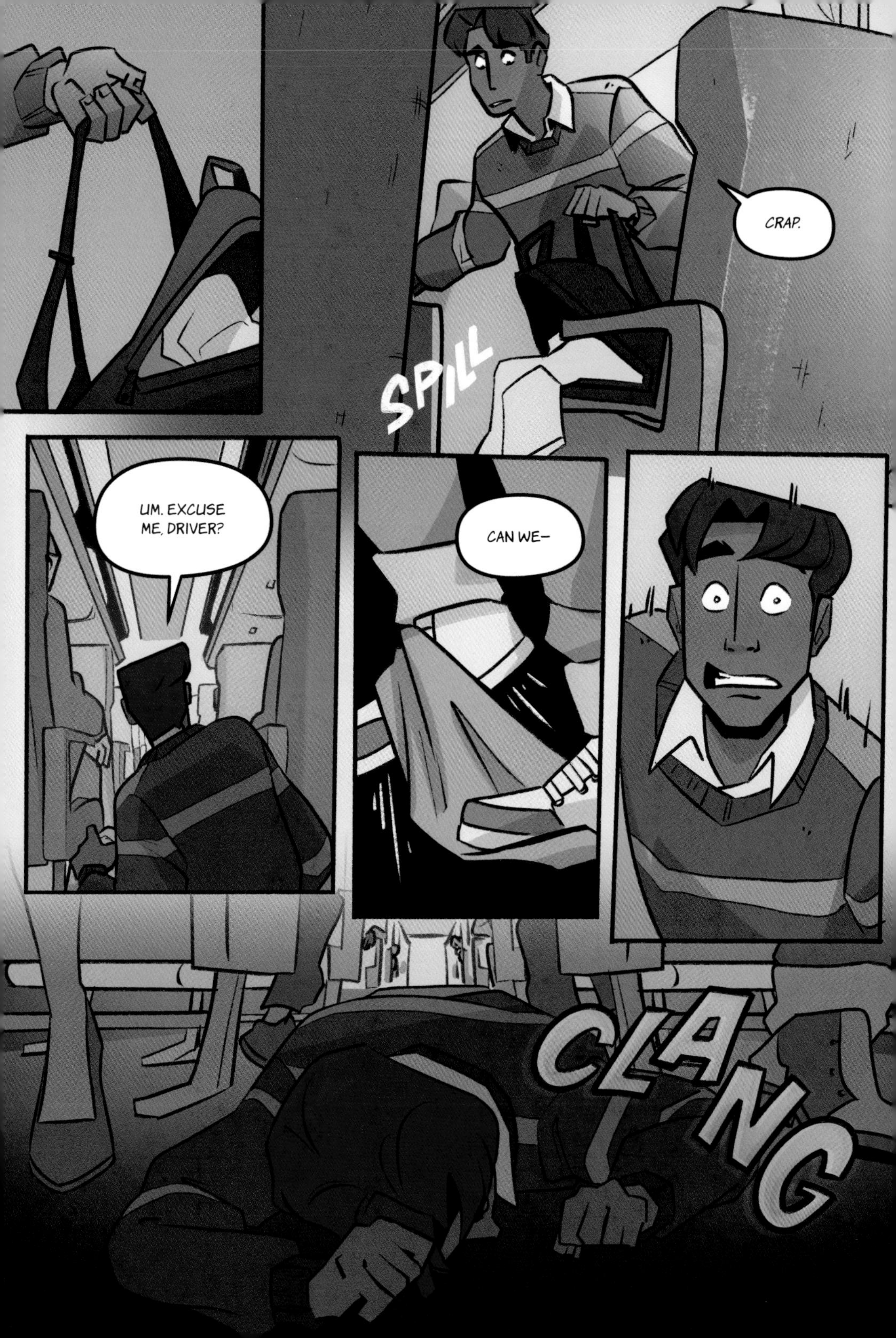
CRAP.
SPILL
UM. EXCUSE ME, DRIVER?
CAN WE–
CLANG

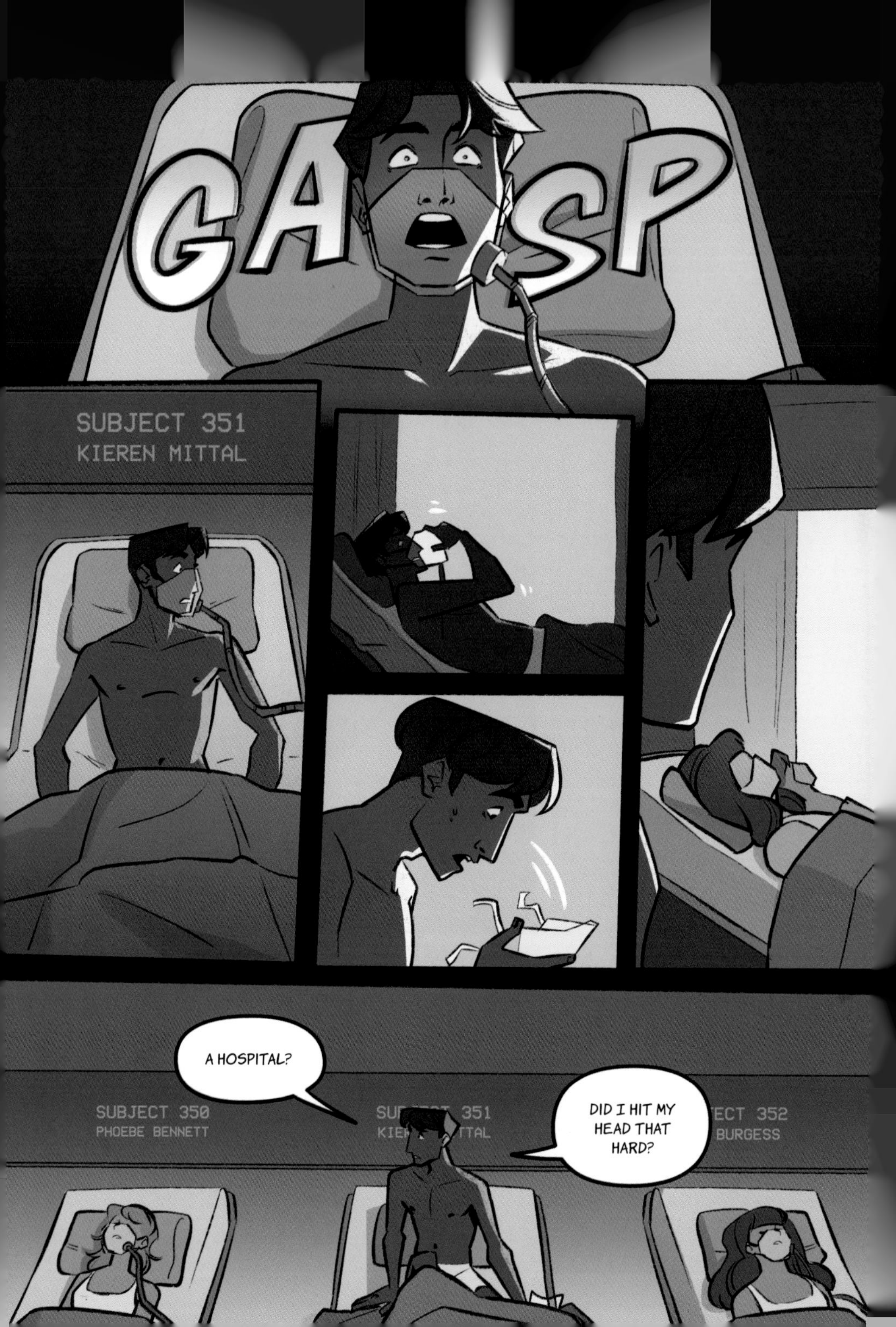
GASP
SUBJECT 351
KIEREN MITTAL
A HOSPITAL?
SUBJECT 350
PHOEBE BENNETT
DID I HIT MY HEAD THAT HARD?
BURGESS

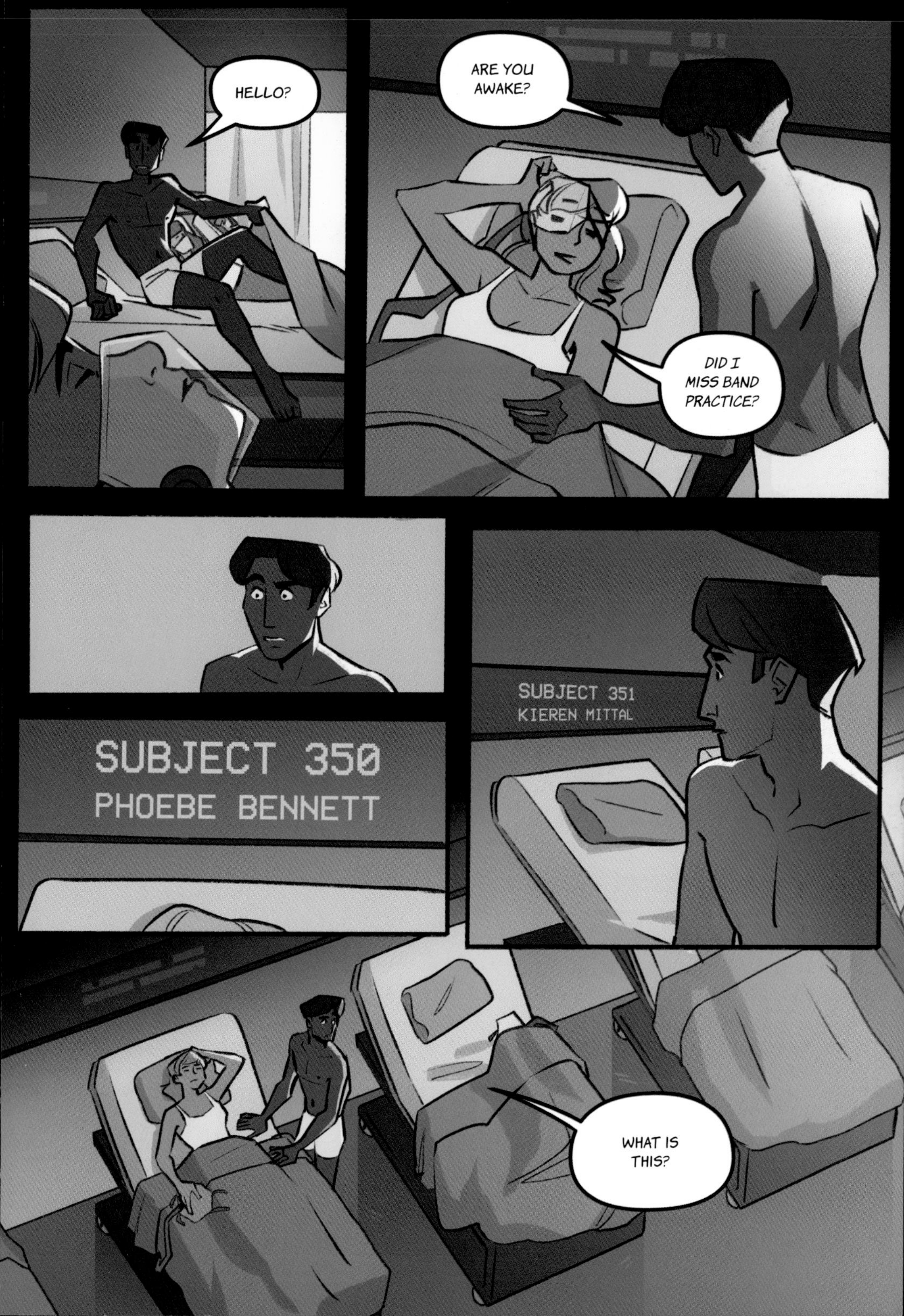
HELLO?
ARE YOU AWAKE?
DID I MISS BAND PRACTICE?
SUBJECT 350
PHOEBE BENNETT
SUBJECT 351
KIEREN MITTAL
WHAT IS THIS?

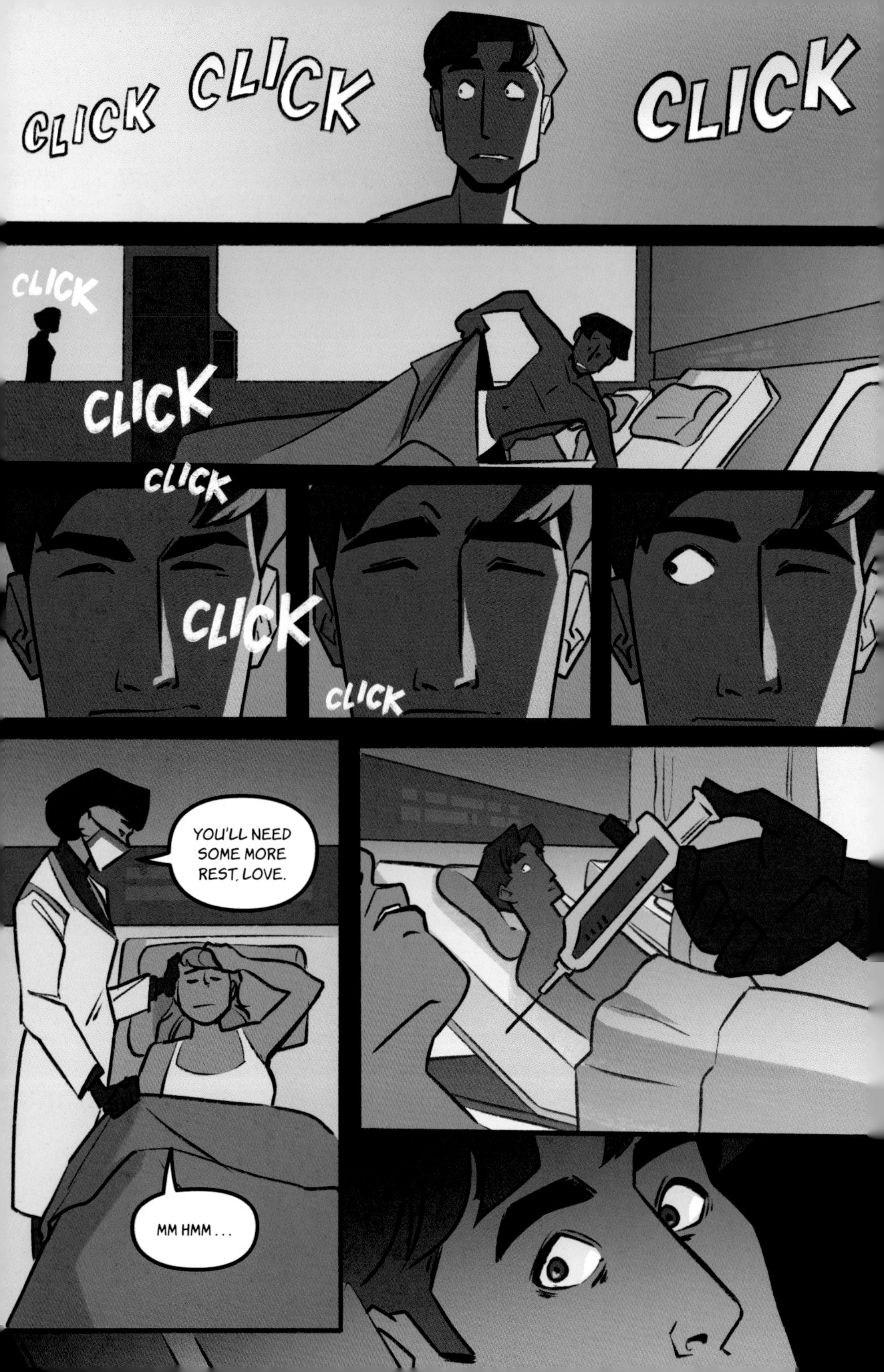

CLICK
CLICK
CLICK
CLICK
CLICK
CLICK
CLICK
CLICK
YOU'LL NEED SOME MORE REST, LOVE.
MM HMM . . .

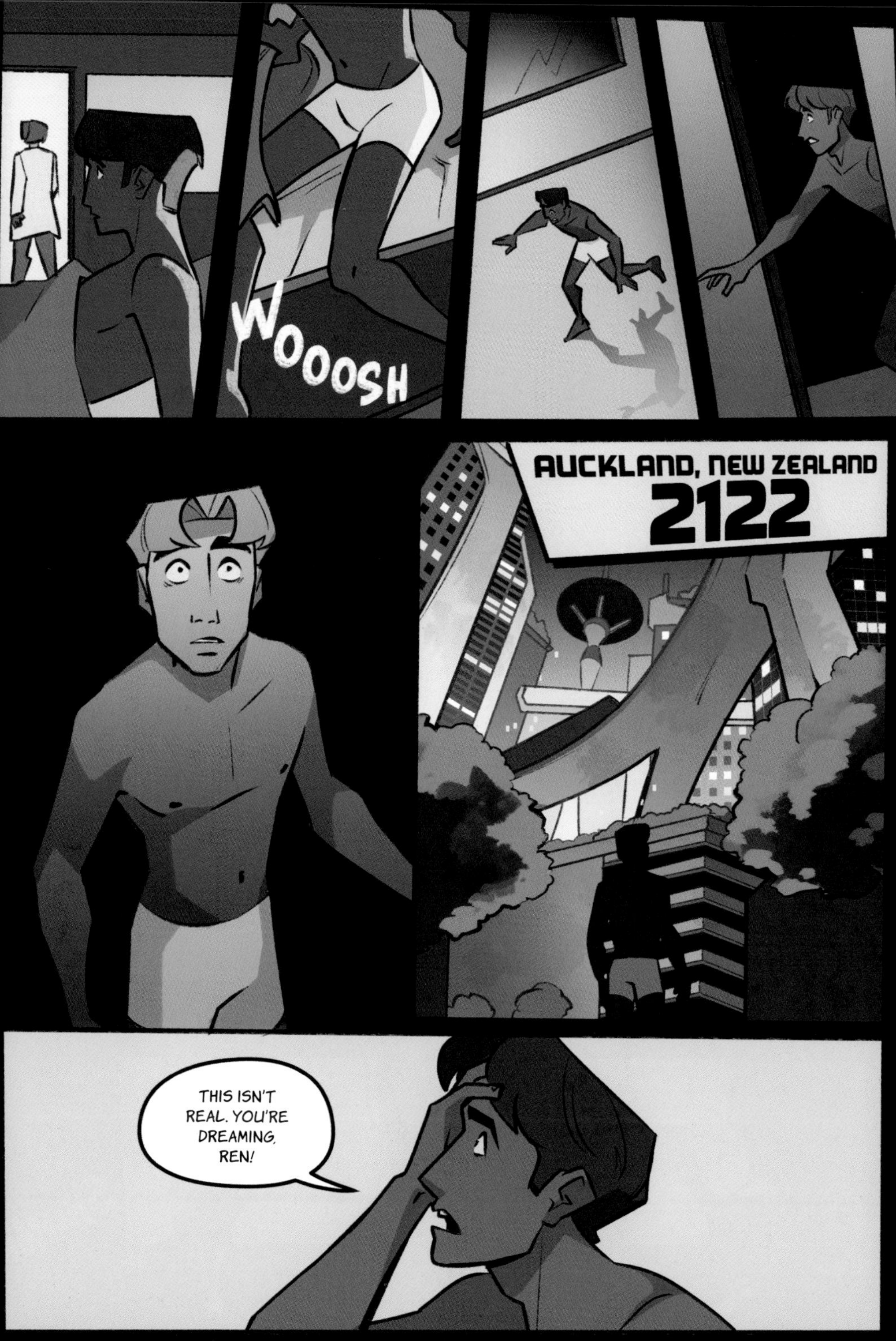
WOOOSH
AUCKLAND, NEW ZEALAND
2122
THIS ISN'T REAL. YOU'RE DREAMING, REN!

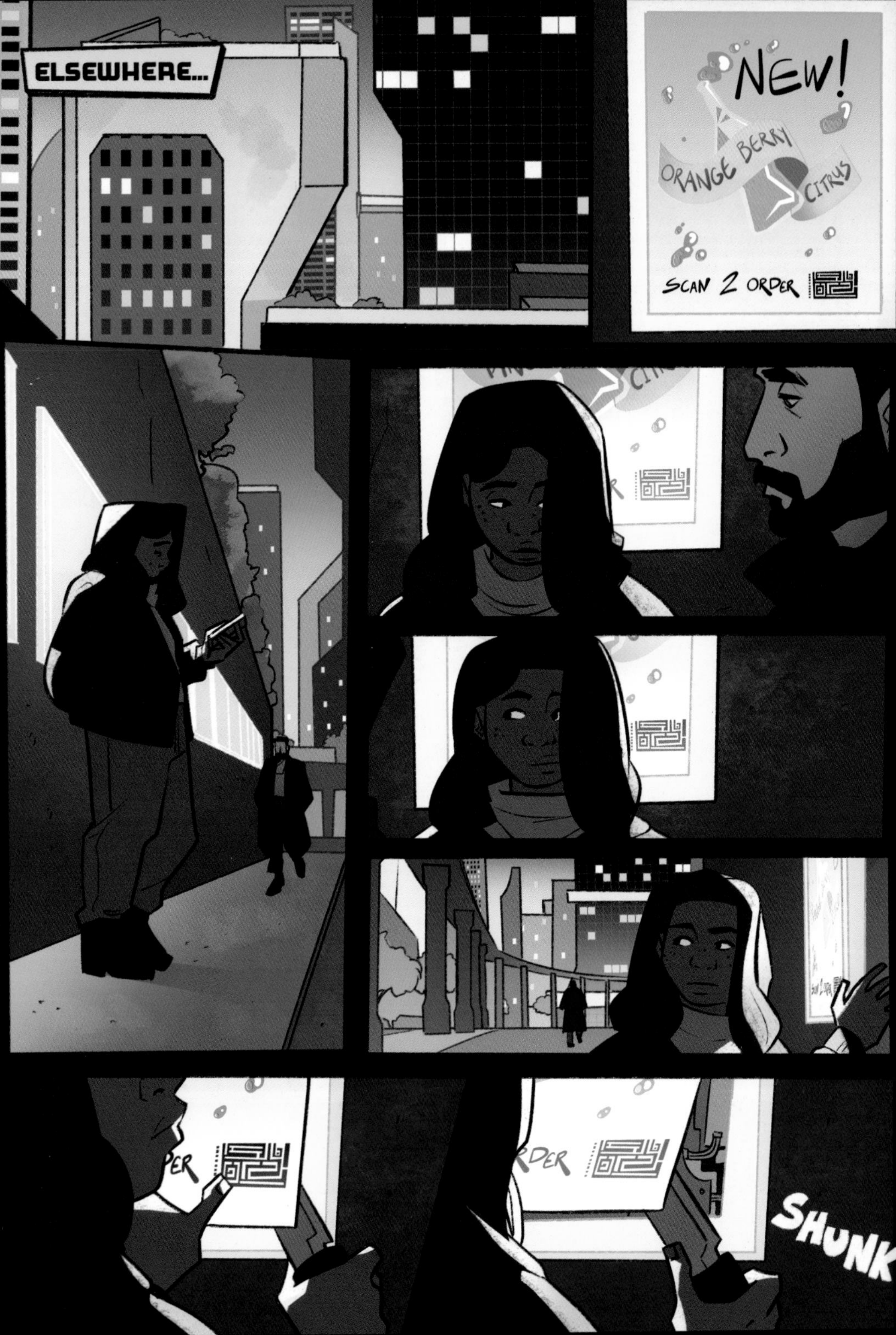
ELSEWHERE...
NEW!
ORANGE BERRY
CITRUS
SCAN 2 ORDER
SHUNK

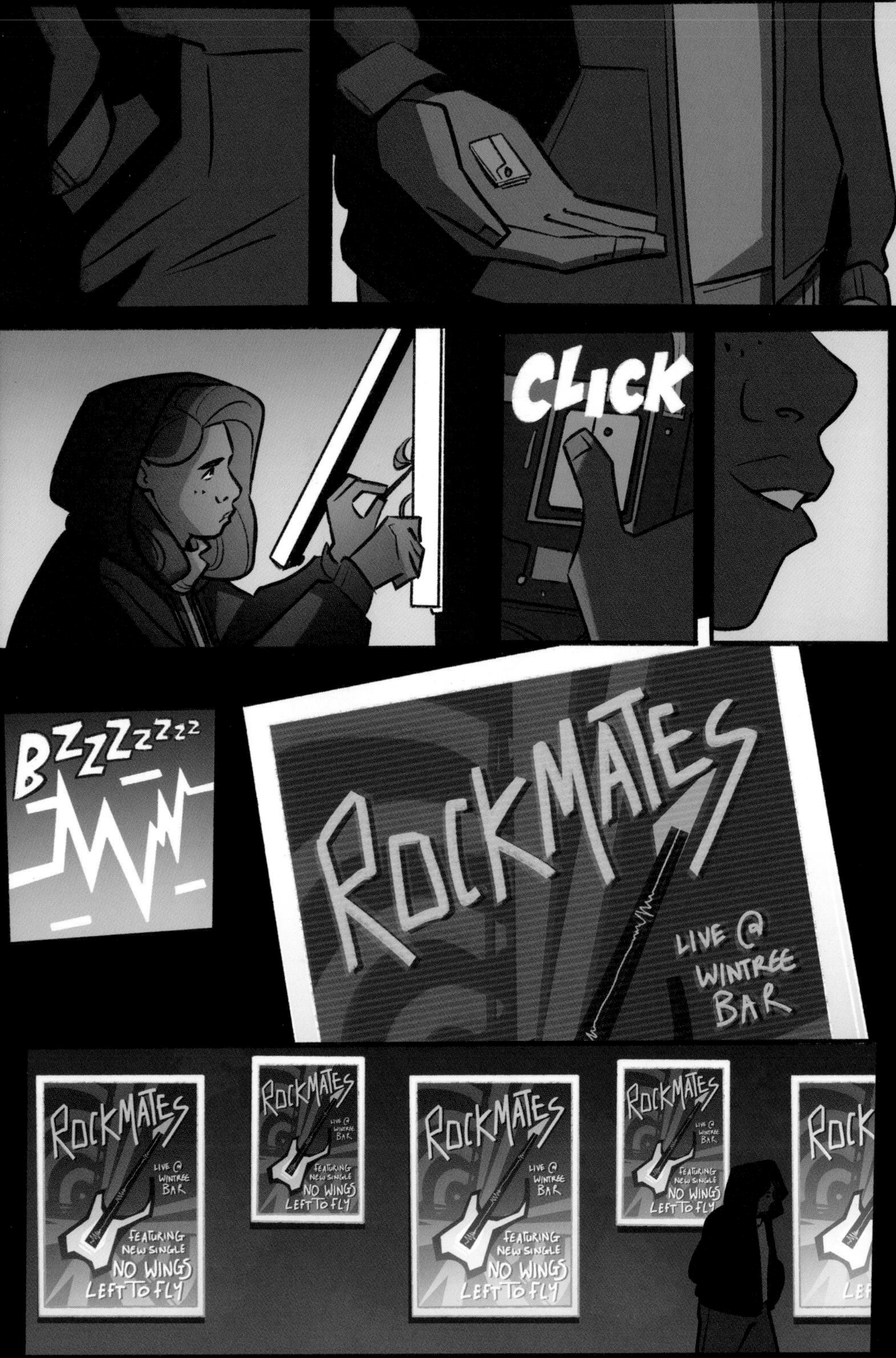
CLICK
BZZZzzzz
ROCKMATES
LIVE @
WINTREE
BAR
ROCKMATES
LIVE @
WINTREE
BAR
FEATURING
NEW SINGLE
NO WINGS
LEFT TO FLY

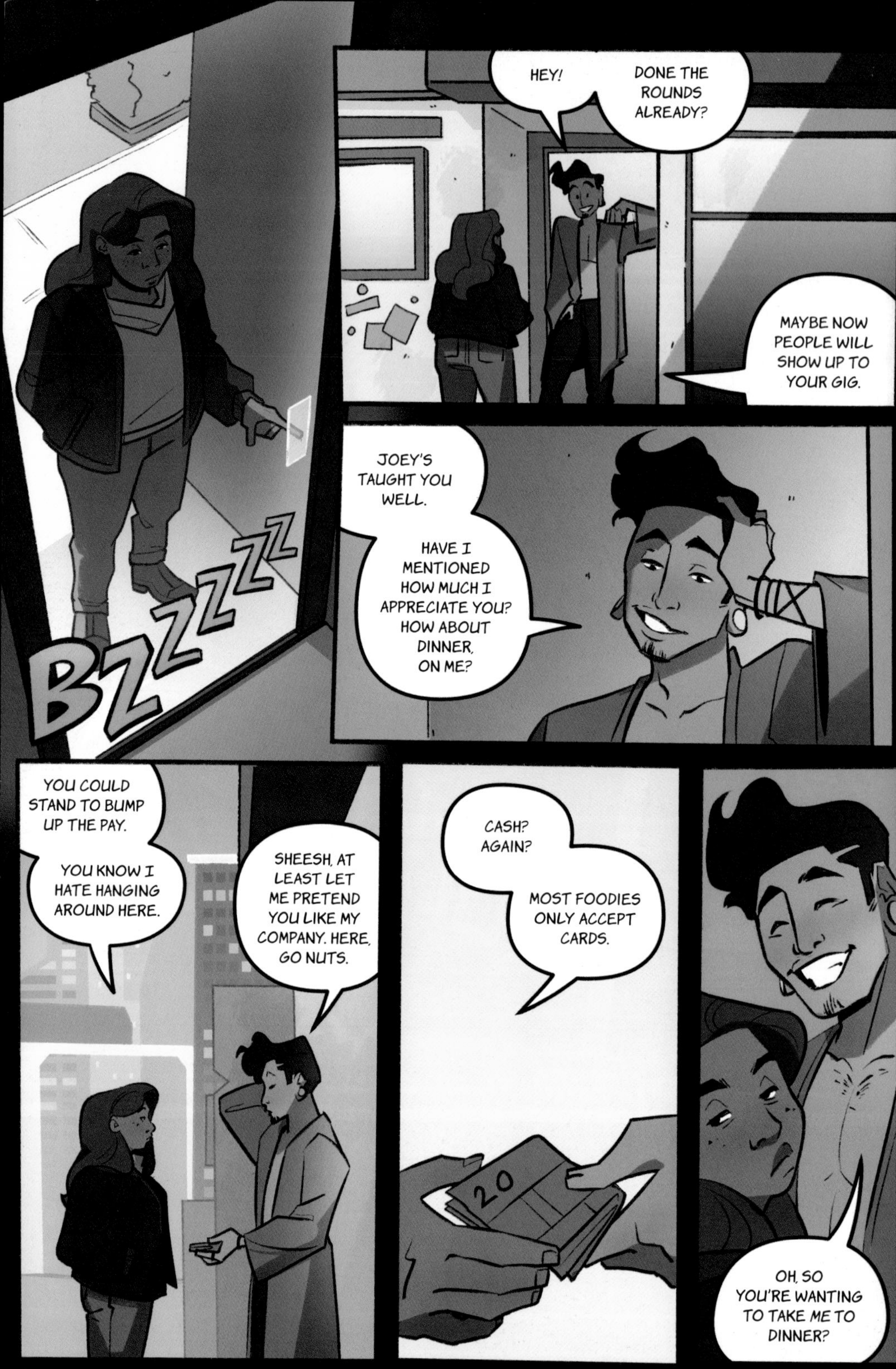
BZZZZZ
HEY!
DONE THE ROUNDS ALREADY?
MAYBE NOW PEOPLE WILL SHOW UP TO YOUR GIG.
JOEY'S TAUGHT YOU WELL.
HAVE I MENTIONED HOW MUCH I APPRECIATE YOU? HOW ABOUT DINNER, ON ME?
YOU COULD STAND TO BUMP UP THE PAY.
YOU KNOW I HATE HANGING AROUND HERE.
SHEESH, AT LEAST LET ME PRETEND YOU LIKE MY COMPANY. HERE, GO NUTS.
CASH? AGAIN?
MOST FOODIES ONLY ACCEPT CARDS.
20
OH, SO YOU'RE WANTING TO TAKE ME TO DINNER?

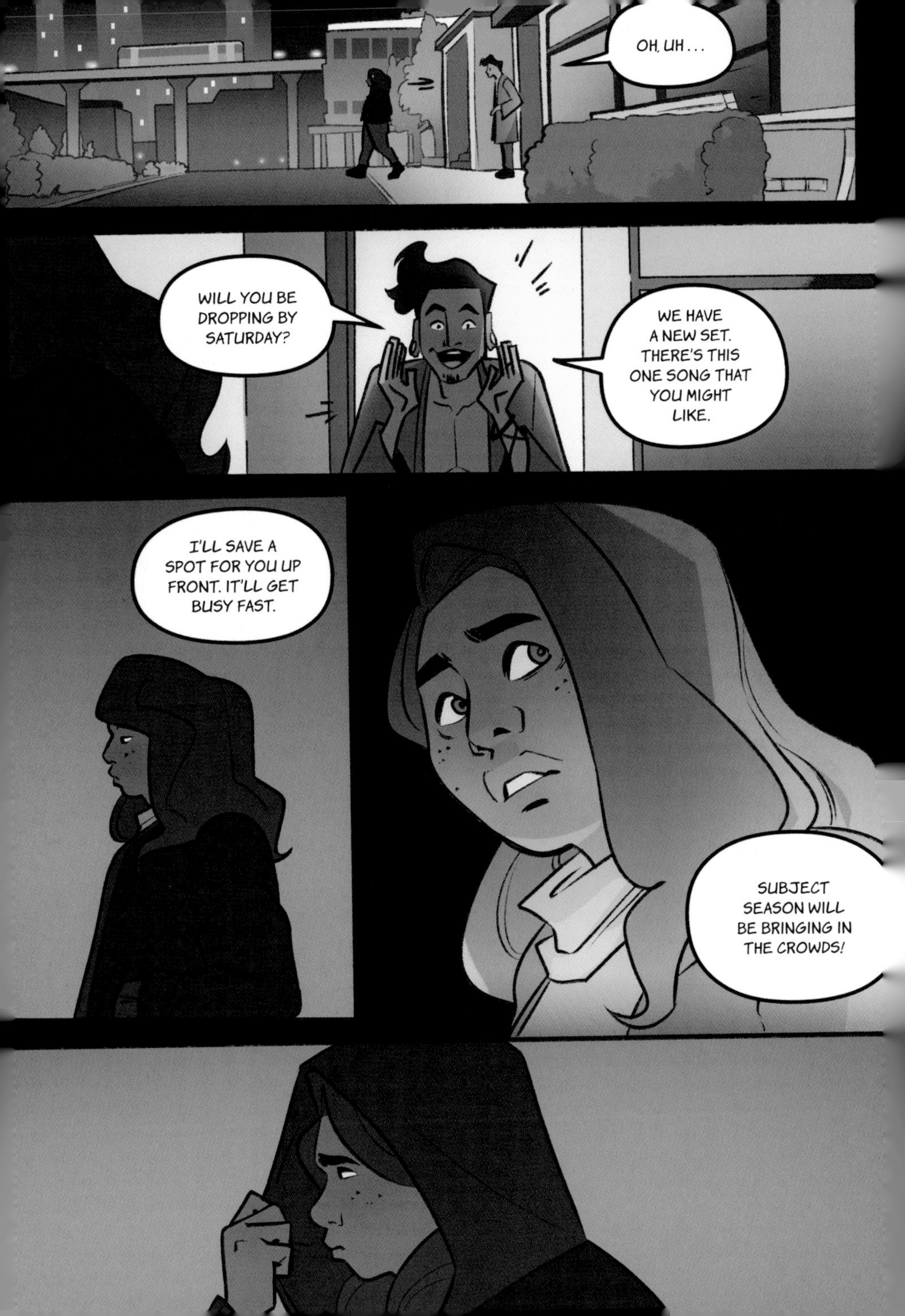
OH, UH . . .
WILL YOU BE DROPPING BY SATURDAY?
WE HAVE A NEW SET. THERE'S THIS ONE SONG THAT YOU MIGHT LIKE.
I'LL SAVE A SPOT FOR YOU UP FRONT. IT'LL GET BUSY FAST.
SUBJECT SEASON WILL BE BRINGING IN THE CROWDS!

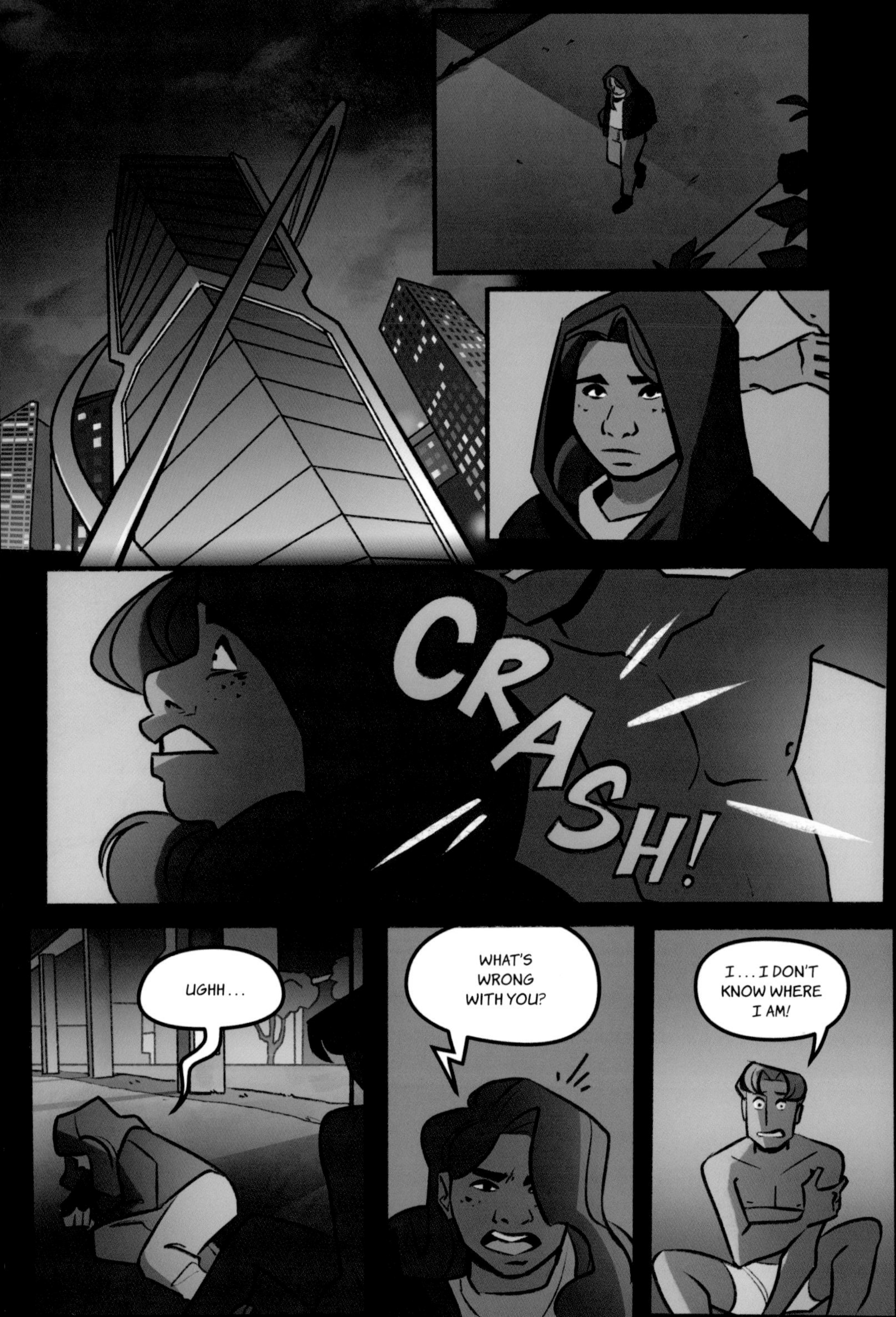
CRASH!
UGHH . . .
WHAT'S WRONG WITH YOU?
I . . . I DON'T KNOW WHERE I AM!

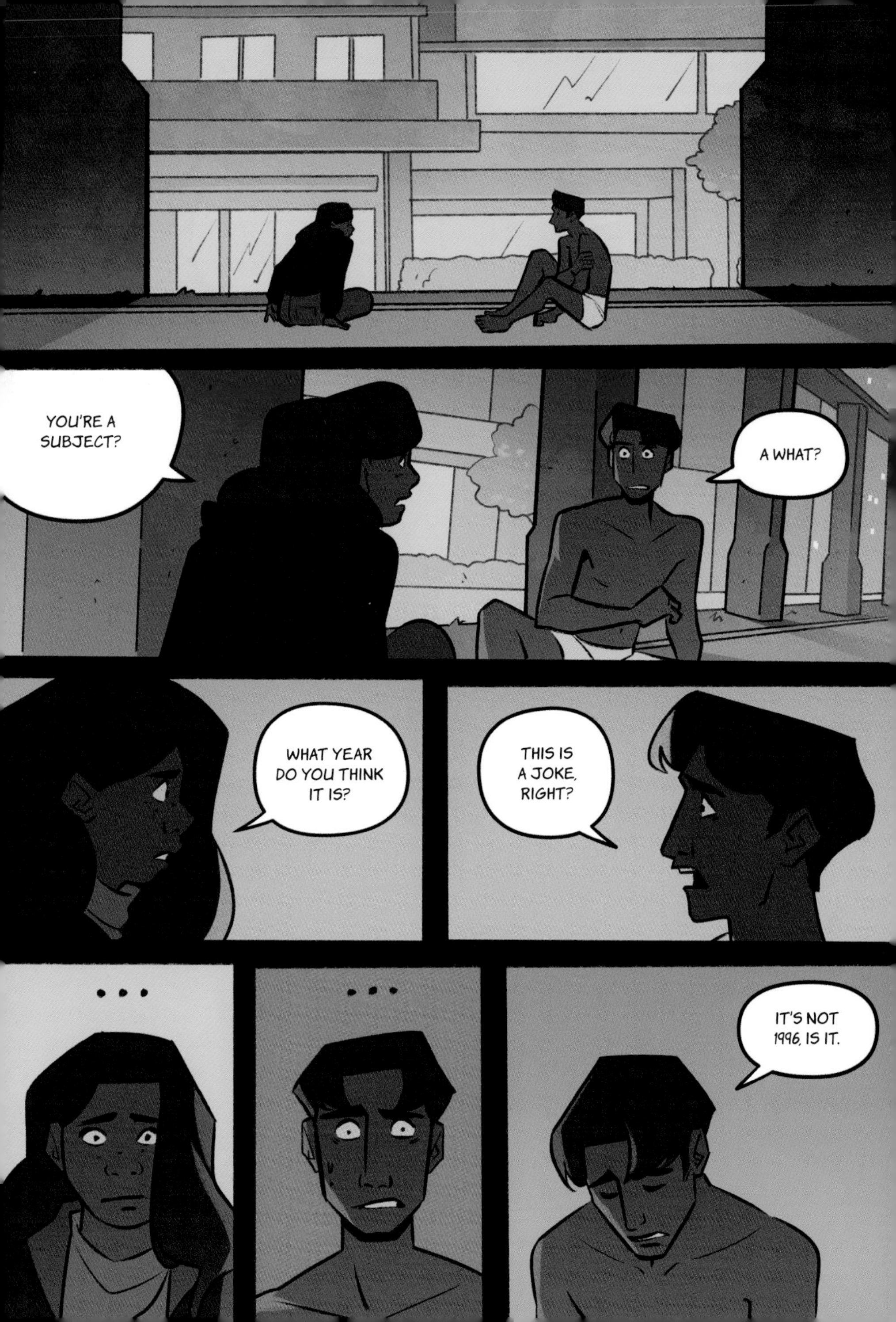

YOU'RE A SUBJECT?
A WHAT?
WHAT YEAR DO YOU THINK IT IS?
THIS IS A JOKE, RIGHT?
...
...
IT'S NOT 1996, IS IT.

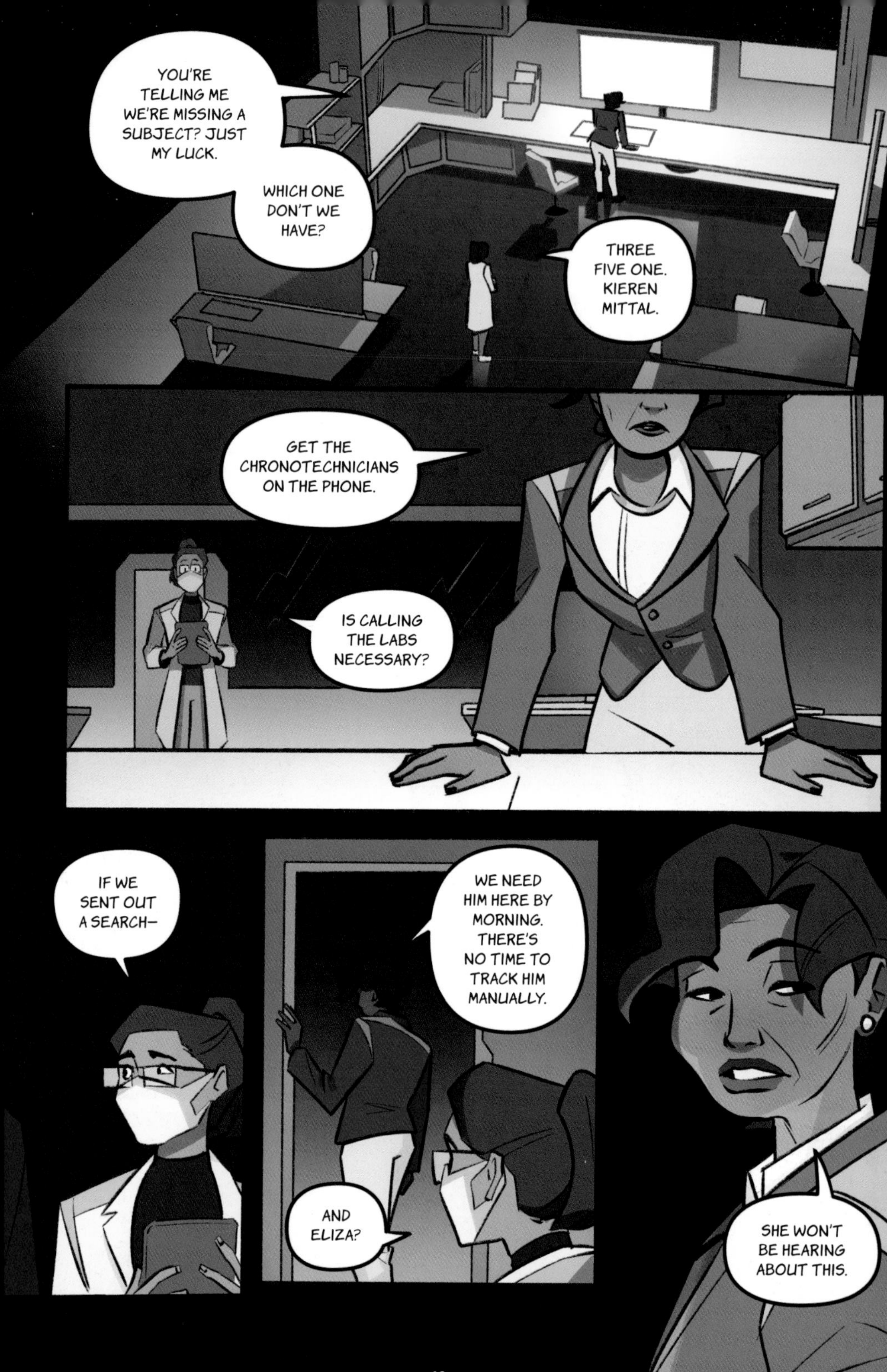
YOU'RE TELLING ME WE'RE MISSING A SUBJECT? JUST MY LUCK.
WHICH ONE DON'T WE HAVE?
THREE FIVE ONE. KIEREN MITTAL.
GET THE CHRONOTECHNICIANS ON THE PHONE.
IS CALLING THE LABS NECESSARY?
IF WE SENT OUT A SEARCH—
WE NEED HIM HERE BY MORNING. THERE'S NO TIME TO TRACK HIM MANUALLY.
AND ELIZA?
SHE WON'T BE HEARING ABOUT THIS.

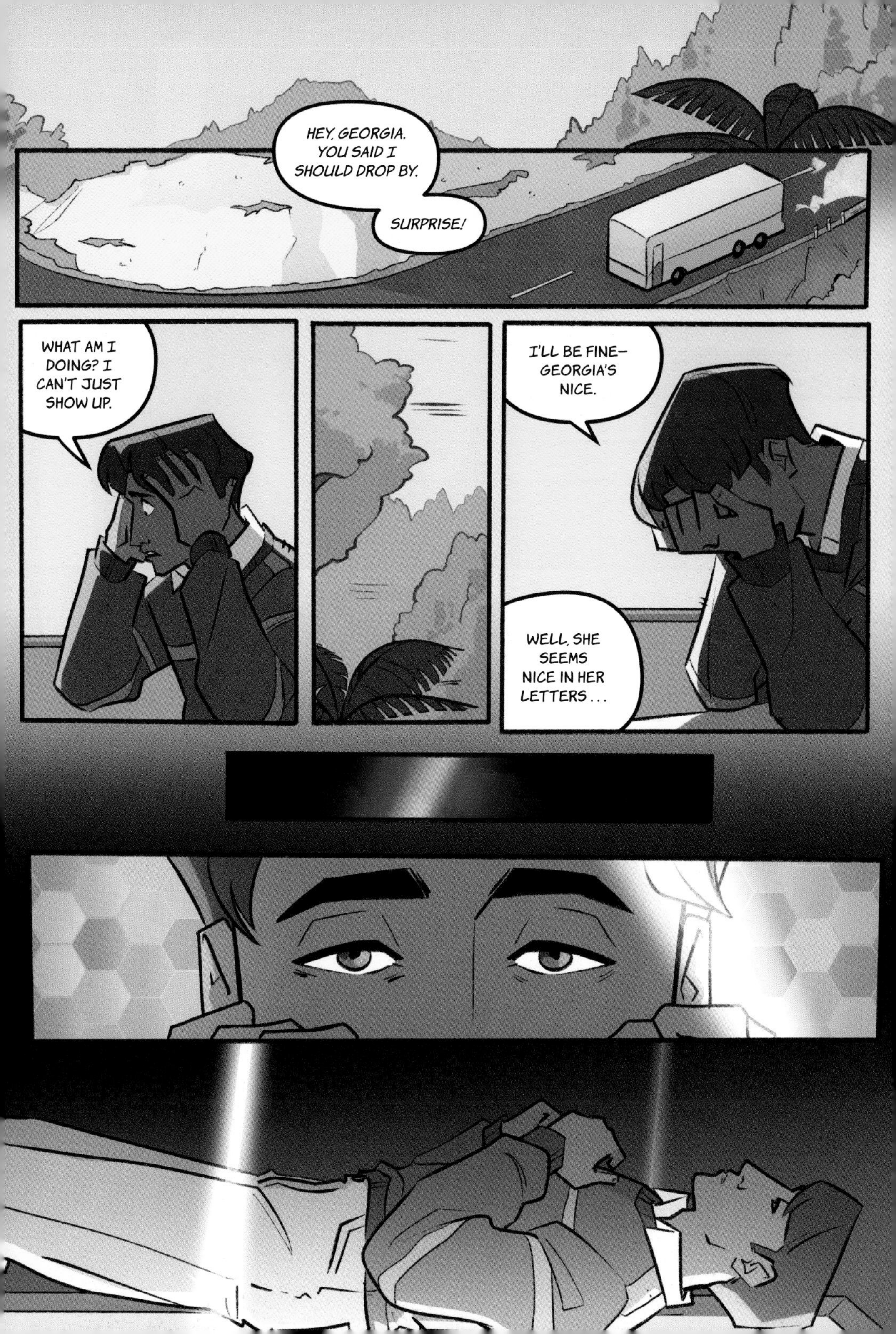
HEY, GEORGIA. YOU SAID I SHOULD DROP BY.
SURPRISE!
WHAT AM I DOING? I CAN'T JUST SHOW UP.
I'LL BE FINE— GEORGIA'S NICE.
WELL, SHE SEEMS NICE IN HER LETTERS . . .

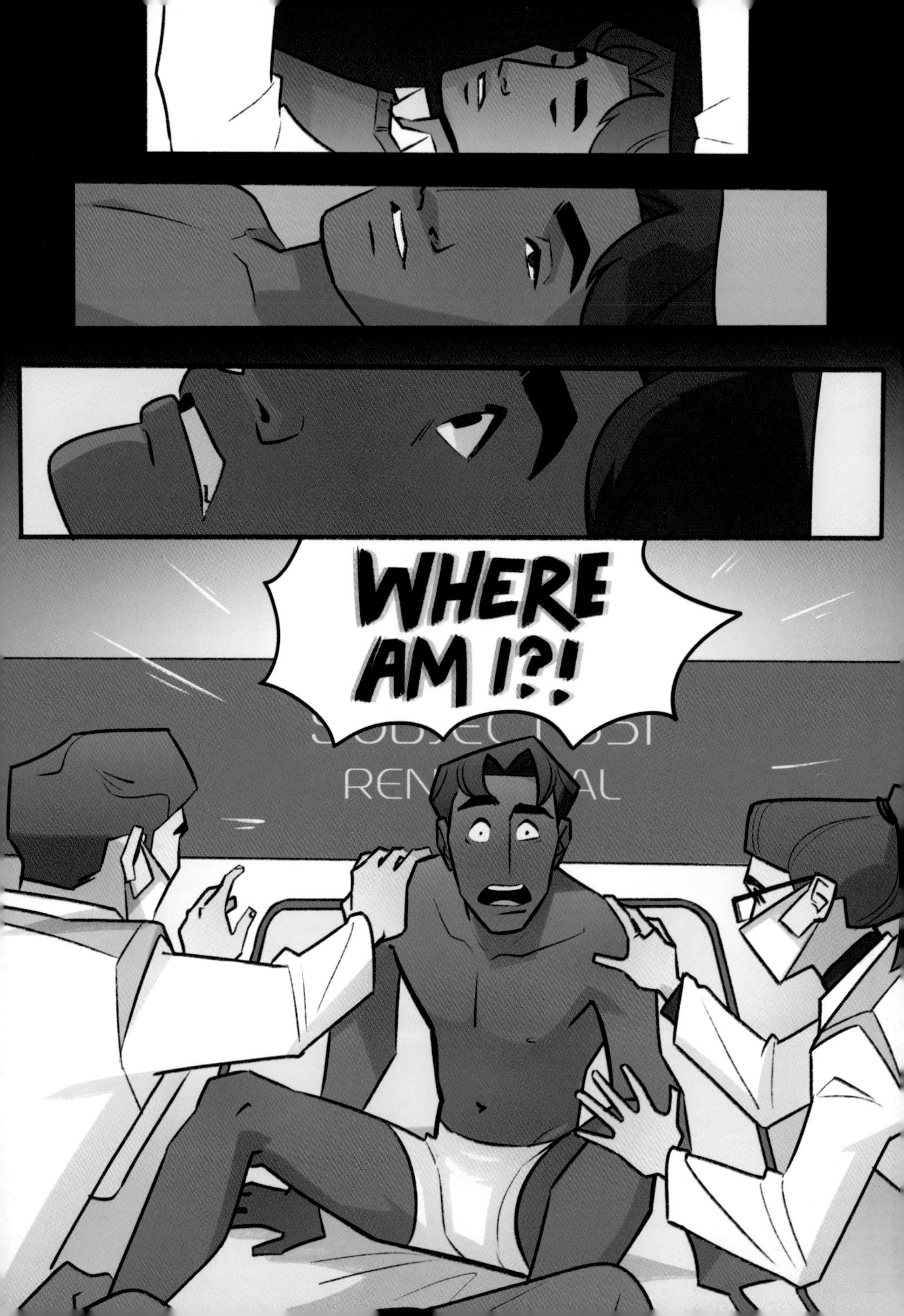
WHERE AM I?!

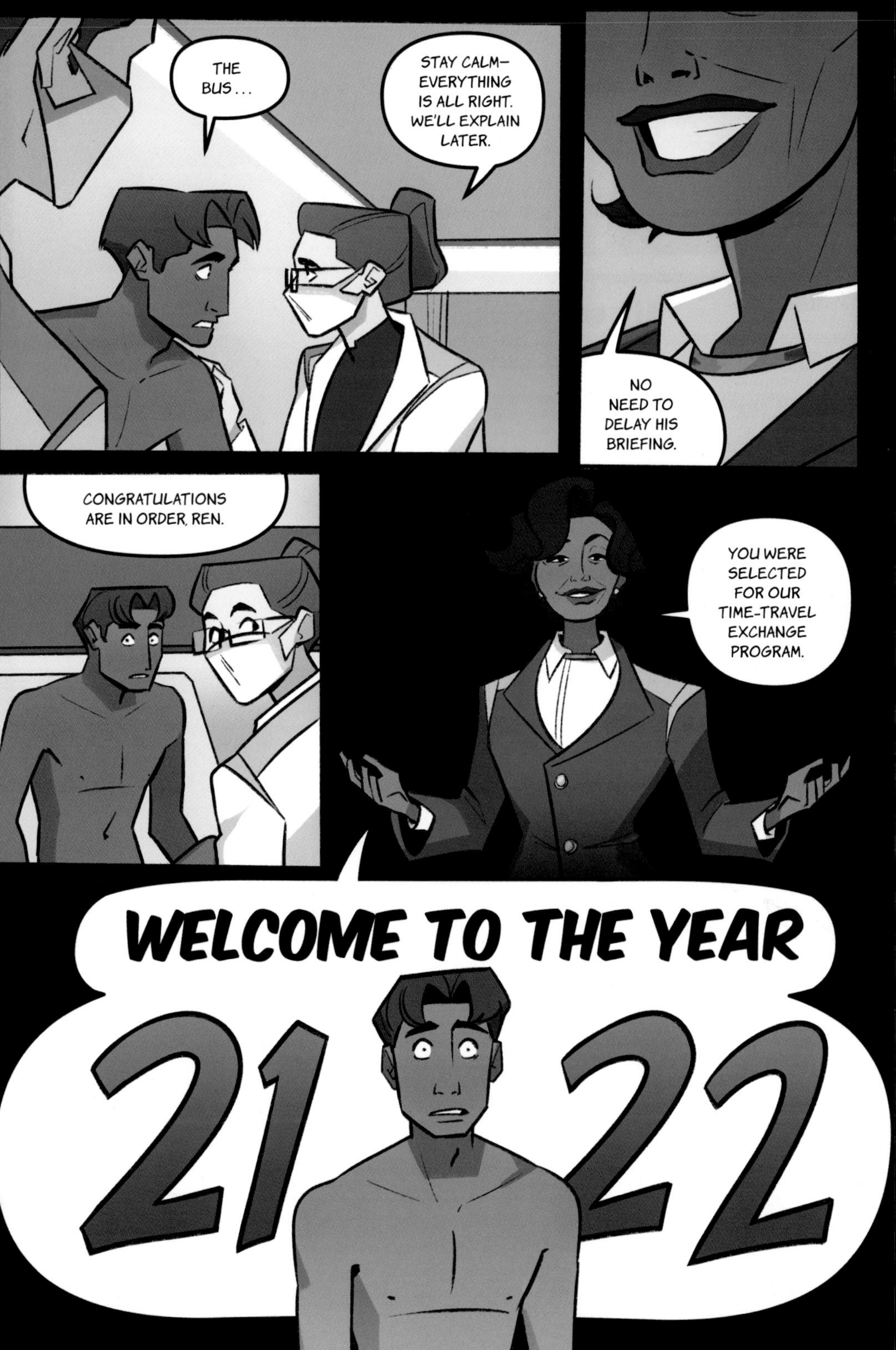
THE BUS . . .
STAY CALM— EVERYTHING IS ALL RIGHT. WE'LL EXPLAIN LATER.
NO NEED TO DELAY HIS BRIEFING.
CONGRATULATIONS ARE IN ORDER, REN.
YOU WERE SELECTED FOR OUR TIME-TRAVEL EXCHANGE PROGRAM.
WELCOME TO THE YEAR
2122

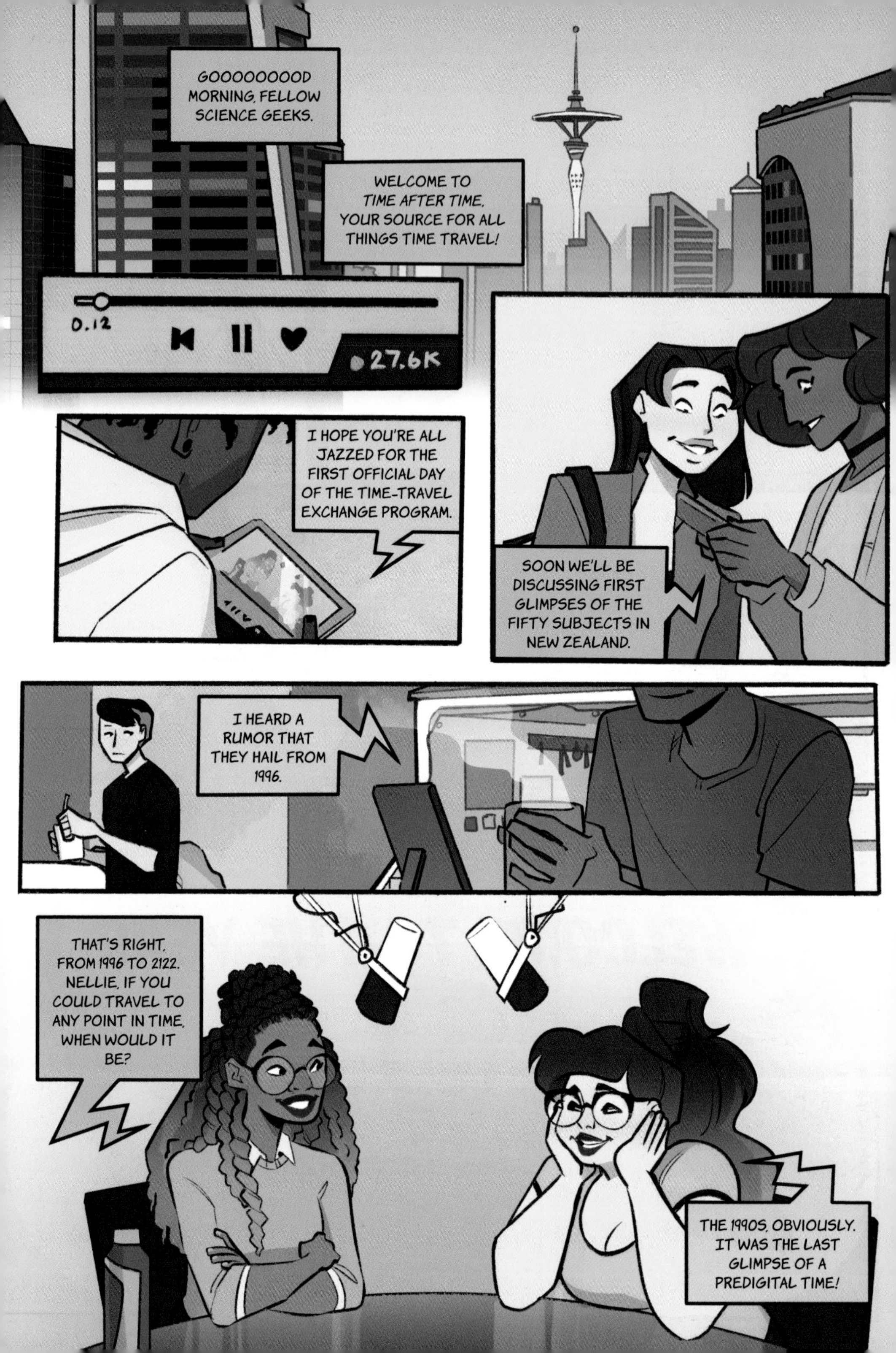
GOOOOOOOOD MORNING, FELLOW SCIENCE GEEKS.
WELCOME TO TIME AFTER TIME, YOUR SOURCE FOR ALL THINGS TIME TRAVEL!
0.12
27.6K
I HOPE YOU'RE ALL JAZZED FOR THE FIRST OFFICIAL DAY OF THE TIME-TRAVEL EXCHANGE PROGRAM.
SOON WE'LL BE DISCUSSING FIRST GLIMPSES OF THE FIFTY SUBJECTS IN NEW ZEALAND.
I HEARD A RUMOR THAT THEY HAIL FROM 1996.
THAT'S RIGHT, FROM 1996 TO 2122. NELLIE, IF YOU COULD TRAVEL TO ANY POINT IN TIME, WHEN WOULD IT BE?
THE 1990S, OBVIOUSLY. IT WAS THE LAST GLIMPSE OF A PREDIGITAL TIME!

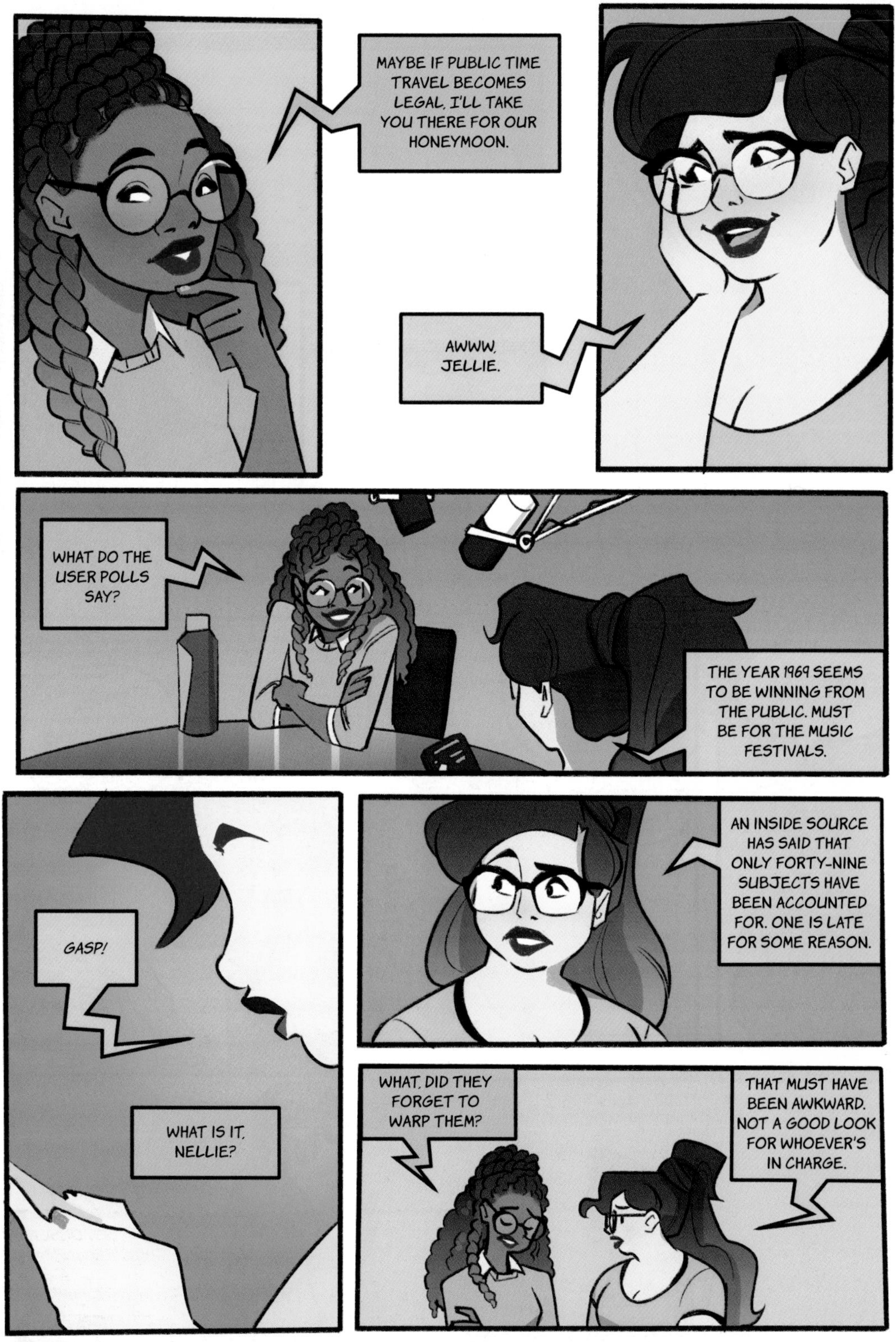
MAYBE IF PUBLIC TIME TRAVEL BECOMES LEGAL, I'LL TAKE YOU THERE FOR OUR HONEYMOON.
AWWW, JELLIE.
WHAT DO THE USER POLLS SAY?
THE YEAR 1969 SEEMS TO BE WINNING FROM THE PUBLIC. MUST BE FOR THE MUSIC FESTIVALS.
GASP!
WHAT IS IT, NELLIE?
AN INSIDE SOURCE HAS SAID THAT ONLY FORTY-NINE SUBJECTS HAVE BEEN ACCOUNTED FOR. ONE IS LATE FOR SOME REASON.
WHAT, DID THEY FORGET TO WARP THEM?
THAT MUST HAVE BEEN AWKWARD. NOT A GOOD LOOK FOR WHOEVER'S IN CHARGE.

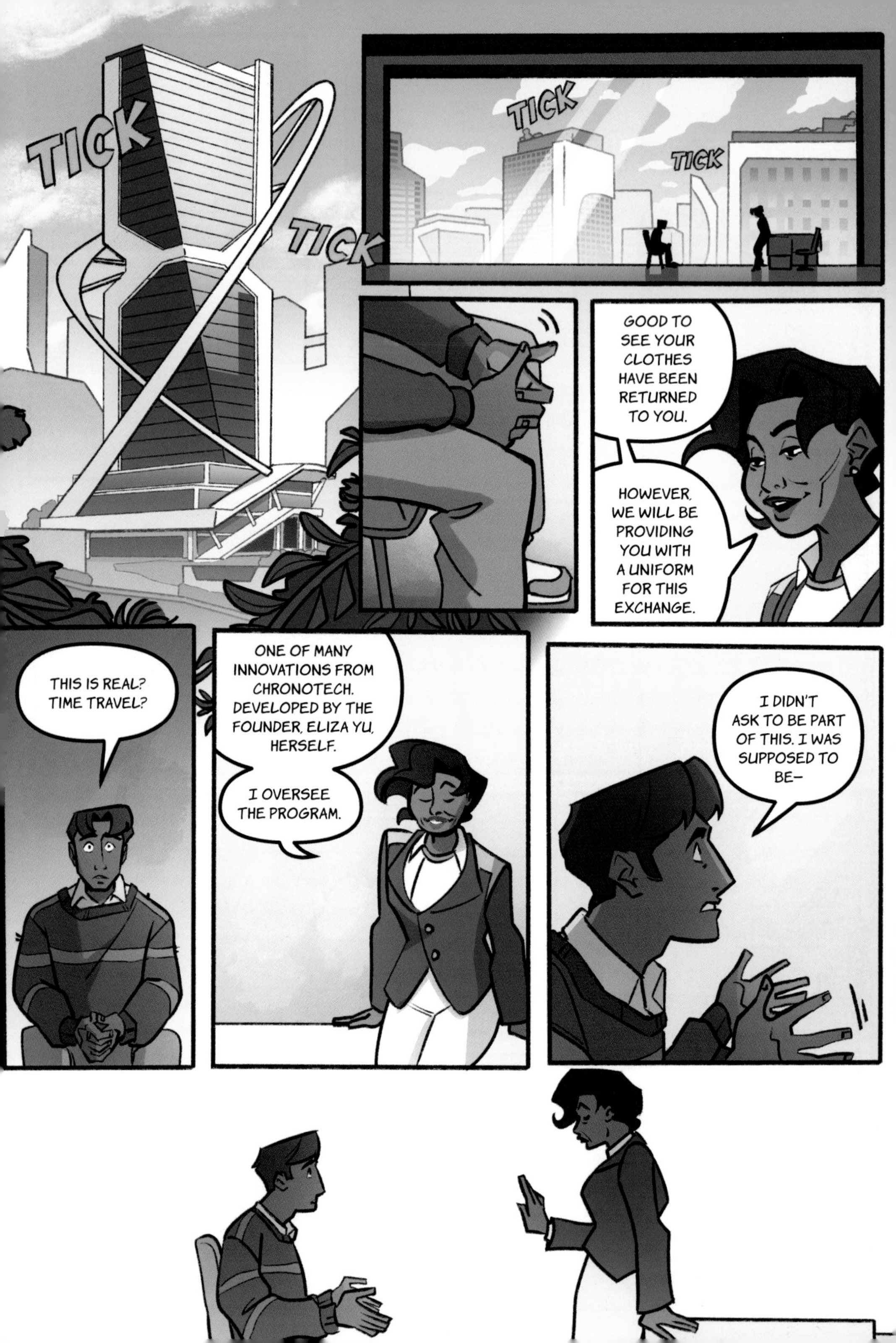
TICK
TICK
TICK
TICK
GOOD TO SEE YOUR CLOTHES HAVE BEEN RETURNED TO YOU.
HOWEVER, WE WILL BE PROVIDING YOU WITH A UNIFORM FOR THIS EXCHANGE.
THIS IS REAL? TIME TRAVEL?
ONE OF MANY INNOVATIONS FROM CHRONOTECH. DEVELOPED BY THE FOUNDER, ELIZA YU, HERSELF.
I OVERSEE THE PROGRAM.
I DIDN'T ASK TO BE PART OF THIS. I WAS SUPPOSED TO BE—

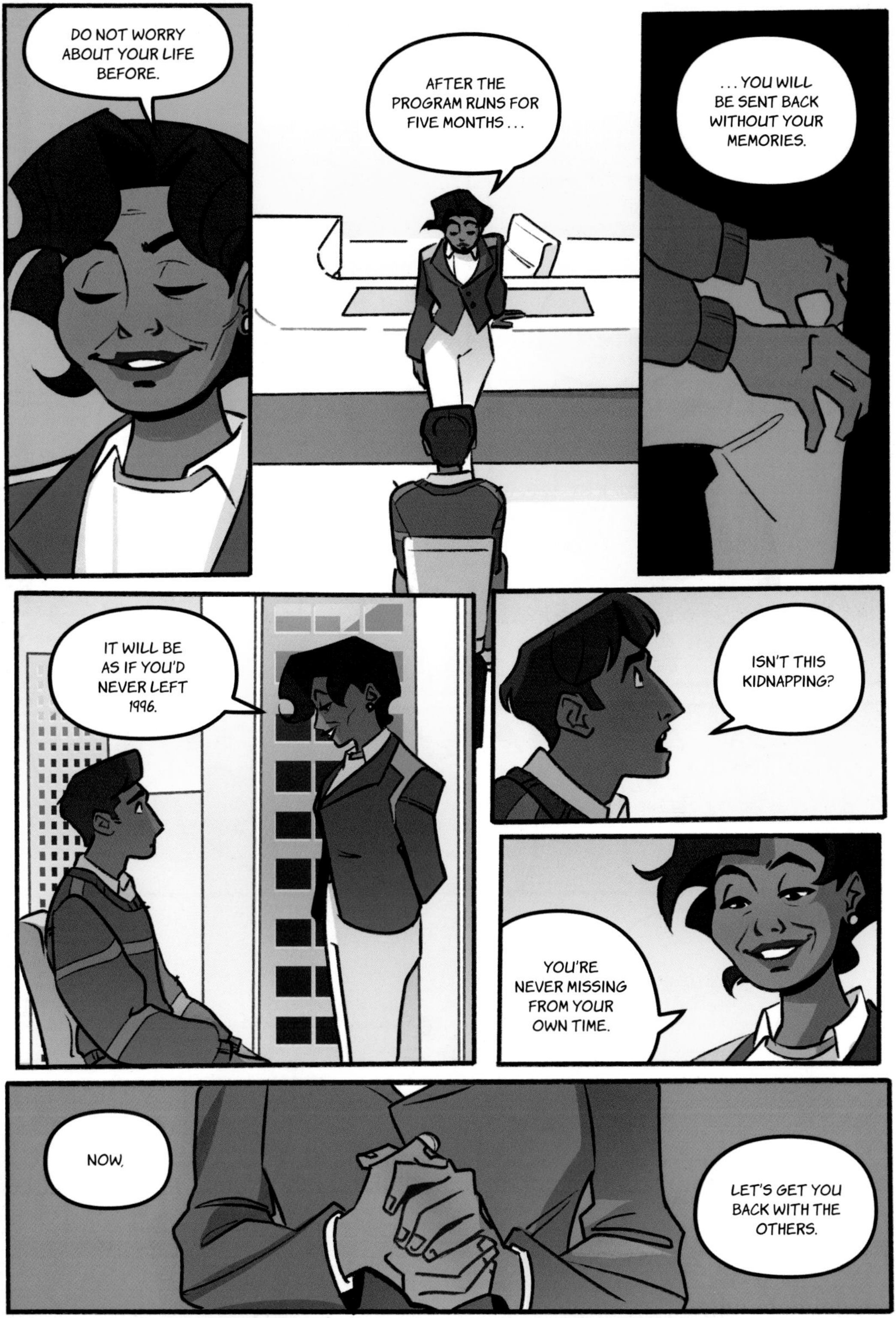
DO NOT WORRY ABOUT YOUR LIFE BEFORE.
AFTER THE PROGRAM RUNS FOR FIVE MONTHS . . .
. . . YOU WILL BE SENT BACK WITHOUT YOUR MEMORIES.
IT WILL BE AS IF YOU'D NEVER LEFT 1996.
ISN'T THIS KIDNAPPING?
YOU'RE NEVER MISSING FROM YOUR OWN TIME.
NOW,
LET'S GET YOU BACK WITH THE OTHERS.

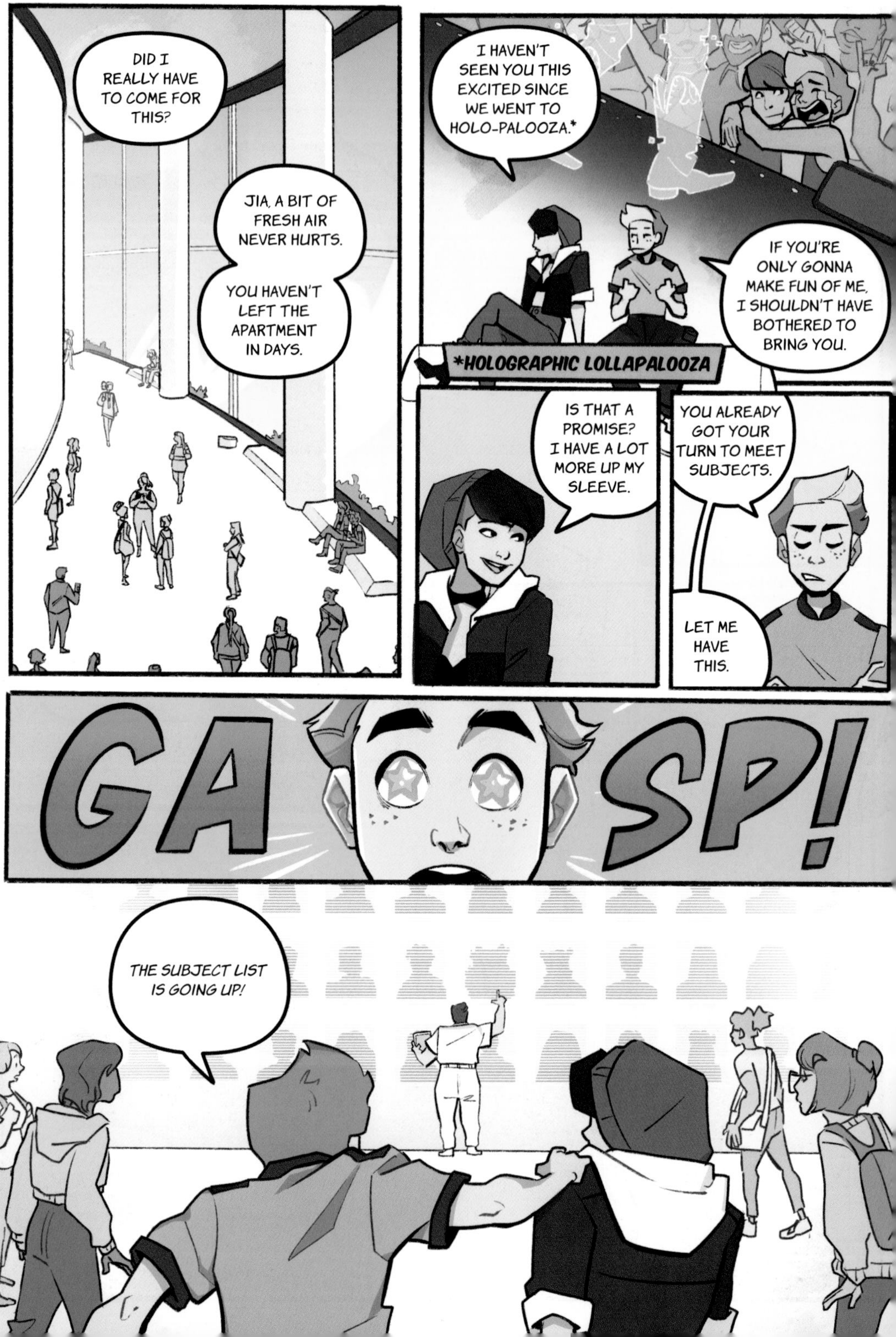
DID I REALLY HAVE TO COME FOR THIS?
JIA, A BIT OF FRESH AIR NEVER HURTS.
YOU HAVEN'T LEFT THE APARTMENT IN DAYS.
I HAVEN'T SEEN YOU THIS EXCITED SINCE WE WENT TO HOLO-PALOOZA.*
IF YOU'RE ONLY GONNA MAKE FUN OF ME, I SHOULDN'T HAVE BOTHERED TO BRING YOU.
*HOLOGRAPHIC LOLLAPALOOZA
IS THAT A PROMISE? I HAVE A LOT MORE UP MY SLEEVE.
YOU ALREADY GOT YOUR TURN TO MEET SUBJECTS.
LET ME HAVE THIS.
GASP!
THE SUBJECT LIST IS GOING UP!

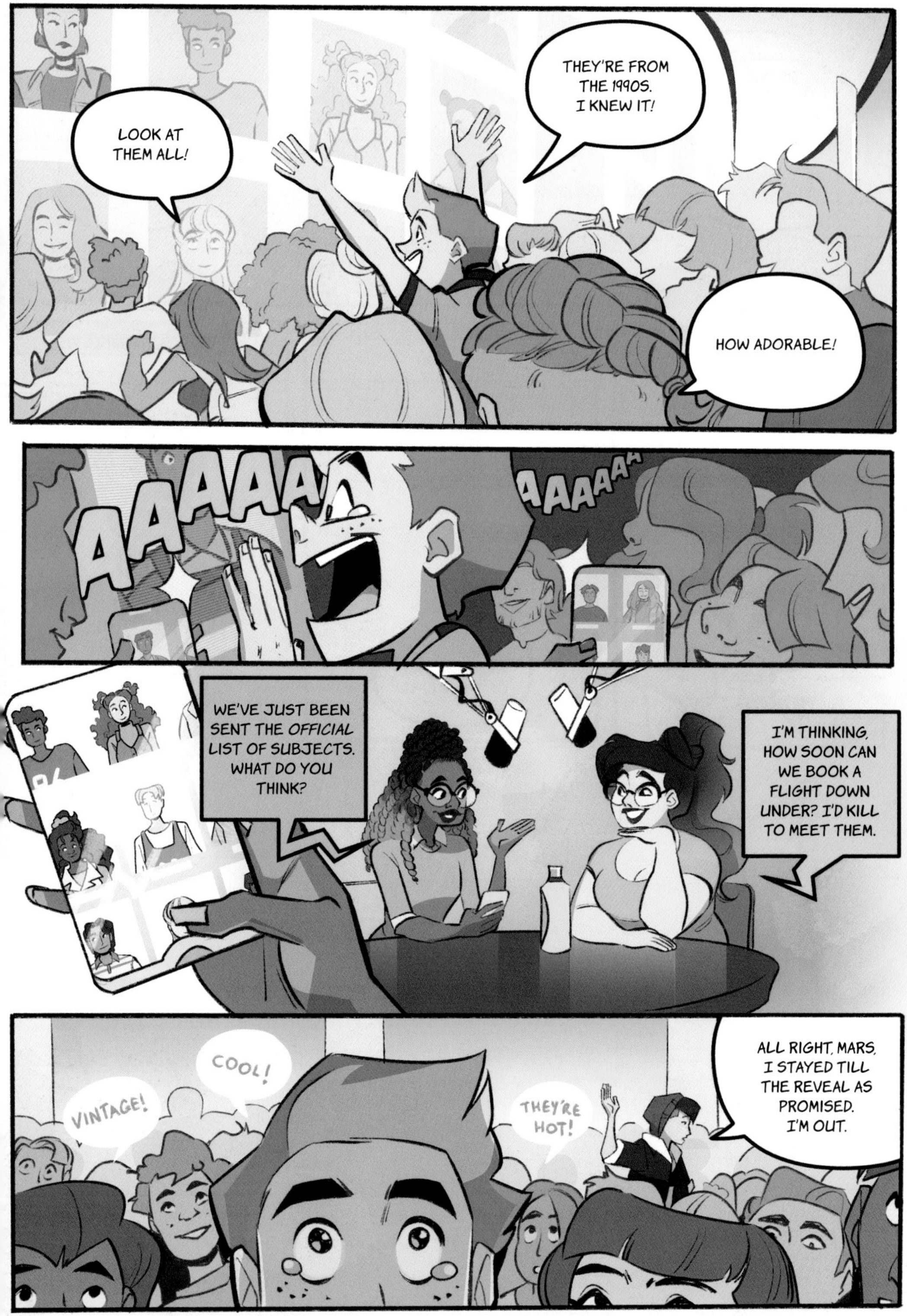
LOOK AT THEM ALL!
THEY'RE FROM THE 1990S. I KNEW IT!
HOW ADORABLE!
AAAAAA
AAAAAA
WE'VE JUST BEEN SENT THE *OFFICIAL* LIST OF SUBJECTS. WHAT DO YOU THINK?
I'M THINKING, HOW SOON CAN WE BOOK A FLIGHT DOWN UNDER? I'D KILL TO MEET THEM.
VINTAGE!
COOL!
THEY'RE HOT!
ALL RIGHT, MARS, I STAYED TILL THE REVEAL AS PROMISED. I'M OUT.

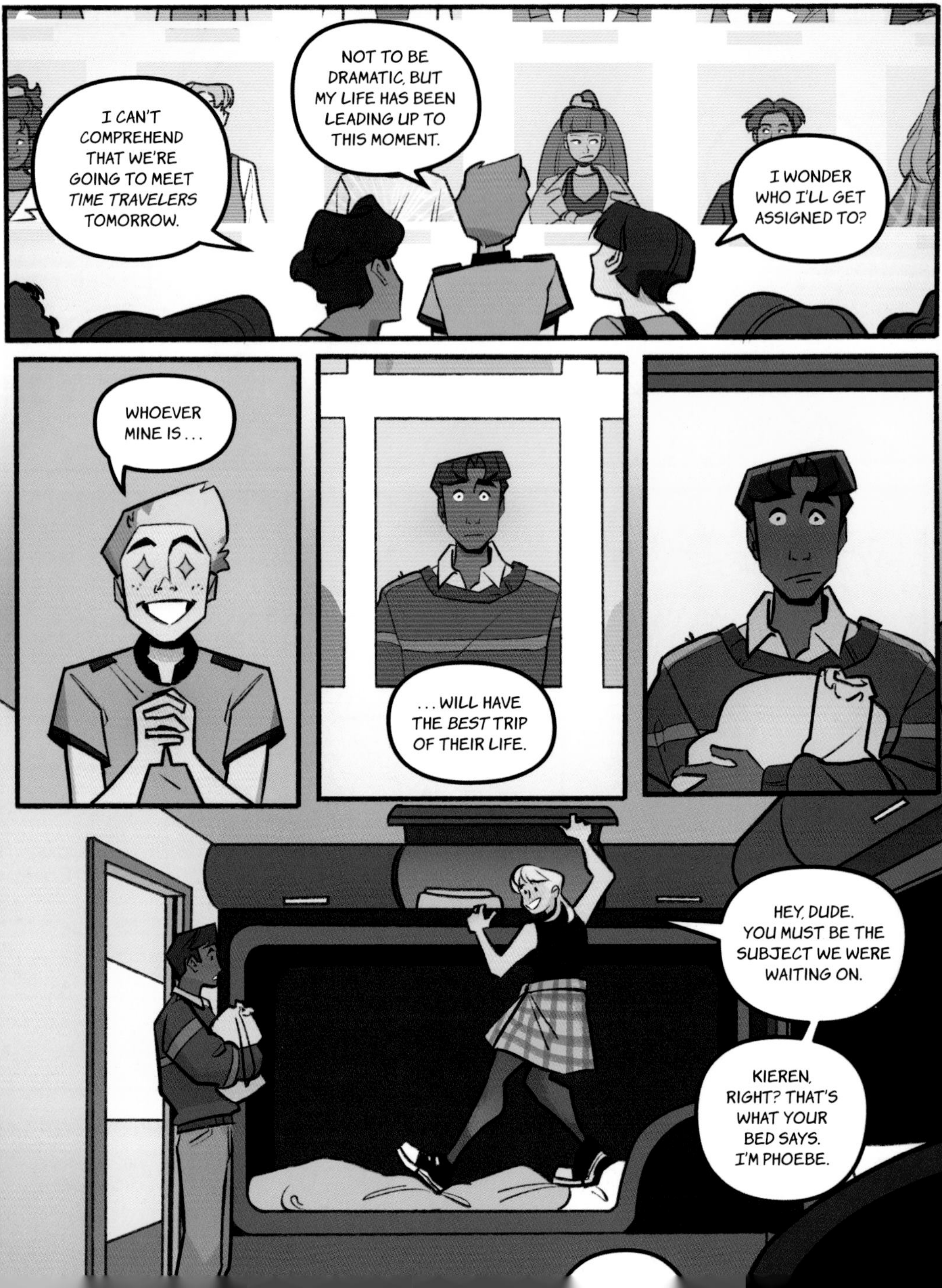
I CAN'T COMPREHEND THAT WE'RE GOING TO MEET *TIME TRAVELERS* TOMORROW.
NOT TO BE DRAMATIC, BUT MY LIFE HAS BEEN LEADING UP TO THIS MOMENT.
I WONDER WHO I'LL GET ASSIGNED TO?
WHOEVER MINE IS . . .
. . . WILL HAVE THE *BEST* TRIP OF THEIR LIFE.
HEY, DUDE. YOU MUST BE THE SUBJECT WE WERE WAITING ON.
KIEREN, RIGHT? THAT'S WHAT YOUR BED SAYS. I'M PHOEBE.

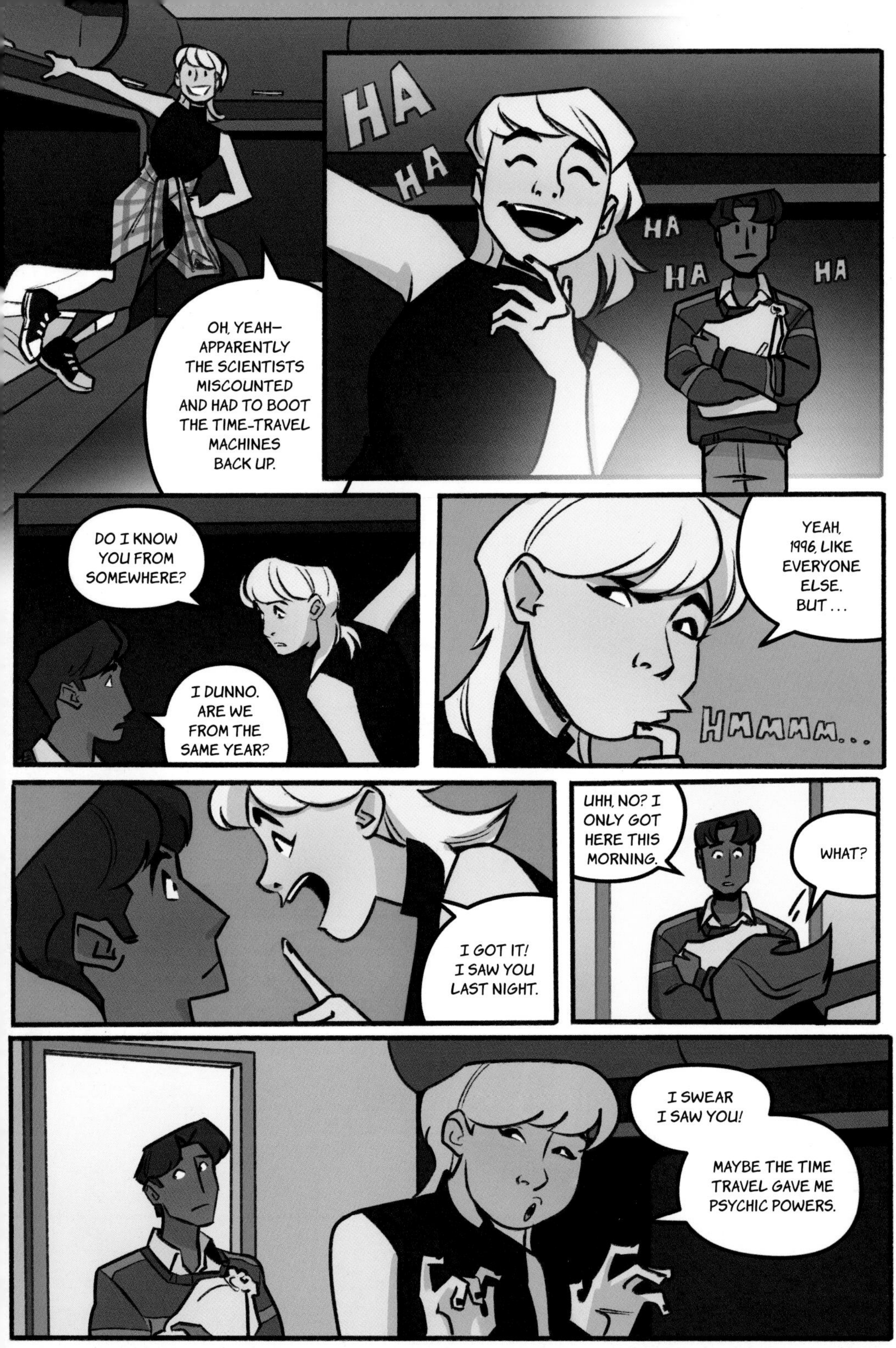

OH, YEAH— APPARENTLY THE SCIENTISTS MISCOUNTED AND HAD TO BOOT THE TIME-TRAVEL MACHINES BACK UP.
HA HA
HA HA HA
DO I KNOW YOU FROM SOMEWHERE?
I DUNNO. ARE WE FROM THE SAME YEAR?
YEAH, 1996, LIKE EVERYONE ELSE. BUT . . .
HMMMM. . .
I GOT IT! I SAW YOU LAST NIGHT.
UHH, NO? I ONLY GOT HERE THIS MORNING.
WHAT?
I SWEAR I SAW YOU!
MAYBE THE TIME TRAVEL GAVE ME PSYCHIC POWERS.

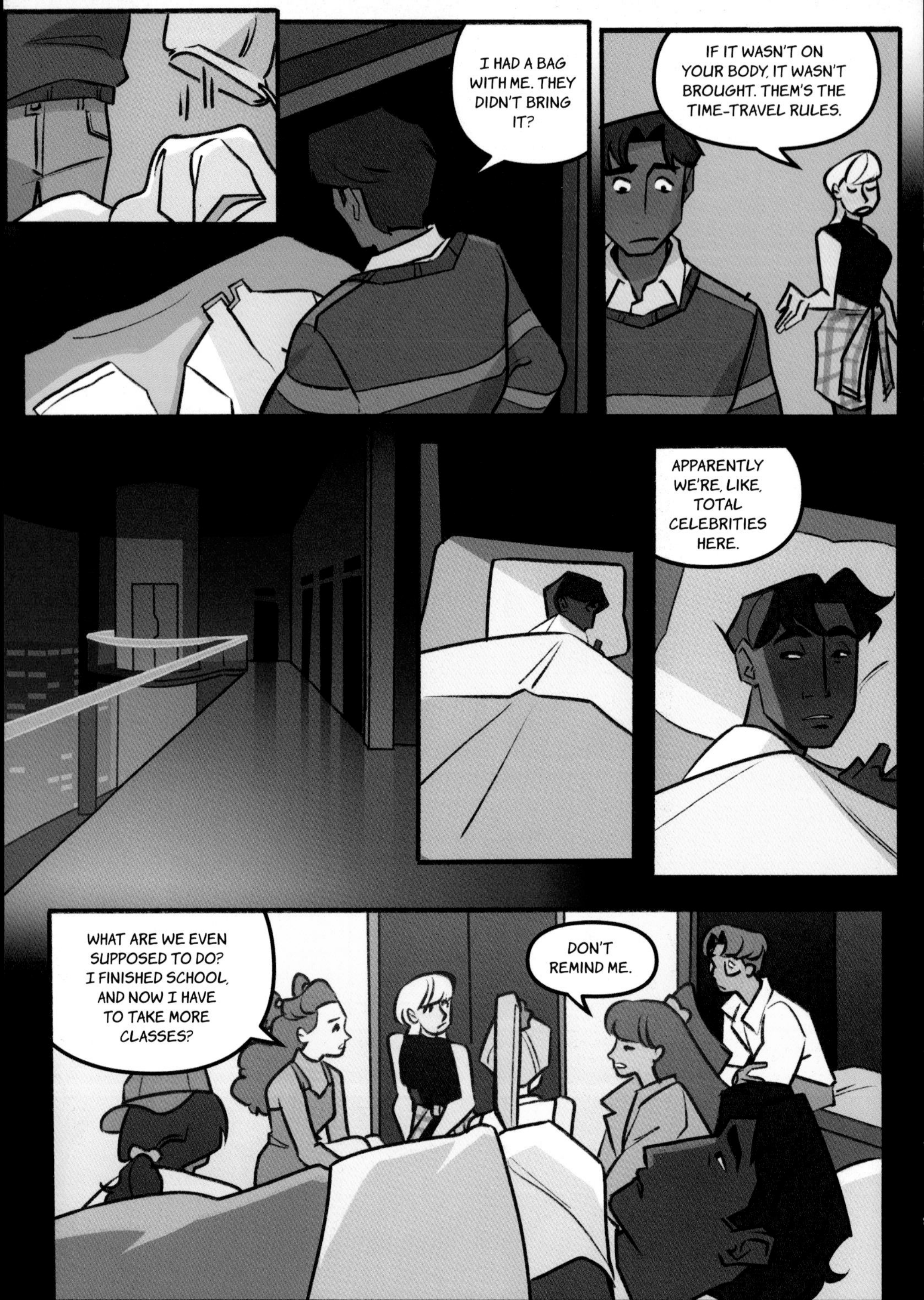
I HAD A BAG WITH ME. THEY DIDN'T BRING IT?
IF IT WASN'T ON YOUR BODY, IT WASN'T BROUGHT. THEM'S THE TIME-TRAVEL RULES.
APPARENTLY WE'RE, LIKE, TOTAL CELEBRITIES HERE.
WHAT ARE WE EVEN SUPPOSED TO DO? I FINISHED SCHOOL, AND NOW I HAVE TO TAKE MORE CLASSES?
DON'T REMIND ME.

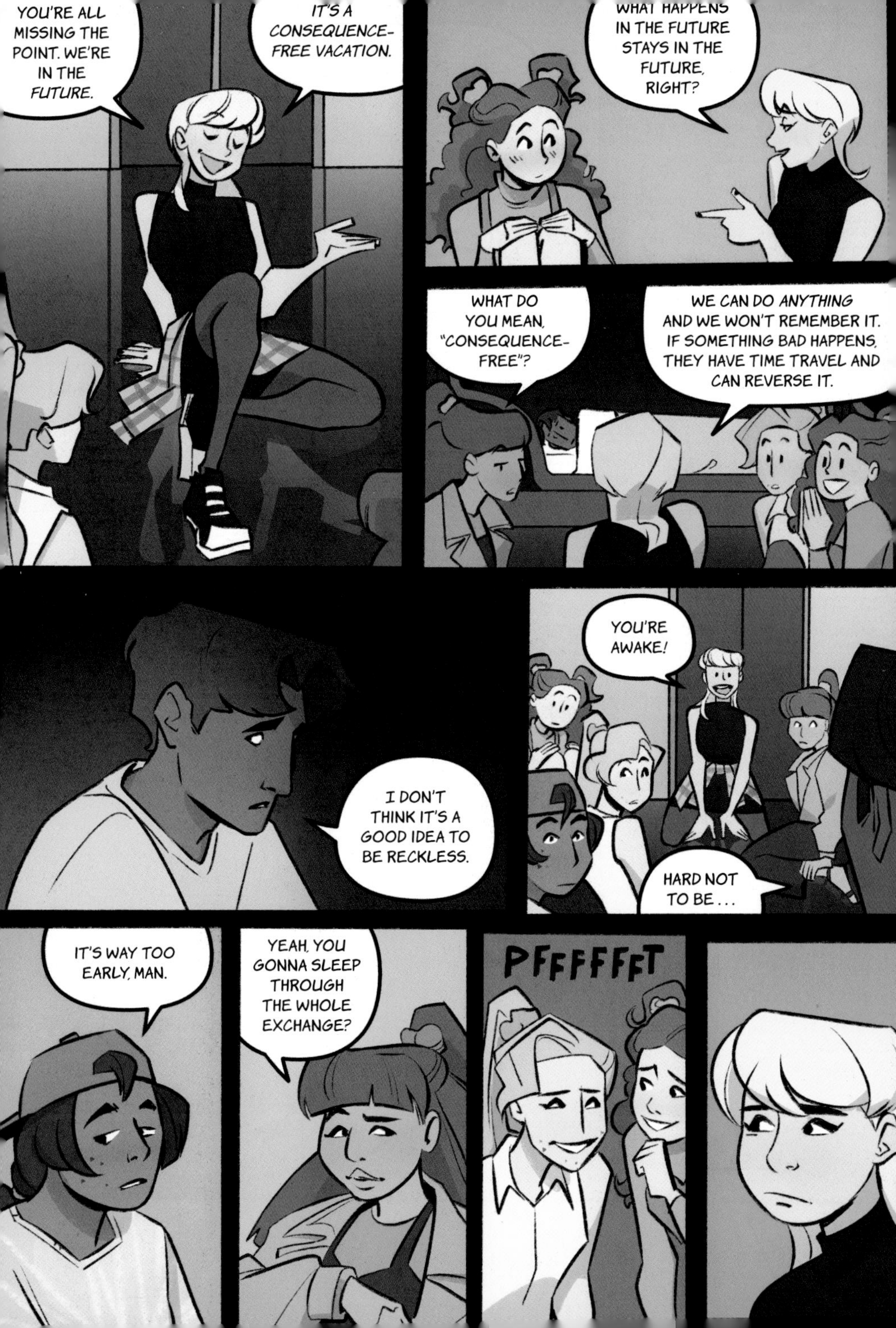
YOU'RE ALL MISSING THE POINT. WE'RE IN THE *FUTURE*.
IT'S A CONSEQUENCE-FREE VACATION.
WHAT HAPPENS IN THE FUTURE STAYS IN THE FUTURE, RIGHT?
WHAT DO YOU MEAN, "CONSEQUENCE-FREE"?
WE CAN DO *ANYTHING* AND WE WON'T REMEMBER IT. IF SOMETHING BAD HAPPENS, THEY HAVE TIME TRAVEL AND CAN REVERSE IT.
I DON'T THINK IT'S A GOOD IDEA TO BE RECKLESS.
YOU'RE AWAKE!
HARD NOT TO BE . . .
IT'S WAY TOO EARLY, MAN.
YEAH, YOU GONNA SLEEP THROUGH THE WHOLE EXCHANGE?
PFFFFFFT

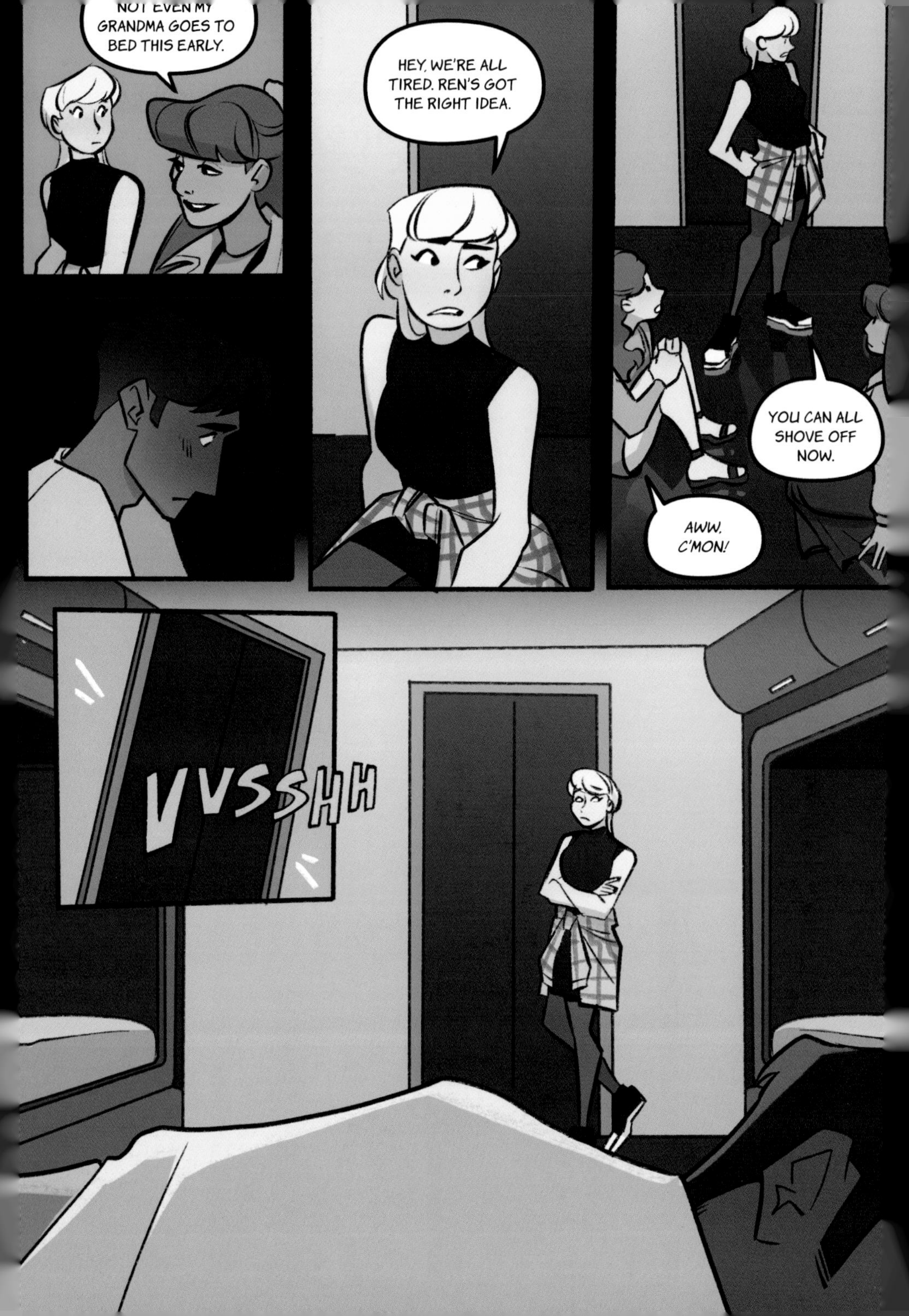
NOT EVEN MY GRANDMA GOES TO BED THIS EARLY.
HEY, WE'RE ALL TIRED. REN'S GOT THE RIGHT IDEA.
YOU CAN ALL SHOVE OFF NOW.
AWW. C'MON!
VVSSHH

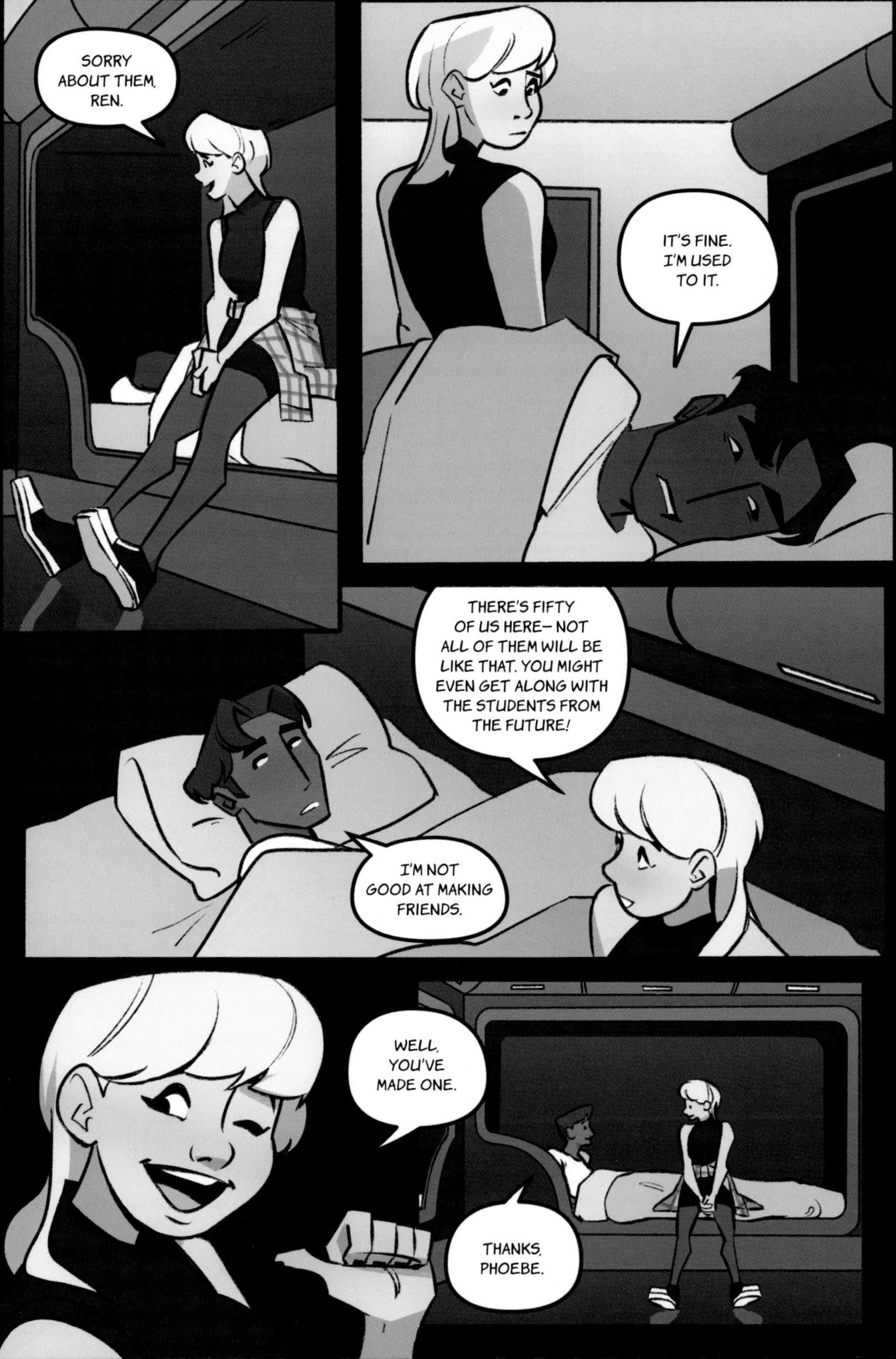
SORRY ABOUT THEM, REN.
IT'S FINE. I'M USED TO IT.
THERE'S FIFTY OF US HERE— NOT ALL OF THEM WILL BE LIKE THAT. YOU MIGHT EVEN GET ALONG WITH THE STUDENTS FROM THE FUTURE!
I'M NOT GOOD AT MAKING FRIENDS.
WELL, YOU'VE MADE ONE.
THANKS, PHOEBE.

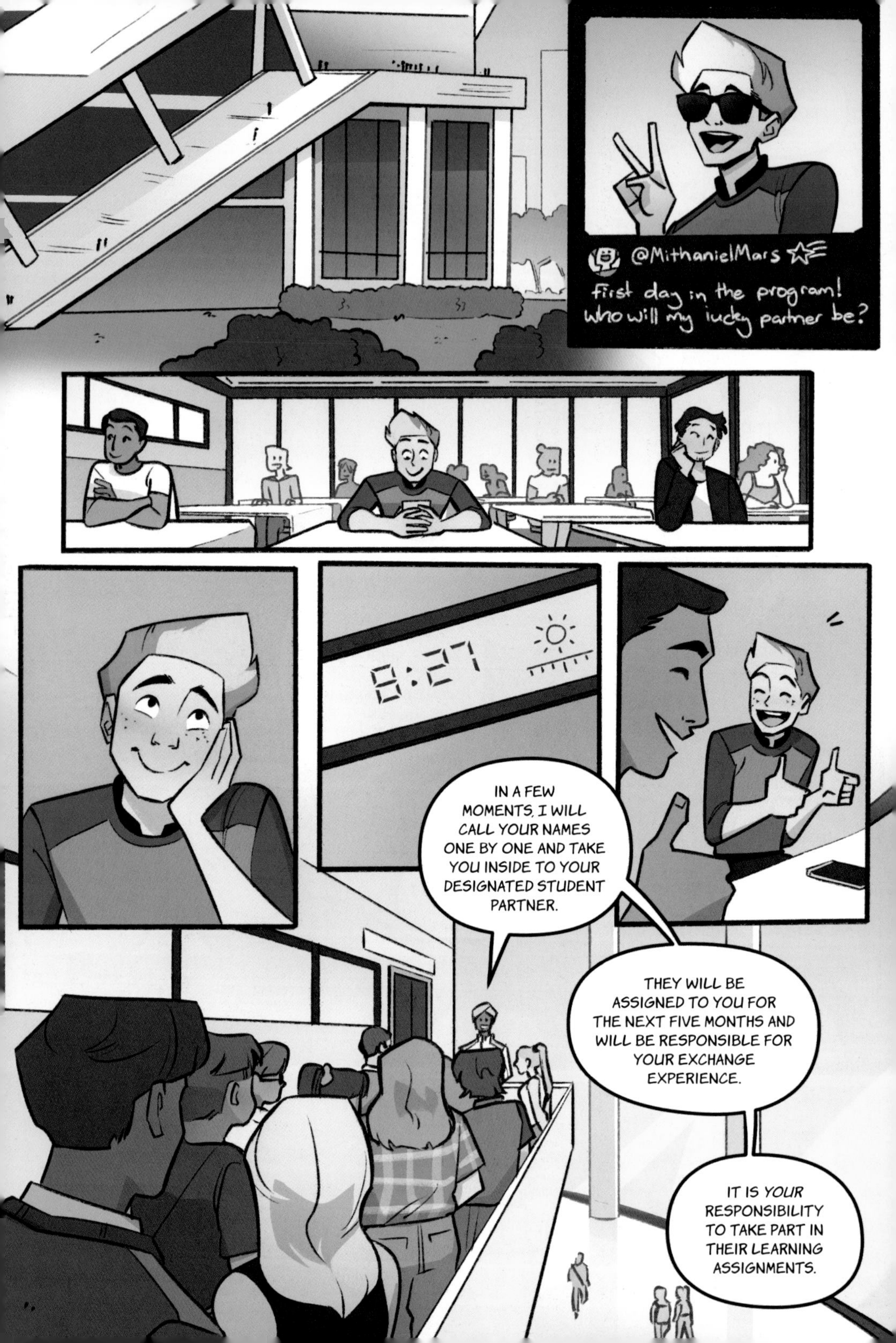
@MithanielMars
first day in the program! who will my lucky partner be?
8:27
IN A FEW MOMENTS, I WILL CALL YOUR NAMES ONE BY ONE AND TAKE YOU INSIDE TO YOUR DESIGNATED STUDENT PARTNER.
THEY WILL BE ASSIGNED TO YOU FOR THE NEXT FIVE MONTHS AND WILL BE RESPONSIBLE FOR YOUR EXCHANGE EXPERIENCE.
IT IS *YOUR* RESPONSIBILITY TO TAKE PART IN THEIR LEARNING ASSIGNMENTS.

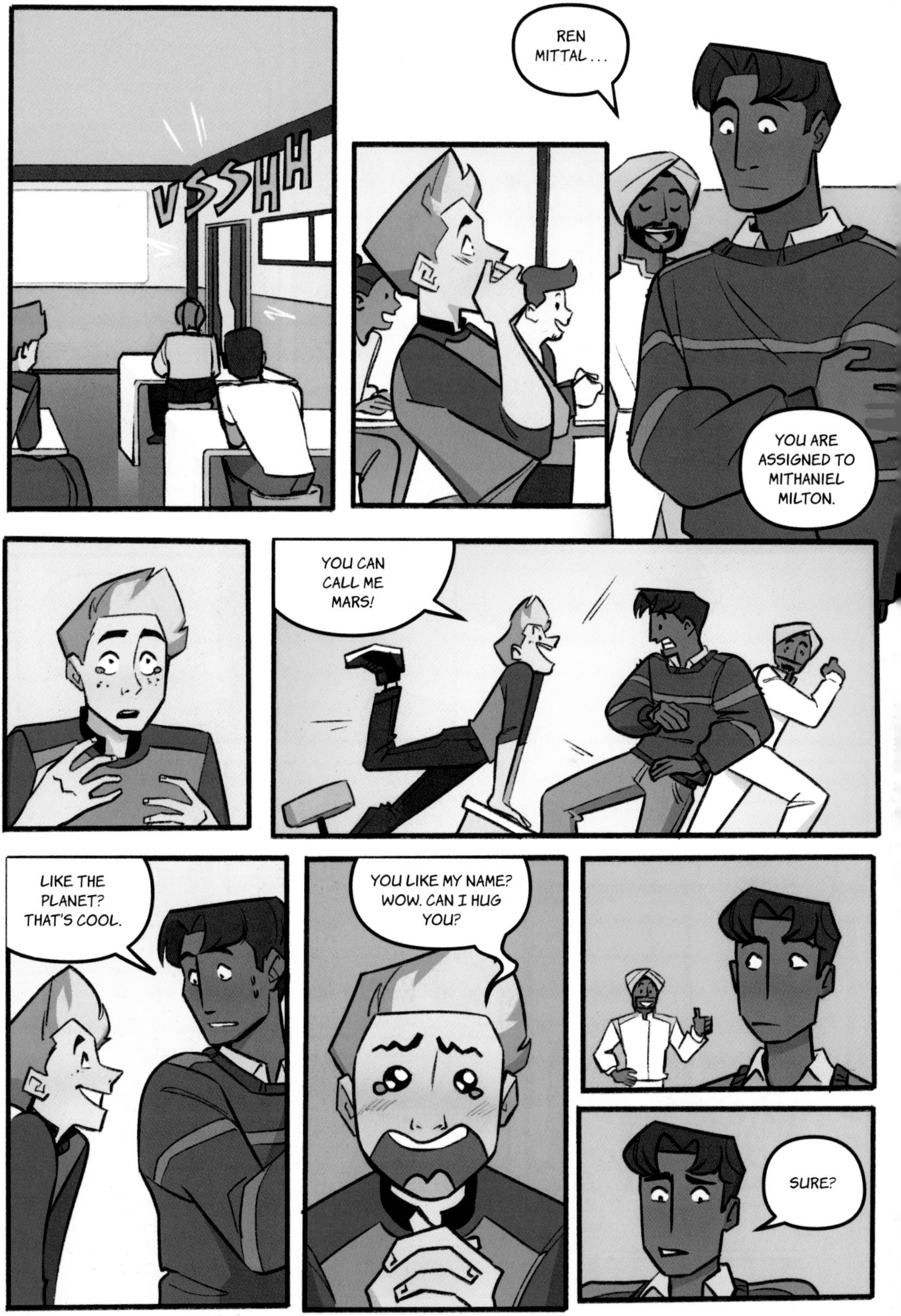
VSSHH
REN MITTAL . . .
YOU ARE ASSIGNED TO MITHANIEL MILTON.
YOU CAN CALL ME MARS!
LIKE THE PLANET? THAT'S COOL.
YOU LIKE MY NAME? WOW. CAN I HUG YOU?
SURE?

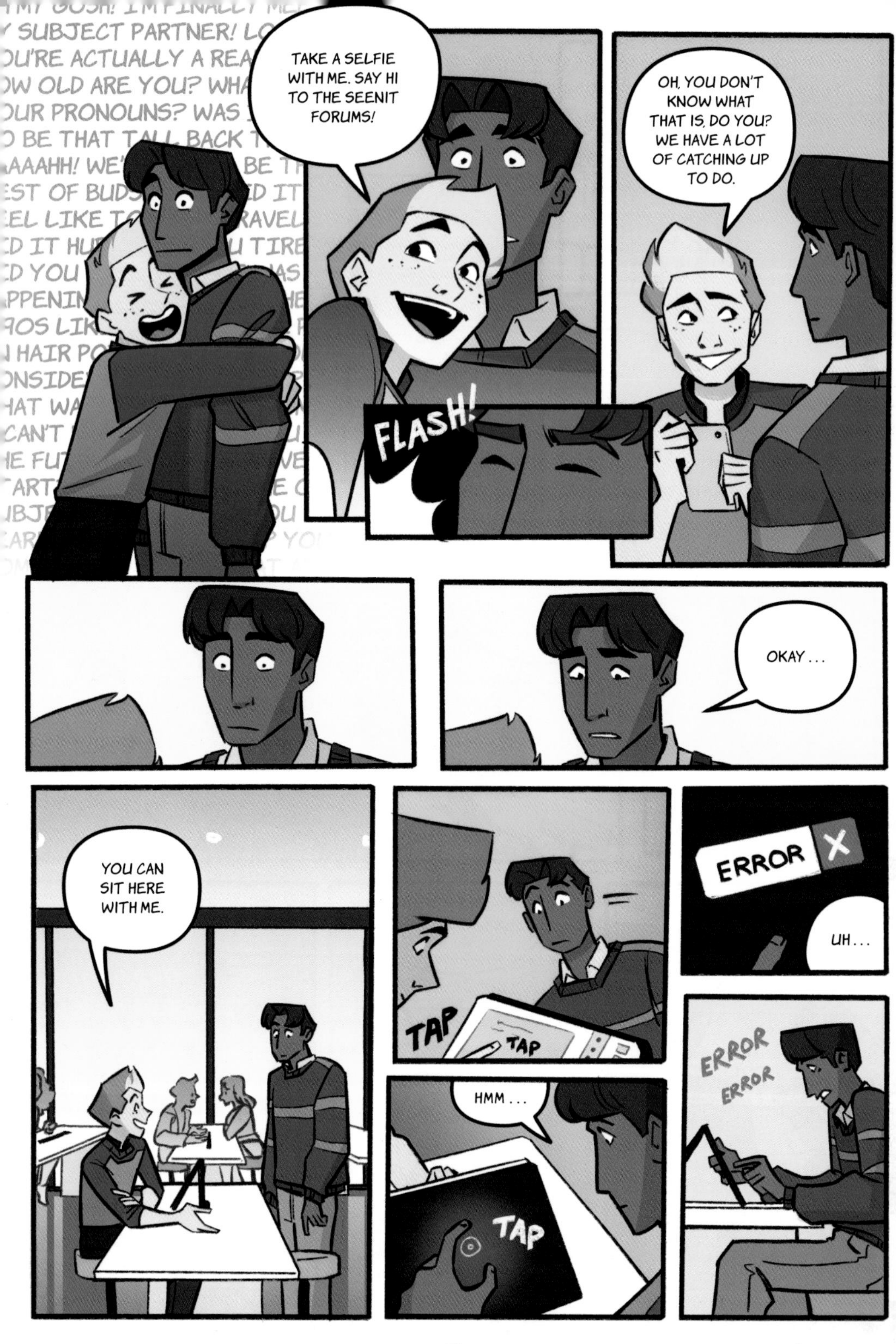
TAKE A SELFIE WITH ME. SAY HI TO THE SEENIT FORUMS!
FLASH!
OH, YOU DON'T KNOW WHAT THAT IS, DO YOU? WE HAVE A LOT OF CATCHING UP TO DO.
OKAY . . .
YOU CAN SIT HERE WITH ME.
TAP
TAP
ERROR
UH . . .
HMM . . .
TAP
ERROR
ERROR

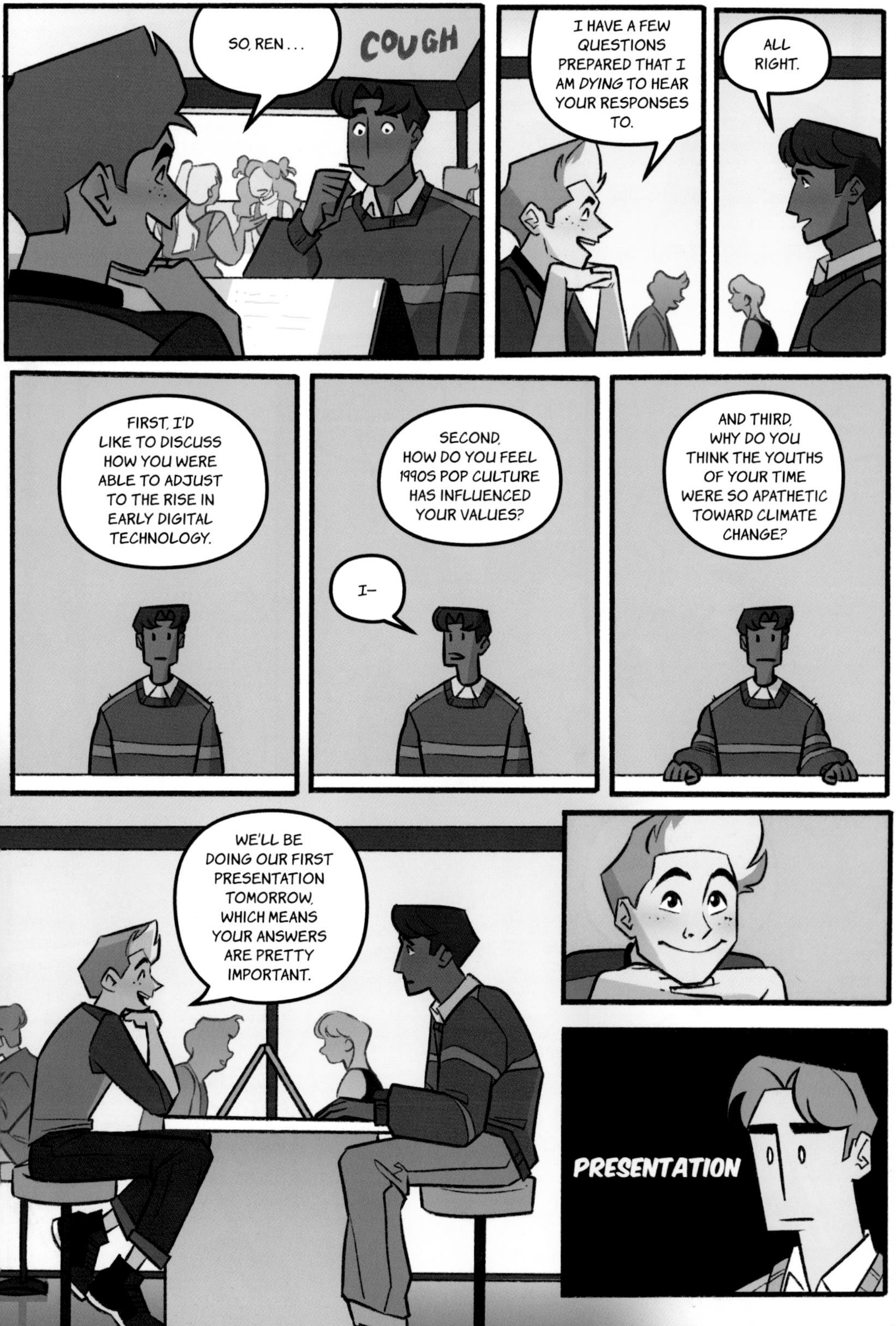
SO, REN . . .
COUGH
I HAVE A FEW QUESTIONS PREPARED THAT I AM *DYING* TO HEAR YOUR RESPONSES TO.
ALL RIGHT.
FIRST, I'D LIKE TO DISCUSS HOW YOU WERE ABLE TO ADJUST TO THE RISE IN EARLY DIGITAL TECHNOLOGY.
SECOND, HOW DO YOU FEEL 1990S POP CULTURE HAS INFLUENCED YOUR VALUES?
I—
AND THIRD, WHY DO YOU THINK THE YOUTHS OF YOUR TIME WERE SO APATHETIC TOWARD CLIMATE CHANGE?
WE'LL BE DOING OUR FIRST PRESENTATION TOMORROW, WHICH MEANS YOUR ANSWERS ARE PRETTY IMPORTANT.
PRESENTATION

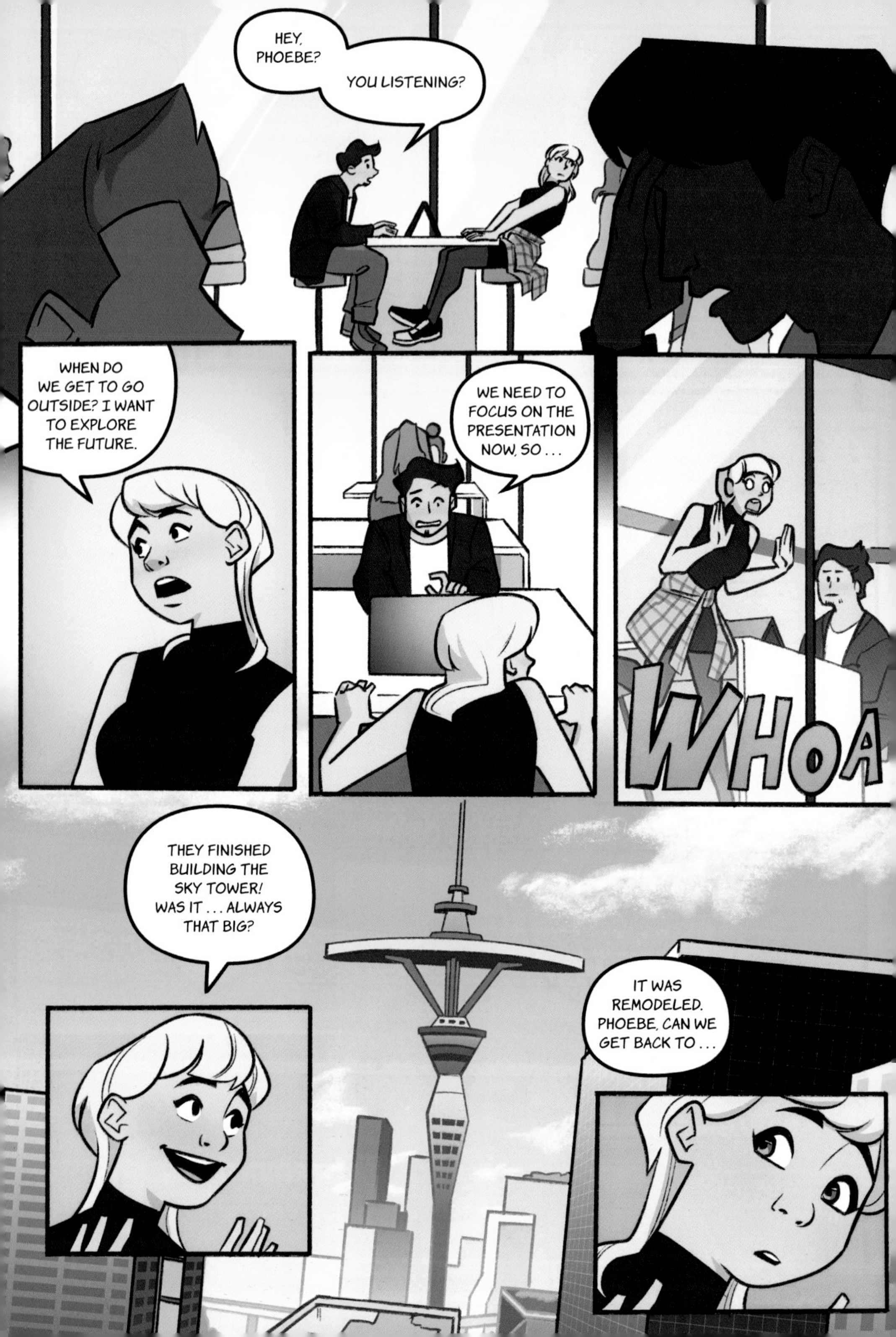
HEY, PHOEBE?
YOU LISTENING?
WHEN DO WE GET TO GO OUTSIDE? I WANT TO EXPLORE THE FUTURE.
WE NEED TO FOCUS ON THE PRESENTATION NOW, SO . . .
WHOA
THEY FINISHED BUILDING THE SKY TOWER! WAS IT . . . ALWAYS THAT BIG?
IT WAS REMODELED. PHOEBE, CAN WE GET BACK TO . . .

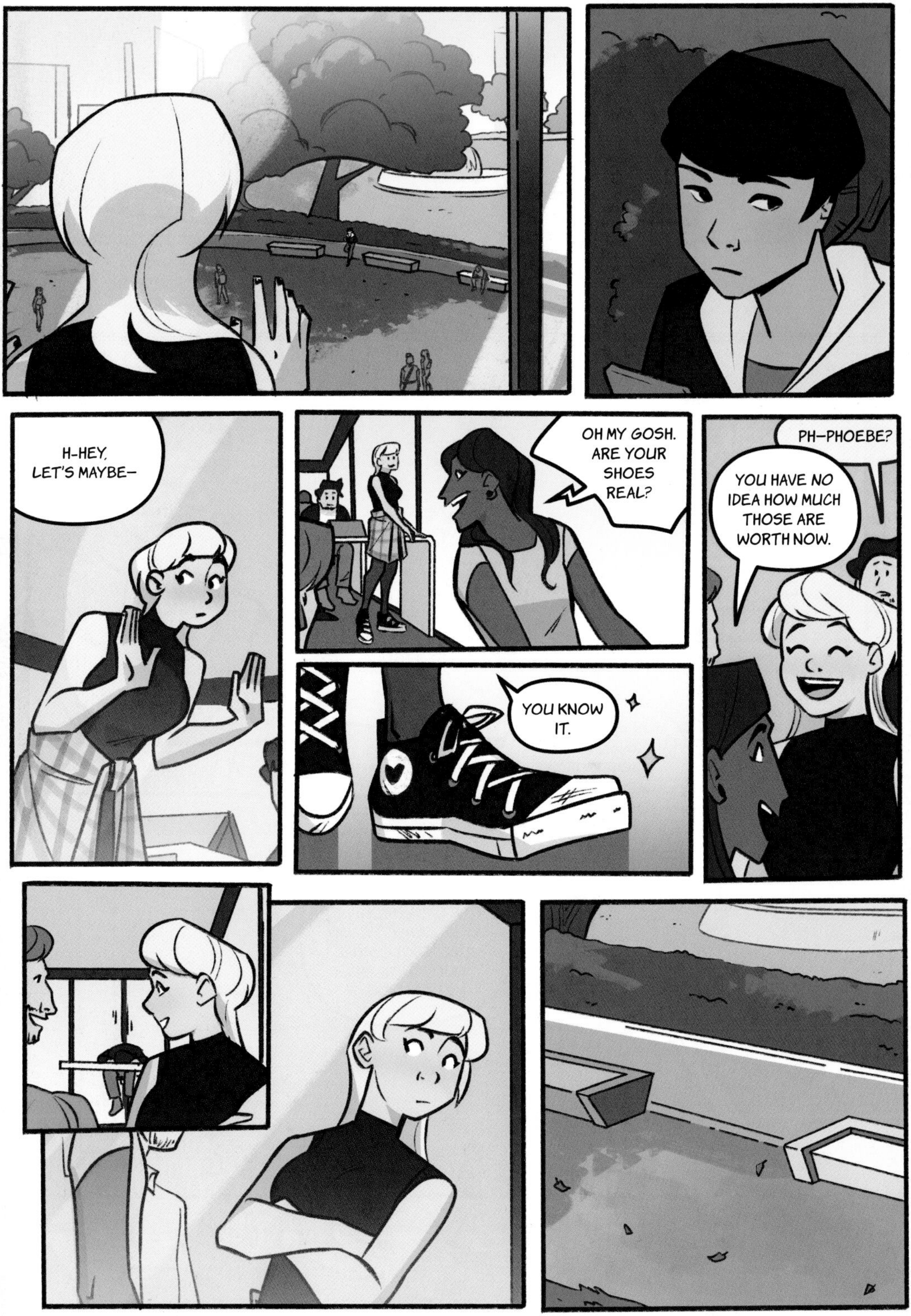
H-HEY, LET'S MAYBE–
OH MY GOSH. ARE YOUR SHOES REAL?
YOU KNOW IT.
PH–PHOEBE?
YOU HAVE NO IDEA HOW MUCH THOSE ARE WORTH NOW.

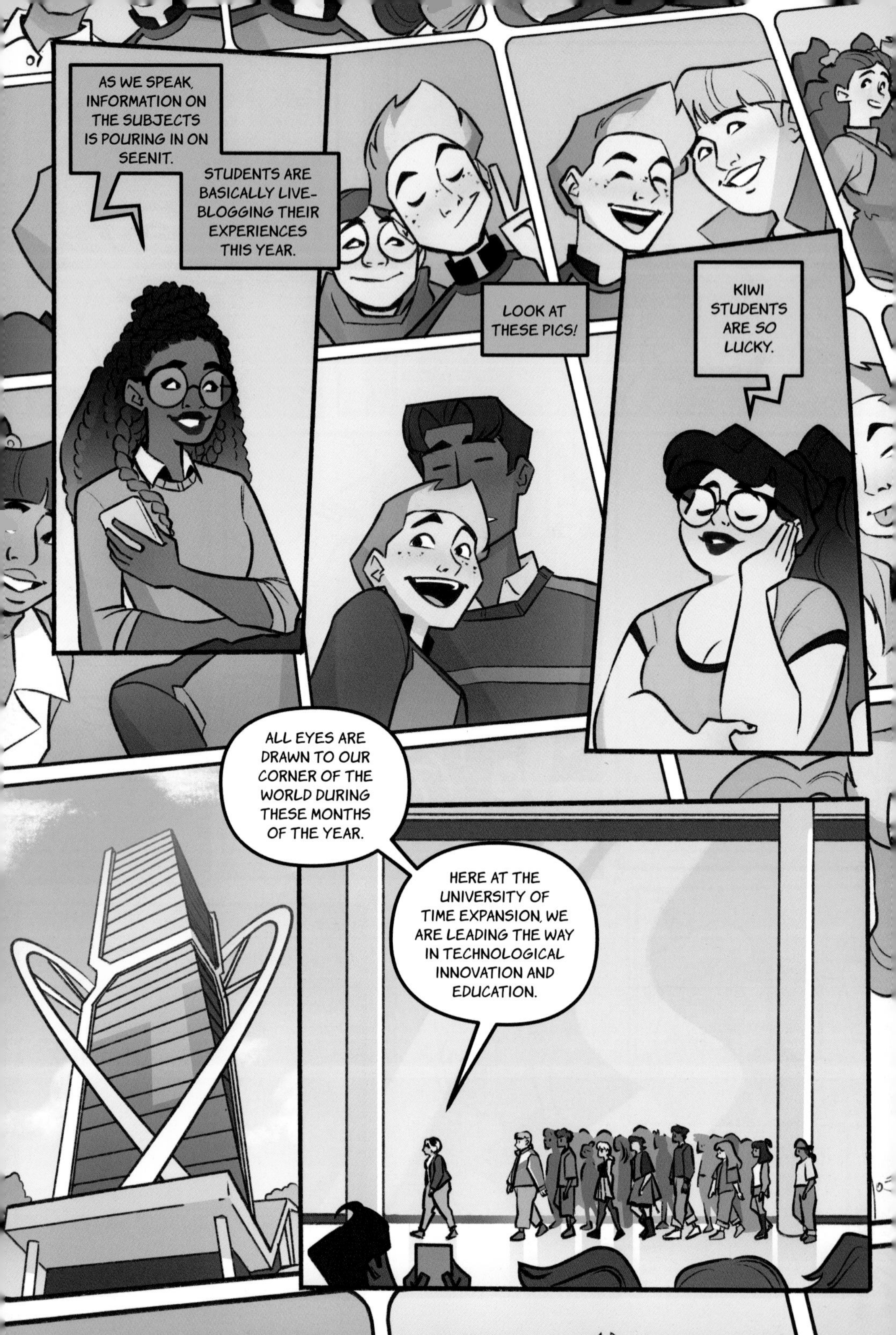
AS WE SPEAK, INFORMATION ON THE SUBJECTS IS POURING IN ON SEENIT.
STUDENTS ARE BASICALLY LIVE-BLOGGING THEIR EXPERIENCES THIS YEAR.
LOOK AT THESE PICS!
KIWI STUDENTS ARE SO LUCKY.
ALL EYES ARE DRAWN TO OUR CORNER OF THE WORLD DURING THESE MONTHS OF THE YEAR.
HERE AT THE UNIVERSITY OF TIME EXPANSION, WE ARE LEADING THE WAY IN TECHNOLOGICAL INNOVATION AND EDUCATION.

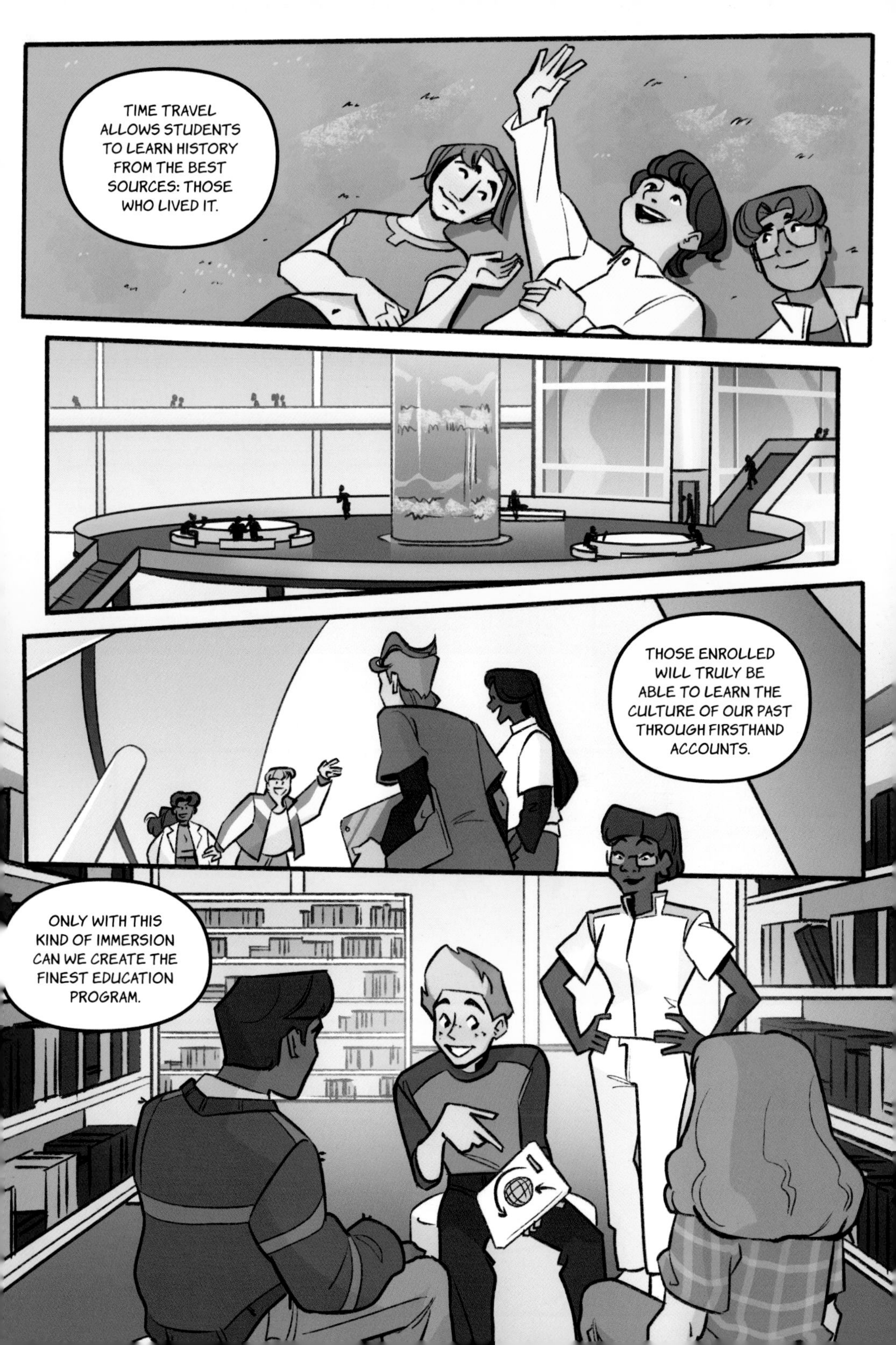
TIME TRAVEL ALLOWS STUDENTS TO LEARN HISTORY FROM THE BEST SOURCES: THOSE WHO LIVED IT.
THOSE ENROLLED WILL TRULY BE ABLE TO LEARN THE CULTURE OF OUR PAST THROUGH FIRSTHAND ACCOUNTS.
ONLY WITH THIS KIND OF IMMERSION CAN WE CREATE THE FINEST EDUCATION PROGRAM.

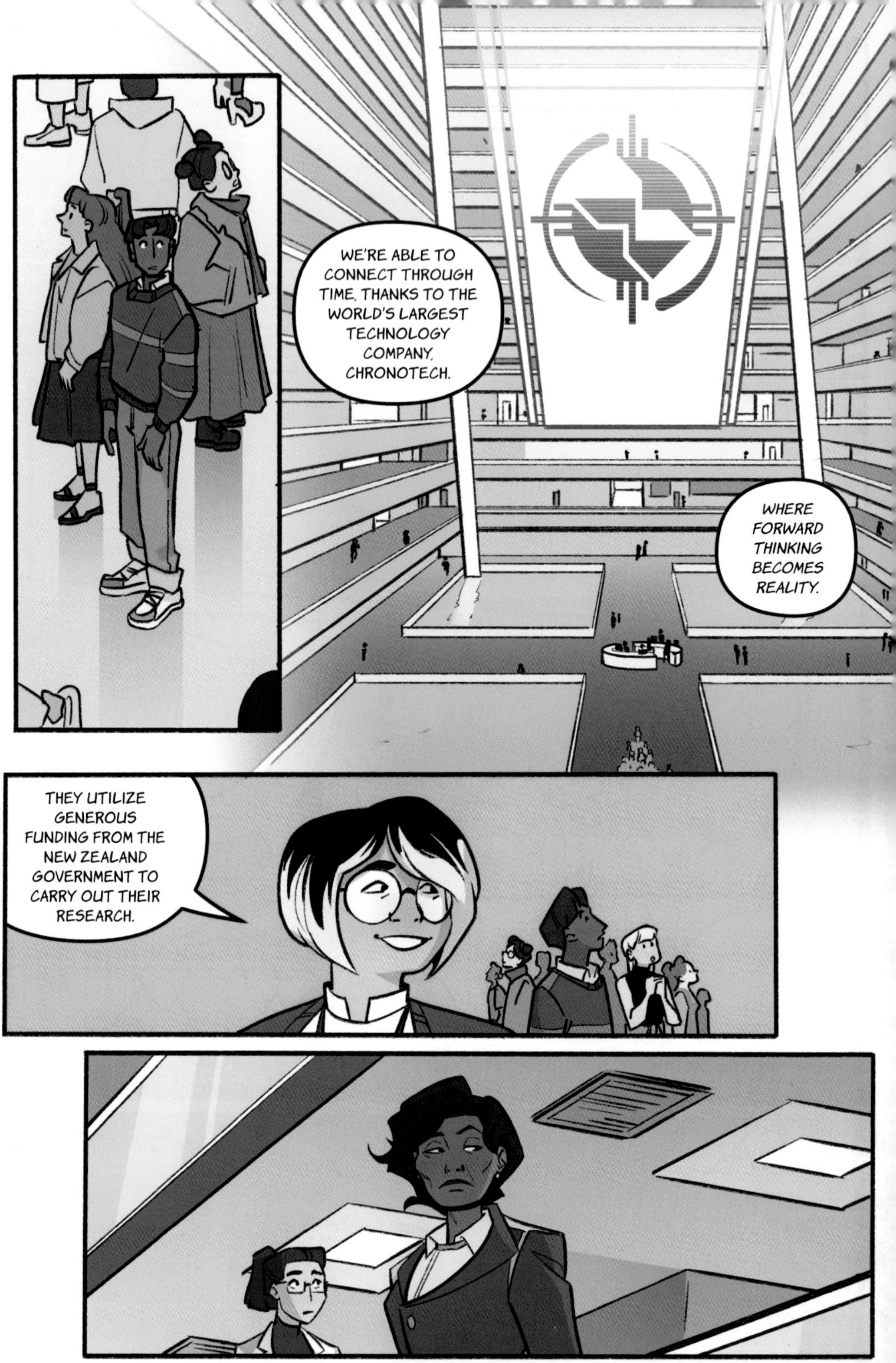
WE'RE ABLE TO CONNECT THROUGH TIME, THANKS TO THE WORLD'S LARGEST TECHNOLOGY COMPANY, CHRONOTECH.
WHERE FORWARD THINKING BECOMES REALITY.
THEY UTILIZE GENEROUS FUNDING FROM THE NEW ZEALAND GOVERNMENT TO CARRY OUT THEIR RESEARCH.

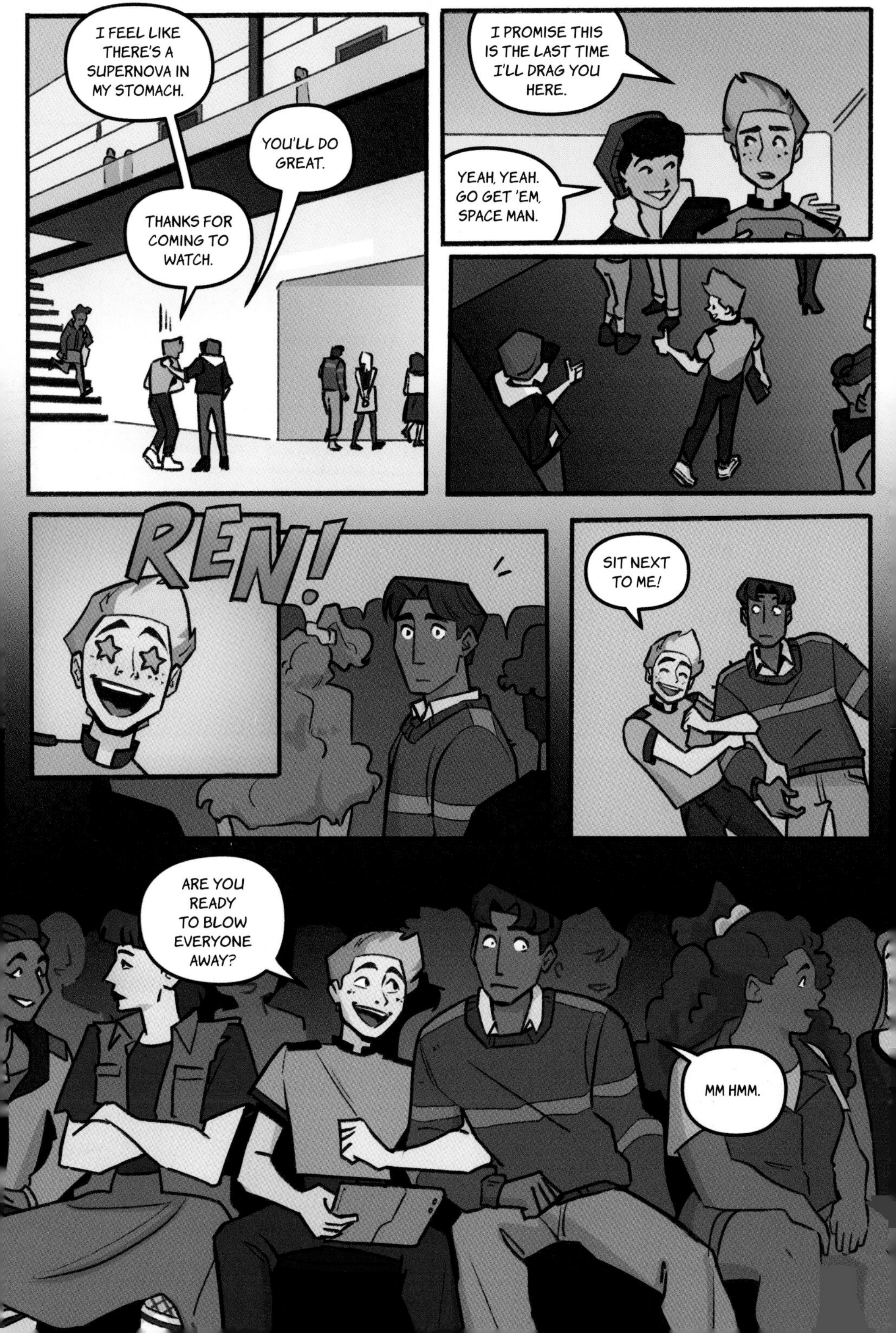

I FEEL LIKE THERE'S A SUPERNOVA IN MY STOMACH.
YOU'LL DO GREAT.
THANKS FOR COMING TO WATCH.
I PROMISE THIS IS THE LAST TIME I'LL DRAG YOU HERE.
YEAH, YEAH. GO GET 'EM, SPACE MAN.
REN!
SIT NEXT TO ME!
ARE YOU READY TO BLOW EVERYONE AWAY?
MM HMM.

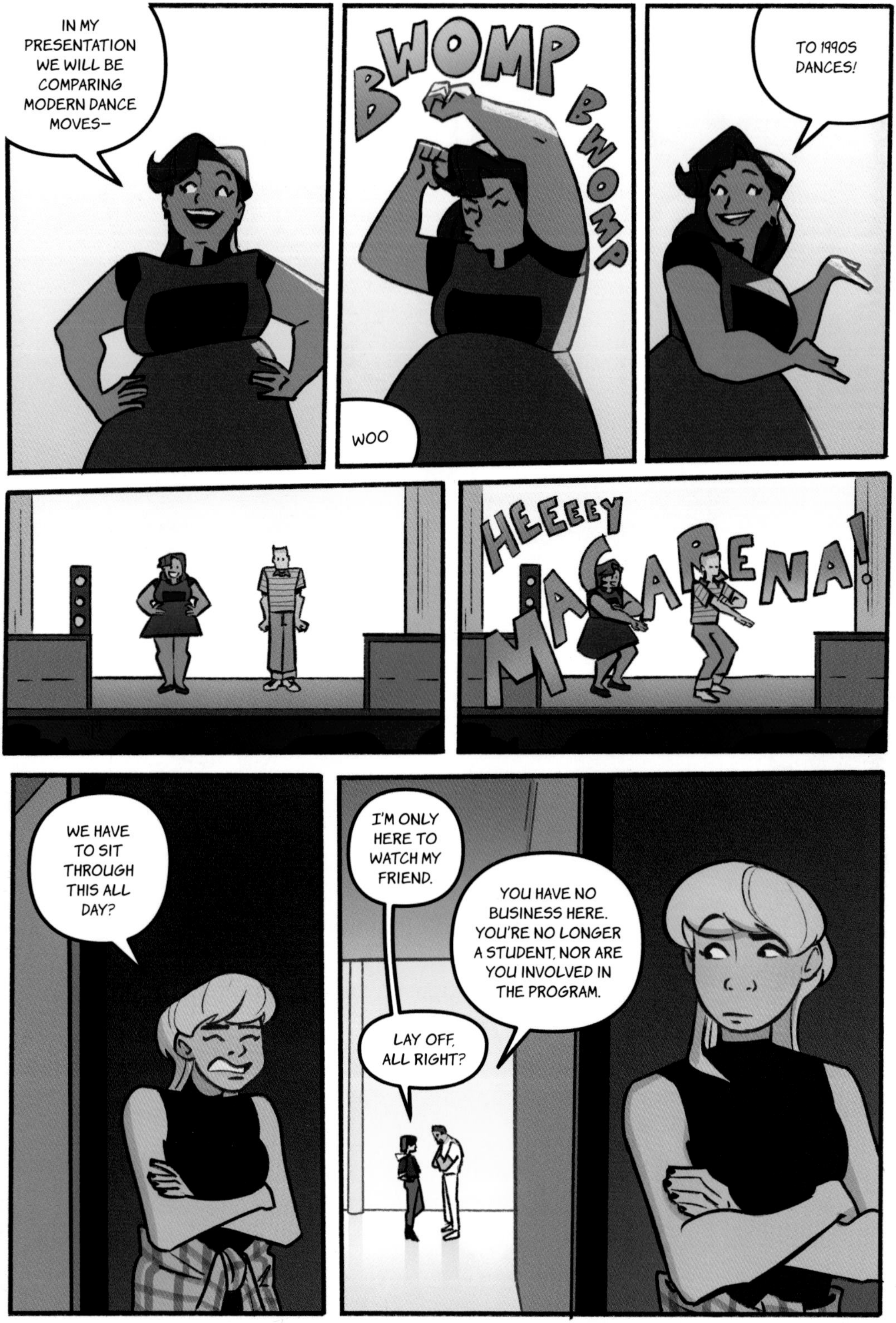
IN MY PRESENTATION WE WILL BE COMPARING MODERN DANCE MOVES—
BWOMP
BWOMP BWOMP
WOO
TO 1990S DANCES!
HEEEEY
MACARENA!
WE HAVE TO SIT THROUGH THIS ALL DAY?
I'M ONLY HERE TO WATCH MY FRIEND.
LAY OFF, ALL RIGHT?
YOU HAVE NO BUSINESS HERE. YOU'RE NO LONGER A STUDENT, NOR ARE YOU INVOLVED IN THE PROGRAM.

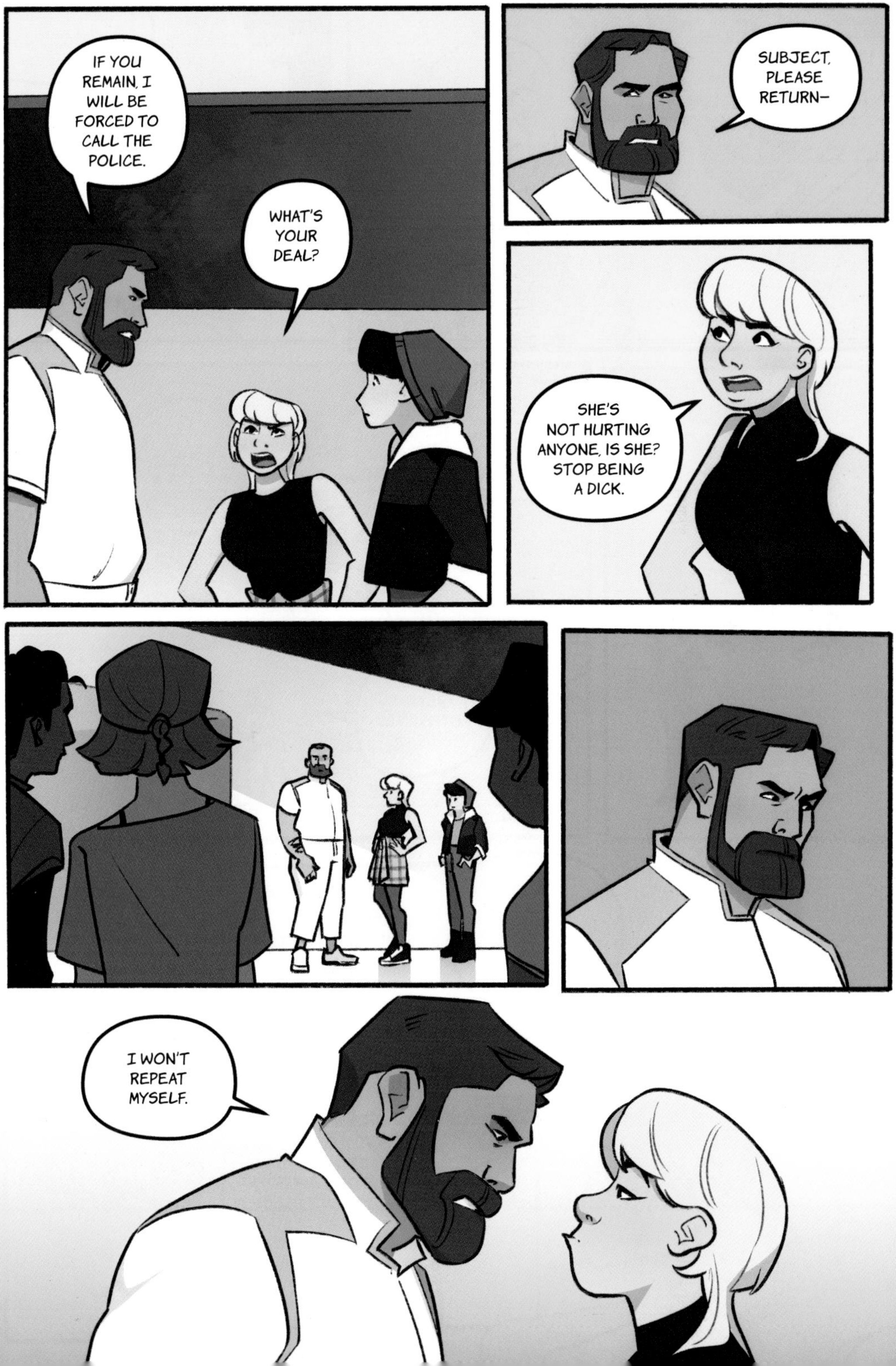
IF YOU REMAIN, I WILL BE FORCED TO CALL THE POLICE.
WHAT'S YOUR DEAL?
SUBJECT, PLEASE RETURN–
SHE'S NOT HURTING ANYONE, IS SHE? STOP BEING A DICK.
I WON'T REPEAT MYSELF.

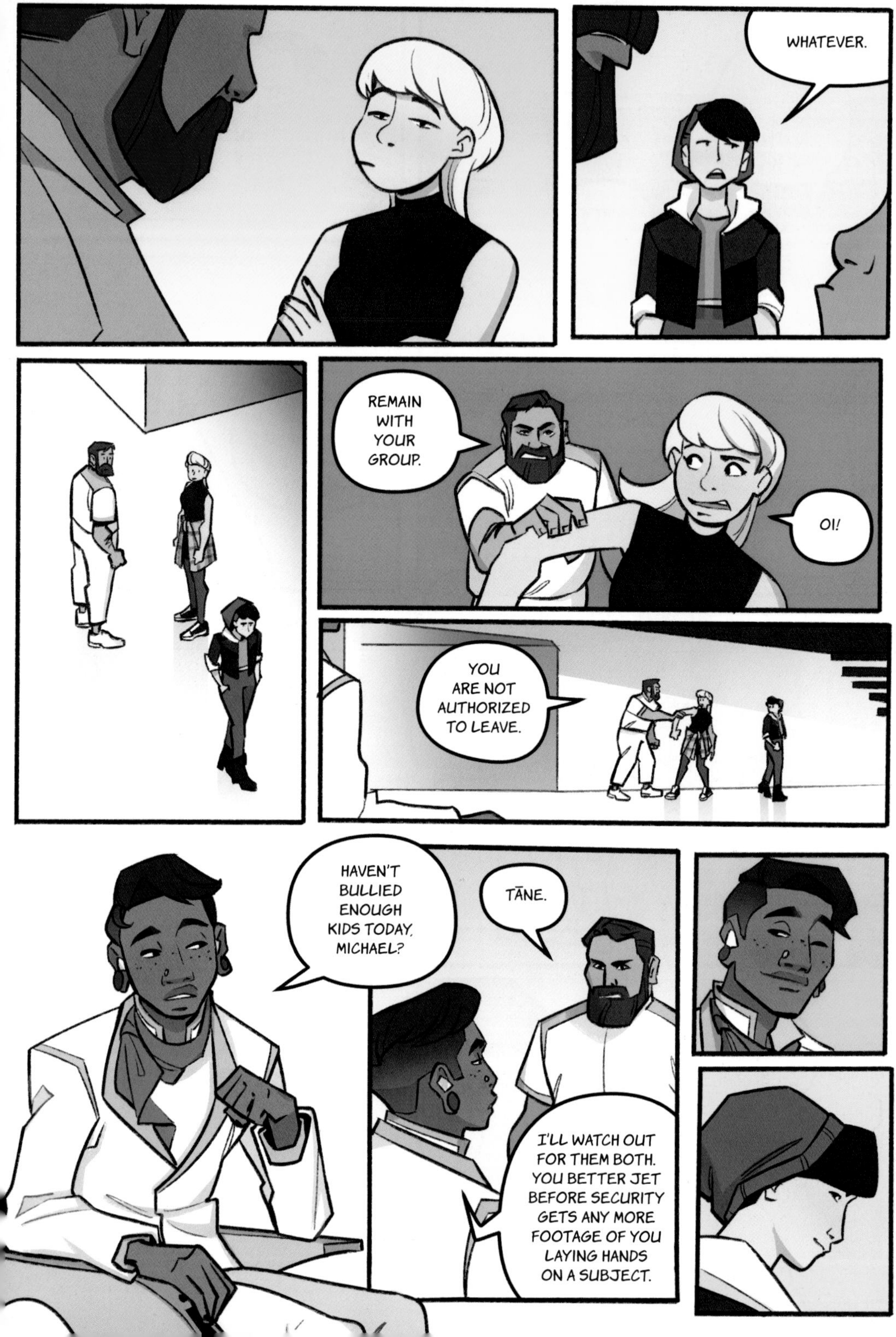
WHATEVER.
REMAIN WITH YOUR GROUP.
OI!
YOU ARE NOT AUTHORIZED TO LEAVE.
HAVEN'T BULLIED ENOUGH KIDS TODAY, MICHAEL?
TĀNE.
I'LL WATCH OUT FOR THEM BOTH. YOU BETTER JET BEFORE SECURITY GETS ANY MORE FOOTAGE OF YOU LAYING HANDS ON A SUBJECT.

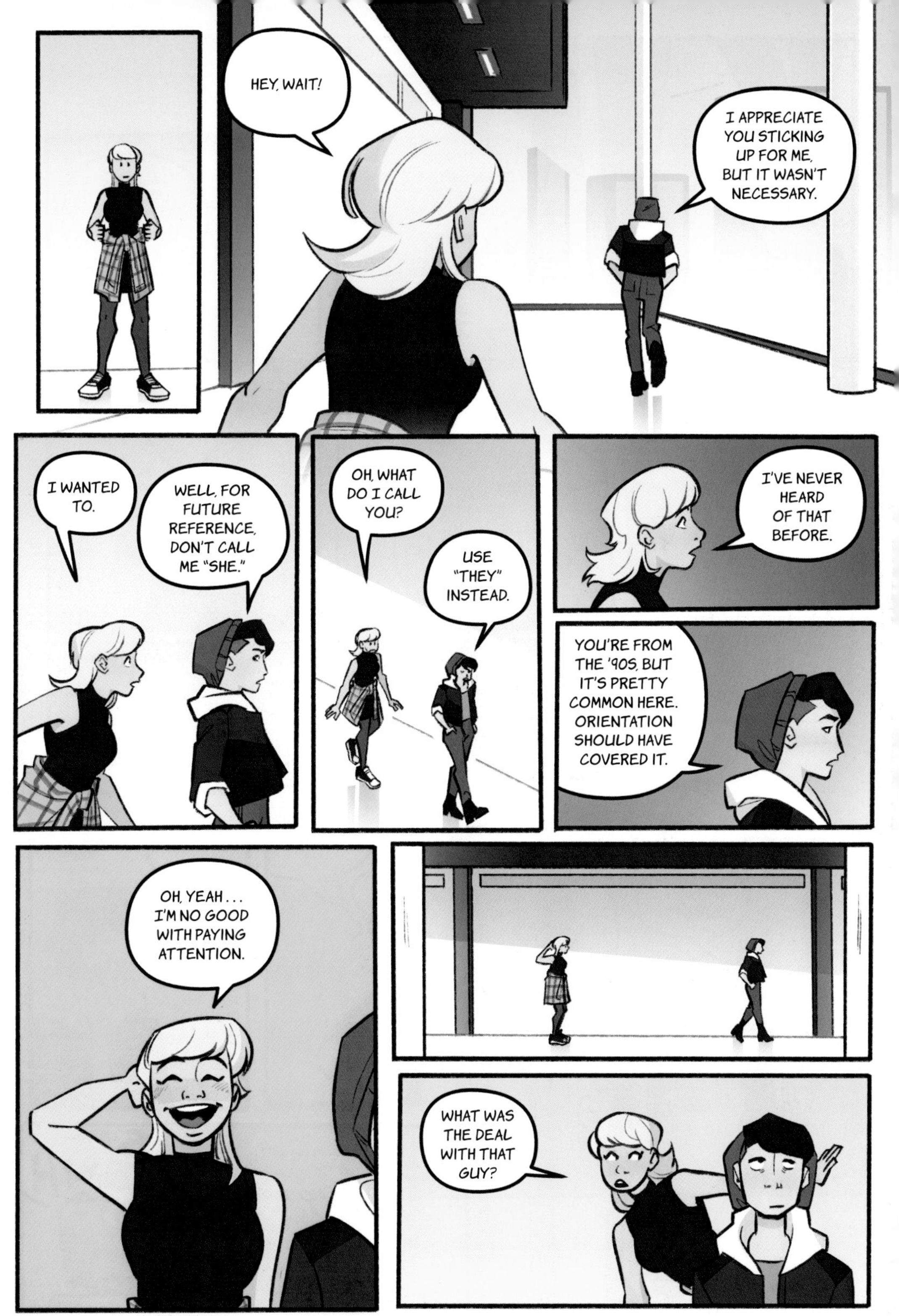
HEY, WAIT!
I APPRECIATE YOU STICKING UP FOR ME, BUT IT WASN'T NECESSARY.
I WANTED TO.
WELL, FOR FUTURE REFERENCE, DON'T CALL ME "SHE."
OH, WHAT DO I CALL YOU?
USE "THEY" INSTEAD.
I'VE NEVER HEARD OF THAT BEFORE.
YOU'RE FROM THE '90S, BUT IT'S PRETTY COMMON HERE. ORIENTATION SHOULD HAVE COVERED IT.
OH, YEAH . . . I'M NO GOOD WITH PAYING ATTENTION.
WHAT WAS THE DEAL WITH THAT GUY?

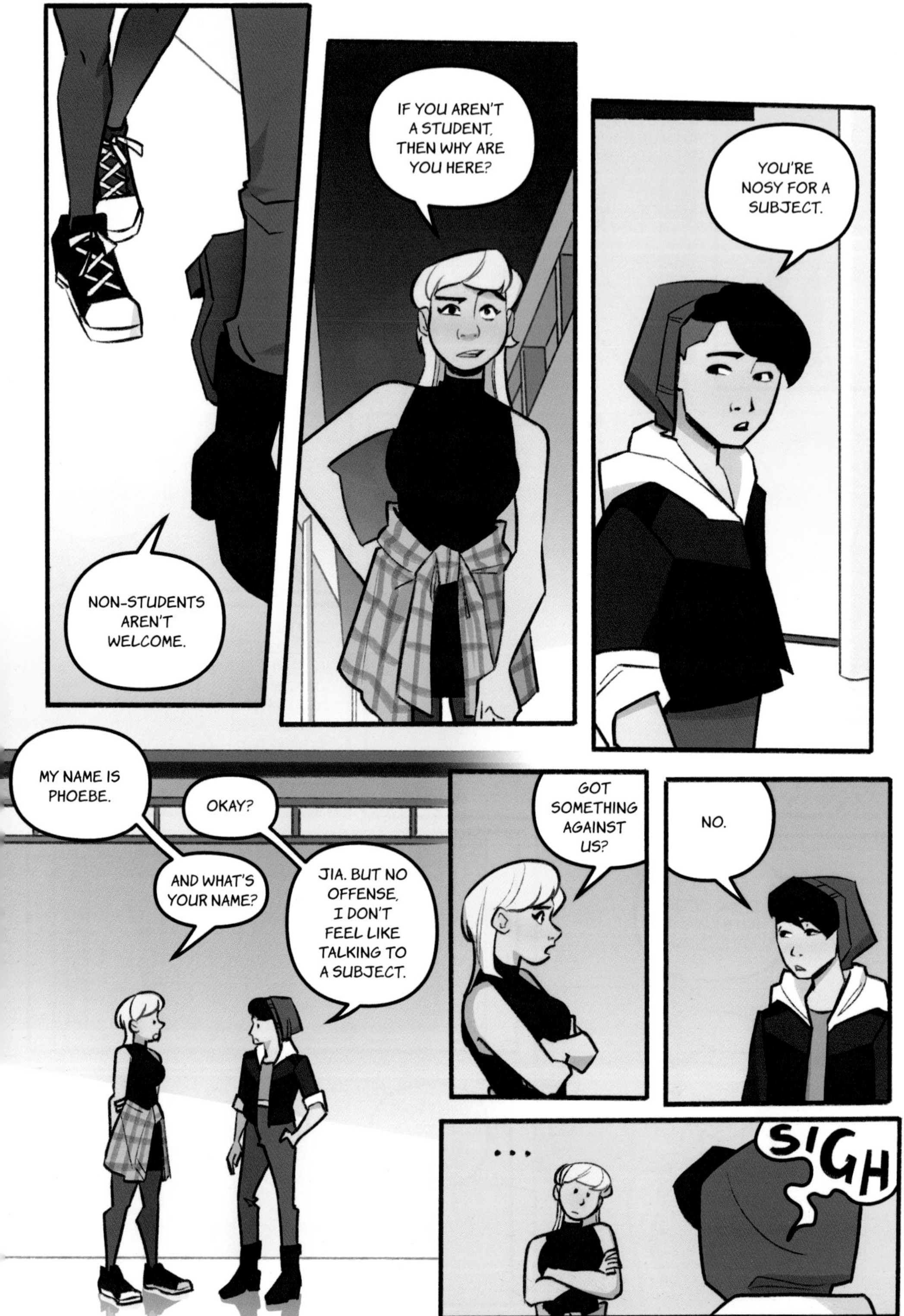
NON-STUDENTS AREN'T WELCOME.
IF YOU AREN'T A STUDENT, THEN WHY ARE YOU HERE?
YOU'RE NOSY FOR A SUBJECT.
MY NAME IS PHOEBE.
OKAY?
AND WHAT'S YOUR NAME?
JIA. BUT NO OFFENSE, I DON'T FEEL LIKE TALKING TO A SUBJECT.
GOT SOMETHING AGAINST US?
NO.
...
SIGH

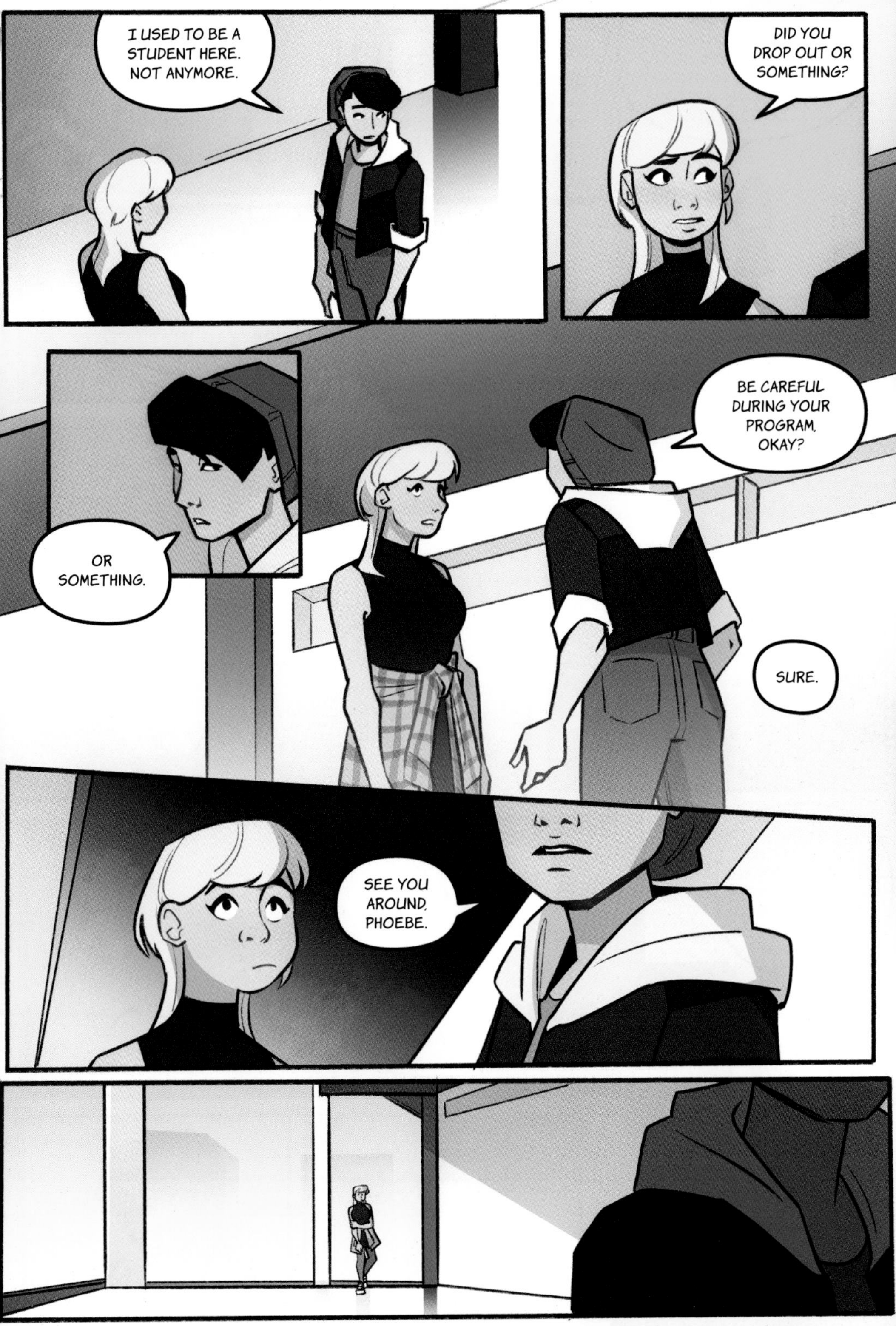
I USED TO BE A STUDENT HERE. NOT ANYMORE.
DID YOU DROP OUT OR SOMETHING?
OR SOMETHING.
BE CAREFUL DURING YOUR PROGRAM, OKAY?
SURE.
SEE YOU AROUND, PHOEBE.

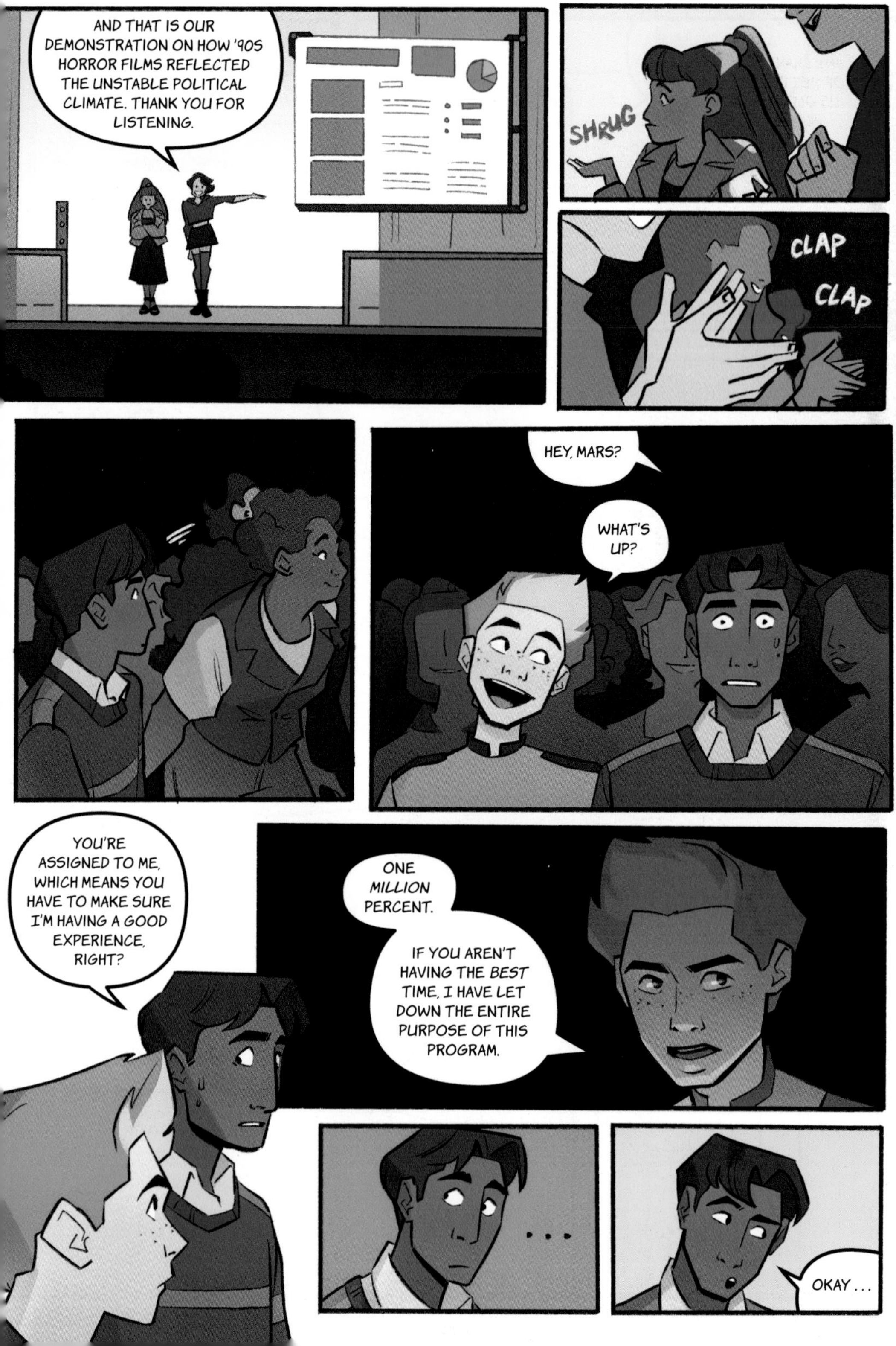
AND THAT IS OUR DEMONSTRATION ON HOW '90S HORROR FILMS REFLECTED THE UNSTABLE POLITICAL CLIMATE. THANK YOU FOR LISTENING.
SHRUG
CLAP
CLAP
HEY, MARS?
WHAT'S UP?
YOU'RE ASSIGNED TO ME, WHICH MEANS YOU HAVE TO MAKE SURE I'M HAVING A GOOD EXPERIENCE, RIGHT?
ONE *MILLION* PERCENT.
IF YOU AREN'T HAVING THE *BEST* TIME, I HAVE LET DOWN THE ENTIRE PURPOSE OF THIS PROGRAM.
. . .
OKAY . . .

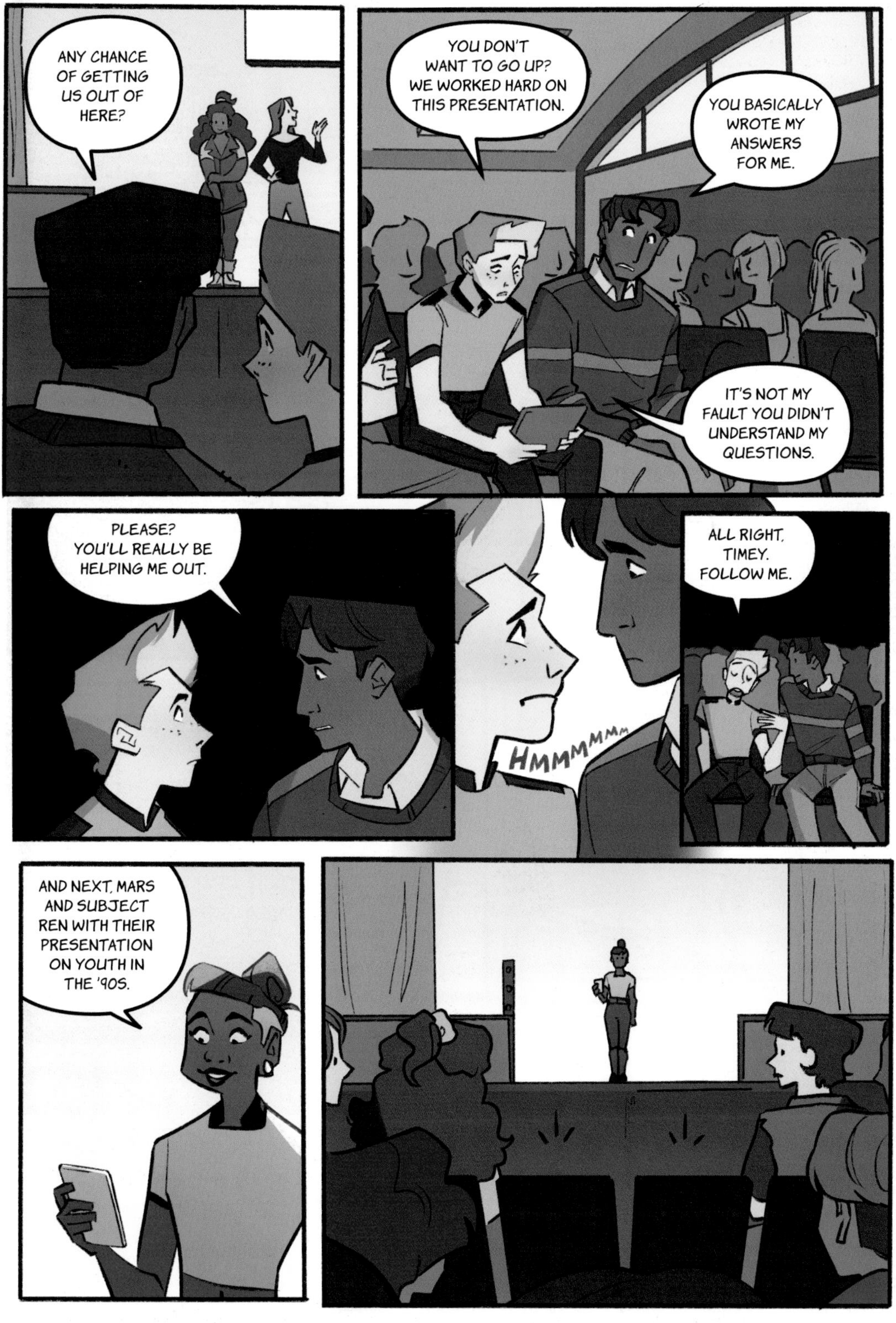
ANY CHANCE OF GETTING US OUT OF HERE?
YOU DON'T WANT TO GO UP? WE WORKED HARD ON THIS PRESENTATION.
YOU BASICALLY WROTE MY ANSWERS FOR ME.
IT'S NOT MY FAULT YOU DIDN'T UNDERSTAND MY QUESTIONS.
PLEASE? YOU'LL REALLY BE HELPING ME OUT.
HMMMMMM
ALL RIGHT, TIMEY. FOLLOW ME.
AND NEXT, MARS AND SUBJECT REN WITH THEIR PRESENTATION ON YOUTH IN THE '90S.

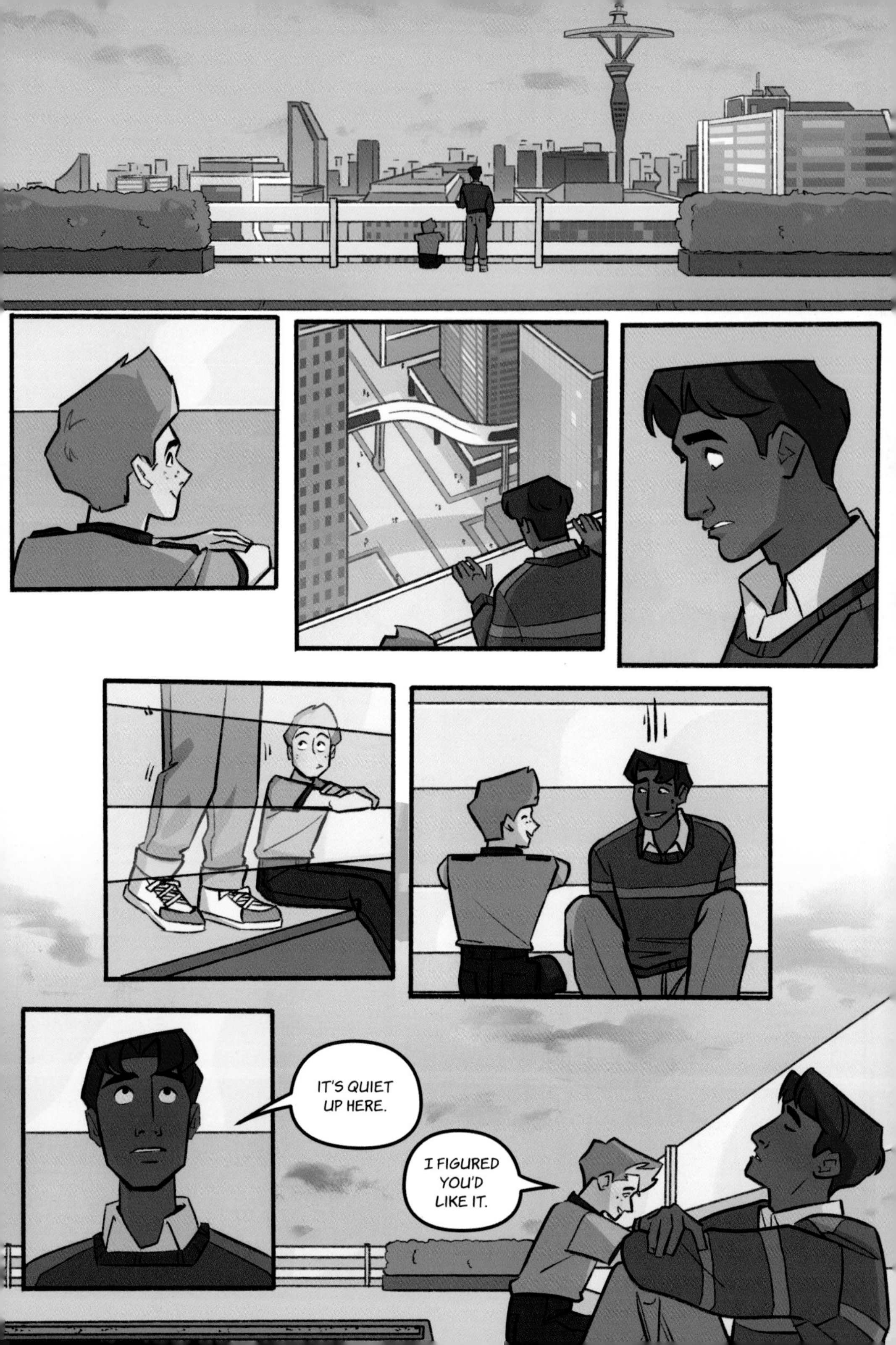
IT'S QUIET UP HERE.
I FIGURED YOU'D LIKE IT.

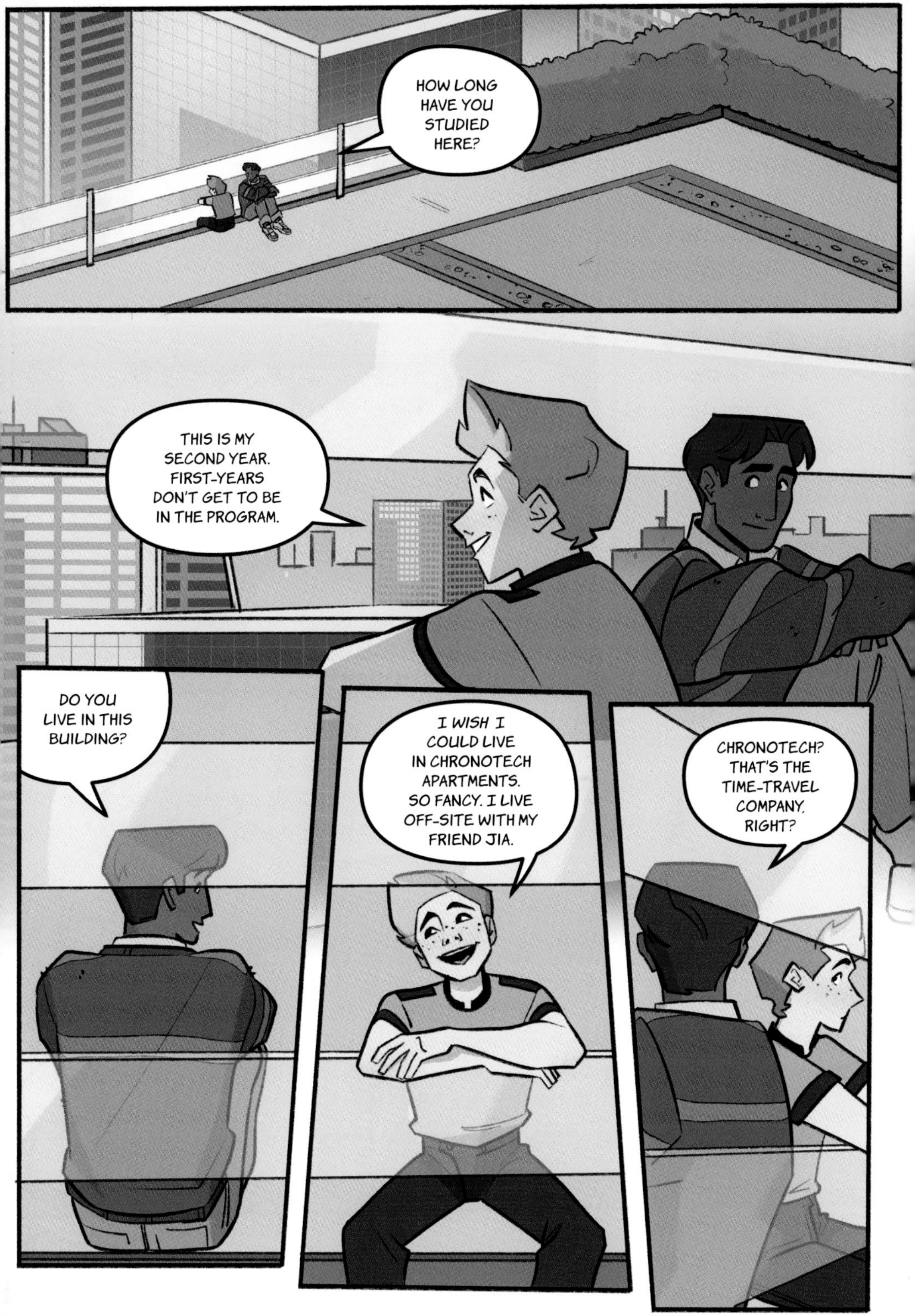
HOW LONG HAVE YOU STUDIED HERE?
THIS IS MY SECOND YEAR. FIRST-YEARS DON'T GET TO BE IN THE PROGRAM.
DO YOU LIVE IN THIS BUILDING?
I WISH I COULD LIVE IN CHRONOTECH APARTMENTS. SO FANCY. I LIVE OFF-SITE WITH MY FRIEND JIA.
CHRONOTECH? THAT'S THE TIME-TRAVEL COMPANY, RIGHT?

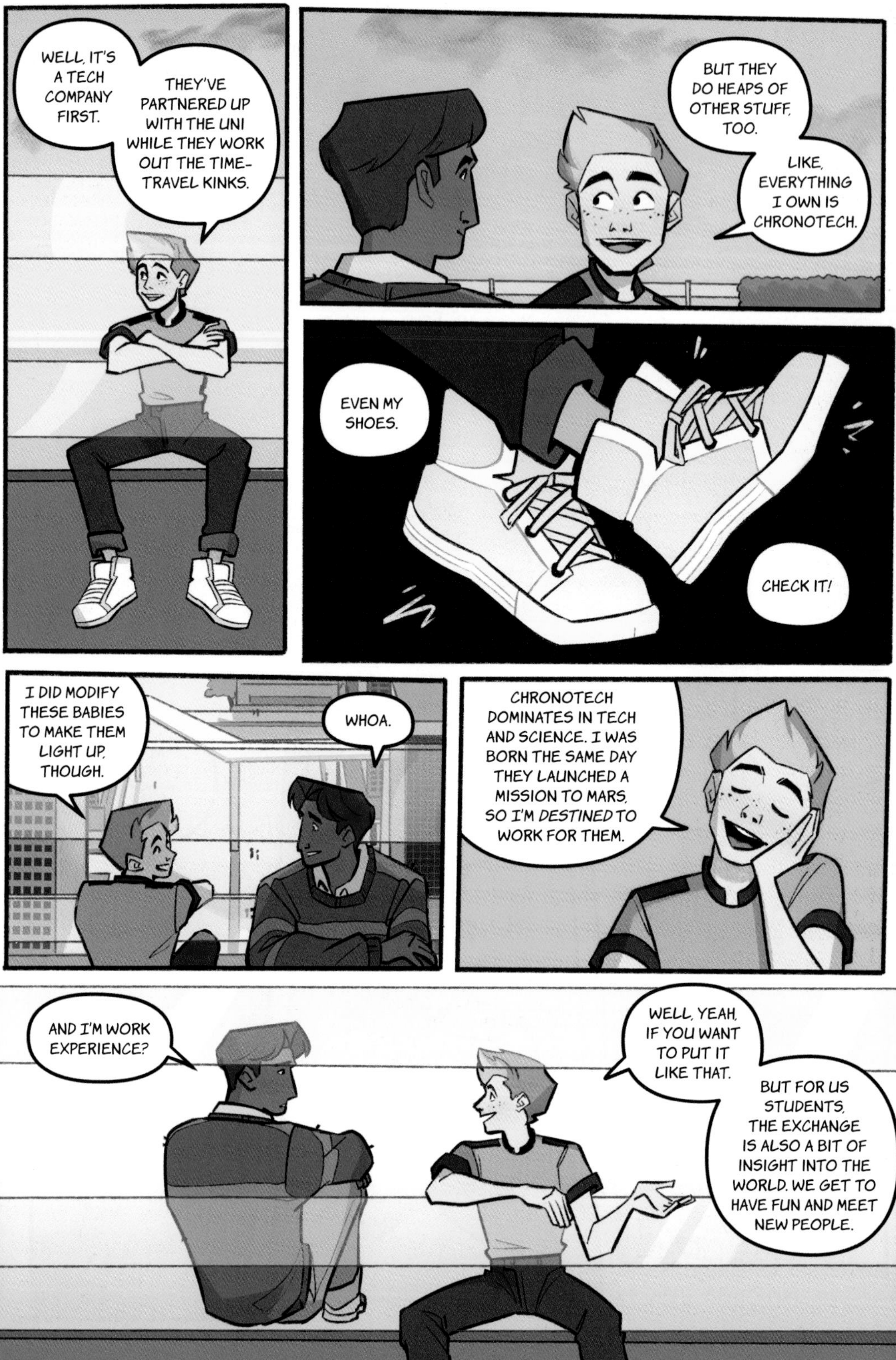
WELL, IT'S A TECH COMPANY FIRST.
THEY'VE PARTNERED UP WITH THE UNI WHILE THEY WORK OUT THE TIME-TRAVEL KINKS.
BUT THEY DO HEAPS OF OTHER STUFF, TOO.
LIKE, EVERYTHING I OWN IS CHRONOTECH.
EVEN MY SHOES.
CHECK IT!
I DID MODIFY THESE BABIES TO MAKE THEM LIGHT UP, THOUGH.
WHOA.
CHRONOTECH DOMINATES IN TECH AND SCIENCE. I WAS BORN THE SAME DAY THEY LAUNCHED A MISSION TO MARS, SO I'M *DESTINED* TO WORK FOR THEM.
AND I'M WORK EXPERIENCE?
WELL, YEAH, IF YOU WANT TO PUT IT LIKE THAT.
BUT FOR US STUDENTS, THE EXCHANGE IS ALSO A BIT OF INSIGHT INTO THE WORLD. WE GET TO HAVE FUN AND MEET NEW PEOPLE.

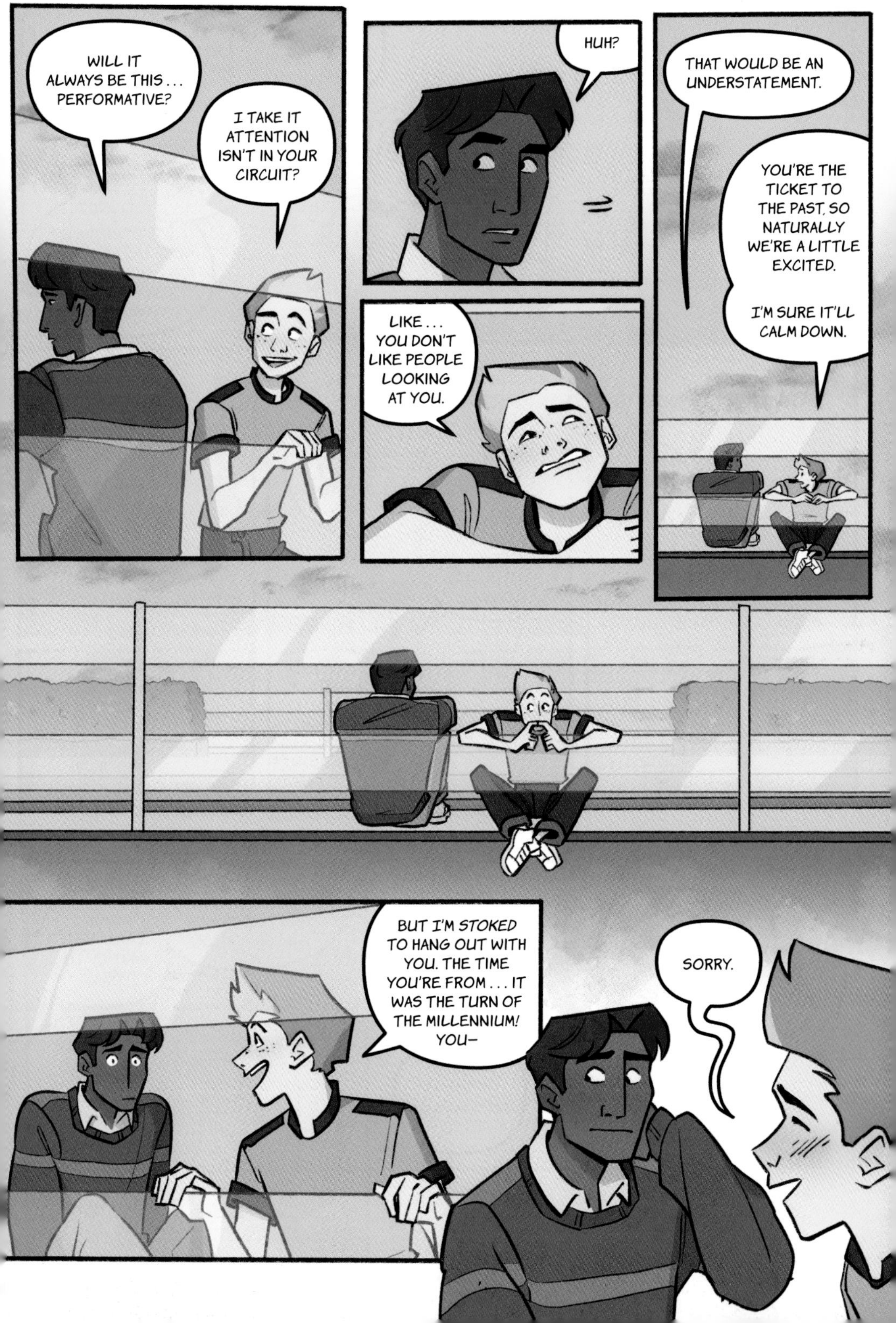
WILL IT ALWAYS BE THIS . . . PERFORMATIVE?
I TAKE IT ATTENTION ISN'T IN YOUR CIRCUIT?
HUH?
LIKE . . . YOU DON'T LIKE PEOPLE LOOKING AT YOU.
THAT WOULD BE AN UNDERSTATEMENT.
YOU'RE THE TICKET TO THE PAST, SO NATURALLY WE'RE A LITTLE EXCITED.
I'M SURE IT'LL CALM DOWN.
BUT I'M *STOKED* TO HANG OUT WITH YOU. THE TIME YOU'RE FROM . . . IT WAS THE TURN OF THE MILLENNIUM! YOU—
SORRY.

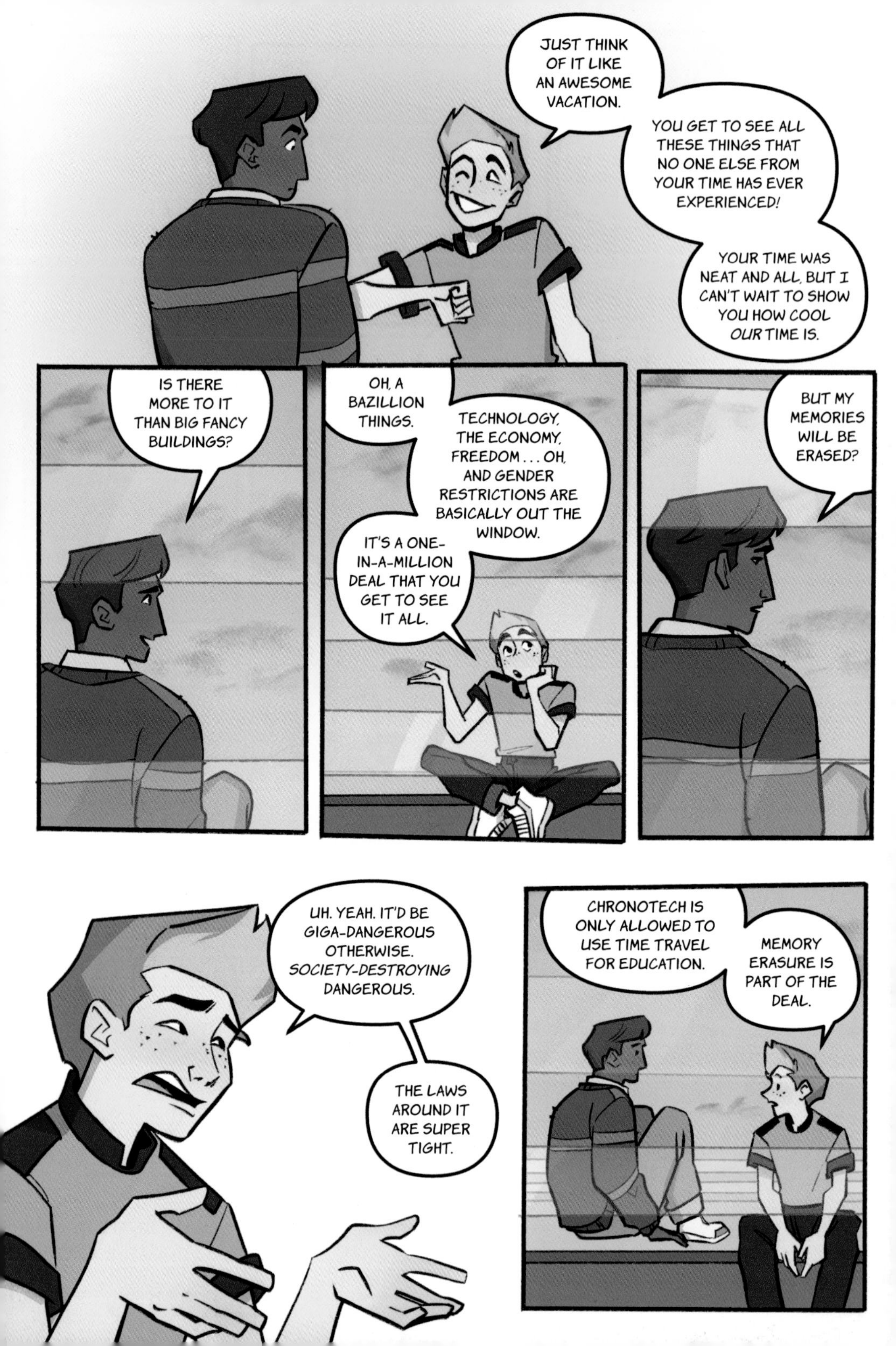
JUST THINK OF IT LIKE AN AWESOME VACATION.
YOU GET TO SEE ALL THESE THINGS THAT NO ONE ELSE FROM YOUR TIME HAS EVER EXPERIENCED!
YOUR TIME WAS NEAT AND ALL, BUT I CAN'T WAIT TO SHOW YOU HOW COOL *OUR* TIME IS.
IS THERE MORE TO IT THAN BIG FANCY BUILDINGS?
OH, A BAZILLION THINGS.
TECHNOLOGY, THE ECONOMY, FREEDOM . . . OH, AND GENDER RESTRICTIONS ARE BASICALLY OUT THE WINDOW.
IT'S A ONE-IN-A-MILLION DEAL THAT YOU GET TO SEE IT ALL.
BUT MY MEMORIES WILL BE ERASED?
UH. YEAH. IT'D BE GIGA-DANGEROUS OTHERWISE. *SOCIETY-DESTROYING* DANGEROUS.
THE LAWS AROUND IT ARE SUPER TIGHT.
CHRONOTECH IS ONLY ALLOWED TO USE TIME TRAVEL FOR EDUCATION.
MEMORY ERASURE IS PART OF THE DEAL.

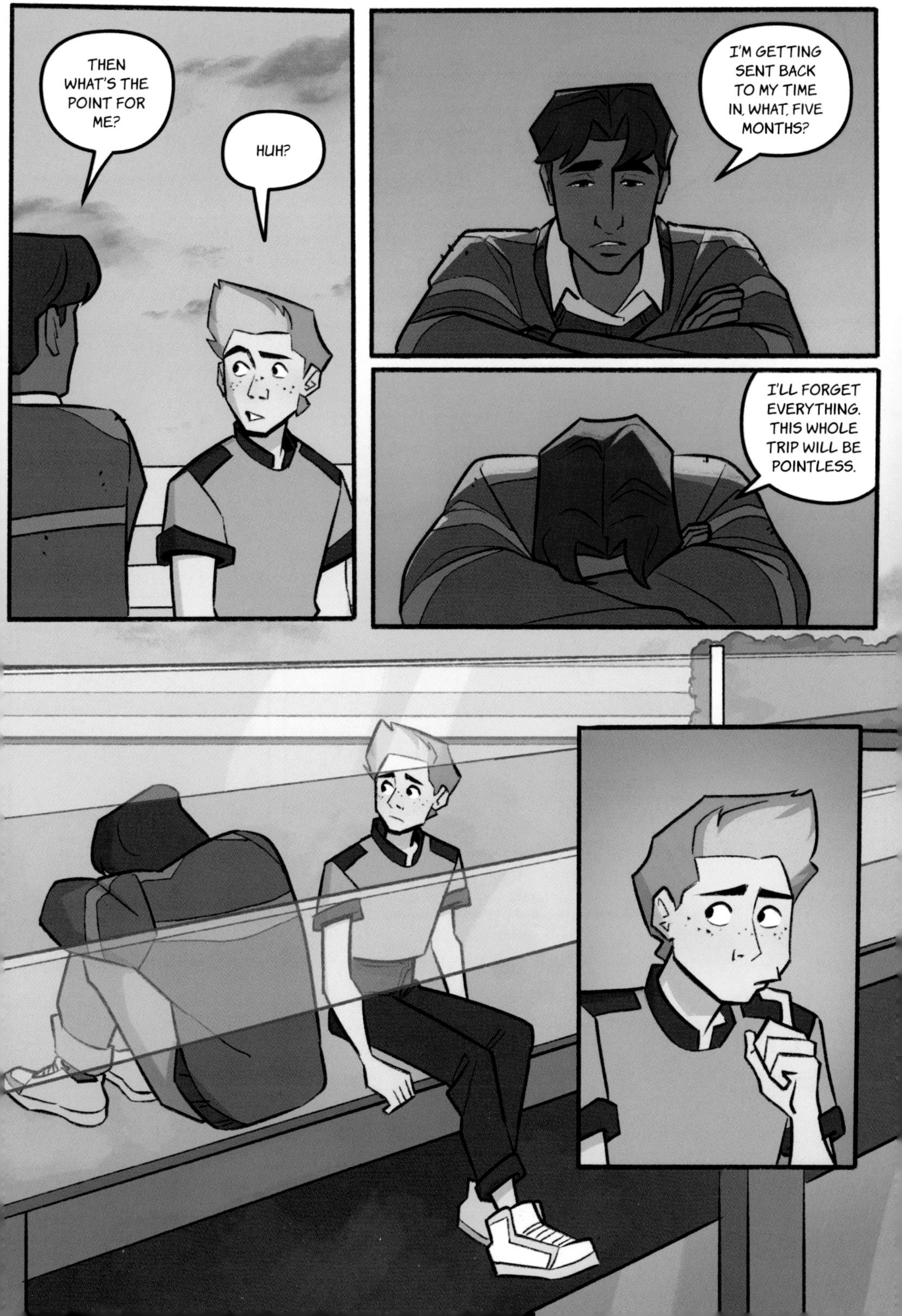
THEN WHAT'S THE POINT FOR ME?
HUH?
I'M GETTING SENT BACK TO MY TIME IN, WHAT, FIVE MONTHS?
I'LL FORGET EVERYTHING. THIS WHOLE TRIP WILL BE POINTLESS.

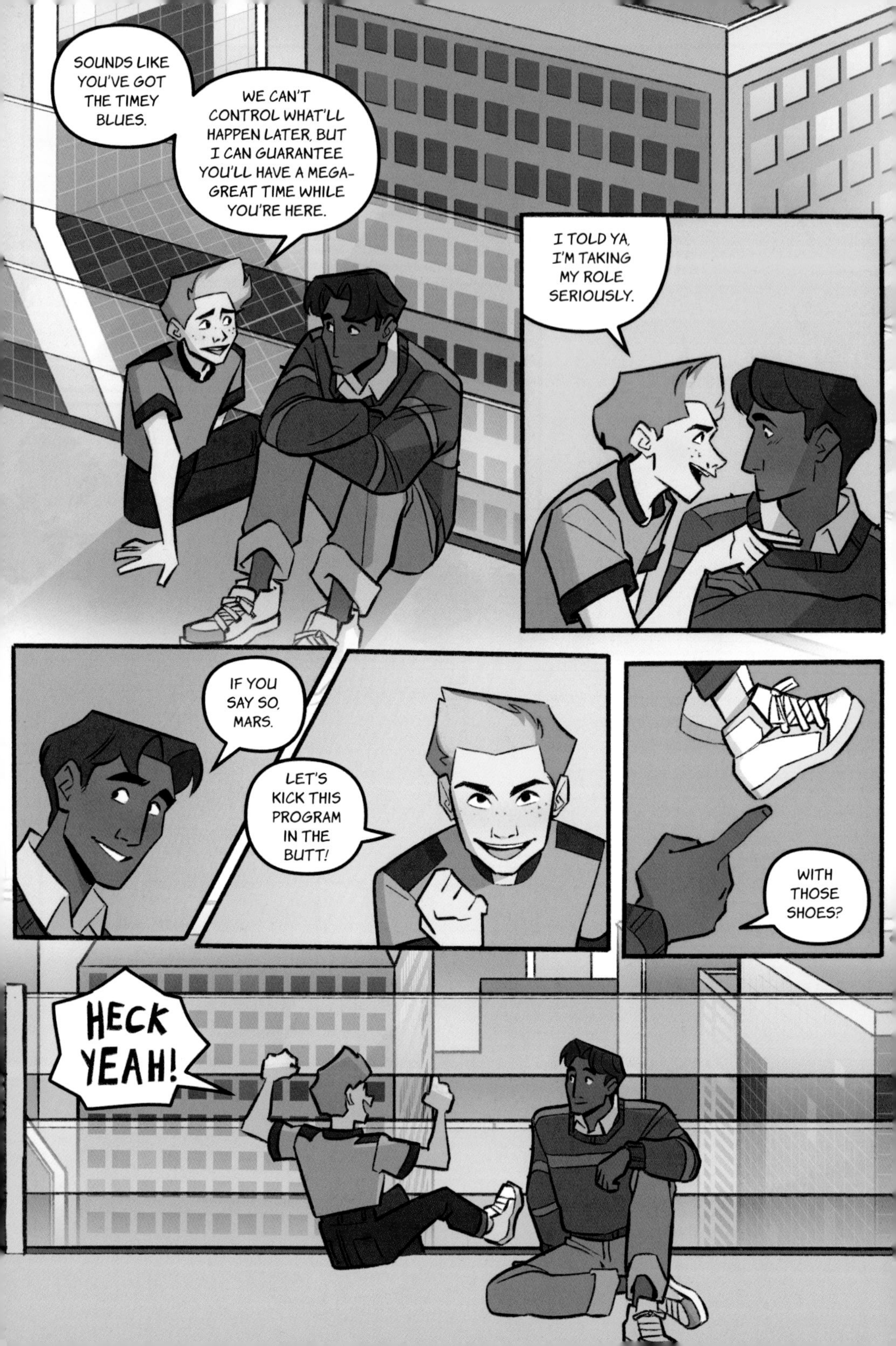
SOUNDS LIKE YOU'VE GOT THE TIMEY BLUES.
WE CAN'T CONTROL WHAT'LL HAPPEN LATER, BUT I CAN GUARANTEE YOU'LL HAVE A MEGA-GREAT TIME WHILE YOU'RE HERE.
I TOLD YA, I'M TAKING MY ROLE SERIOUSLY.
IF YOU SAY SO, MARS.
LET'S KICK THIS PROGRAM IN THE BUTT!
WITH THOSE SHOES?
HECK YEAH!

CHAPTER TWO

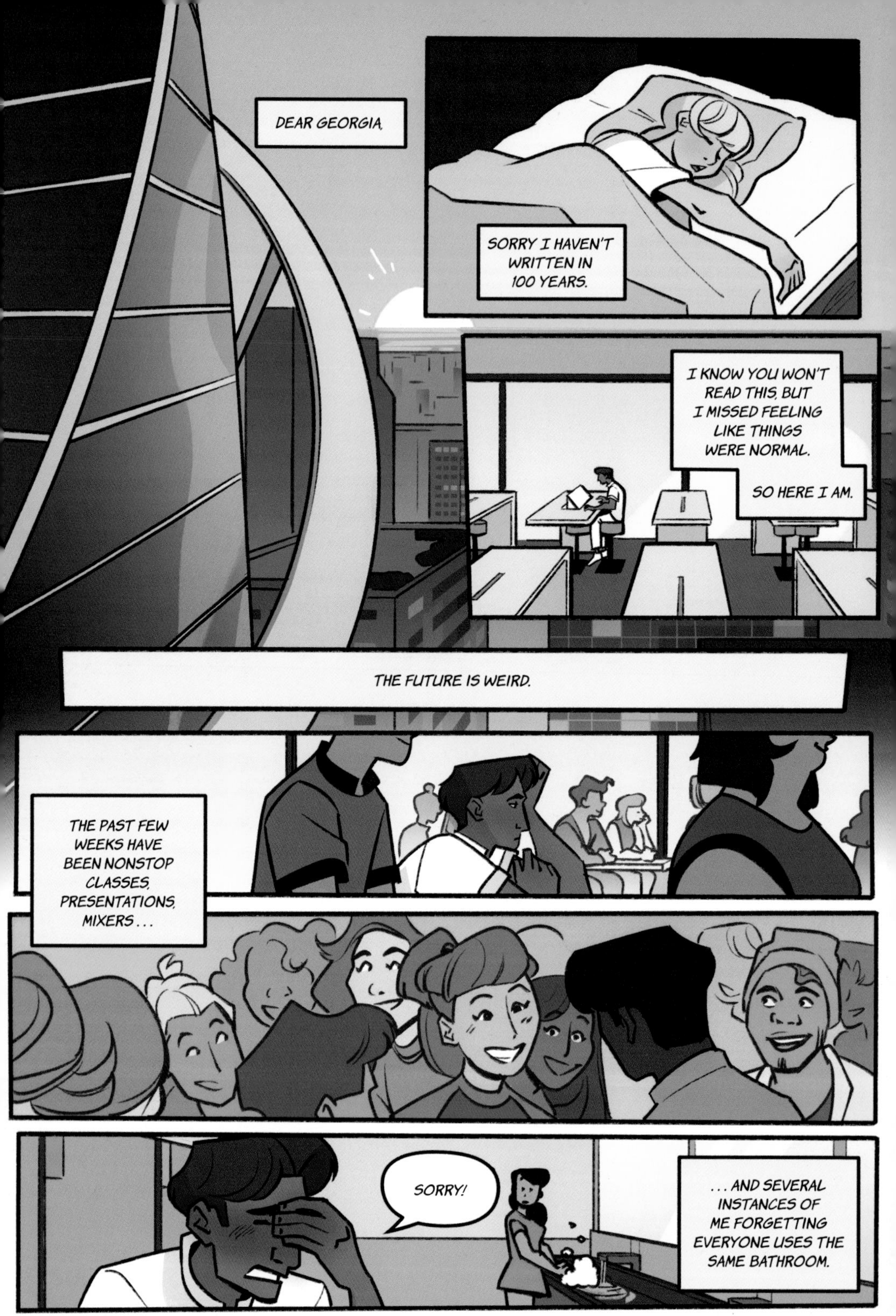
DEAR GEORGIA,
SORRY I HAVEN'T WRITTEN IN 100 YEARS.
I KNOW YOU WON'T READ THIS, BUT I MISSED FEELING LIKE THINGS WERE NORMAL.
SO HERE I AM.
THE FUTURE IS WEIRD.
THE PAST FEW WEEKS HAVE BEEN NONSTOP CLASSES, PRESENTATIONS, MIXERS . . .
SORRY!
. . . AND SEVERAL INSTANCES OF ME FORGETTING EVERYONE USES THE SAME BATHROOM.

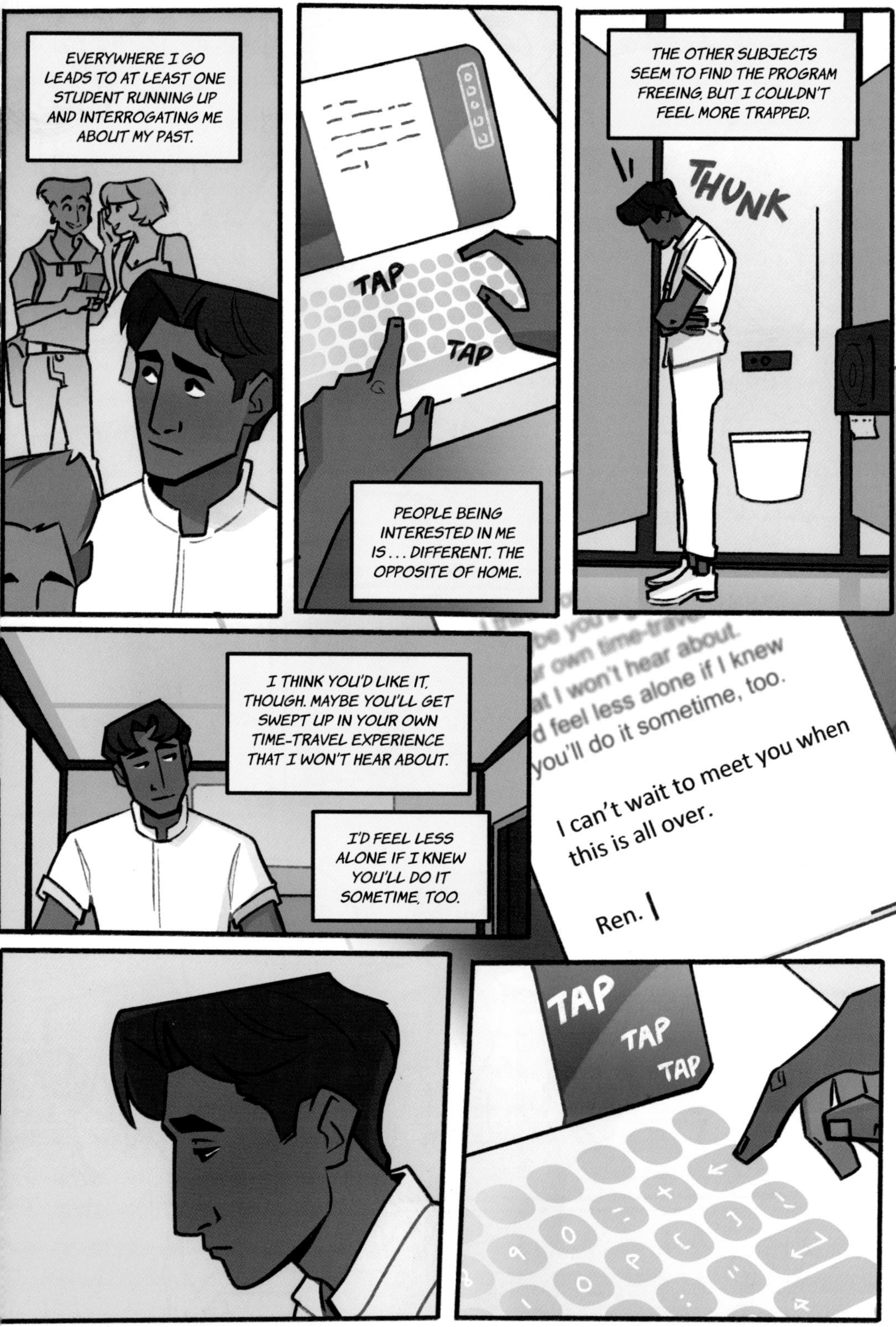
EVERYWHERE I GO LEADS TO AT LEAST ONE STUDENT RUNNING UP AND INTERROGATING ME ABOUT MY PAST.
TAP
TAP
PEOPLE BEING INTERESTED IN ME IS . . . DIFFERENT. THE OPPOSITE OF HOME.
THE OTHER SUBJECTS SEEM TO FIND THE PROGRAM FREEING, BUT I COULDN'T FEEL MORE TRAPPED.
THUNK
I THINK YOU'D LIKE IT, THOUGH. MAYBE YOU'LL GET SWEPT UP IN YOUR OWN TIME-TRAVEL EXPERIENCE THAT I WON'T HEAR ABOUT.
I'D FEEL LESS ALONE IF I KNEW YOU'LL DO IT SOMETIME, TOO.
I can't wait to meet you when this is all over.
Ren.
TAP
TAP
TAP

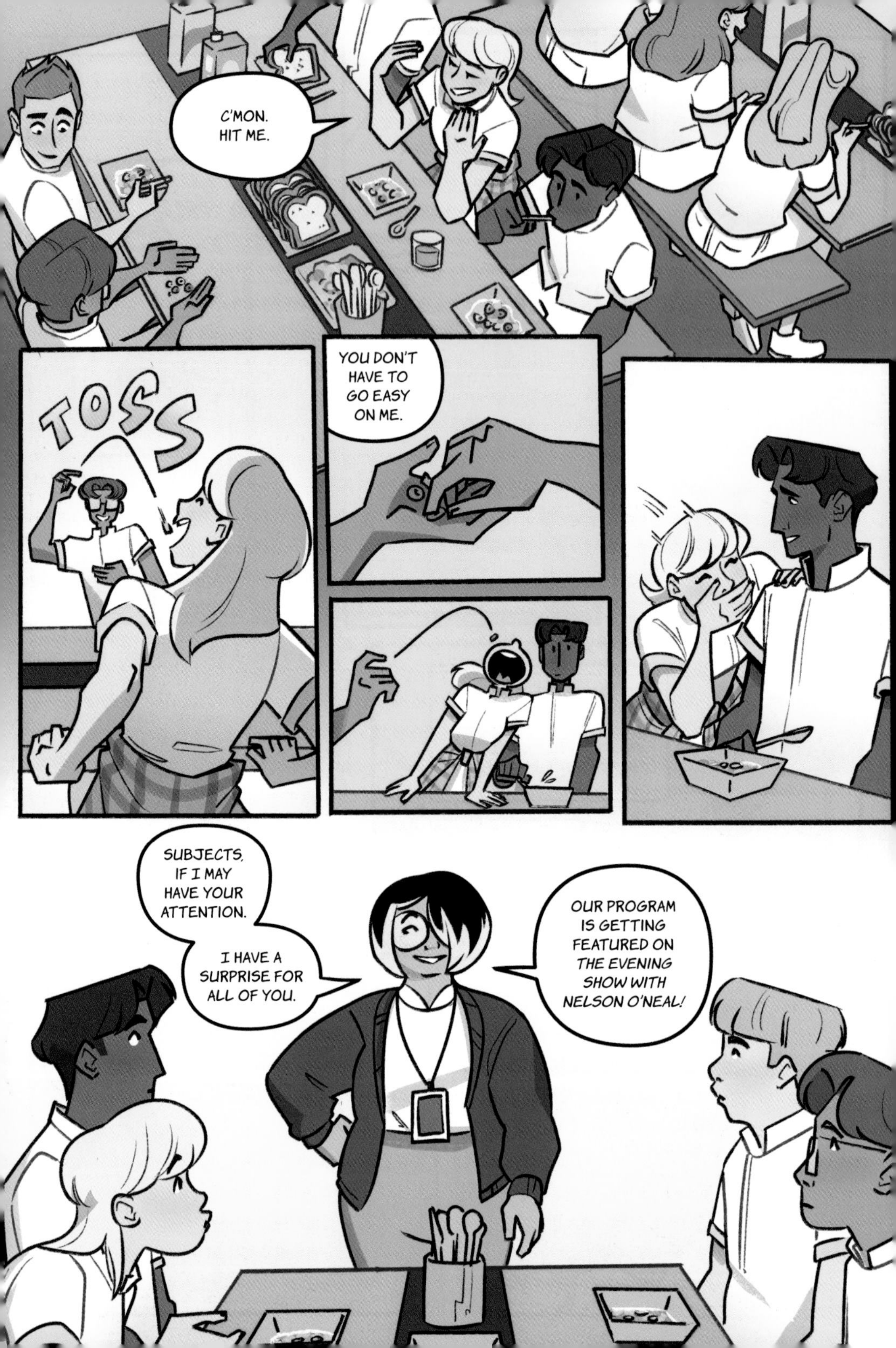
C'MON. HIT ME.
TOSS
YOU DON'T HAVE TO GO EASY ON ME.
SUBJECTS, IF I MAY HAVE YOUR ATTENTION.
I HAVE A SURPRISE FOR ALL OF YOU.
OUR PROGRAM IS GETTING FEATURED ON THE EVENING SHOW WITH NELSON O'NEAL!

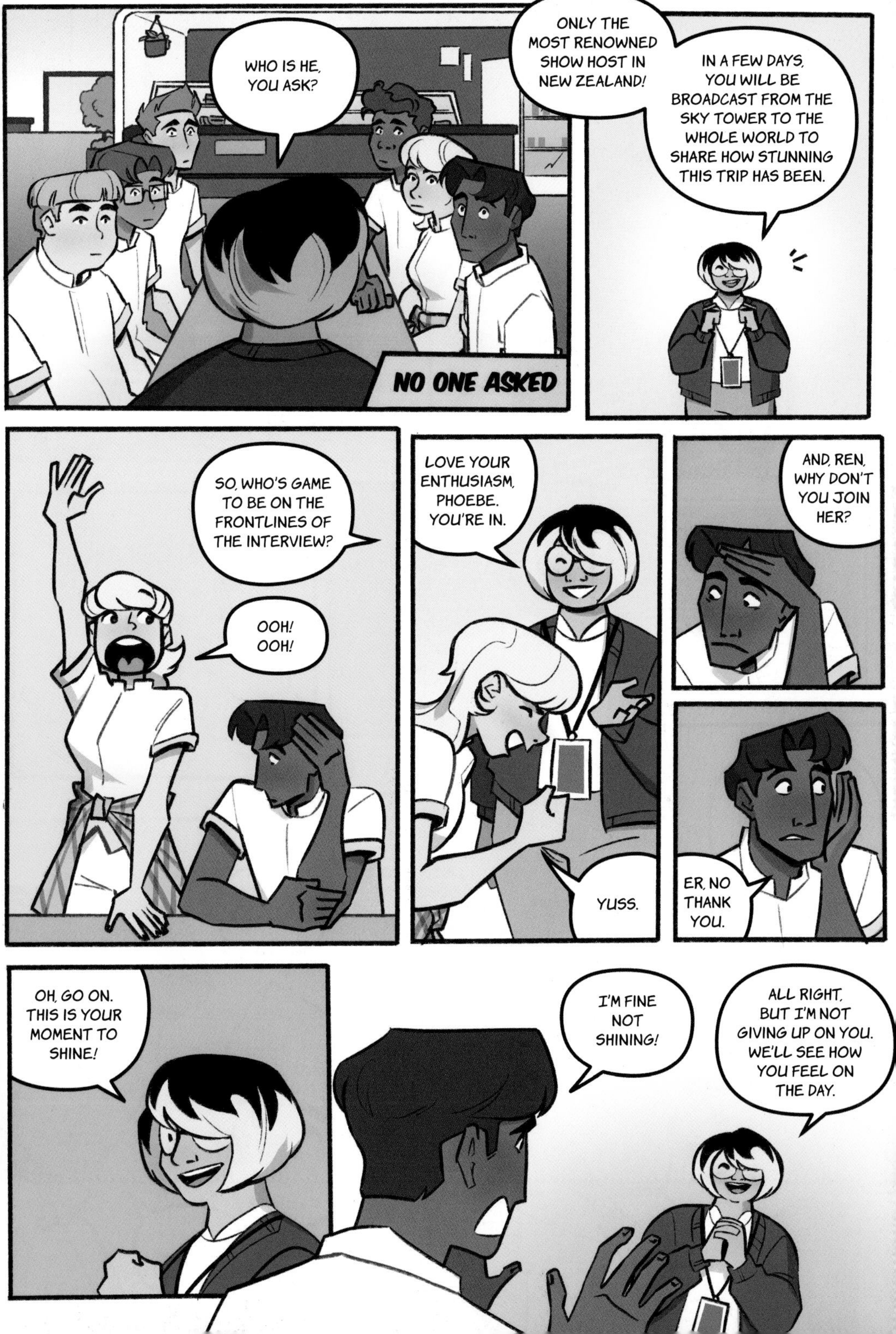
WHO IS HE, YOU ASK?
NO ONE ASKED
ONLY THE MOST RENOWNED SHOW HOST IN NEW ZEALAND!
IN A FEW DAYS, YOU WILL BE BROADCAST FROM THE SKY TOWER TO THE WHOLE WORLD TO SHARE HOW STUNNING THIS TRIP HAS BEEN.
SO, WHO'S GAME TO BE ON THE FRONTLINES OF THE INTERVIEW?
OOH! OOH!
LOVE YOUR ENTHUSIASM, PHOEBE. YOU'RE IN.
YUSS.
AND, REN, WHY DON'T YOU JOIN HER?
ER, NO THANK YOU.
OH, GO ON. THIS IS YOUR MOMENT TO SHINE!
I'M FINE NOT SHINING!
ALL RIGHT, BUT I'M NOT GIVING UP ON YOU. WE'LL SEE HOW YOU FEEL ON THE DAY.

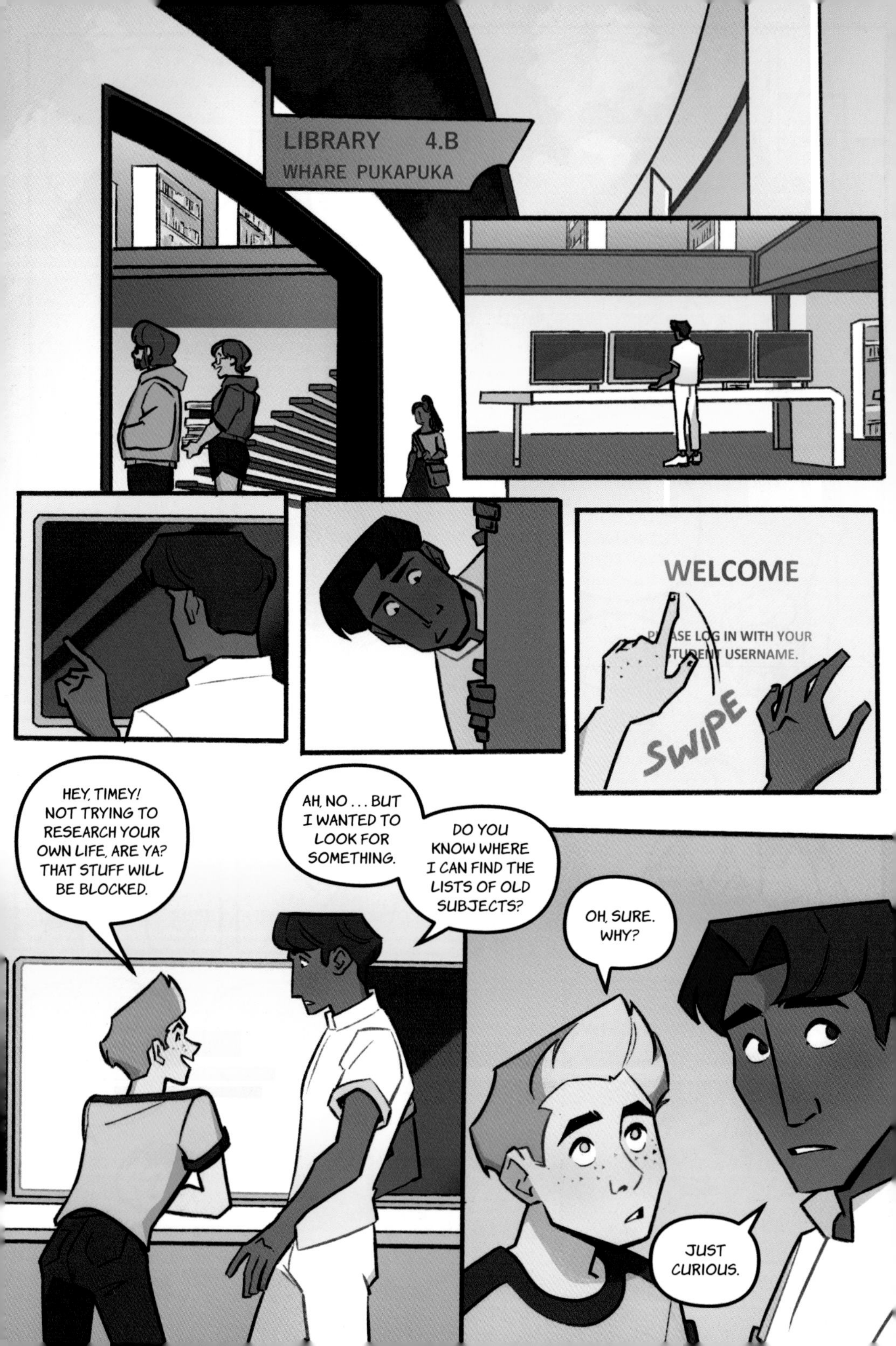
LIBRARY 4.B
WHARE PUKAPUKA
WELCOME
SWIPE
HEY, TIMEY! NOT TRYING TO RESEARCH YOUR OWN LIFE, ARE YA? THAT STUFF WILL BE BLOCKED.
AH, NO . . . BUT I WANTED TO LOOK FOR SOMETHING.
DO YOU KNOW WHERE I CAN FIND THE LISTS OF OLD SUBJECTS?
OH, SURE. WHY?
JUST CURIOUS.

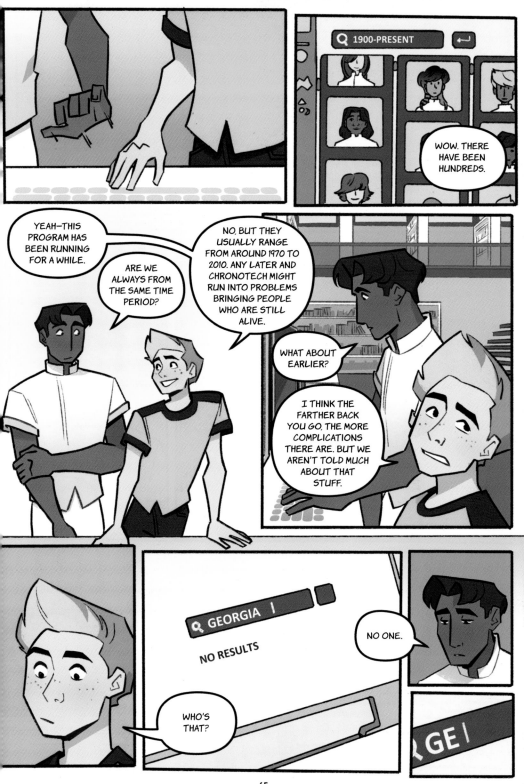

Q 1900-PRESENT

WOW. THERE HAVE BEEN HUNDREDS.

YEAH—THIS PROGRAM HAS BEEN RUNNING FOR A WHILE.

ARE WE ALWAYS FROM THE SAME TIME PERIOD?

NO, BUT THEY USUALLY RANGE FROM AROUND 1970 TO 2010. ANY LATER AND CHRONOTECH MIGHT RUN INTO PROBLEMS BRINGING PEOPLE WHO ARE STILL ALIVE.

WHAT ABOUT EARLIER?

I THINK THE FARTHER BACK YOU GO, THE MORE COMPLICATIONS THERE ARE. BUT WE AREN'T TOLD MUCH ABOUT THAT STUFF.

Q GEORGIA

NO RESULTS

NO ONE.

WHO'S THAT?

RGE

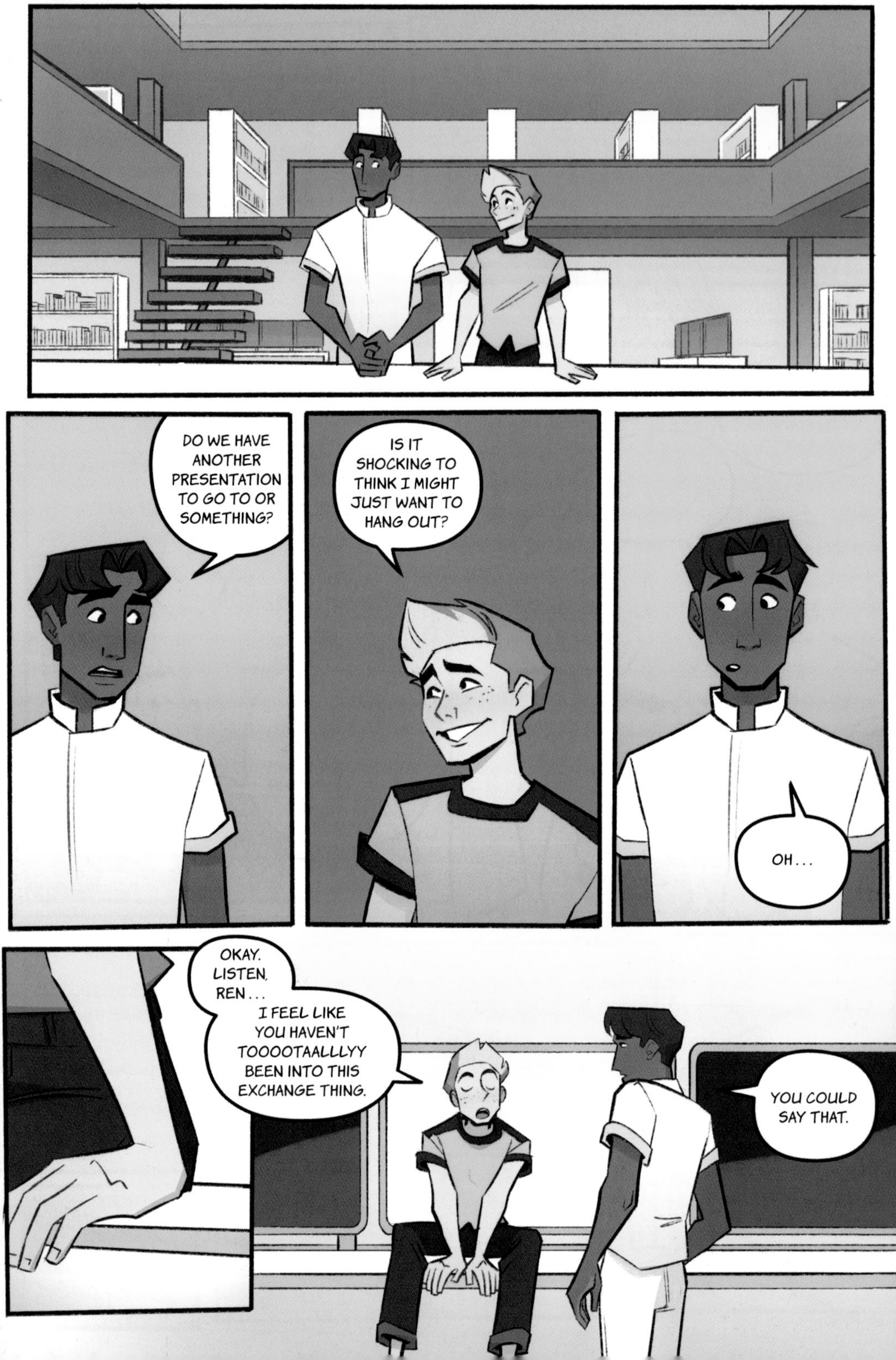
DO WE HAVE ANOTHER PRESENTATION TO GO TO OR SOMETHING?
IS IT SHOCKING TO THINK I MIGHT JUST WANT TO HANG OUT?
OH . . .
OKAY. LISTEN, REN . . .
I FEEL LIKE YOU HAVEN'T TOOOOTAALLLYY BEEN INTO THIS EXCHANGE THING.
YOU COULD SAY THAT.

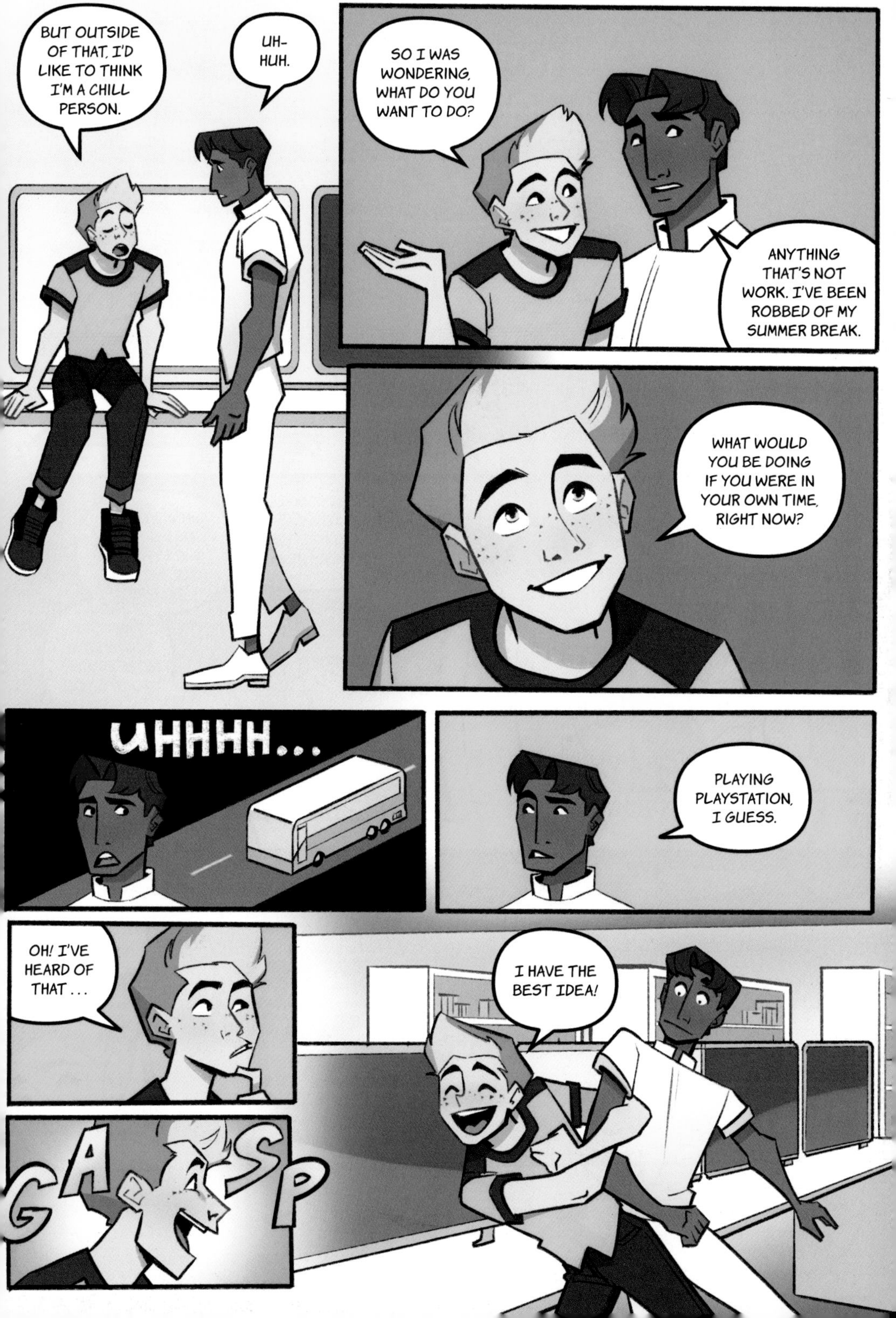
BUT OUTSIDE OF THAT, I'D LIKE TO THINK I'M A CHILL PERSON.
UH-HUH.
SO I WAS WONDERING, WHAT DO YOU WANT TO DO?
ANYTHING THAT'S NOT WORK. I'VE BEEN ROBBED OF MY SUMMER BREAK.
WHAT WOULD YOU BE DOING IF YOU WERE IN YOUR OWN TIME, RIGHT NOW?
UHHHH...
PLAYING PLAYSTATION, I GUESS.
OH! I'VE HEARD OF THAT . . .
GASP
I HAVE THE BEST IDEA!

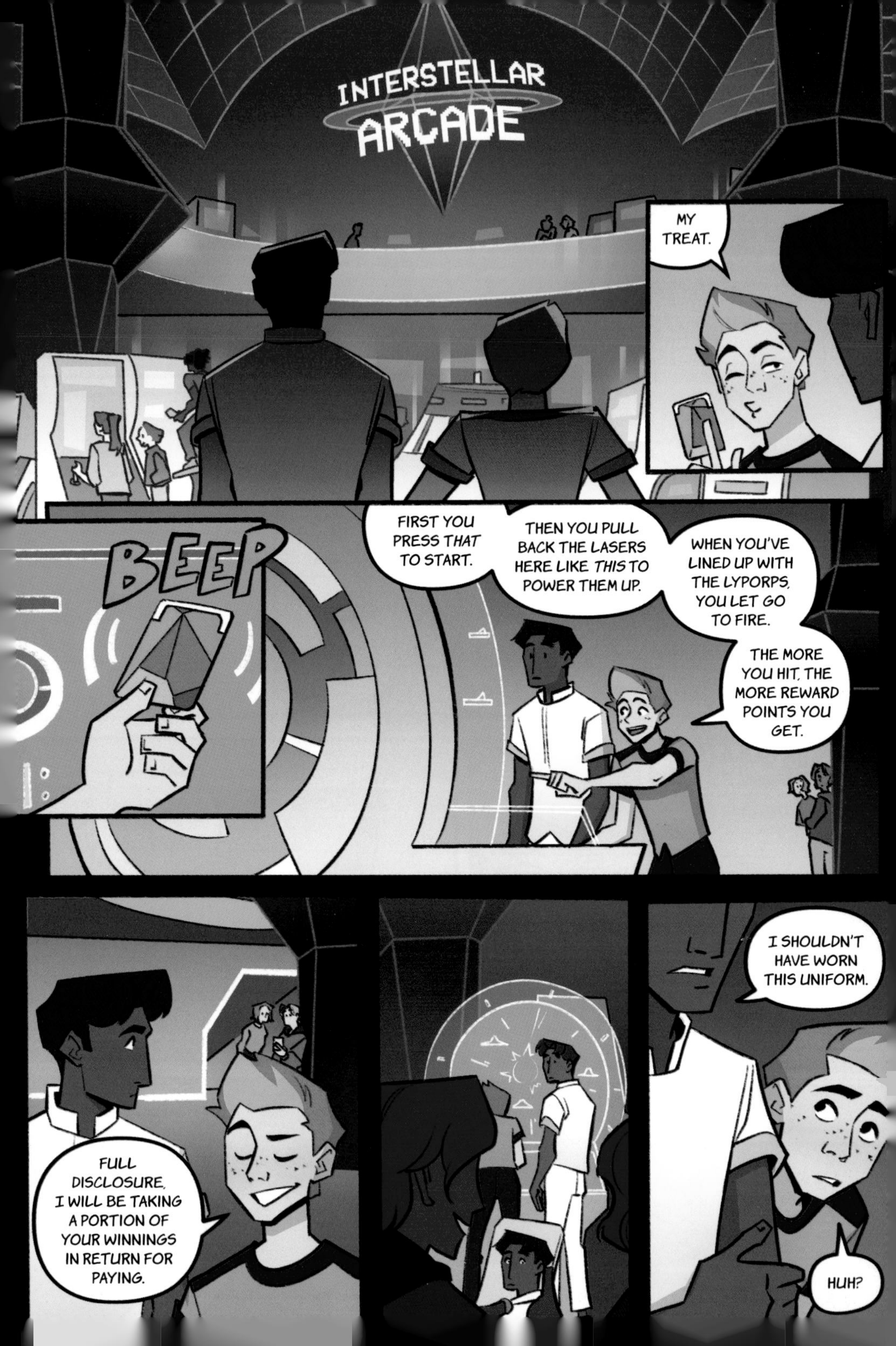
INTERSTELLAR ARCADE
MY TREAT.
BEEP
FIRST YOU PRESS THAT TO START.
THEN YOU PULL BACK THE LASERS HERE LIKE *THIS* TO POWER THEM UP.
WHEN YOU'VE LINED UP WITH THE LYPORPS, YOU LET GO TO FIRE.
THE MORE YOU HIT, THE MORE REWARD POINTS YOU GET.
FULL DISCLOSURE, I WILL BE TAKING A PORTION OF YOUR WINNINGS IN RETURN FOR PAYING.
I SHOULDN'T HAVE WORN THIS UNIFORM.
HUH?

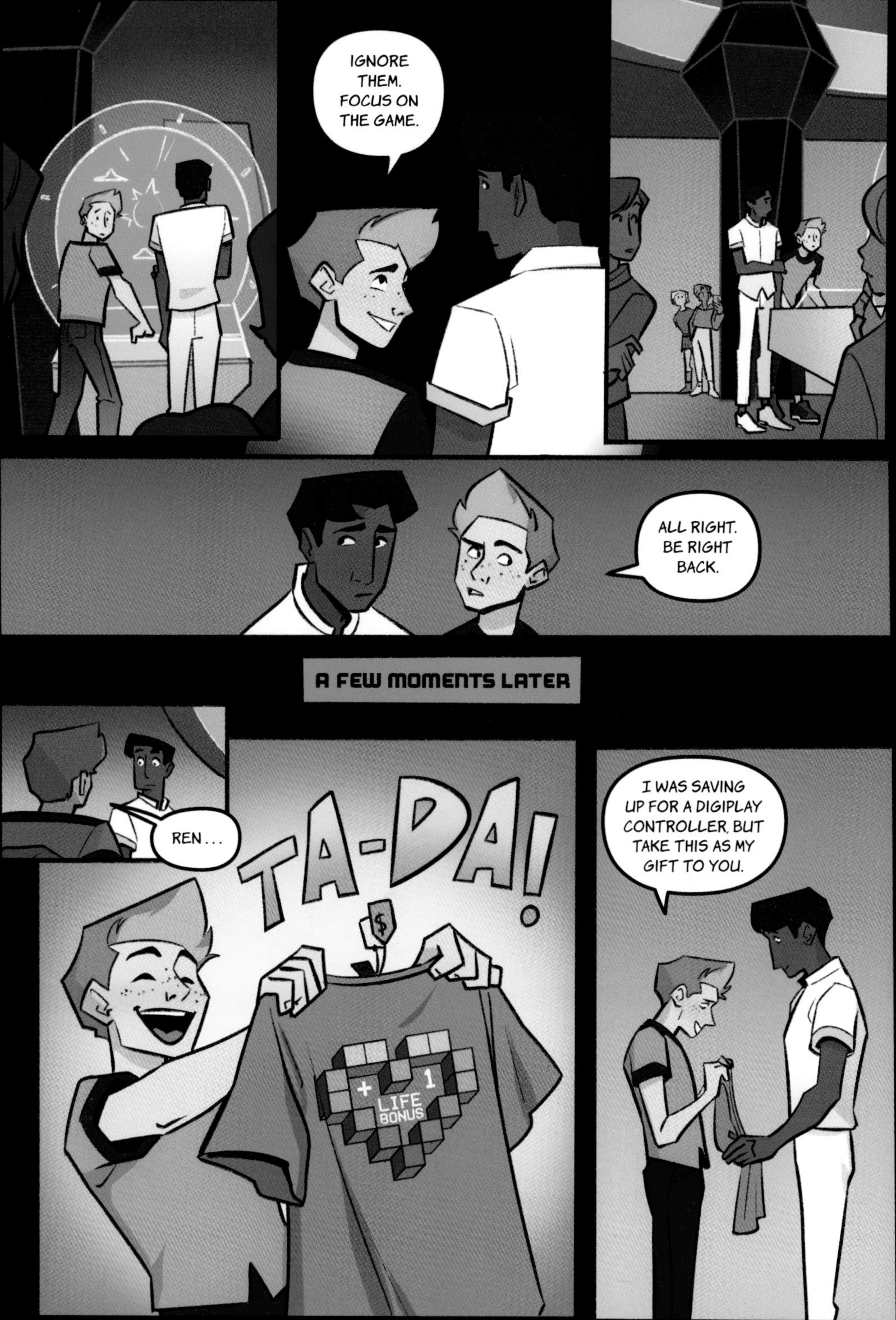
IGNORE THEM. FOCUS ON THE GAME.
ALL RIGHT. BE RIGHT BACK.
A FEW MOMENTS LATER
REN . . .
TA-DA!
+1 LIFE BONUS
I WAS SAVING UP FOR A DIGIPLAY CONTROLLER, BUT TAKE THIS AS MY GIFT TO YOU.

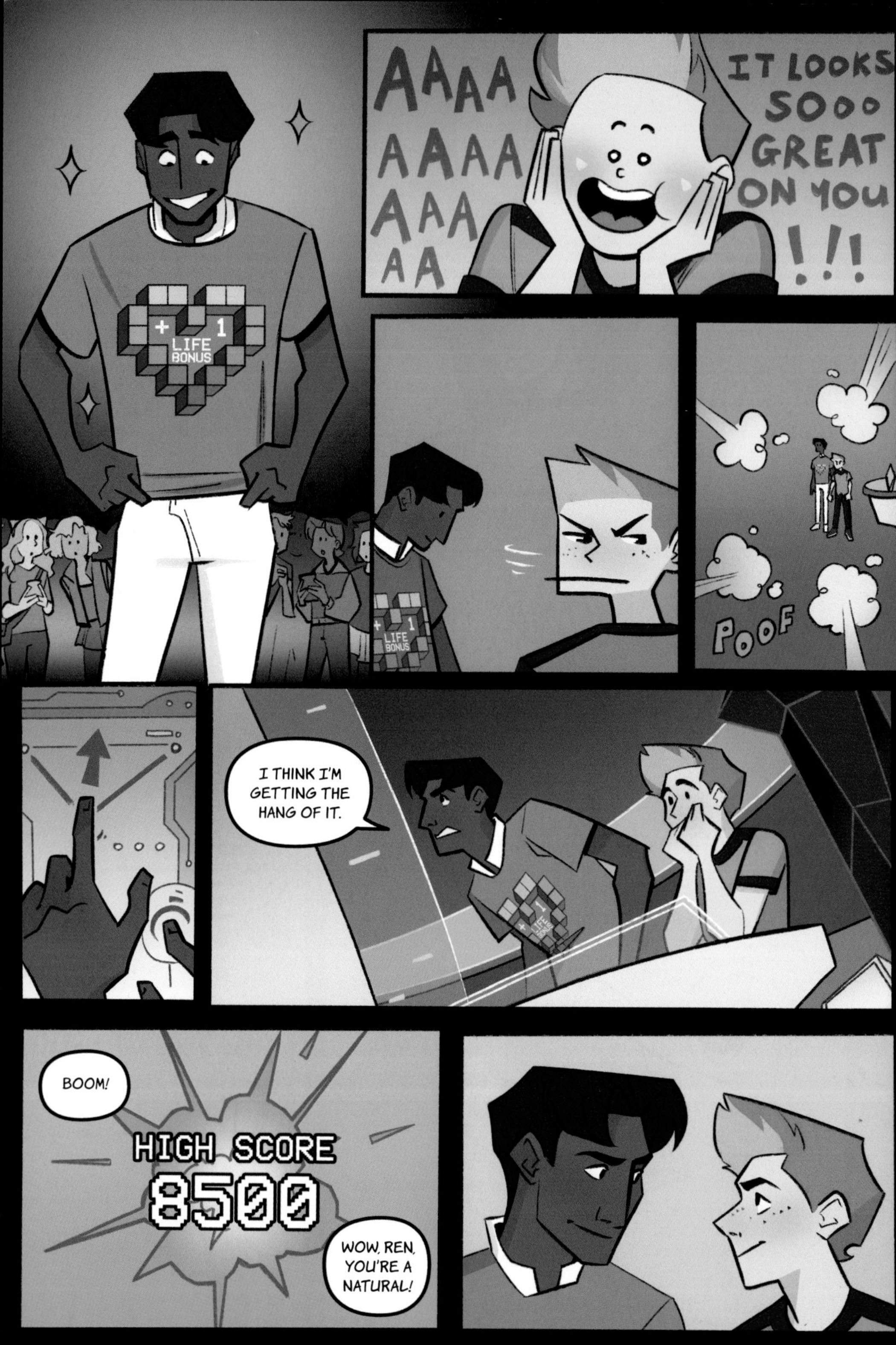
+1 LIFE BONUS
AAAA AAAA AAA AA
IT LOOKS SOooo GREAT ON YOU !!!
POOF
I THINK I'M GETTING THE HANG OF IT.
BOOM!
HIGH SCORE
8500
WOW, REN, YOU'RE A NATURAL!

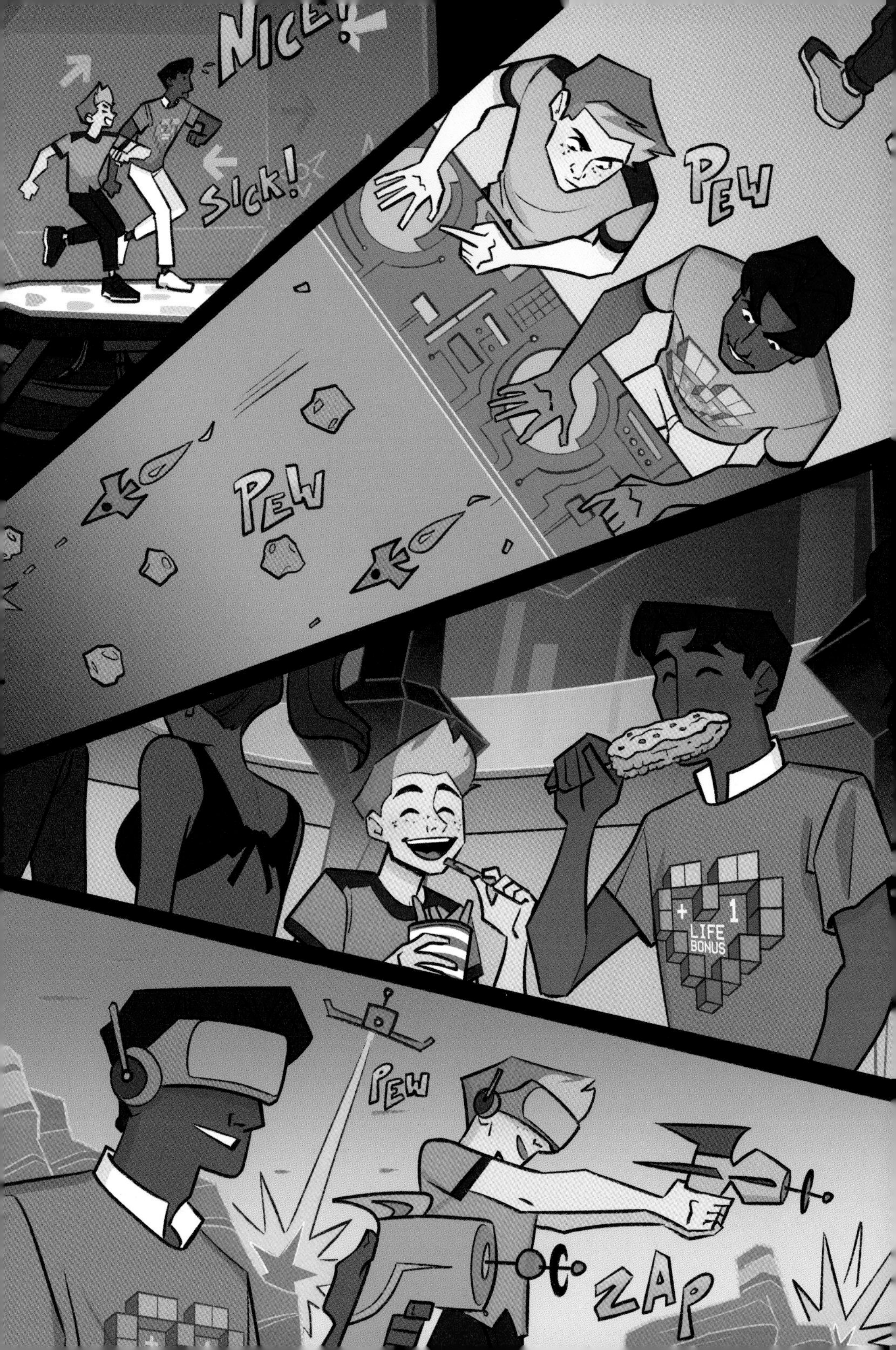
NICE!
SICK!
PEW
PEW
+ 1
LIFE
BONUS
PEW
ZAP

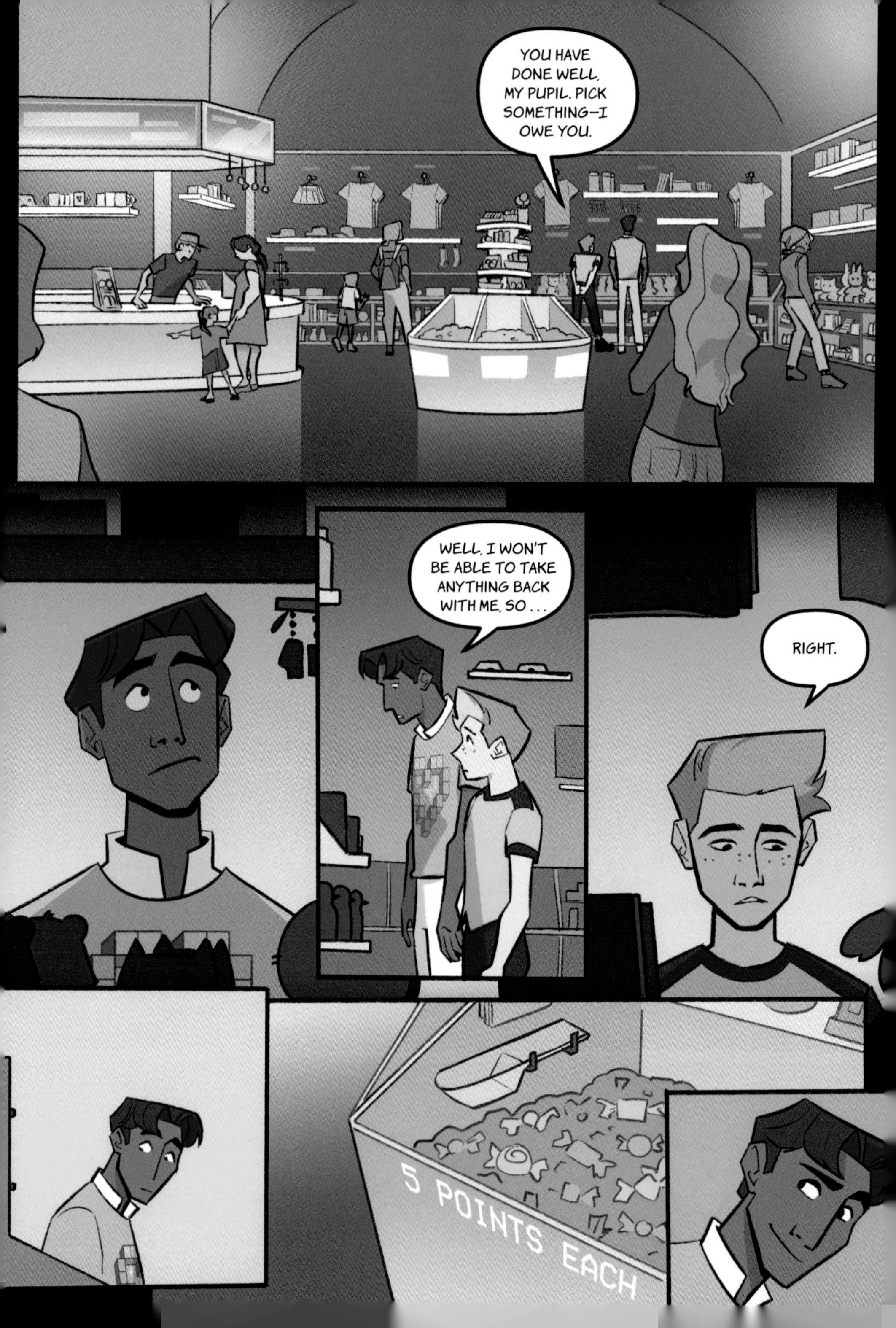
YOU HAVE DONE WELL, MY PUPIL. PICK SOMETHING—I OWE YOU.
WELL, I WON'T BE ABLE TO TAKE ANYTHING BACK WITH ME, SO . . .
RIGHT.
5 POINTS EACH

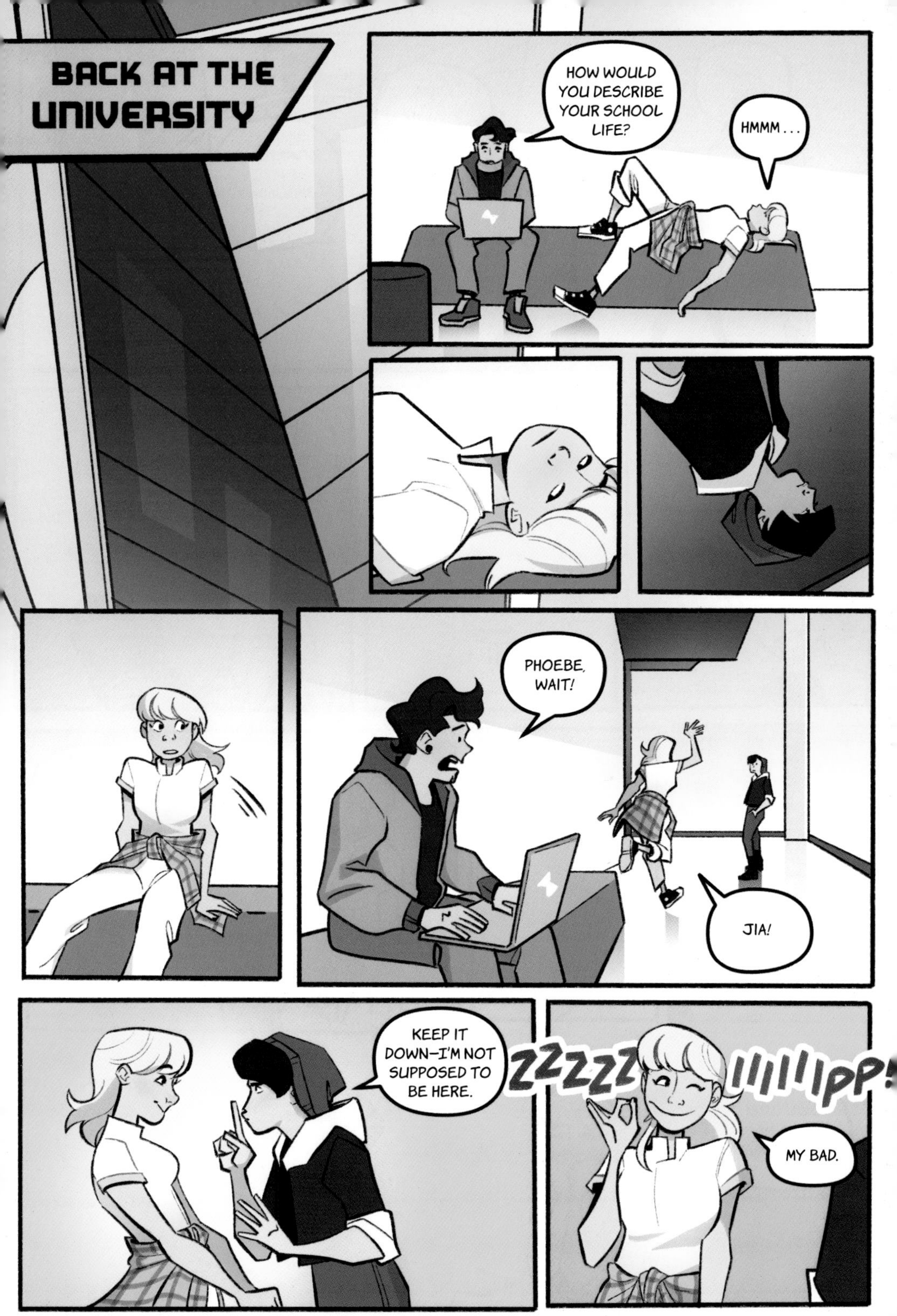
BACK AT THE UNIVERSITY
HOW WOULD YOU DESCRIBE YOUR SCHOOL LIFE?
HMMM . . .
PHOEBE, WAIT!
JIA!
KEEP IT DOWN—I'M NOT SUPPOSED TO BE HERE.
ZZZZZ
IIIIIPP!
MY BAD.

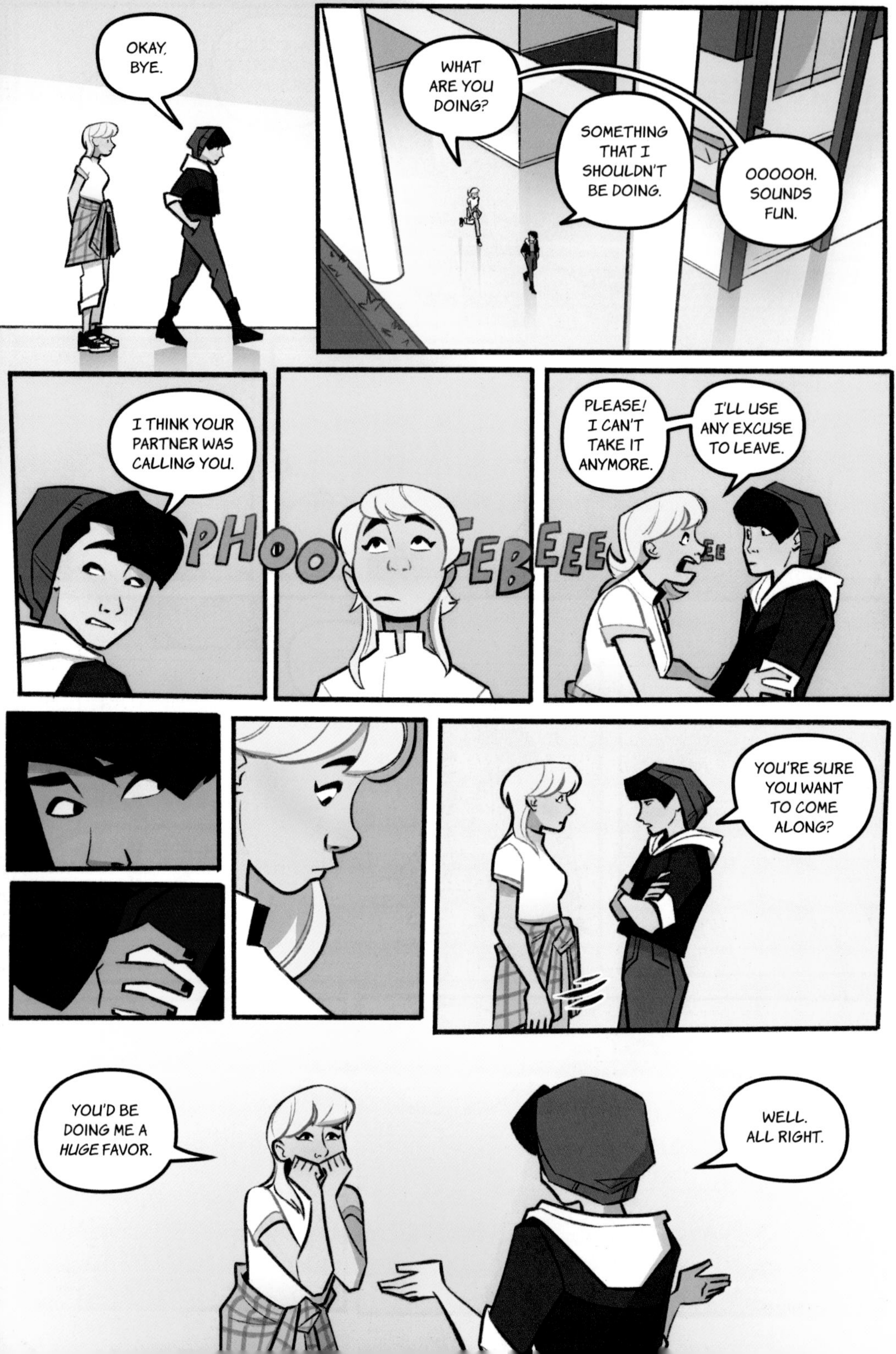
OKAY, BYE.
WHAT ARE YOU DOING?
SOMETHING THAT I SHOULDN'T BE DOING.
OOOOOH. SOUNDS FUN.
I THINK YOUR PARTNER WAS CALLING YOU.
PHOO
EEBEEE
PLEASE! I CAN'T TAKE IT ANYMORE.
I'LL USE ANY EXCUSE TO LEAVE.
YOU'RE SURE YOU WANT TO COME ALONG?
YOU'D BE DOING ME A HUGE FAVOR.
WELL. ALL RIGHT.

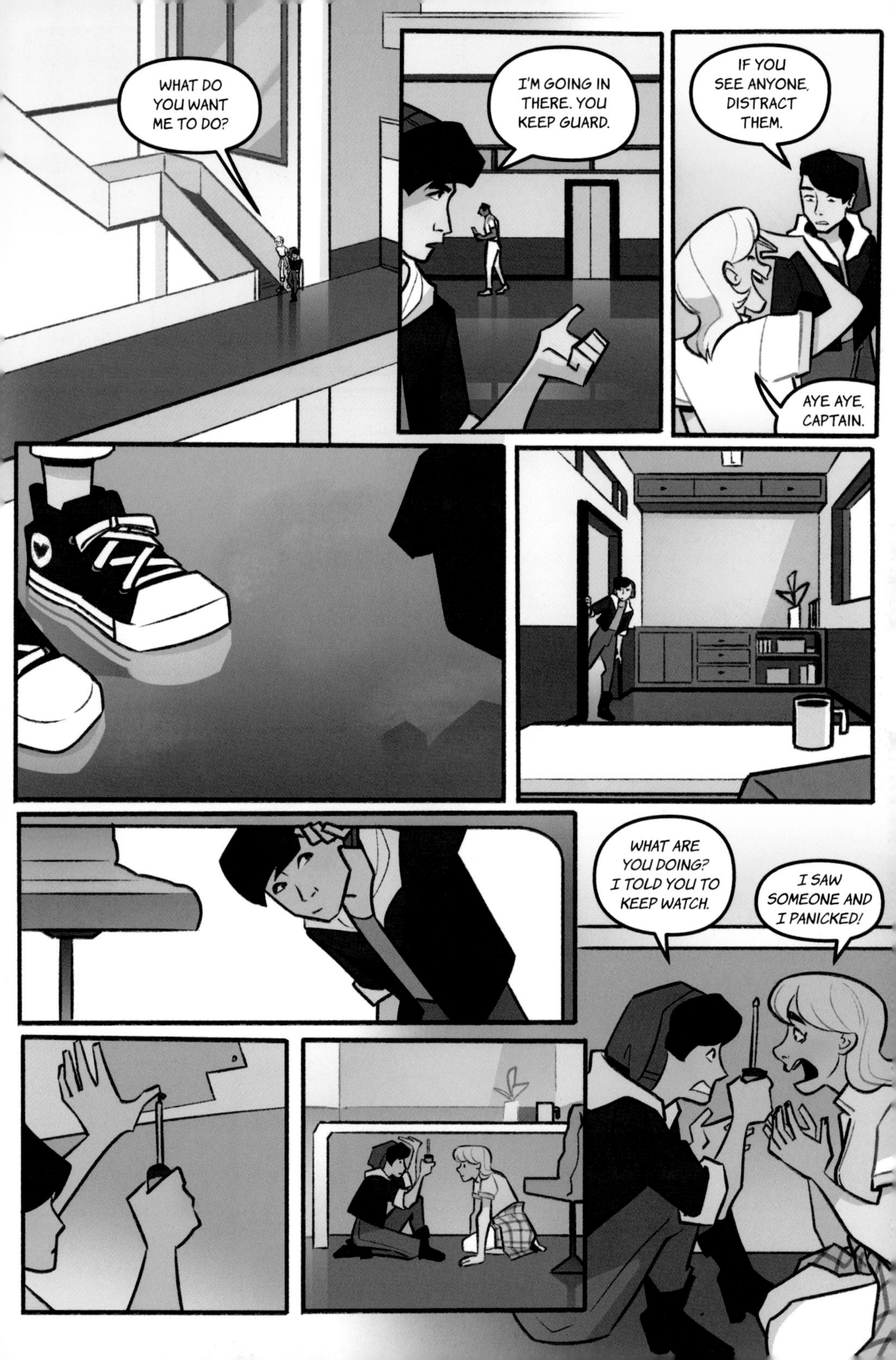
WHAT DO YOU WANT ME TO DO?
I'M GOING IN THERE. YOU KEEP GUARD.
IF YOU SEE ANYONE, DISTRACT THEM.
AYE AYE, CAPTAIN.
WHAT ARE YOU DOING? I TOLD YOU TO KEEP WATCH.
I SAW SOMEONE AND I PANICKED!

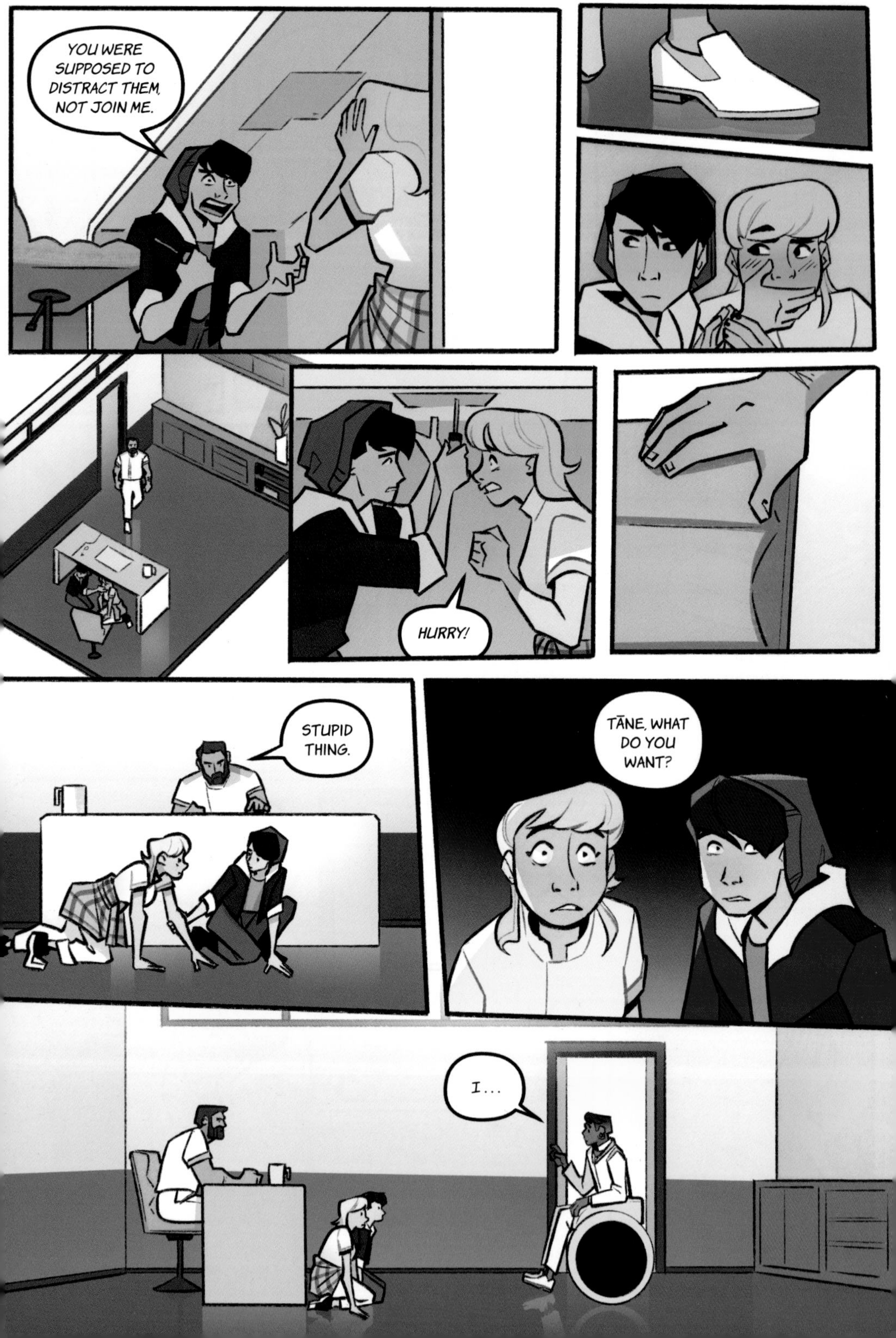
YOU WERE SUPPOSED TO DISTRACT THEM, NOT JOIN ME.
HURRY!
STUPID THING.
TĀNE, WHAT DO YOU WANT?
I...

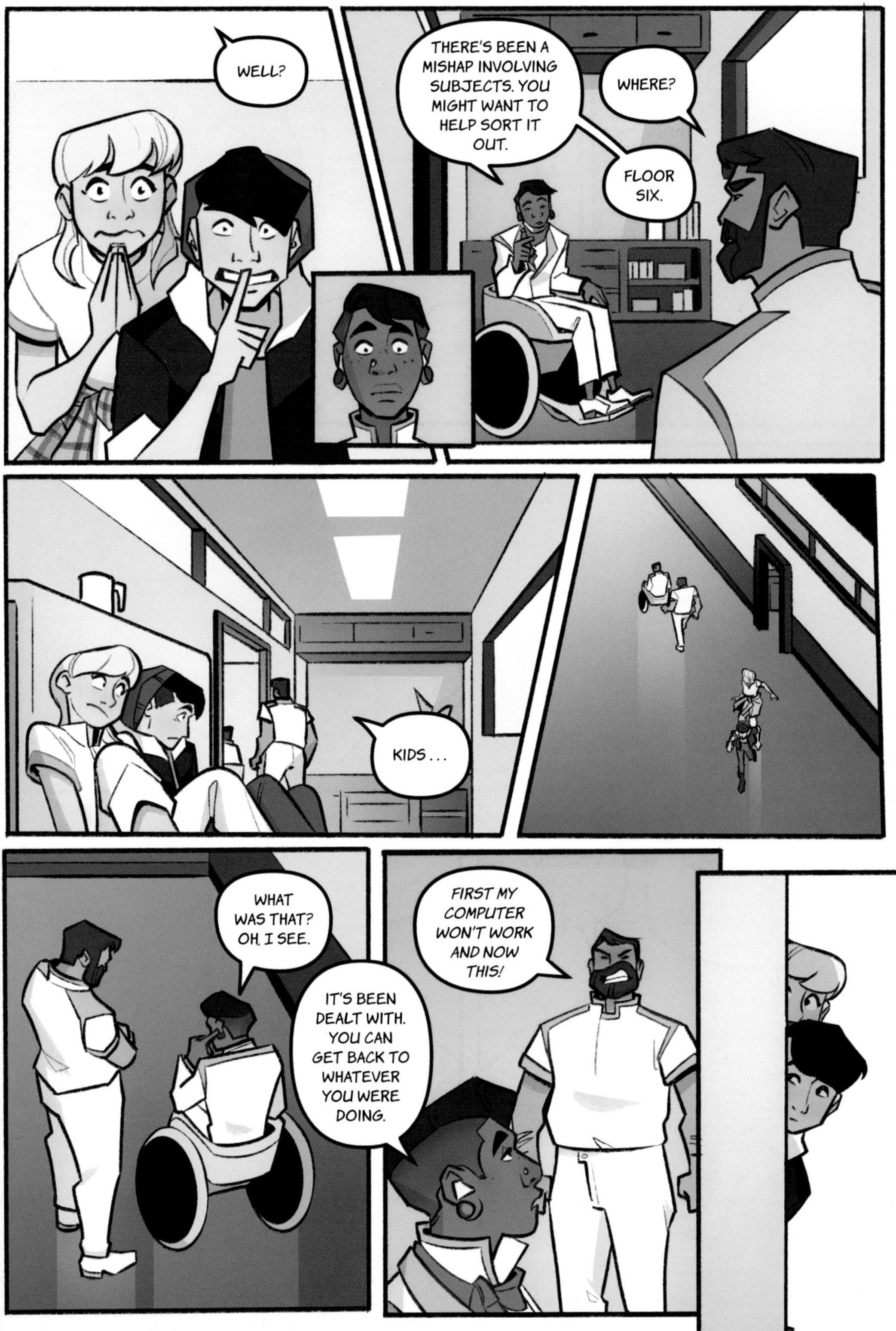
WELL?
THERE'S BEEN A MISHAP INVOLVING SUBJECTS. YOU MIGHT WANT TO HELP SORT IT OUT.
WHERE?
FLOOR SIX.
KIDS . . .
WHAT WAS THAT? OH, I SEE.
FIRST MY COMPUTER WON'T WORK AND NOW THIS!
IT'S BEEN DEALT WITH. YOU CAN GET BACK TO WHATEVER YOU WERE DOING.

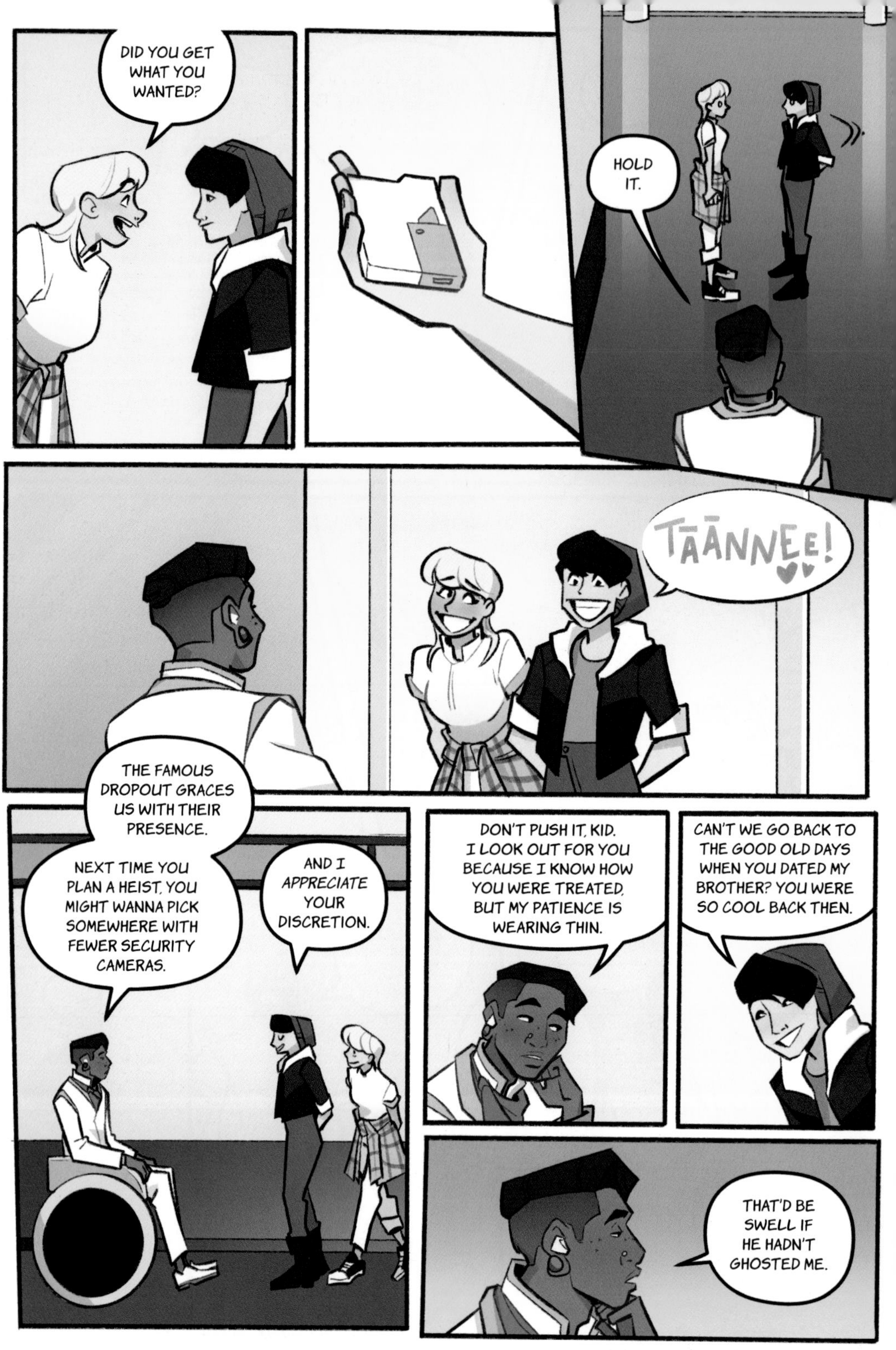
DID YOU GET WHAT YOU WANTED?
HOLD IT.
TAANNEE!
THE FAMOUS DROPOUT GRACES US WITH THEIR PRESENCE.
NEXT TIME YOU PLAN A HEIST, YOU MIGHT WANNA PICK SOMEWHERE WITH FEWER SECURITY CAMERAS.
AND I APPRECIATE YOUR DISCRETION.
DON'T PUSH IT, KID. I LOOK OUT FOR YOU BECAUSE I KNOW HOW YOU WERE TREATED, BUT MY PATIENCE IS WEARING THIN.
CAN'T WE GO BACK TO THE GOOD OLD DAYS WHEN YOU DATED MY BROTHER? YOU WERE SO COOL BACK THEN.
THAT'D BE SWELL IF HE HADN'T GHOSTED ME.

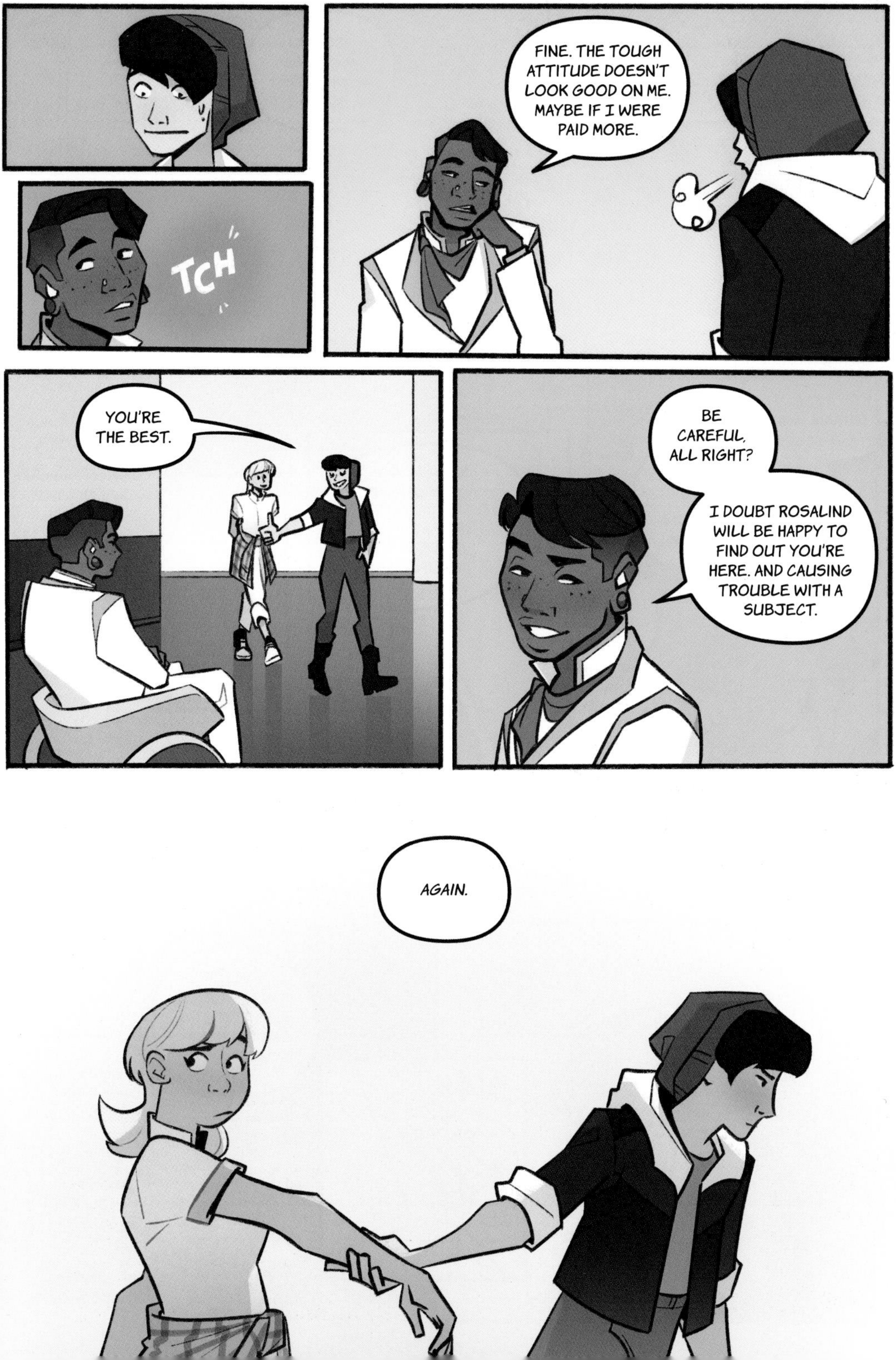
TCH
FINE. THE TOUGH ATTITUDE DOESN'T LOOK GOOD ON ME. MAYBE IF I WERE PAID MORE.
YOU'RE THE BEST.
BE CAREFUL, ALL RIGHT?
I DOUBT ROSALIND WILL BE HAPPY TO FIND OUT YOU'RE HERE. AND CAUSING TROUBLE WITH A SUBJECT.
AGAIN.

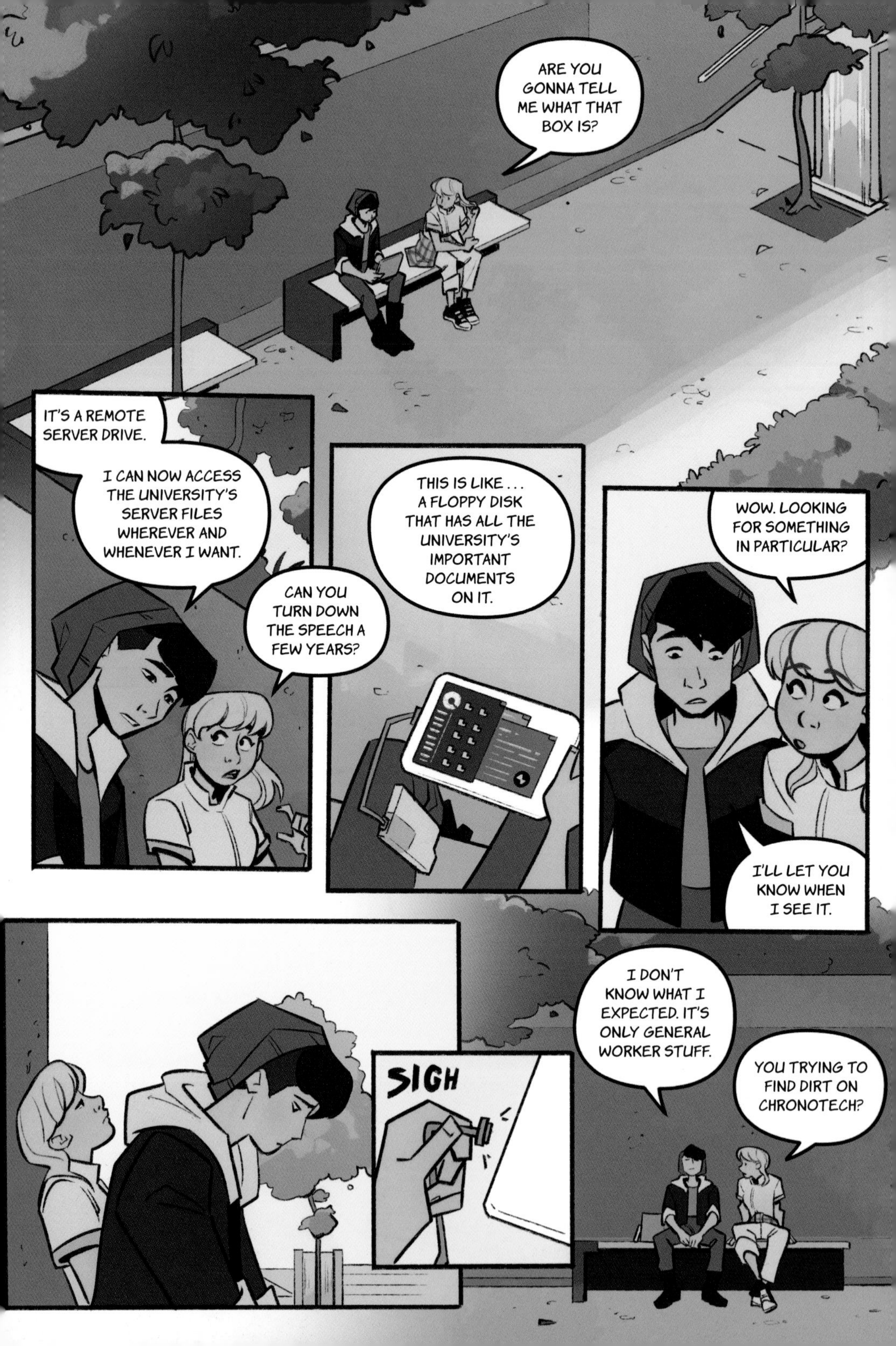
ARE YOU GONNA TELL ME WHAT THAT BOX IS?
IT'S A REMOTE SERVER DRIVE.
I CAN NOW ACCESS THE UNIVERSITY'S SERVER FILES WHEREVER AND WHENEVER I WANT.
CAN YOU TURN DOWN THE SPEECH A FEW YEARS?
THIS IS LIKE . . . A FLOPPY DISK THAT HAS ALL THE UNIVERSITY'S IMPORTANT DOCUMENTS ON IT.
WOW. LOOKING FOR SOMETHING IN PARTICULAR?
I'LL LET YOU KNOW WHEN I SEE IT.
SIGH
I DON'T KNOW WHAT I EXPECTED. IT'S ONLY GENERAL WORKER STUFF.
YOU TRYING TO FIND DIRT ON CHRONOTECH?

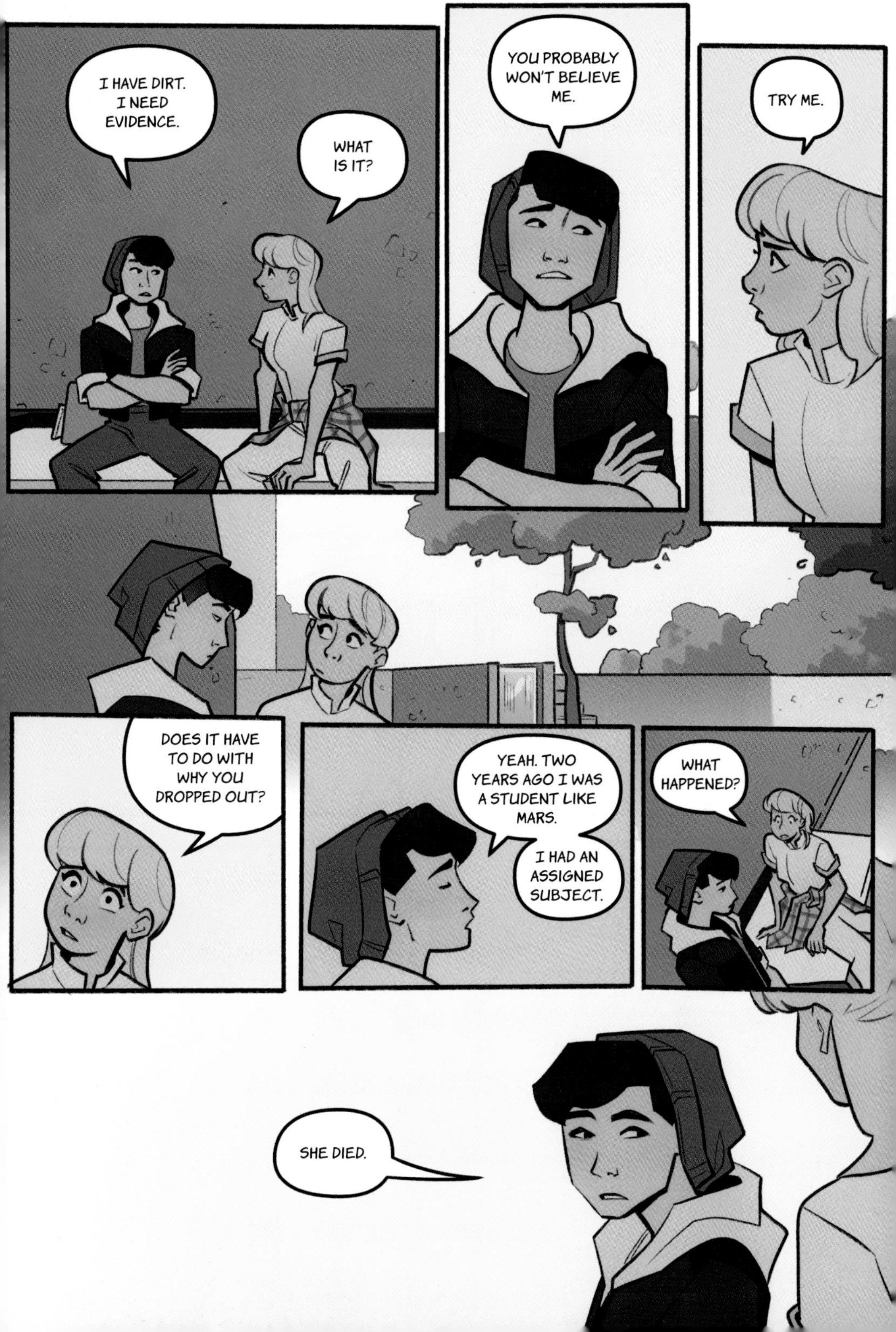

I HAVE DIRT. I NEED EVIDENCE.
WHAT IS IT?
YOU PROBABLY WON'T BELIEVE ME.
TRY ME.
DOES IT HAVE TO DO WITH WHY YOU DROPPED OUT?
YEAH. TWO YEARS AGO I WAS A STUDENT LIKE MARS.
I HAD AN ASSIGNED SUBJECT.
WHAT HAPPENED?
SHE DIED.

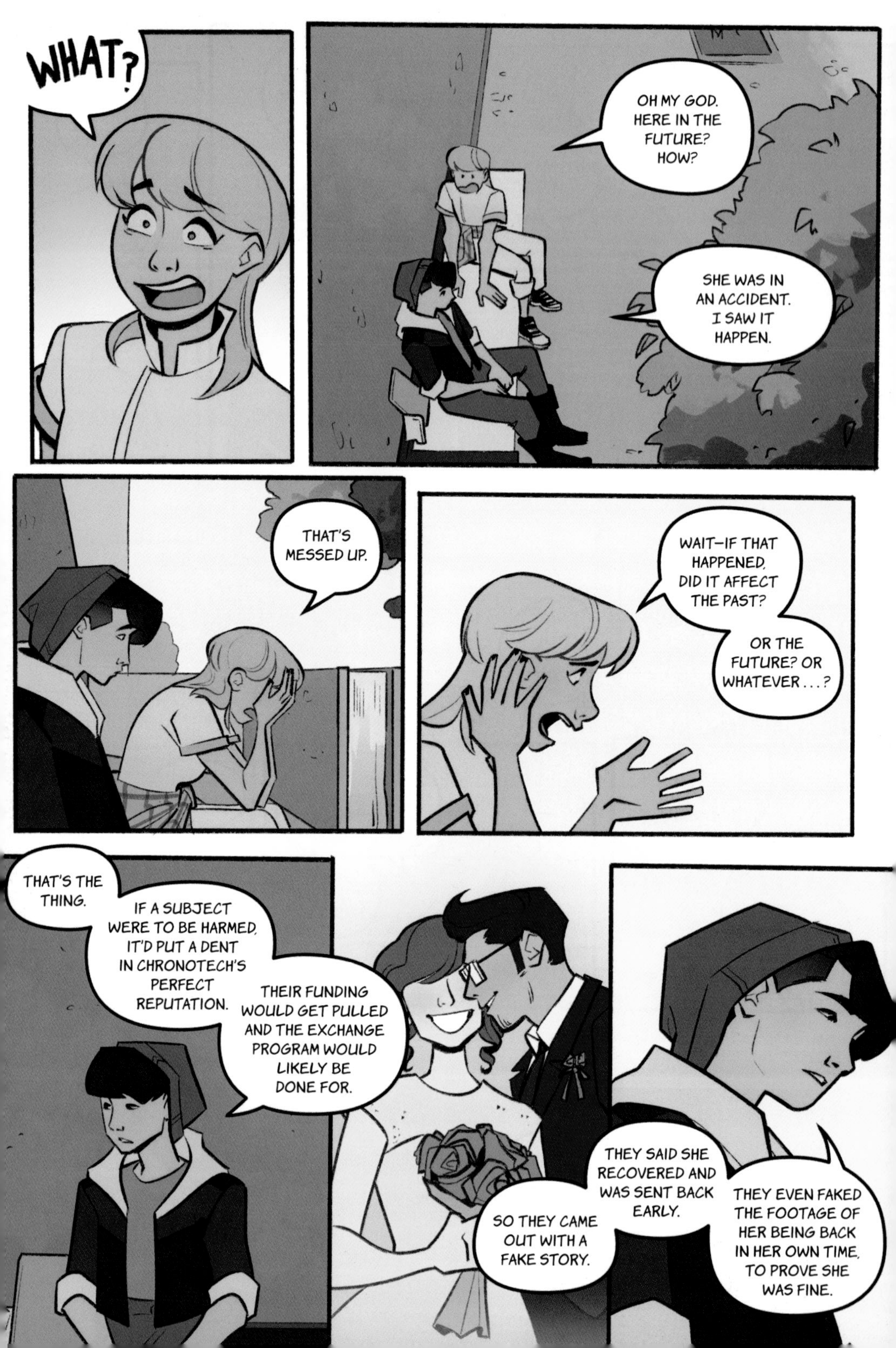
WHAT?
OH MY GOD. HERE IN THE FUTURE? HOW?
SHE WAS IN AN ACCIDENT. I SAW IT HAPPEN.
THAT'S MESSED UP.
WAIT—IF THAT HAPPENED, DID IT AFFECT THE PAST?
OR THE FUTURE? OR WHATEVER . . . ?
THAT'S THE THING.
IF A SUBJECT WERE TO BE HARMED, IT'D PUT A DENT IN CHRONOTECH'S PERFECT REPUTATION.
THEIR FUNDING WOULD GET PULLED AND THE EXCHANGE PROGRAM WOULD LIKELY BE DONE FOR.
SO THEY CAME OUT WITH A FAKE STORY.
THEY SAID SHE RECOVERED AND WAS SENT BACK EARLY.
THEY EVEN FAKED THE FOOTAGE OF HER BEING BACK IN HER OWN TIME, TO PROVE SHE WAS FINE.

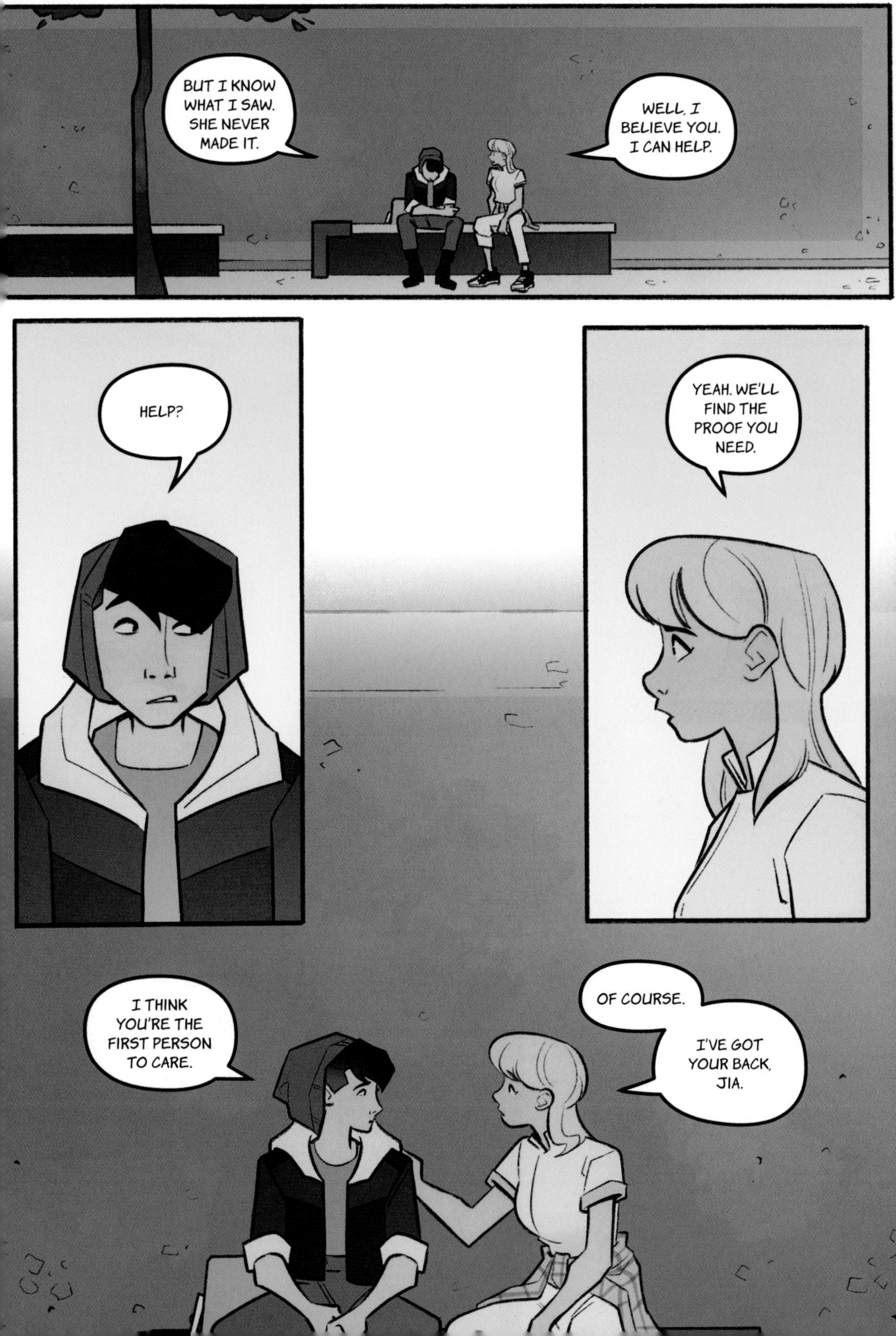
BUT I KNOW WHAT I SAW. SHE NEVER MADE IT.
WELL, I BELIEVE YOU. I CAN HELP.
HELP?
YEAH. WE'LL FIND THE PROOF YOU NEED.
I THINK YOU'RE THE FIRST PERSON TO CARE.
OF COURSE.
I'VE GOT YOUR BACK, JIA.

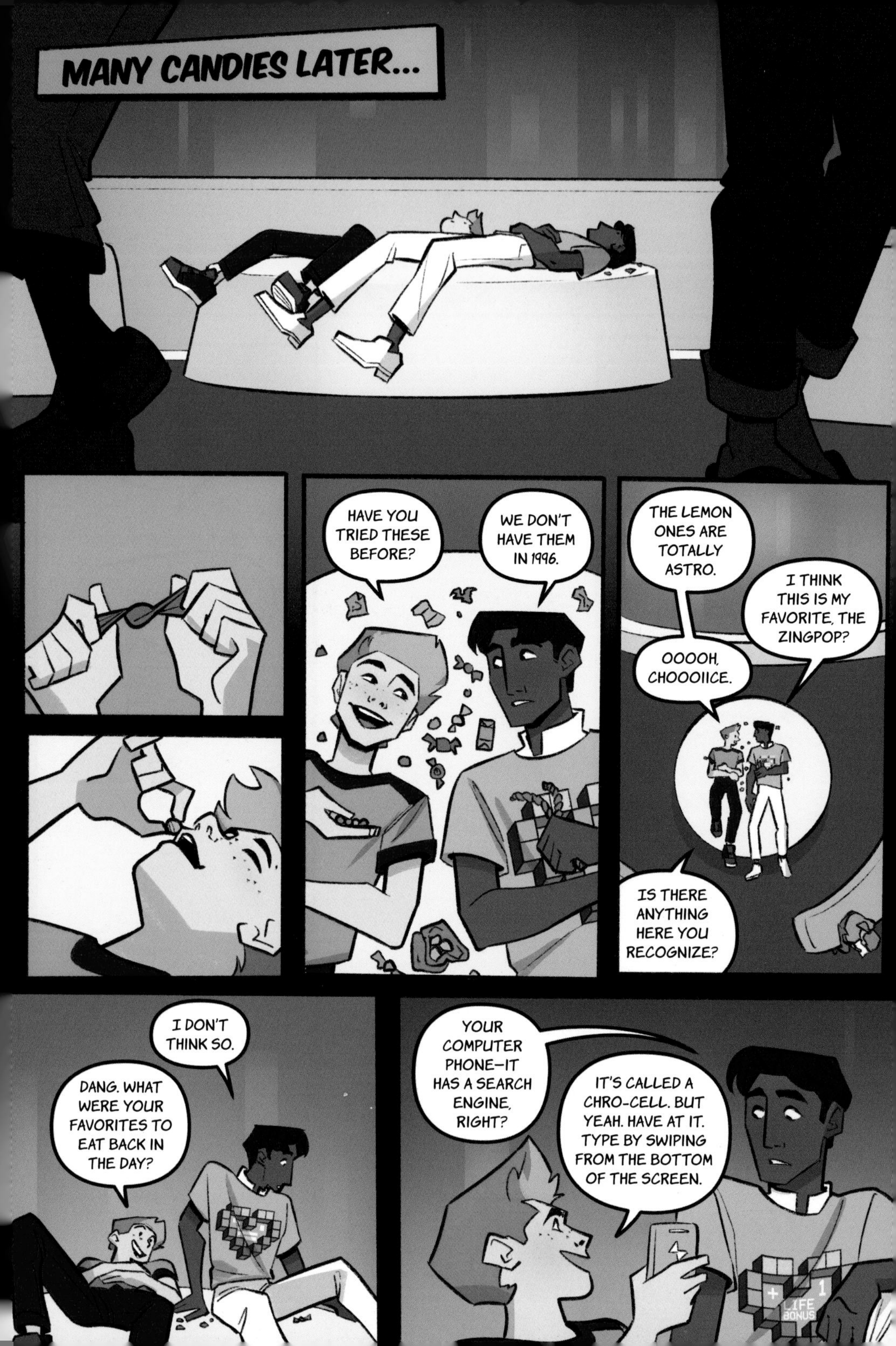
MANY CANDIES LATER...
HAVE YOU TRIED THESE BEFORE?
WE DON'T HAVE THEM IN 1996.
THE LEMON ONES ARE TOTALLY ASTRO.
OOOOH, CHOOOIICE.
I THINK THIS IS MY FAVORITE, THE ZINGPOP?
IS THERE ANYTHING HERE YOU RECOGNIZE?
I DON'T THINK SO.
DANG. WHAT WERE YOUR FAVORITES TO EAT BACK IN THE DAY?
YOUR COMPUTER PHONE—IT HAS A SEARCH ENGINE, RIGHT?
IT'S CALLED A CHRO-CELL. BUT YEAH. HAVE AT IT. TYPE BY SWIPING FROM THE BOTTOM OF THE SCREEN.
+1 LIFE BONUS

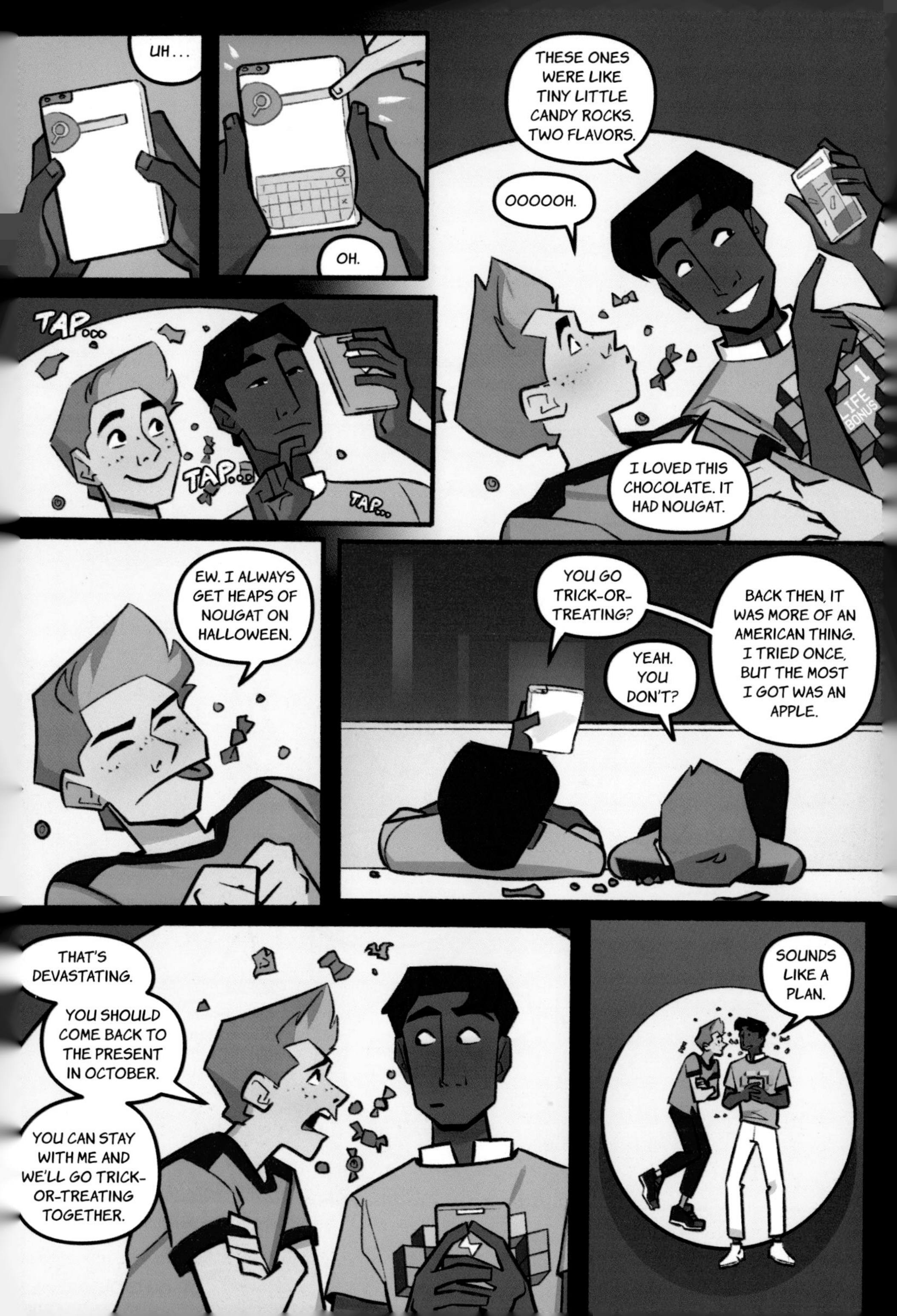
UH...
OH.
THESE ONES WERE LIKE TINY LITTLE CANDY ROCKS. TWO FLAVORS.
OOOOOH.
TAP...
TAP...
TAP...
1 LIFE BONUS
I LOVED THIS CHOCOLATE. IT HAD NOUGAT.
EW. I ALWAYS GET HEAPS OF NOUGAT ON HALLOWEEN.
YOU GO TRICK-OR-TREATING?
YEAH. YOU DON'T?
BACK THEN, IT WAS MORE OF AN AMERICAN THING. I TRIED ONCE, BUT THE MOST I GOT WAS AN APPLE.
THAT'S DEVASTATING.
YOU SHOULD COME BACK TO THE PRESENT IN OCTOBER.
YOU CAN STAY WITH ME AND WE'LL GO TRICK-OR-TREATING TOGETHER.
SOUNDS LIKE A PLAN.

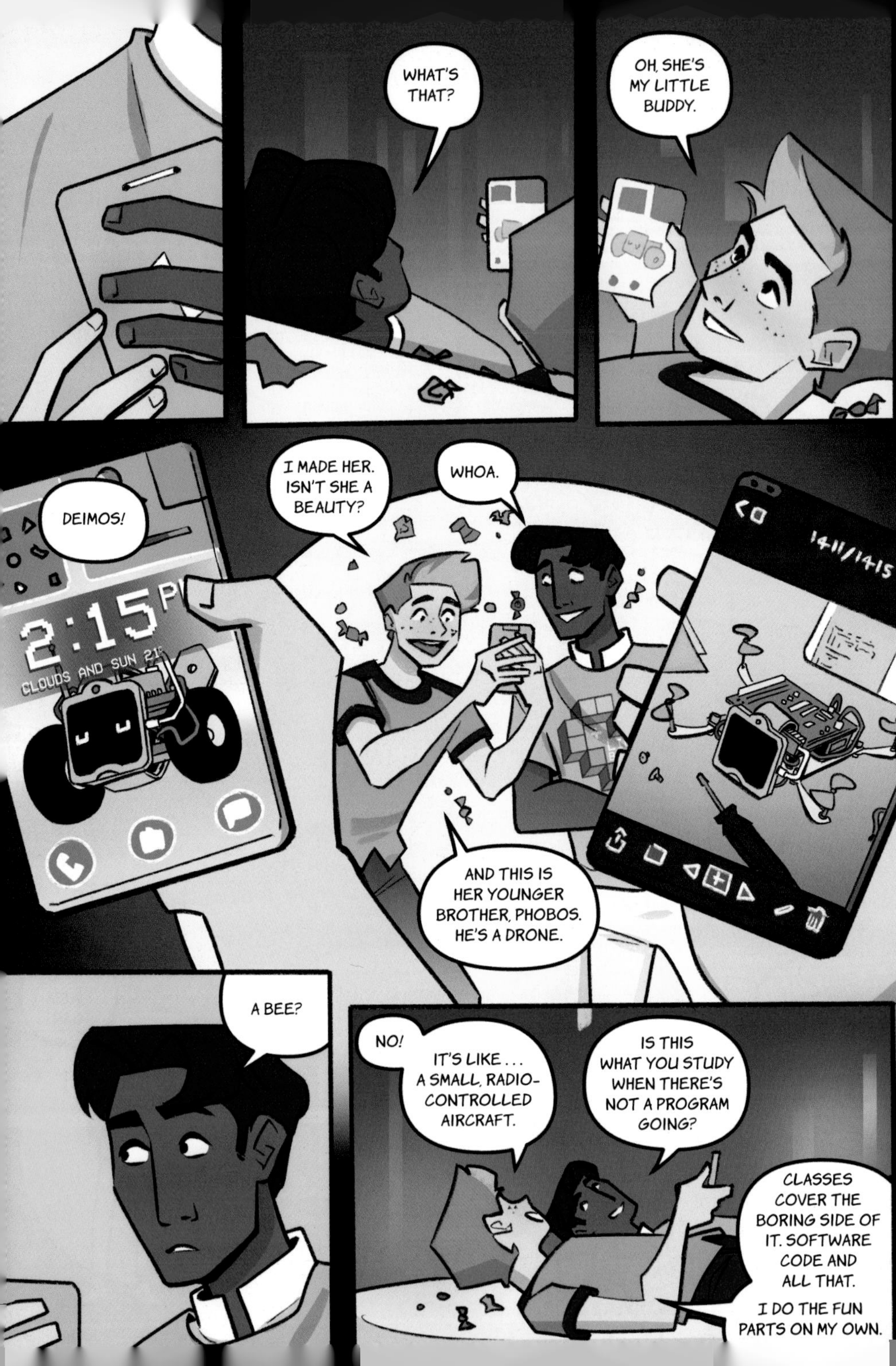

WHAT'S THAT?
OH, SHE'S MY LITTLE BUDDY.
DEIMOS!
2:15
CLOUDS AND SUN
I MADE HER. ISN'T SHE A BEAUTY?
WHOA.
AND THIS IS HER YOUNGER BROTHER, PHOBOS. HE'S A DRONE.
A BEE?
NO!
IT'S LIKE . . . A SMALL, RADIO-CONTROLLED AIRCRAFT.
IS THIS WHAT YOU STUDY WHEN THERE'S NOT A PROGRAM GOING?
CLASSES COVER THE BORING SIDE OF IT. SOFTWARE CODE AND ALL THAT.
I DO THE FUN PARTS ON MY OWN.

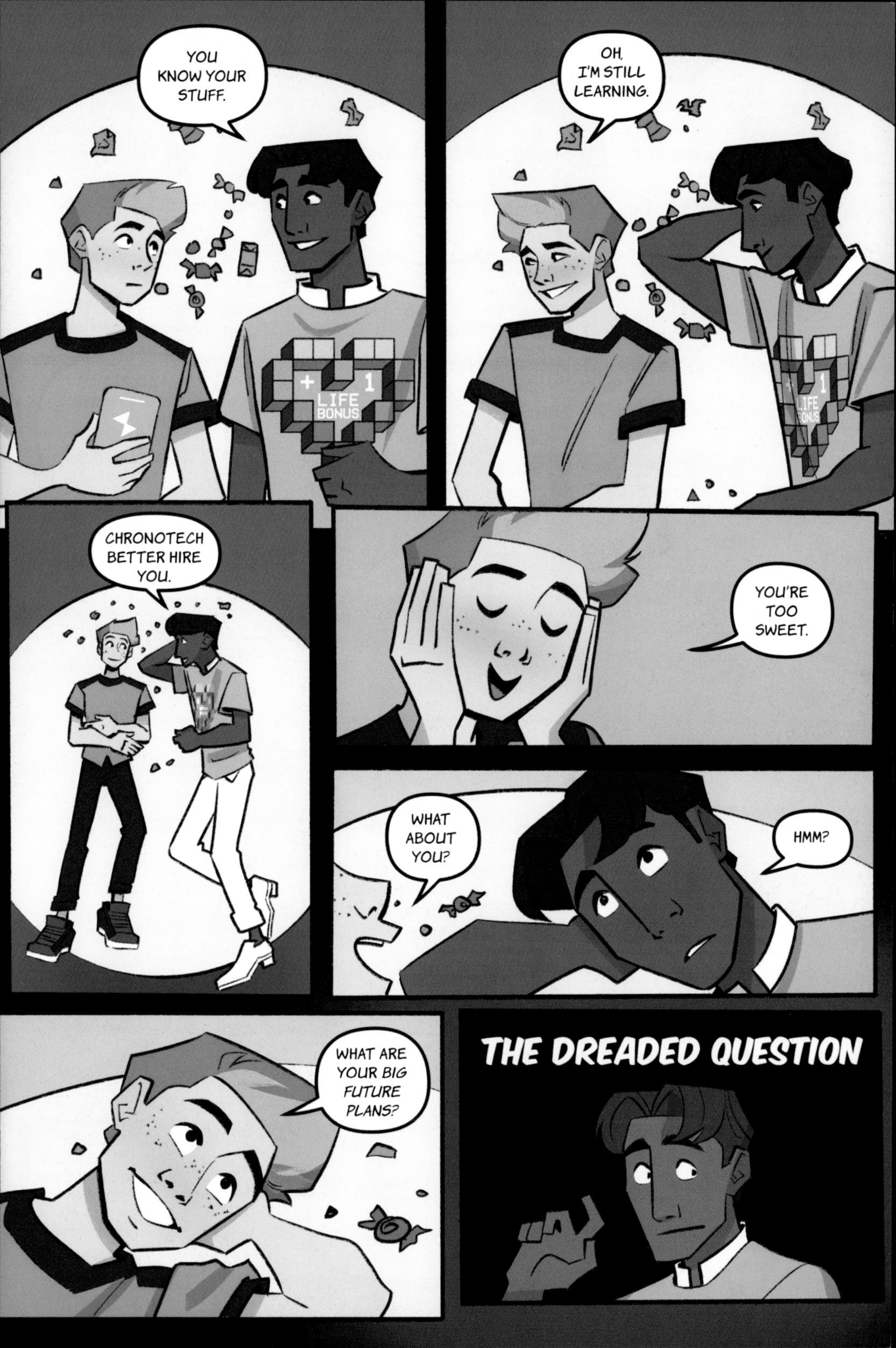
YOU KNOW YOUR STUFF.
+1
LIFE BONUS
OH, I'M STILL LEARNING.
CHRONOTECH BETTER HIRE YOU.
YOU'RE TOO SWEET.
WHAT ABOUT YOU?
HMM?
WHAT ARE YOUR BIG FUTURE PLANS?
THE DREADED QUESTION

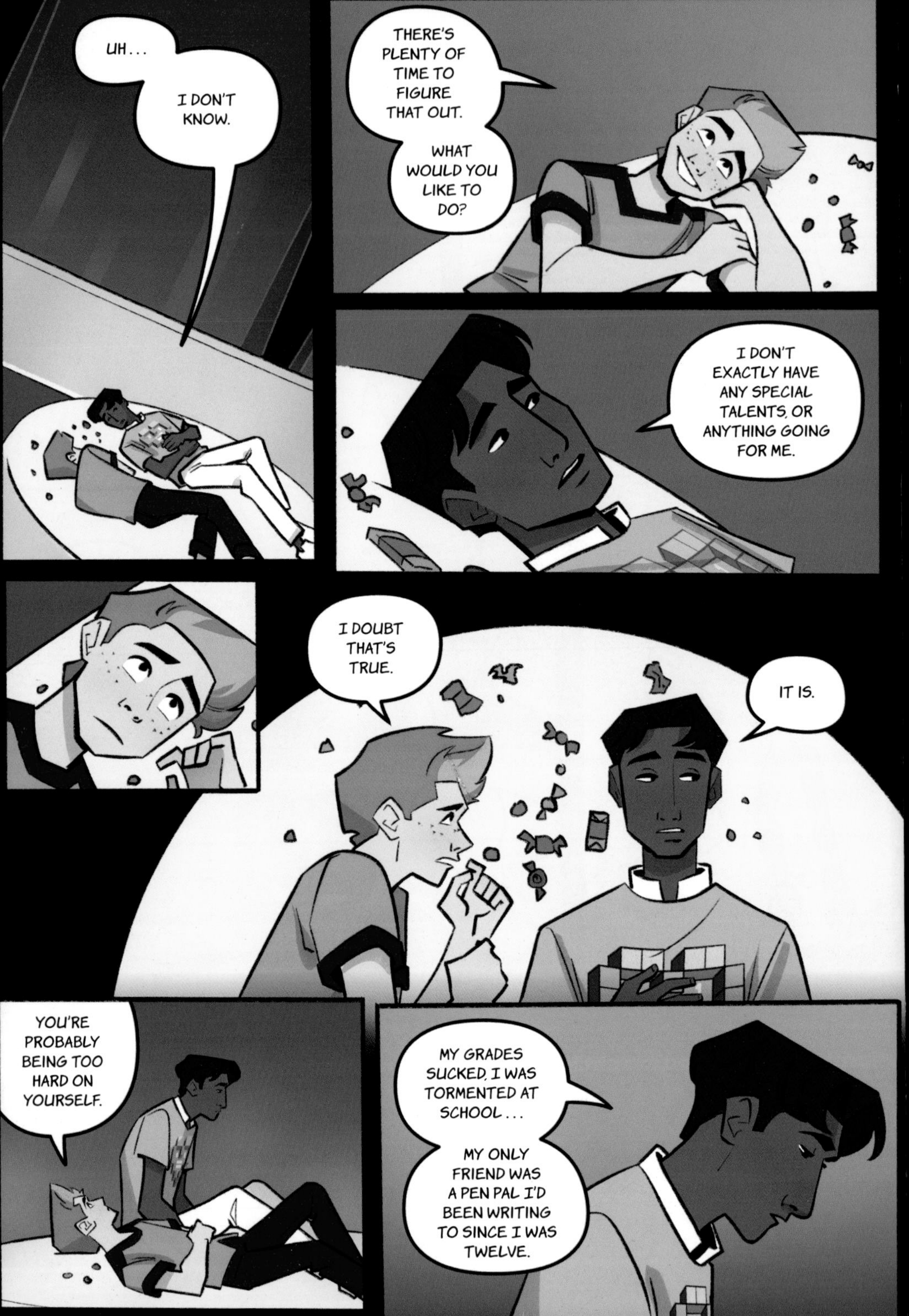
UH . . .
I DON'T KNOW.
THERE'S PLENTY OF TIME TO FIGURE THAT OUT.
WHAT WOULD YOU LIKE TO DO?
I DON'T EXACTLY HAVE ANY SPECIAL TALENTS, OR ANYTHING GOING FOR ME.
I DOUBT THAT'S TRUE.
IT IS.
YOU'RE PROBABLY BEING TOO HARD ON YOURSELF.
MY GRADES SUCKED, I WAS TORMENTED AT SCHOOL . . .
MY ONLY FRIEND WAS A PEN PAL I'D BEEN WRITING TO SINCE I WAS TWELVE.

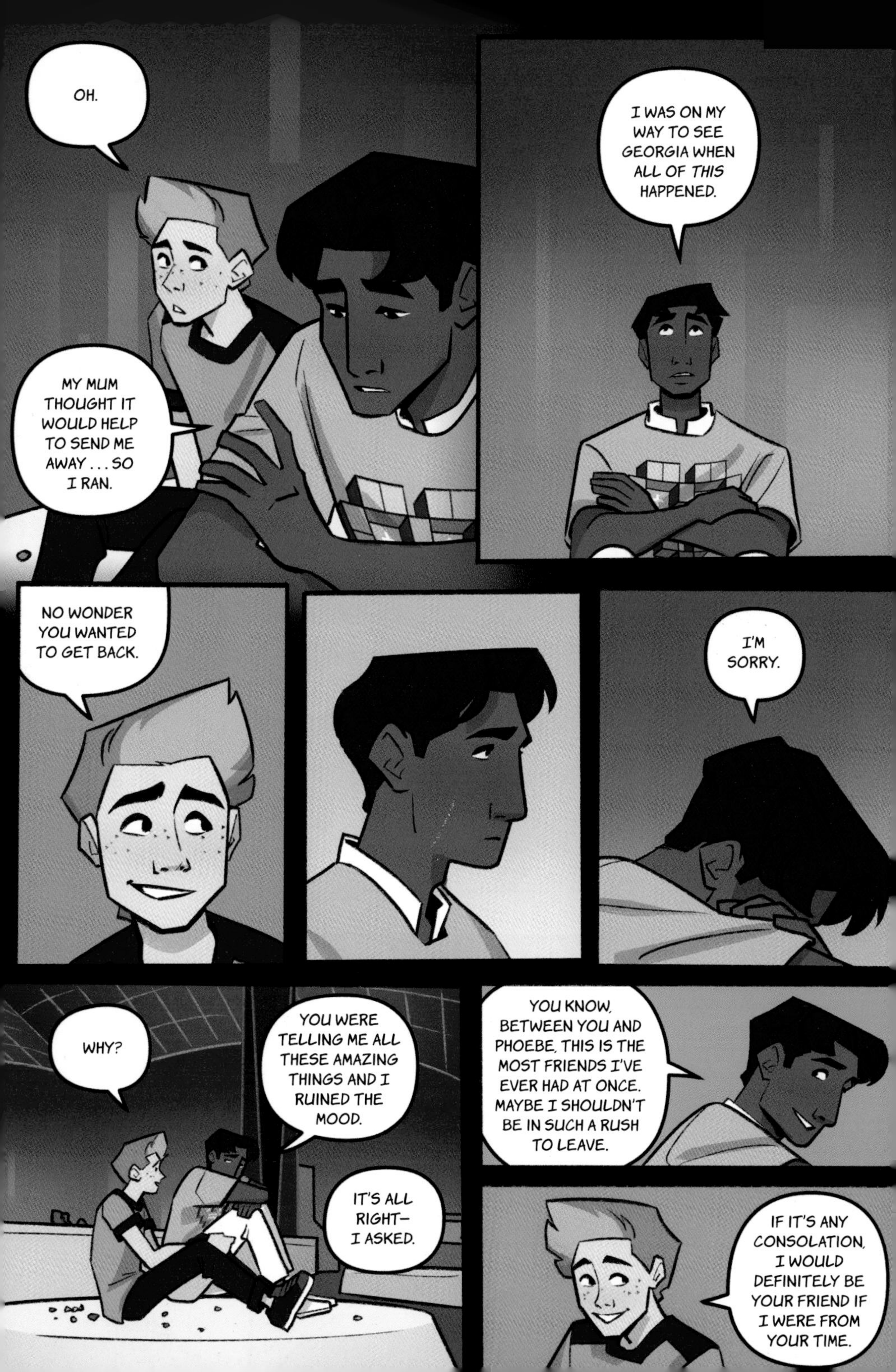
OH.
MY MUM THOUGHT IT WOULD HELP TO SEND ME AWAY . . . SO I RAN.
I WAS ON MY WAY TO SEE GEORGIA WHEN ALL OF THIS HAPPENED.
NO WONDER YOU WANTED TO GET BACK.
I'M SORRY.
WHY?
YOU WERE TELLING ME ALL THESE AMAZING THINGS AND I RUINED THE MOOD.
IT'S ALL RIGHT— I ASKED.
YOU KNOW, BETWEEN YOU AND PHOEBE, THIS IS THE MOST FRIENDS I'VE EVER HAD AT ONCE. MAYBE I SHOULDN'T BE IN SUCH A RUSH TO LEAVE.
IF IT'S ANY CONSOLATION, I WOULD DEFINITELY BE YOUR FRIEND IF I WERE FROM YOUR TIME.

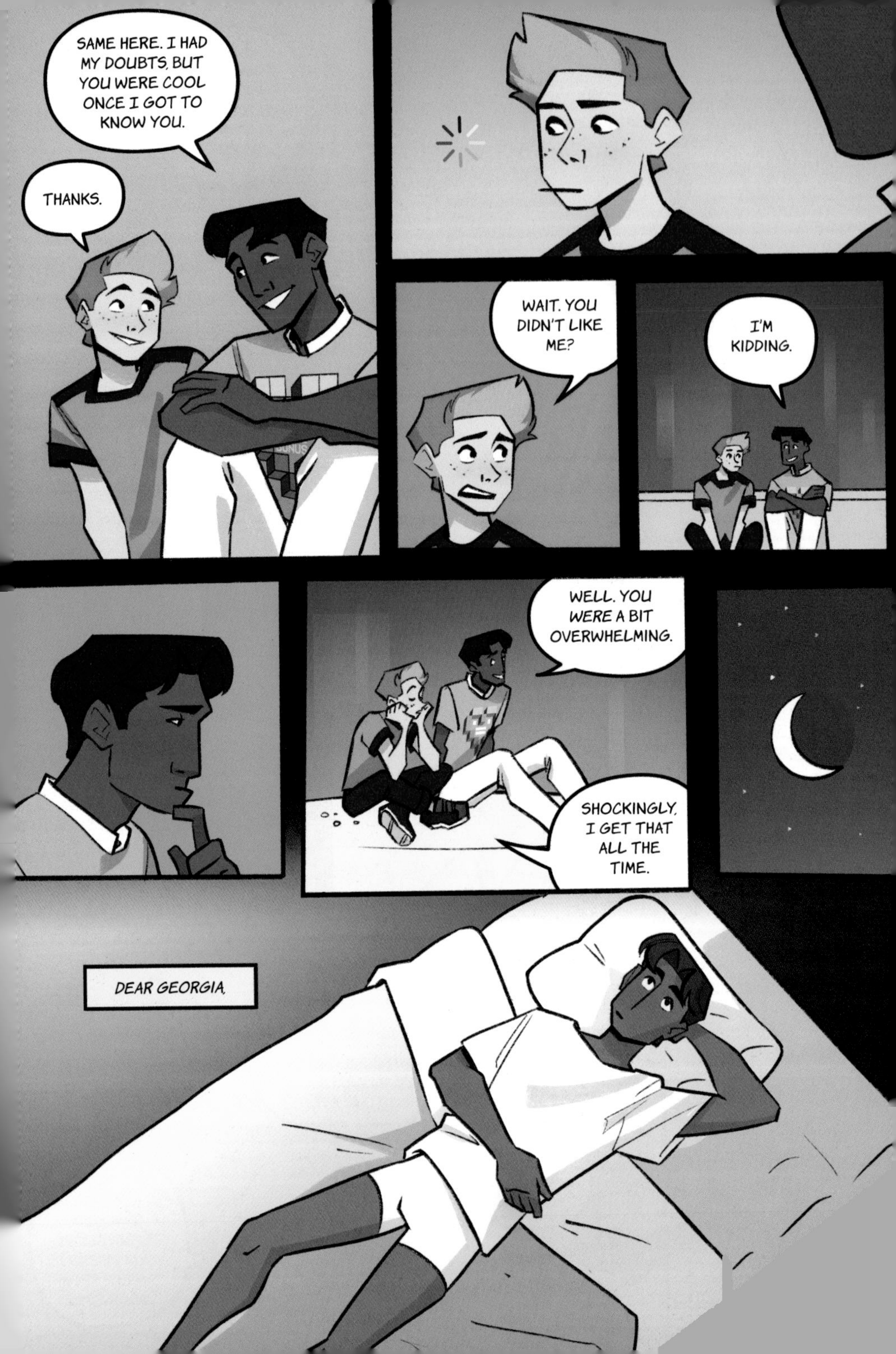
SAME HERE. I HAD MY DOUBTS, BUT YOU WERE COOL ONCE I GOT TO KNOW YOU.
THANKS.
WAIT. YOU DIDN'T LIKE ME?
I'M KIDDING.
WELL. YOU WERE A BIT OVERWHELMING.
SHOCKINGLY, I GET THAT ALL THE TIME.
DEAR GEORGIA,

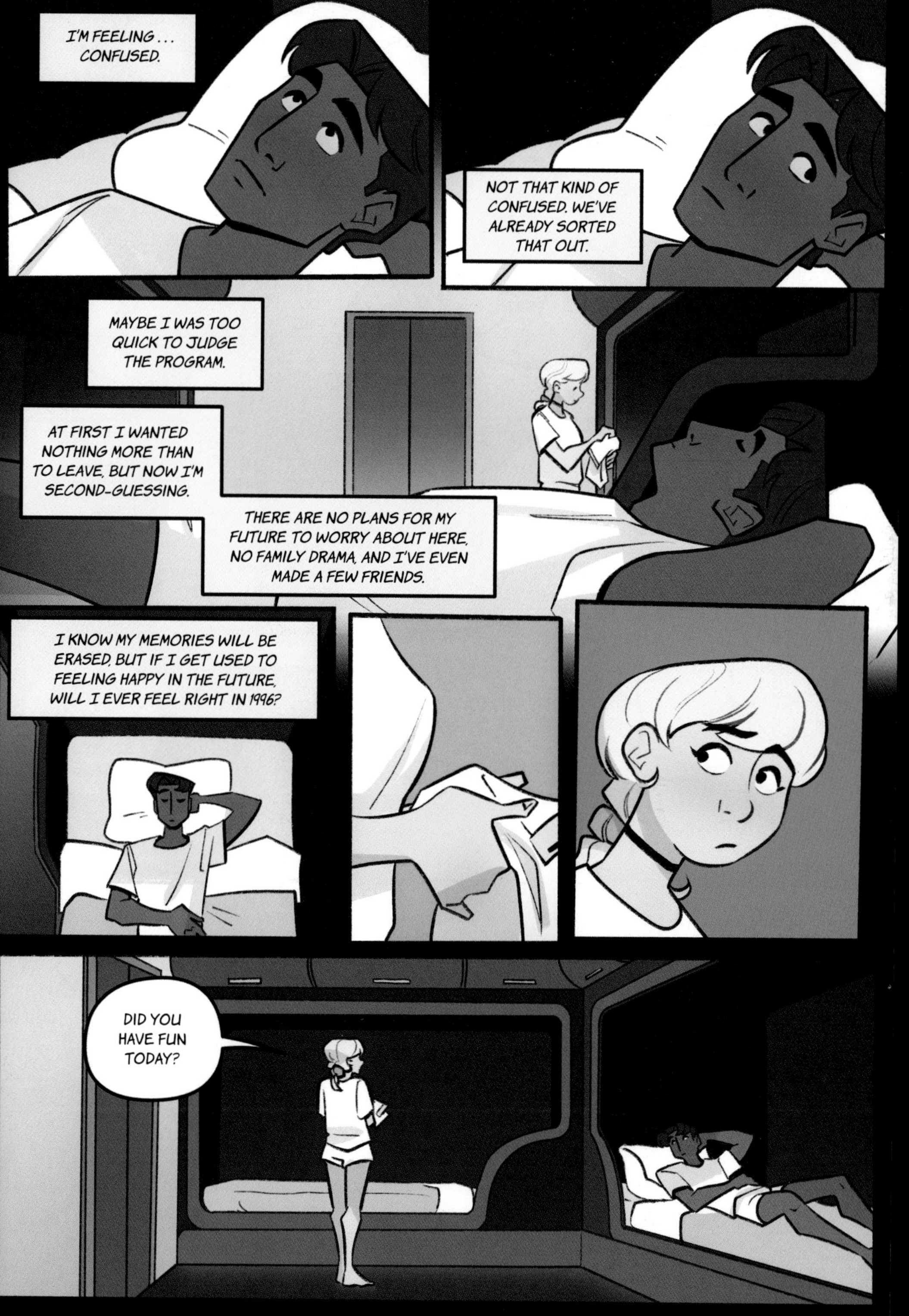
I'M FEELING . . . CONFUSED.
NOT THAT KIND OF CONFUSED. WE'VE ALREADY SORTED THAT OUT.
MAYBE I WAS TOO QUICK TO JUDGE THE PROGRAM.
AT FIRST I WANTED NOTHING MORE THAN TO LEAVE, BUT NOW I'M SECOND-GUESSING.
THERE ARE NO PLANS FOR MY FUTURE TO WORRY ABOUT HERE, NO FAMILY DRAMA, AND I'VE EVEN MADE A FEW FRIENDS.
I KNOW MY MEMORIES WILL BE ERASED, BUT IF I GET USED TO FEELING HAPPY IN THE FUTURE, WILL I EVER FEEL RIGHT IN 1996?
DID YOU HAVE FUN TODAY?

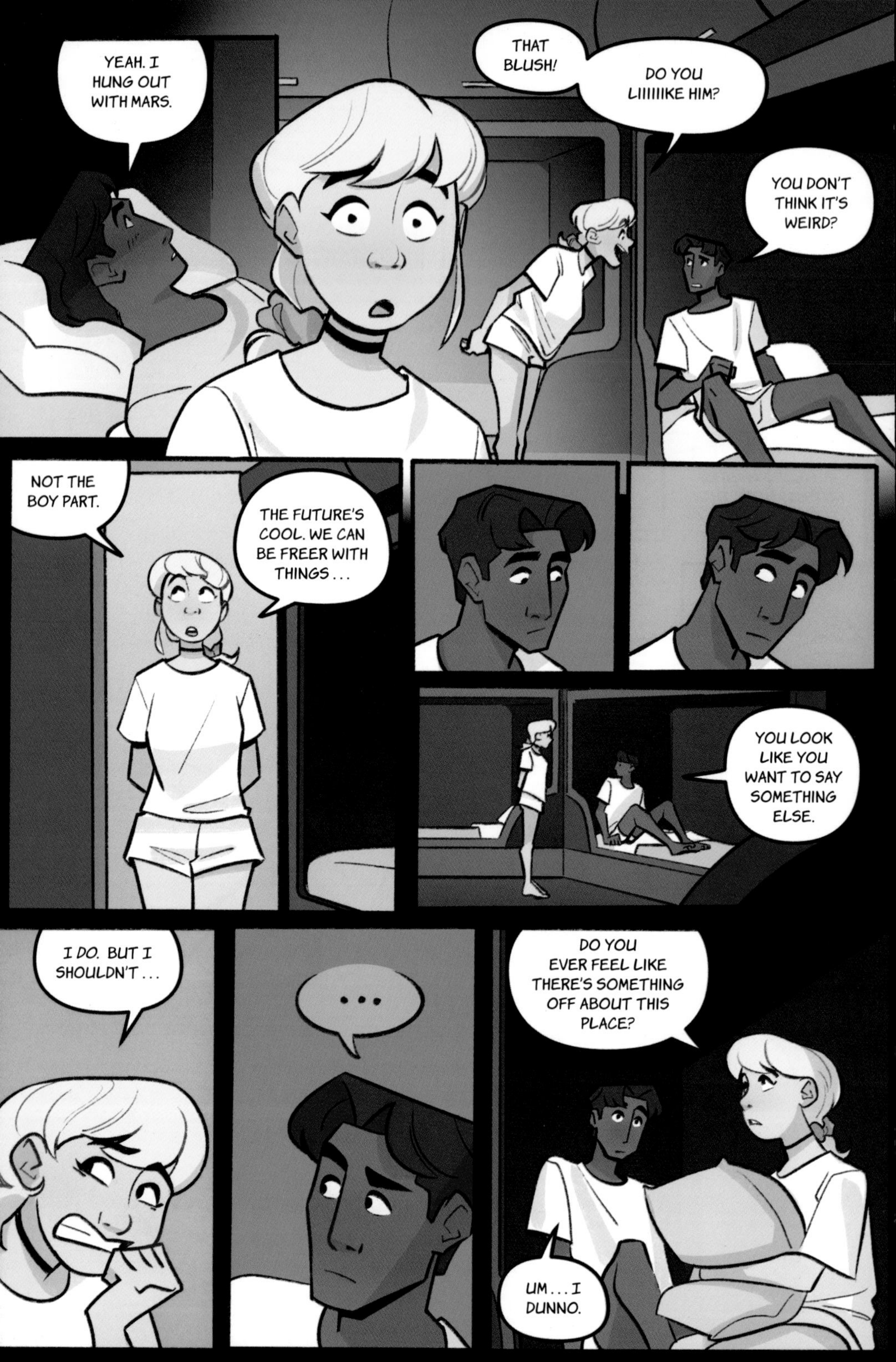
YEAH. I HUNG OUT WITH MARS.
THAT BLUSH!
DO YOU LIIIIIKE HIM?
YOU DON'T THINK IT'S WEIRD?
NOT THE BOY PART.
THE FUTURE'S COOL. WE CAN BE FREER WITH THINGS . . .
YOU LOOK LIKE YOU WANT TO SAY SOMETHING ELSE.
I DO. BUT I SHOULDN'T . . .
. . .
DO YOU EVER FEEL LIKE THERE'S SOMETHING OFF ABOUT THIS PLACE?
UM . . . I DUNNO.

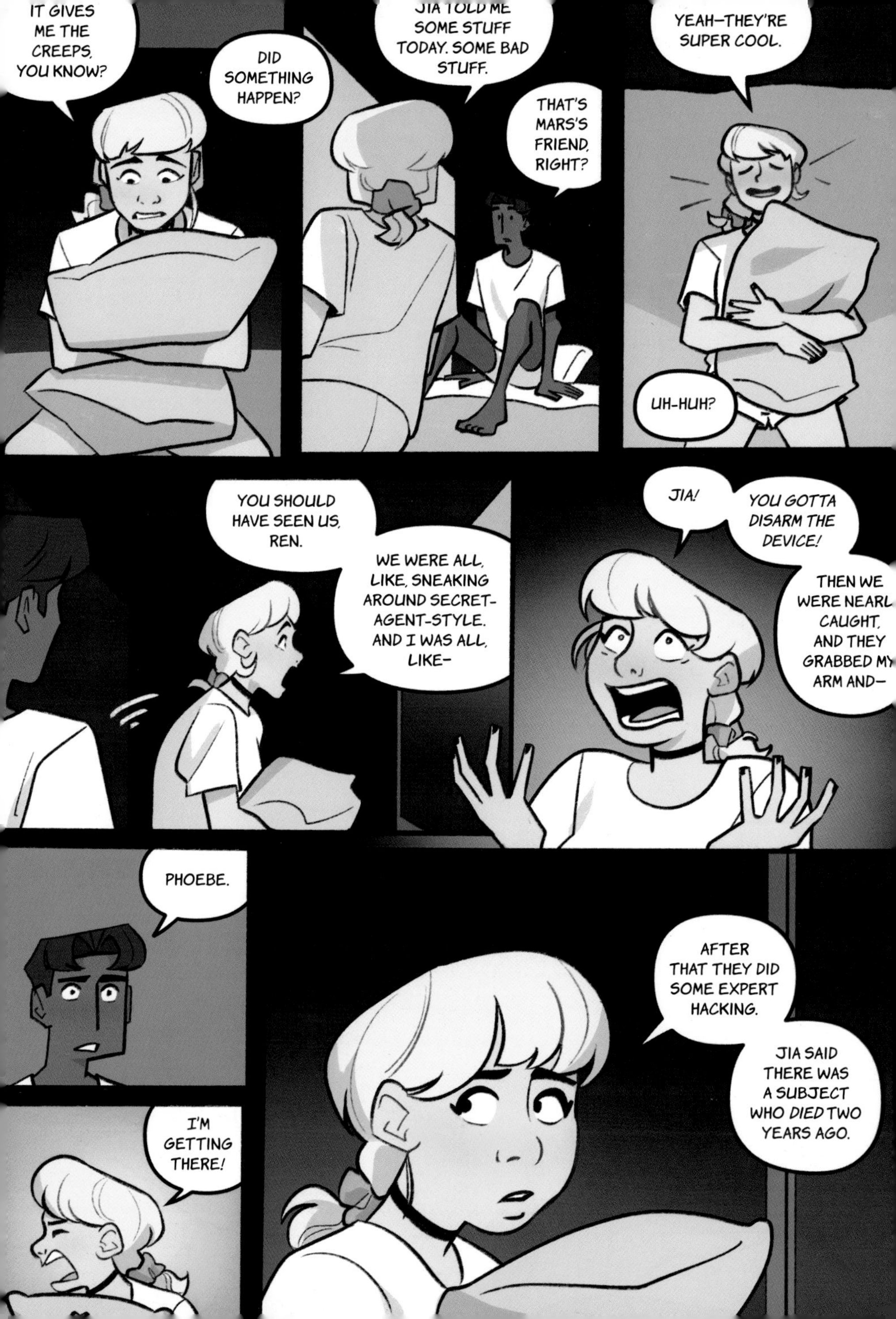

IT GIVES ME THE CREEPS, YOU KNOW?
DID SOMETHING HAPPEN?
JIA TOLD ME SOME STUFF TODAY. SOME BAD STUFF.
THAT'S MARS'S FRIEND, RIGHT?
YEAH—THEY'RE SUPER COOL.
UH-HUH?
YOU SHOULD HAVE SEEN US, REN.
WE WERE ALL, LIKE, SNEAKING AROUND SECRET-AGENT-STYLE. AND I WAS ALL, LIKE-
JIA!
YOU GOTTA DISARM THE DEVICE!
THEN WE WERE NEARL CAUGHT, AND THEY GRABBED MY ARM AND—
PHOEBE.
I'M GETTING THERE!
AFTER THAT THEY DID SOME EXPERT HACKING.
JIA SAID THERE WAS A SUBJECT WHO DIED TWO YEARS AGO.

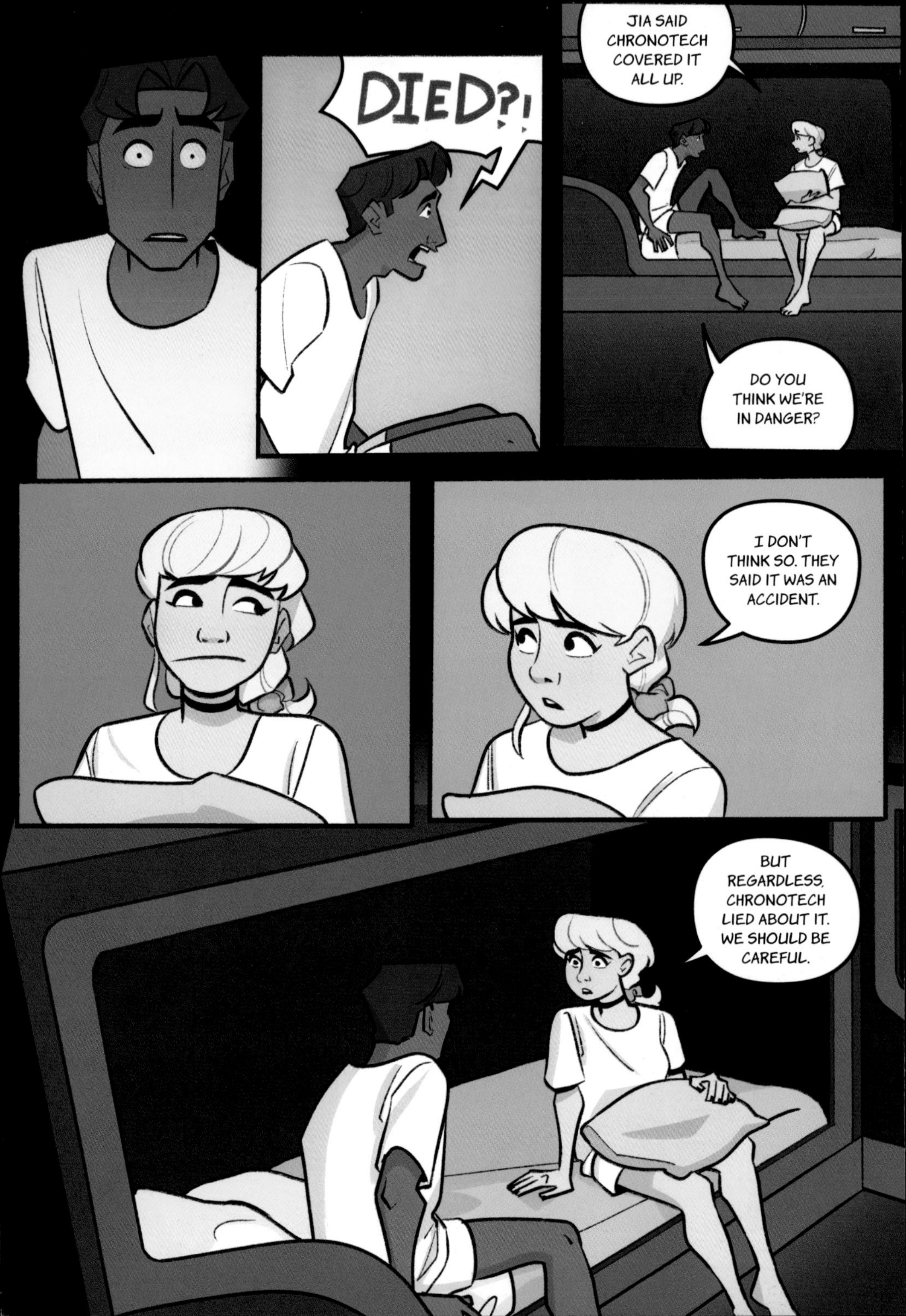
DIED?!
JIA SAID CHRONOTECH COVERED IT ALL UP.
DO YOU THINK WE'RE IN DANGER?
I DON'T THINK SO. THEY SAID IT WAS AN ACCIDENT.
BUT REGARDLESS, CHRONOTECH LIED ABOUT IT. WE SHOULD BE CAREFUL.

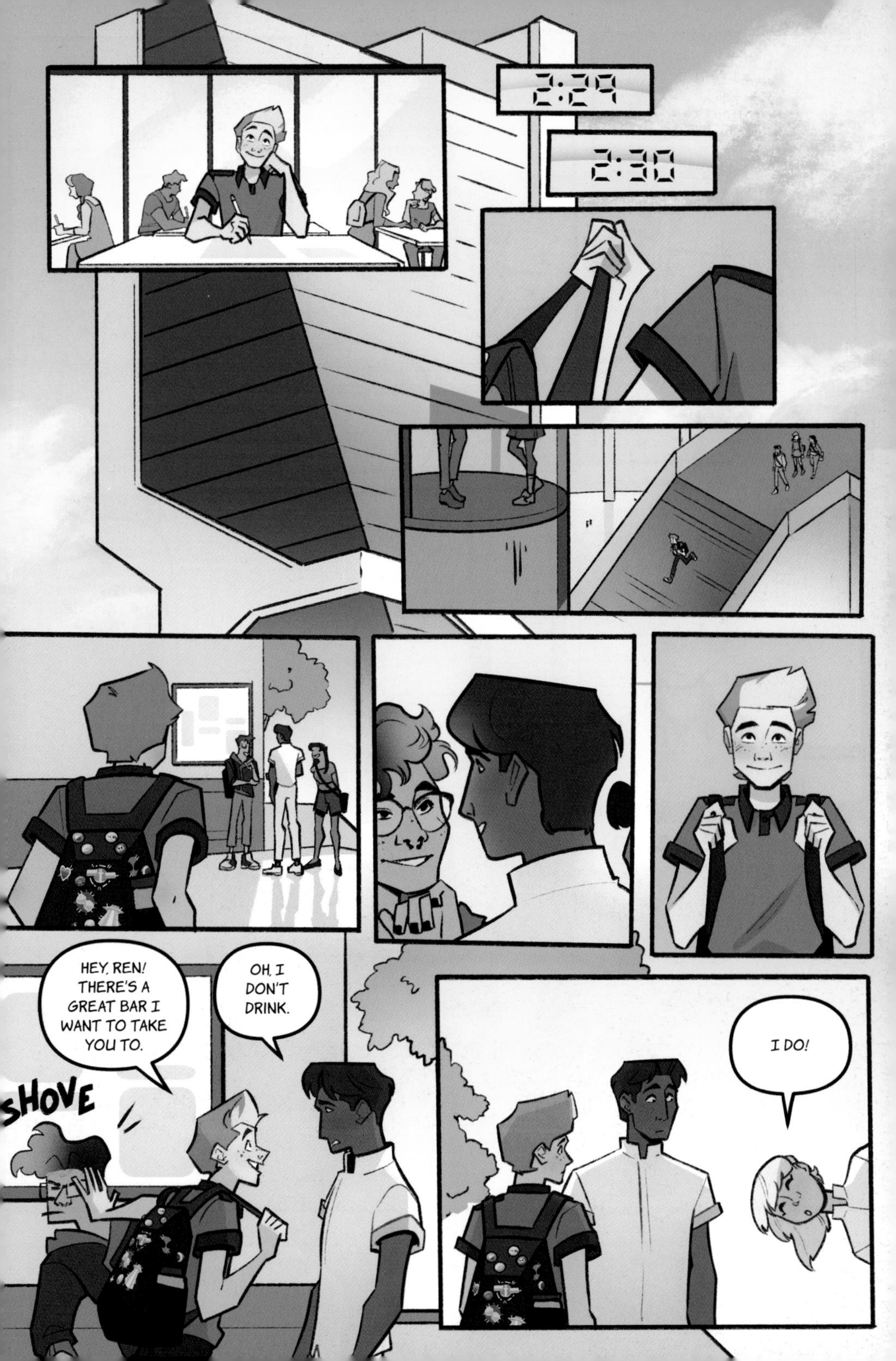
2:29
2:30
HEY, REN! THERE'S A GREAT BAR I WANT TO TAKE YOU TO.
OH, I DON'T DRINK.
SHOVE
I DO!

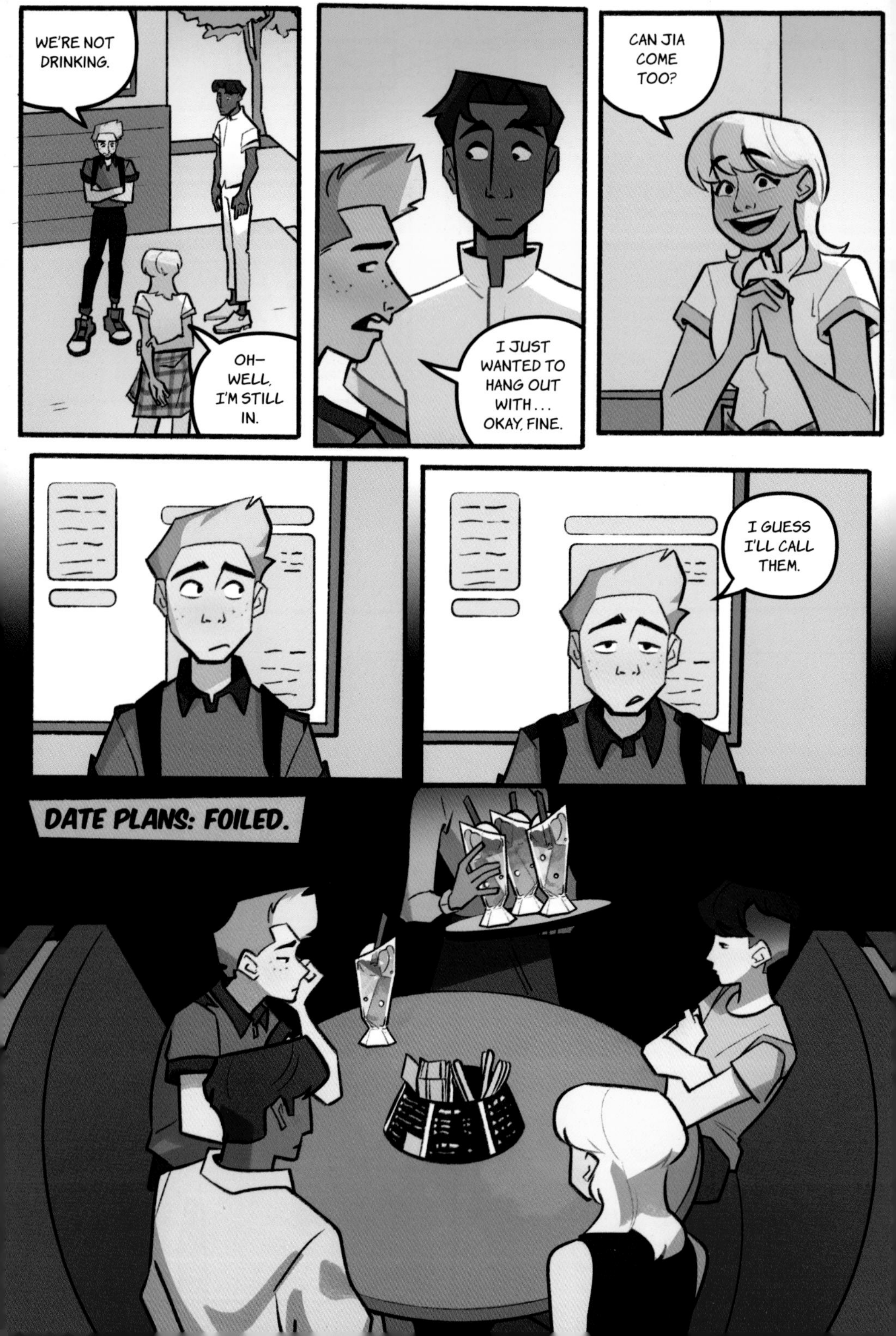
WE'RE NOT DRINKING.
OH— WELL, I'M STILL IN.
I JUST WANTED TO HANG OUT WITH . . . OKAY, FINE.
CAN JIA COME TOO?
I GUESS I'LL CALL THEM.
DATE PLANS: FOILED.

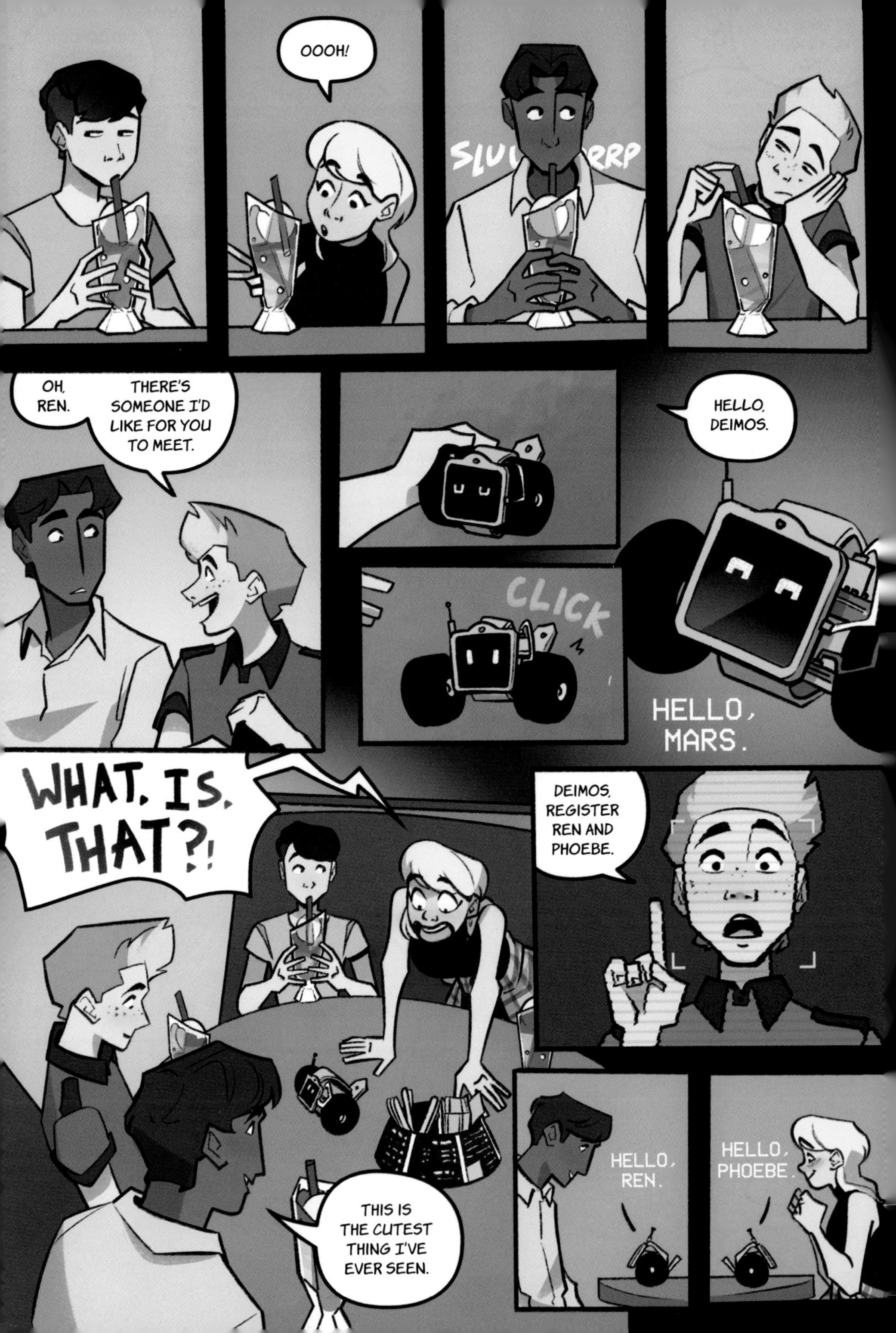
OOOH!
SLU RRP
OH, REN.
THERE'S SOMEONE I'D LIKE FOR YOU TO MEET.
HELLO, DEIMOS.
CLICK
HELLO, MARS.
WHAT. IS. THAT?!
DEIMOS, REGISTER REN AND PHOEBE.
THIS IS THE CUTEST THING I'VE EVER SEEN.
HELLO, REN.
HELLO, PHOEBE.

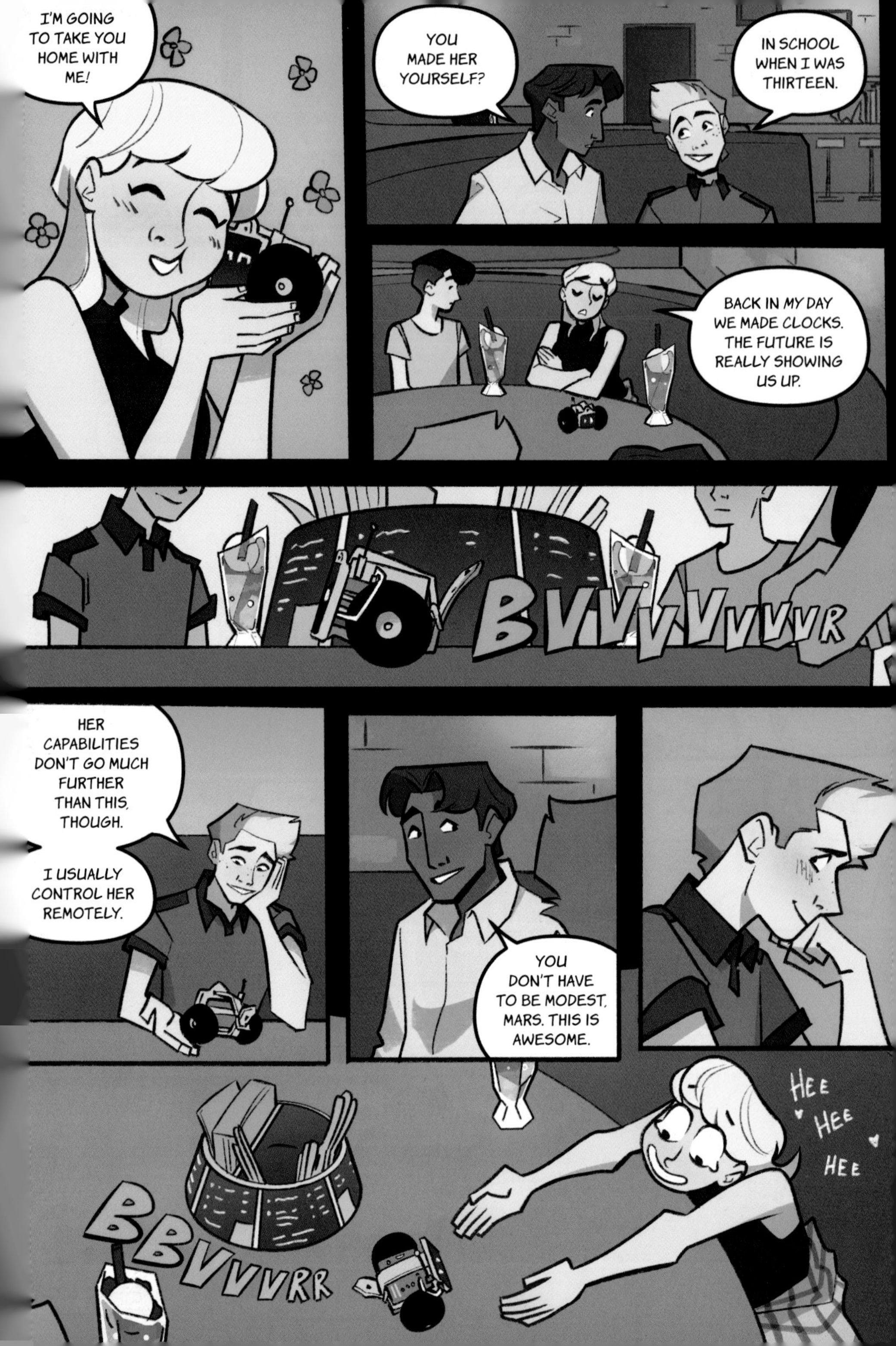
I'M GOING TO TAKE YOU HOME WITH ME!
YOU MADE HER YOURSELF?
IN SCHOOL WHEN I WAS THIRTEEN.
BACK IN MY DAY WE MADE CLOCKS. THE FUTURE IS REALLY SHOWING US UP.
BVVVVVVVVR
HER CAPABILITIES DON'T GO MUCH FURTHER THAN THIS, THOUGH.
I USUALLY CONTROL HER REMOTELY.
YOU DON'T HAVE TO BE MODEST, MARS. THIS IS AWESOME.
BBVVVVRR
HEE
HEE
HEE

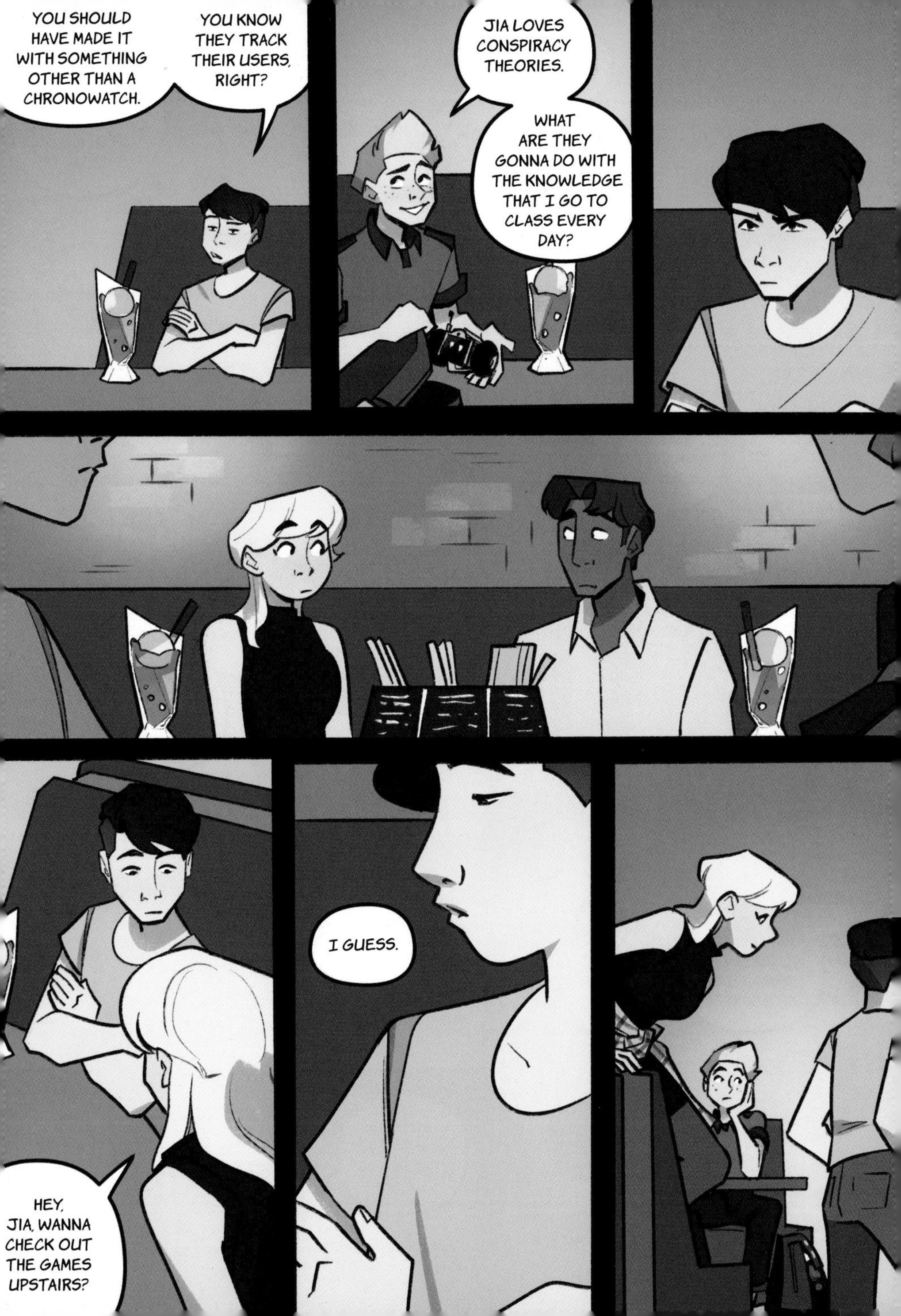
YOU SHOULD HAVE MADE IT WITH SOMETHING OTHER THAN A CHRONOWATCH.
YOU KNOW THEY TRACK THEIR USERS, RIGHT?
JIA LOVES CONSPIRACY THEORIES.
WHAT ARE THEY GONNA DO WITH THE KNOWLEDGE THAT I GO TO CLASS EVERY DAY?
I GUESS.
HEY, JIA, WANNA CHECK OUT THE GAMES UPSTAIRS?

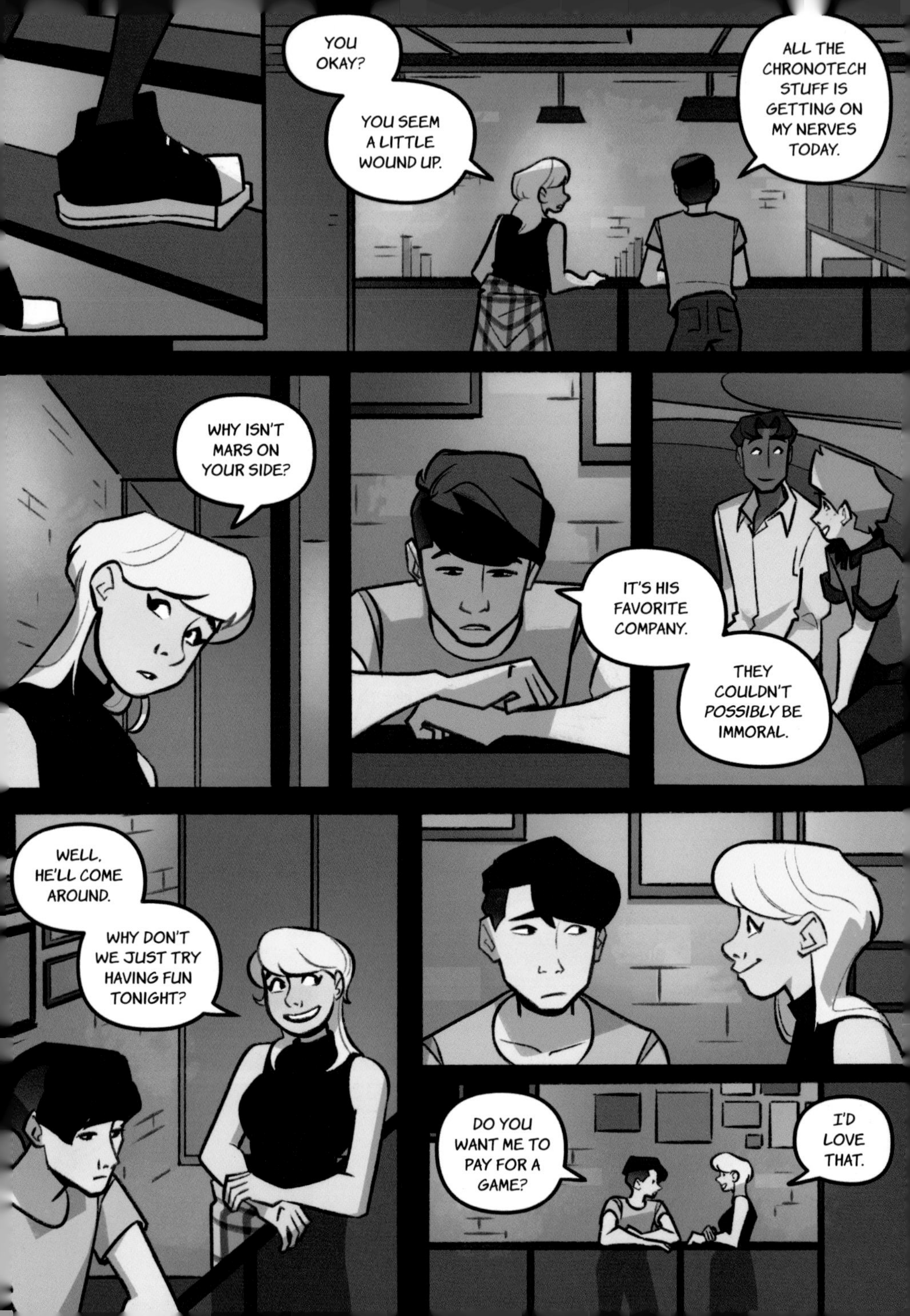
YOU OKAY?
YOU SEEM A LITTLE WOUND UP.
ALL THE CHRONOTECH STUFF IS GETTING ON MY NERVES TODAY.
WHY ISN'T MARS ON YOUR SIDE?
IT'S HIS FAVORITE COMPANY.
THEY COULDN'T *POSSIBLY* BE IMMORAL.
WELL, HE'LL COME AROUND.
WHY DON'T WE JUST TRY HAVING FUN TONIGHT?
DO YOU WANT ME TO PAY FOR A GAME?
I'D LOVE THAT.

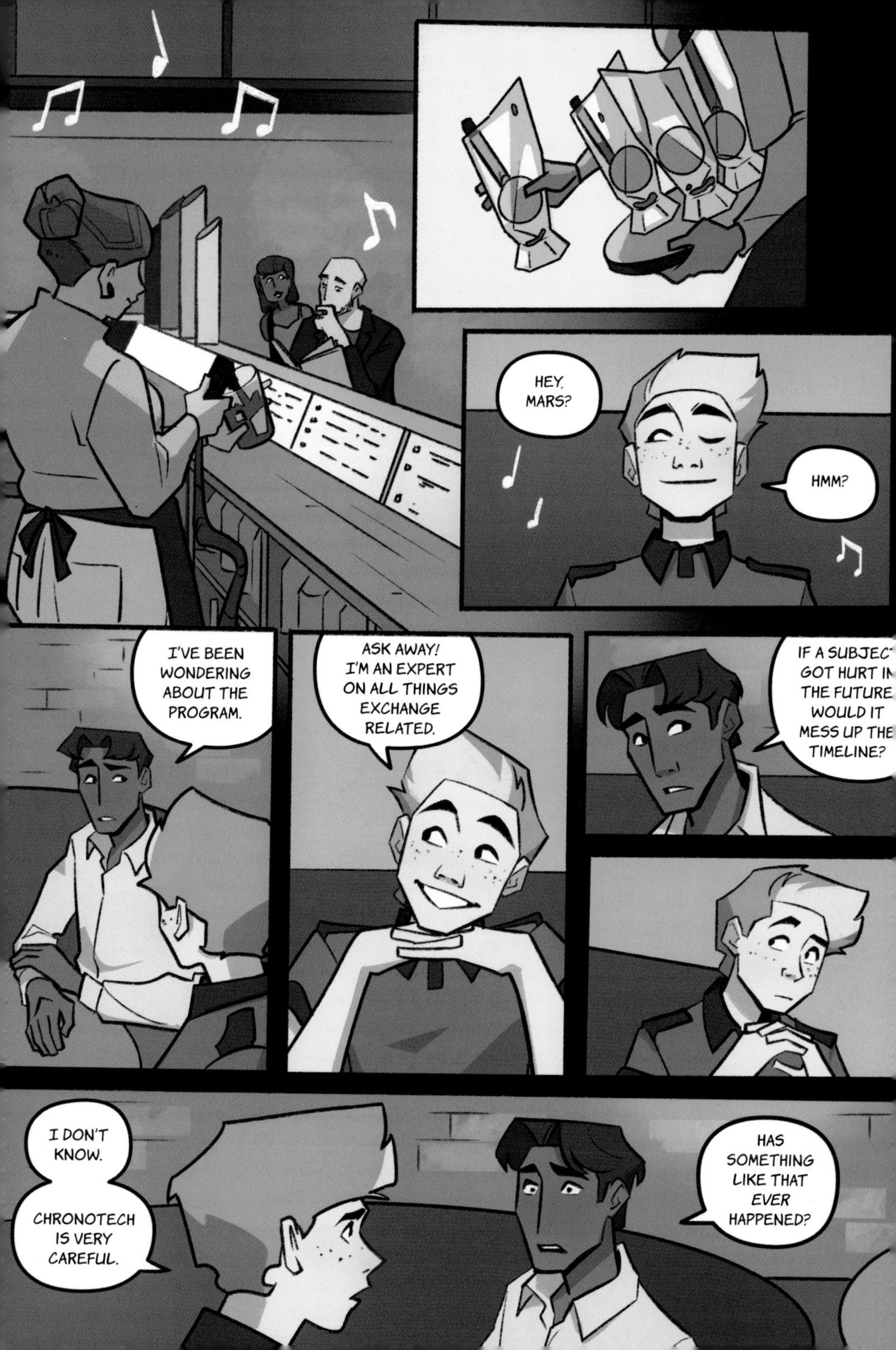
HEY, MARS?
HMM?
I'VE BEEN WONDERING ABOUT THE PROGRAM.
ASK AWAY! I'M AN EXPERT ON ALL THINGS EXCHANGE RELATED.
IF A SUBJEC GOT HURT IN THE FUTURE WOULD IT MESS UP THE TIMELINE?
I DON'T KNOW.
CHRONOTECH IS VERY CAREFUL.
HAS SOMETHING LIKE THAT *EVER* HAPPENED?

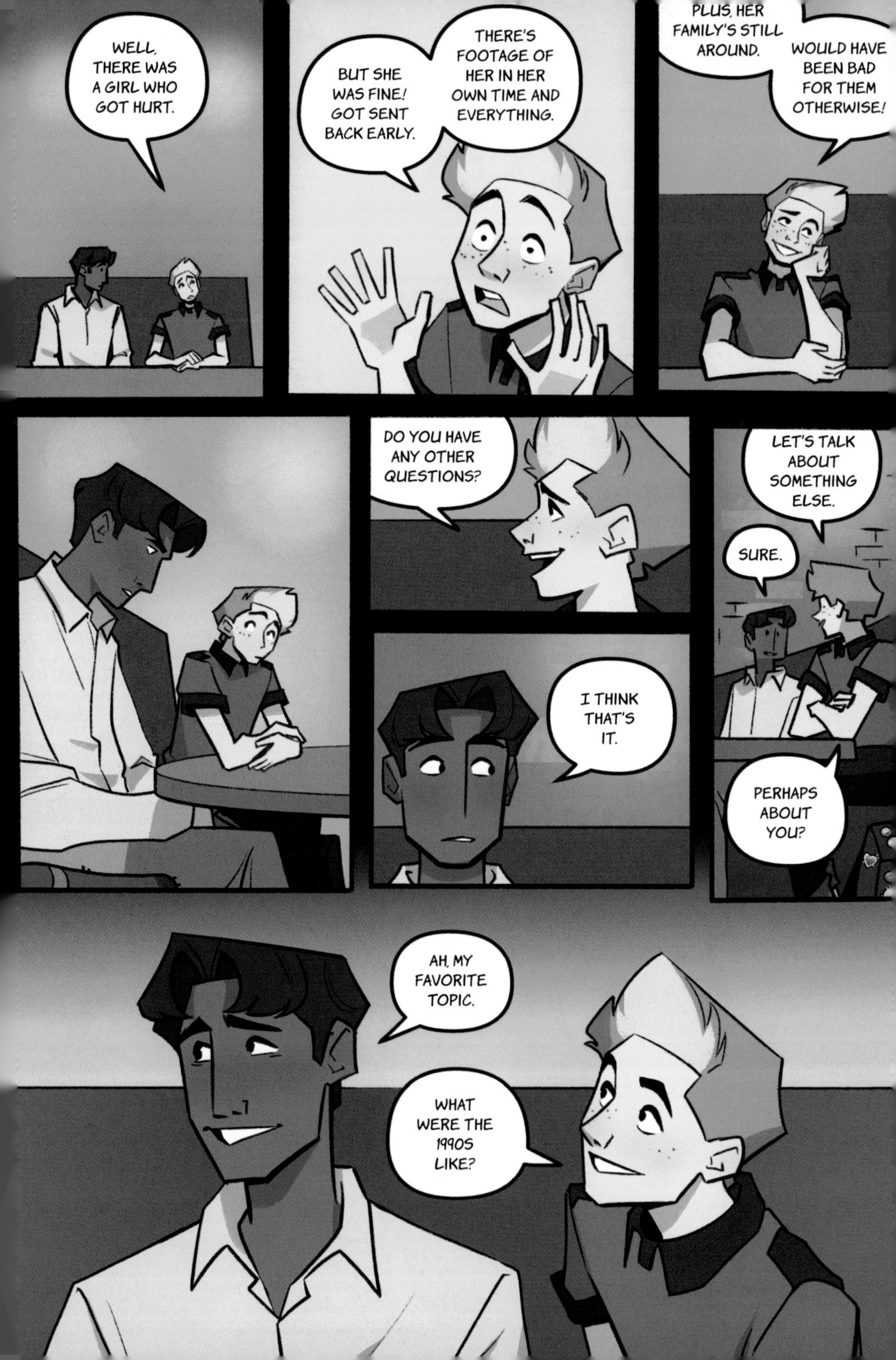
WELL, THERE WAS A GIRL WHO GOT HURT.
BUT SHE WAS FINE! GOT SENT BACK EARLY.
THERE'S FOOTAGE OF HER IN HER OWN TIME AND EVERYTHING.
PLUS, HER FAMILY'S STILL AROUND.
WOULD HAVE BEEN BAD FOR THEM OTHERWISE!
DO YOU HAVE ANY OTHER QUESTIONS?
I THINK THAT'S IT.
LET'S TALK ABOUT SOMETHING ELSE.
SURE.
PERHAPS ABOUT YOU?
AH, MY FAVORITE TOPIC.
WHAT WERE THE 1990S LIKE?

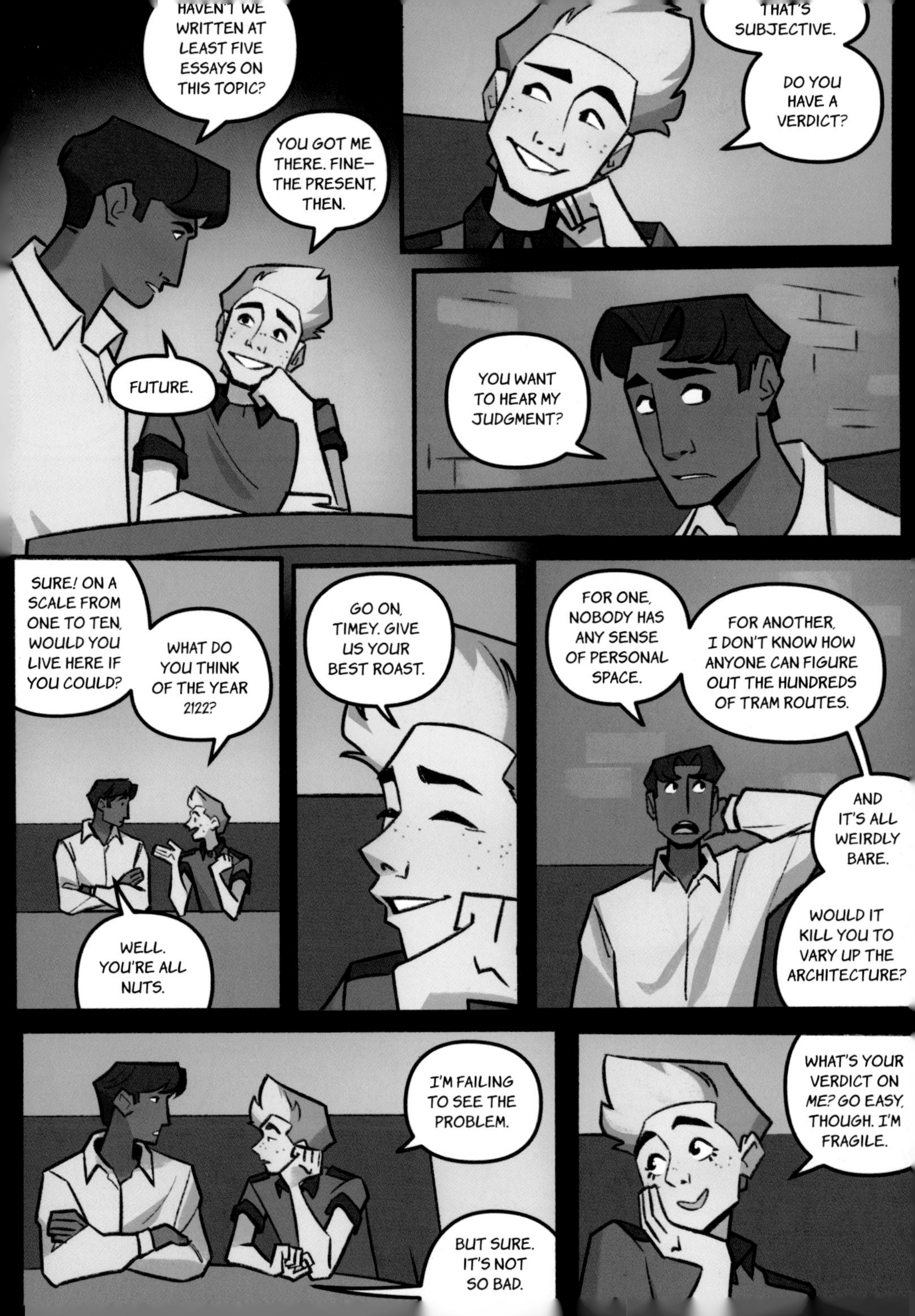
HAVEN'T WE WRITTEN AT LEAST FIVE ESSAYS ON THIS TOPIC?
YOU GOT ME THERE. FINE– THE PRESENT, THEN.
FUTURE.
THAT'S SUBJECTIVE.
DO YOU HAVE A VERDICT?
YOU WANT TO HEAR MY JUDGMENT?
SURE! ON A SCALE FROM ONE TO TEN, WOULD YOU LIVE HERE IF YOU COULD?
WHAT DO YOU THINK OF THE YEAR 2122?
WELL. YOU'RE ALL NUTS.
GO ON, TIMEY. GIVE US YOUR BEST ROAST.
FOR ONE, NOBODY HAS ANY SENSE OF PERSONAL SPACE.
FOR ANOTHER, I DON'T KNOW HOW ANYONE CAN FIGURE OUT THE HUNDREDS OF TRAM ROUTES.
AND IT'S ALL WEIRDLY BARE.
WOULD IT KILL YOU TO VARY UP THE ARCHITECTURE?
I'M FAILING TO SEE THE PROBLEM.
BUT SURE. IT'S NOT SO BAD.
WHAT'S YOUR VERDICT ON ME? GO EASY, THOUGH. I'M FRAGILE.

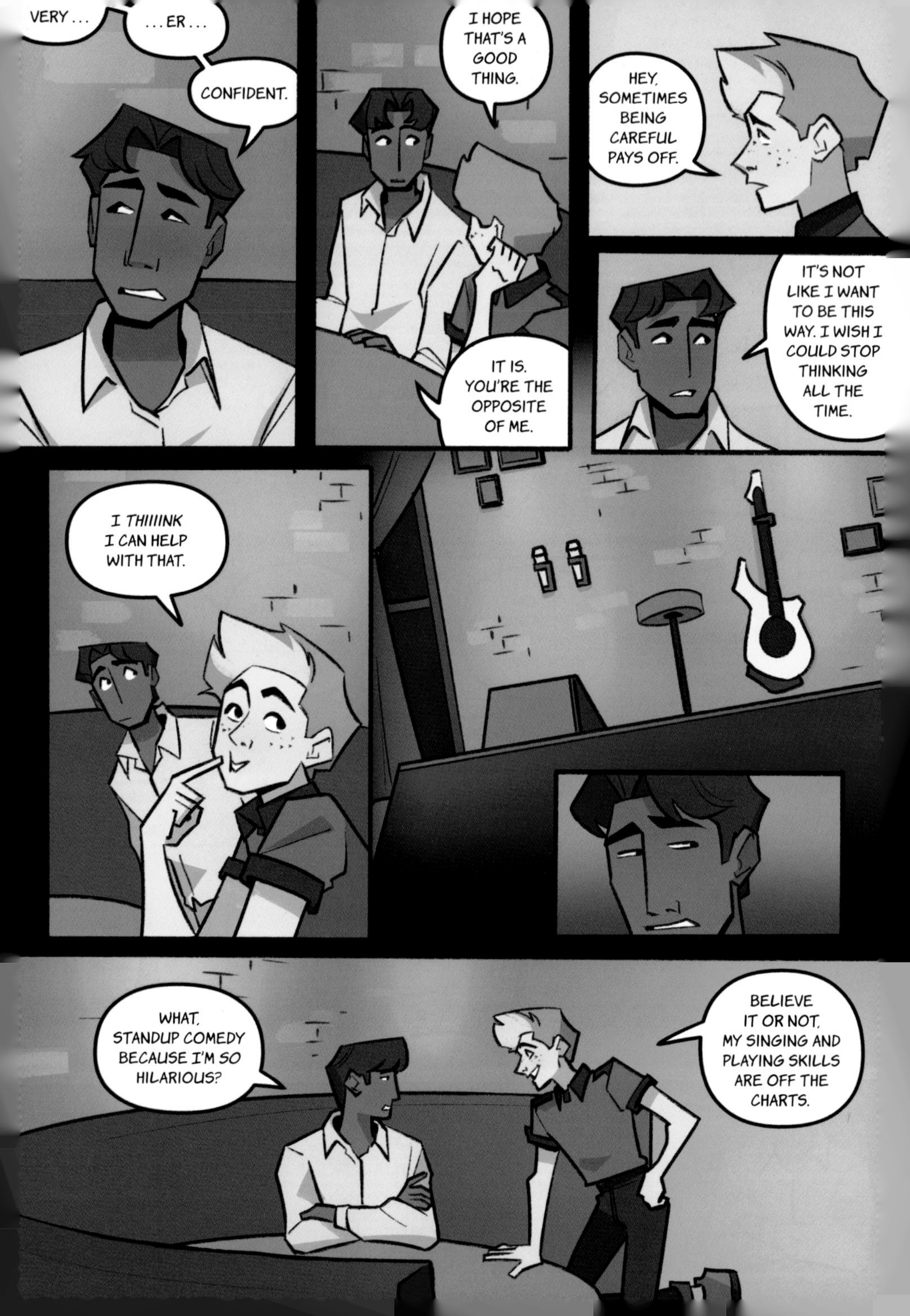
VERY . . .
. . . ER . . .
CONFIDENT.
I HOPE THAT'S A GOOD THING.
IT IS. YOU'RE THE OPPOSITE OF ME.
HEY, SOMETIMES BEING CAREFUL PAYS OFF.
IT'S NOT LIKE I WANT TO BE THIS WAY. I WISH I COULD STOP THINKING ALL THE TIME.
I THIIIINK I CAN HELP WITH THAT.
WHAT, STANDUP COMEDY BECAUSE I'M SO HILARIOUS?
BELIEVE IT OR NOT, MY SINGING AND PLAYING SKILLS ARE OFF THE CHARTS.

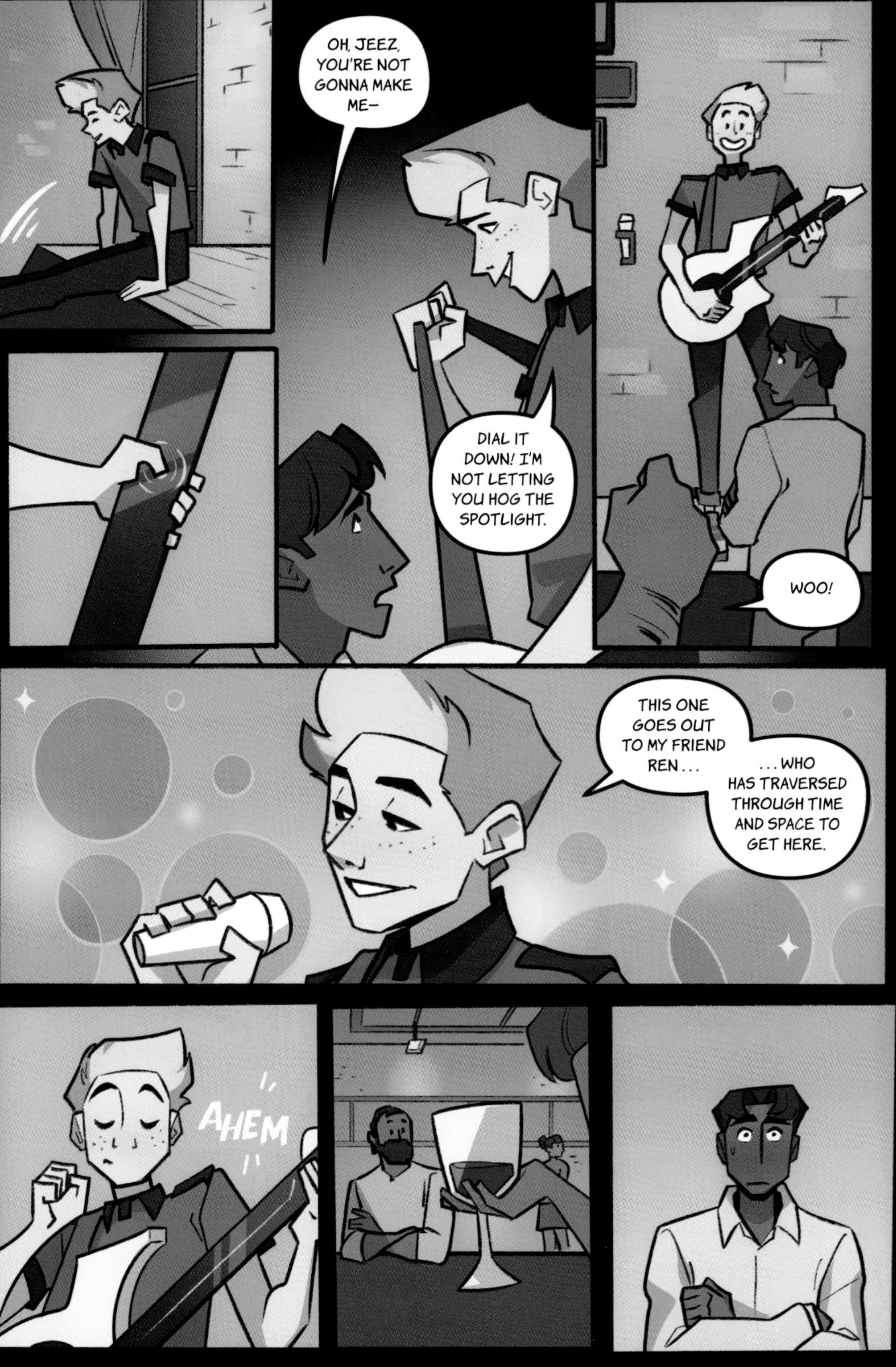
OH, JEEZ, YOU'RE NOT GONNA MAKE ME—
DIAL IT DOWN! I'M NOT LETTING YOU HOG THE SPOTLIGHT.
WOO!
THIS ONE GOES OUT TO MY FRIEND REN . . .
. . . WHO HAS TRAVERSED THROUGH TIME AND SPACE TO GET HERE.
AHEM

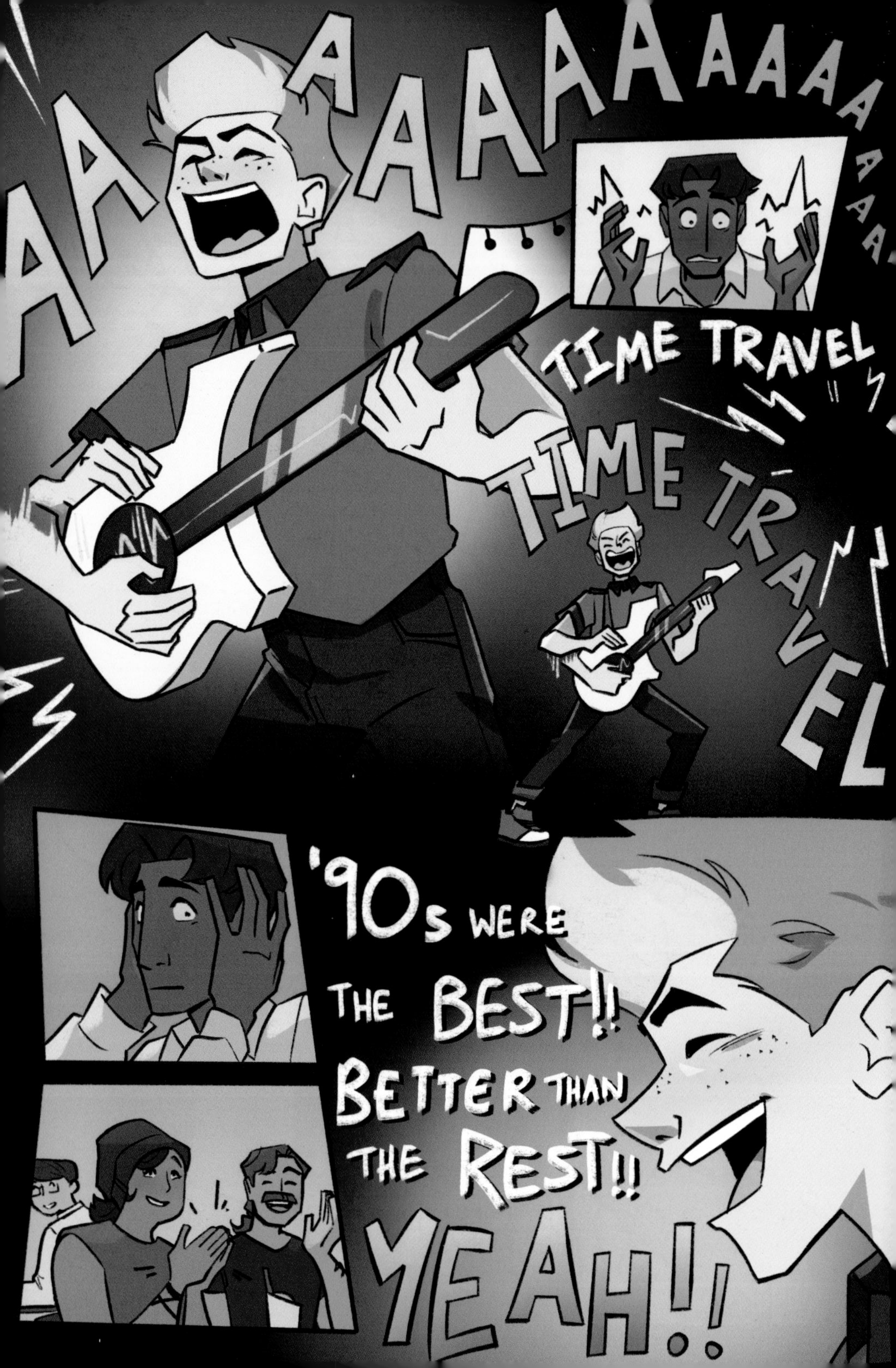
AAAAAAAAAAAAAAA
TIME TRAVEL
TIME TRAVEL
'90s WERE
THE BEST!!
BETTER THAN
THE REST!!
YEAH!!

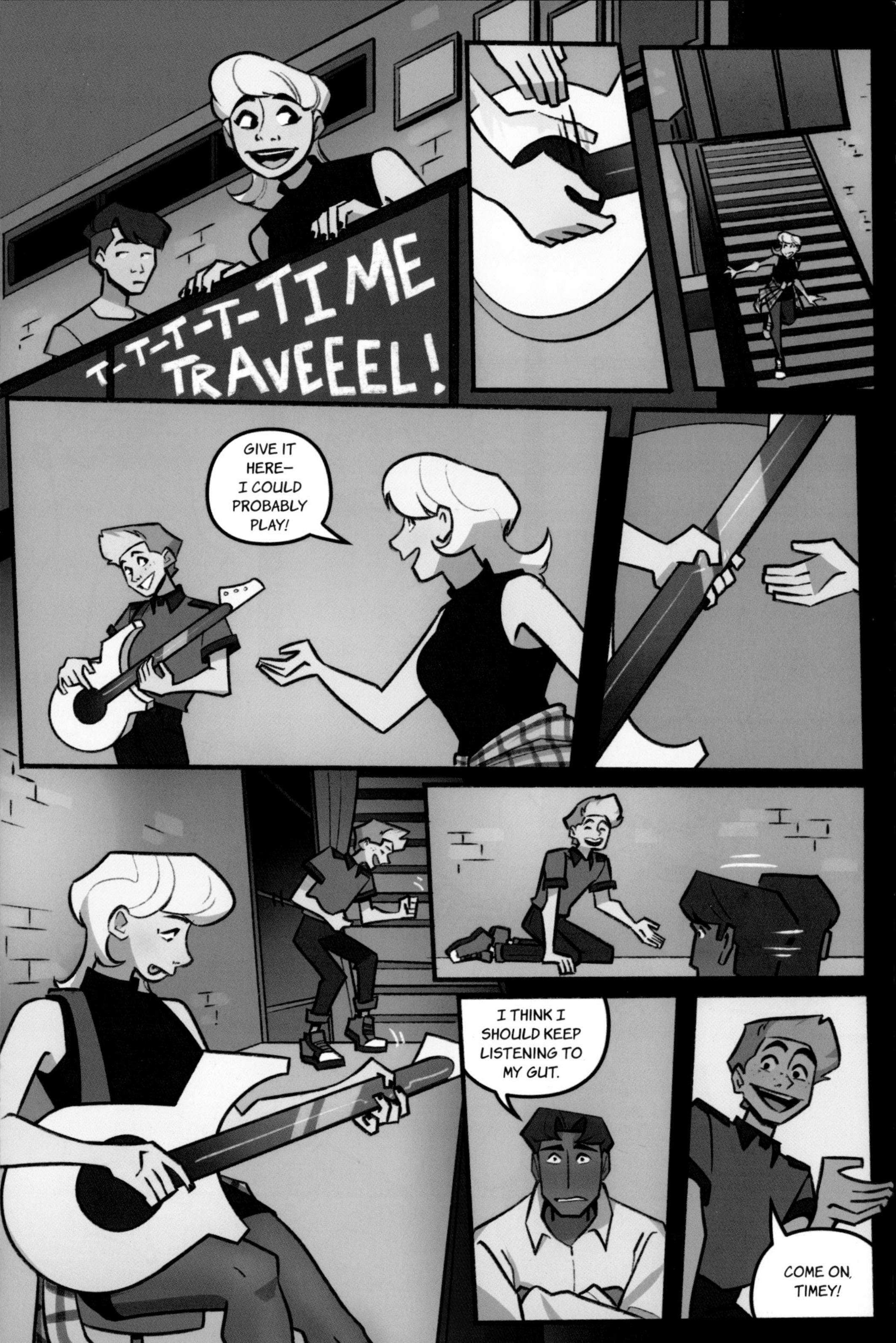
T-T-T-T-TIME TRAVEEEL!
GIVE IT HERE— I COULD PROBABLY PLAY!
I THINK I SHOULD KEEP LISTENING TO MY GUT.
COME ON, TIMEY!

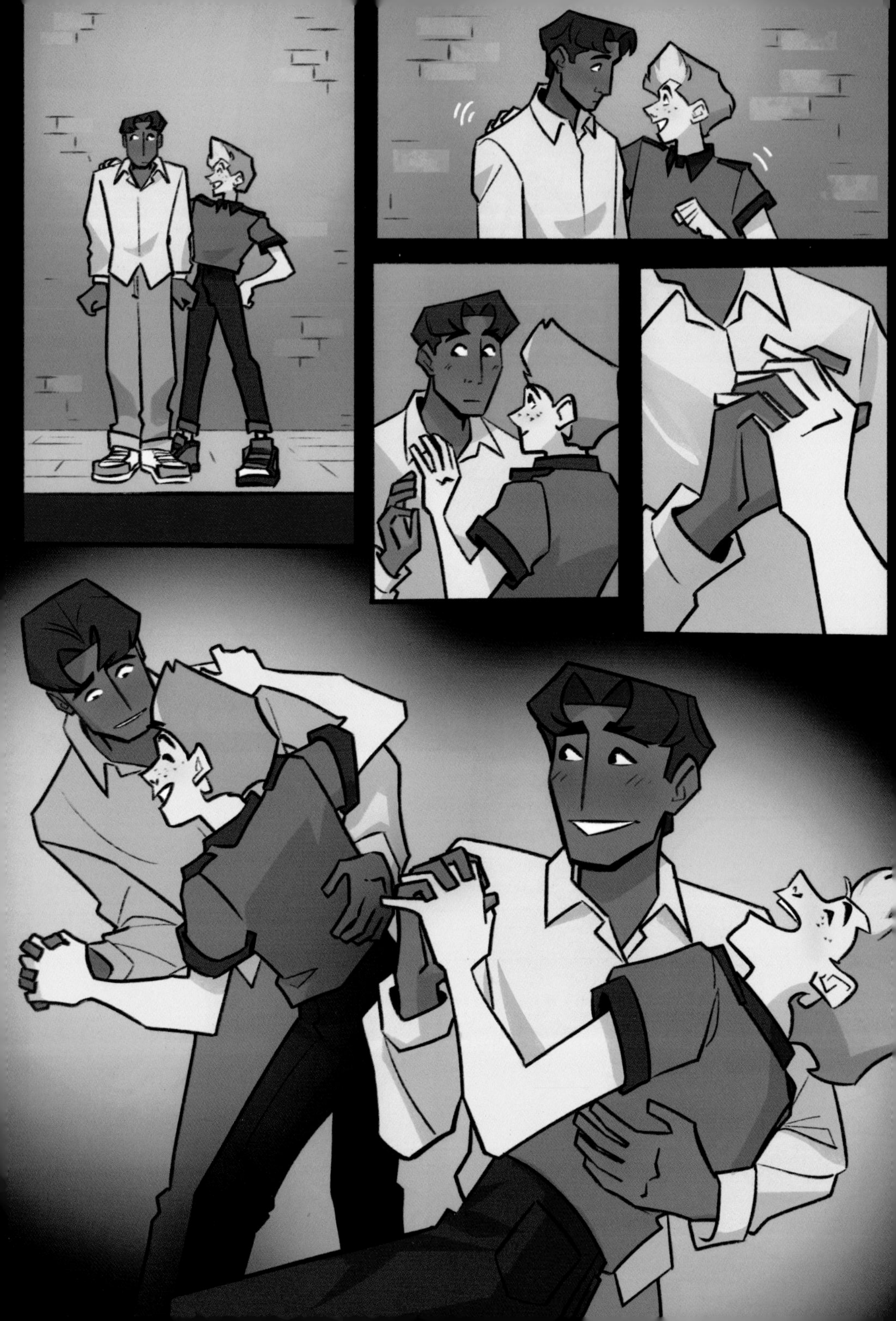

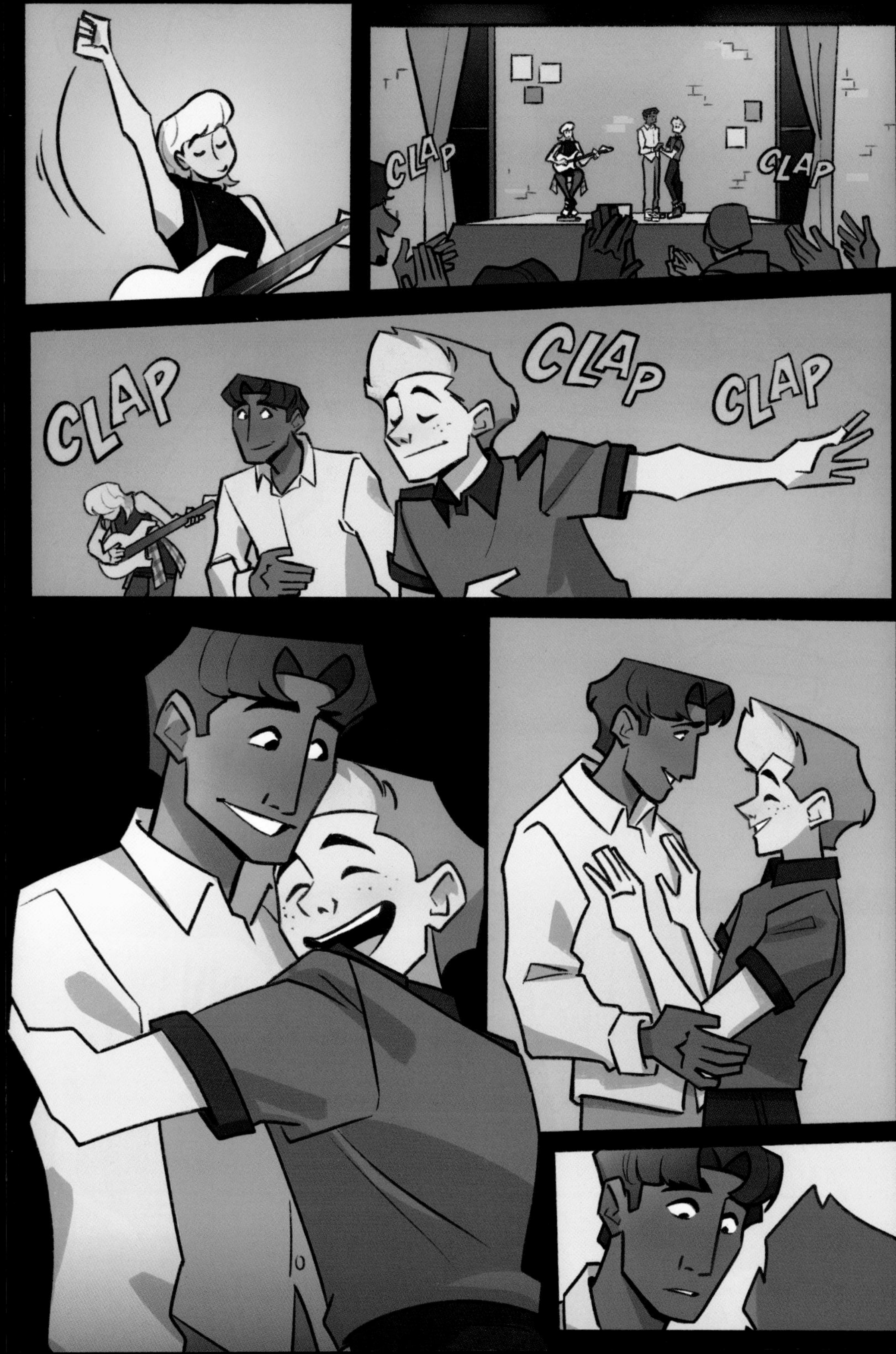
CLAP
CLAP
CLAP
CLAP
CLAP

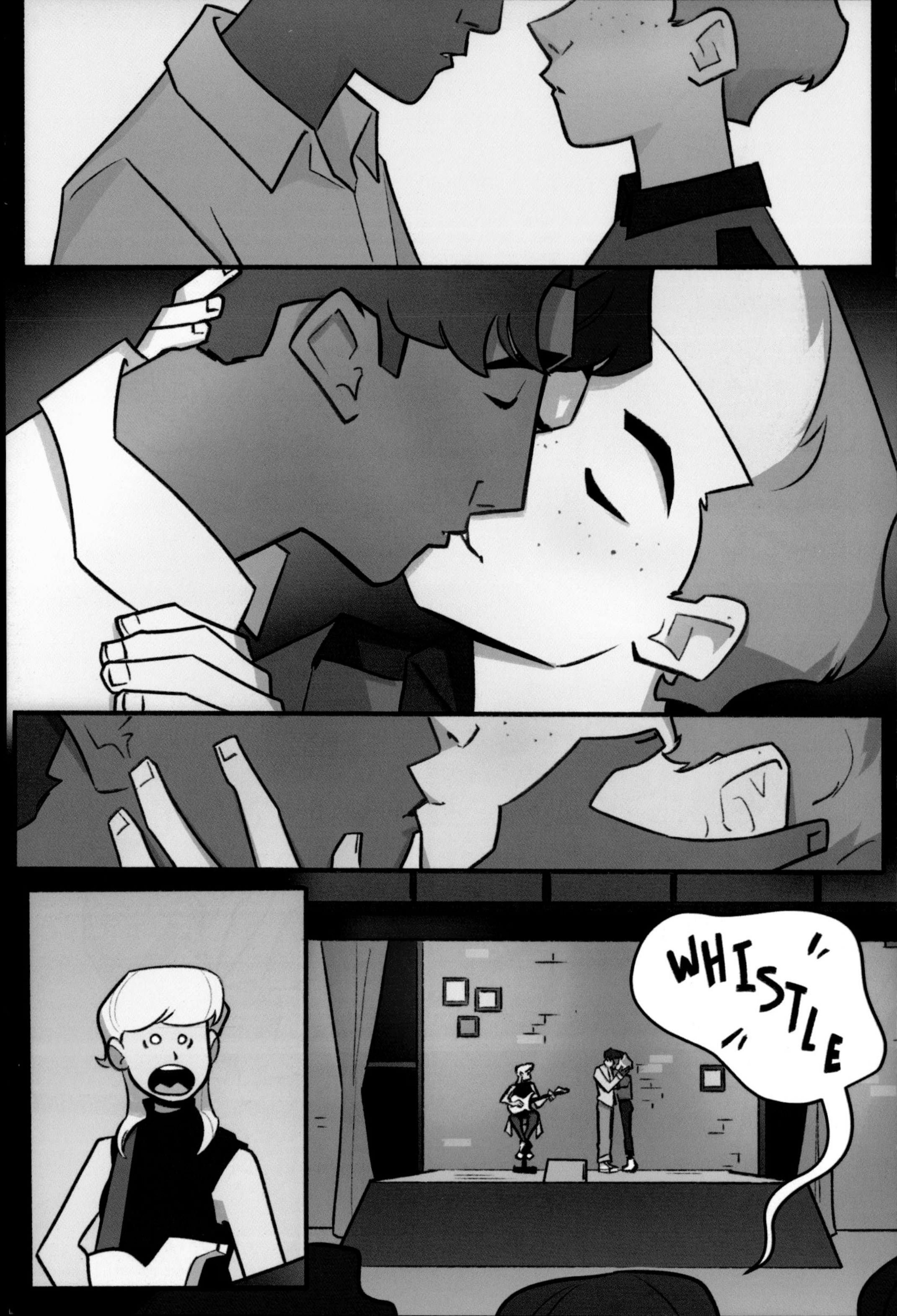
WHISTLE

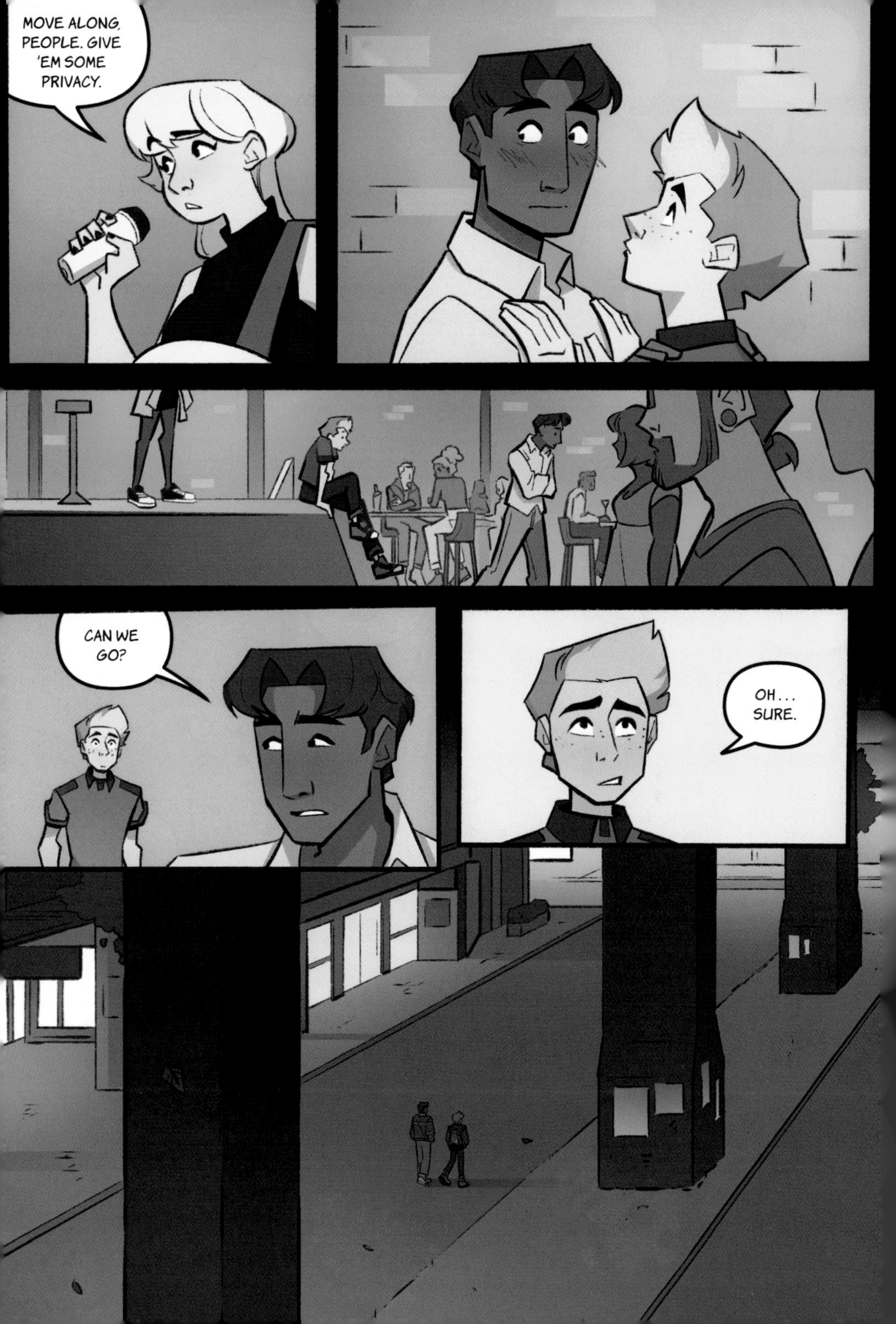

MOVE ALONG, PEOPLE. GIVE 'EM SOME PRIVACY.
CAN WE GO?
OH... SURE.

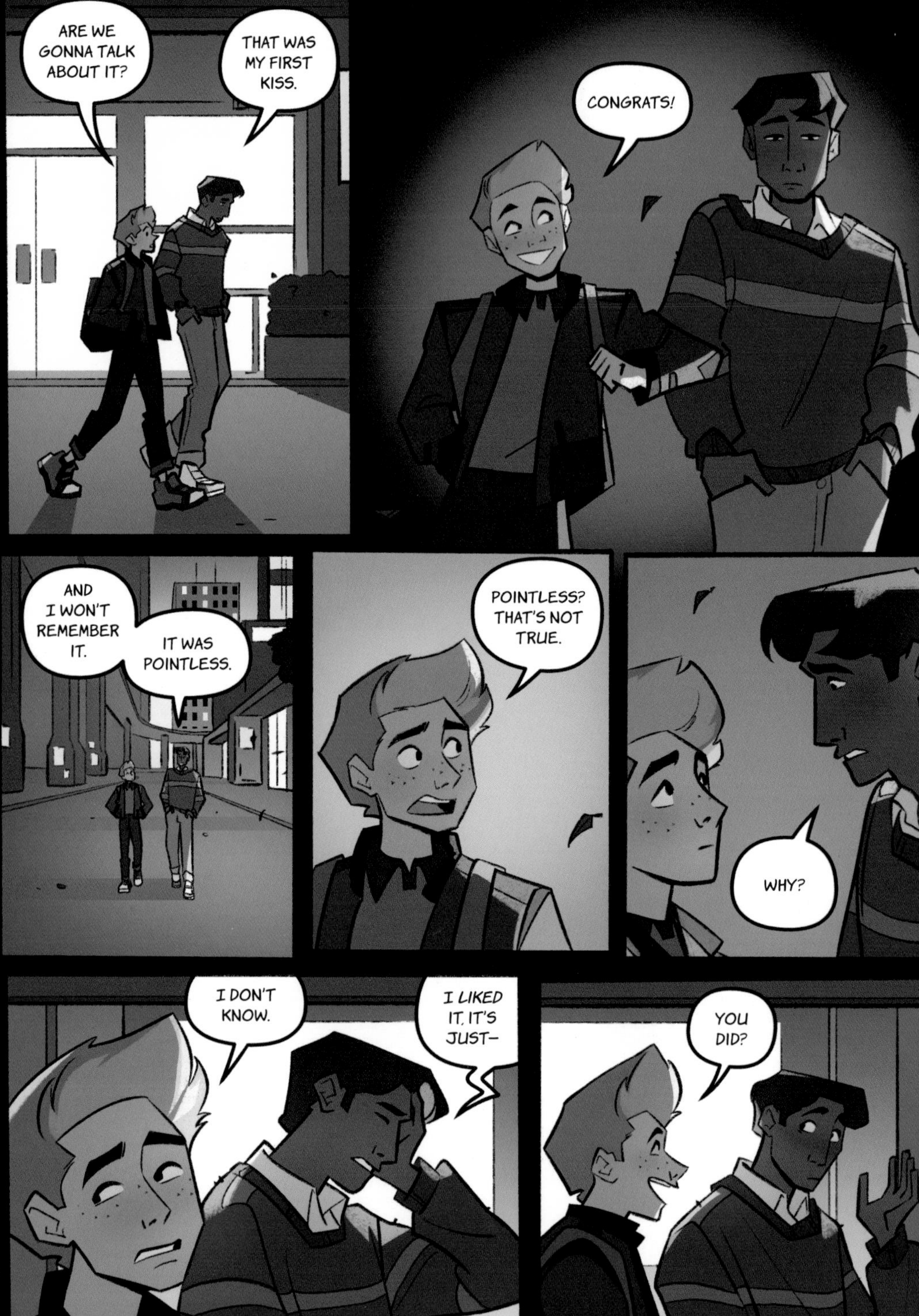
ARE WE GONNA TALK ABOUT IT?
THAT WAS MY FIRST KISS.
CONGRATS!
AND I WON'T REMEMBER IT.
IT WAS POINTLESS.
POINTLESS? THAT'S NOT TRUE.
WHY?
I DON'T KNOW.
I LIKED IT, IT'S JUST—
YOU DID?

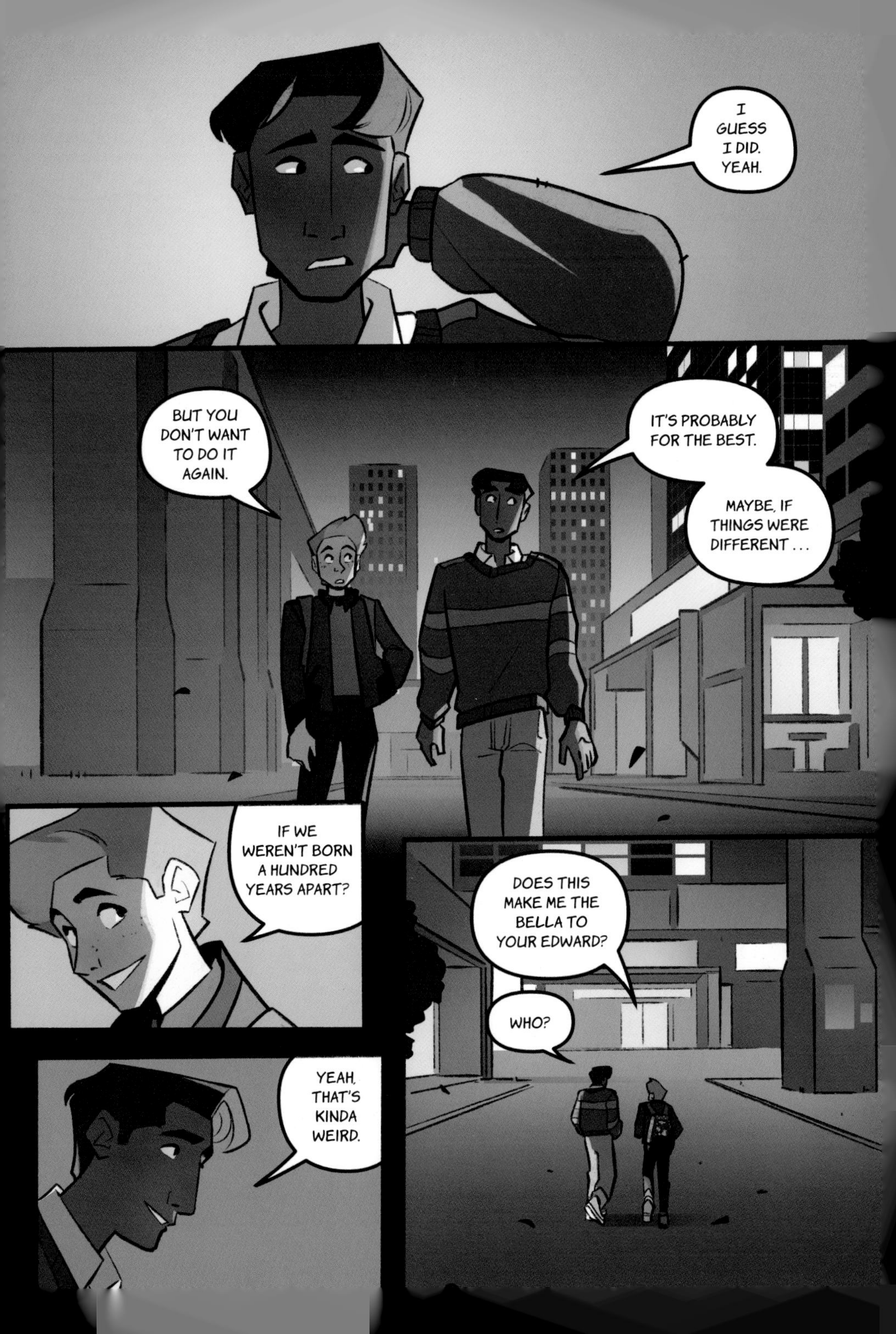
I GUESS I DID. YEAH.
BUT YOU DON'T WANT TO DO IT AGAIN.
IT'S PROBABLY FOR THE BEST.
MAYBE, IF THINGS WERE DIFFERENT . . .
IF WE WEREN'T BORN A HUNDRED YEARS APART?
YEAH, THAT'S KINDA WEIRD.
DOES THIS MAKE ME THE BELLA TO YOUR EDWARD?
WHO?

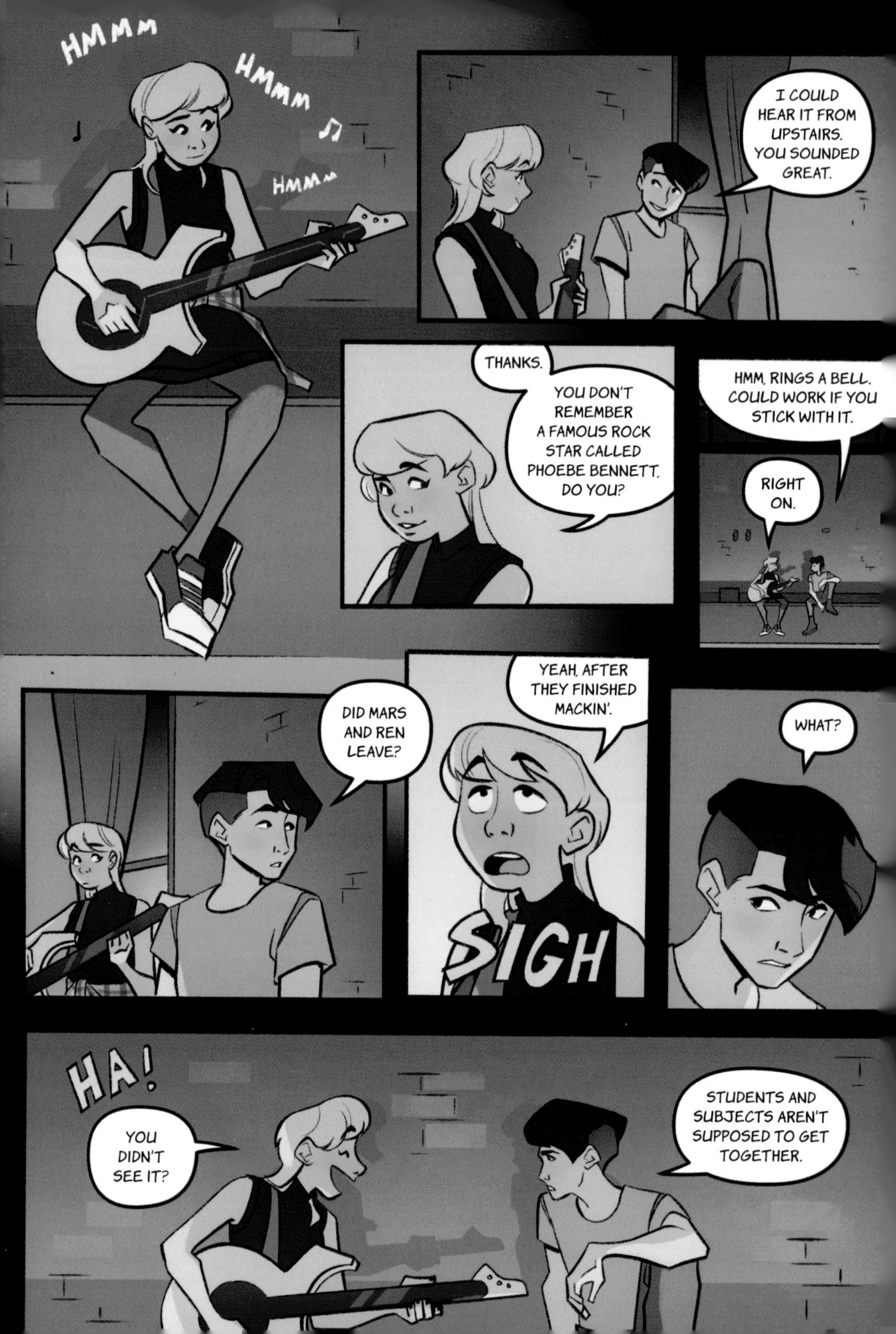
HMMM
HMMM
HMMM
I COULD HEAR IT FROM UPSTAIRS. YOU SOUNDED GREAT.
THANKS.
YOU DON'T REMEMBER A FAMOUS ROCK STAR CALLED PHOEBE BENNETT, DO YOU?
HMM, RINGS A BELL. COULD WORK IF YOU STICK WITH IT.
RIGHT ON.
DID MARS AND REN LEAVE?
YEAH, AFTER THEY FINISHED MACKIN'.
SIGH
WHAT?
HA!
YOU DIDN'T SEE IT?
STUDENTS AND SUBJECTS AREN'T SUPPOSED TO GET TOGETHER.

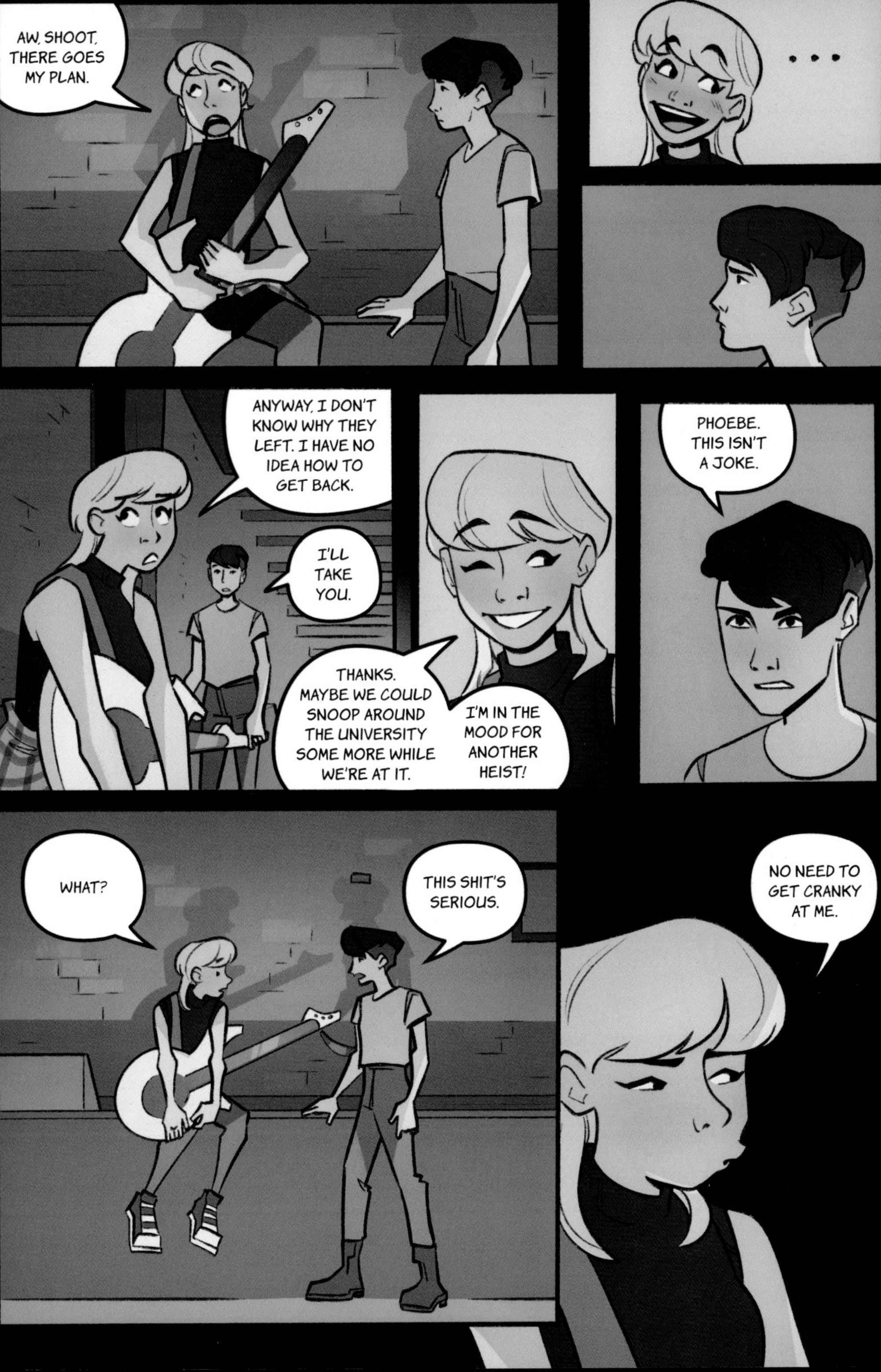
AW, SHOOT, THERE GOES MY PLAN.
. . .
ANYWAY, I DON'T KNOW WHY THEY LEFT. I HAVE NO IDEA HOW TO GET BACK.
I'LL TAKE YOU.
THANKS. MAYBE WE COULD SNOOP AROUND THE UNIVERSITY SOME MORE WHILE WE'RE AT IT.
I'M IN THE MOOD FOR ANOTHER HEIST!
PHOEBE. THIS ISN'T A JOKE.
WHAT?
THIS SHIT'S SERIOUS.
NO NEED TO GET CRANKY AT ME.

MAYBE I GOT CARRIED AWAY.

BUT YOU DIDN'T EXACTLY TELL ME MUCH.

THE GIRL THAT DIED.

I LOVED HER.

I THOUGHT STUDENTS CAN'T ROMANCE SUBJECTS?

DIDN'T STOP ME FROM WANTING TO.

I'M SORRY.

IT'S OKAY. YOU DIDN'T KNOW.

I CAN'T IMAGINE WHAT YOU WENT THROUGH.

THE WORST PART IS, I NEVER GOT TO MOURN FOR HER.

NOT PROPERLY.

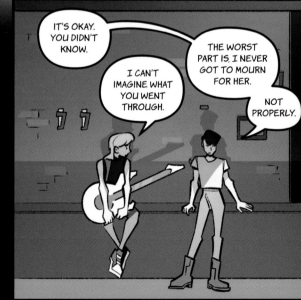

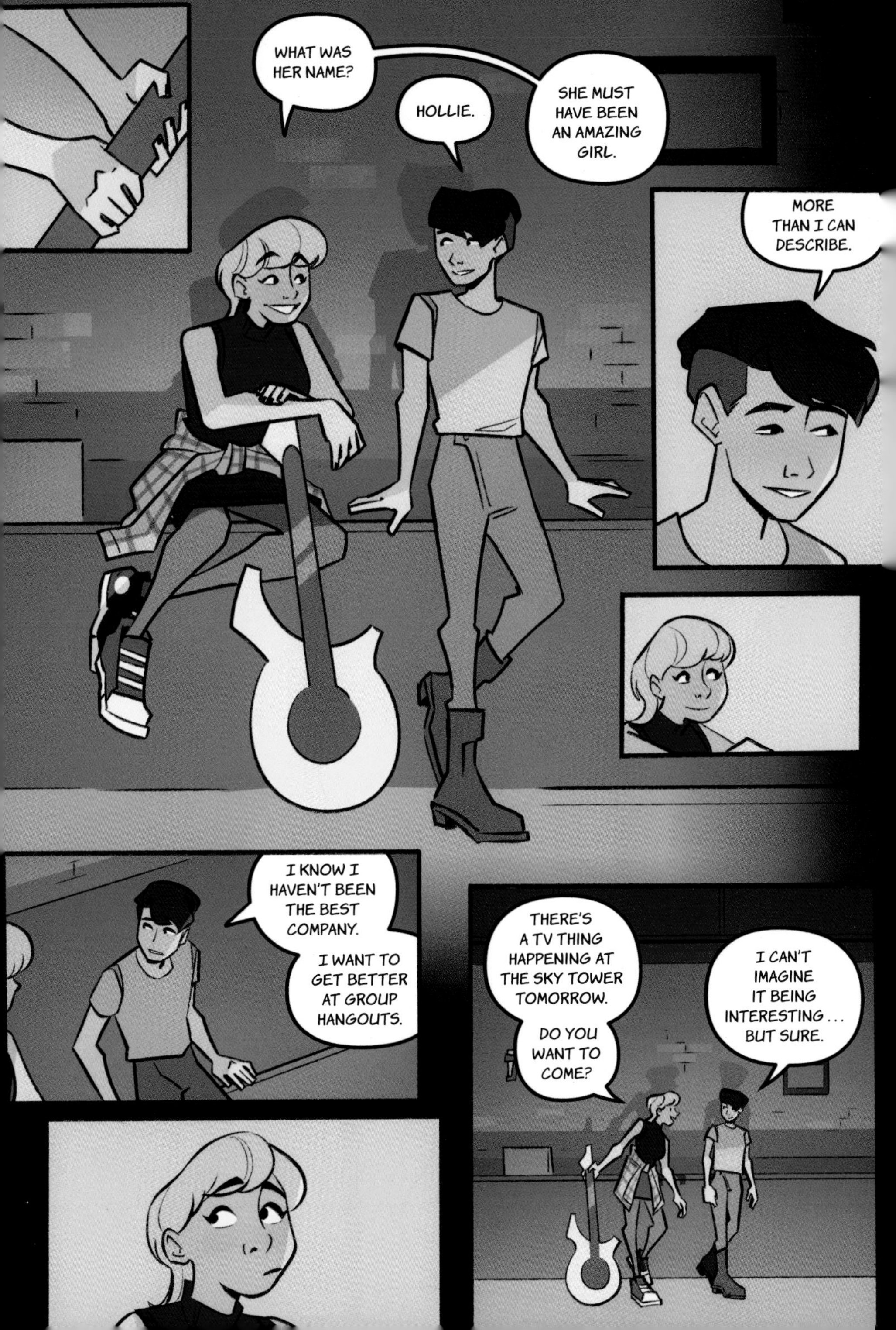
WHAT WAS HER NAME?
HOLLIE.
SHE MUST HAVE BEEN AN AMAZING GIRL.
MORE THAN I CAN DESCRIBE.
I KNOW I HAVEN'T BEEN THE BEST COMPANY.
I WANT TO GET BETTER AT GROUP HANGOUTS.
THERE'S A TV THING HAPPENING AT THE SKY TOWER TOMORROW.
DO YOU WANT TO COME?
I CAN'T IMAGINE IT BEING INTERESTING . . . BUT SURE.

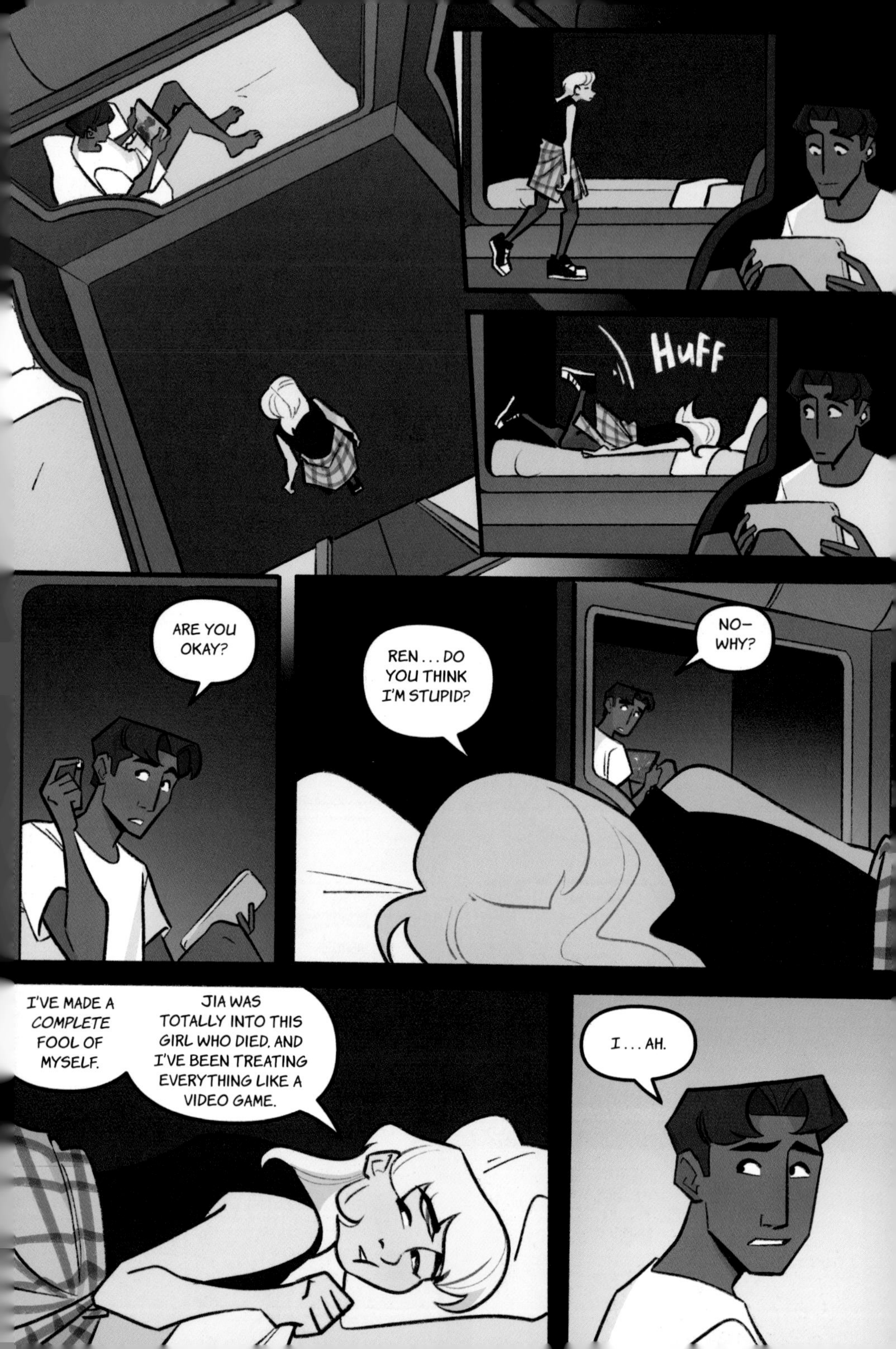
HUFF
ARE YOU OKAY?
REN . . . DO YOU THINK I'M STUPID?
NO— WHY?
I'VE MADE A COMPLETE FOOL OF MYSELF.
JIA WAS TOTALLY INTO THIS GIRL WHO DIED, AND I'VE BEEN TREATING EVERYTHING LIKE A VIDEO GAME.
I . . . AH.

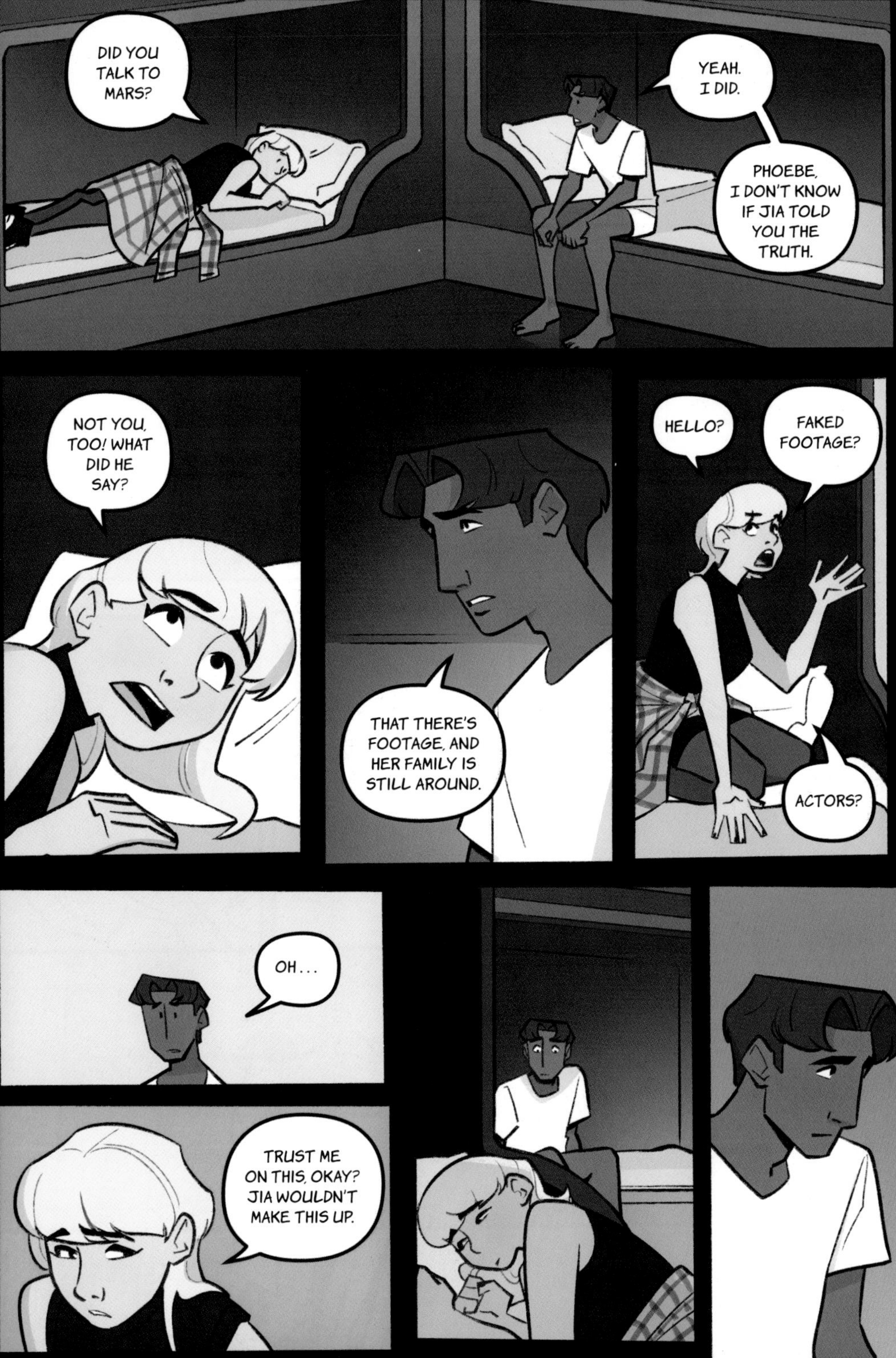
DID YOU TALK TO MARS?
YEAH. I DID.
PHOEBE, I DON'T KNOW IF JIA TOLD YOU THE TRUTH.
NOT YOU, TOO! WHAT DID HE SAY?
THAT THERE'S FOOTAGE, AND HER FAMILY IS STILL AROUND.
HELLO?
FAKED FOOTAGE?
ACTORS?
OH...
TRUST ME ON THIS, OKAY? JIA WOULDN'T MAKE THIS UP.

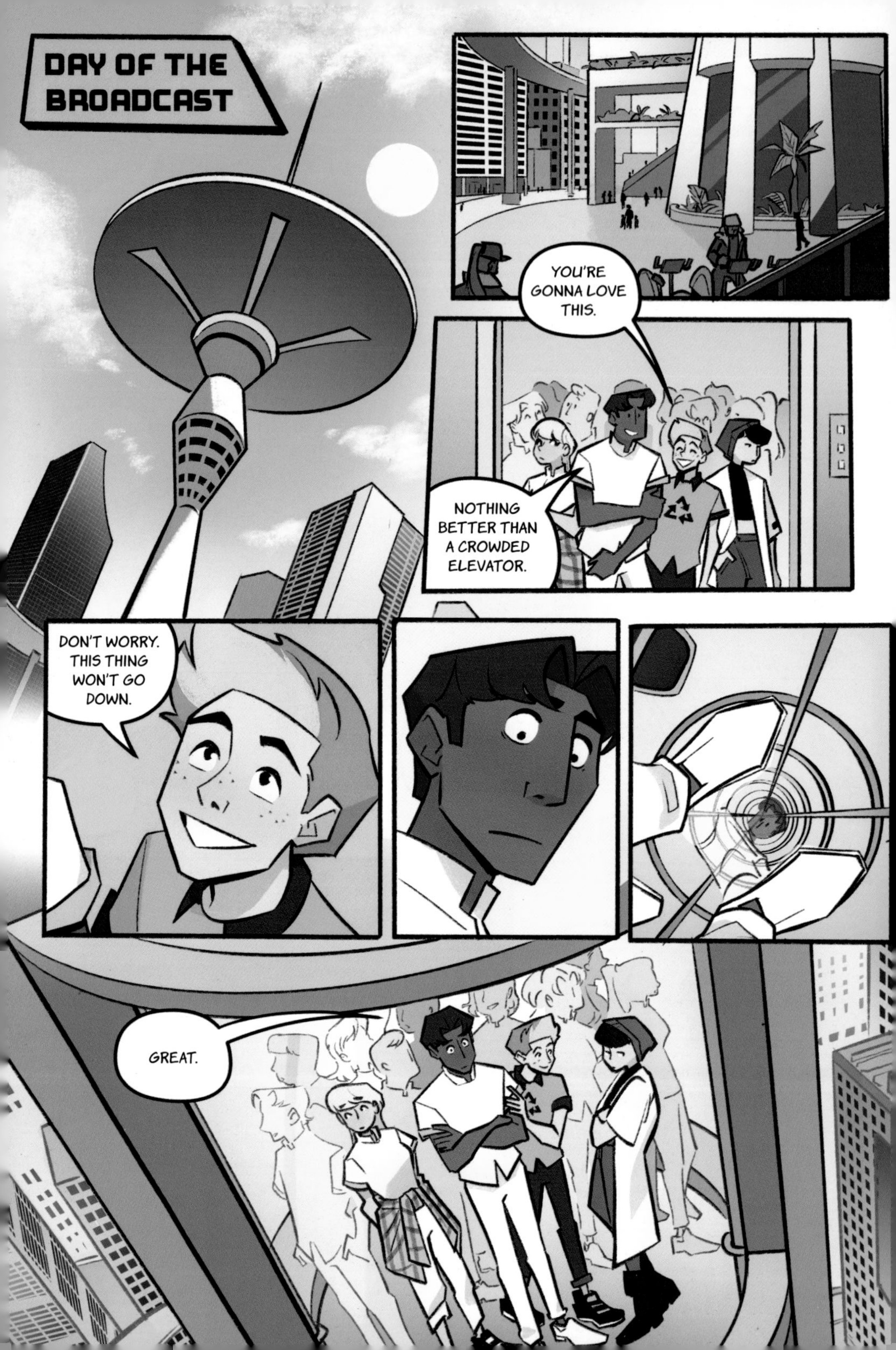
DAY OF THE BROADCAST
YOU'RE GONNA LOVE THIS.
NOTHING BETTER THAN A CROWDED ELEVATOR.
DON'T WORRY. THIS THING WON'T GO DOWN.
GREAT.

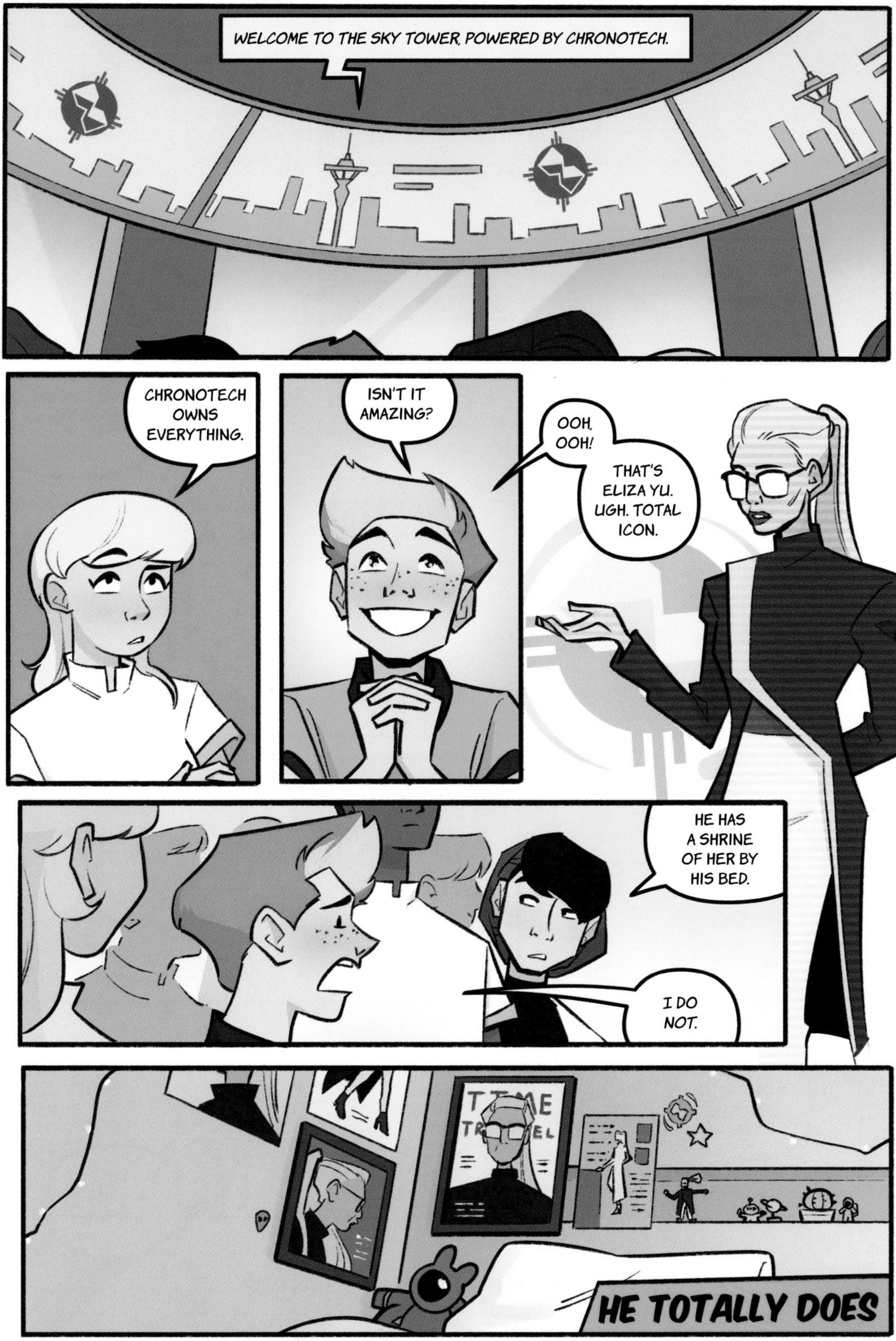
WELCOME TO THE SKY TOWER, POWERED BY CHRONOTECH.
CHRONOTECH OWNS EVERYTHING.
ISN'T IT AMAZING?
OOH, OOH!
THAT'S ELIZA YU. UGH. TOTAL ICON.
HE HAS A SHRINE OF HER BY HIS BED.
I DO NOT.
TIME TRAVEL
HE TOTALLY DOES

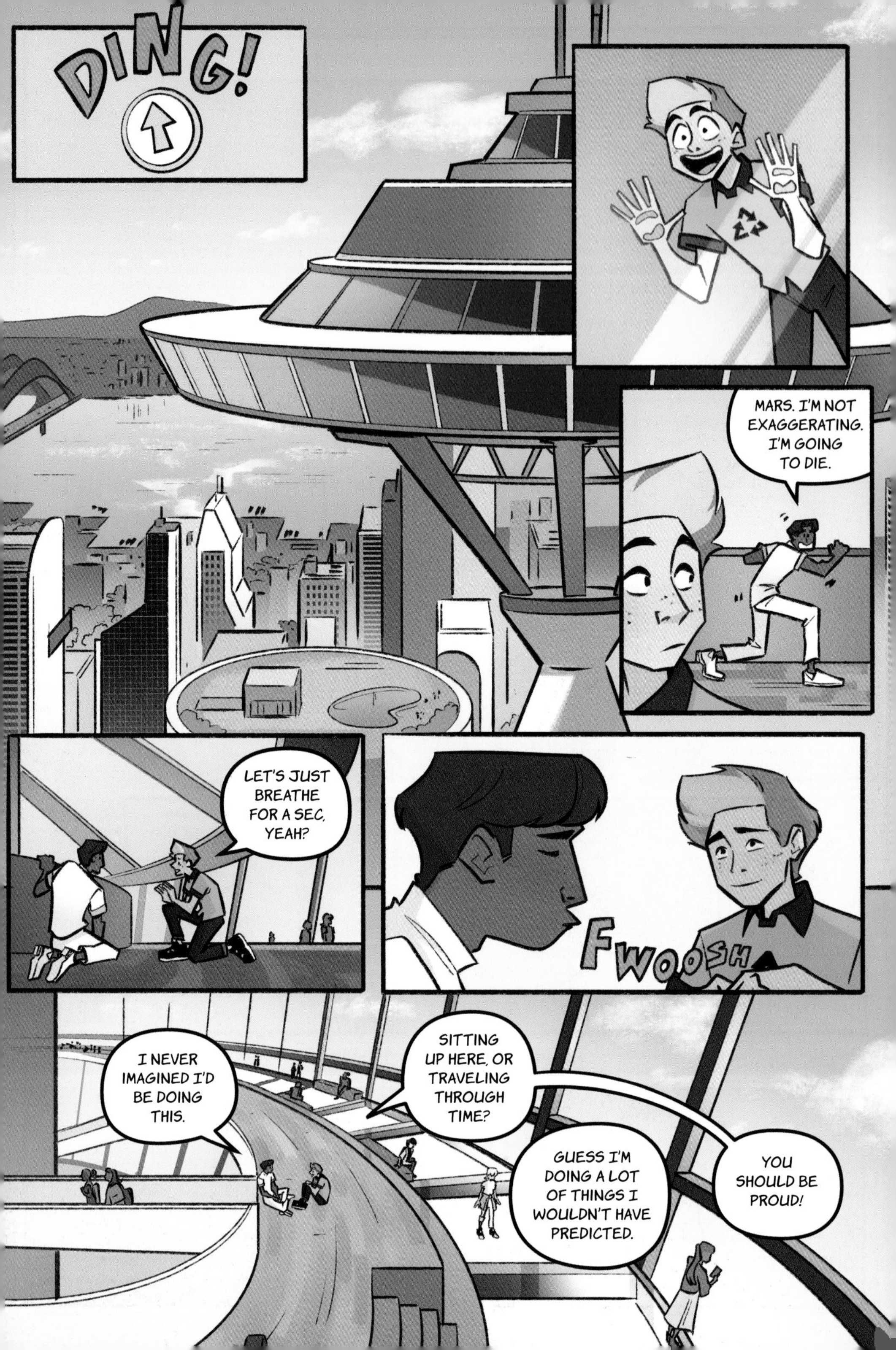
DING!
MARS. I'M NOT EXAGGERATING. I'M GOING TO DIE.
LET'S JUST BREATHE FOR A SEC, YEAH?
FWOOSH
I NEVER IMAGINED I'D BE DOING THIS.
SITTING UP HERE, OR TRAVELING THROUGH TIME?
GUESS I'M DOING A LOT OF THINGS I WOULDN'T HAVE PREDICTED.
YOU SHOULD BE PROUD!

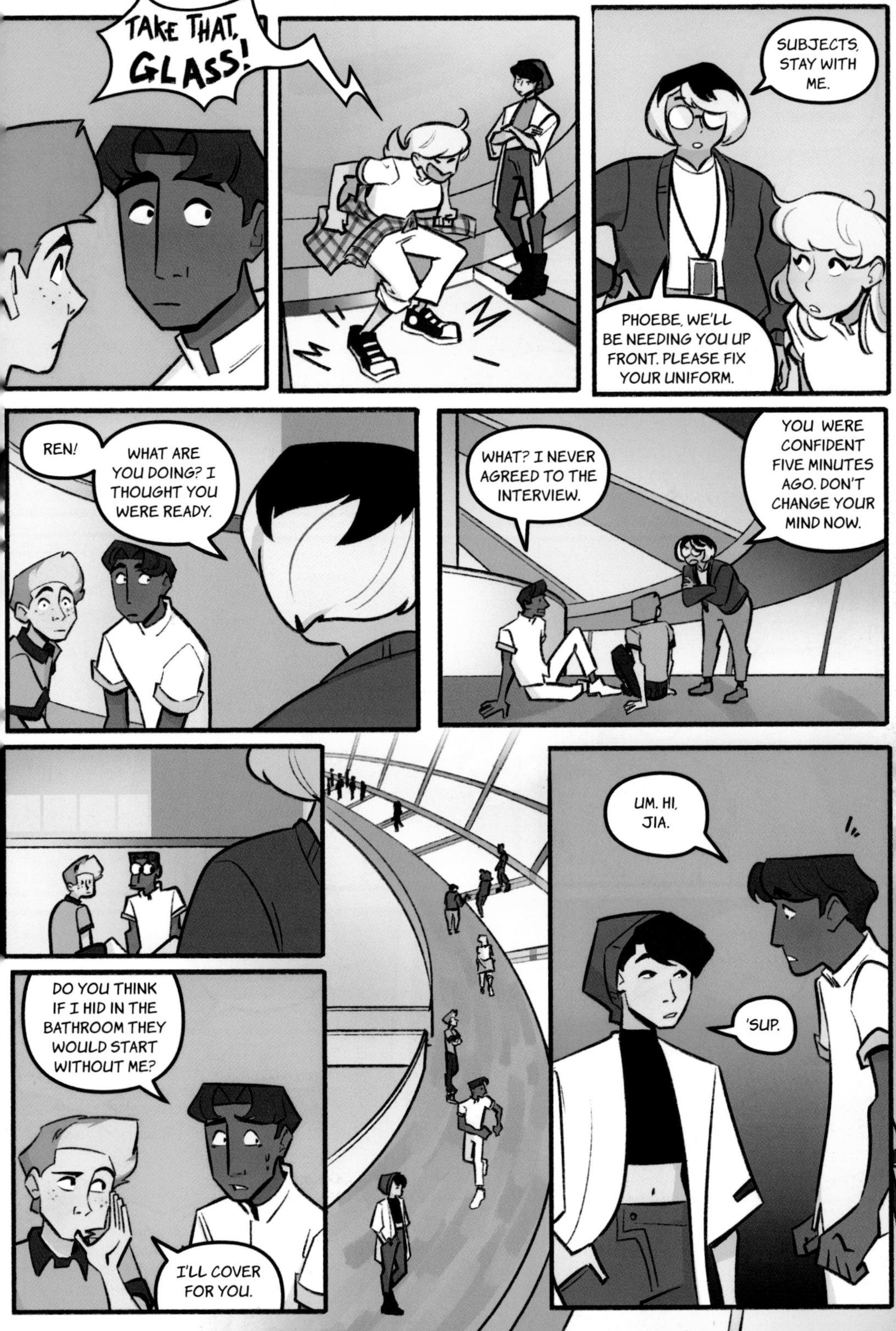
TAKE THAT, GLASS!
SUBJECTS, STAY WITH ME.
PHOEBE, WE'LL BE NEEDING YOU UP FRONT. PLEASE FIX YOUR UNIFORM.
REN!
WHAT ARE YOU DOING? I THOUGHT YOU WERE READY.
WHAT? I NEVER AGREED TO THE INTERVIEW.
YOU WERE CONFIDENT FIVE MINUTES AGO. DON'T CHANGE YOUR MIND NOW.
DO YOU THINK IF I HID IN THE BATHROOM THEY WOULD START WITHOUT ME?
I'LL COVER FOR YOU.
UM. HI, JIA.
'SUP.

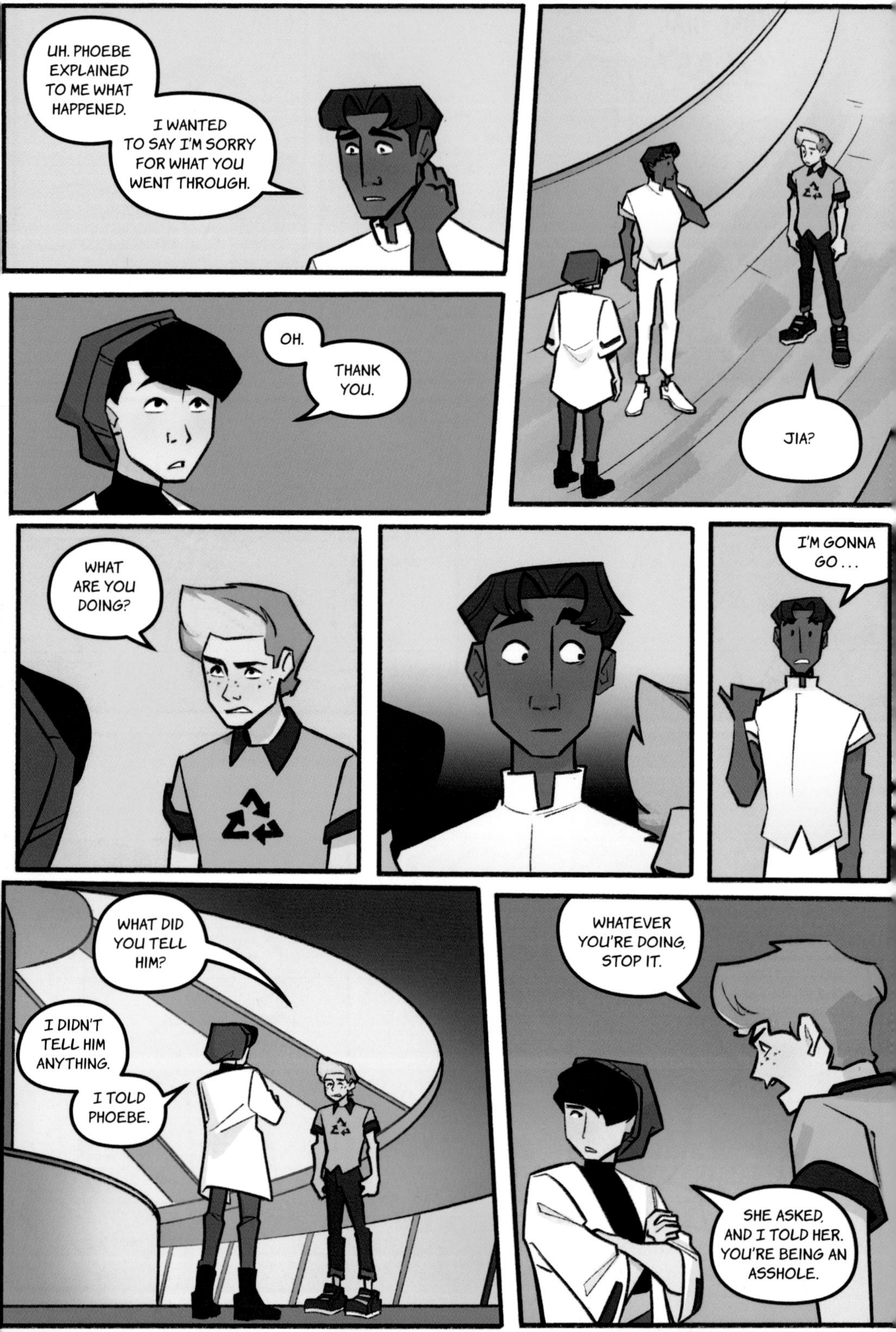
UH. PHOEBE EXPLAINED TO ME WHAT HAPPENED.
I WANTED TO SAY I'M SORRY FOR WHAT YOU WENT THROUGH.
OH.
THANK YOU.
JIA?
WHAT ARE YOU DOING?
I'M GONNA GO . . .
WHAT DID YOU TELL HIM?
I DIDN'T TELL HIM ANYTHING.
I TOLD PHOEBE.
WHATEVER YOU'RE DOING, STOP IT.
SHE ASKED, AND I TOLD HER. YOU'RE BEING AN ASSHOLE.

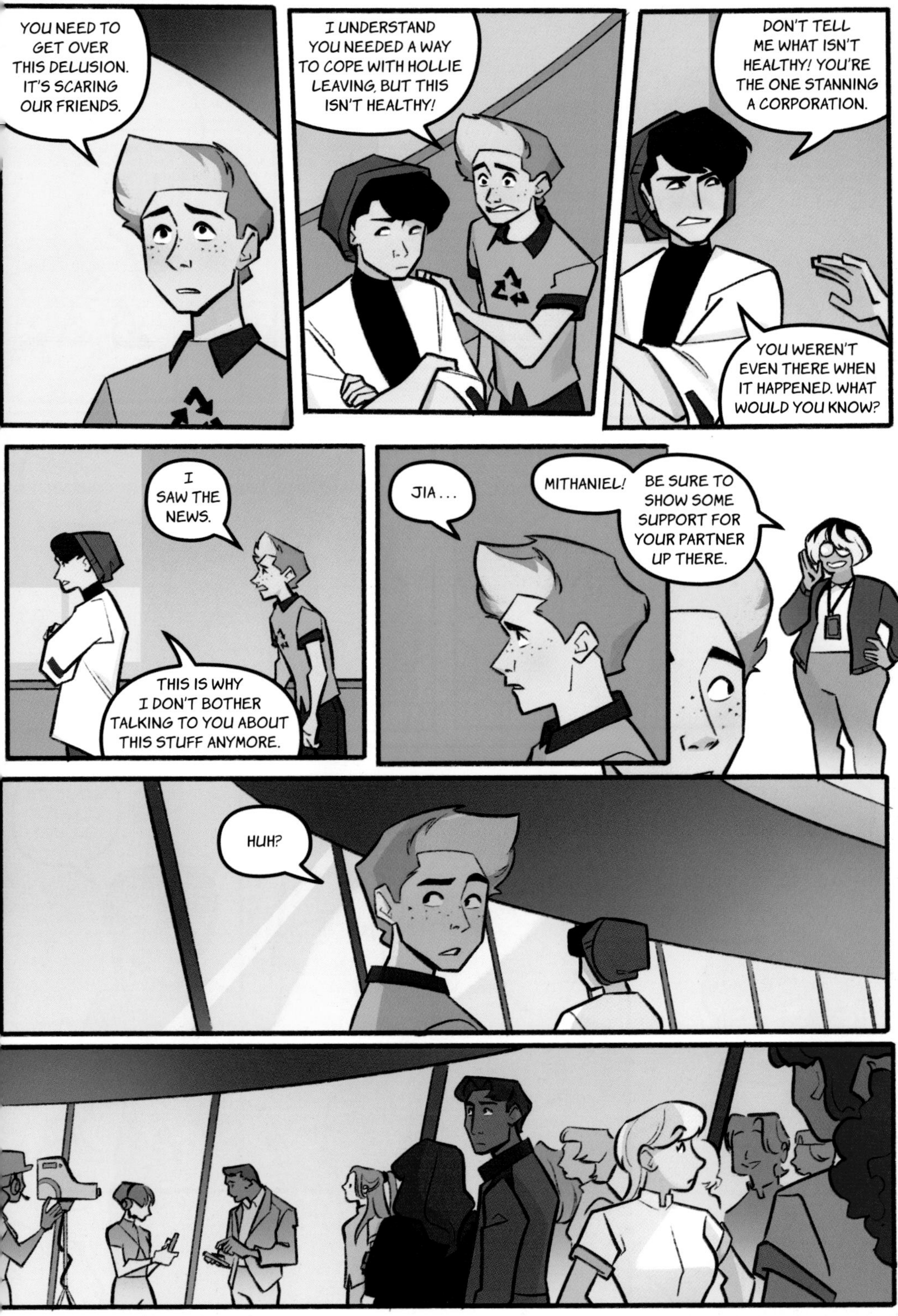
YOU NEED TO GET OVER THIS DELUSION. IT'S SCARING OUR FRIENDS.
I UNDERSTAND YOU NEEDED A WAY TO COPE WITH HOLLIE LEAVING, BUT THIS ISN'T HEALTHY!
DON'T TELL ME WHAT ISN'T HEALTHY! YOU'RE THE ONE STANNING A CORPORATION.
YOU WEREN'T EVEN THERE WHEN IT HAPPENED. WHAT WOULD YOU KNOW?
I SAW THE NEWS.
THIS IS WHY I DON'T BOTHER TALKING TO YOU ABOUT THIS STUFF ANYMORE.
JIA . . .
MITHANIEL!
BE SURE TO SHOW SOME SUPPORT FOR YOUR PARTNER UP THERE.
HUH?

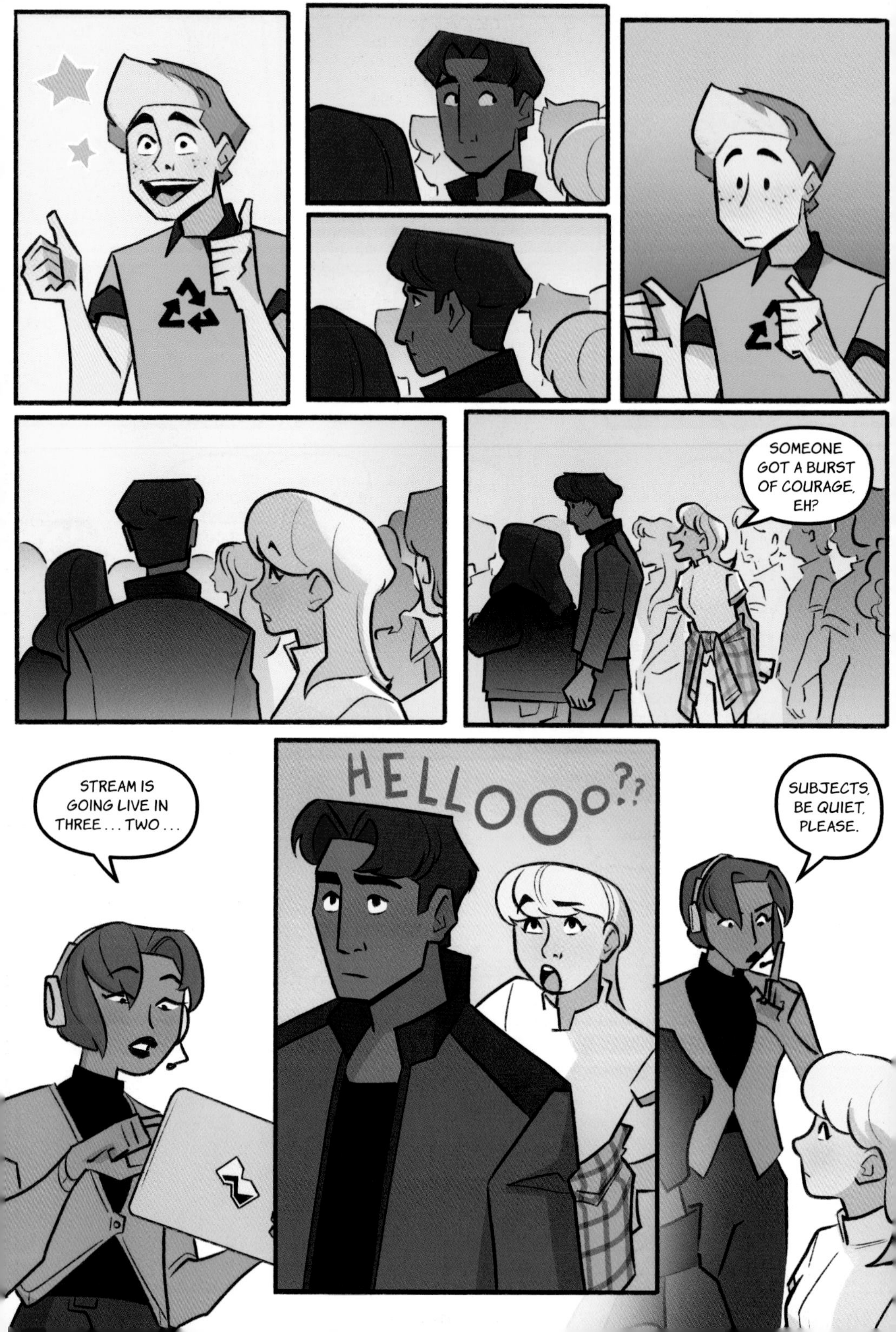
SOMEONE GOT A BURST OF COURAGE, EH?
STREAM IS GOING LIVE IN THREE . . . TWO . . .
HELLOOo??
SUBJECTS, BE QUIET, PLEASE.

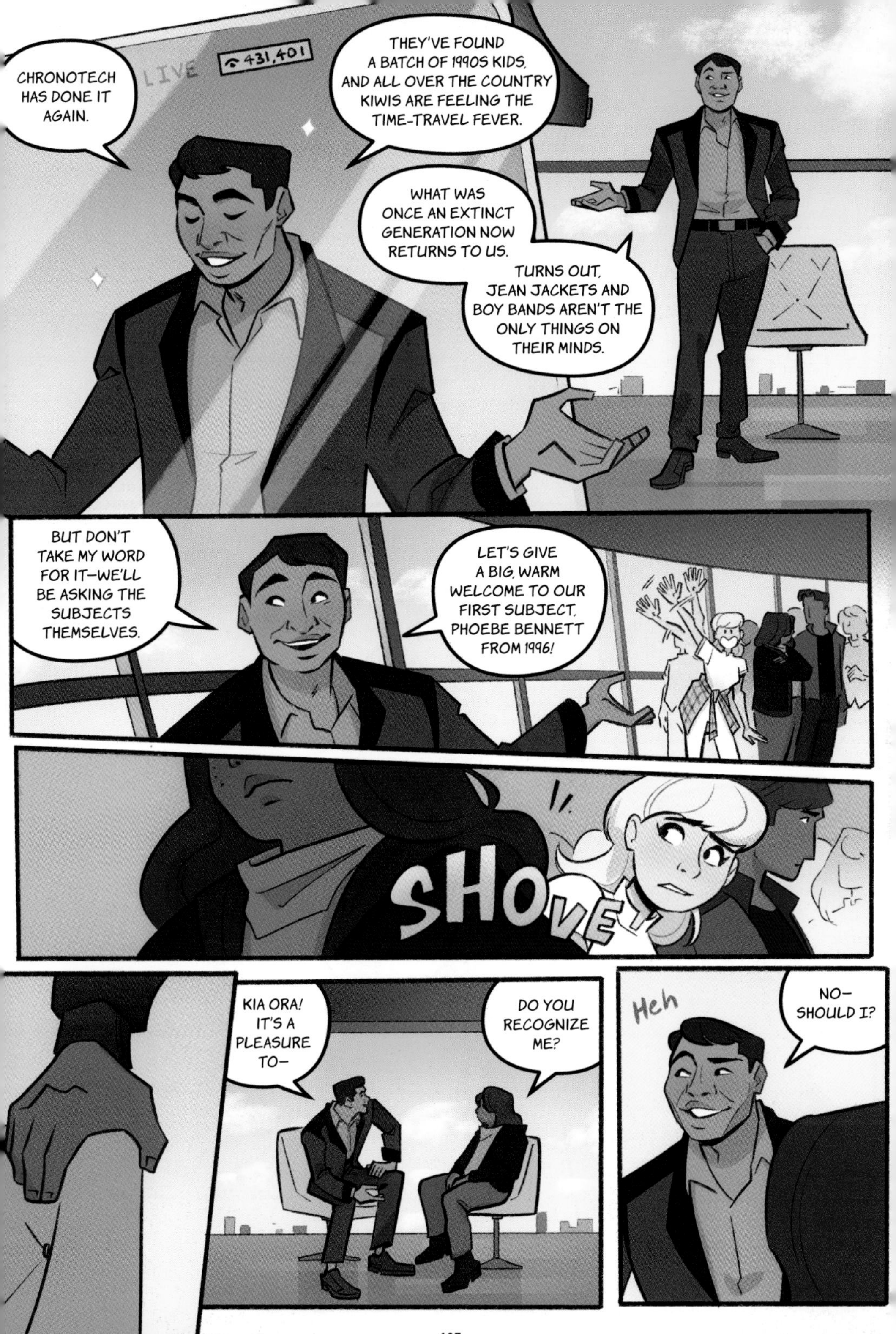
LIVE
431,401
CHRONOTECH HAS DONE IT AGAIN.
THEY'VE FOUND A BATCH OF 1990S KIDS, AND ALL OVER THE COUNTRY KIWIS ARE FEELING THE TIME-TRAVEL FEVER.
WHAT WAS ONCE AN EXTINCT GENERATION NOW RETURNS TO US.
TURNS OUT, JEAN JACKETS AND BOY BANDS AREN'T THE ONLY THINGS ON THEIR MINDS.
BUT DON'T TAKE MY WORD FOR IT—WE'LL BE ASKING THE SUBJECTS THEMSELVES.
LET'S GIVE A BIG, WARM WELCOME TO OUR FIRST SUBJECT, PHOEBE BENNETT FROM 1996!
SHOVE!
KIA ORA! IT'S A PLEASURE TO—
DO YOU RECOGNIZE ME?
Heh
NO—SHOULD I?

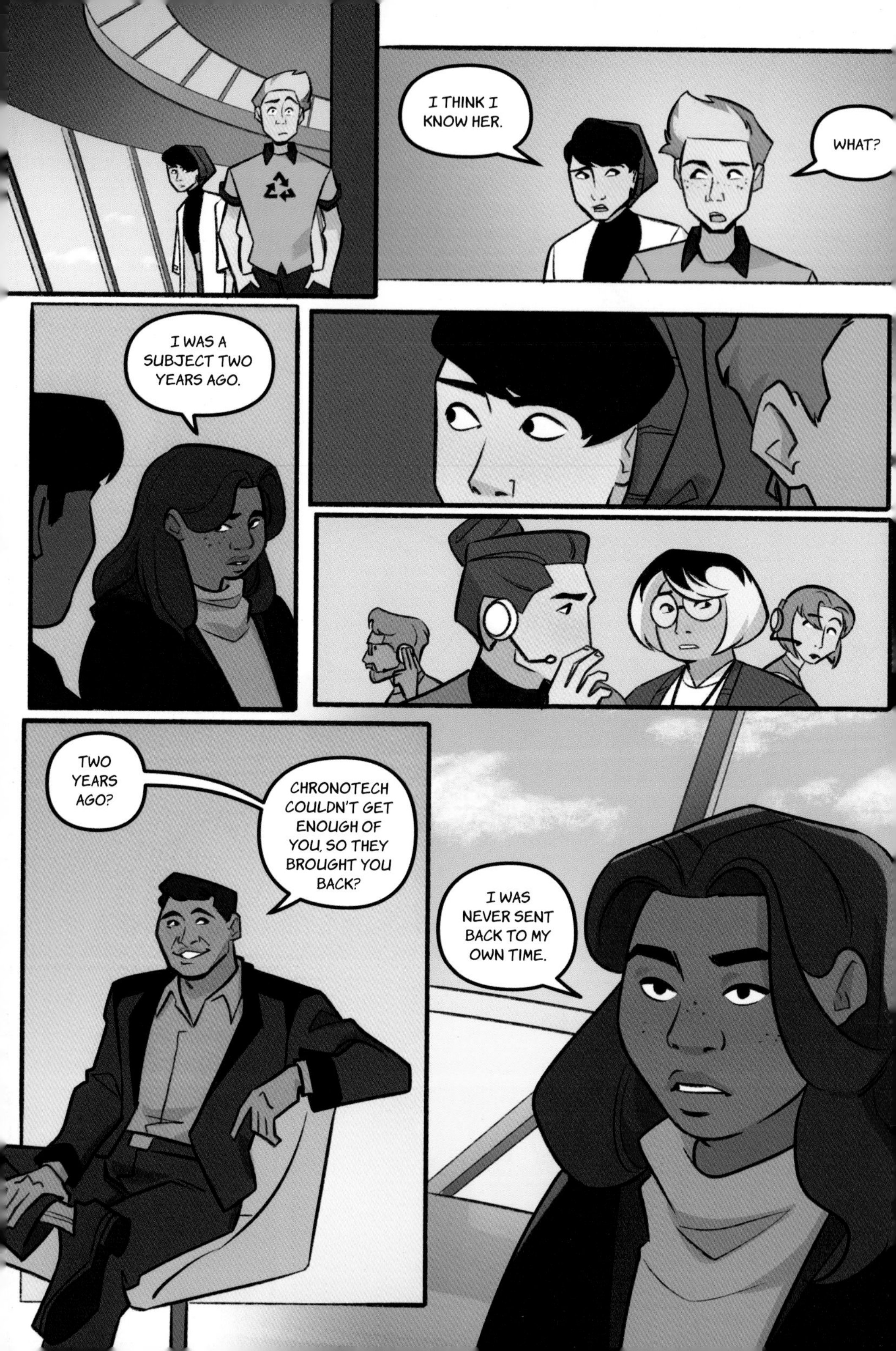
I THINK I KNOW HER.
WHAT?
I WAS A SUBJECT TWO YEARS AGO.
TWO YEARS AGO?
CHRONOTECH COULDN'T GET ENOUGH OF YOU, SO THEY BROUGHT YOU BACK?
I WAS NEVER SENT BACK TO MY OWN TIME.

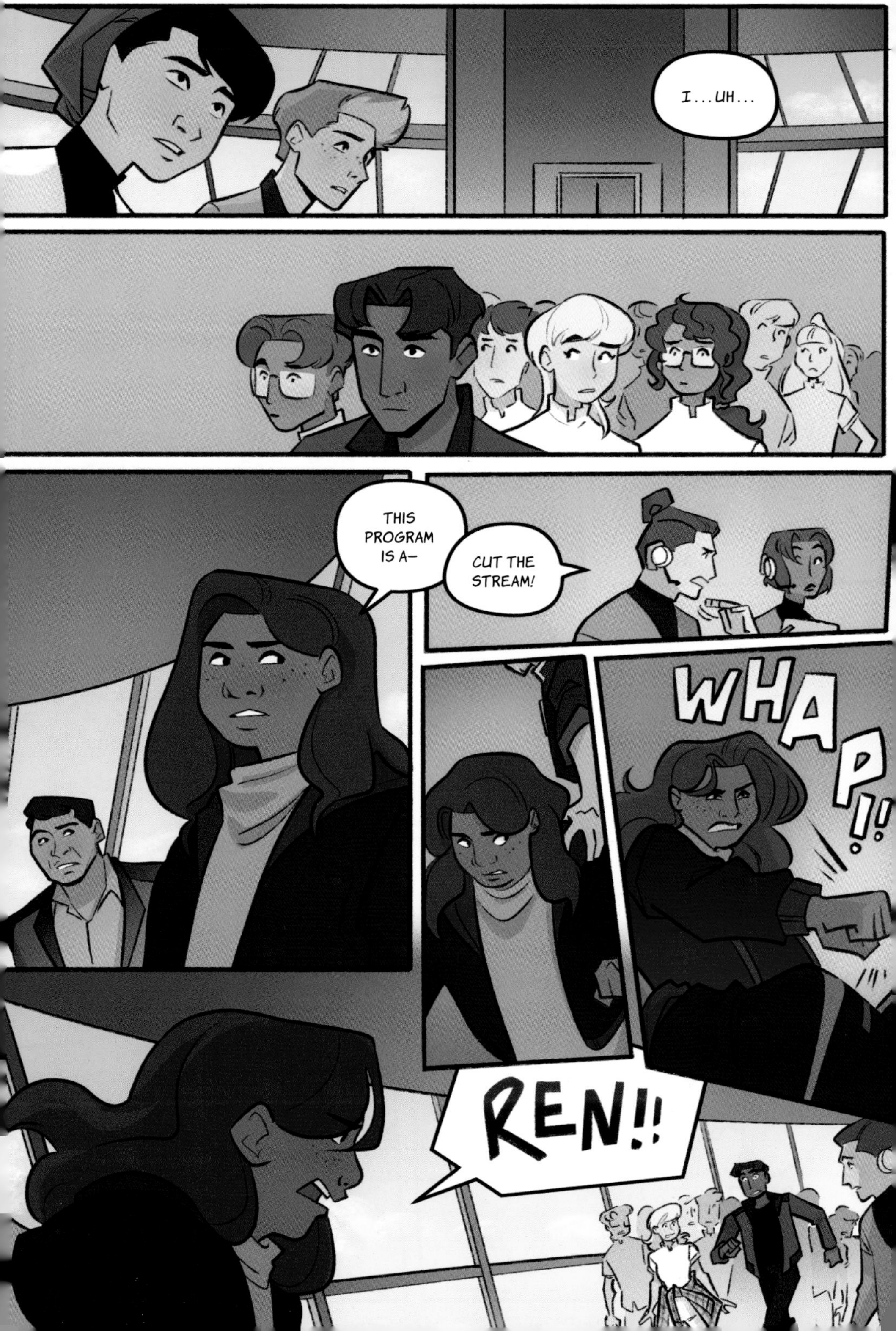
I...UH...
THIS PROGRAM IS A—
CUT THE STREAM!
WHAP!!
REN!!

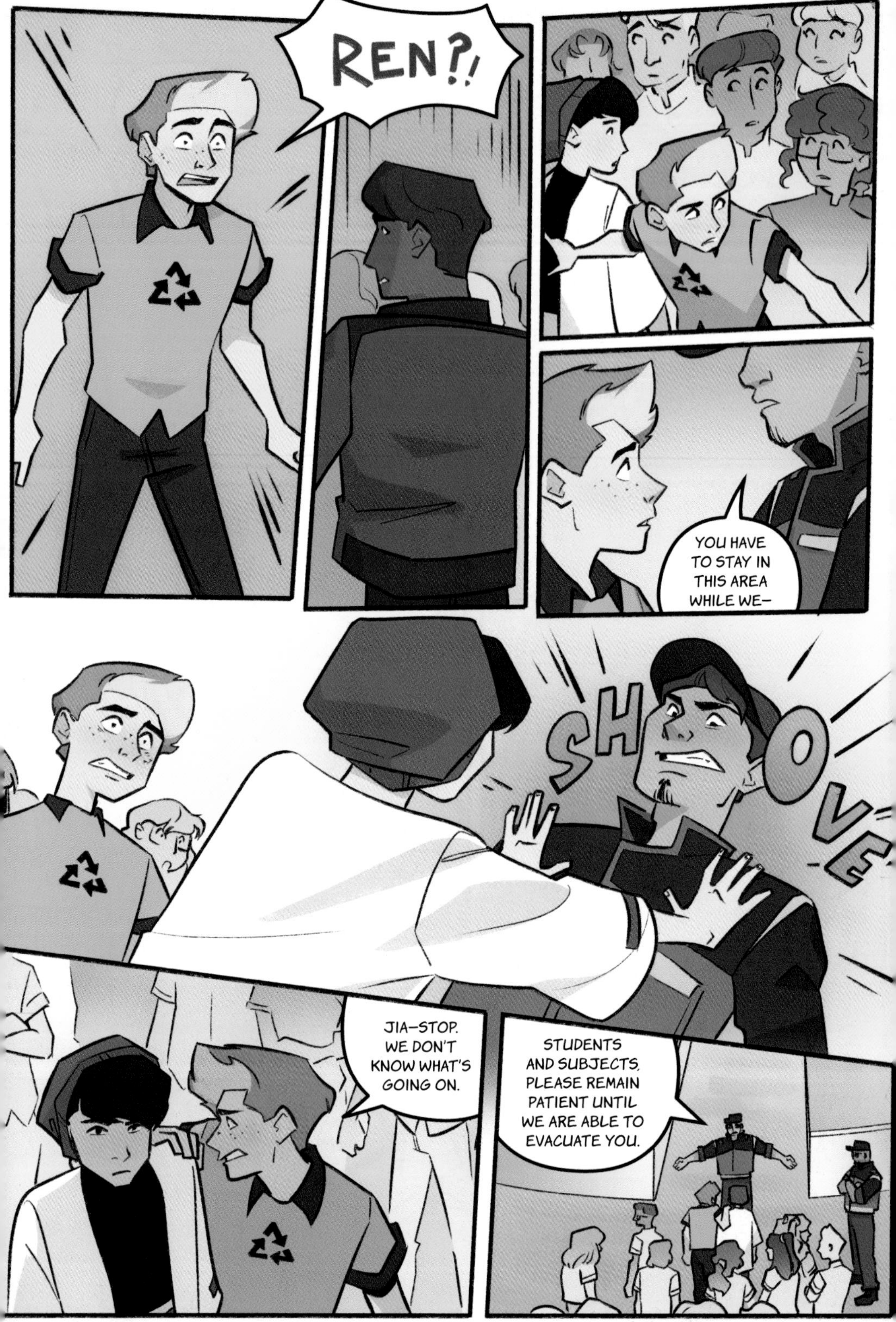
REN?!
YOU HAVE TO STAY IN THIS AREA WHILE WE—
SHOVE
JIA—STOP. WE DON'T KNOW WHAT'S GOING ON.
STUDENTS AND SUBJECTS, PLEASE REMAIN PATIENT UNTIL WE ARE ABLE TO EVACUATE YOU.

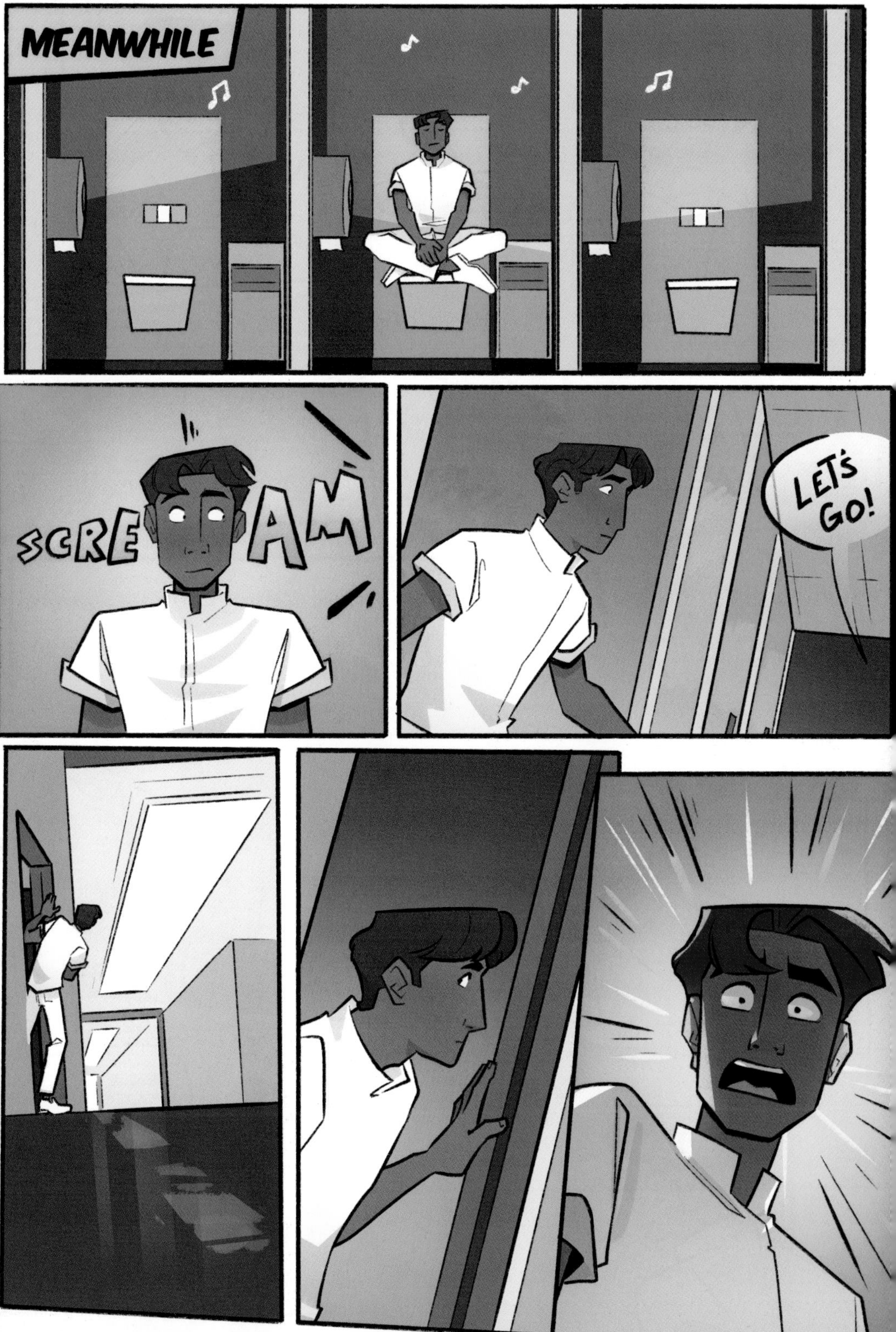
MEANWHILE
SCREAM
LET'S GO!

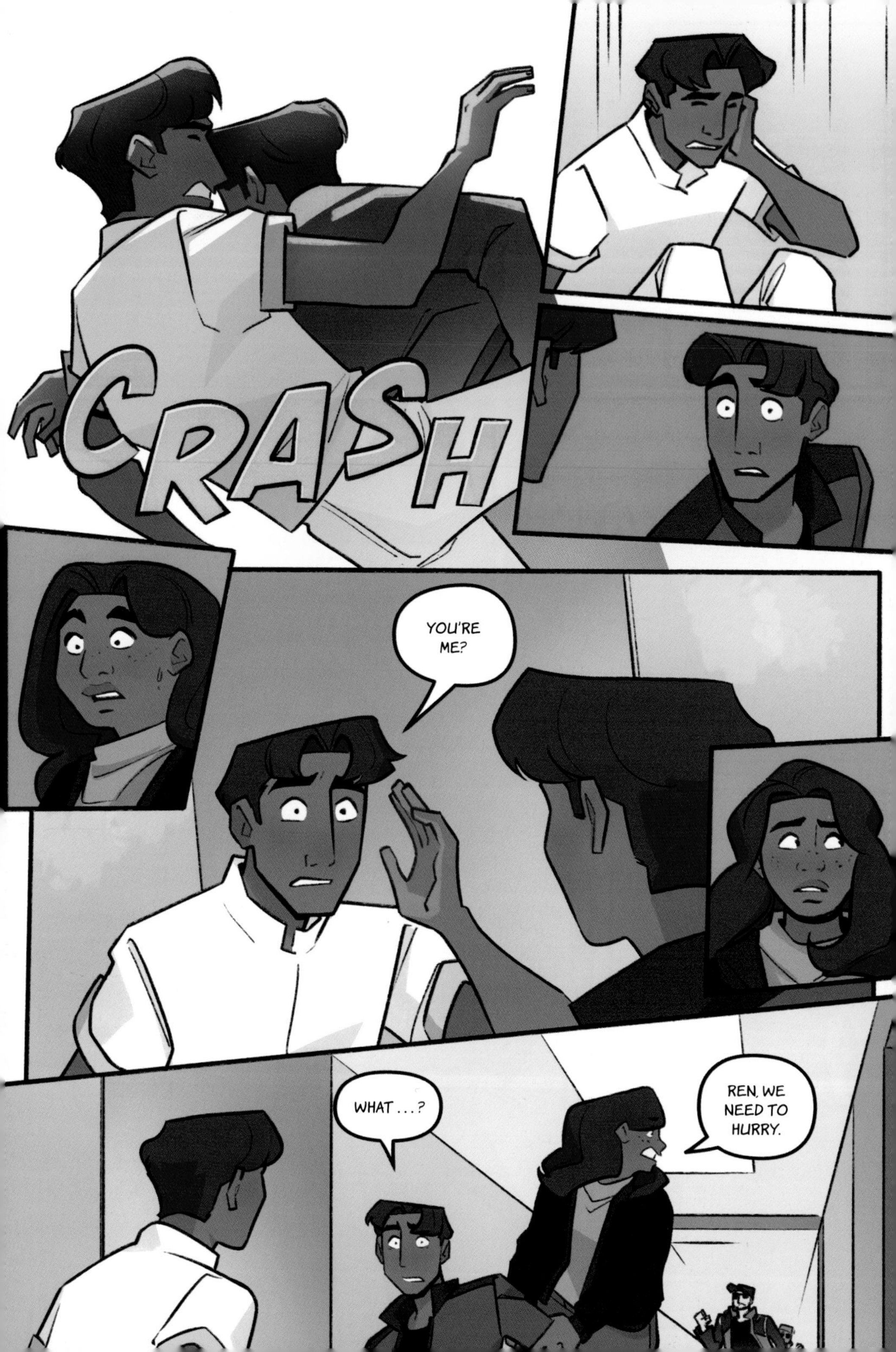
CRASH
YOU'RE ME?
WHAT . . . ?
REN, WE NEED TO HURRY.

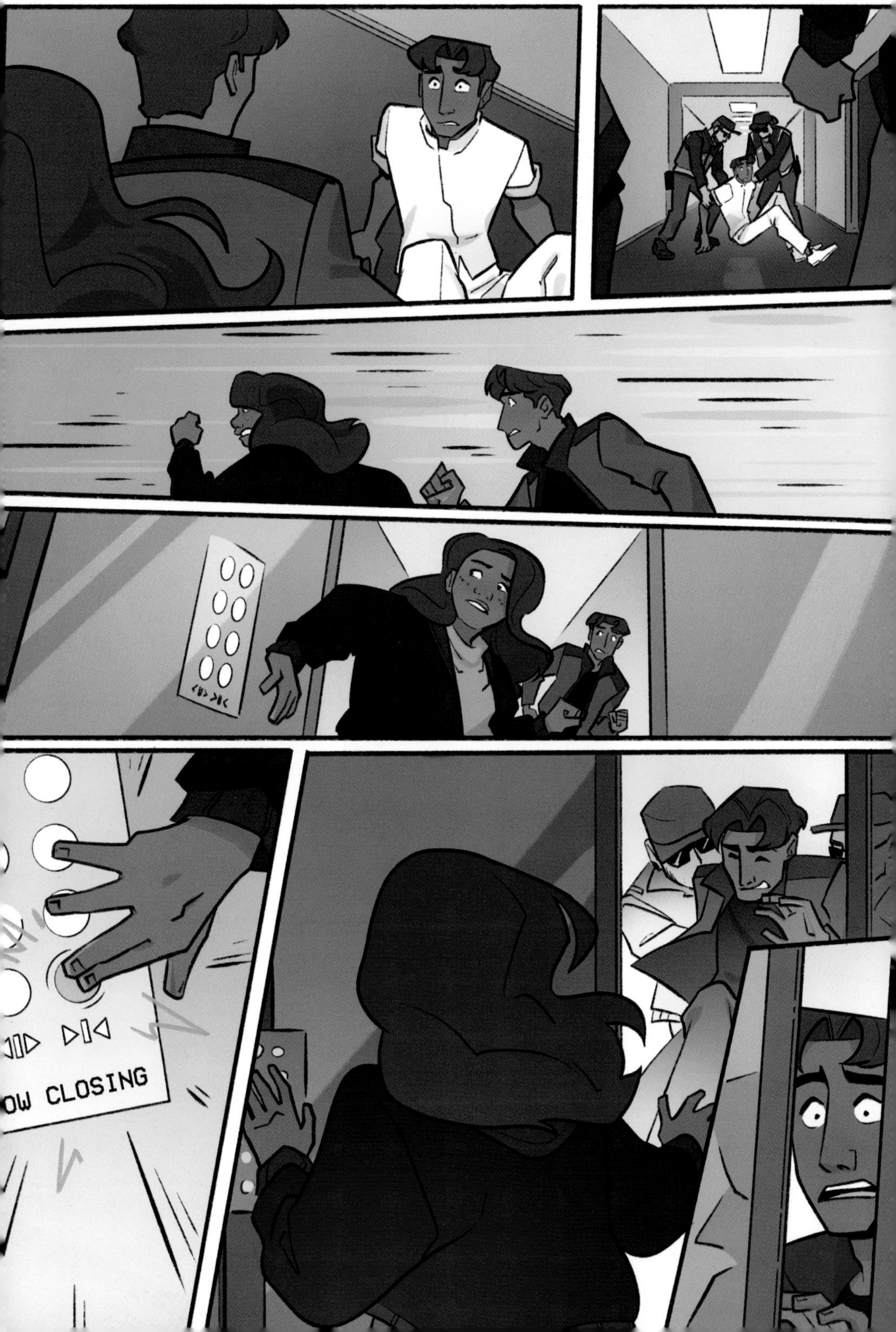

OW CLOSING

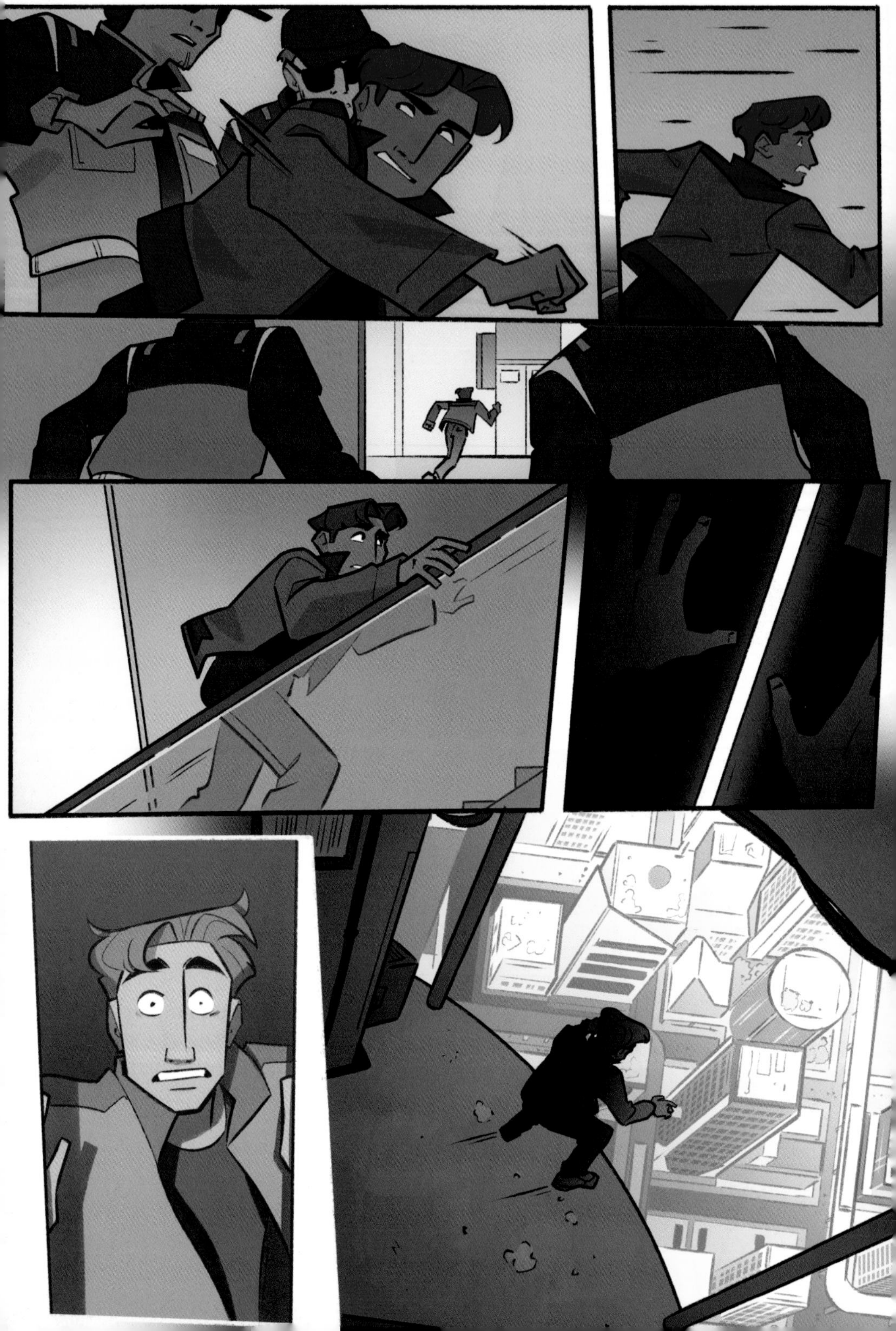

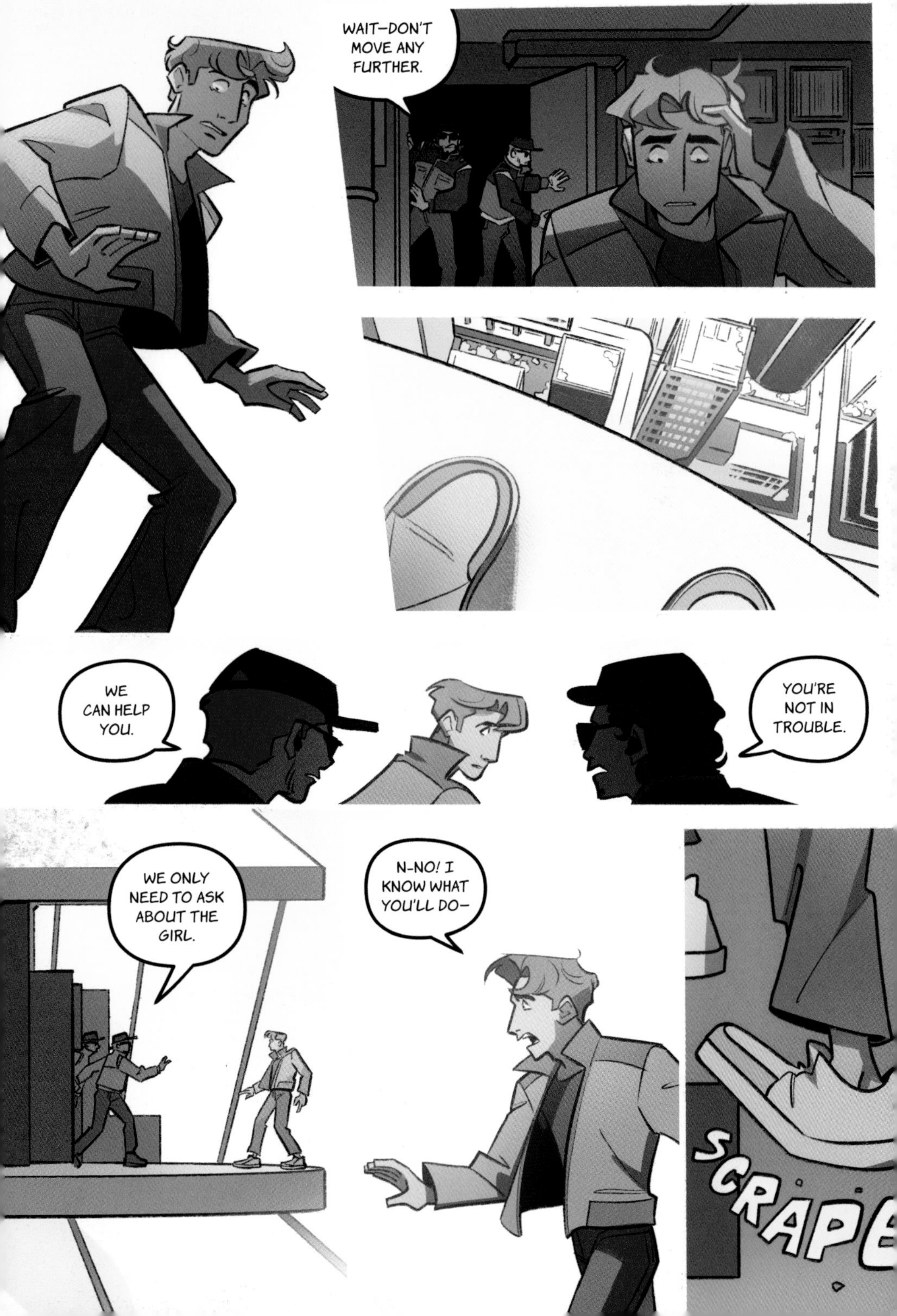
WAIT—DON'T MOVE ANY FURTHER.
WE CAN HELP YOU.
YOU'RE NOT IN TROUBLE.
WE ONLY NEED TO ASK ABOUT THE GIRL.
N-NO! I KNOW WHAT YOU'LL DO—
SCRAPE

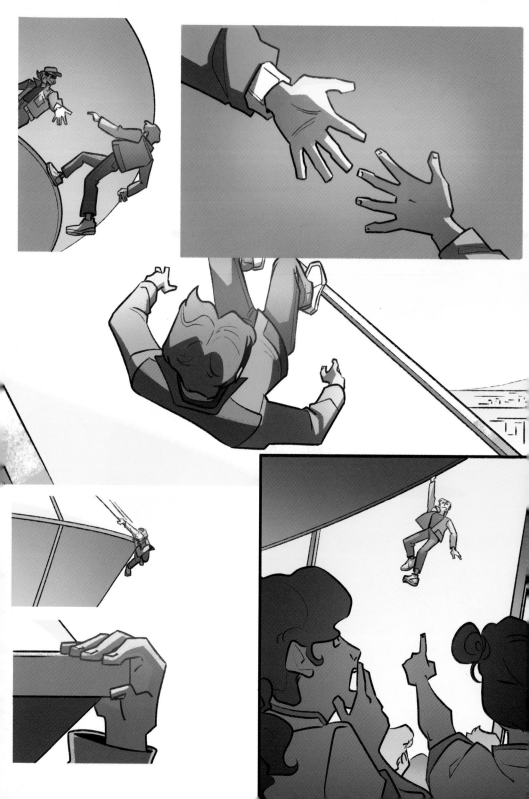

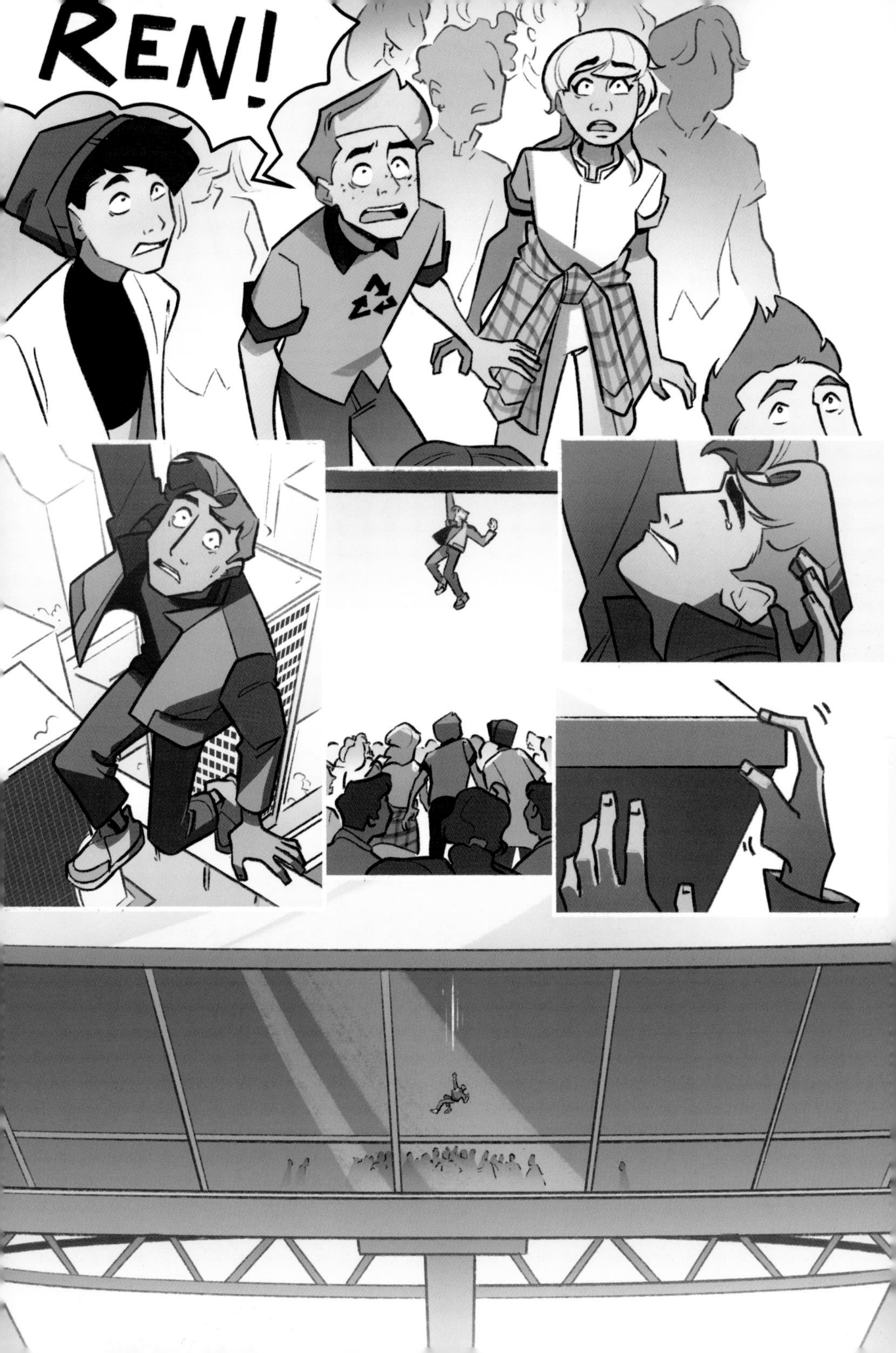
REN!

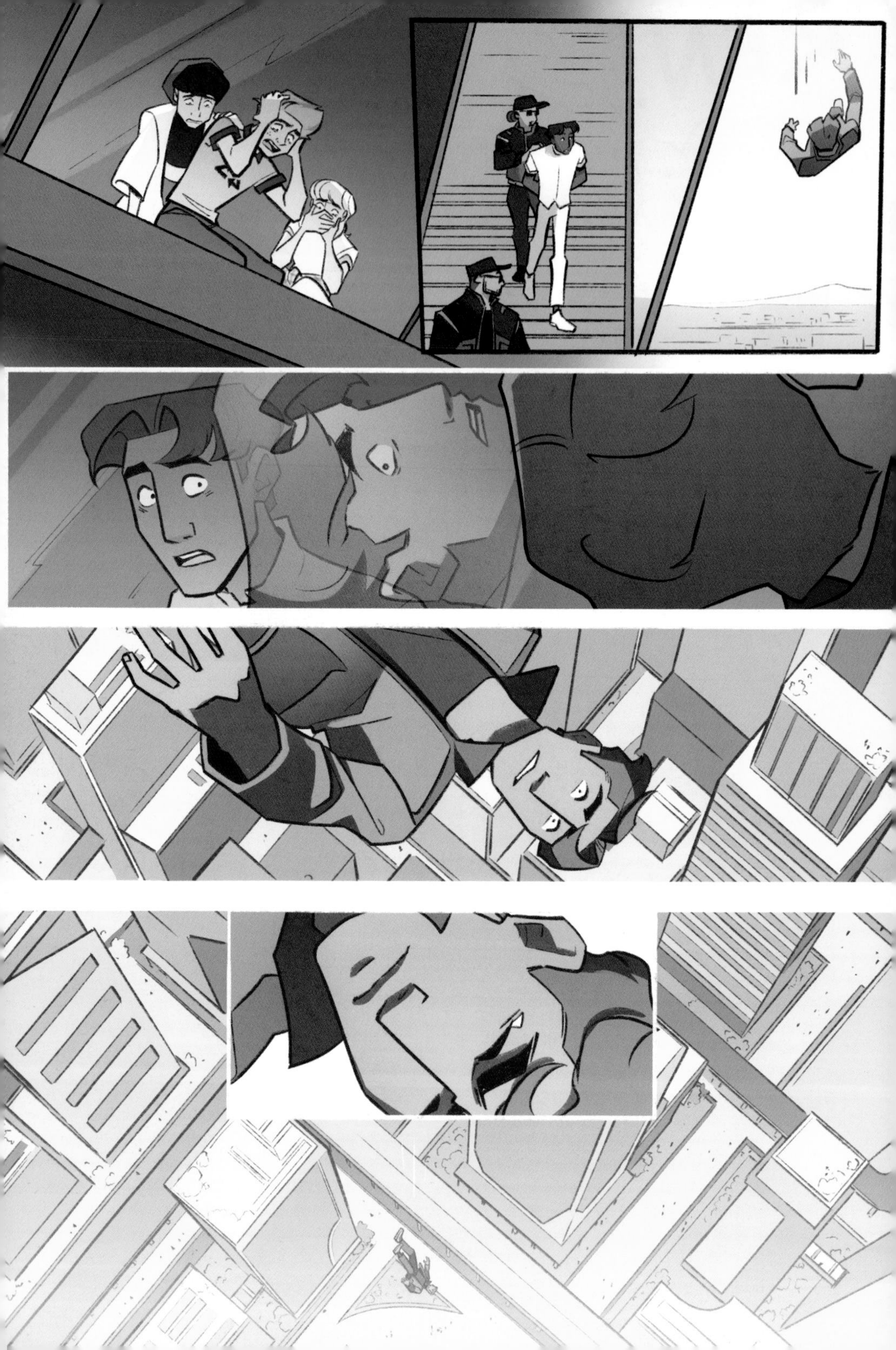

CHAPTER THREE

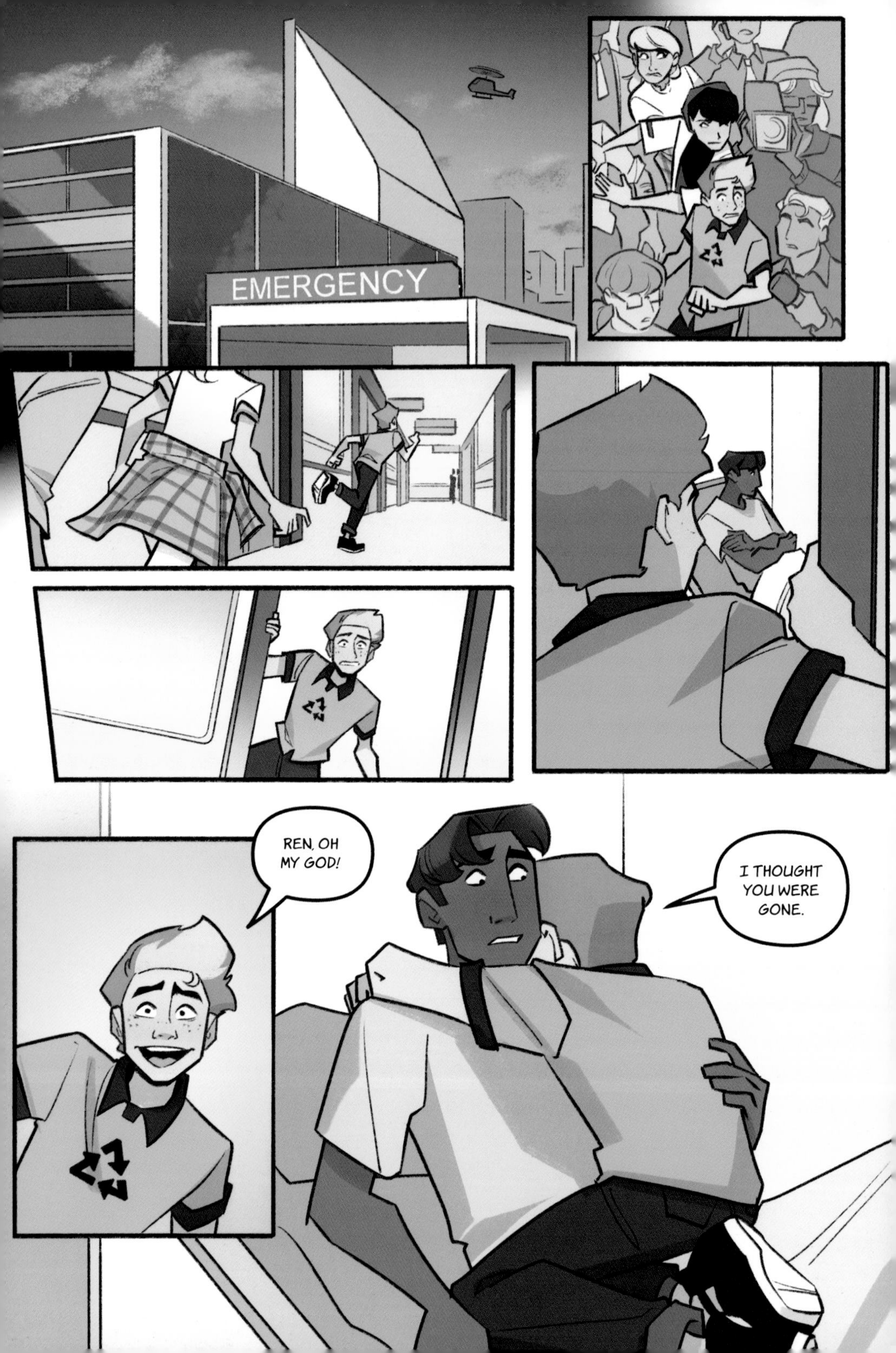
EMERGENCY
REN, OH MY GOD!
I THOUGHT YOU WERE GONE.

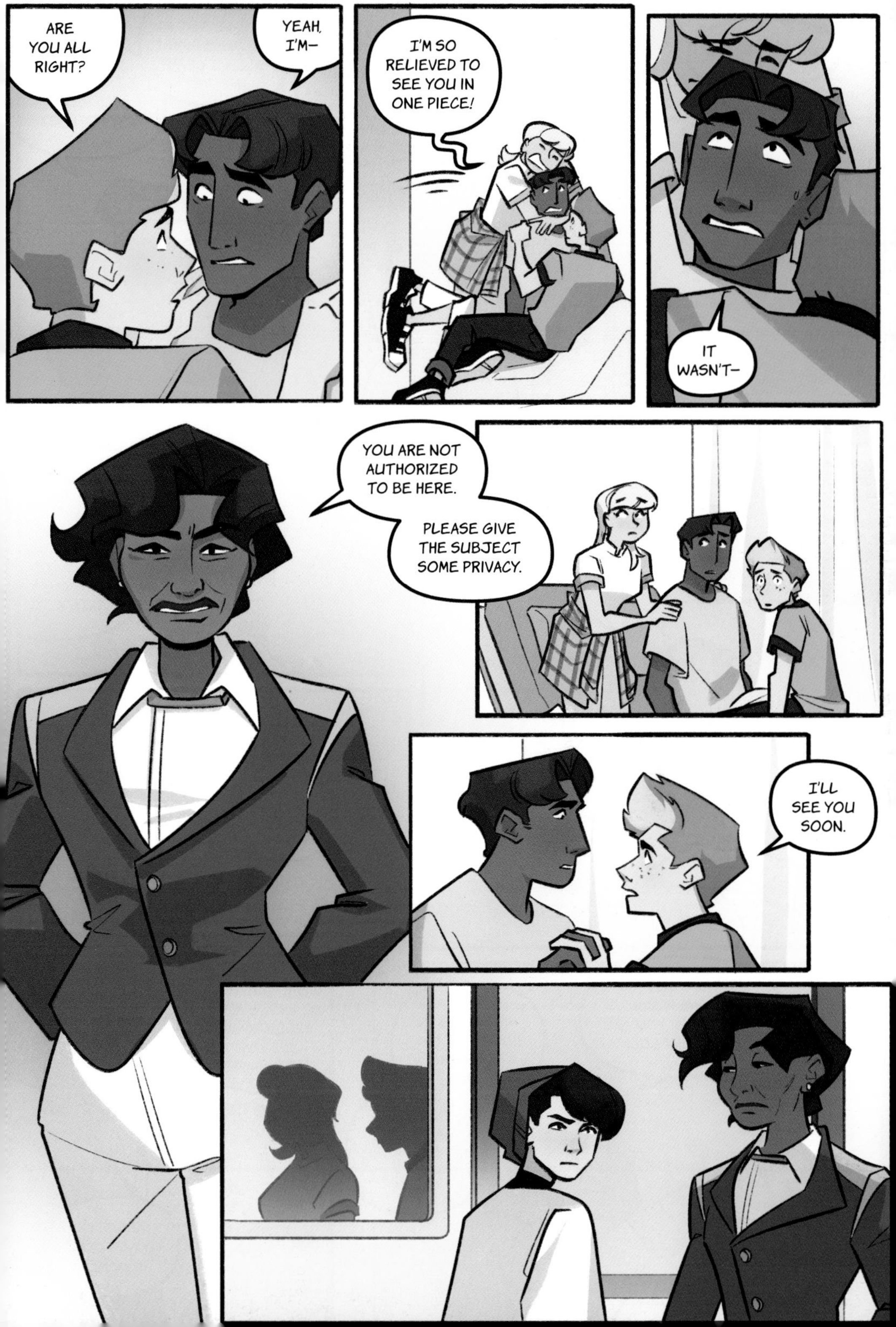
ARE YOU ALL RIGHT?
YEAH, I'M—
I'M SO RELIEVED TO SEE YOU IN ONE PIECE!
IT WASN'T—
YOU ARE NOT AUTHORIZED TO BE HERE.
PLEASE GIVE THE SUBJECT SOME PRIVACY.
I'LL SEE YOU SOON.

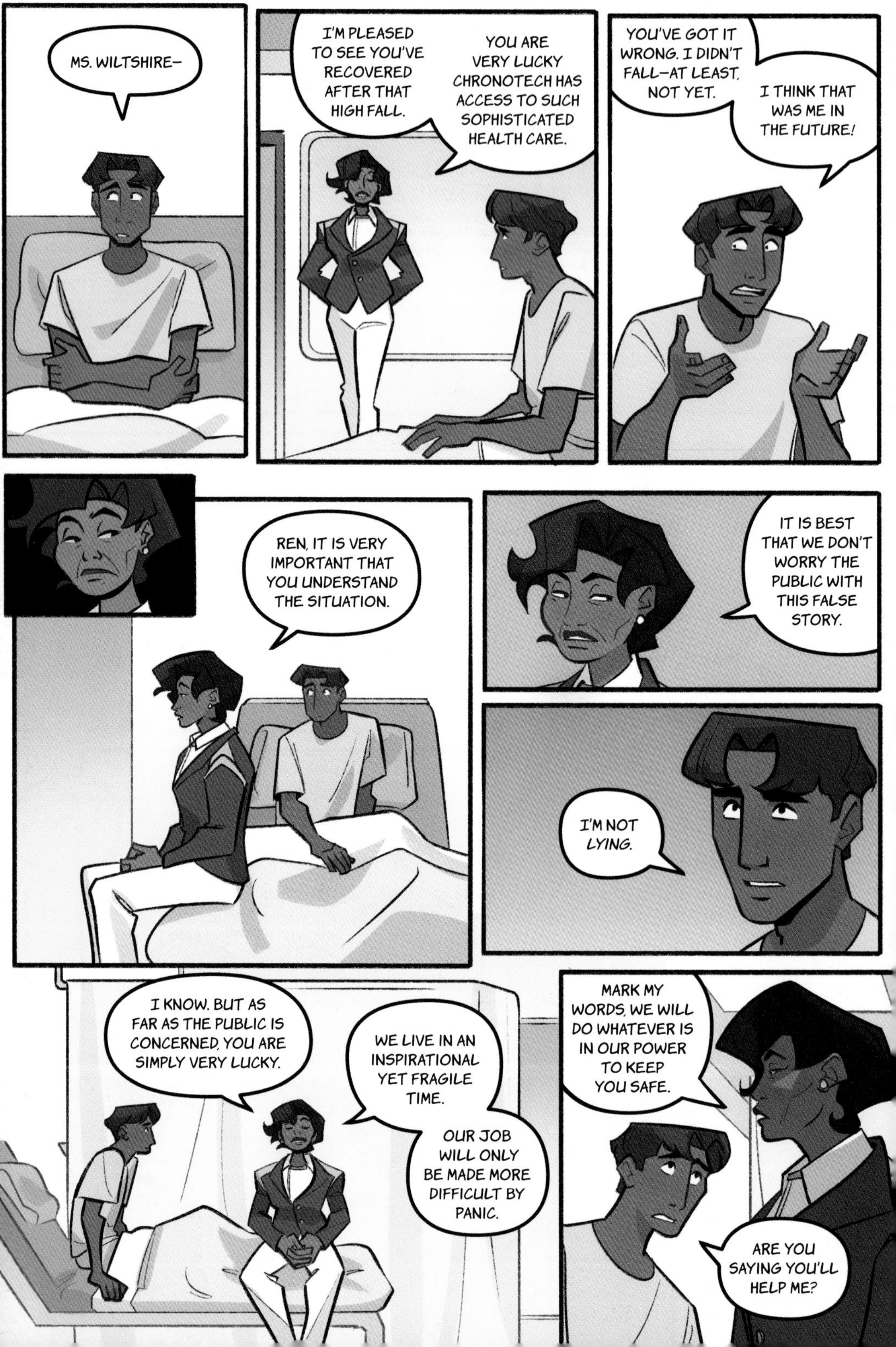
MS. WILTSHIRE—
I'M PLEASED TO SEE YOU'VE RECOVERED AFTER THAT HIGH FALL.
YOU ARE VERY LUCKY CHRONOTECH HAS ACCESS TO SUCH SOPHISTICATED HEALTH CARE.
YOU'VE GOT IT WRONG. I DIDN'T FALL—AT LEAST, NOT YET.
I THINK THAT WAS ME IN THE FUTURE!
REN, IT IS VERY IMPORTANT THAT YOU UNDERSTAND THE SITUATION.
IT IS BEST THAT WE DON'T WORRY THE PUBLIC WITH THIS FALSE STORY.
I'M NOT LYING.
I KNOW. BUT AS FAR AS THE PUBLIC IS CONCERNED, YOU ARE SIMPLY VERY LUCKY.
WE LIVE IN AN INSPIRATIONAL YET FRAGILE TIME.
OUR JOB WILL ONLY BE MADE MORE DIFFICULT BY PANIC.
MARK MY WORDS, WE WILL DO WHATEVER IS IN OUR POWER TO KEEP YOU SAFE.
ARE YOU SAYING YOU'LL HELP ME?

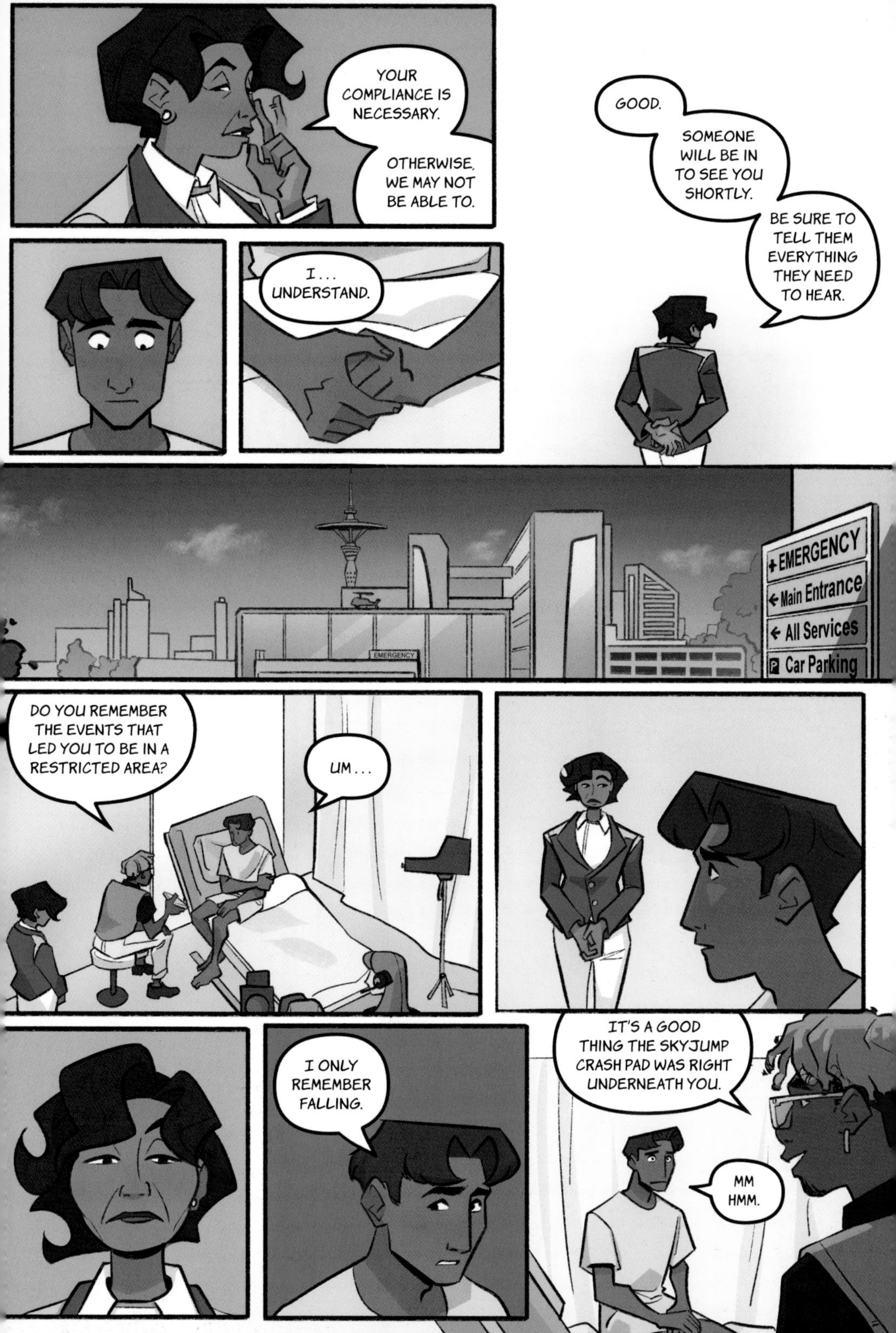
YOUR COMPLIANCE IS NECESSARY.
OTHERWISE, WE MAY NOT BE ABLE TO.
GOOD.
SOMEONE WILL BE IN TO SEE YOU SHORTLY.
BE SURE TO TELL THEM EVERYTHING THEY NEED TO HEAR.
I... UNDERSTAND.
EMERGENCY
EMERGENCY
Main Entrance
All Services
Car Parking
DO YOU REMEMBER THE EVENTS THAT LED YOU TO BE IN A RESTRICTED AREA?
UM...
I ONLY REMEMBER FALLING.
IT'S A GOOD THING THE SKYJUMP CRASH PAD WAS RIGHT UNDERNEATH YOU.
MM HMM.

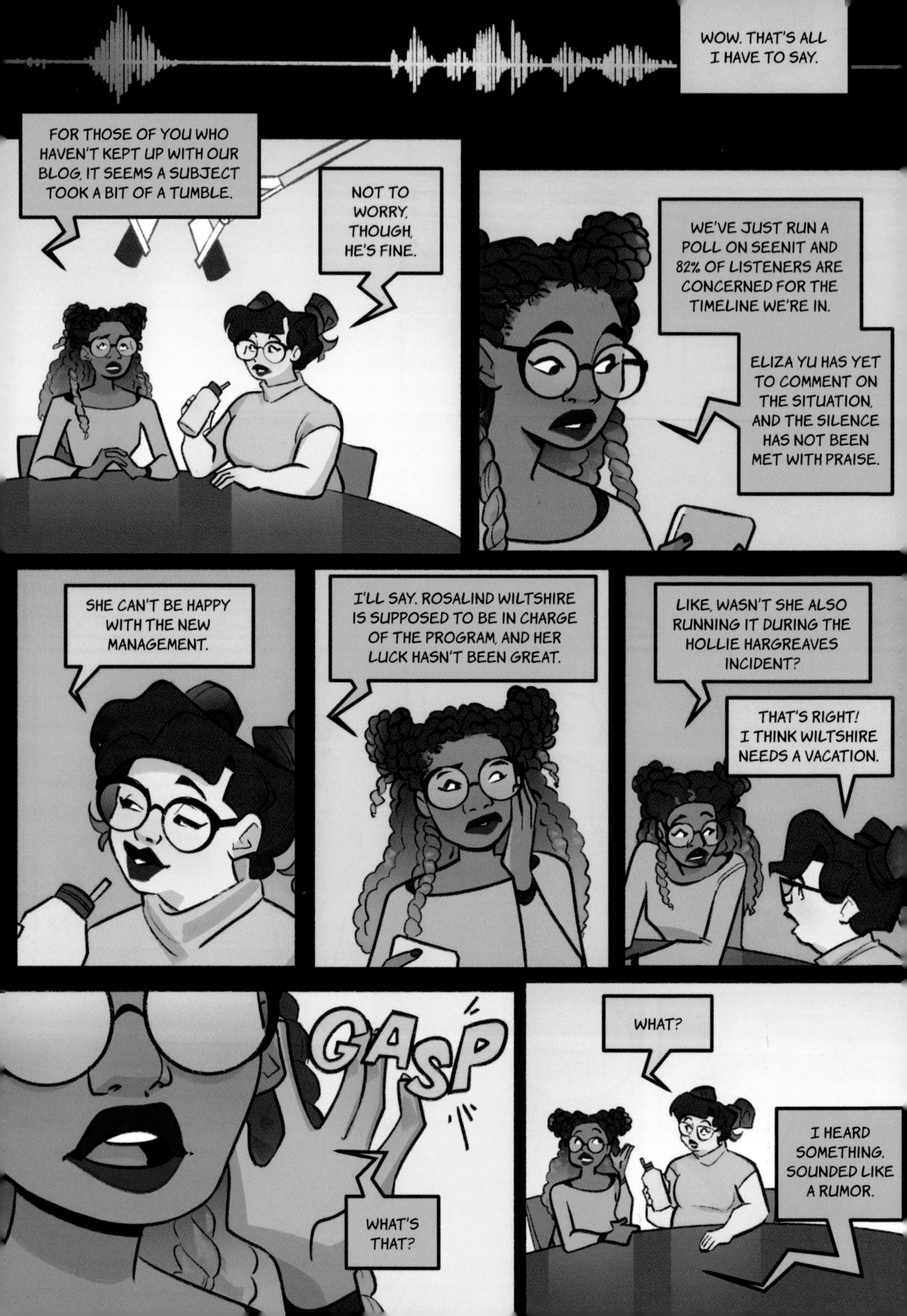
WOW. THAT'S ALL I HAVE TO SAY.
FOR THOSE OF YOU WHO HAVEN'T KEPT UP WITH OUR BLOG, IT SEEMS A SUBJECT TOOK A BIT OF A TUMBLE.
NOT TO WORRY, THOUGH, HE'S FINE.
WE'VE JUST RUN A POLL ON SEENIT AND 82% OF LISTENERS ARE CONCERNED FOR THE TIMELINE WE'RE IN.
ELIZA YU HAS YET TO COMMENT ON THE SITUATION, AND THE SILENCE HAS NOT BEEN MET WITH PRAISE.
SHE CAN'T BE HAPPY WITH THE NEW MANAGEMENT.
I'LL SAY. ROSALIND WILTSHIRE IS SUPPOSED TO BE IN CHARGE OF THE PROGRAM, AND HER LUCK HASN'T BEEN GREAT.
LIKE, WASN'T SHE ALSO RUNNING IT DURING THE HOLLIE HARGREAVES INCIDENT?
THAT'S RIGHT! I THINK WILTSHIRE NEEDS A VACATION.
GASP
WHAT'S THAT?
WHAT?
I HEARD SOMETHING. SOUNDED LIKE A RUMOR.

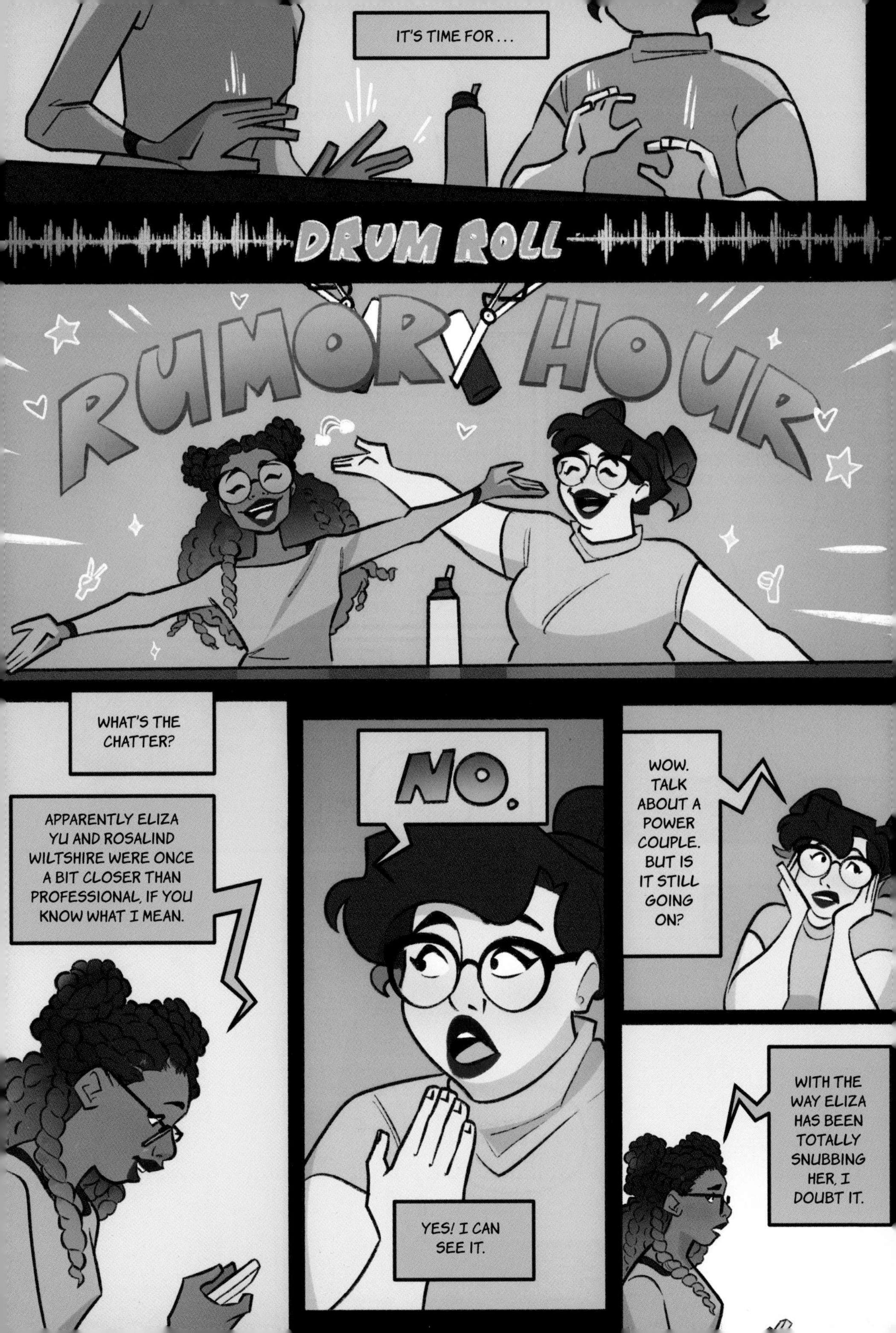
IT'S TIME FOR . . .
DRUM ROLL
RUMOR HOUR
WHAT'S THE CHATTER?
APPARENTLY ELIZA YU AND ROSALIND WILTSHIRE WERE ONCE A BIT CLOSER THAN PROFESSIONAL, IF YOU KNOW WHAT I MEAN.
NO.
YES! I CAN SEE IT.
WOW. TALK ABOUT A POWER COUPLE. BUT IS IT STILL GOING ON?
WITH THE WAY ELIZA HAS BEEN TOTALLY SNUBBING HER, I DOUBT IT.

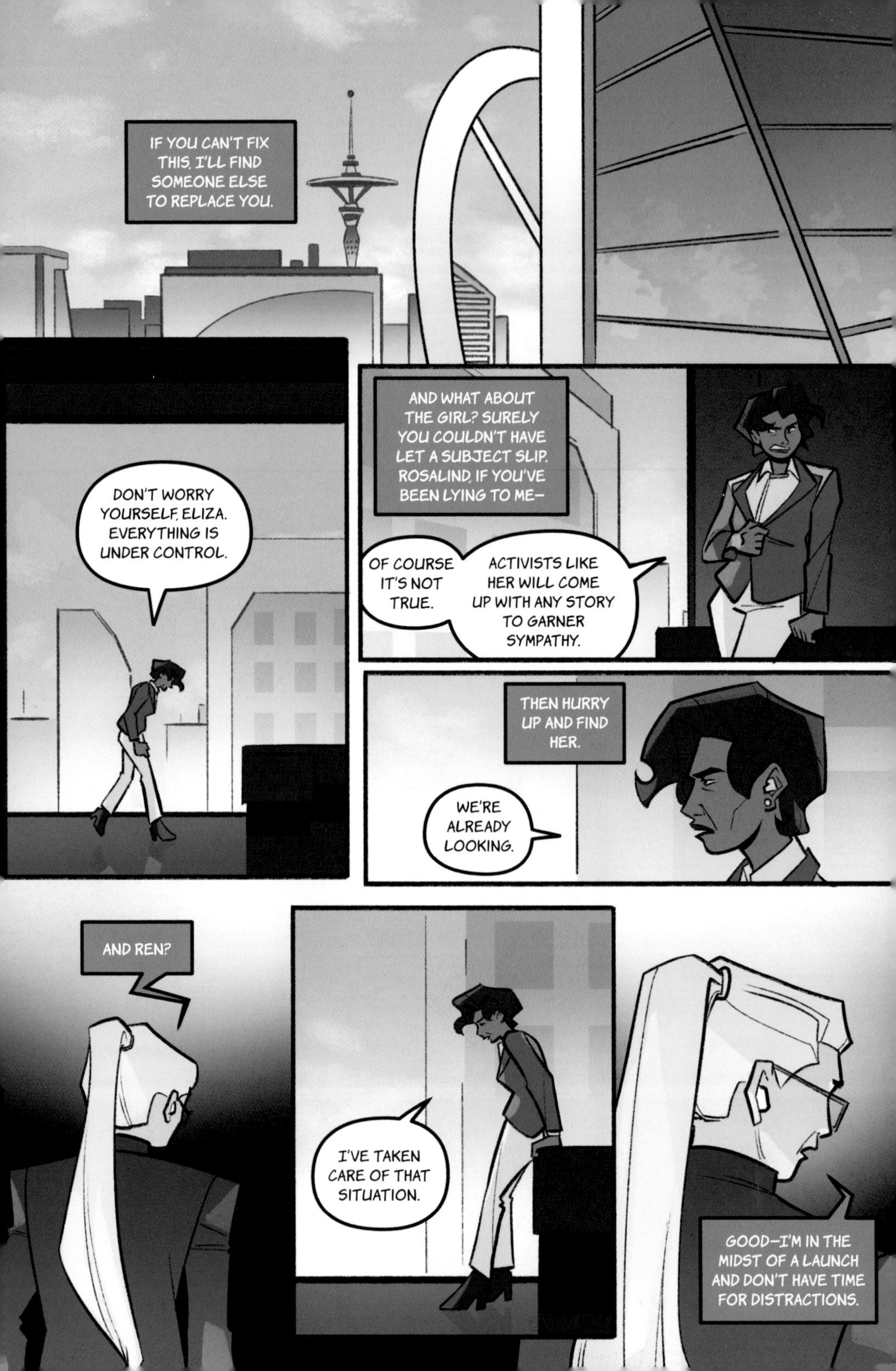
IF YOU CAN'T FIX THIS, I'LL FIND SOMEONE ELSE TO REPLACE YOU.
DON'T WORRY YOURSELF, ELIZA. EVERYTHING IS UNDER CONTROL.
AND WHAT ABOUT THE GIRL? SURELY YOU COULDN'T HAVE LET A SUBJECT SLIP. ROSALIND, IF YOU'VE BEEN LYING TO ME—
OF COURSE IT'S NOT TRUE.
ACTIVISTS LIKE HER WILL COME UP WITH ANY STORY TO GARNER SYMPATHY.
THEN HURRY UP AND FIND HER.
WE'RE ALREADY LOOKING.
AND REN?
I'VE TAKEN CARE OF THAT SITUATION.
GOOD—I'M IN THE MIDST OF A LAUNCH AND DON'T HAVE TIME FOR DISTRACTIONS.

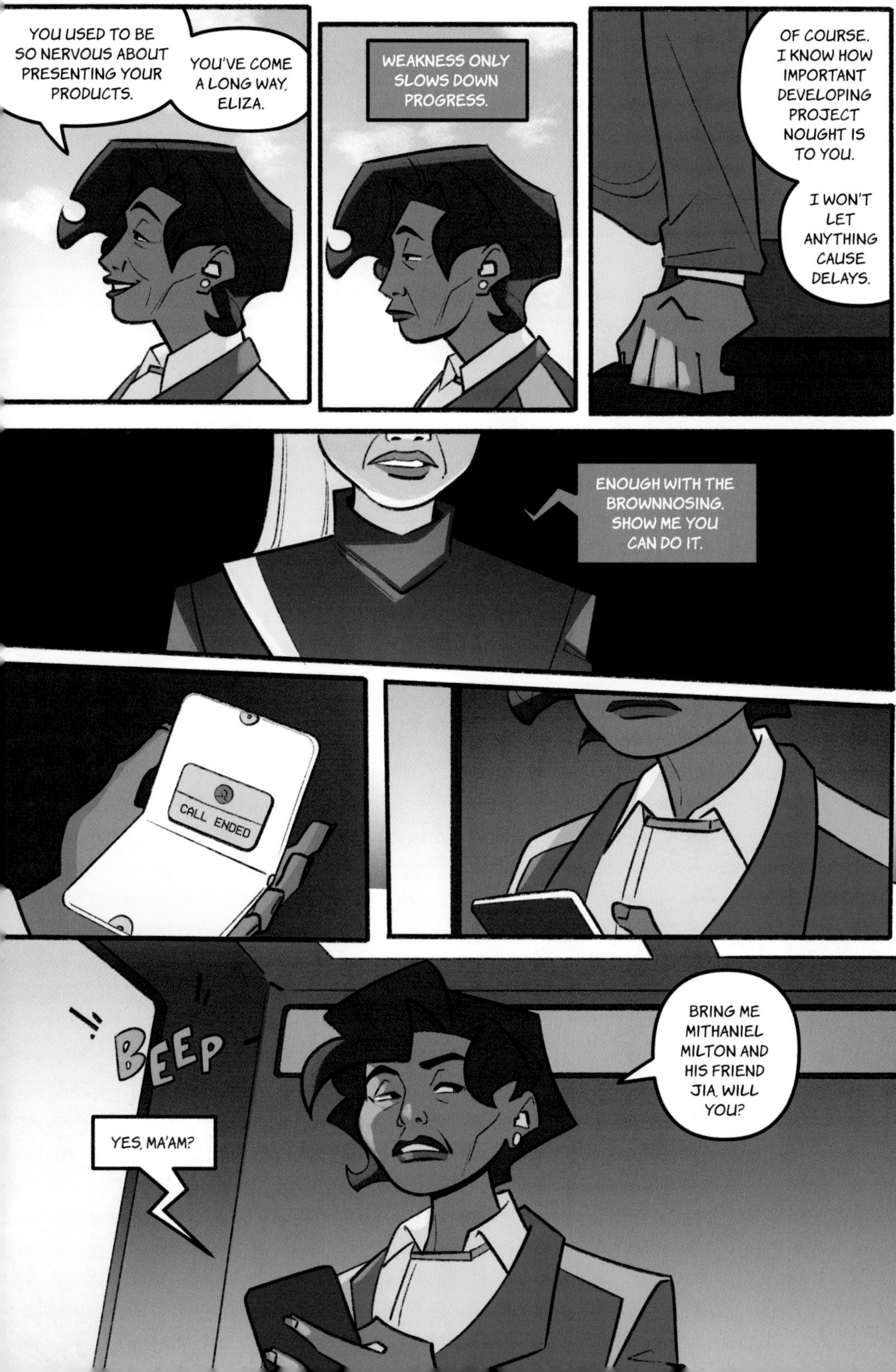
YOU USED TO BE SO NERVOUS ABOUT PRESENTING YOUR PRODUCTS.
YOU'VE COME A LONG WAY, ELIZA.
WEAKNESS ONLY SLOWS DOWN PROGRESS.
OF COURSE. I KNOW HOW IMPORTANT DEVELOPING PROJECT NOUGHT IS TO YOU.
I WON'T LET ANYTHING CAUSE DELAYS.
ENOUGH WITH THE BROWNNOSING. SHOW ME YOU CAN DO IT.
CALL ENDED
BEEP
YES, MA'AM?
BRING ME MITHANIEL MILTON AND HIS FRIEND JIA, WILL YOU?

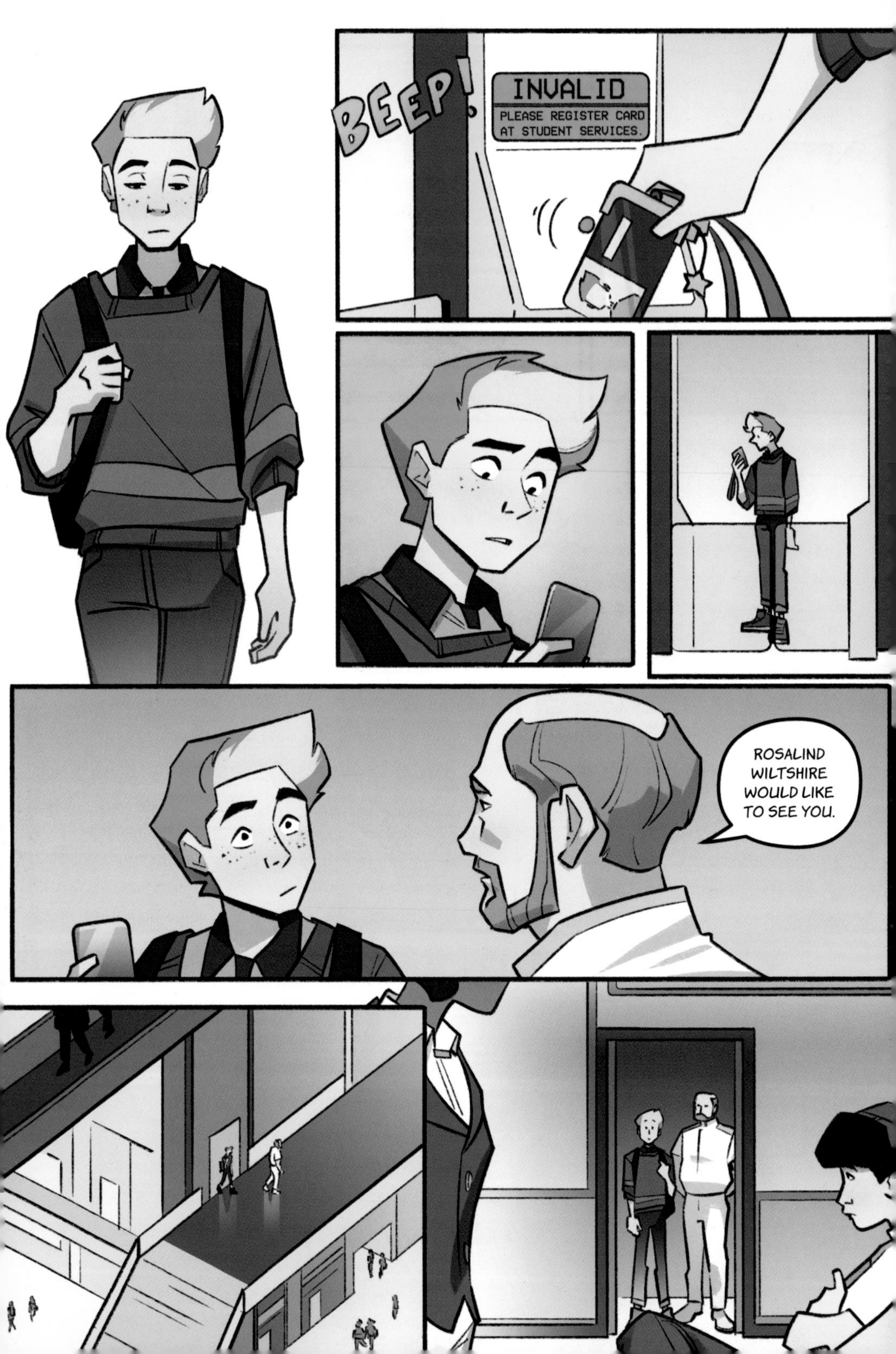
BEEP!
INVALID
PLEASE REGISTER CARD AT STUDENT SERVICES.
ROSALIND WILTSHIRE WOULD LIKE TO SEE YOU.

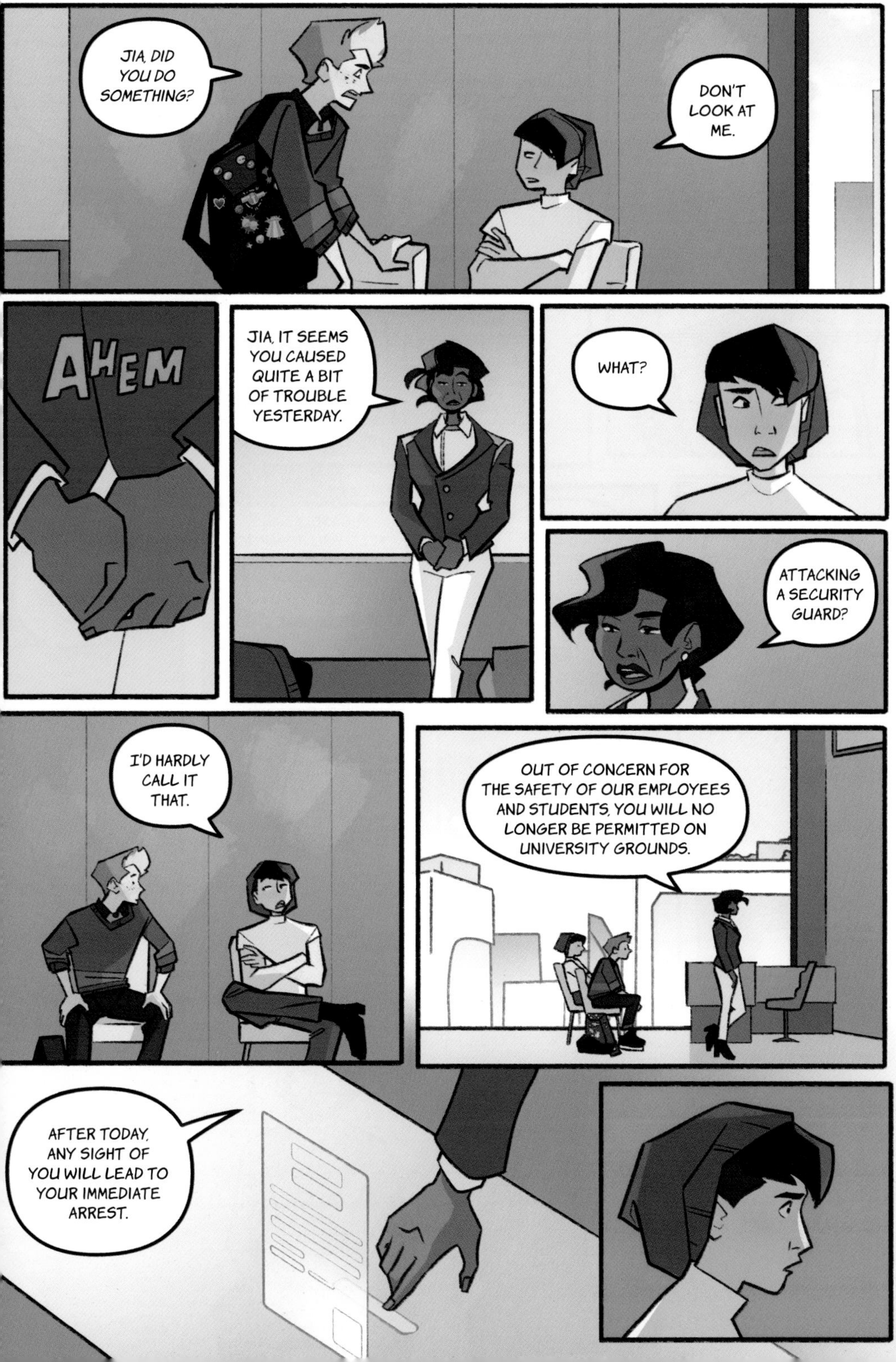

JIA, DID YOU DO SOMETHING?
DON'T LOOK AT ME.
AHEM
JIA, IT SEEMS YOU CAUSED QUITE A BIT OF TROUBLE YESTERDAY.
WHAT?
ATTACKING A SECURITY GUARD?
I'D HARDLY CALL IT THAT.
OUT OF CONCERN FOR THE SAFETY OF OUR EMPLOYEES AND STUDENTS, YOU WILL NO LONGER BE PERMITTED ON UNIVERSITY GROUNDS.
AFTER TODAY, ANY SIGHT OF YOU WILL LEAD TO YOUR IMMEDIATE ARREST.

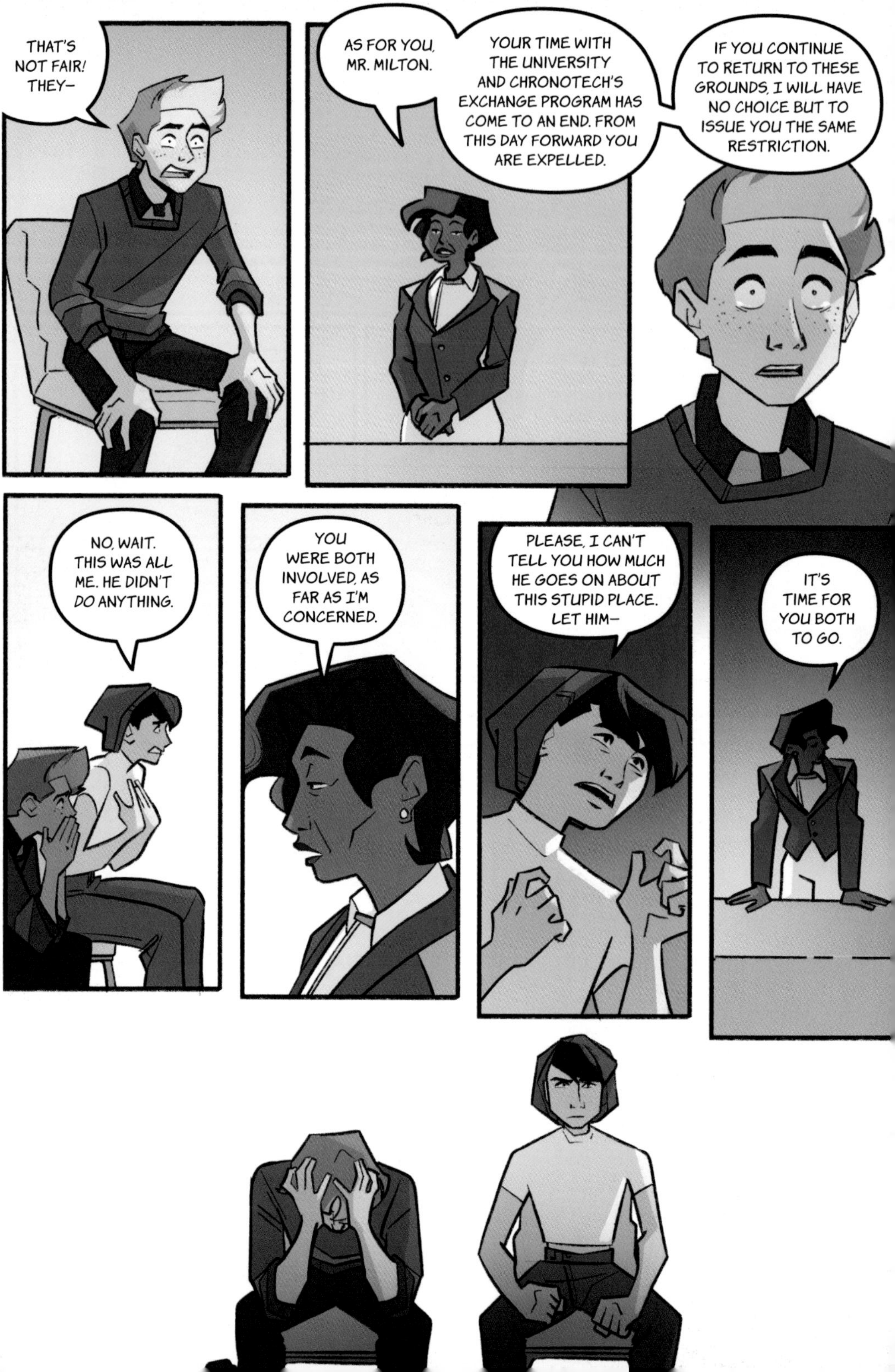
THAT'S NOT FAIR! THEY—
AS FOR YOU, MR. MILTON.
YOUR TIME WITH THE UNIVERSITY AND CHRONOTECH'S EXCHANGE PROGRAM HAS COME TO AN END. FROM THIS DAY FORWARD YOU ARE EXPELLED.
IF YOU CONTINUE TO RETURN TO THESE GROUNDS, I WILL HAVE NO CHOICE BUT TO ISSUE YOU THE SAME RESTRICTION.
NO, WAIT. THIS WAS ALL ME. HE DIDN'T DO ANYTHING.
YOU WERE BOTH INVOLVED, AS FAR AS I'M CONCERNED.
PLEASE, I CAN'T TELL YOU HOW MUCH HE GOES ON ABOUT THIS STUPID PLACE. LET HIM—
IT'S TIME FOR YOU BOTH TO GO.

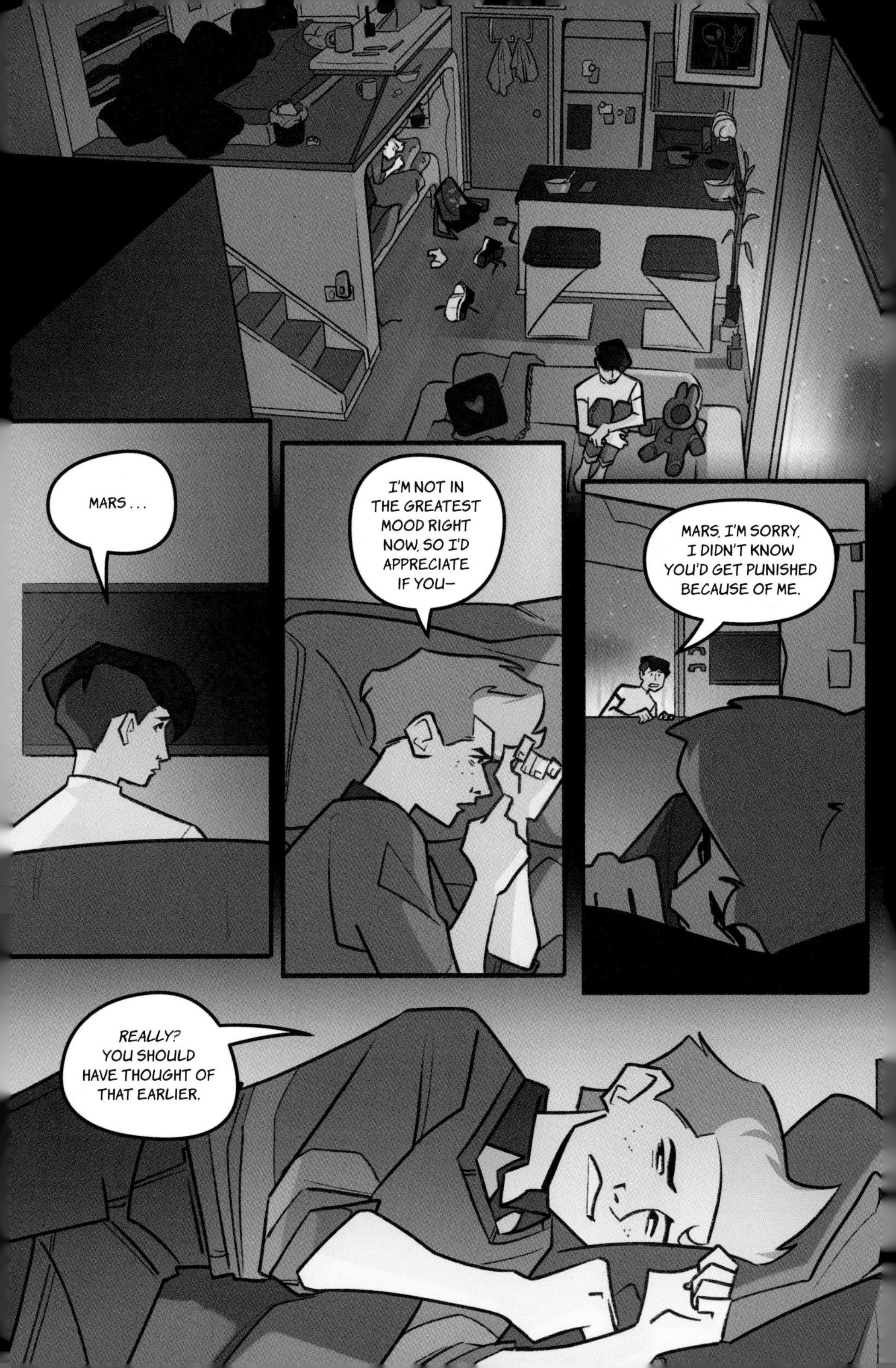
MARS . . .
I'M NOT IN THE GREATEST MOOD RIGHT NOW, SO I'D APPRECIATE IF YOU—
MARS, I'M SORRY, I DIDN'T KNOW YOU'D GET PUNISHED BECAUSE OF ME.
REALLY? YOU SHOULD HAVE THOUGHT OF THAT EARLIER.

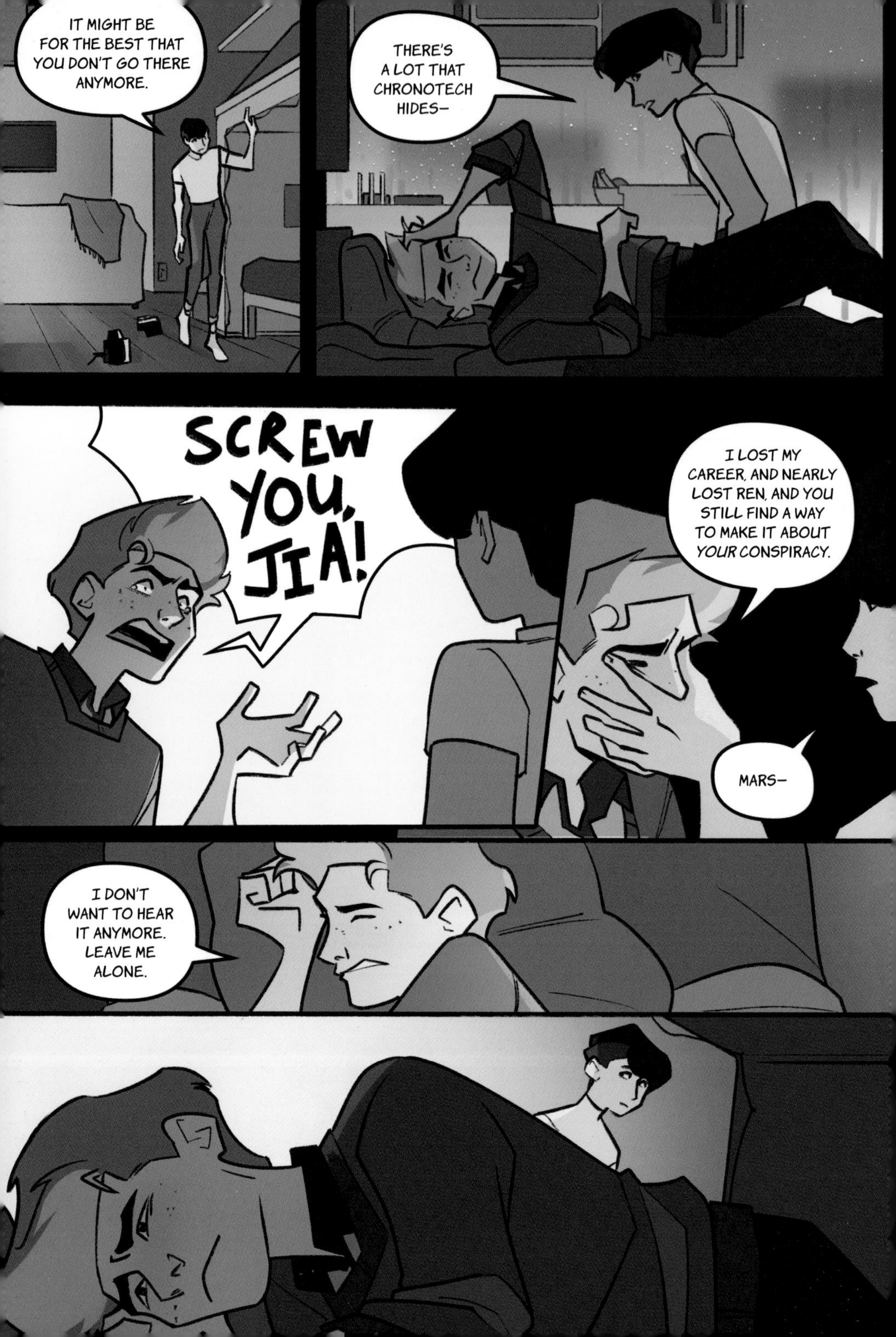
IT MIGHT BE FOR THE BEST THAT YOU DON'T GO THERE ANYMORE.
THERE'S A LOT THAT CHRONOTECH HIDES—
SCREW YOU, JIA!
I LOST MY CAREER, AND NEARLY LOST REN, AND YOU STILL FIND A WAY TO MAKE IT ABOUT *YOUR* CONSPIRACY.
MARS—
I DON'T WANT TO HEAR IT ANYMORE. LEAVE ME ALONE.

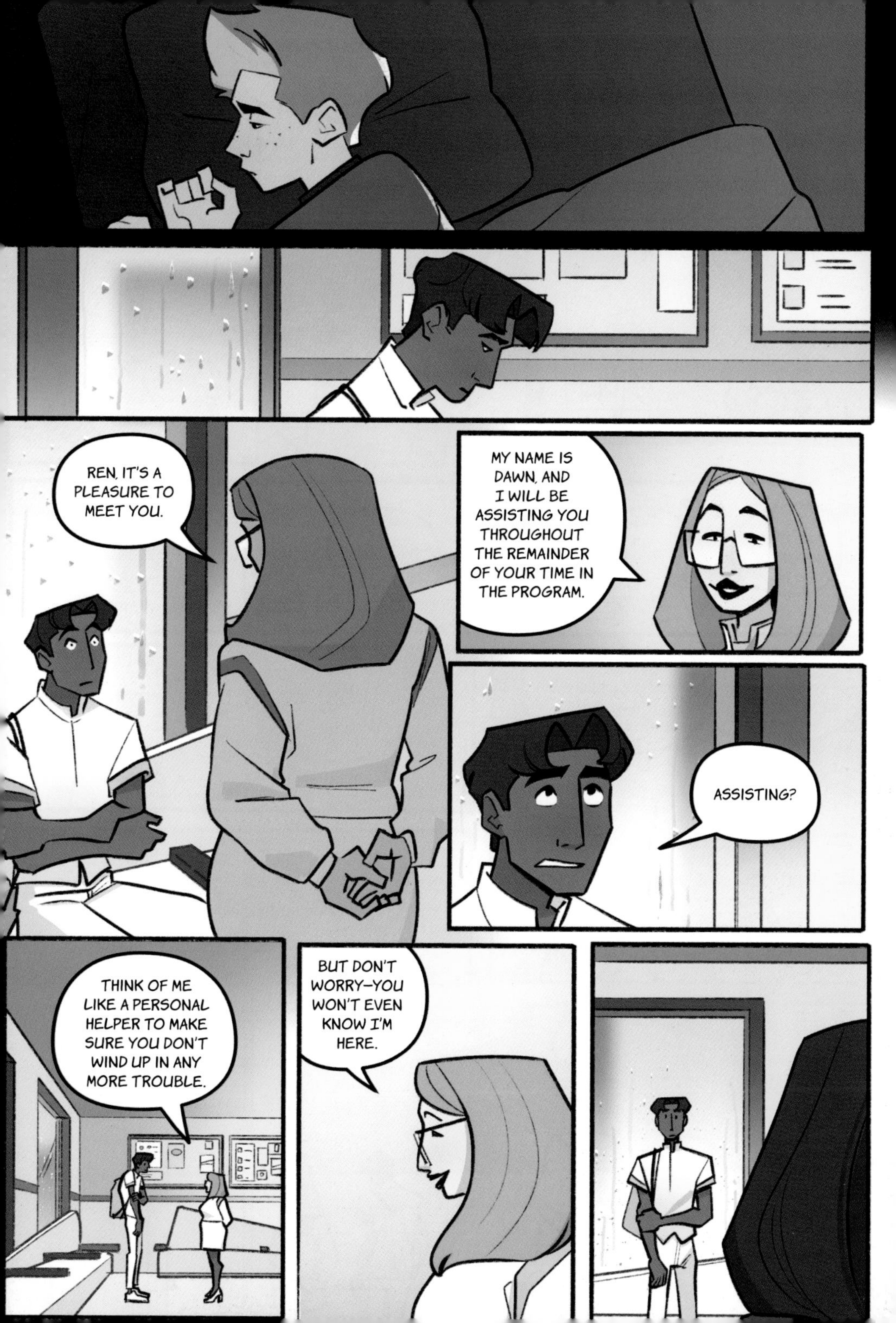
REN, IT'S A PLEASURE TO MEET YOU.
MY NAME IS DAWN, AND I WILL BE ASSISTING YOU THROUGHOUT THE REMAINDER OF YOUR TIME IN THE PROGRAM.
ASSISTING?
THINK OF ME LIKE A PERSONAL HELPER TO MAKE SURE YOU DON'T WIND UP IN ANY MORE TROUBLE.
BUT DON'T WORRY—YOU WON'T EVEN KNOW I'M HERE.

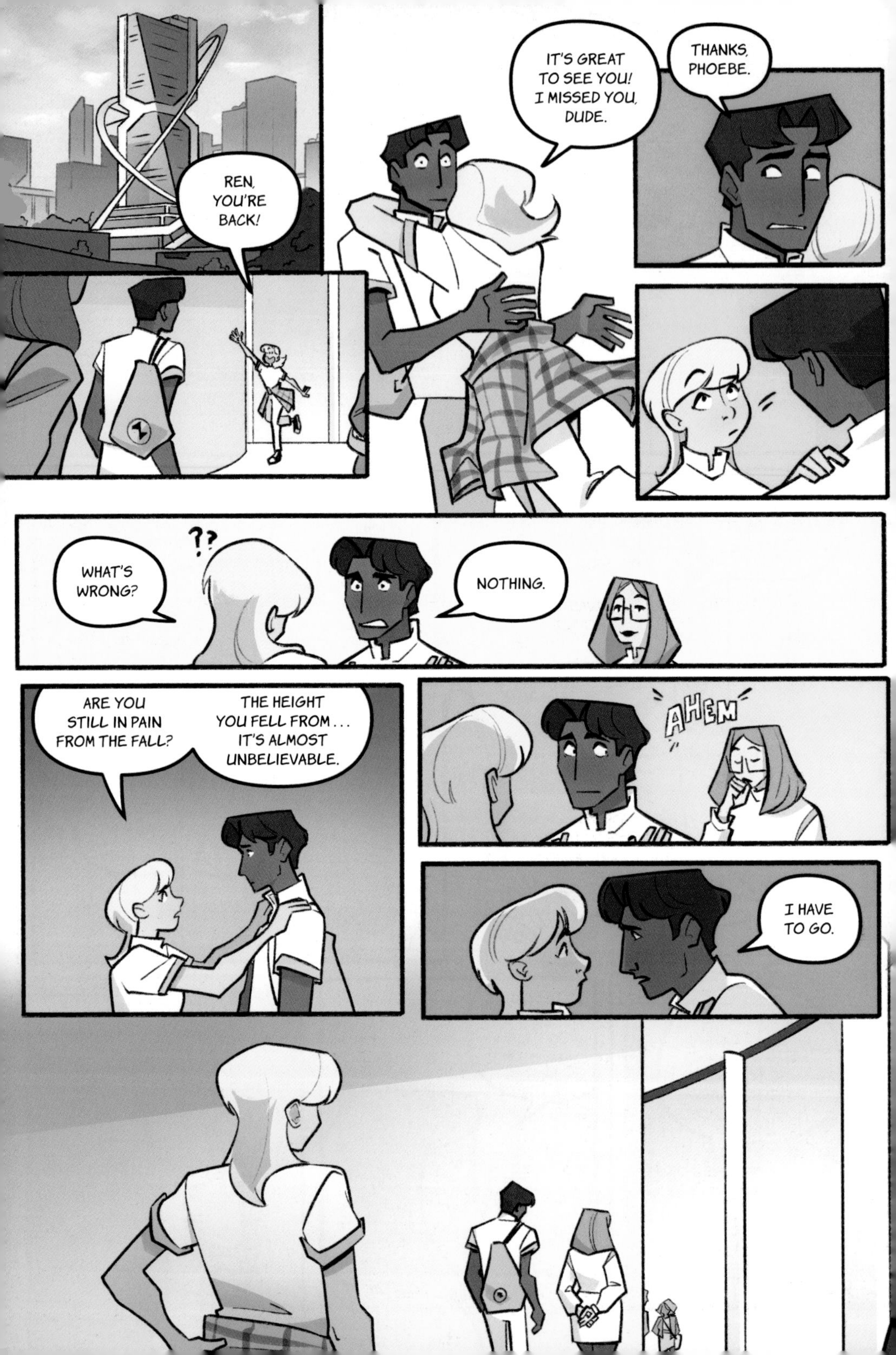
REN, YOU'RE BACK!
IT'S GREAT TO SEE YOU! I MISSED YOU, DUDE.
THANKS, PHOEBE.
??
WHAT'S WRONG?
NOTHING.
ARE YOU STILL IN PAIN FROM THE FALL?
THE HEIGHT YOU FELL FROM . . . IT'S ALMOST UNBELIEVABLE.
AHEM
I HAVE TO GO.

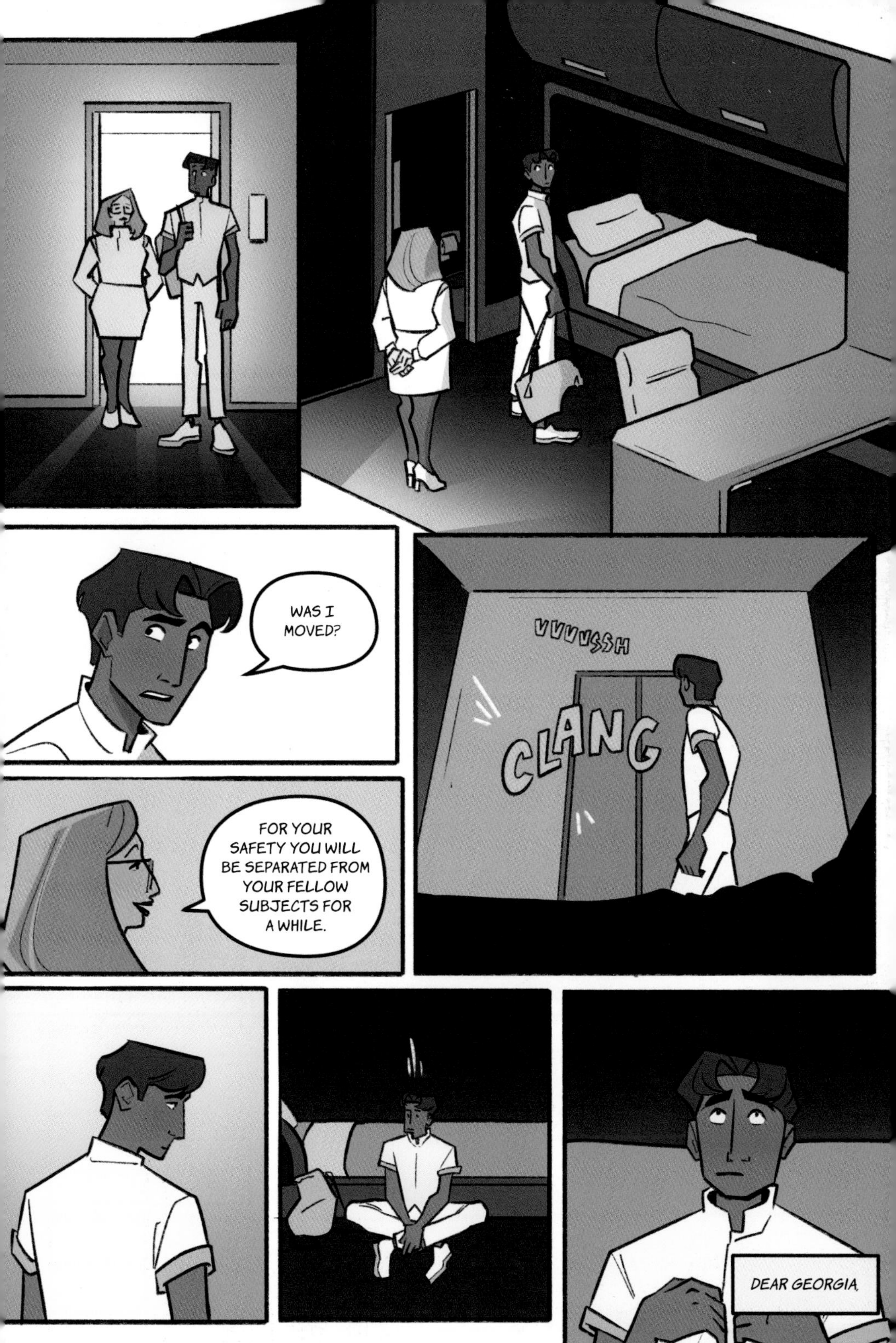
WAS I MOVED?
VVVVSSH
CLANG
FOR YOUR SAFETY YOU WILL BE SEPARATED FROM YOUR FELLOW SUBJECTS FOR A WHILE.
DEAR GEORGIA,

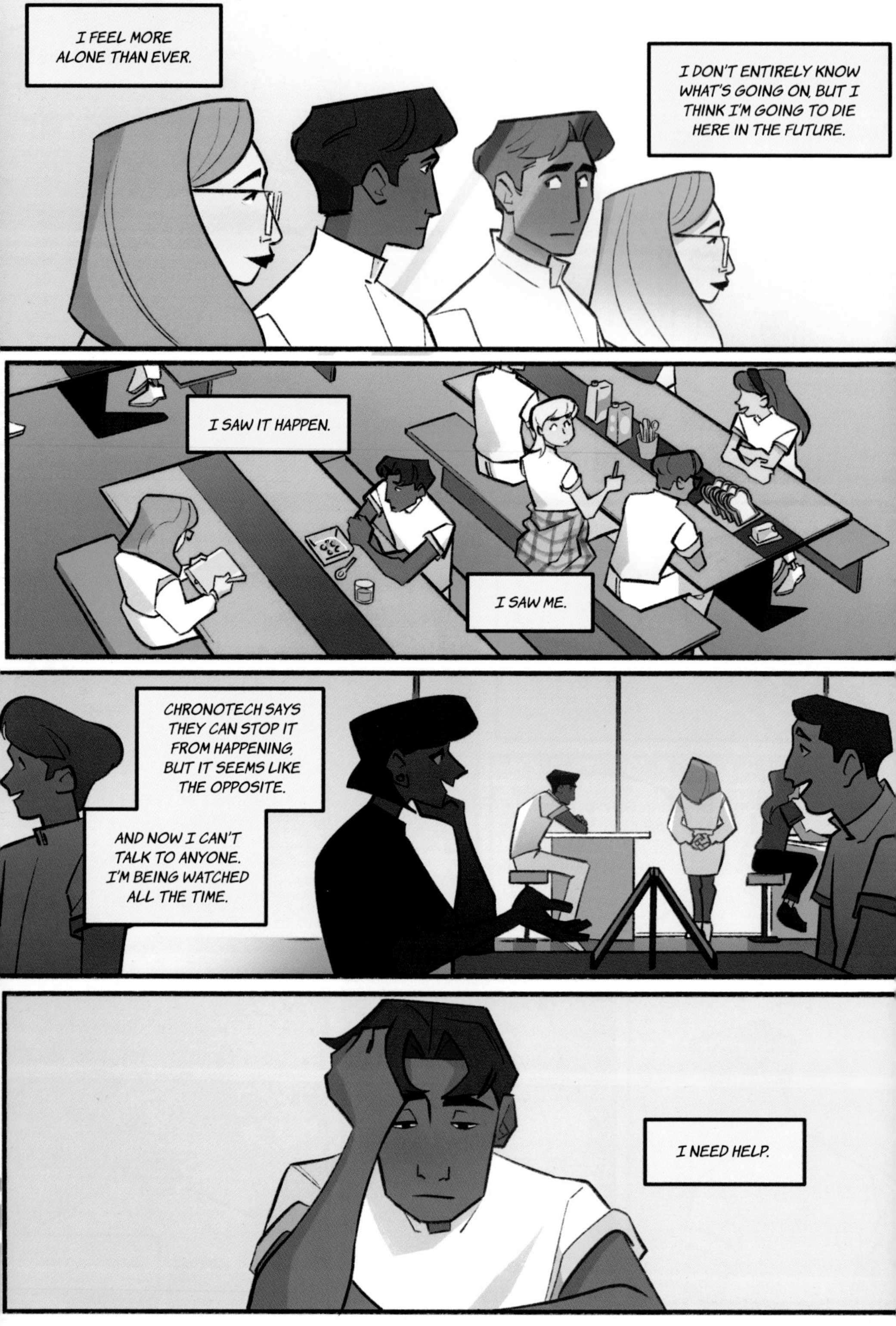
I FEEL MORE ALONE THAN EVER.
I DON'T ENTIRELY KNOW WHAT'S GOING ON, BUT I THINK I'M GOING TO DIE HERE IN THE FUTURE.
I SAW IT HAPPEN.
I SAW ME.
CHRONOTECH SAYS THEY CAN STOP IT FROM HAPPENING, BUT IT SEEMS LIKE THE OPPOSITE.
AND NOW I CAN'T TALK TO ANYONE. I'M BEING WATCHED ALL THE TIME.
I NEED HELP.

PHOEBE!

I THOUGHT I'D FIND A SECOND WHEN YOU WEREN'T WITH YOUR BABYSITTER.

YOU NOTICED, HUH?

EVERYONE HAS. IT'S WEIRD.

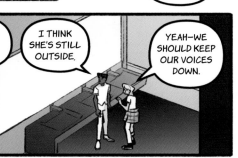

I THINK SHE'S STILL OUTSIDE.

YEAH—WE SHOULD KEEP OUR VOICES DOWN.

DO YOU KNOW WHERE MARS HAS BEEN? HE HASN'T SHOWN UP TO OUR CLASSES.

YOU DON'T KNOW? MARS GOT EXPELLED. JIA'S ALSO BEEN BANNED FROM THE GROUNDS.

WHY?

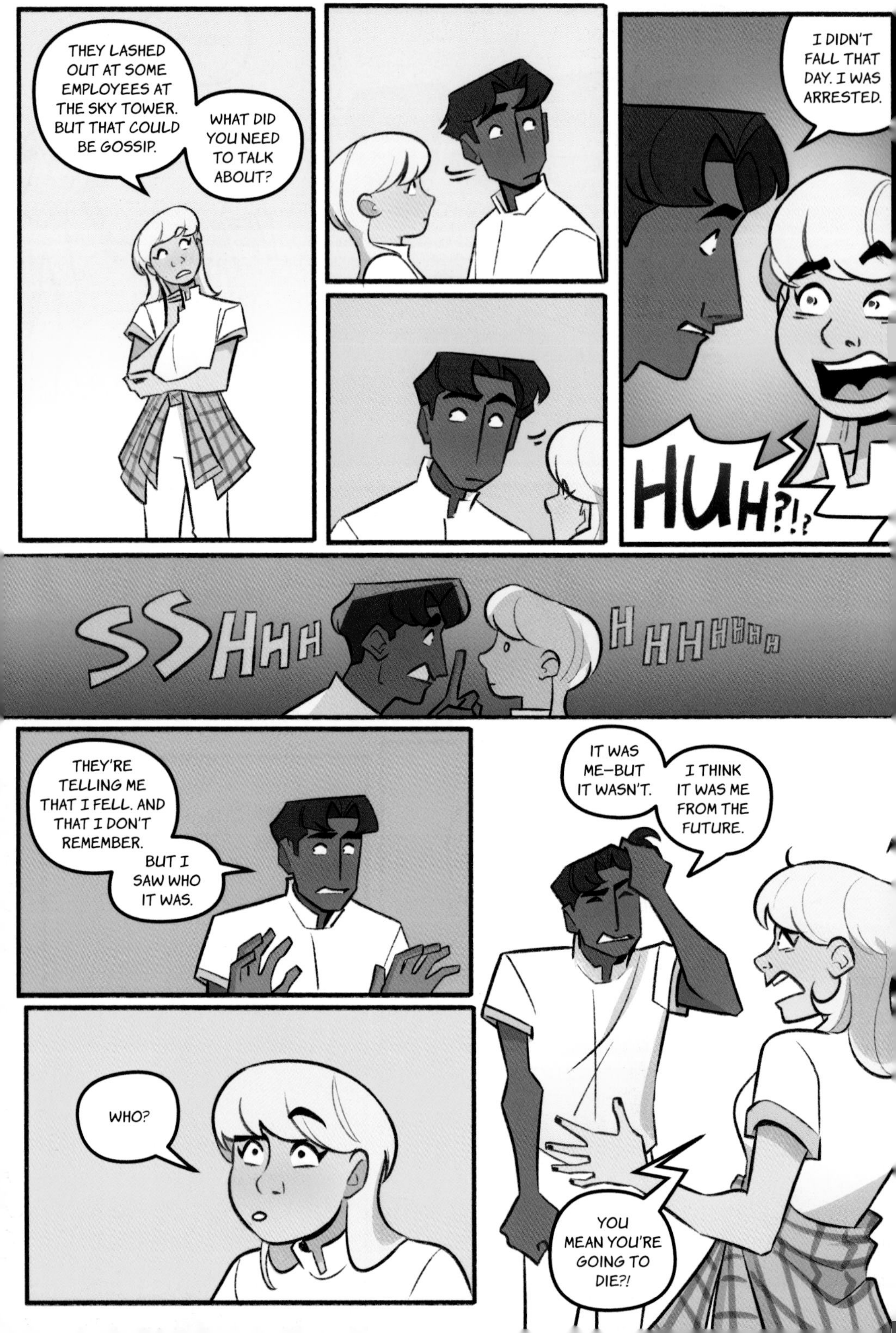
THEY LASHED OUT AT SOME EMPLOYEES AT THE SKY TOWER. BUT THAT COULD BE GOSSIP.
WHAT DID YOU NEED TO TALK ABOUT?
I DIDN'T FALL THAT DAY. I WAS ARRESTED.
HUH?!?
SSHHHH HHHHHHHH
THEY'RE TELLING ME THAT I FELL. AND THAT I DON'T REMEMBER.
BUT I SAW WHO IT WAS.
WHO?
IT WAS ME—BUT IT WASN'T.
I THINK IT WAS ME FROM THE FUTURE.
YOU MEAN YOU'RE GOING TO DIE?!

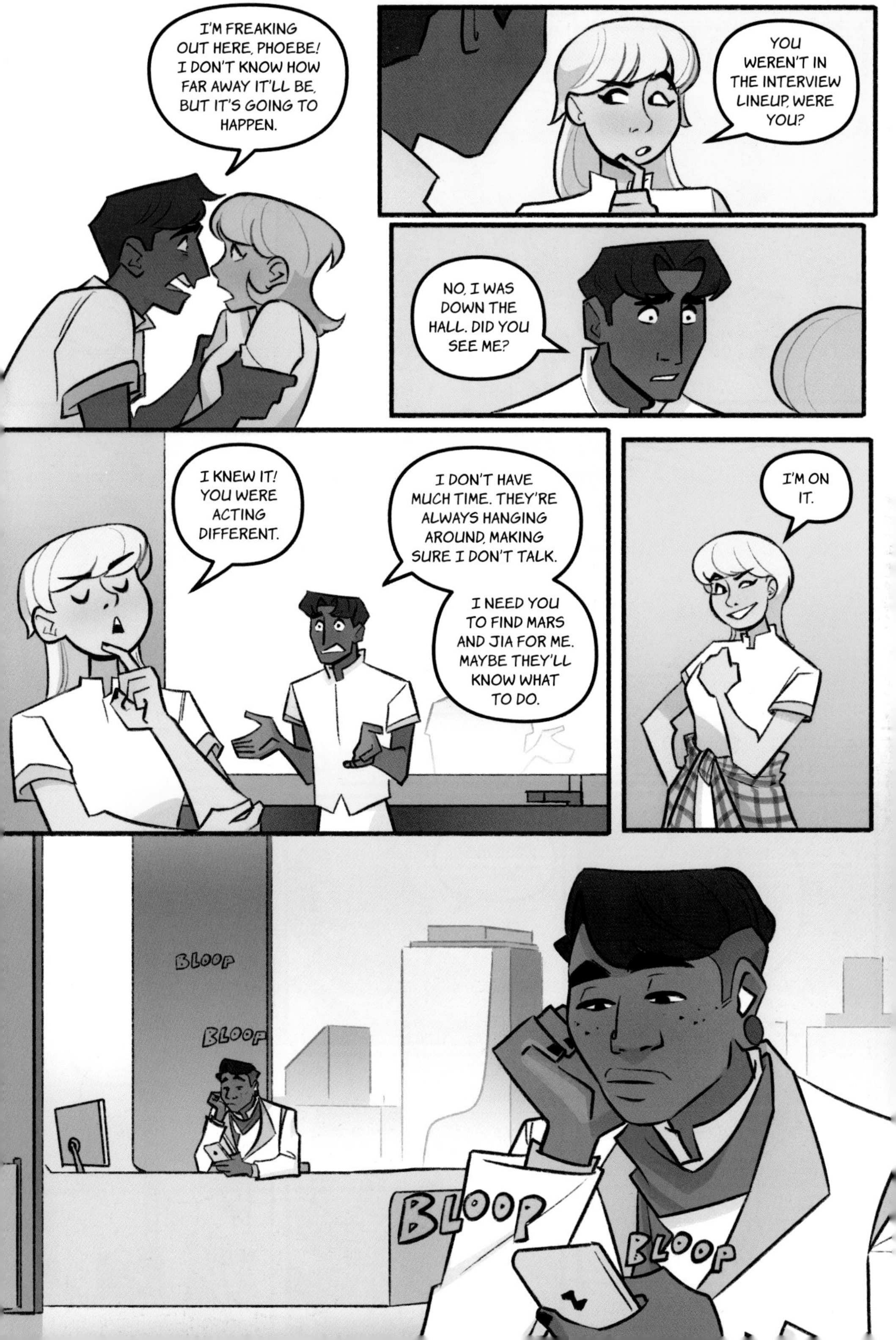

I'M FREAKING OUT HERE, PHOEBE! I DON'T KNOW HOW FAR AWAY IT'LL BE, BUT IT'S GOING TO HAPPEN.
YOU WEREN'T IN THE INTERVIEW LINEUP, WERE YOU?
NO, I WAS DOWN THE HALL. DID YOU SEE ME?
I KNEW IT! YOU WERE ACTING DIFFERENT.
I DON'T HAVE MUCH TIME. THEY'RE ALWAYS HANGING AROUND, MAKING SURE I DON'T TALK.
I NEED YOU TO FIND MARS AND JIA FOR ME. MAYBE THEY'LL KNOW WHAT TO DO.
I'M ON IT.
BLOOP
BLOOP
BLOOP
BLOOP

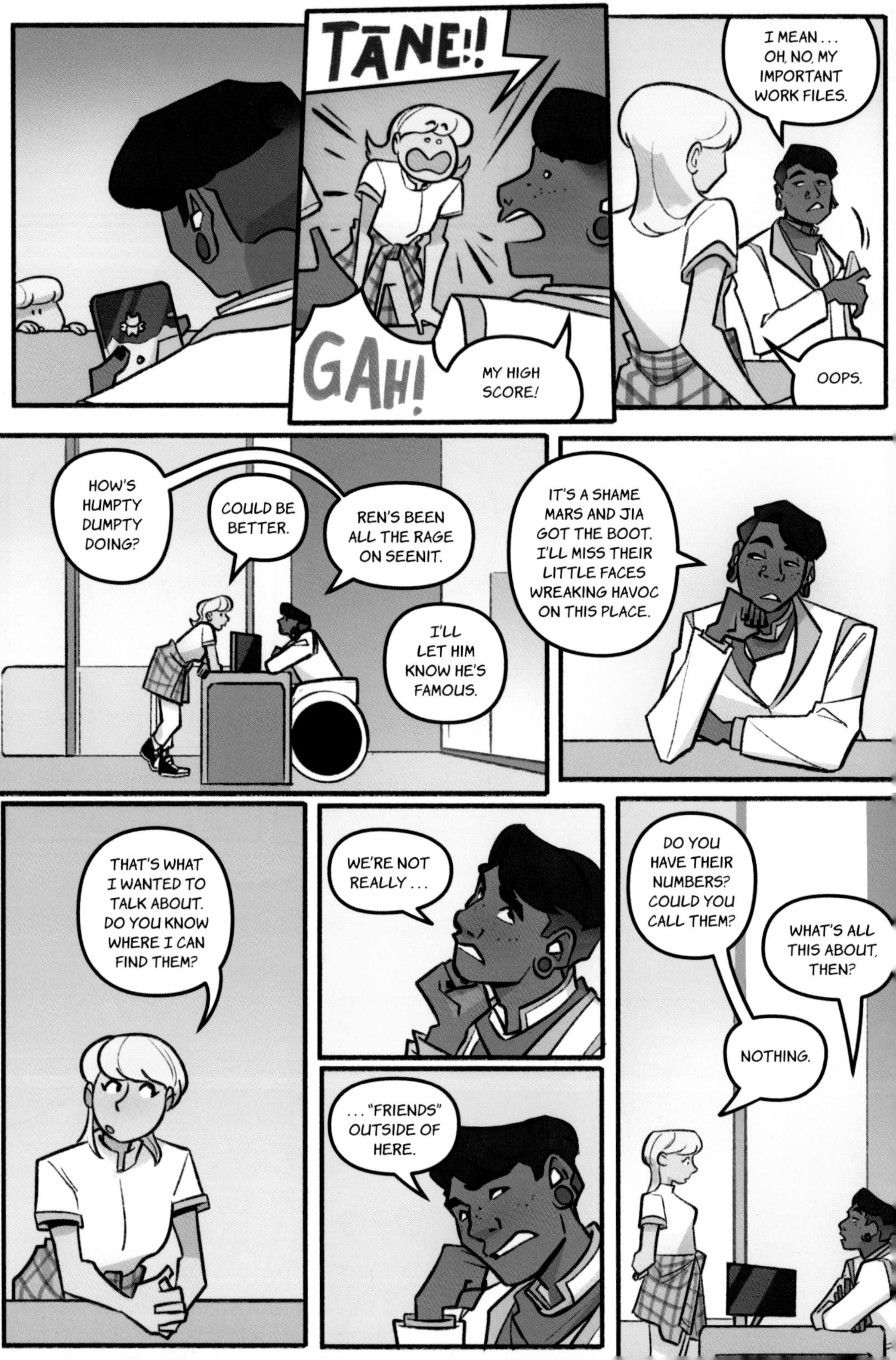
TĀNE!!
GAH!
MY HIGH SCORE!
I MEAN . . . OH, NO, MY IMPORTANT WORK FILES.
OOPS.
HOW'S HUMPTY DUMPTY DOING?
COULD BE BETTER.
REN'S BEEN ALL THE RAGE ON SEENIT.
I'LL LET HIM KNOW HE'S FAMOUS.
IT'S A SHAME MARS AND JIA GOT THE BOOT. I'LL MISS THEIR LITTLE FACES WREAKING HAVOC ON THIS PLACE.
THAT'S WHAT I WANTED TO TALK ABOUT. DO YOU KNOW WHERE I CAN FIND THEM?
WE'RE NOT REALLY . . .
. . . "FRIENDS" OUTSIDE OF HERE.
DO YOU HAVE THEIR NUMBERS? COULD YOU CALL THEM?
WHAT'S ALL THIS ABOUT, THEN?
NOTHING.

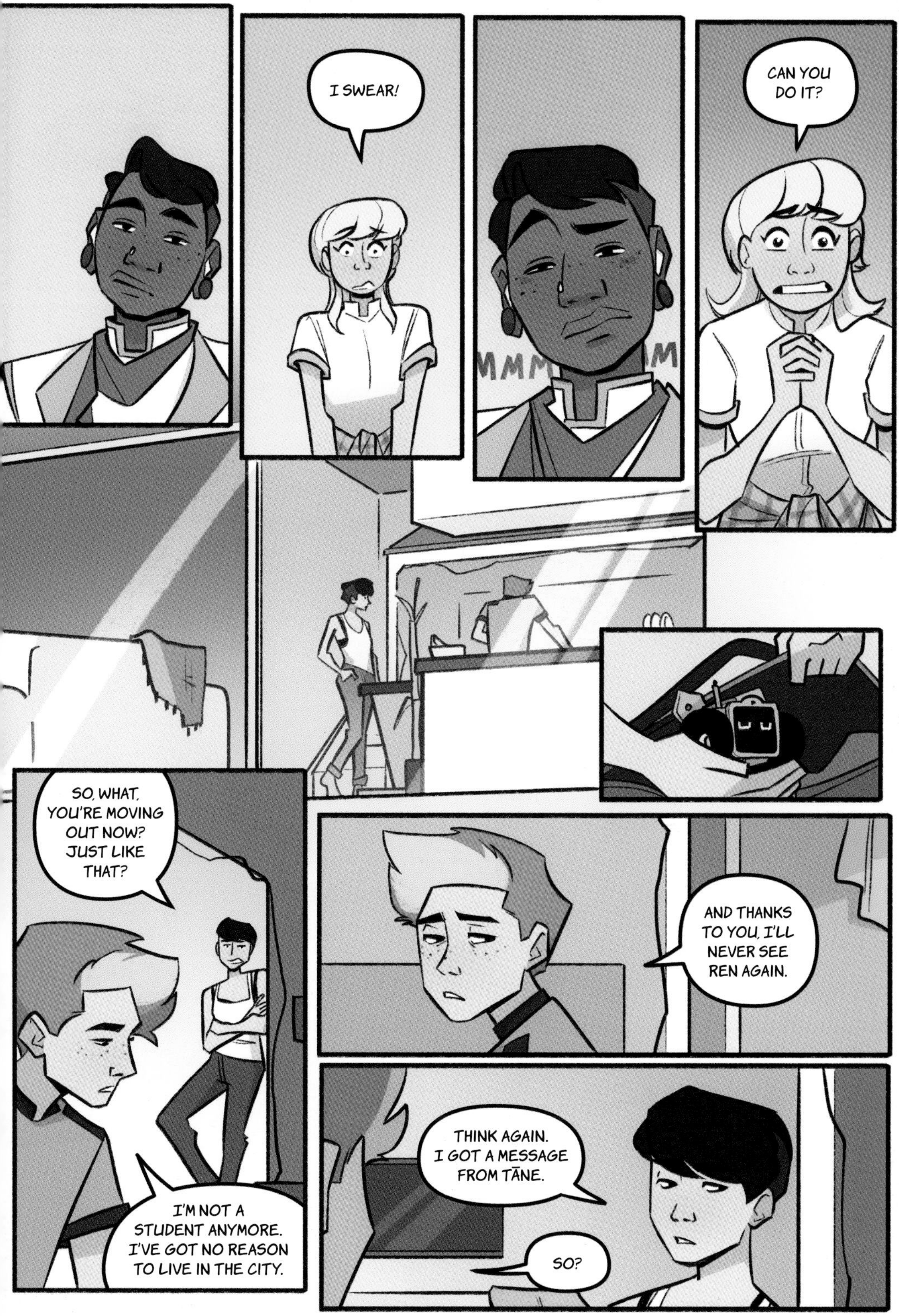
I SWEAR!
MMMMMMM
CAN YOU DO IT?
SO, WHAT, YOU'RE MOVING OUT NOW? JUST LIKE THAT?
I'M NOT A STUDENT ANYMORE. I'VE GOT NO REASON TO LIVE IN THE CITY.
AND THANKS TO YOU, I'LL NEVER SEE REN AGAIN.
THINK AGAIN. I GOT A MESSAGE FROM TĀNE.
SO?

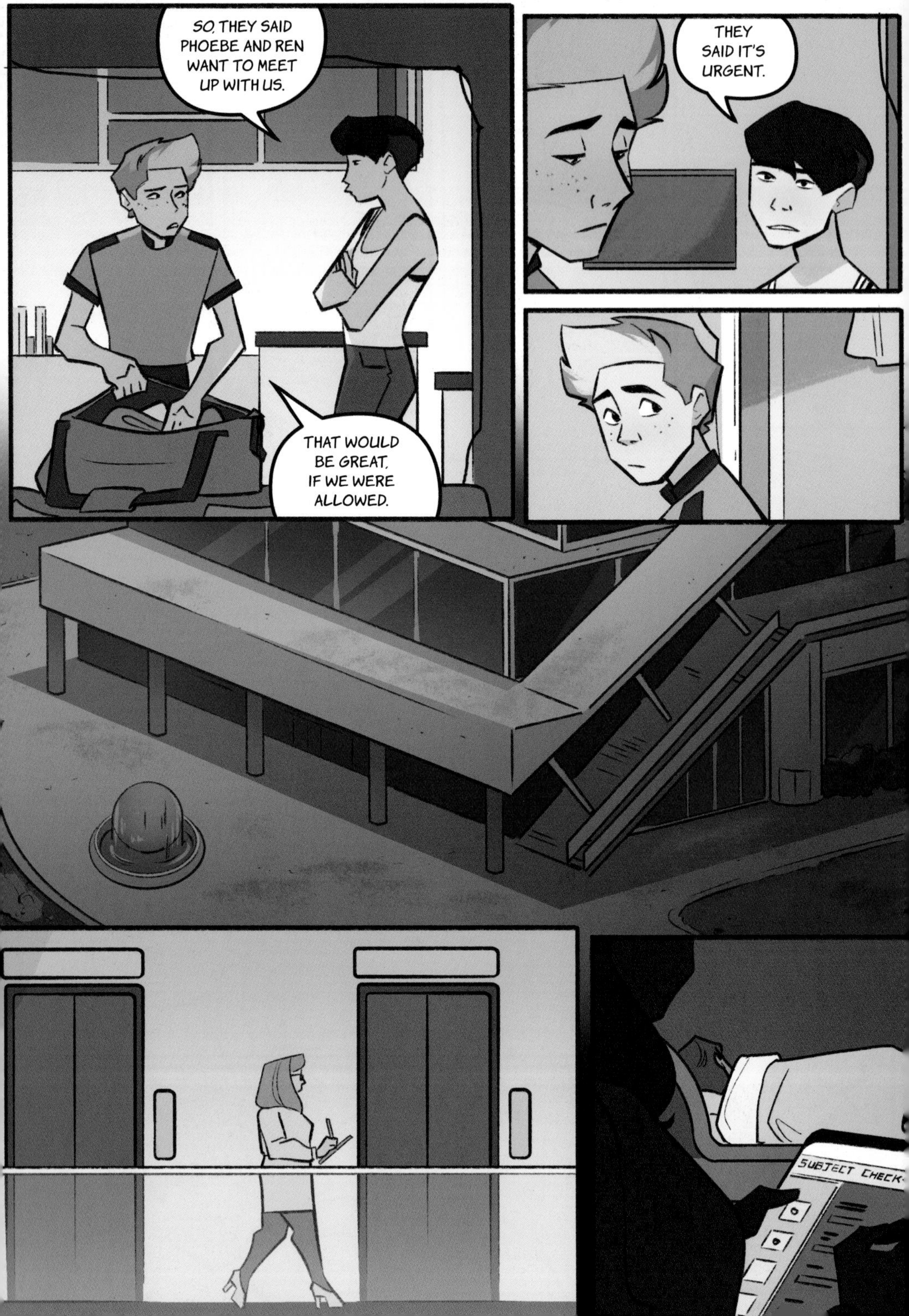
SO, THEY SAID PHOEBE AND REN WANT TO MEET UP WITH US.
THAT WOULD BE GREAT, IF WE WERE ALLOWED.
THEY SAID IT'S URGENT.
SUBJECT CHECK-

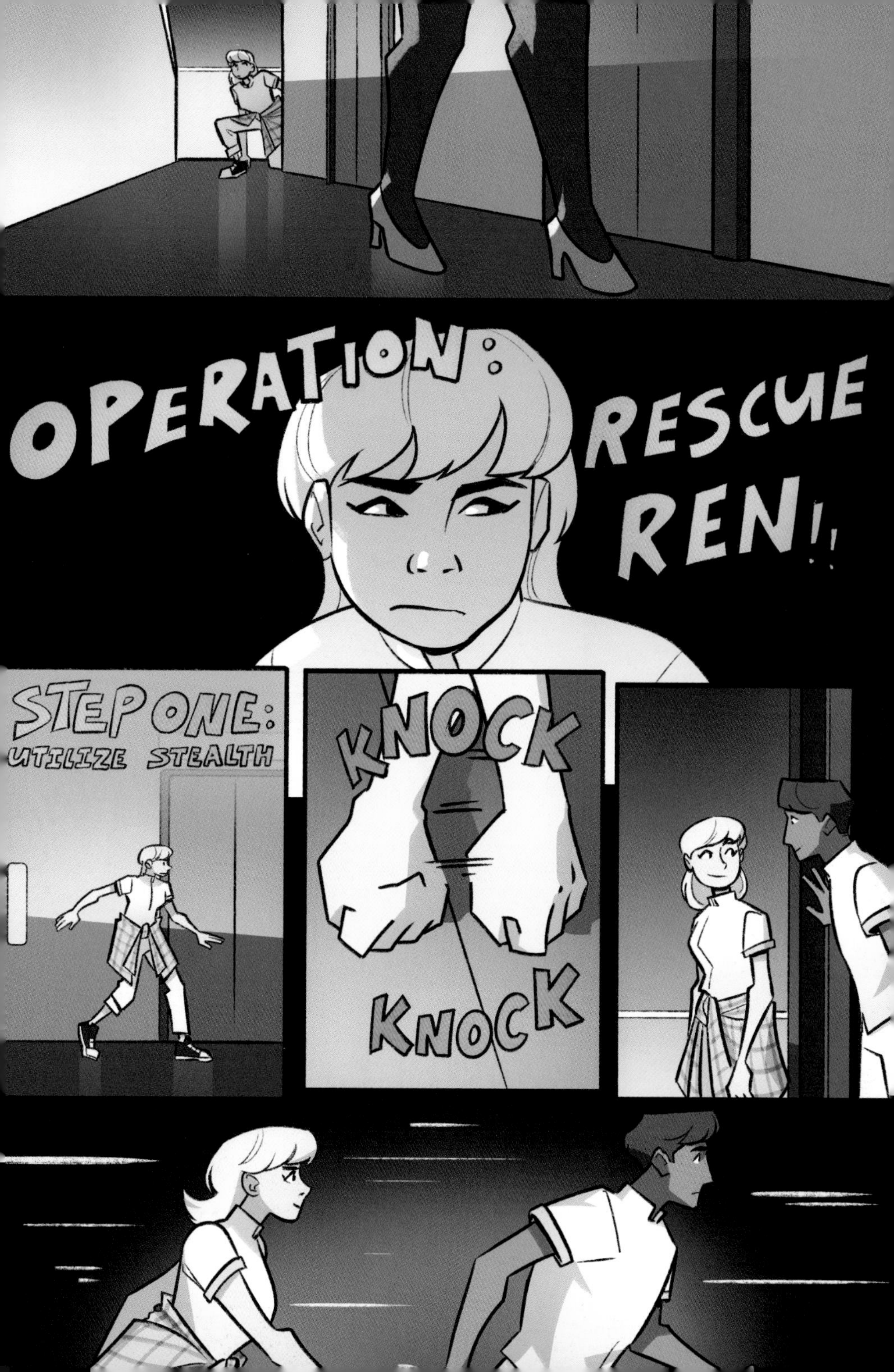
OPERATION: RESCUE REN!!
STEP ONE:
UTILIZE STEALTH
KNOCK
KNOCK

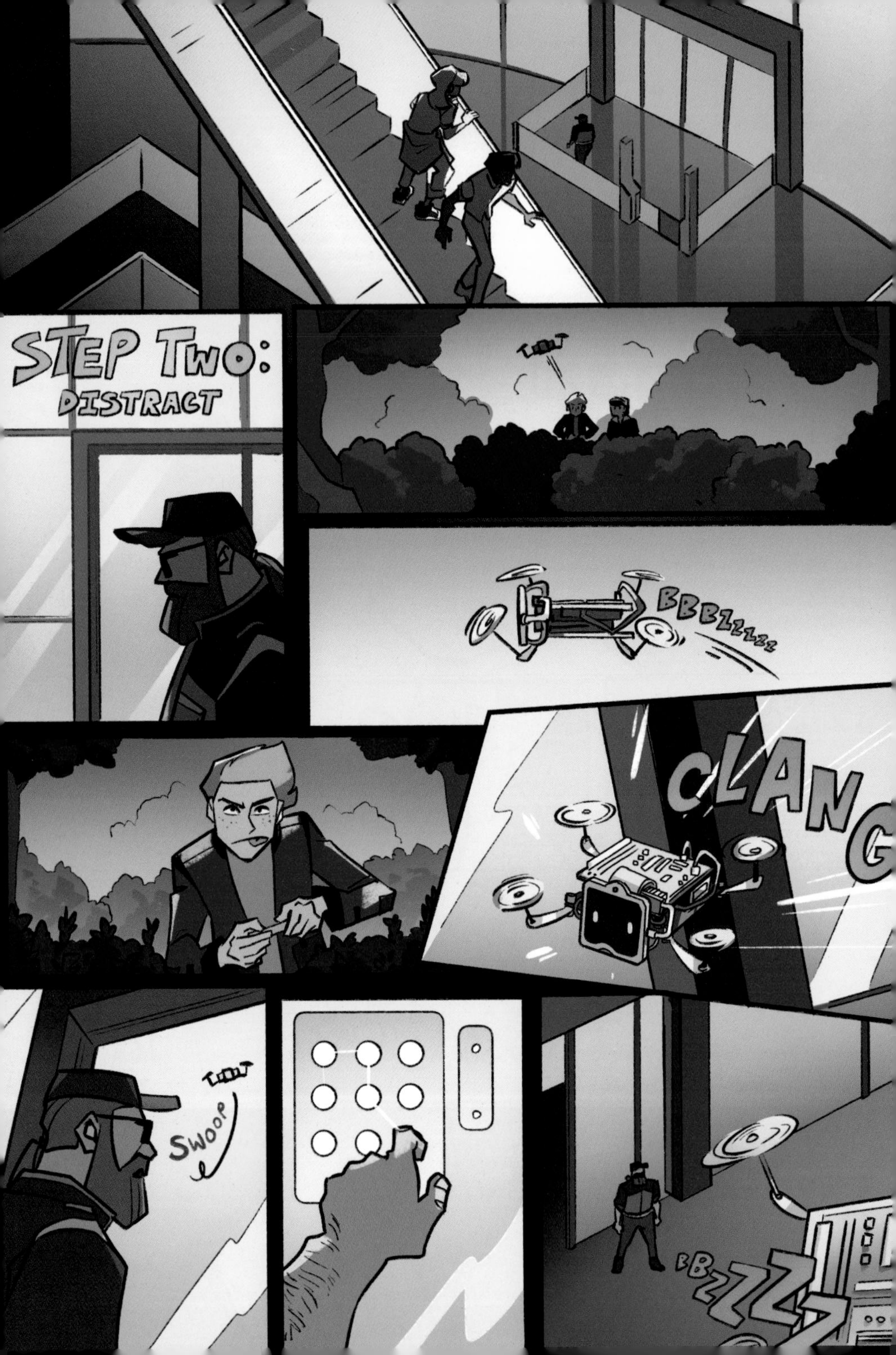
STEP TWO:
DISTRACT
BBBZzzzz
CLANG
SWOOP
BBZZZZ

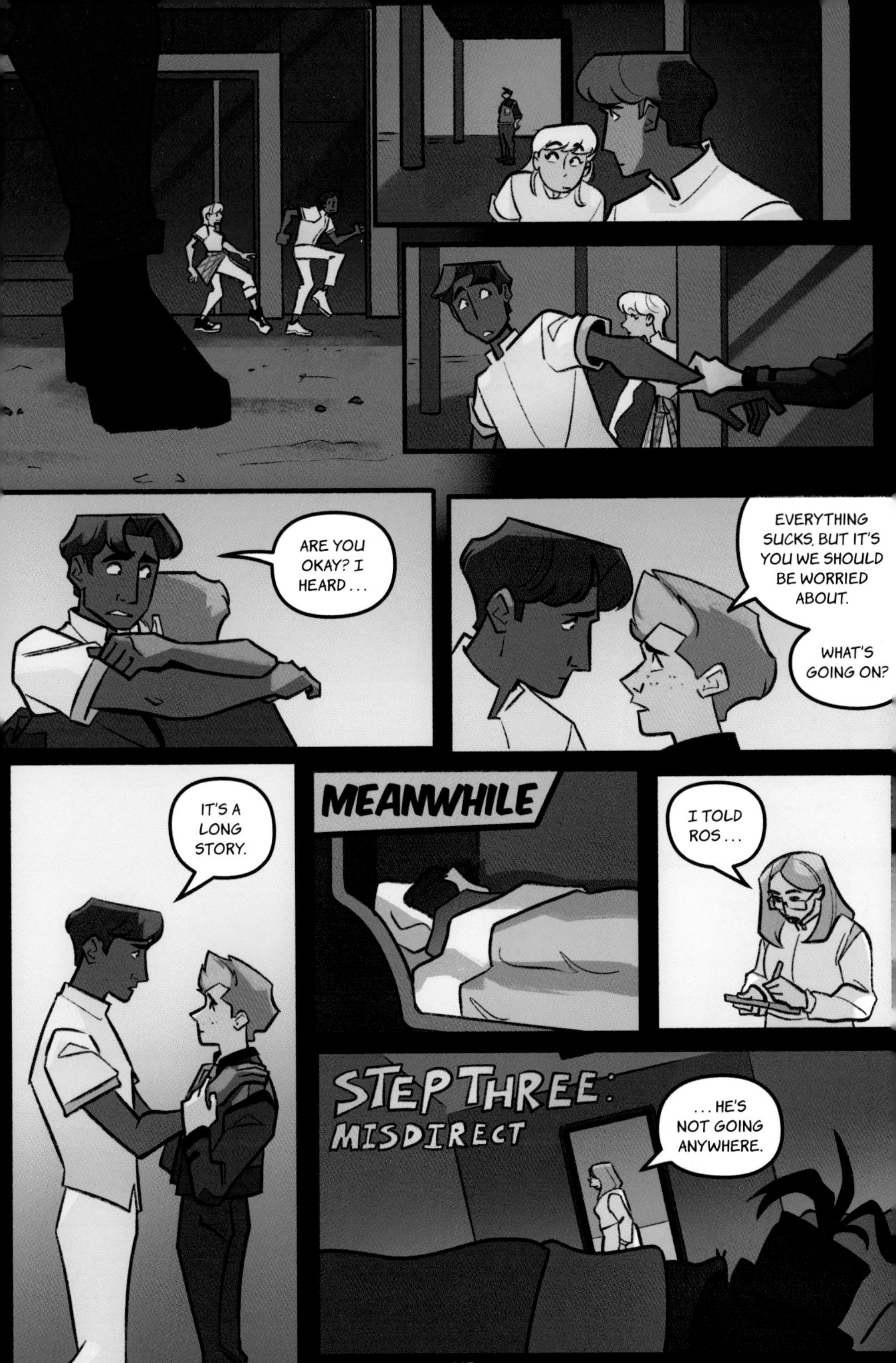
ARE YOU OKAY? I HEARD . . .
EVERYTHING SUCKS, BUT IT'S YOU WE SHOULD BE WORRIED ABOUT.
WHAT'S GOING ON?
IT'S A LONG STORY.
MEANWHILE
I TOLD ROS . . .
STEP THREE: MISDIRECT
. . . HE'S NOT GOING ANYWHERE.

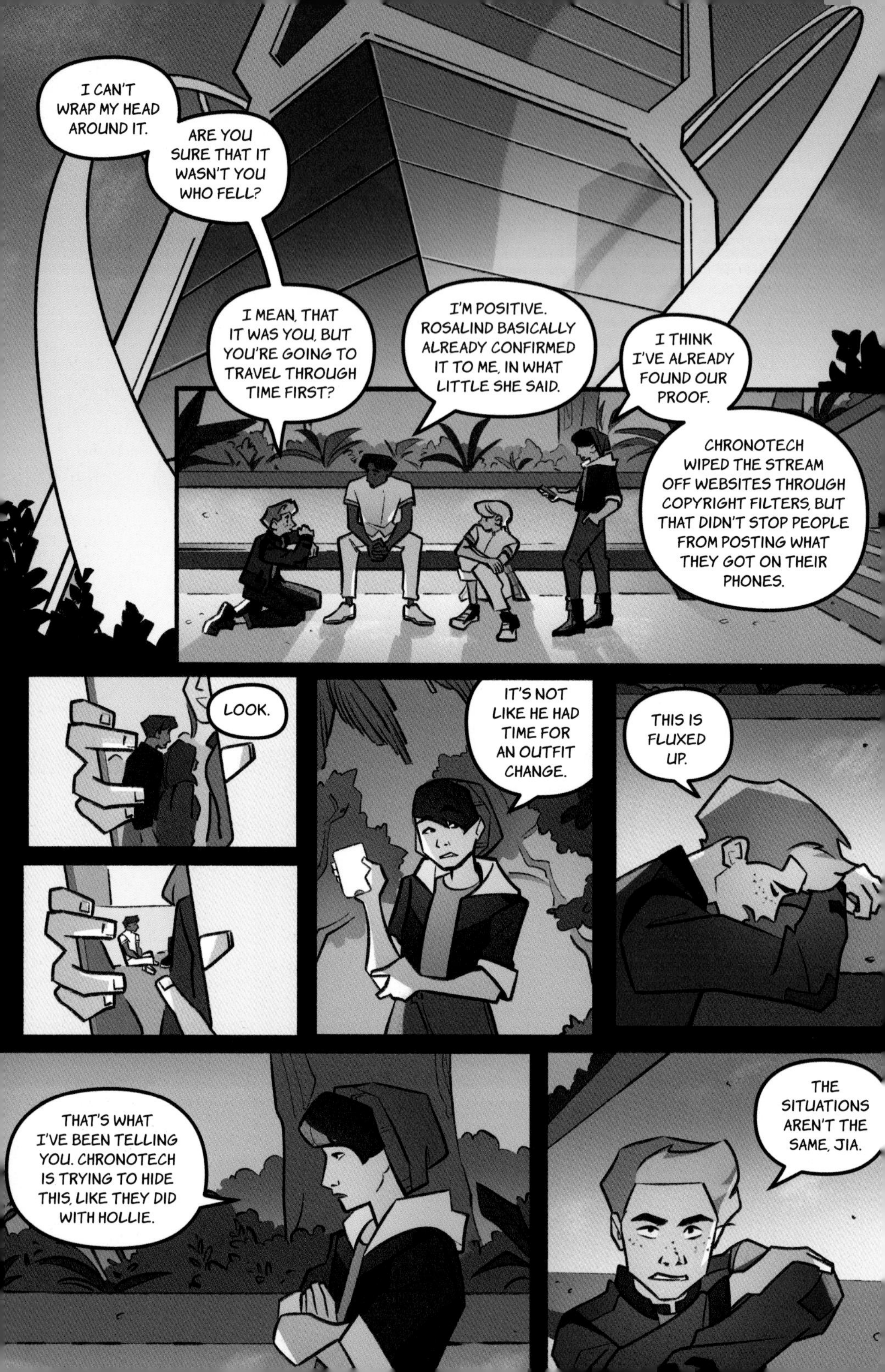
I CAN'T WRAP MY HEAD AROUND IT.
ARE YOU SURE THAT IT WASN'T YOU WHO FELL?
I MEAN, THAT IT WAS YOU, BUT YOU'RE GOING TO TRAVEL THROUGH TIME FIRST?
I'M POSITIVE. ROSALIND BASICALLY ALREADY CONFIRMED IT TO ME, IN WHAT LITTLE SHE SAID.
I THINK I'VE ALREADY FOUND OUR PROOF.
CHRONOTECH WIPED THE STREAM OFF WEBSITES THROUGH COPYRIGHT FILTERS, BUT THAT DIDN'T STOP PEOPLE FROM POSTING WHAT THEY GOT ON THEIR PHONES.
LOOK.
IT'S NOT LIKE HE HAD TIME FOR AN OUTFIT CHANGE.
THIS IS FLUXED UP.
THAT'S WHAT I'VE BEEN TELLING YOU. CHRONOTECH IS TRYING TO HIDE THIS, LIKE THEY DID WITH HOLLIE.
THE SITUATIONS AREN'T THE SAME, JIA.

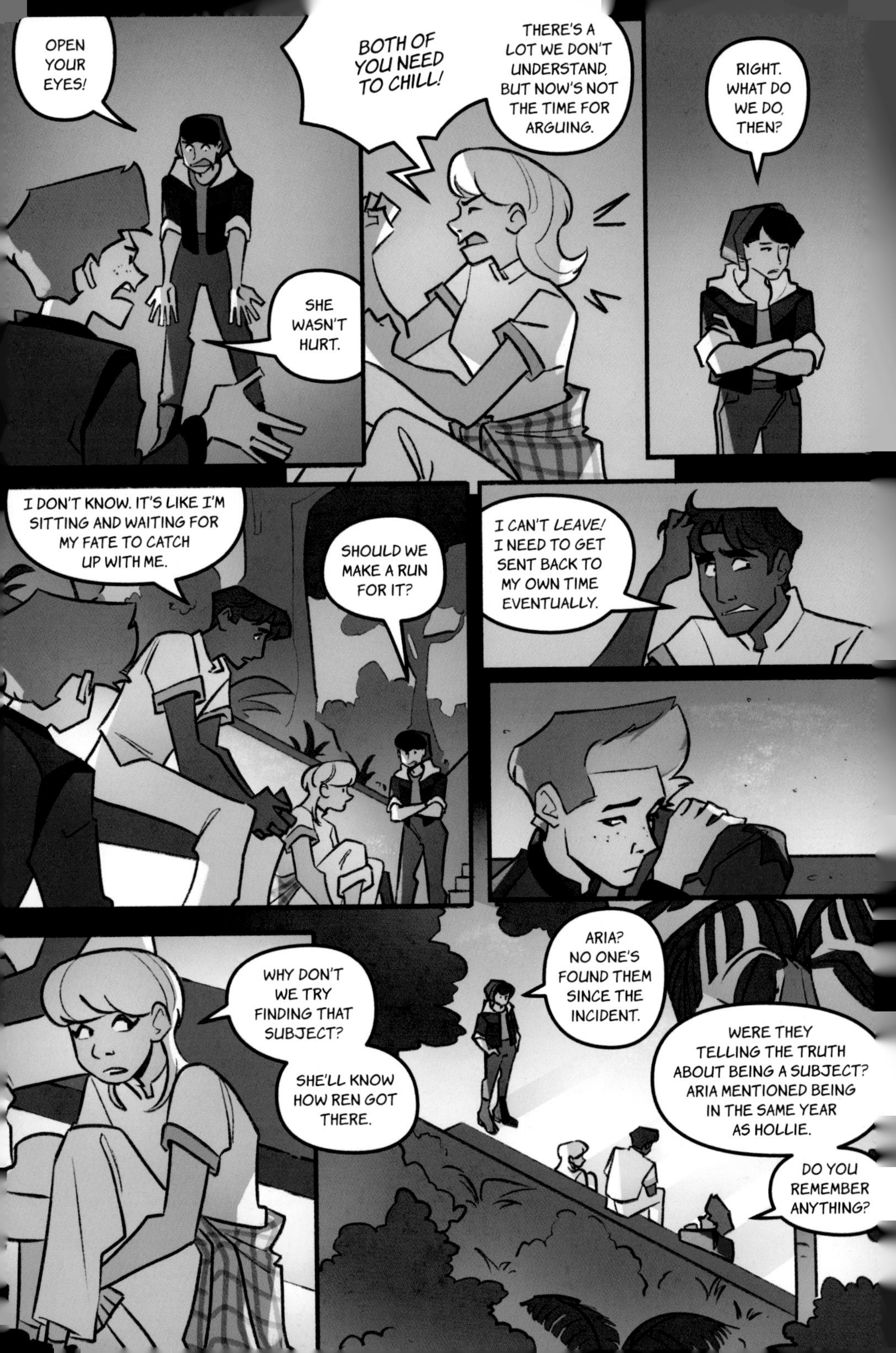
OPEN YOUR EYES!
SHE WASN'T HURT.
BOTH OF YOU NEED TO CHILL!
THERE'S A LOT WE DON'T UNDERSTAND, BUT NOW'S NOT THE TIME FOR ARGUING.
RIGHT. WHAT DO WE DO, THEN?
I DON'T KNOW. IT'S LIKE I'M SITTING AND WAITING FOR MY FATE TO CATCH UP WITH ME.
SHOULD WE MAKE A RUN FOR IT?
I CAN'T LEAVE! I NEED TO GET SENT BACK TO MY OWN TIME EVENTUALLY.
WHY DON'T WE TRY FINDING THAT SUBJECT?
SHE'LL KNOW HOW REN GOT THERE.
ARIA? NO ONE'S FOUND THEM SINCE THE INCIDENT.
WERE THEY TELLING THE TRUTH ABOUT BEING A SUBJECT? ARIA MENTIONED BEING IN THE SAME YEAR AS HOLLIE.
DO YOU REMEMBER ANYTHING?

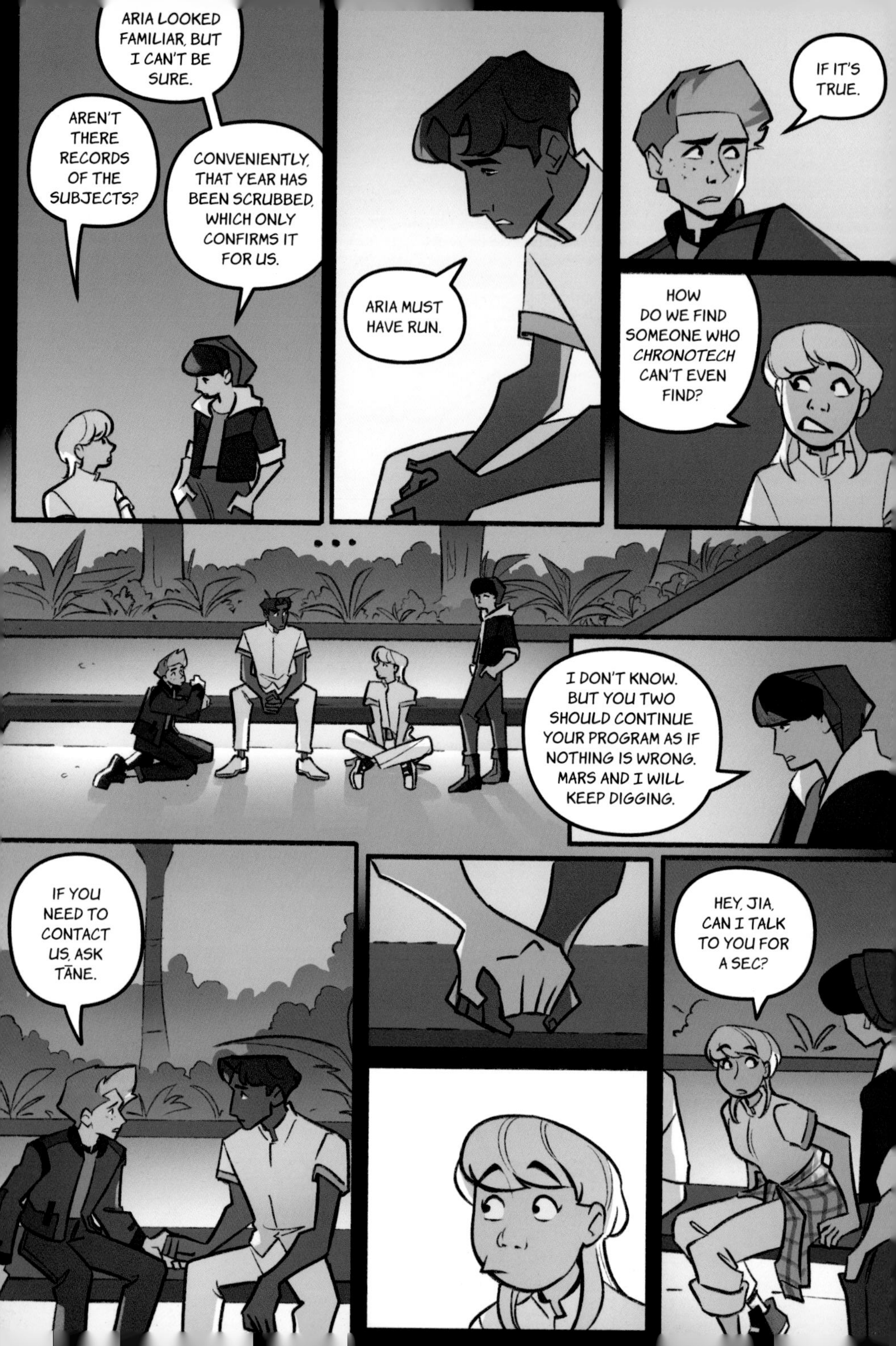
ARIA LOOKED FAMILIAR, BUT I CAN'T BE SURE.
AREN'T THERE RECORDS OF THE SUBJECTS?
CONVENIENTLY, THAT YEAR HAS BEEN SCRUBBED, WHICH ONLY CONFIRMS IT FOR US.
ARIA MUST HAVE RUN.
IF IT'S TRUE.
HOW DO WE FIND SOMEONE WHO CHRONOTECH CAN'T EVEN FIND?
• • •
I DON'T KNOW. BUT YOU TWO SHOULD CONTINUE YOUR PROGRAM AS IF NOTHING IS WRONG. MARS AND I WILL KEEP DIGGING.
IF YOU NEED TO CONTACT US, ASK TĀNE.
HEY, JIA, CAN I TALK TO YOU FOR A SEC?

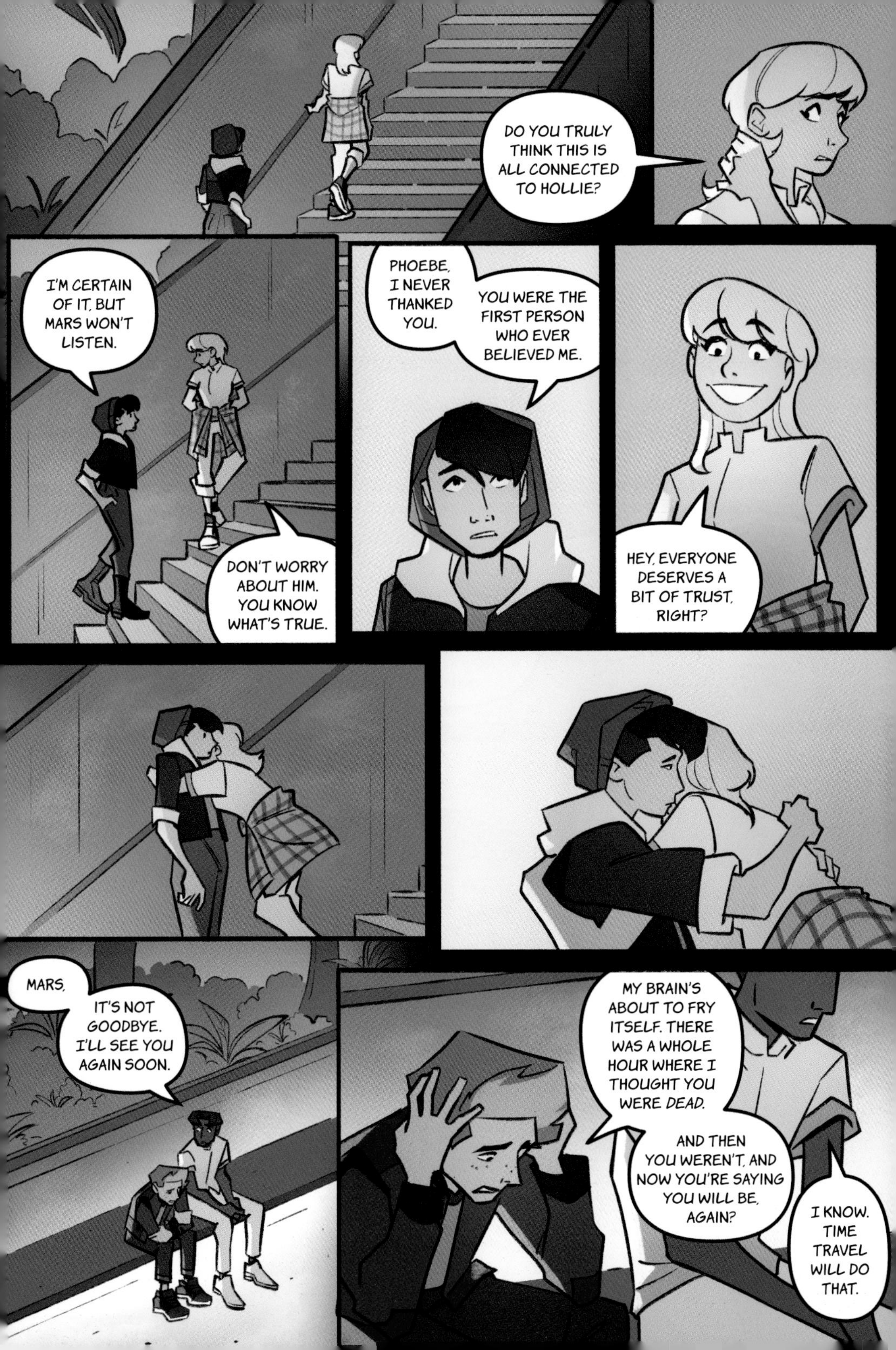
DO YOU TRULY THINK THIS IS ALL CONNECTED TO HOLLIE?
I'M CERTAIN OF IT, BUT MARS WON'T LISTEN.
DON'T WORRY ABOUT HIM. YOU KNOW WHAT'S TRUE.
PHOEBE, I NEVER THANKED YOU.
YOU WERE THE FIRST PERSON WHO EVER BELIEVED ME.
HEY, EVERYONE DESERVES A BIT OF TRUST, RIGHT?
MARS,
IT'S NOT GOODBYE. I'LL SEE YOU AGAIN SOON.
MY BRAIN'S ABOUT TO FRY ITSELF. THERE WAS A WHOLE HOUR WHERE I THOUGHT YOU WERE *DEAD*.
AND THEN YOU WEREN'T, AND NOW YOU'RE SAYING YOU WILL BE, AGAIN?
I KNOW. TIME TRAVEL WILL DO THAT.

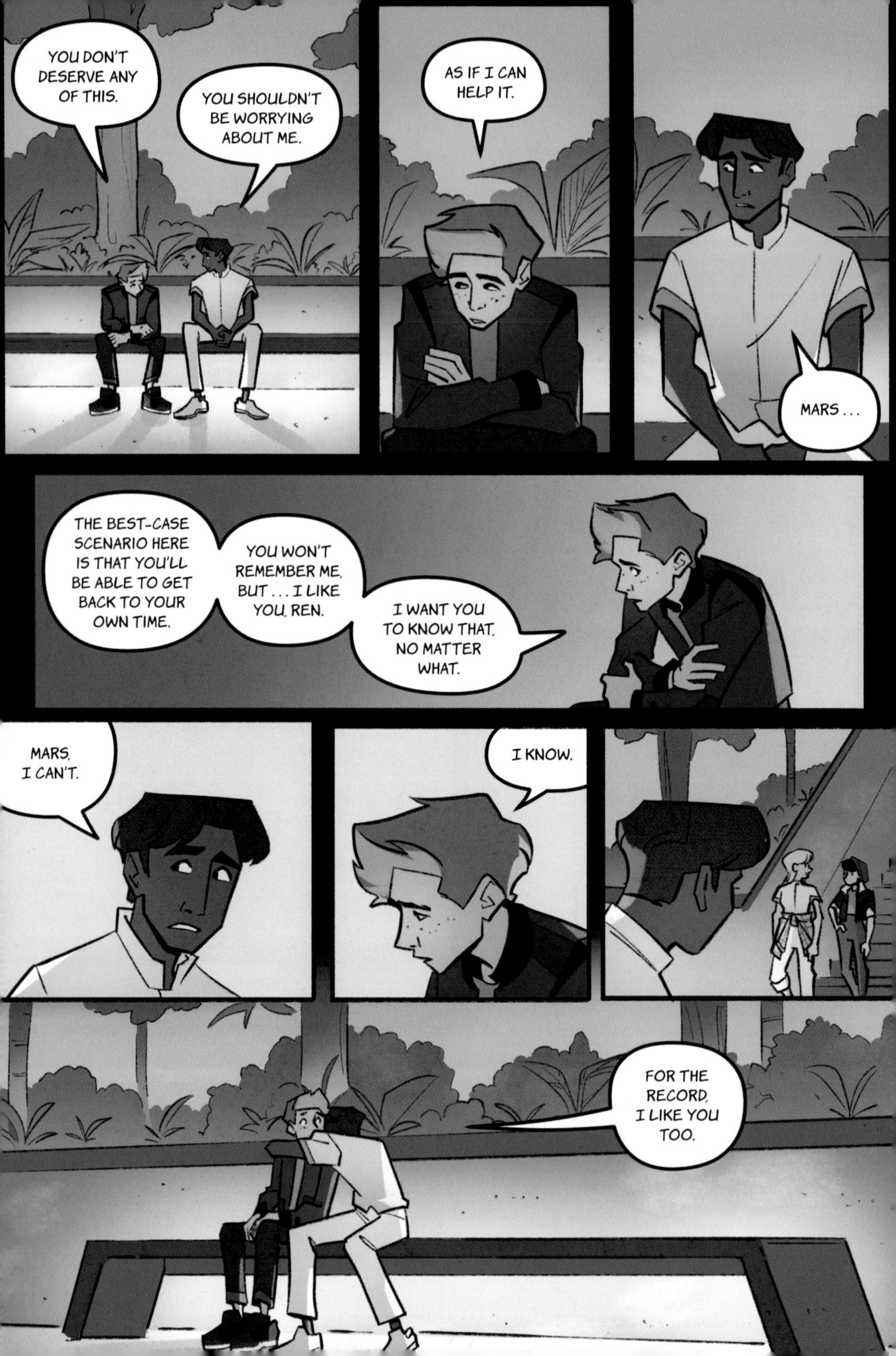
YOU DON'T DESERVE ANY OF THIS.
YOU SHOULDN'T BE WORRYING ABOUT ME.
AS IF I CAN HELP IT.
MARS . . .
THE BEST-CASE SCENARIO HERE IS THAT YOU'LL BE ABLE TO GET BACK TO YOUR OWN TIME.
YOU WON'T REMEMBER ME, BUT . . . I LIKE YOU, REN.
I WANT YOU TO KNOW THAT, NO MATTER WHAT.
MARS, I CAN'T.
I KNOW.
FOR THE RECORD, I LIKE YOU TOO.

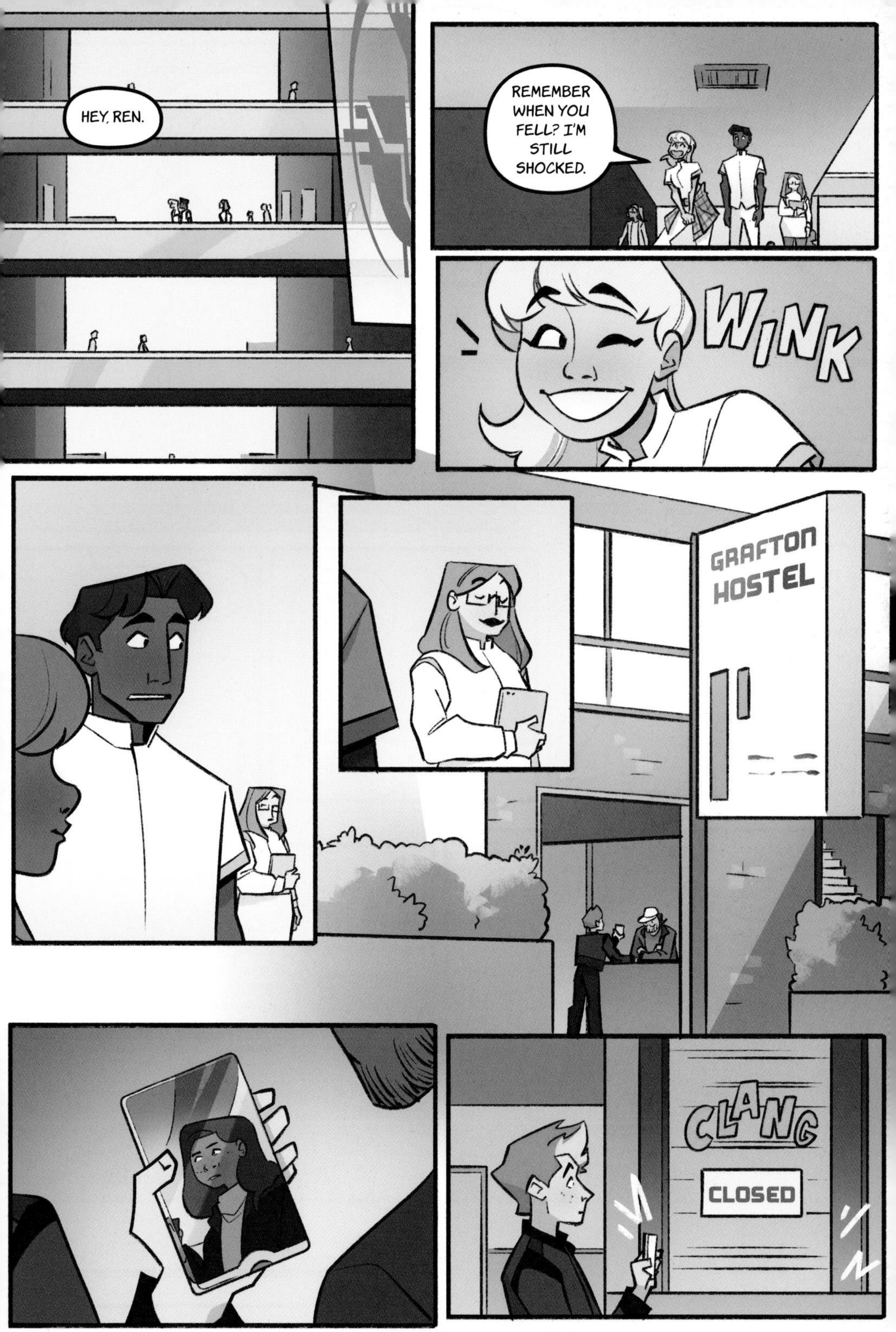
HEY, REN.
REMEMBER WHEN YOU FELL? I'M STILL SHOCKED.
WINK
GRAFTON HOSTEL
CLANG
CLOSED

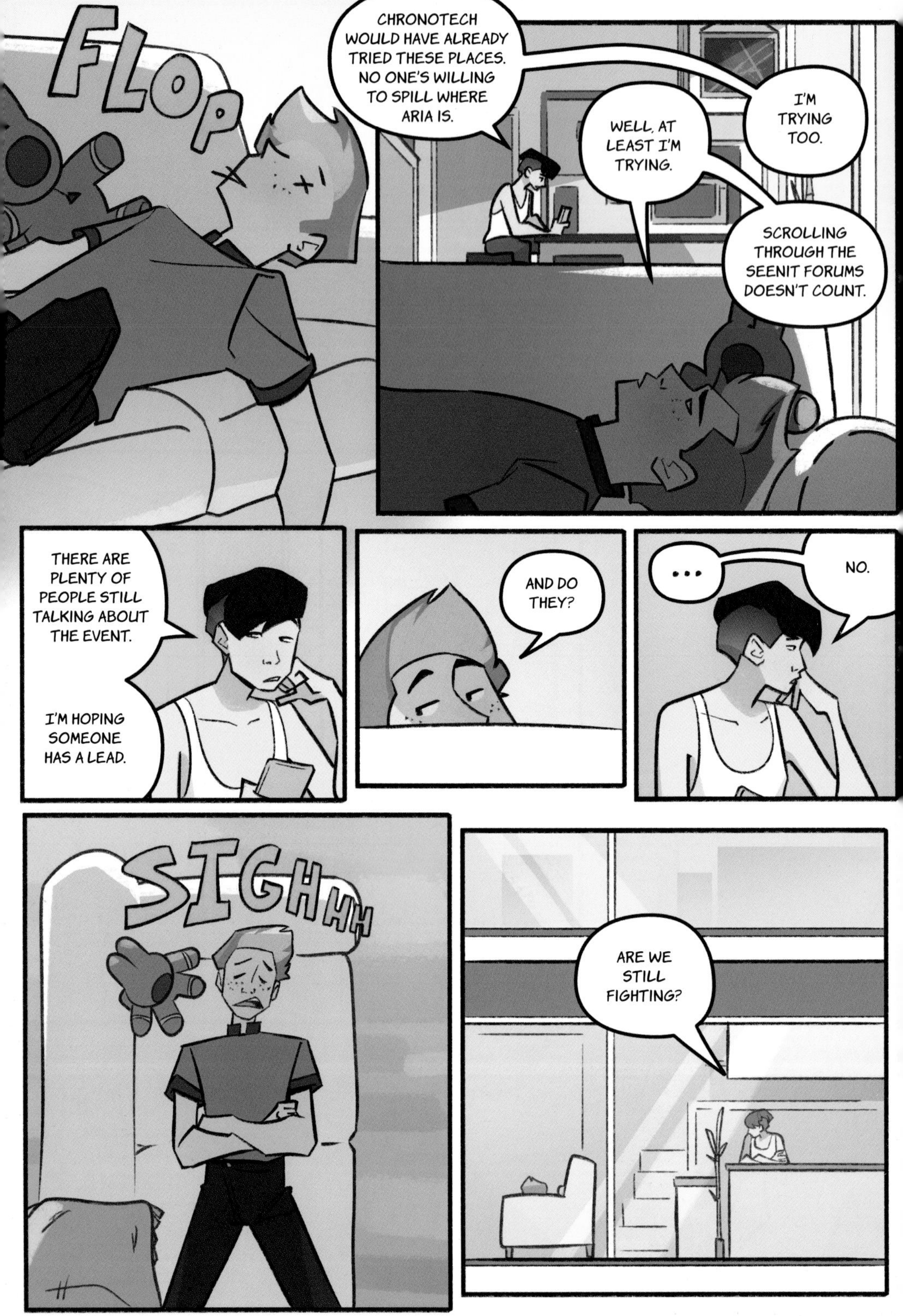
FLOP
CHRONOTECH WOULD HAVE ALREADY TRIED THESE PLACES. NO ONE'S WILLING TO SPILL WHERE ARIA IS.
WELL, AT LEAST I'M TRYING.
I'M TRYING TOO.
SCROLLING THROUGH THE SEENIT FORUMS DOESN'T COUNT.
THERE ARE PLENTY OF PEOPLE STILL TALKING ABOUT THE EVENT.
I'M HOPING SOMEONE HAS A LEAD.
AND DO THEY?
...
NO.
SIGHHH
ARE WE STILL FIGHTING?

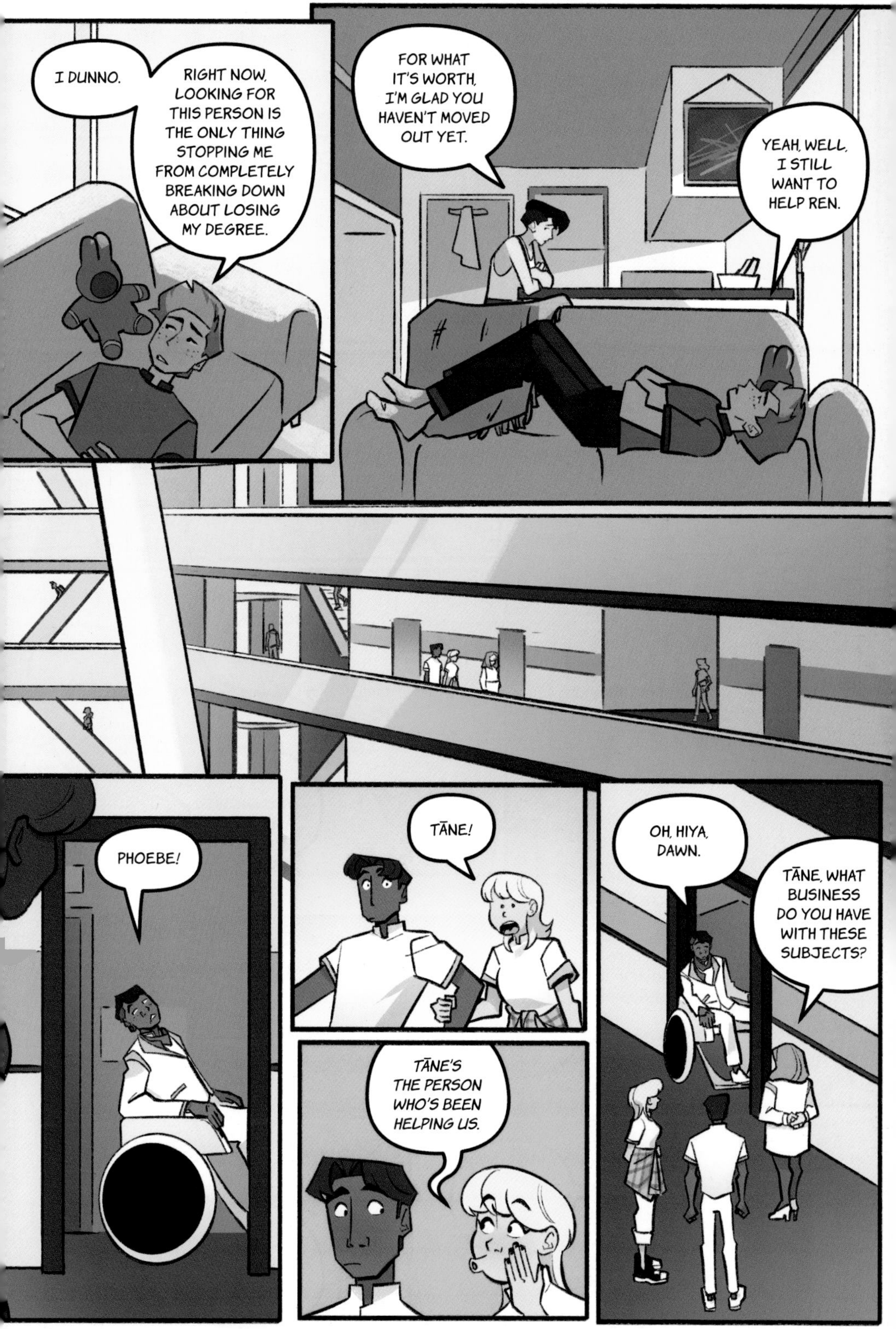
I DUNNO.
RIGHT NOW, LOOKING FOR THIS PERSON IS THE ONLY THING STOPPING ME FROM COMPLETELY BREAKING DOWN ABOUT LOSING MY DEGREE.
FOR WHAT IT'S WORTH, I'M GLAD YOU HAVEN'T MOVED OUT YET.
YEAH, WELL, I STILL WANT TO HELP REN.
PHOEBE!
TĀNE!
TĀNE'S THE PERSON WHO'S BEEN HELPING US.
OH, HIYA, DAWN.
TĀNE, WHAT BUSINESS DO YOU HAVE WITH THESE SUBJECTS?

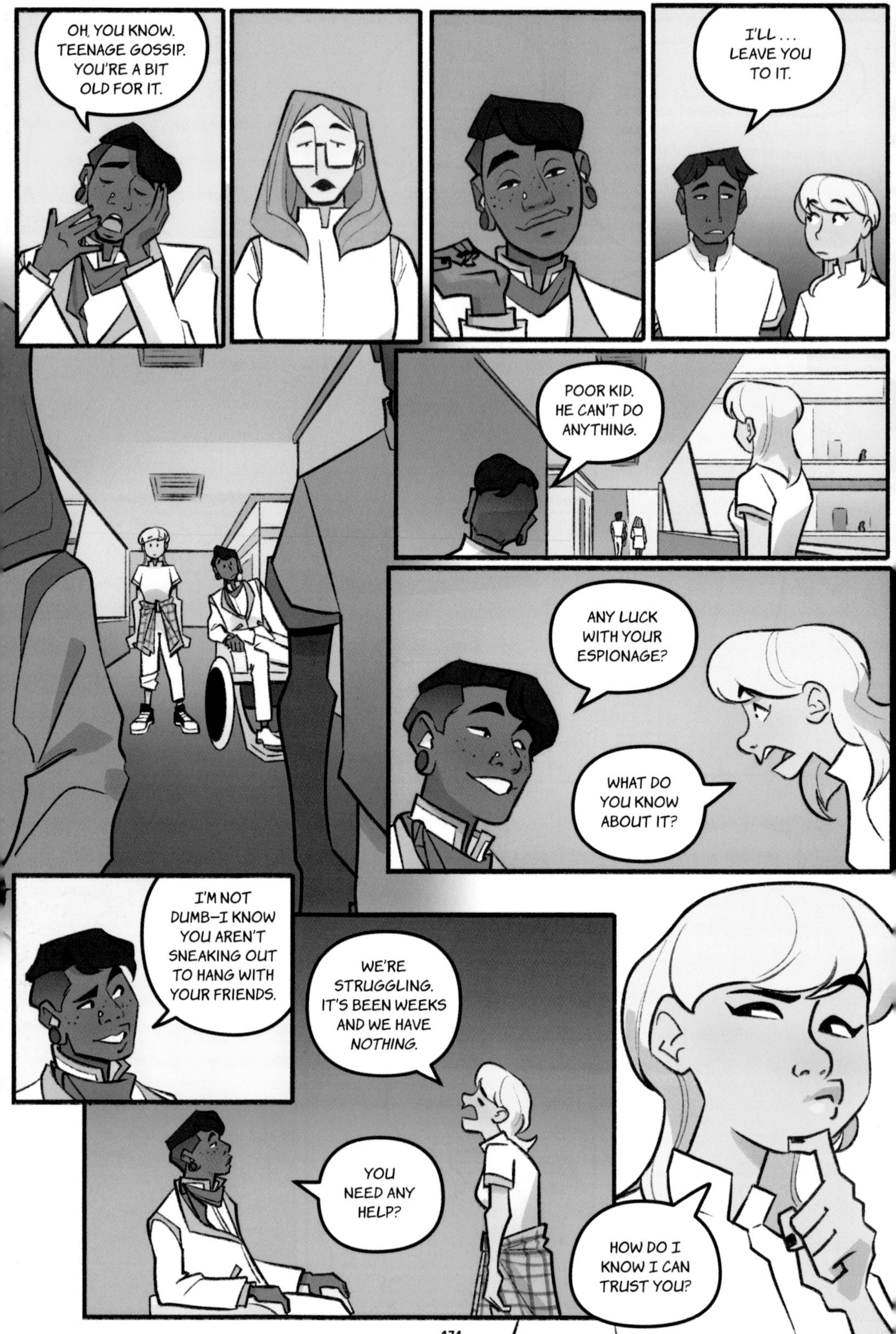
OH, YOU KNOW. TEENAGE GOSSIP. YOU'RE A BIT OLD FOR IT.
I'LL . . . LEAVE YOU TO IT.
POOR KID. HE CAN'T DO ANYTHING.
ANY LUCK WITH YOUR ESPIONAGE?
WHAT DO YOU KNOW ABOUT IT?
I'M NOT DUMB—I KNOW YOU AREN'T SNEAKING OUT TO HANG WITH YOUR FRIENDS.
WE'RE STRUGGLING. IT'S BEEN WEEKS AND WE HAVE NOTHING.
YOU NEED ANY HELP?
HOW DO I KNOW I CAN TRUST YOU?

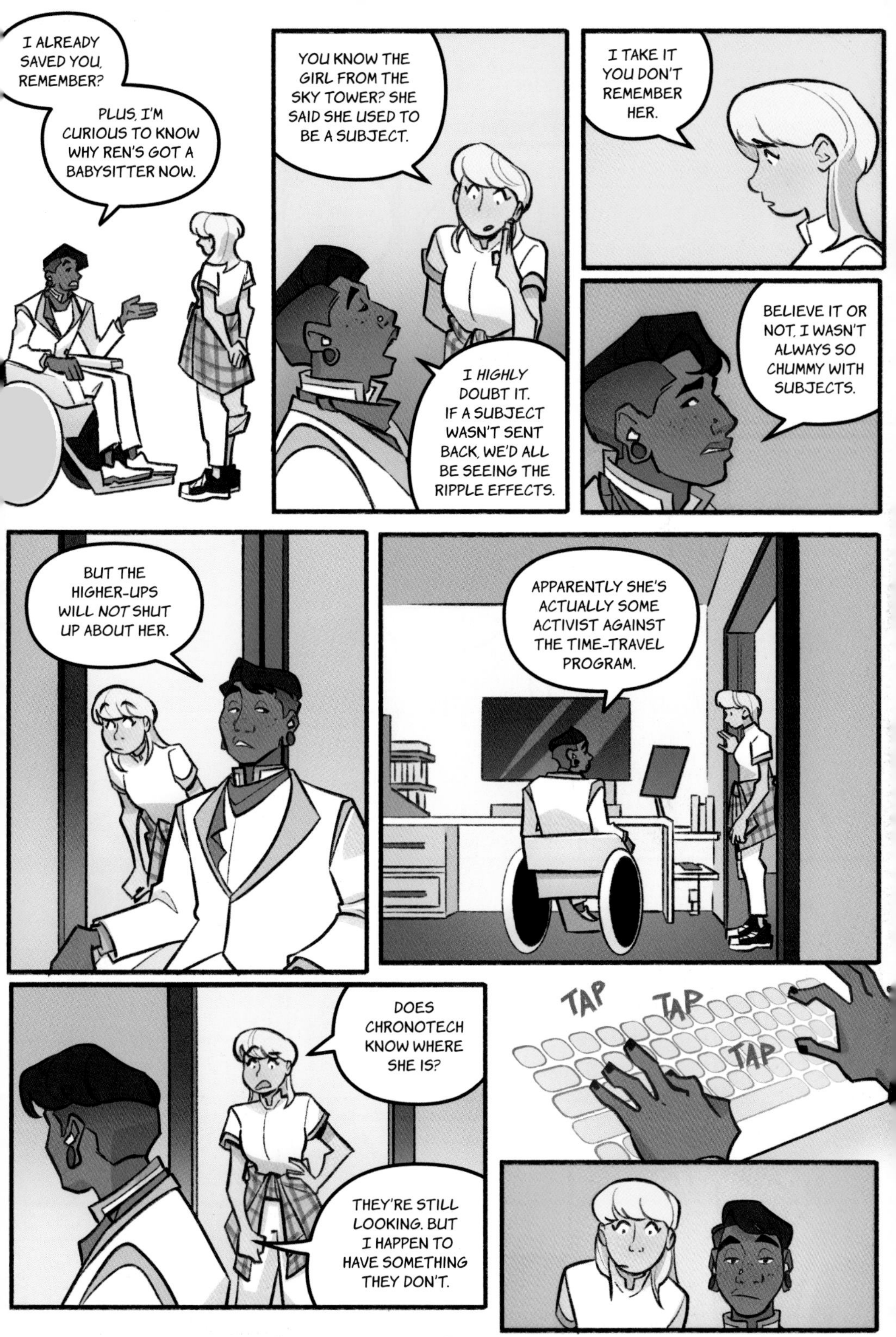

I ALREADY SAVED YOU, REMEMBER?
PLUS, I'M CURIOUS TO KNOW WHY REN'S GOT A BABYSITTER NOW.
YOU KNOW THE GIRL FROM THE SKY TOWER? SHE SAID SHE USED TO BE A SUBJECT.
I HIGHLY DOUBT IT. IF A SUBJECT WASN'T SENT BACK, WE'D ALL BE SEEING THE RIPPLE EFFECTS.
I TAKE IT YOU DON'T REMEMBER HER.
BELIEVE IT OR NOT, I WASN'T ALWAYS SO CHUMMY WITH SUBJECTS.
BUT THE HIGHER-UPS WILL NOT SHUT UP ABOUT HER.
APPARENTLY SHE'S ACTUALLY SOME ACTIVIST AGAINST THE TIME-TRAVEL PROGRAM.
DOES CHRONOTECH KNOW WHERE SHE IS?
THEY'RE STILL LOOKING. BUT I HAPPEN TO HAVE SOMETHING THEY DON'T.
TAP
TAP
TAP

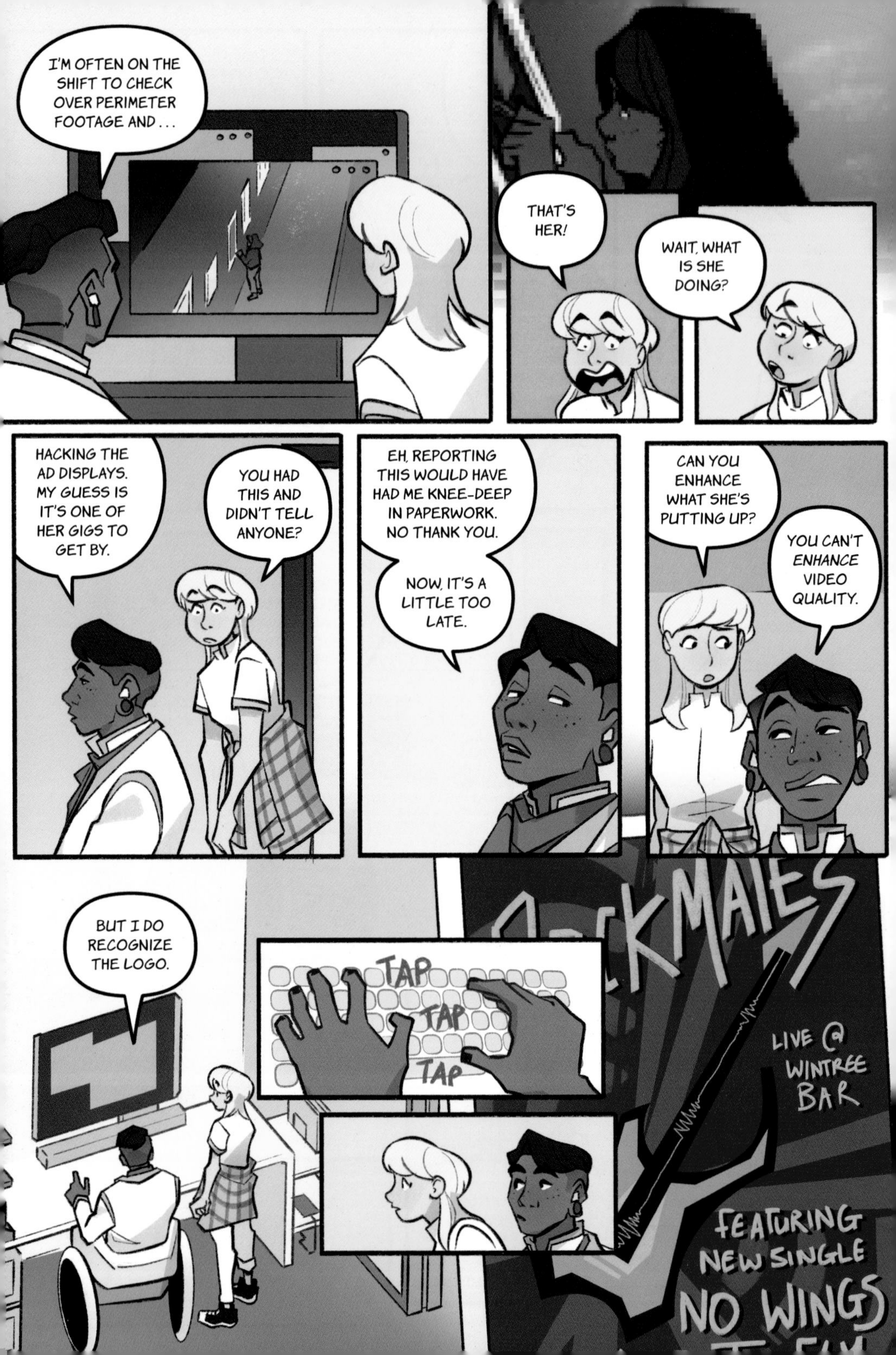

I'M OFTEN ON THE SHIFT TO CHECK OVER PERIMETER FOOTAGE AND . . .
THAT'S HER!
WAIT, WHAT IS SHE DOING?
HACKING THE AD DISPLAYS. MY GUESS IS IT'S ONE OF HER GIGS TO GET BY.
YOU HAD THIS AND DIDN'T TELL ANYONE?
EH, REPORTING THIS WOULD HAVE HAD ME KNEE-DEEP IN PAPERWORK. NO THANK YOU.
NOW, IT'S A LITTLE TOO LATE.
CAN YOU ENHANCE WHAT SHE'S PUTTING UP?
YOU CAN'T ENHANCE VIDEO QUALITY.
BUT I DO RECOGNIZE THE LOGO.
TAP
TAP
TAP
LIVE @ WINTREE BAR
FEATURING NEW SINGLE
NO WINGS

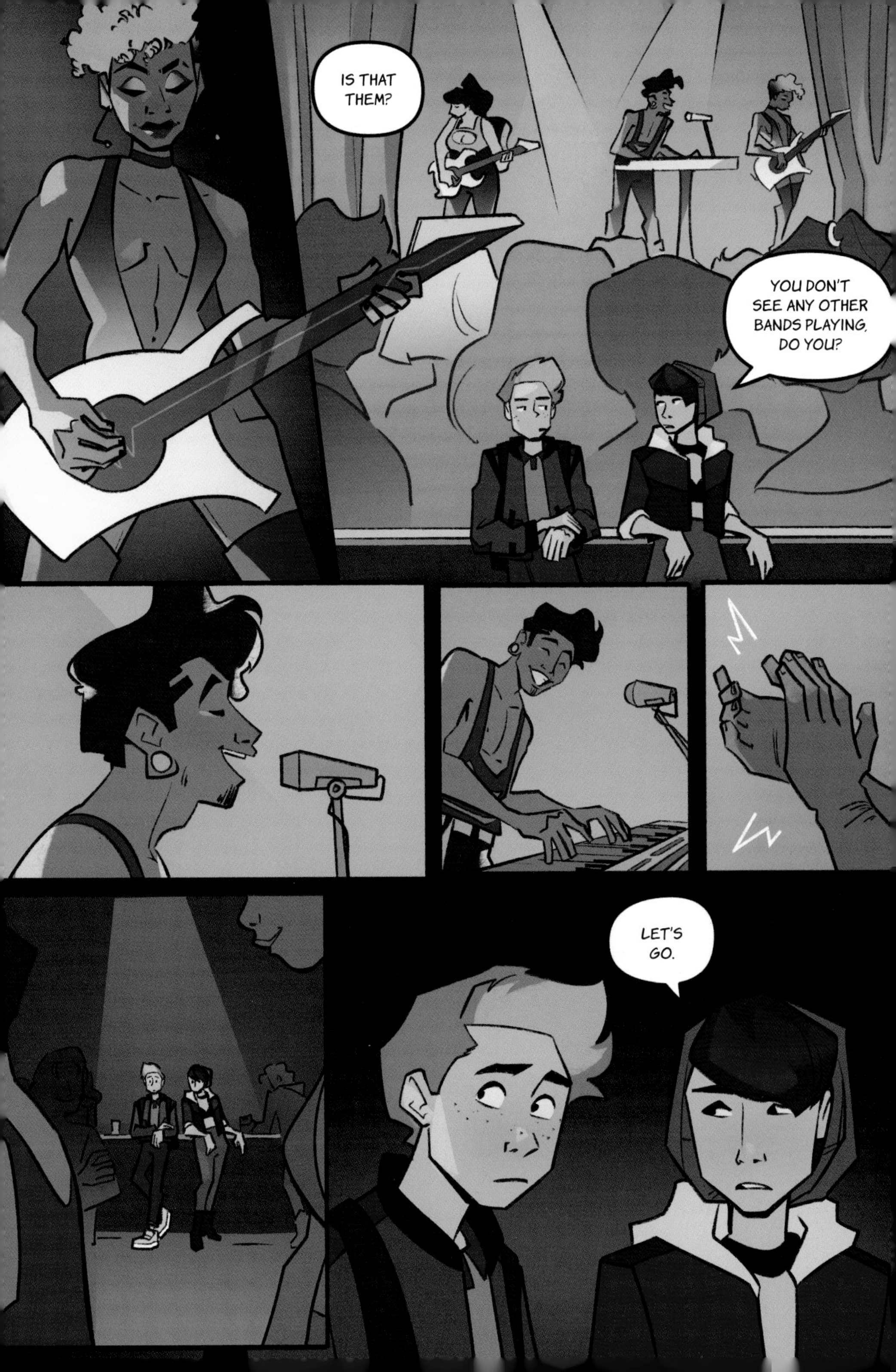
IS THAT THEM?
YOU DON'T SEE ANY OTHER BANDS PLAYING, DO YOU?
LET'S GO.

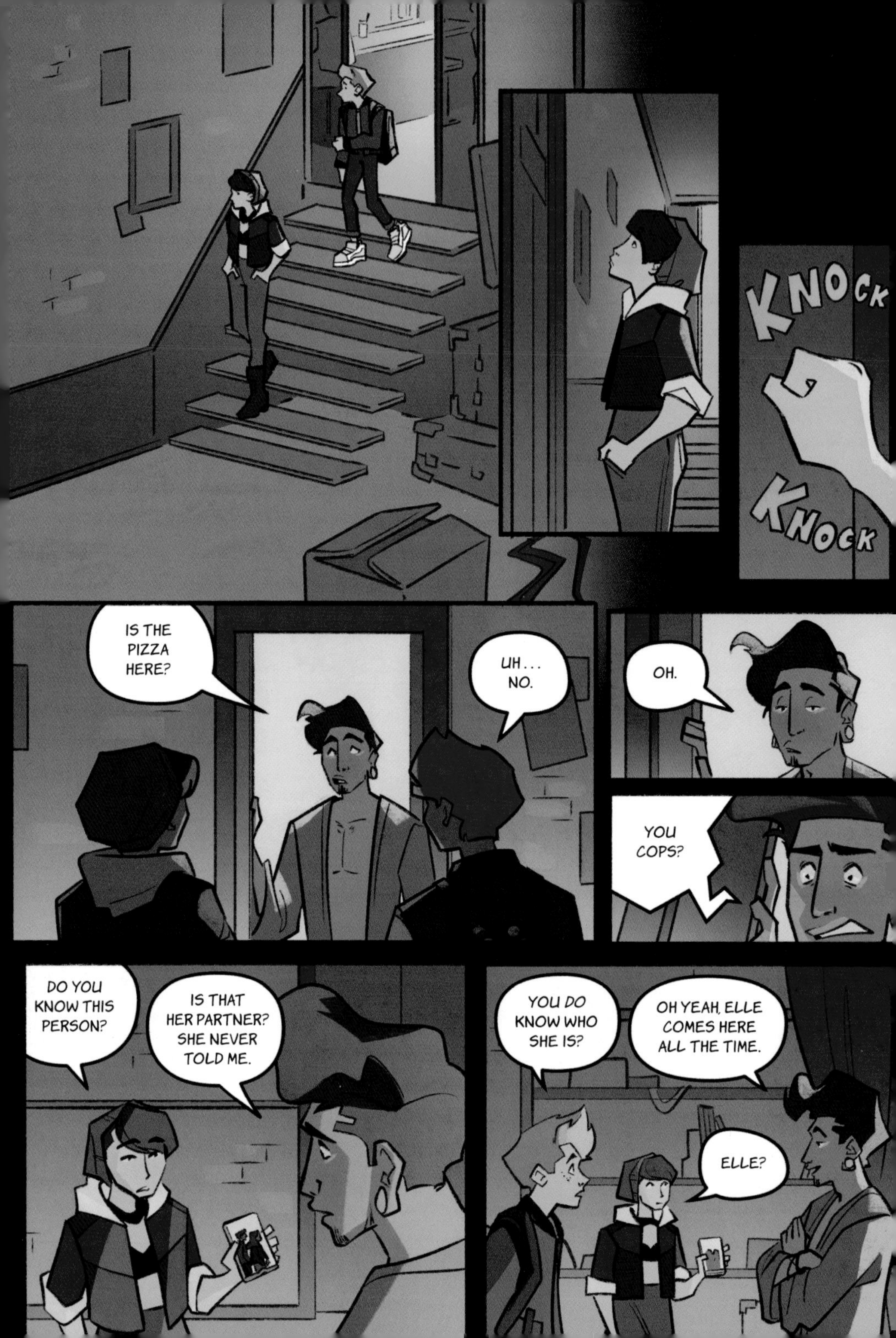
KNOCK
KNOCK
IS THE PIZZA HERE?
UH... NO.
OH.
YOU COPS?
DO YOU KNOW THIS PERSON?
IS THAT HER PARTNER? SHE NEVER TOLD ME.
YOU DO KNOW WHO SHE IS?
OH YEAH, ELLE COMES HERE ALL THE TIME.
ELLE?

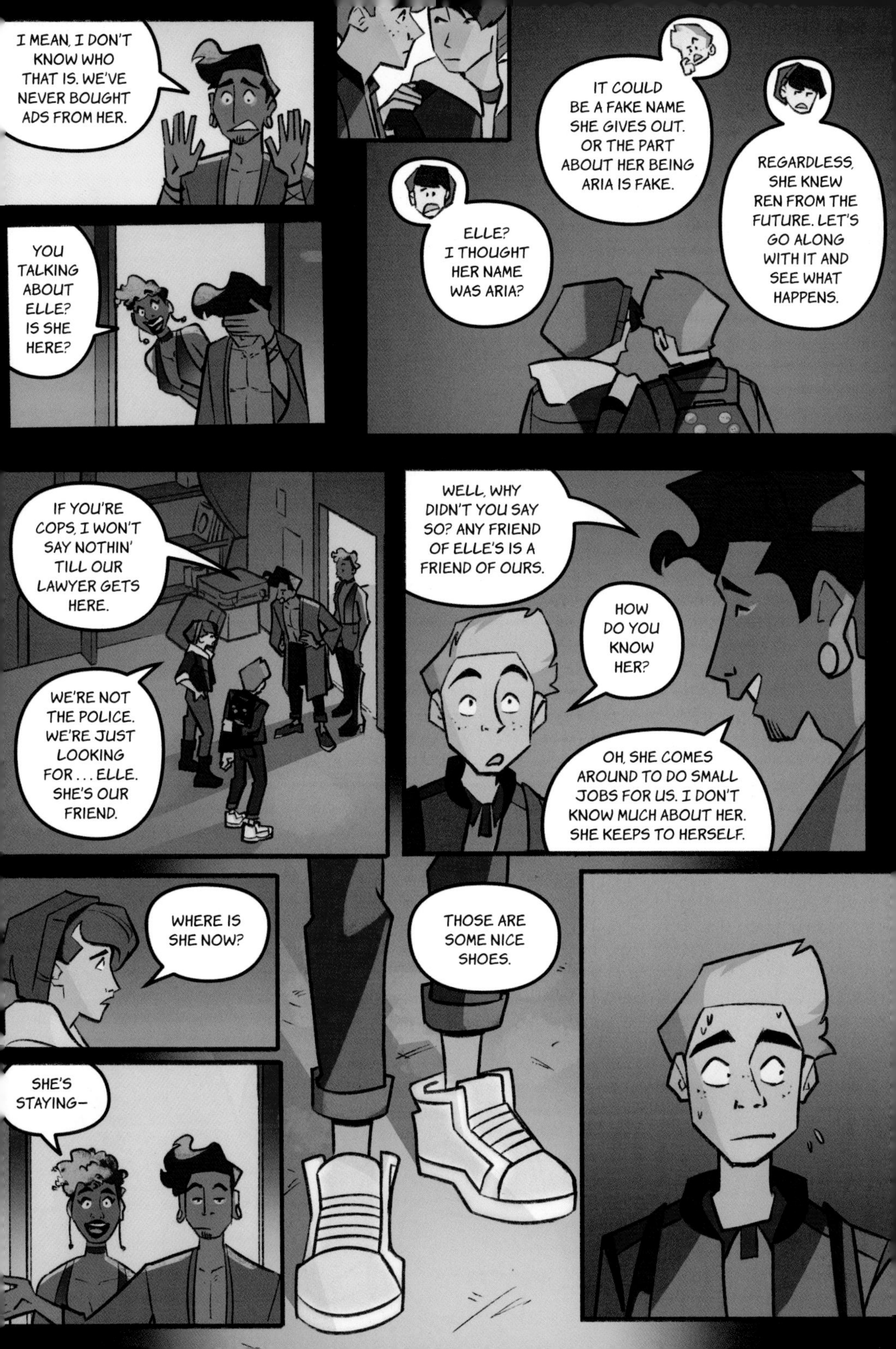
I MEAN, I DON'T KNOW WHO THAT IS. WE'VE NEVER BOUGHT ADS FROM HER.
YOU TALKING ABOUT ELLE? IS SHE HERE?
ELLE? I THOUGHT HER NAME WAS ARIA?
IT COULD BE A FAKE NAME SHE GIVES OUT. OR THE PART ABOUT HER BEING ARIA IS FAKE.
REGARDLESS, SHE KNEW REN FROM THE FUTURE. LET'S GO ALONG WITH IT AND SEE WHAT HAPPENS.
IF YOU'RE COPS, I WON'T SAY NOTHIN' TILL OUR LAWYER GETS HERE.
WE'RE NOT THE POLICE. WE'RE JUST LOOKING FOR . . . ELLE. SHE'S OUR FRIEND.
WELL, WHY DIDN'T YOU SAY SO? ANY FRIEND OF ELLE'S IS A FRIEND OF OURS.
HOW DO YOU KNOW HER?
OH, SHE COMES AROUND TO DO SMALL JOBS FOR US. I DON'T KNOW MUCH ABOUT HER. SHE KEEPS TO HERSELF.
WHERE IS SHE NOW?
SHE'S STAYING—
THOSE ARE SOME NICE SHOES.

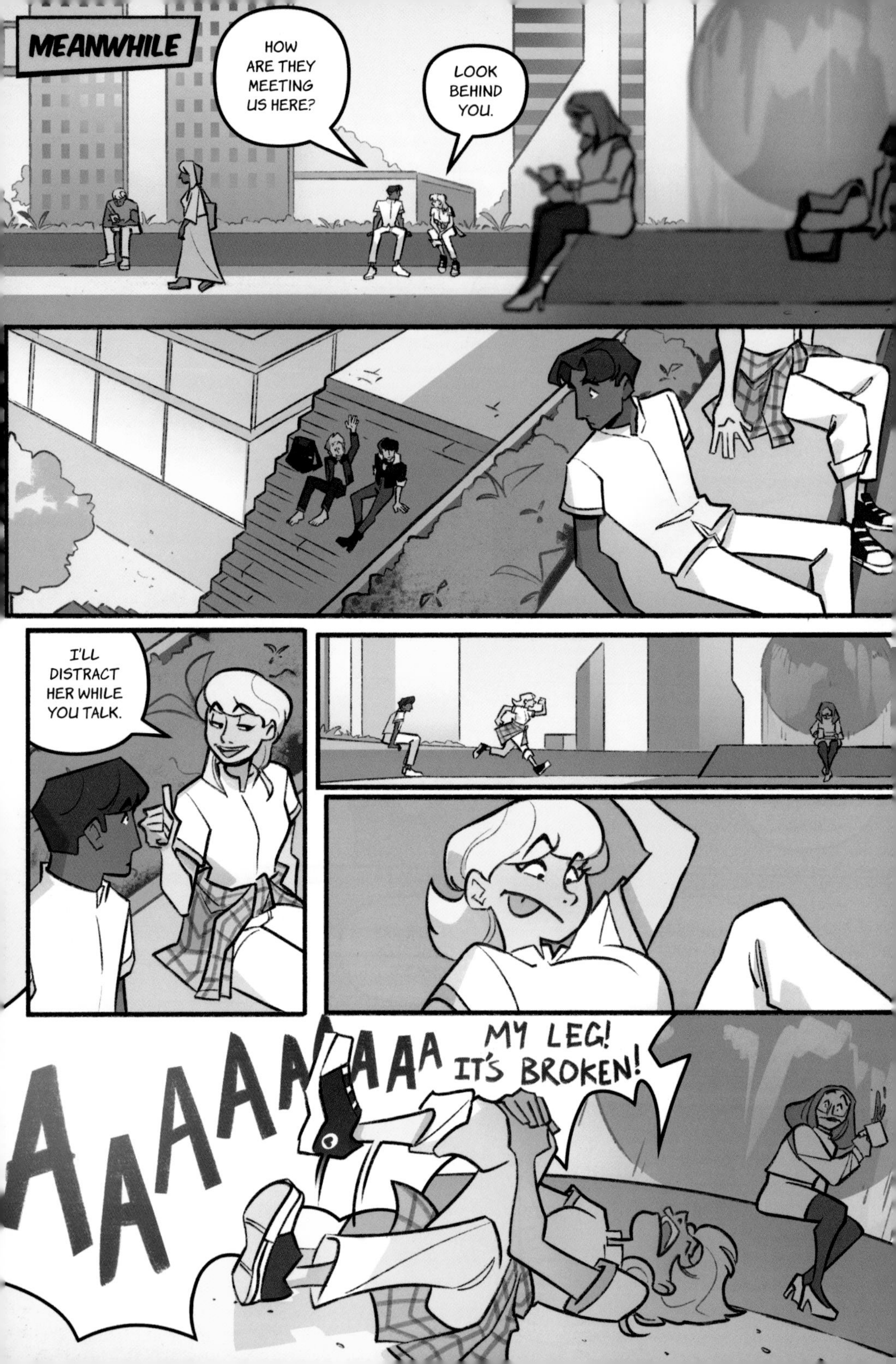
MEANWHILE
HOW ARE THEY MEETING US HERE?
LOOK BEHIND YOU.
I'LL DISTRACT HER WHILE YOU TALK.
AAAAAAAAAA
MY LEG! IT'S BROKEN!

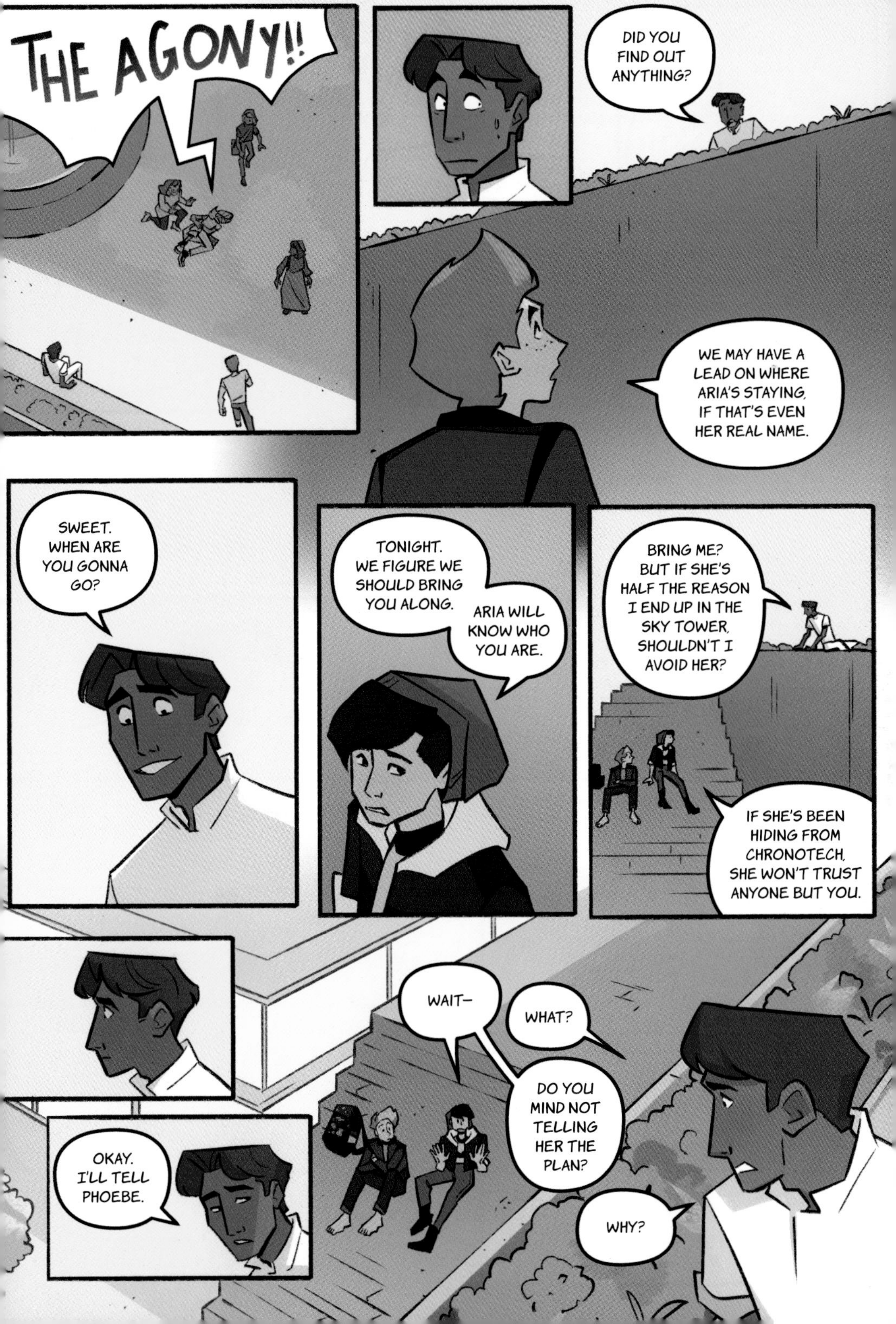
THE AGONY!!
DID YOU FIND OUT ANYTHING?
WE MAY HAVE A LEAD ON WHERE ARIA'S STAYING, IF THAT'S EVEN HER REAL NAME.
SWEET. WHEN ARE YOU GONNA GO?
TONIGHT. WE FIGURE WE SHOULD BRING YOU ALONG.
ARIA WILL KNOW WHO YOU ARE.
BRING ME? BUT IF SHE'S HALF THE REASON I END UP IN THE SKY TOWER, SHOULDN'T I AVOID HER?
IF SHE'S BEEN HIDING FROM CHRONOTECH, SHE WON'T TRUST ANYONE BUT YOU.
OKAY. I'LL TELL PHOEBE.
WAIT—
WHAT?
DO YOU MIND NOT TELLING HER THE PLAN?
WHY?

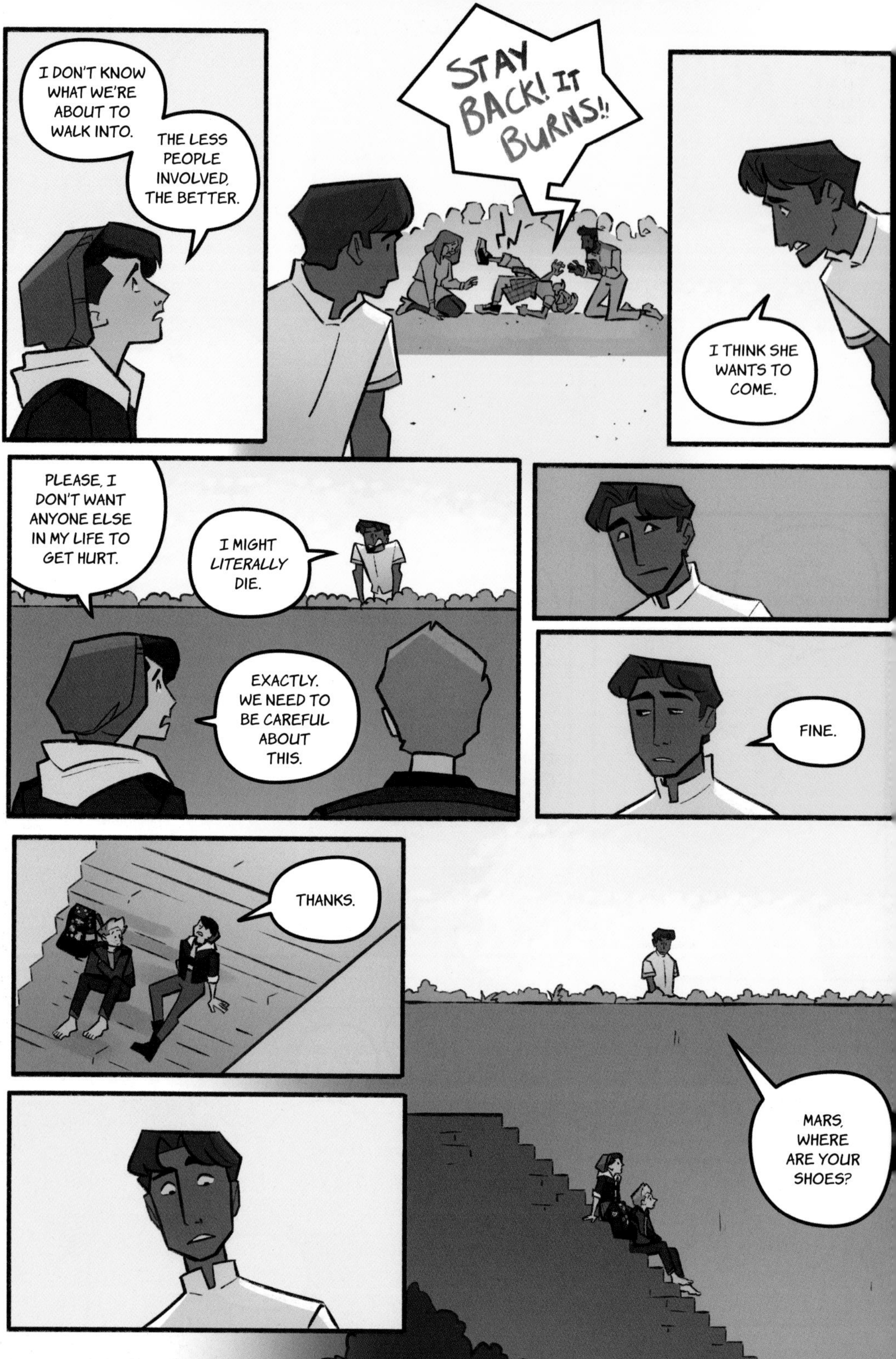
I DON'T KNOW WHAT WE'RE ABOUT TO WALK INTO.
THE LESS PEOPLE INVOLVED, THE BETTER.
STAY BACK! IT BURNS!!
I THINK SHE WANTS TO COME.
PLEASE, I DON'T WANT ANYONE ELSE IN MY LIFE TO GET HURT.
I MIGHT LITERALLY DIE.
EXACTLY. WE NEED TO BE CAREFUL ABOUT THIS.
FINE.
THANKS.
MARS, WHERE ARE YOUR SHOES?

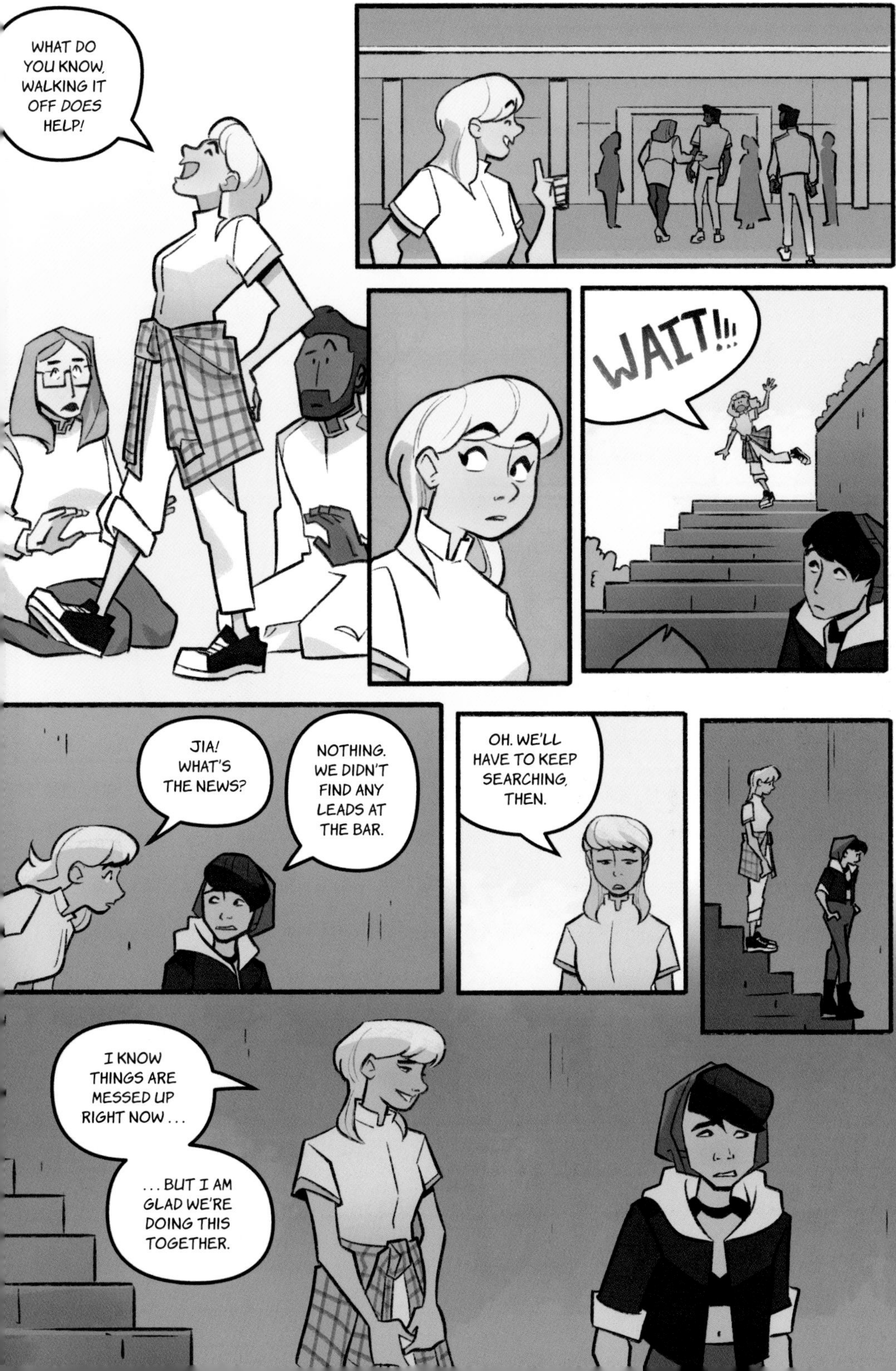
WHAT DO YOU KNOW, WALKING IT OFF DOES HELP!
WAIT!!!
JIA! WHAT'S THE NEWS?
NOTHING. WE DIDN'T FIND ANY LEADS AT THE BAR.
OH. WE'LL HAVE TO KEEP SEARCHING, THEN.
I KNOW THINGS ARE MESSED UP RIGHT NOW . . .
. . . BUT I AM GLAD WE'RE DOING THIS TOGETHER.

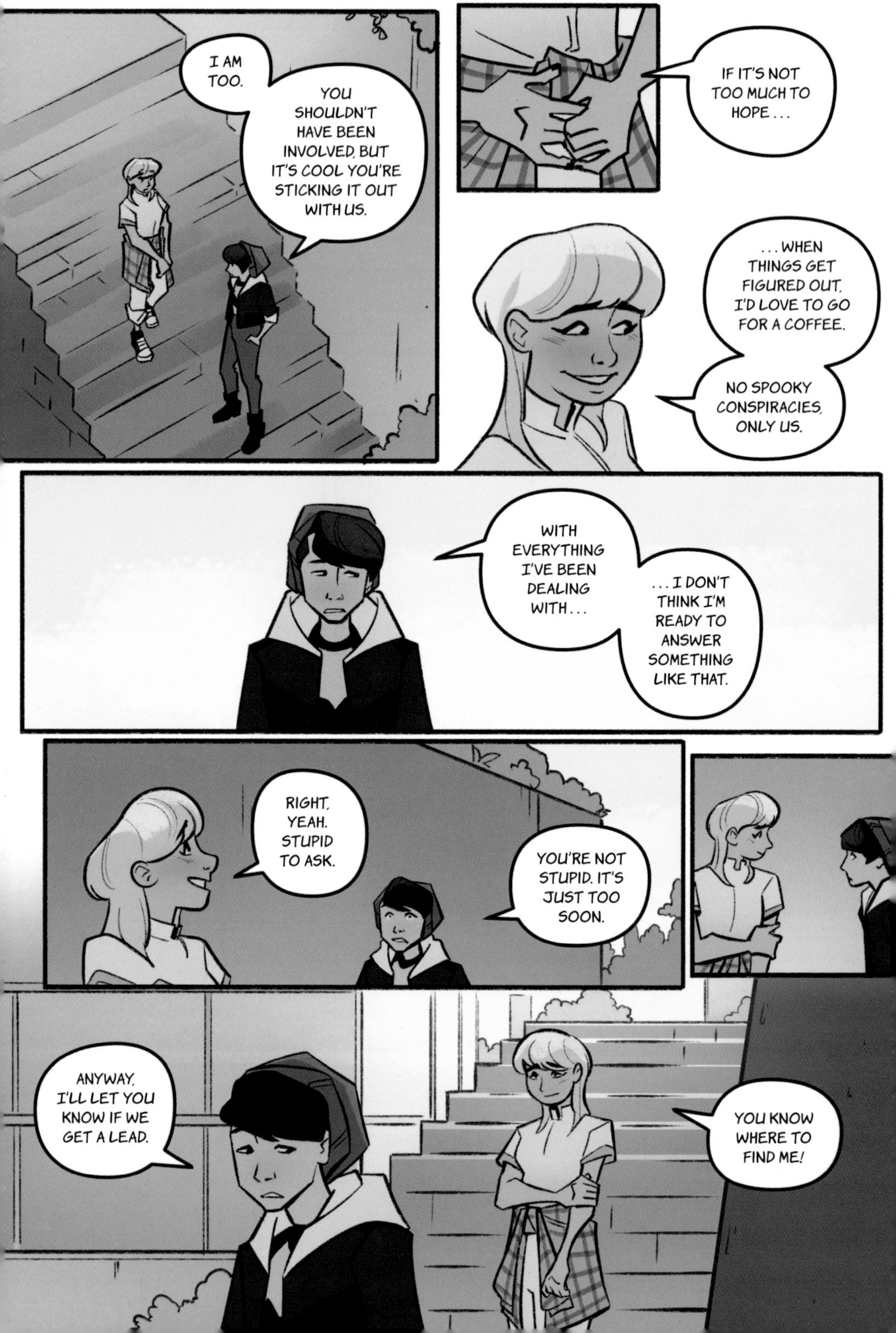
I AM TOO.
YOU SHOULDN'T HAVE BEEN INVOLVED, BUT IT'S COOL YOU'RE STICKING IT OUT WITH US.
IF IT'S NOT TOO MUCH TO HOPE . . .
. . . WHEN THINGS GET FIGURED OUT, I'D LOVE TO GO FOR A COFFEE.
NO SPOOKY CONSPIRACIES, ONLY US.
WITH EVERYTHING I'VE BEEN DEALING WITH . . .
. . . I DON'T THINK I'M READY TO ANSWER SOMETHING LIKE THAT.
RIGHT, YEAH. STUPID TO ASK.
YOU'RE NOT STUPID. IT'S JUST TOO SOON.
ANYWAY, I'LL LET YOU KNOW IF WE GET A LEAD.
YOU KNOW WHERE TO FIND ME!

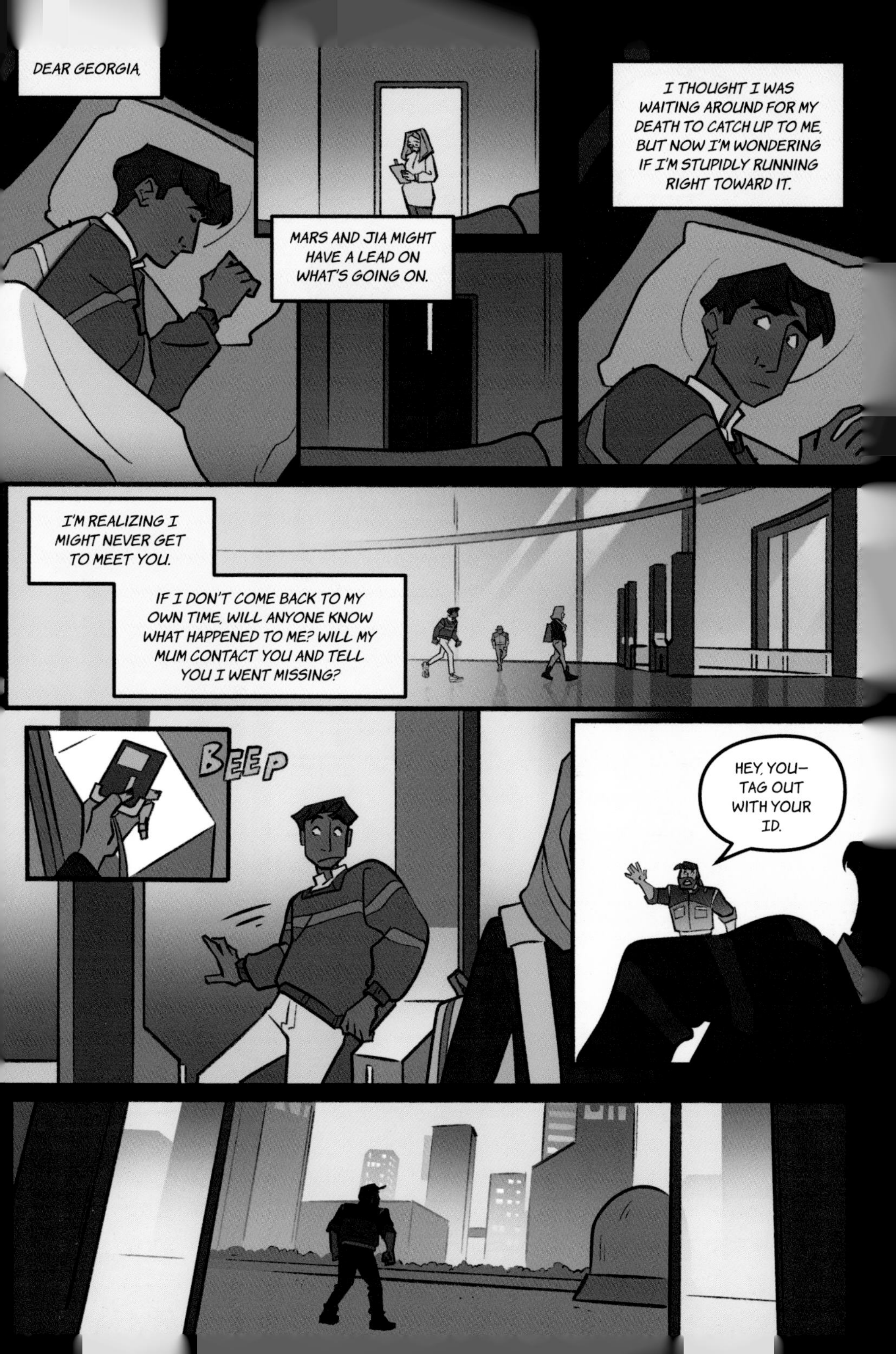
DEAR GEORGIA,
MARS AND JIA MIGHT HAVE A LEAD ON WHAT'S GOING ON.
I THOUGHT I WAS WAITING AROUND FOR MY DEATH TO CATCH UP TO ME, BUT NOW I'M WONDERING IF I'M STUPIDLY RUNNING RIGHT TOWARD IT.
I'M REALIZING I MIGHT NEVER GET TO MEET YOU.
IF I DON'T COME BACK TO MY OWN TIME, WILL ANYONE KNOW WHAT HAPPENED TO ME? WILL MY MUM CONTACT YOU AND TELL YOU I WENT MISSING?
BEEP
HEY, YOU— TAG OUT WITH YOUR ID.

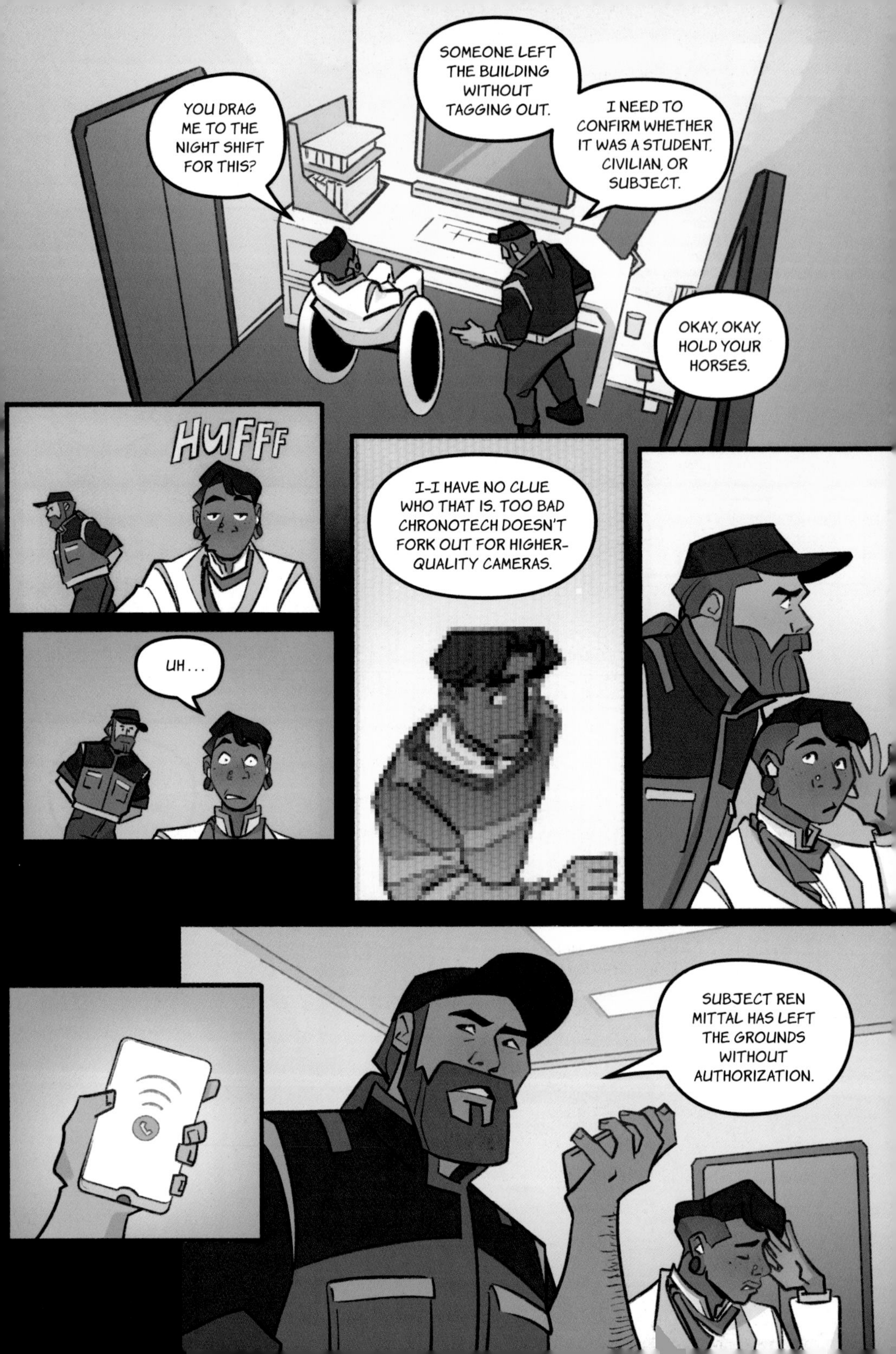
YOU DRAG ME TO THE NIGHT SHIFT FOR THIS?
SOMEONE LEFT THE BUILDING WITHOUT TAGGING OUT.
I NEED TO CONFIRM WHETHER IT WAS A STUDENT, CIVILIAN, OR SUBJECT.
OKAY, OKAY, HOLD YOUR HORSES.
HUFFF
UH...
I-I HAVE NO CLUE WHO THAT IS. TOO BAD CHRONOTECH DOESN'T FORK OUT FOR HIGHER-QUALITY CAMERAS.
SUBJECT REN MITTAL HAS LEFT THE GROUNDS WITHOUT AUTHORIZATION.

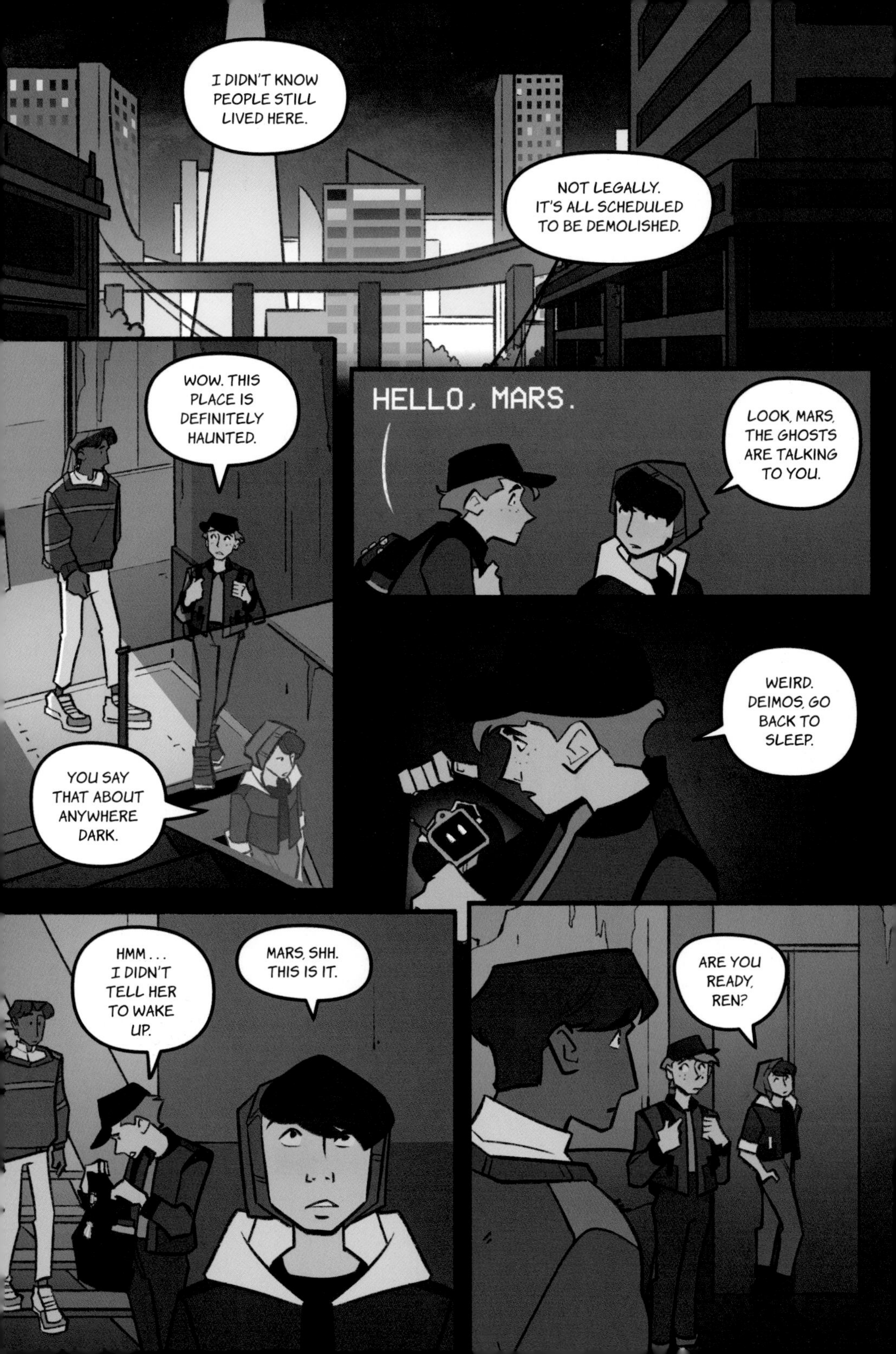
I DIDN'T KNOW PEOPLE STILL LIVED HERE.
NOT LEGALLY. IT'S ALL SCHEDULED TO BE DEMOLISHED.
WOW. THIS PLACE IS DEFINITELY HAUNTED.
YOU SAY THAT ABOUT ANYWHERE DARK.
HELLO, MARS.
LOOK, MARS, THE GHOSTS ARE TALKING TO YOU.
WEIRD. DEIMOS, GO BACK TO SLEEP.
HMM . . . I DIDN'T TELL HER TO WAKE UP.
MARS, SHH. THIS IS IT.
ARE YOU READY, REN?

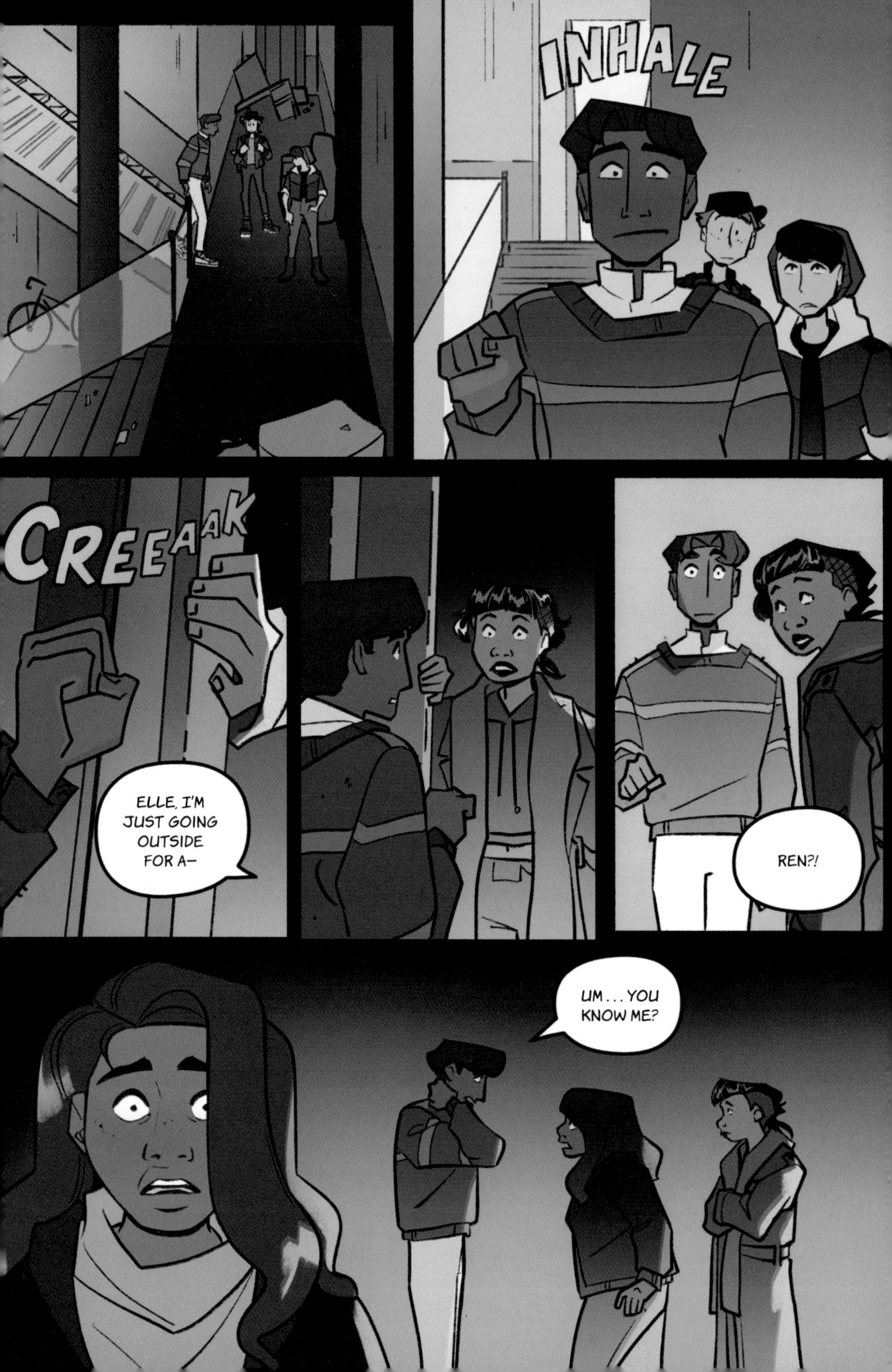
INHALE
CREEAAK
ELLE, I'M JUST GOING OUTSIDE FOR A—
REN?!
UM . . . YOU KNOW ME?

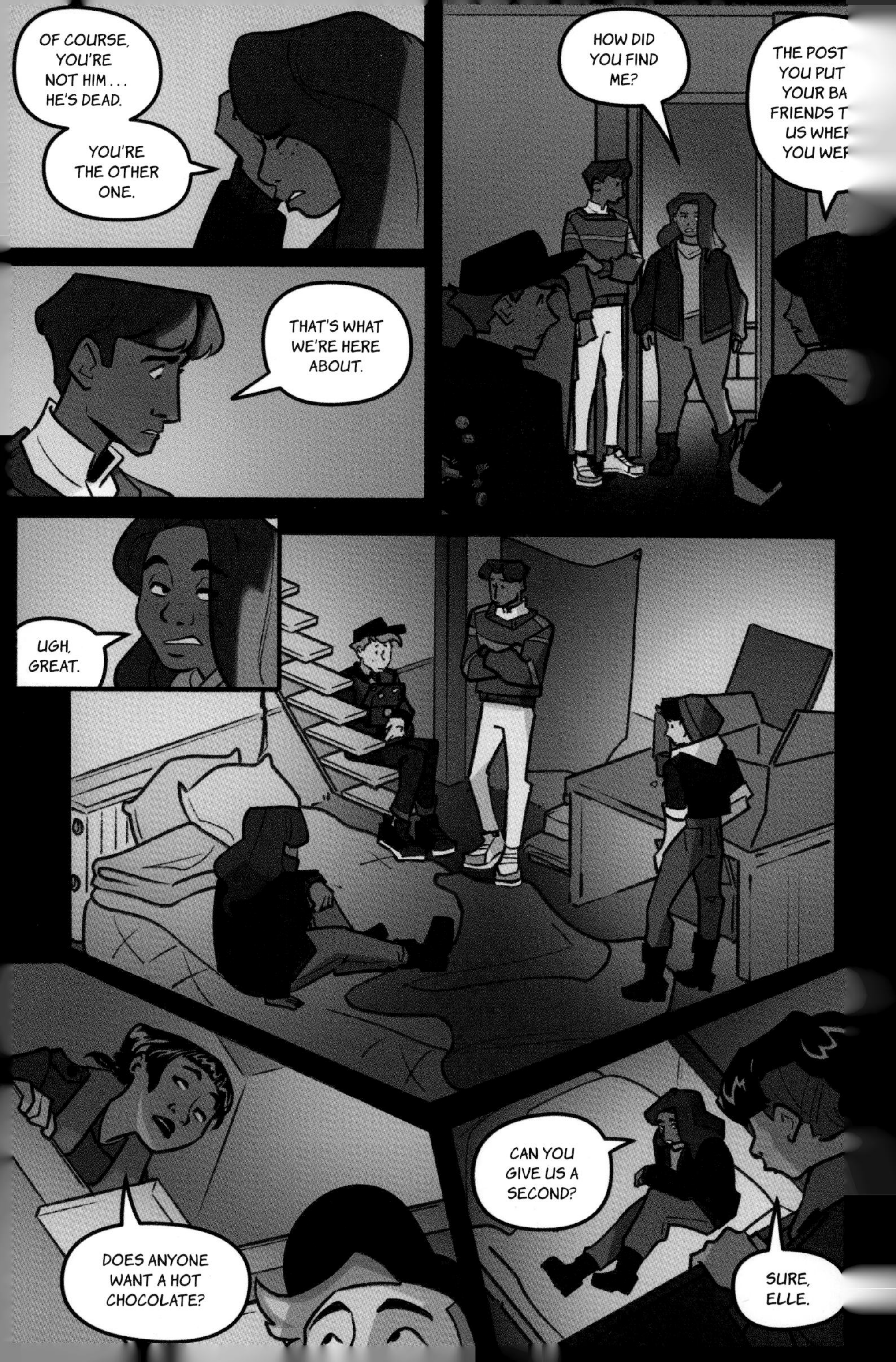
OF COURSE, YOU'RE NOT HIM . . . HE'S DEAD.
YOU'RE THE OTHER ONE.
THAT'S WHAT WE'RE HERE ABOUT.
HOW DID YOU FIND ME?
THE POST YOU PUT YOUR BA FRIENDS T US WHEF YOU WEF
UGH, GREAT.
DOES ANYONE WANT A HOT CHOCOLATE?
CAN YOU GIVE US A SECOND?
SURE, ELLE.

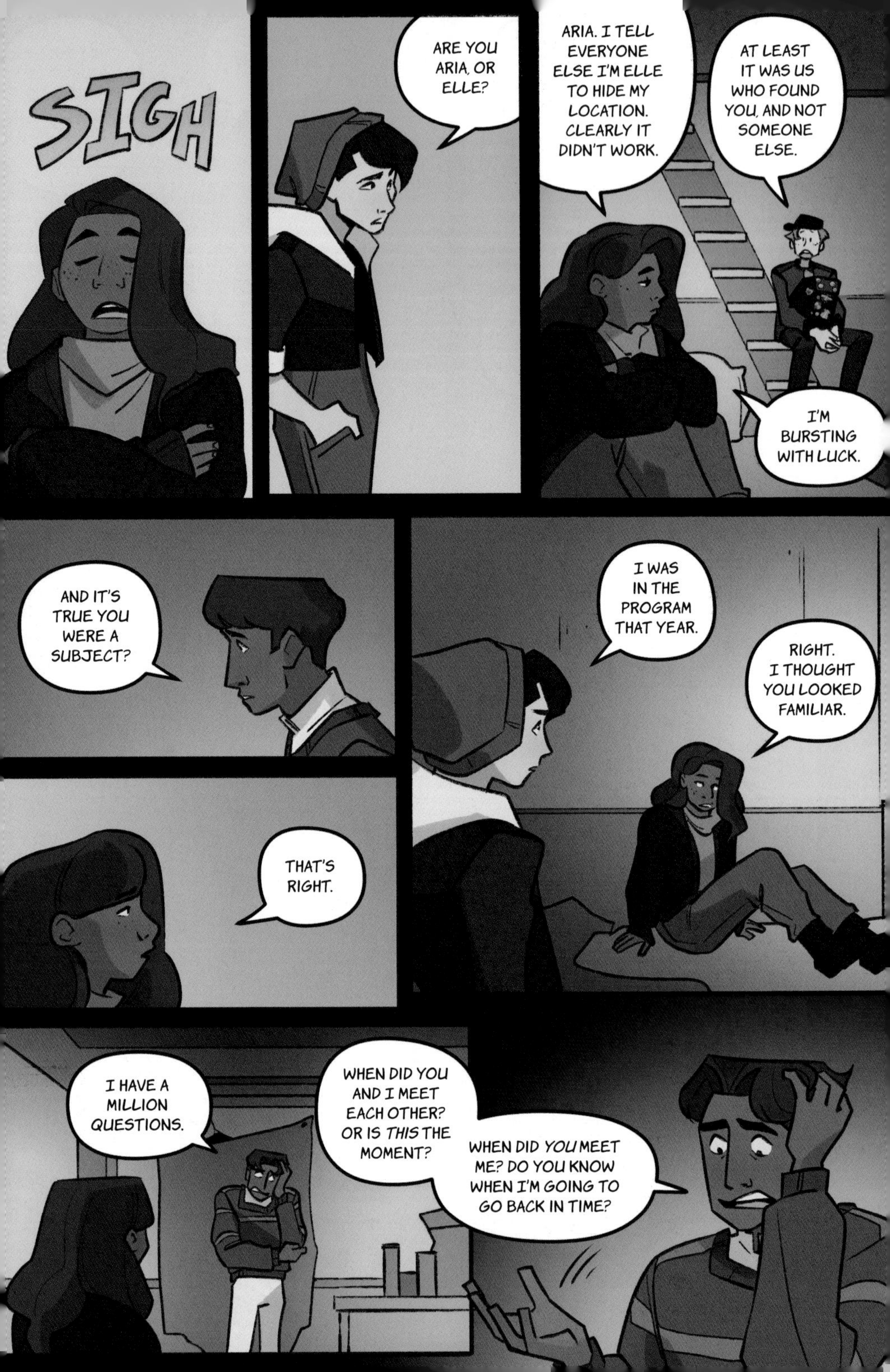
SIGH
ARE YOU ARIA, OR ELLE?
ARIA. I TELL EVERYONE ELSE I'M ELLE TO HIDE MY LOCATION. CLEARLY IT DIDN'T WORK.
AT LEAST IT WAS US WHO FOUND YOU, AND NOT SOMEONE ELSE.
I'M BURSTING WITH LUCK.
AND IT'S TRUE YOU WERE A SUBJECT?
THAT'S RIGHT.
I WAS IN THE PROGRAM THAT YEAR.
RIGHT. I THOUGHT YOU LOOKED FAMILIAR.
I HAVE A MILLION QUESTIONS.
WHEN DID YOU AND I MEET EACH OTHER? OR IS *THIS* THE MOMENT?
WHEN DID *YOU* MEET ME? DO YOU KNOW WHEN I'M GOING TO GO BACK IN TIME?

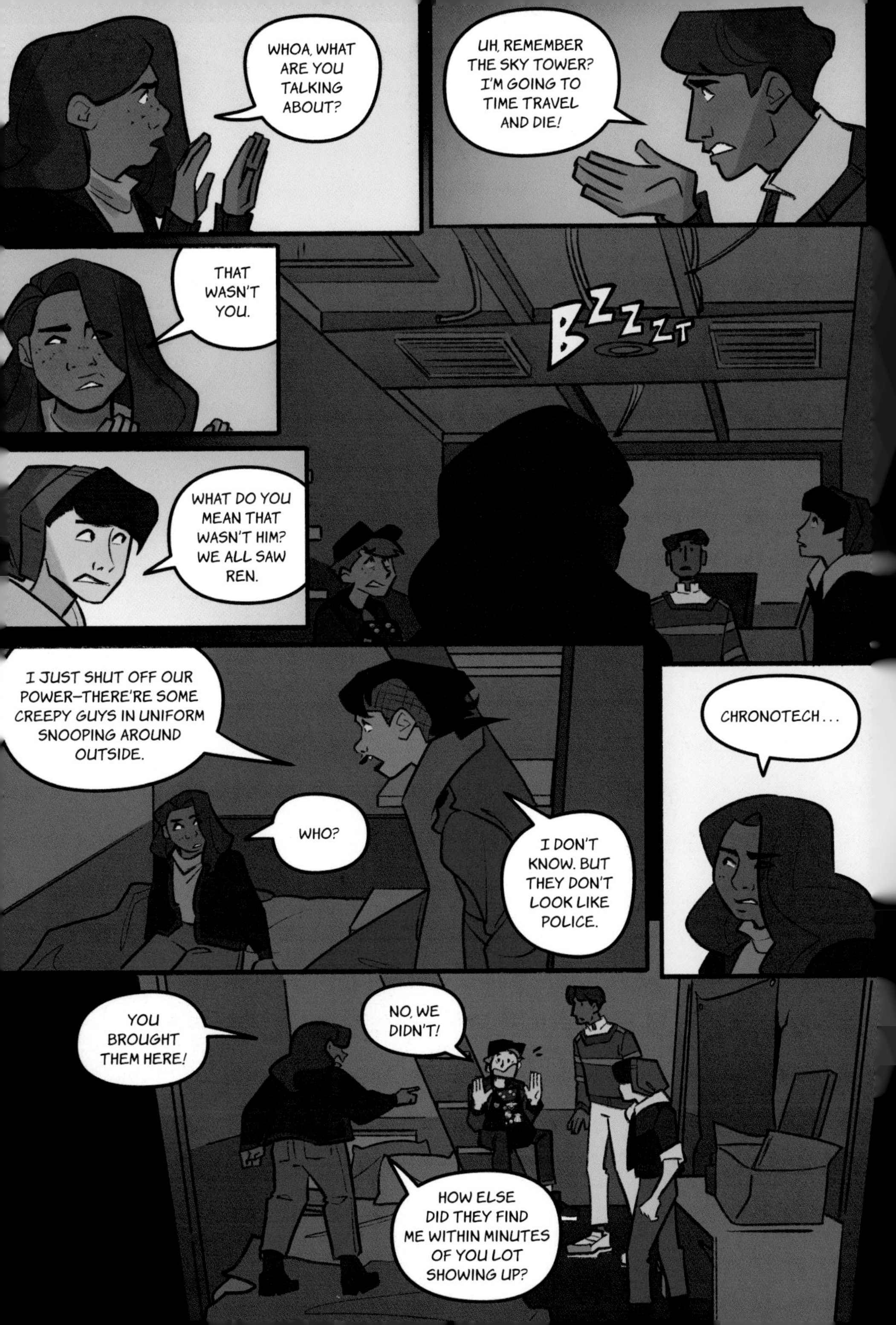
WHOA, WHAT ARE YOU TALKING ABOUT?
UH, REMEMBER THE SKY TOWER? I'M GOING TO TIME TRAVEL AND DIE!
THAT WASN'T YOU.
BZZZZT
WHAT DO YOU MEAN THAT WASN'T HIM? WE ALL SAW REN.
I JUST SHUT OFF OUR POWER—THERE'RE SOME CREEPY GUYS IN UNIFORM SNOOPING AROUND OUTSIDE.
WHO?
I DON'T KNOW. BUT THEY DON'T LOOK LIKE POLICE.
CHRONOTECH . . .
YOU BROUGHT THEM HERE!
NO, WE DIDN'T!
HOW ELSE DID THEY FIND ME WITHIN MINUTES OF YOU LOT SHOWING UP?

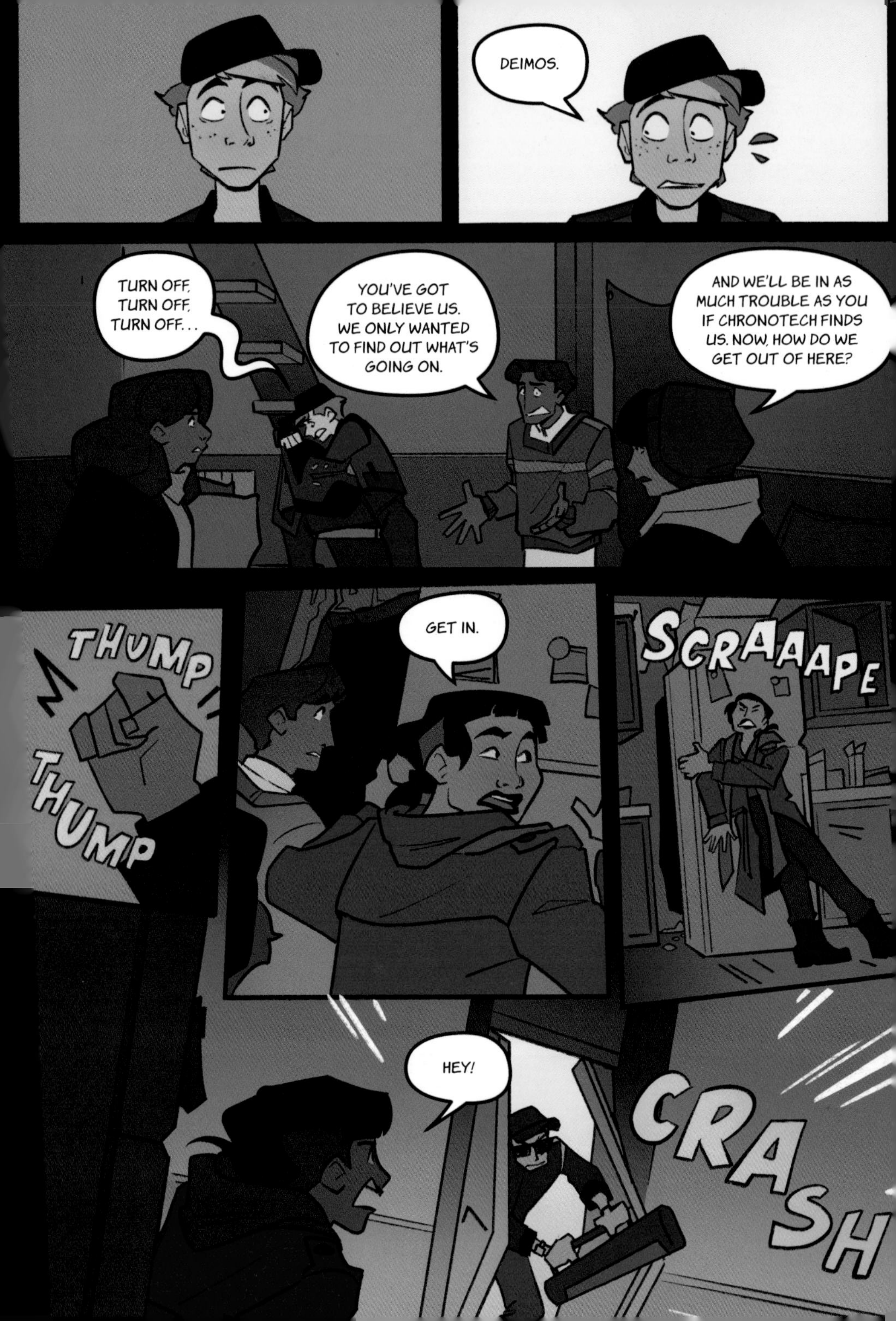
DEIMOS.
TURN OFF, TURN OFF, TURN OFF. . .
YOU'VE GOT TO BELIEVE US. WE ONLY WANTED TO FIND OUT WHAT'S GOING ON.
AND WE'LL BE IN AS MUCH TROUBLE AS YOU IF CHRONOTECH FINDS US. NOW, HOW DO WE GET OUT OF HERE?
THUMP
THUMP
GET IN.
SCRAAAPE
HEY!
CRASH

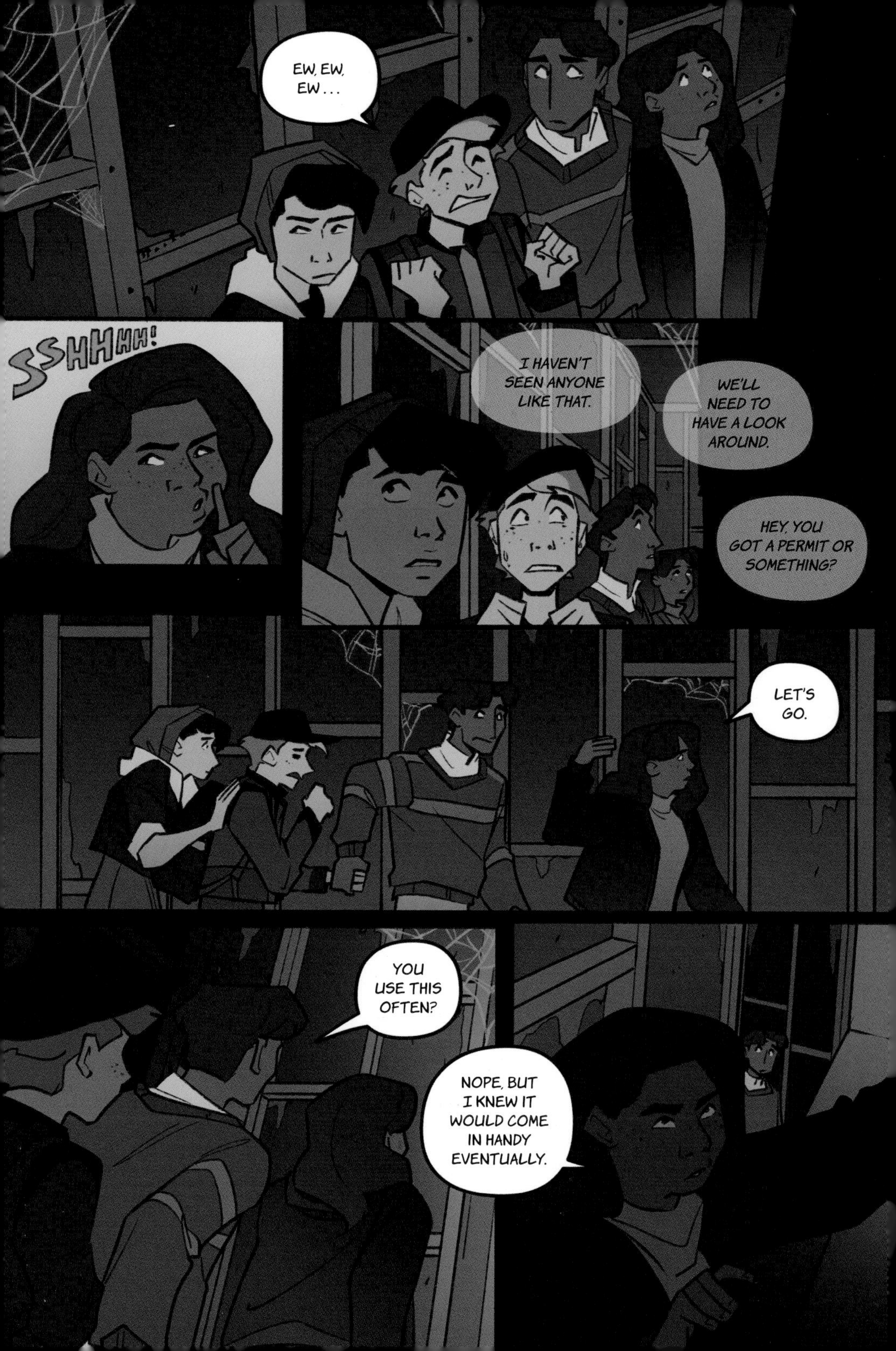

EW, EW, EW . . .
SSHHHH!
I HAVEN'T SEEN ANYONE LIKE THAT.
WE'LL NEED TO HAVE A LOOK AROUND.
HEY, YOU GOT A PERMIT OR SOMETHING?
LET'S GO.
YOU USE THIS OFTEN?
NOPE, BUT I KNEW IT WOULD COME IN HANDY EVENTUALLY.

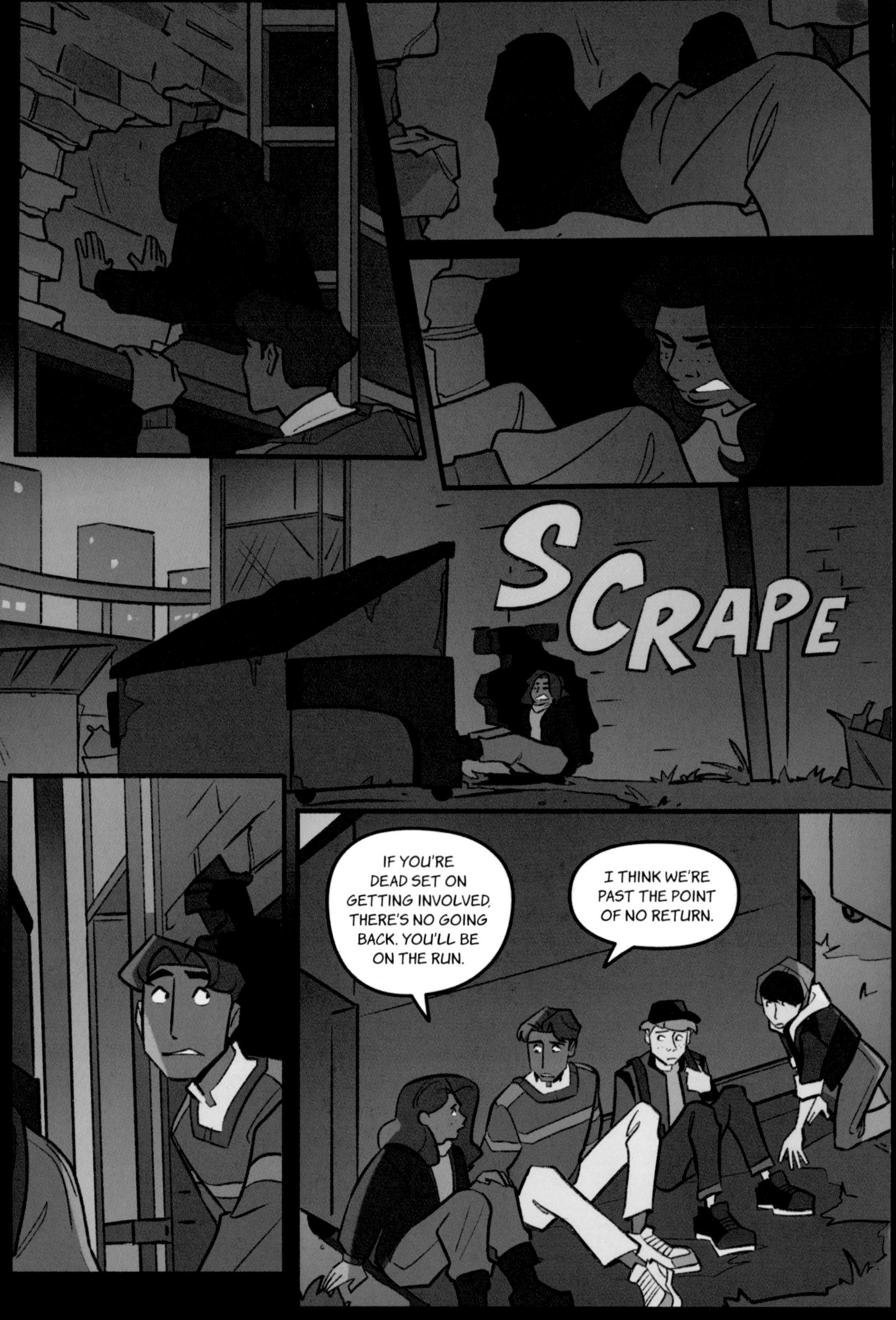
SCRAPE
IF YOU'RE DEAD SET ON GETTING INVOLVED, THERE'S NO GOING BACK. YOU'LL BE ON THE RUN.
I THINK WE'RE PAST THE POINT OF NO RETURN.

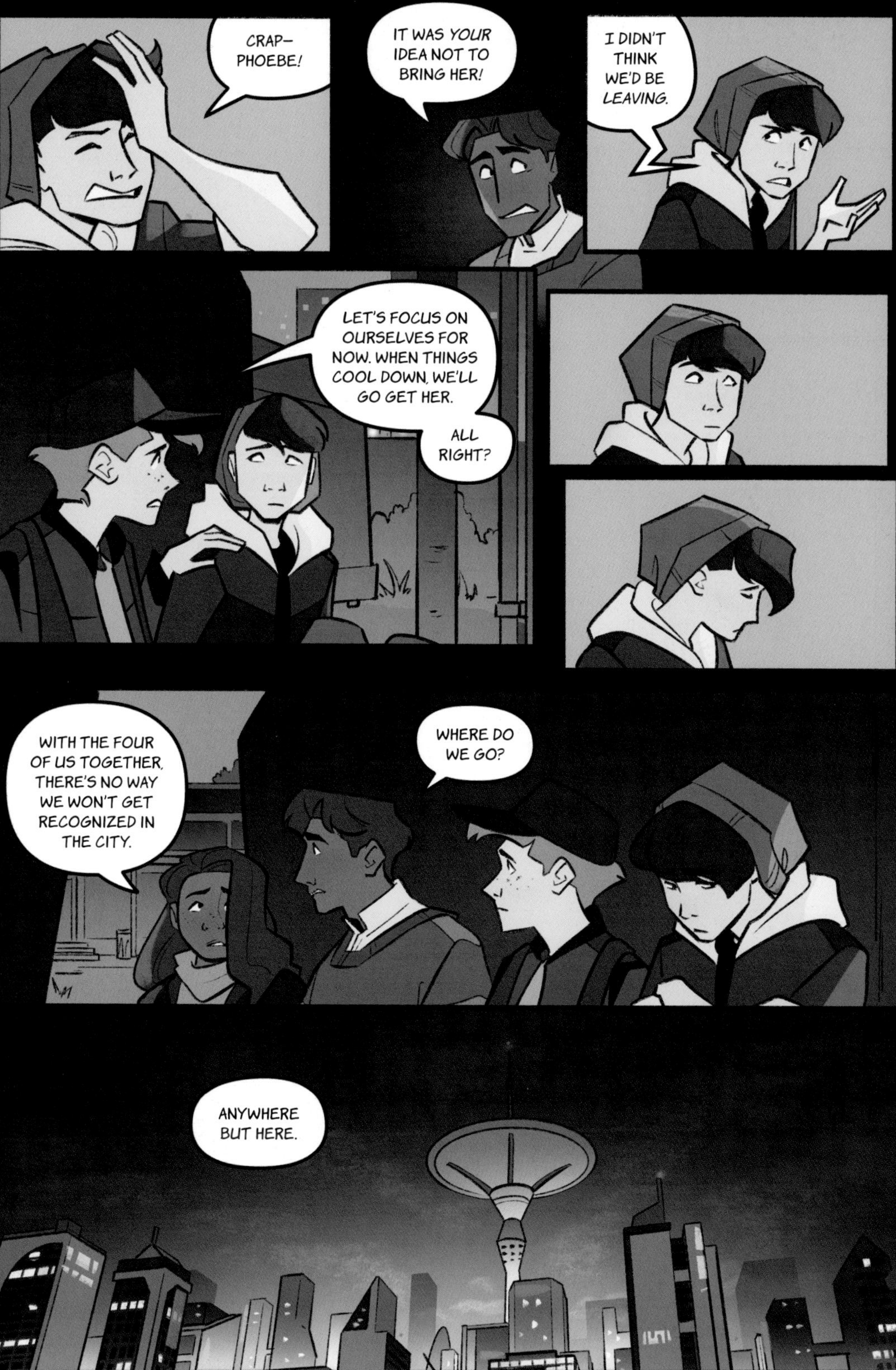
CRAP—
PHOEBE!
IT WAS *YOUR* IDEA NOT TO BRING HER!
I DIDN'T THINK WE'D BE *LEAVING*.
LET'S FOCUS ON OURSELVES FOR NOW. WHEN THINGS COOL DOWN, WE'LL GO GET HER.
ALL RIGHT?
WITH THE FOUR OF US TOGETHER, THERE'S NO WAY WE WON'T GET RECOGNIZED IN THE CITY.
WHERE DO WE GO?
ANYWHERE BUT HERE.

CHAPTER FOUR

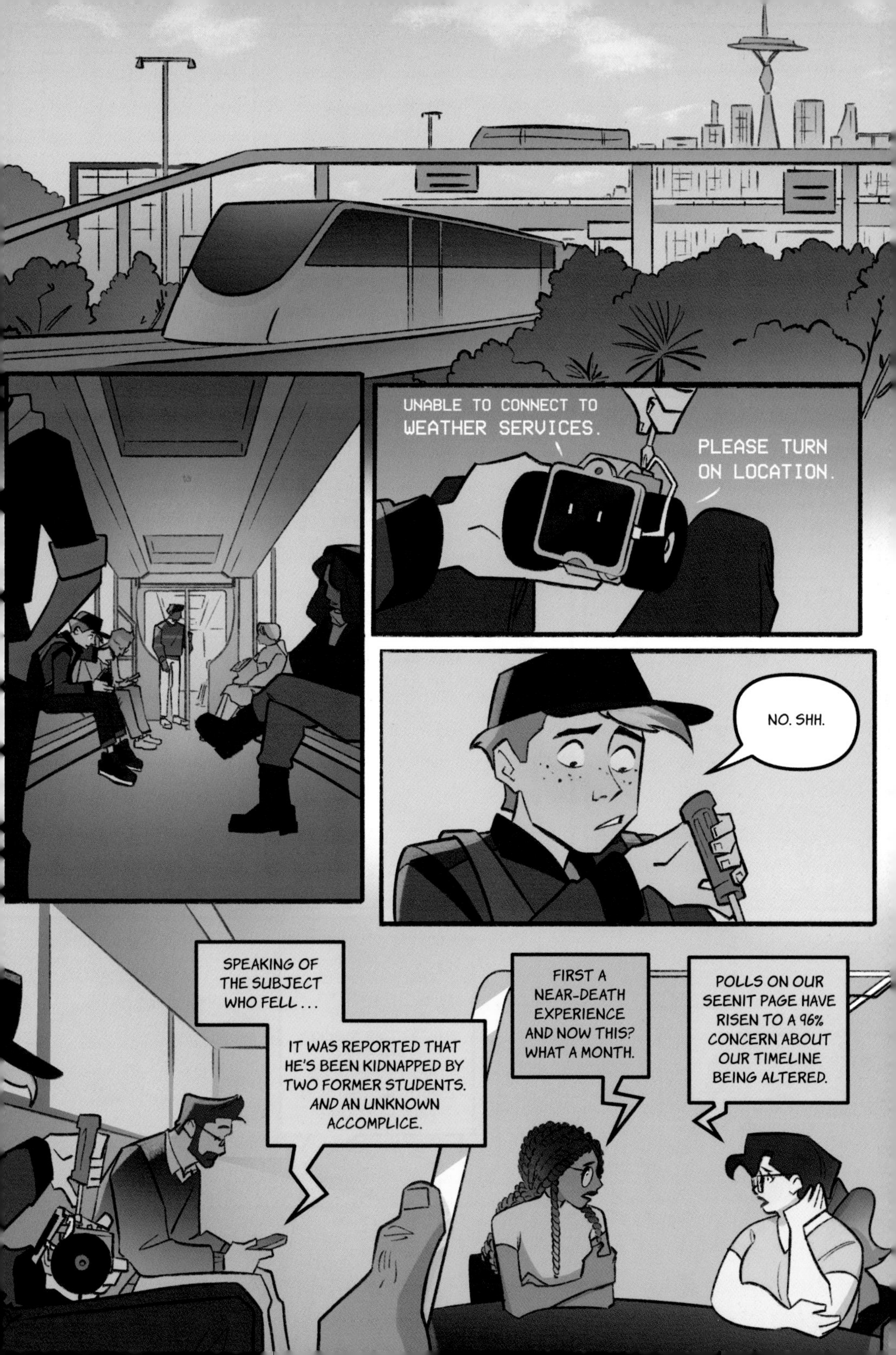
UNABLE TO CONNECT TO WEATHER SERVICES.
PLEASE TURN ON LOCATION.
NO. SHH.
SPEAKING OF THE SUBJECT WHO FELL . . .
IT WAS REPORTED THAT HE'S BEEN KIDNAPPED BY TWO FORMER STUDENTS. AND AN UNKNOWN ACCOMPLICE.
FIRST A NEAR-DEATH EXPERIENCE AND NOW THIS? WHAT A MONTH.
POLLS ON OUR SEENIT PAGE HAVE RISEN TO A 96% CONCERN ABOUT OUR TIMELINE BEING ALTERED.

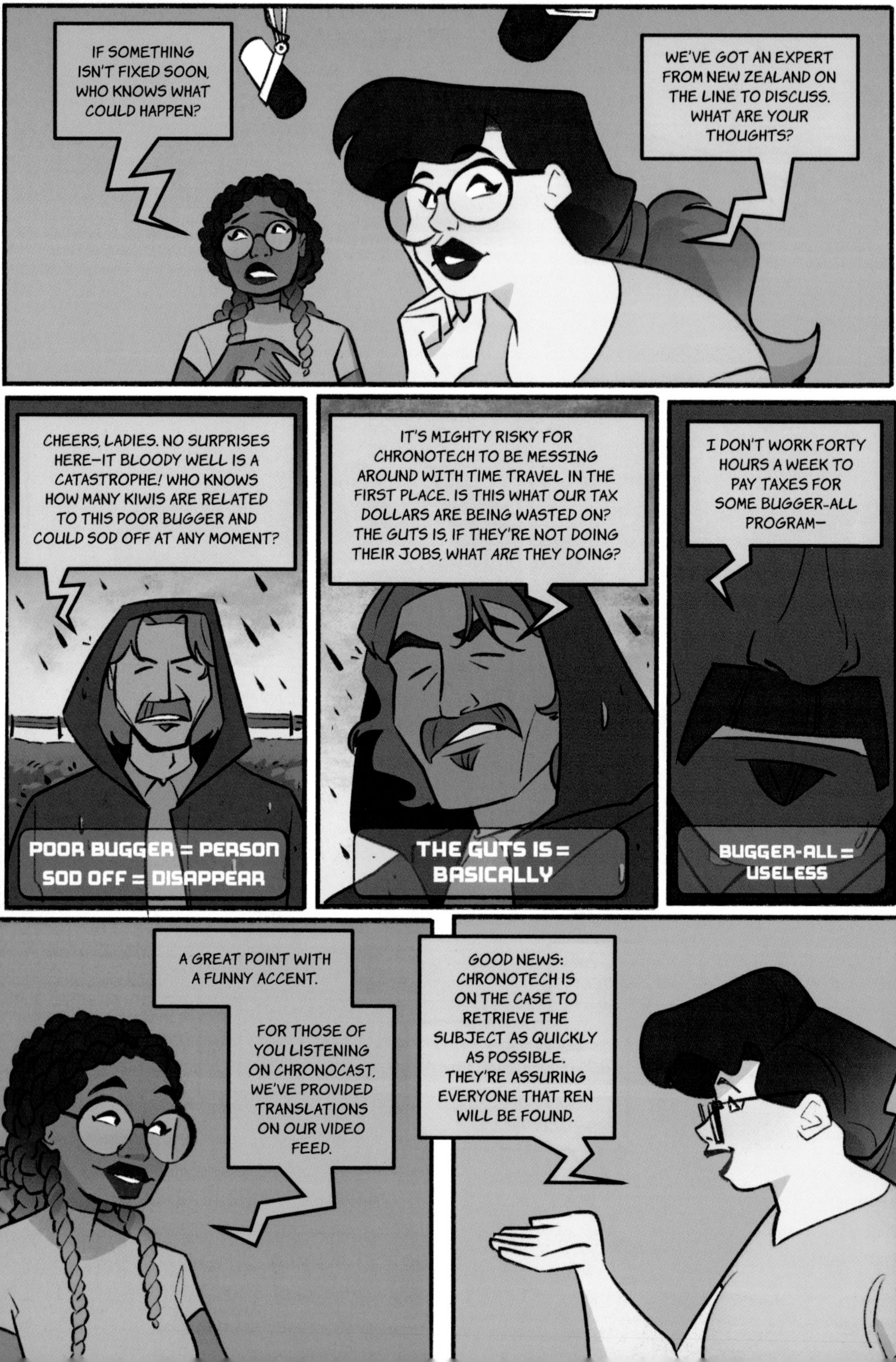
IF SOMETHING ISN'T FIXED SOON, WHO KNOWS WHAT COULD HAPPEN?
WE'VE GOT AN EXPERT FROM NEW ZEALAND ON THE LINE TO DISCUSS. WHAT ARE YOUR THOUGHTS?
CHEERS, LADIES. NO SURPRISES HERE—IT BLOODY WELL IS A CATASTROPHE! WHO KNOWS HOW MANY KIWIS ARE RELATED TO THIS POOR BUGGER AND COULD SOD OFF AT ANY MOMENT?
POOR BUGGER = PERSON
SOD OFF = DISAPPEAR
IT'S MIGHTY RISKY FOR CHRONOTECH TO BE MESSING AROUND WITH TIME TRAVEL IN THE FIRST PLACE. IS THIS WHAT OUR TAX DOLLARS ARE BEING WASTED ON? THE GUTS IS, IF THEY'RE NOT DOING THEIR JOBS, WHAT *ARE* THEY DOING?
THE GUTS IS = BASICALLY
I DON'T WORK FORTY HOURS A WEEK TO PAY TAXES FOR SOME BUGGER-ALL PROGRAM—
BUGGER-ALL = USELESS
A GREAT POINT WITH A FUNNY ACCENT.
FOR THOSE OF YOU LISTENING ON CHRONOCAST, WE'VE PROVIDED TRANSLATIONS ON OUR VIDEO FEED.
GOOD NEWS: CHRONOTECH IS ON THE CASE TO RETRIEVE THE SUBJECT AS QUICKLY AS POSSIBLE. THEY'RE ASSURING EVERYONE THAT REN WILL BE FOUND.

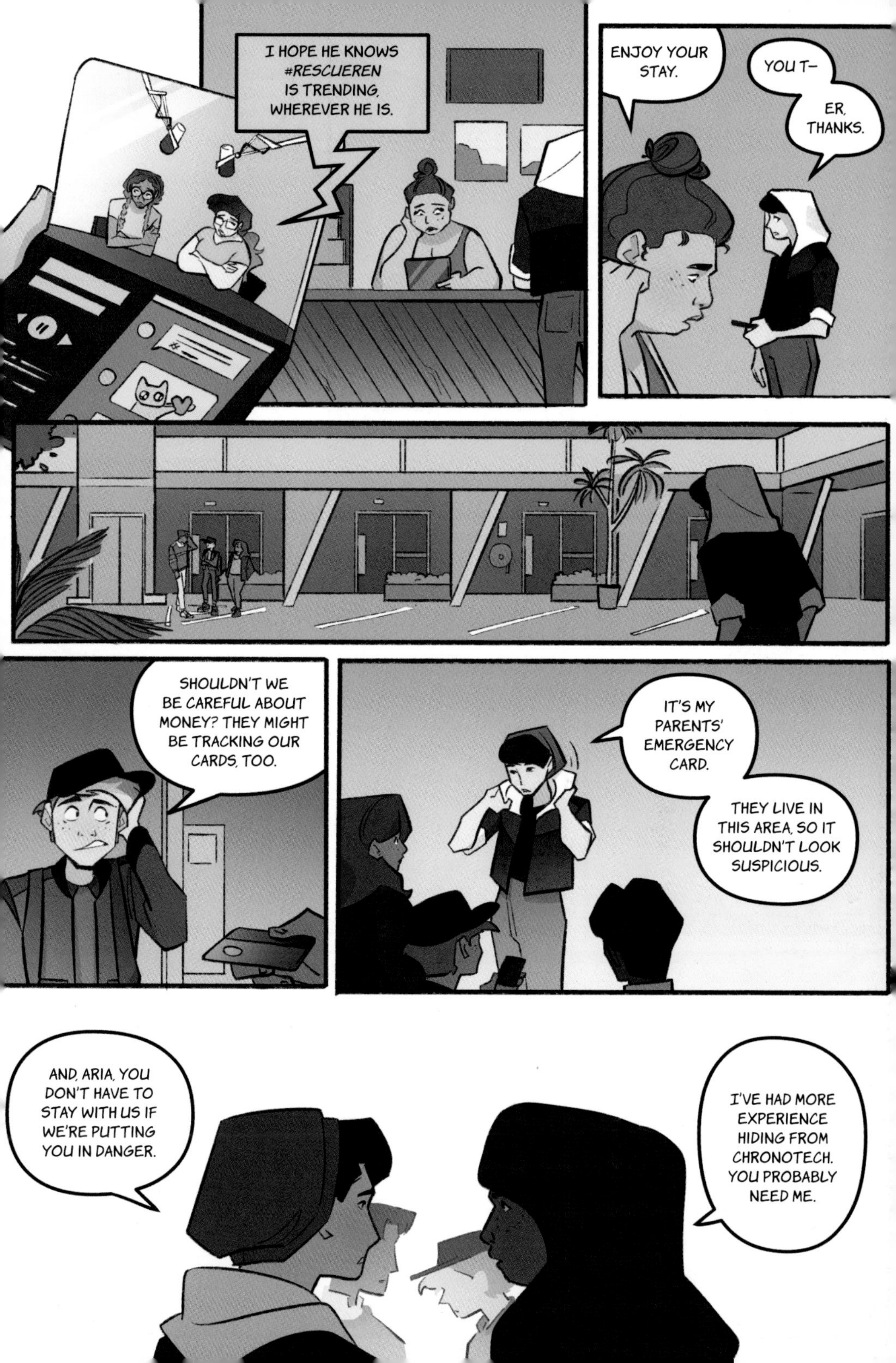
I HOPE HE KNOWS #RESCUEREN IS TRENDING, WHEREVER HE IS.
ENJOY YOUR STAY.
YOU T—
ER, THANKS.
SHOULDN'T WE BE CAREFUL ABOUT MONEY? THEY MIGHT BE TRACKING OUR CARDS, TOO.
IT'S MY PARENTS' EMERGENCY CARD.
THEY LIVE IN THIS AREA, SO IT SHOULDN'T LOOK SUSPICIOUS.
AND, ARIA, YOU DON'T HAVE TO STAY WITH US IF WE'RE PUTTING YOU IN DANGER.
I'VE HAD MORE EXPERIENCE HIDING FROM CHRONOTECH. YOU PROBABLY NEED ME.

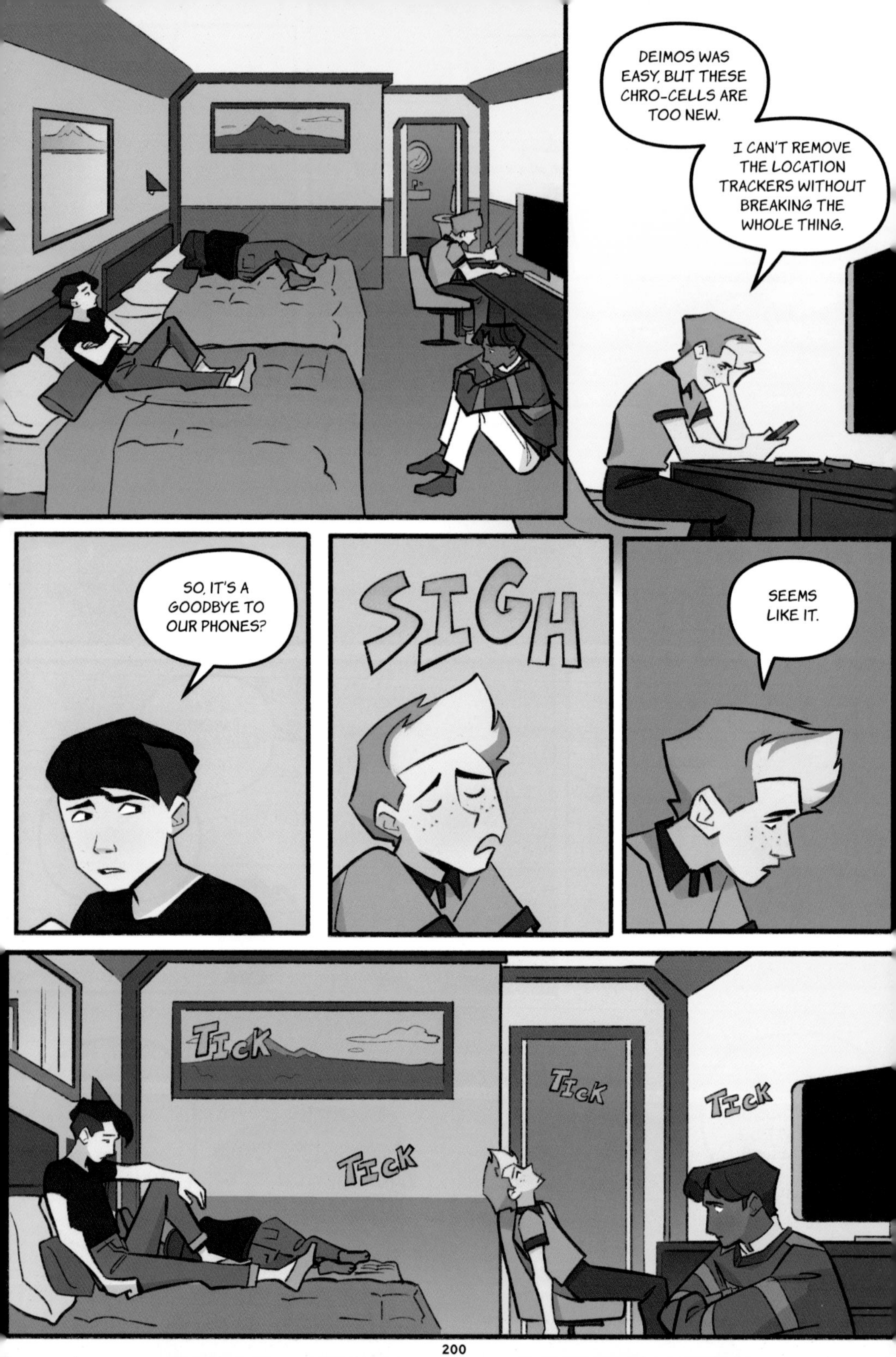

DEIMOS WAS EASY, BUT THESE CHRO-CELLS ARE TOO NEW.
I CAN'T REMOVE THE LOCATION TRACKERS WITHOUT BREAKING THE WHOLE THING.
SO, IT'S A GOODBYE TO OUR PHONES?
SIGH
SEEMS LIKE IT.
TICK
TICK
TICK
TICK

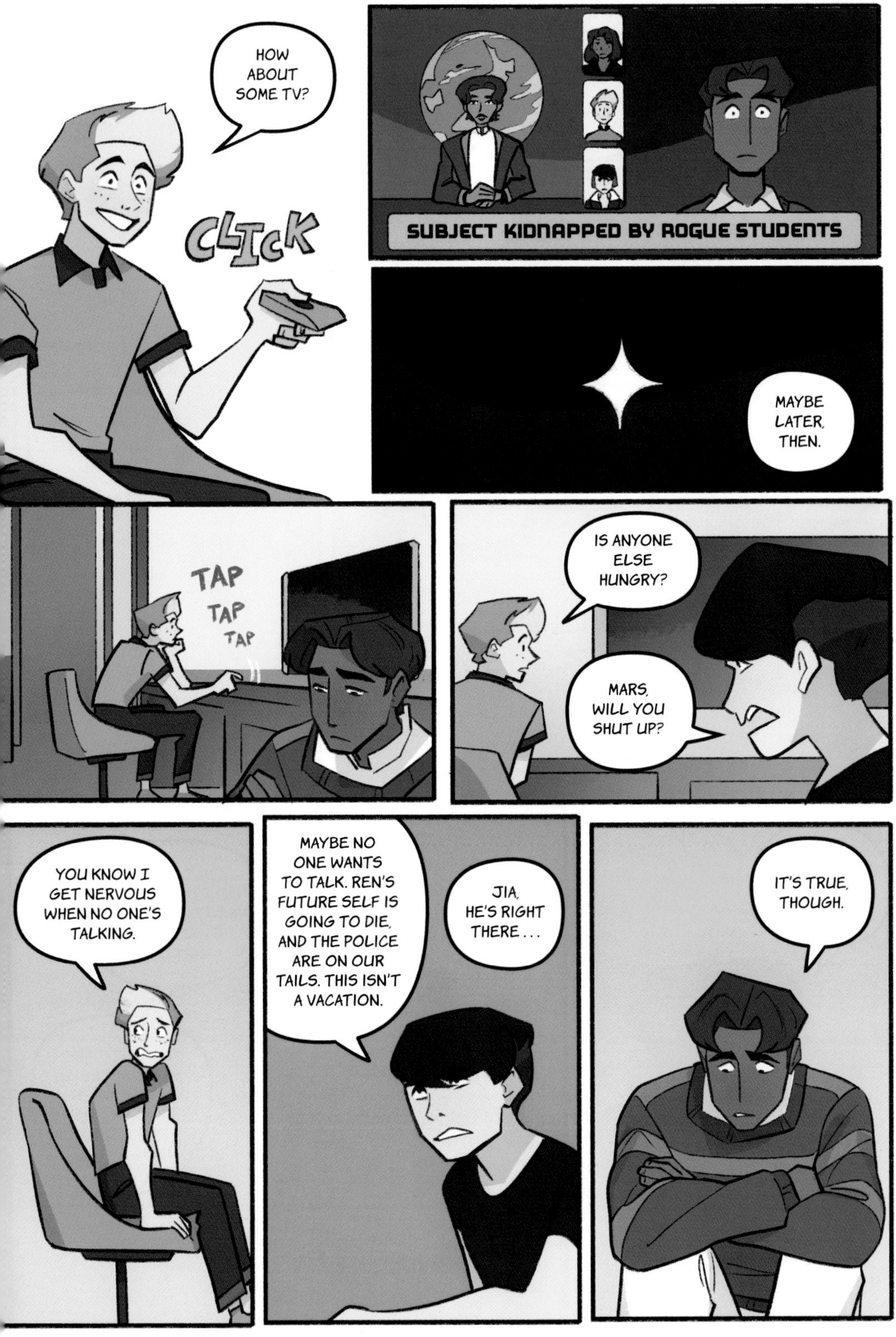
HOW ABOUT SOME TV?
CLICK
SUBJECT KIDNAPPED BY ROGUE STUDENTS
MAYBE LATER, THEN.
TAP TAP TAP
IS ANYONE ELSE HUNGRY?
MARS, WILL YOU SHUT UP?
YOU KNOW I GET NERVOUS WHEN NO ONE'S TALKING.
MAYBE NO ONE WANTS TO TALK. REN'S FUTURE SELF IS GOING TO DIE, AND THE POLICE ARE ON OUR TAILS. THIS ISN'T A VACATION.
JIA, HE'S RIGHT THERE . . .
IT'S TRUE, THOUGH.

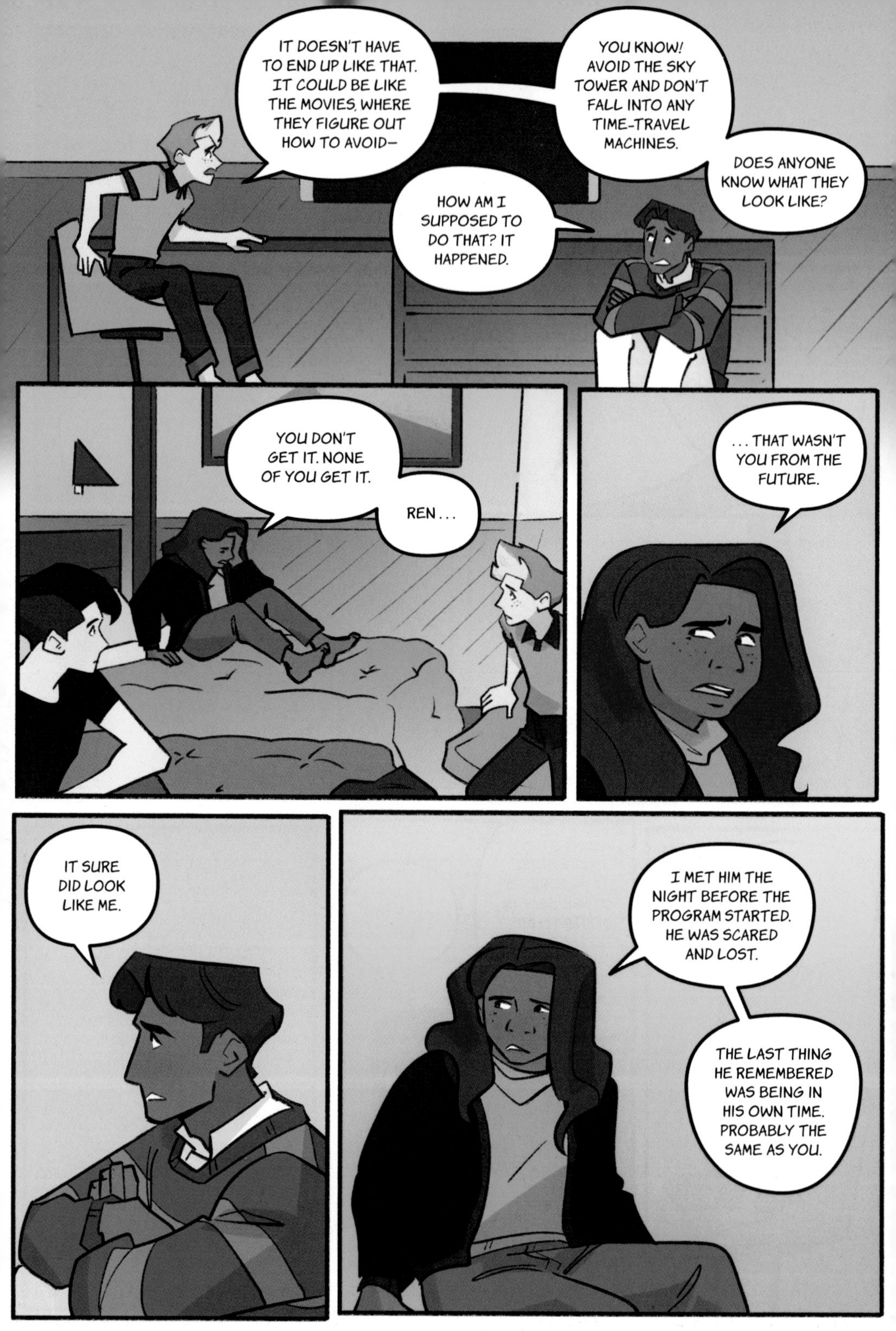
IT DOESN'T HAVE TO END UP LIKE THAT. IT COULD BE LIKE THE MOVIES, WHERE THEY FIGURE OUT HOW TO AVOID—
YOU KNOW! AVOID THE SKY TOWER AND DON'T FALL INTO ANY TIME-TRAVEL MACHINES.
DOES ANYONE KNOW WHAT THEY LOOK LIKE?
HOW AM I SUPPOSED TO DO THAT? IT HAPPENED.
YOU DON'T GET IT. NONE OF YOU GET IT.
REN . . .
. . . THAT WASN'T YOU FROM THE FUTURE.
IT SURE DID LOOK LIKE ME.
I MET HIM THE NIGHT BEFORE THE PROGRAM STARTED. HE WAS SCARED AND LOST.
THE LAST THING HE REMEMBERED WAS BEING IN HIS OWN TIME. PROBABLY THE SAME AS YOU.

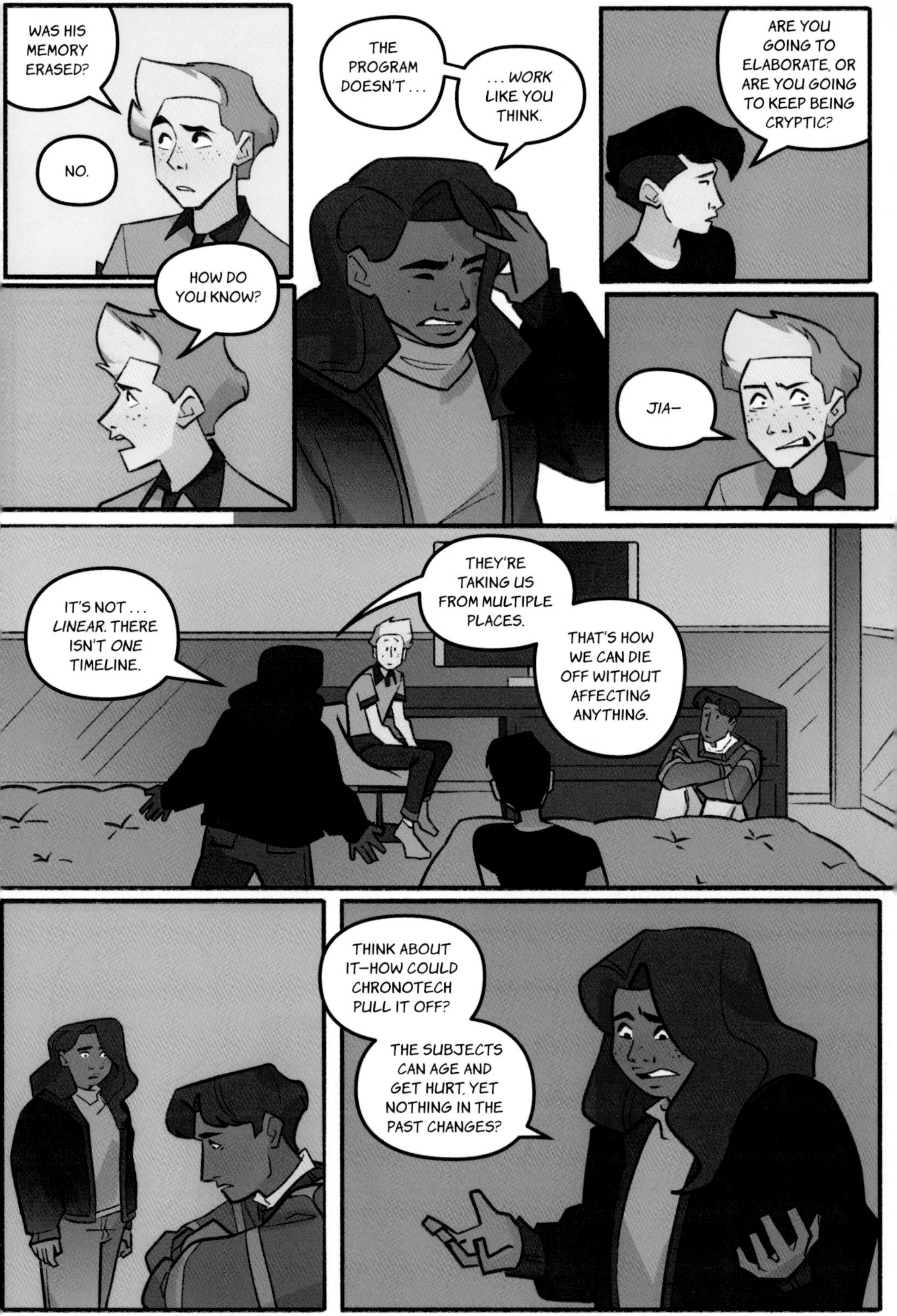
WAS HIS MEMORY ERASED?
NO.
THE PROGRAM DOESN'T . . .
. . . WORK LIKE YOU THINK.
ARE YOU GOING TO ELABORATE, OR ARE YOU GOING TO KEEP BEING CRYPTIC?
HOW DO YOU KNOW?
JIA—
IT'S NOT . . . LINEAR. THERE ISN'T ONE TIMELINE.
THEY'RE TAKING US FROM MULTIPLE PLACES.
THAT'S HOW WE CAN DIE OFF WITHOUT AFFECTING ANYTHING.
THINK ABOUT IT—HOW COULD CHRONOTECH PULL IT OFF?
THE SUBJECTS CAN AGE AND GET HURT, YET NOTHING IN THE PAST CHANGES?

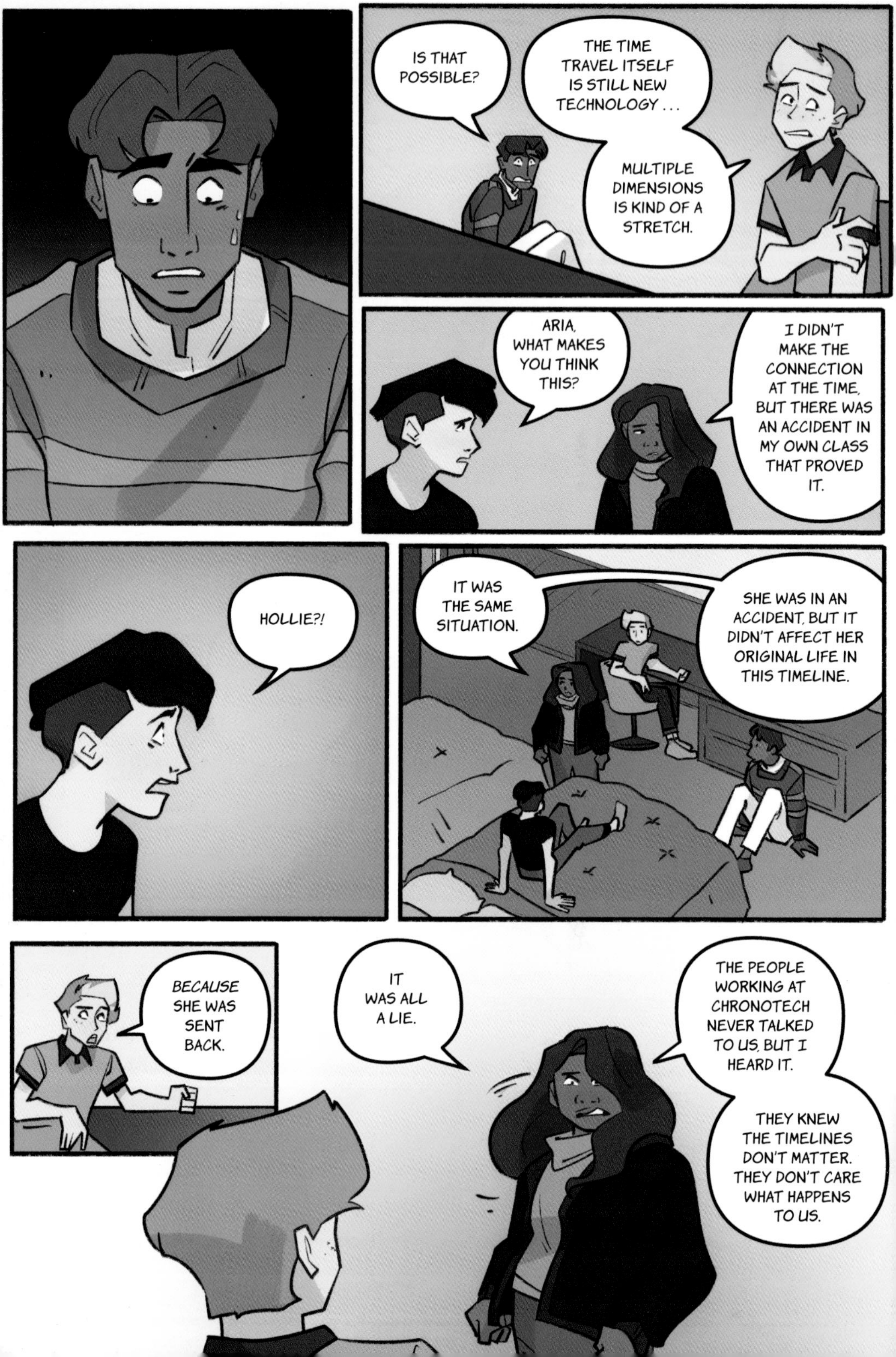
IS THAT POSSIBLE?
THE TIME TRAVEL ITSELF IS STILL NEW TECHNOLOGY . . .
MULTIPLE DIMENSIONS IS KIND OF A STRETCH.
ARIA, WHAT MAKES YOU THINK THIS?
I DIDN'T MAKE THE CONNECTION AT THE TIME, BUT THERE WAS AN ACCIDENT IN MY OWN CLASS THAT PROVED IT.
HOLLIE?!
IT WAS THE SAME SITUATION.
SHE WAS IN AN ACCIDENT, BUT IT DIDN'T AFFECT HER ORIGINAL LIFE IN THIS TIMELINE.
BECAUSE SHE WAS SENT BACK.
IT WAS ALL A LIE.
THE PEOPLE WORKING AT CHRONOTECH NEVER TALKED TO US, BUT I HEARD IT.
THEY KNEW THE TIMELINES DON'T MATTER. THEY DON'T CARE WHAT HAPPENS TO US.

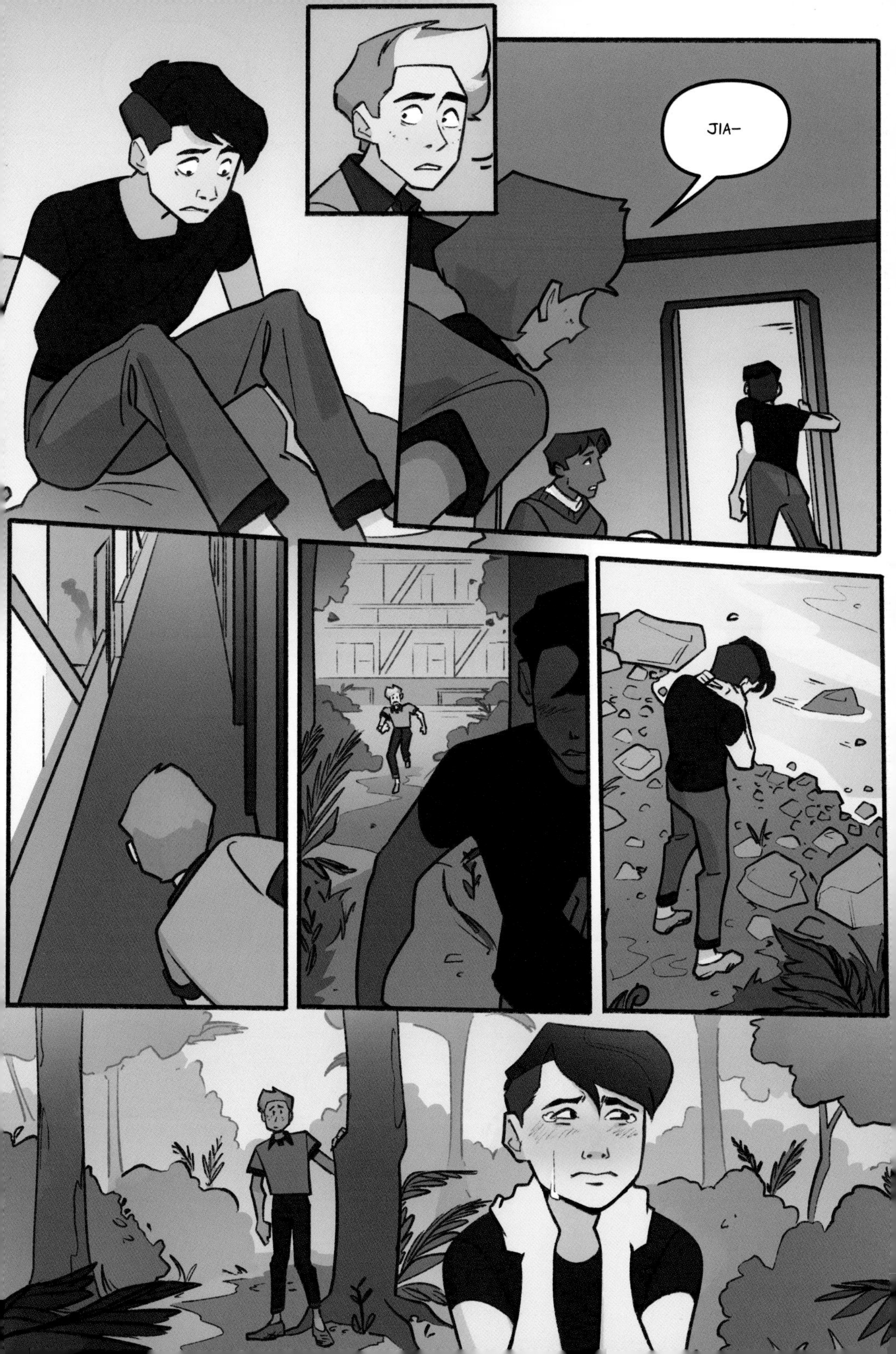
JIA–

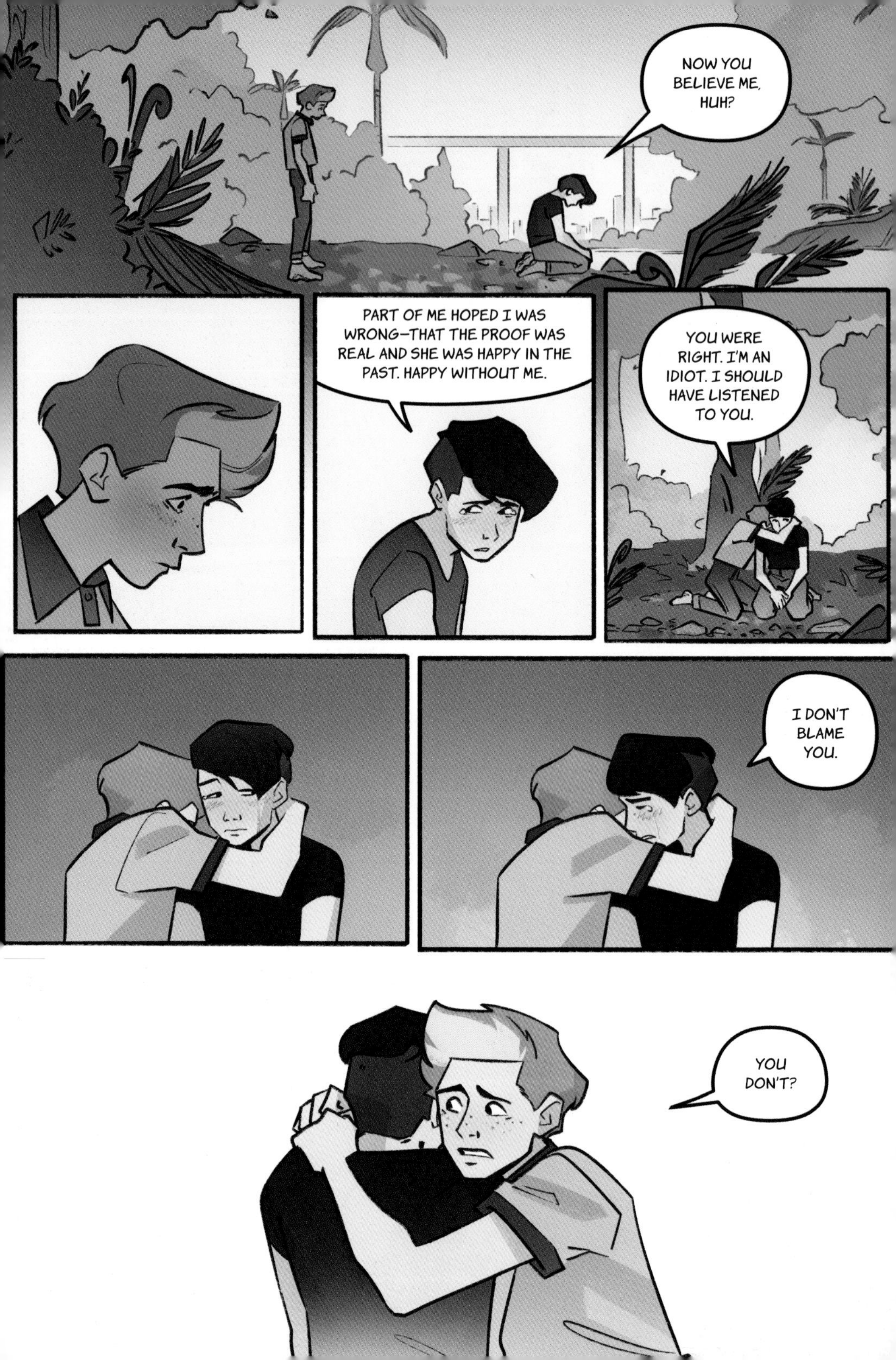
NOW YOU BELIEVE ME, HUH?
PART OF ME HOPED I WAS WRONG—THAT THE PROOF WAS REAL AND SHE WAS HAPPY IN THE PAST. HAPPY WITHOUT ME.
YOU WERE RIGHT. I'M AN IDIOT. I SHOULD HAVE LISTENED TO YOU.
I DON'T BLAME YOU.
YOU DON'T?

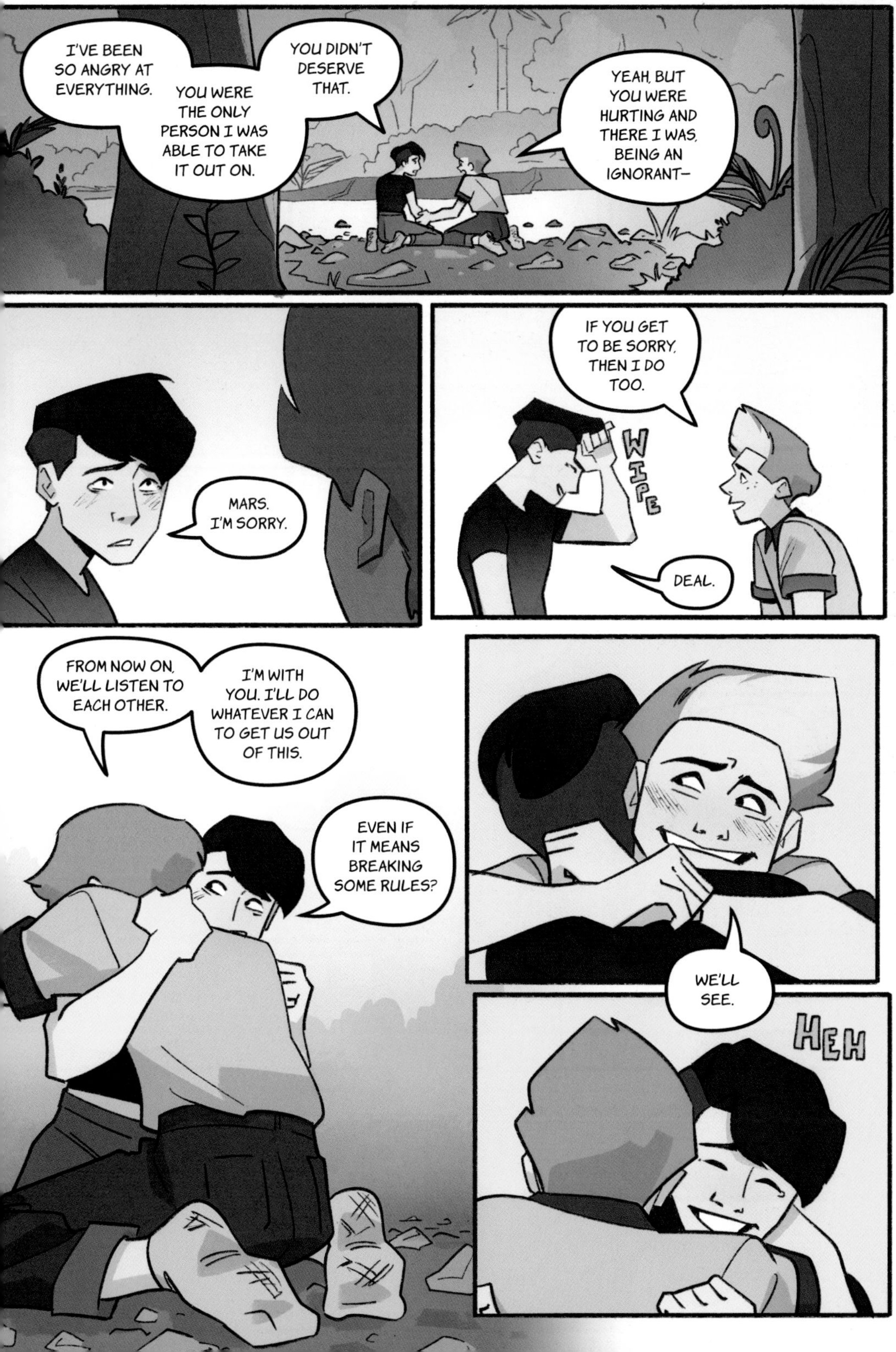
I'VE BEEN SO ANGRY AT EVERYTHING.
YOU WERE THE ONLY PERSON I WAS ABLE TO TAKE IT OUT ON.
YOU DIDN'T DESERVE THAT.
YEAH, BUT YOU WERE HURTING AND THERE I WAS, BEING AN IGNORANT—
MARS. I'M SORRY.
IF YOU GET TO BE SORRY, THEN I DO TOO.
WIPE
DEAL.
FROM NOW ON, WE'LL LISTEN TO EACH OTHER.
I'M WITH YOU. I'LL DO WHATEVER I CAN TO GET US OUT OF THIS.
EVEN IF IT MEANS BREAKING SOME RULES?
WE'LL SEE.
HEH

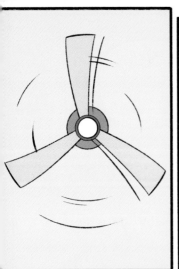

SO I'M NOT GOING TO DIE AFTER ALL . . .

DON'T GET TOO COMFORTABLE.

ALTERNATE DIMENSIONS. I CAN'T BELIEVE IT.

THEY BROUGHT TWO DIFFERENT VERSIONS OF ME HERE?

I GUESS I SHOULD BE RELIEVED THAT I'M NOT IN DANGER. BUT . . . IT'S SCARY THAT HE'S GONE.

YOU'RE VERY LUCKY, REN. IT STILL COULD HAVE BEEN YOU.

HOW DID YOU CONVINCE HIM TO HELP YOU EXPOSE CHRONOTECH?

IT WAS HIM THAT CONVINCED ME.

I'VE BEEN SO CAUGHT UP IN TRYING TO LIE LOW AND SURVIVE THAT I DIDN'T STOP TO CONSIDER THAT CHRONOTECH WENT UNPUNISHED FOR LYING.

REN HELPED ME SEE WE COULD DO SOMETHING. HE WAS BRAVE.

THAT'S AN ALTERNATE REALITY, ALL RIGHT.

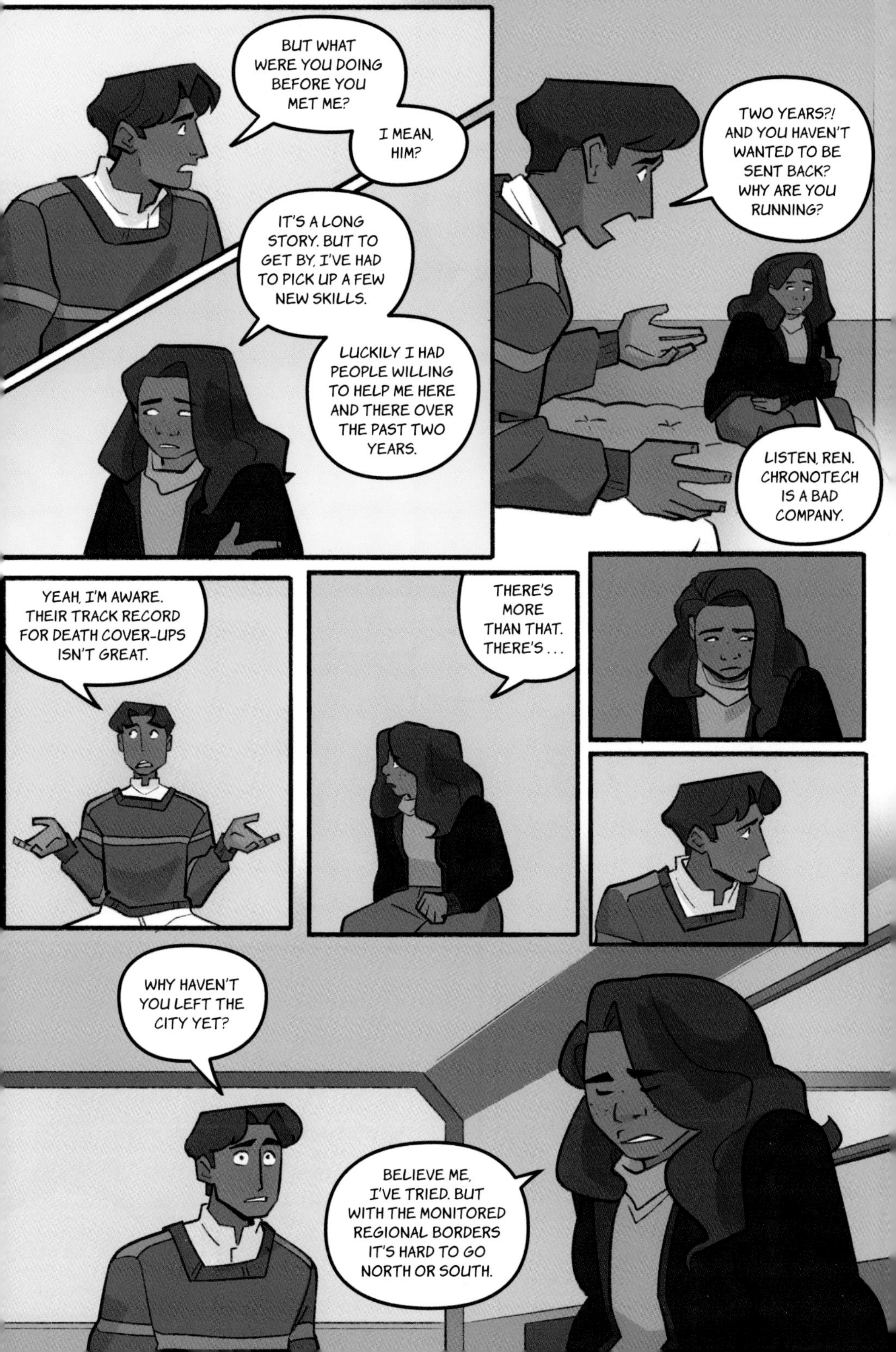
BUT WHAT WERE YOU DOING BEFORE YOU MET ME?
I MEAN, HIM?
IT'S A LONG STORY. BUT TO GET BY, I'VE HAD TO PICK UP A FEW NEW SKILLS.
LUCKILY I HAD PEOPLE WILLING TO HELP ME HERE AND THERE OVER THE PAST TWO YEARS.
TWO YEARS?! AND YOU HAVEN'T WANTED TO BE SENT BACK? WHY ARE YOU RUNNING?
LISTEN, REN. CHRONOTECH IS A BAD COMPANY.
YEAH, I'M AWARE. THEIR TRACK RECORD FOR DEATH COVER-UPS ISN'T GREAT.
THERE'S MORE THAN THAT. THERE'S . . .
WHY HAVEN'T YOU LEFT THE CITY YET?
BELIEVE ME, I'VE TRIED. BUT WITH THE MONITORED REGIONAL BORDERS IT'S HARD TO GO NORTH OR SOUTH.

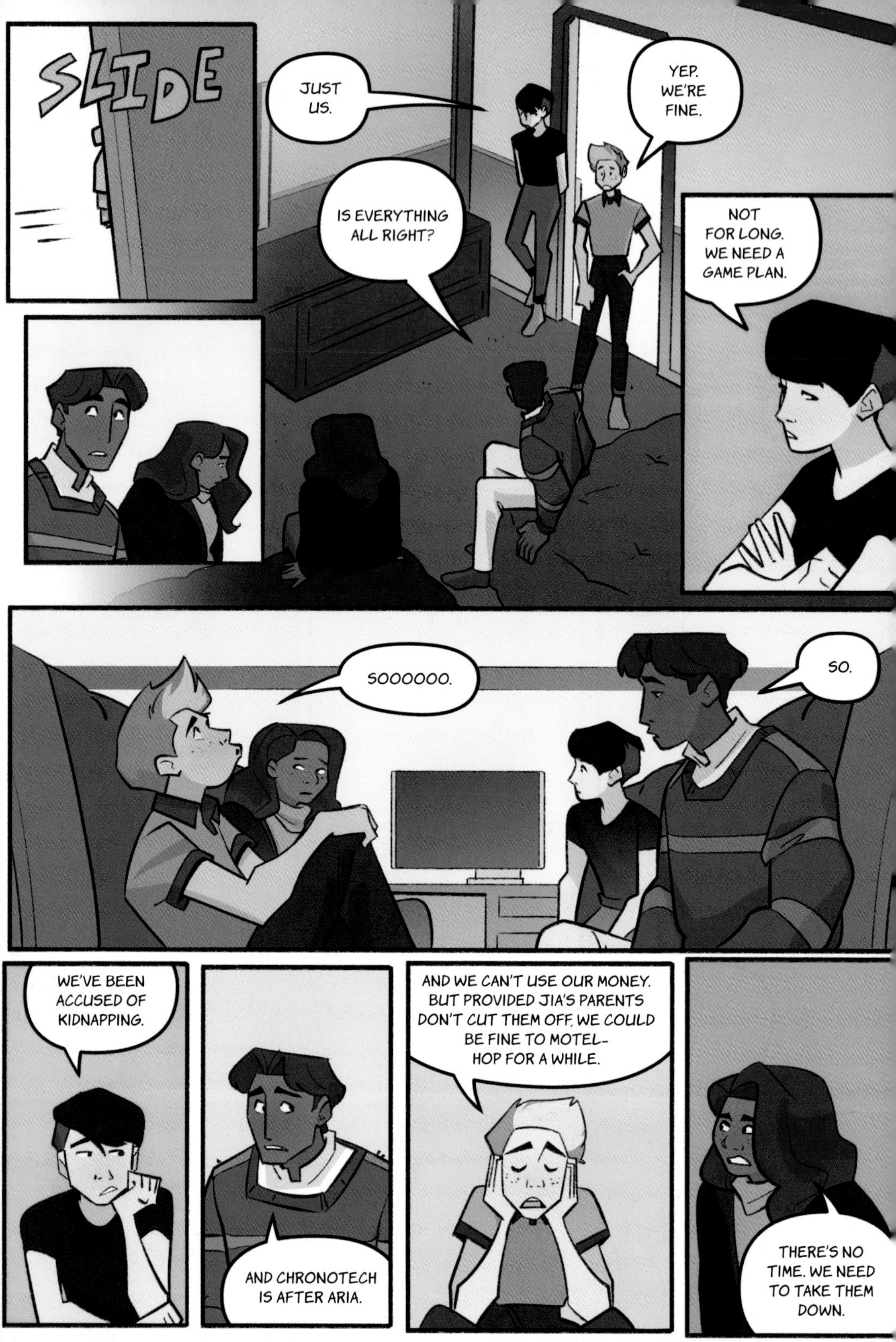
SLIDE
JUST US.
YEP. WE'RE FINE.
IS EVERYTHING ALL RIGHT?
NOT FOR LONG. WE NEED A GAME PLAN.
SOOOOOO.
SO.
WE'VE BEEN ACCUSED OF KIDNAPPING.
AND CHRONOTECH IS AFTER ARIA.
AND WE CAN'T USE OUR MONEY. BUT PROVIDED JIA'S PARENTS DON'T CUT THEM OFF, WE COULD BE FINE TO MOTEL-HOP FOR A WHILE.
THERE'S NO TIME. WE NEED TO TAKE THEM DOWN.

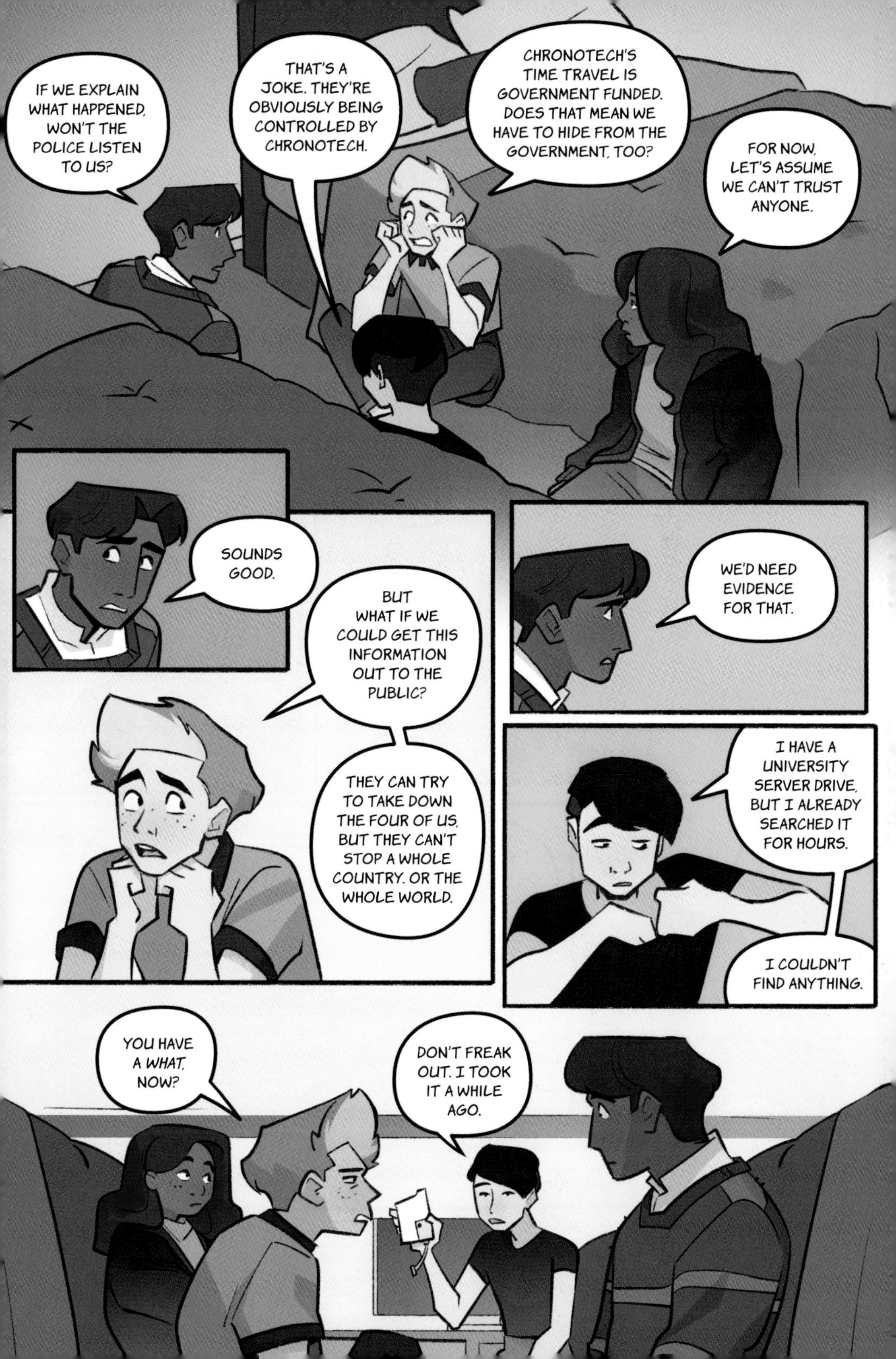
IF WE EXPLAIN WHAT HAPPENED, WON'T THE POLICE LISTEN TO US?
THAT'S A JOKE. THEY'RE OBVIOUSLY BEING CONTROLLED BY CHRONOTECH.
CHRONOTECH'S TIME TRAVEL IS GOVERNMENT FUNDED. DOES THAT MEAN WE HAVE TO HIDE FROM THE GOVERNMENT, TOO?
FOR NOW, LET'S ASSUME WE CAN'T TRUST ANYONE.
SOUNDS GOOD.
BUT WHAT IF WE COULD GET THIS INFORMATION OUT TO THE PUBLIC?
THEY CAN TRY TO TAKE DOWN THE FOUR OF US, BUT THEY CAN'T STOP A WHOLE COUNTRY. OR THE WHOLE WORLD.
WE'D NEED EVIDENCE FOR THAT.
I HAVE A UNIVERSITY SERVER DRIVE, BUT I ALREADY SEARCHED IT FOR HOURS.
I COULDN'T FIND ANYTHING.
YOU HAVE A *WHAT*, NOW?
DON'T FREAK OUT. I TOOK IT A WHILE AGO.

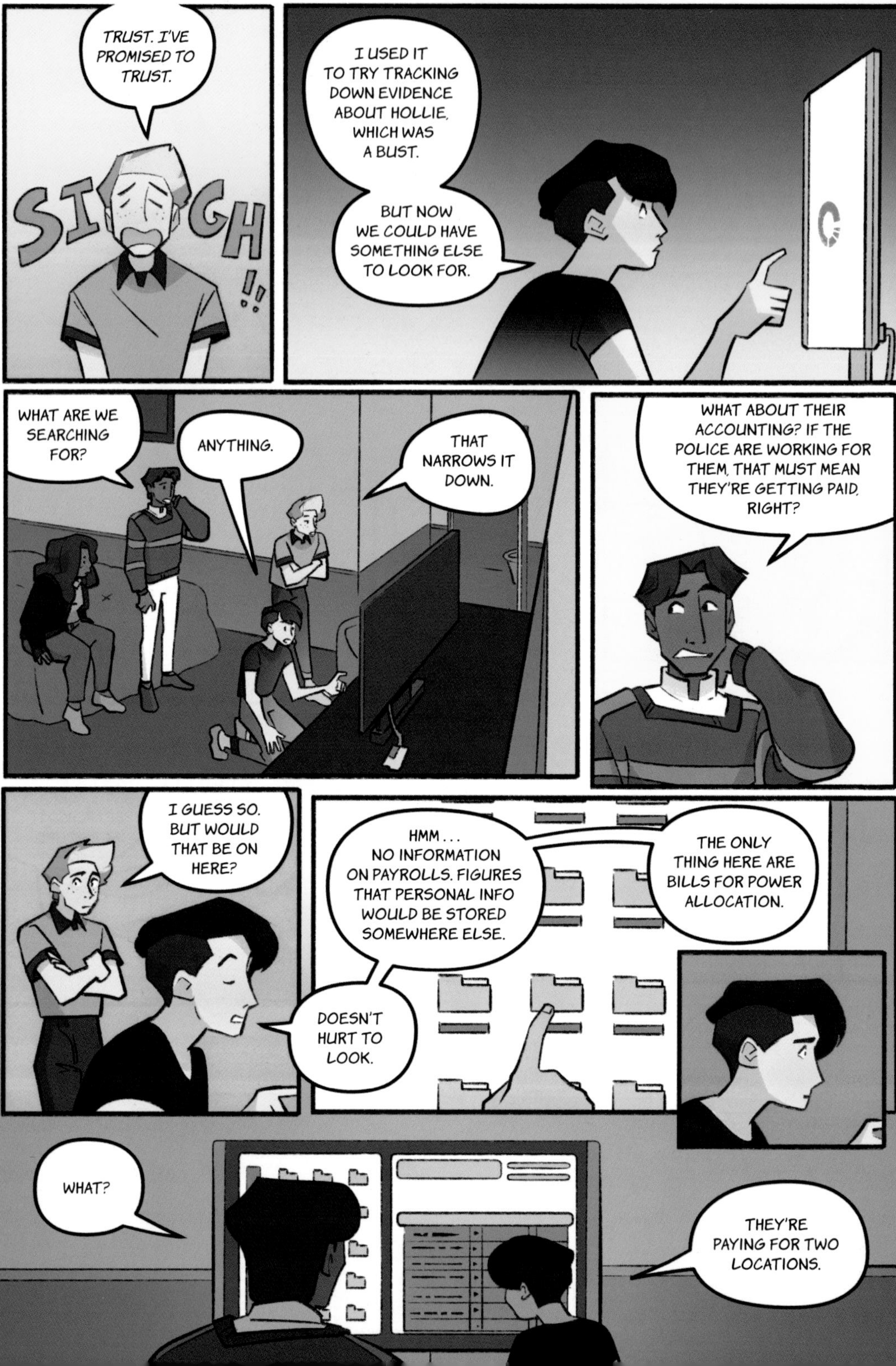
TRUST. I'VE PROMISED TO TRUST.
SIGH!!
I USED IT TO TRY TRACKING DOWN EVIDENCE ABOUT HOLLIE, WHICH WAS A BUST.
BUT NOW WE COULD HAVE SOMETHING ELSE TO LOOK FOR.
WHAT ARE WE SEARCHING FOR?
ANYTHING.
THAT NARROWS IT DOWN.
WHAT ABOUT THEIR ACCOUNTING? IF THE POLICE ARE WORKING FOR THEM, THAT MUST MEAN THEY'RE GETTING PAID, RIGHT?
I GUESS SO. BUT WOULD THAT BE ON HERE?
DOESN'T HURT TO LOOK.
HMM . . . NO INFORMATION ON PAYROLLS. FIGURES THAT PERSONAL INFO WOULD BE STORED SOMEWHERE ELSE.
THE ONLY THING HERE ARE BILLS FOR POWER ALLOCATION.
WHAT?
THEY'RE PAYING FOR TWO LOCATIONS.

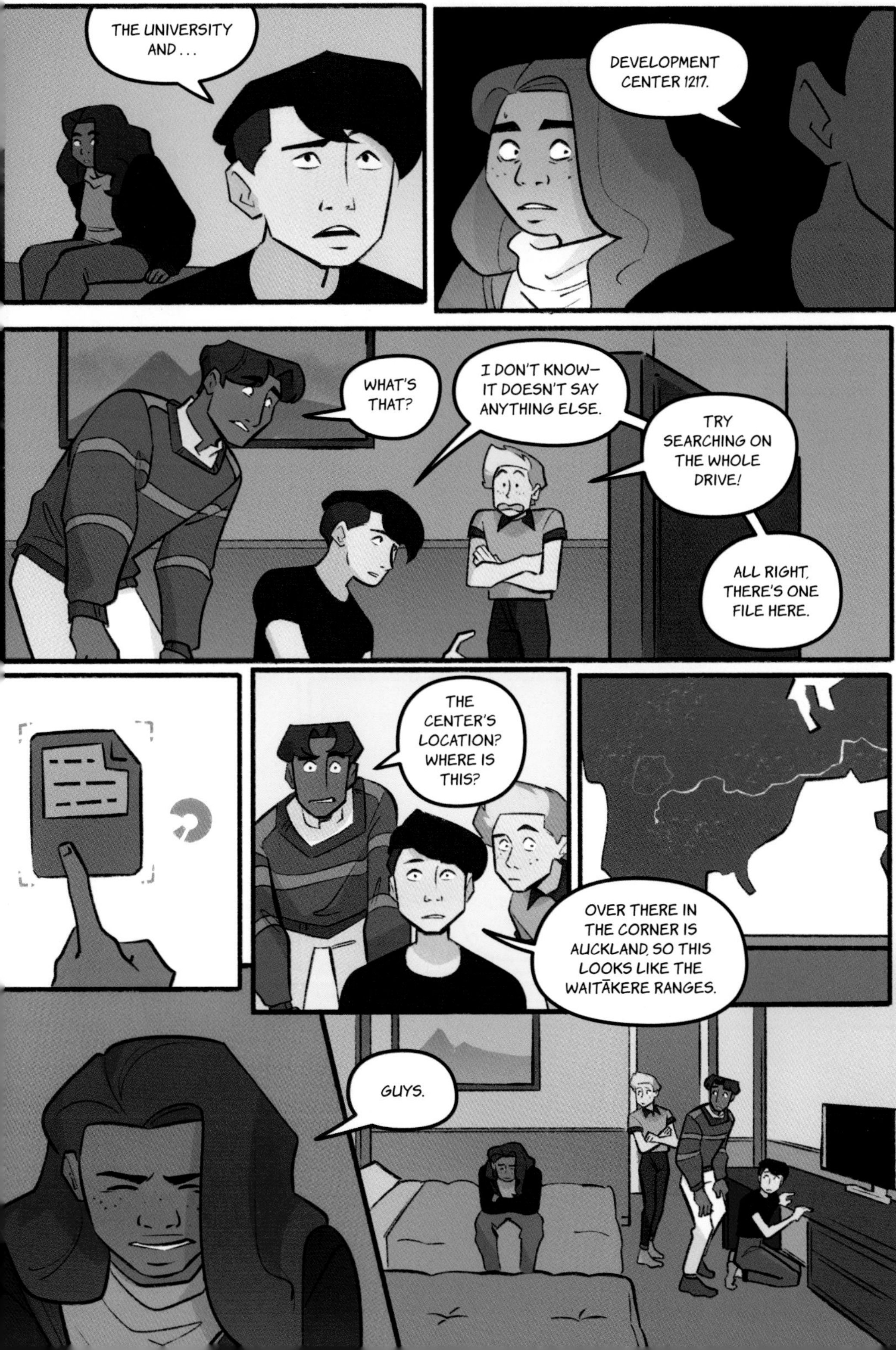
THE UNIVERSITY AND . . .
DEVELOPMENT CENTER 1217.
WHAT'S THAT?
I DON'T KNOW— IT DOESN'T SAY ANYTHING ELSE.
TRY SEARCHING ON THE WHOLE DRIVE!
ALL RIGHT, THERE'S ONE FILE HERE.
THE CENTER'S LOCATION? WHERE IS THIS?
OVER THERE IN THE CORNER IS AUCKLAND, SO THIS LOOKS LIKE THE WAITĀKERE RANGES.
GUYS.

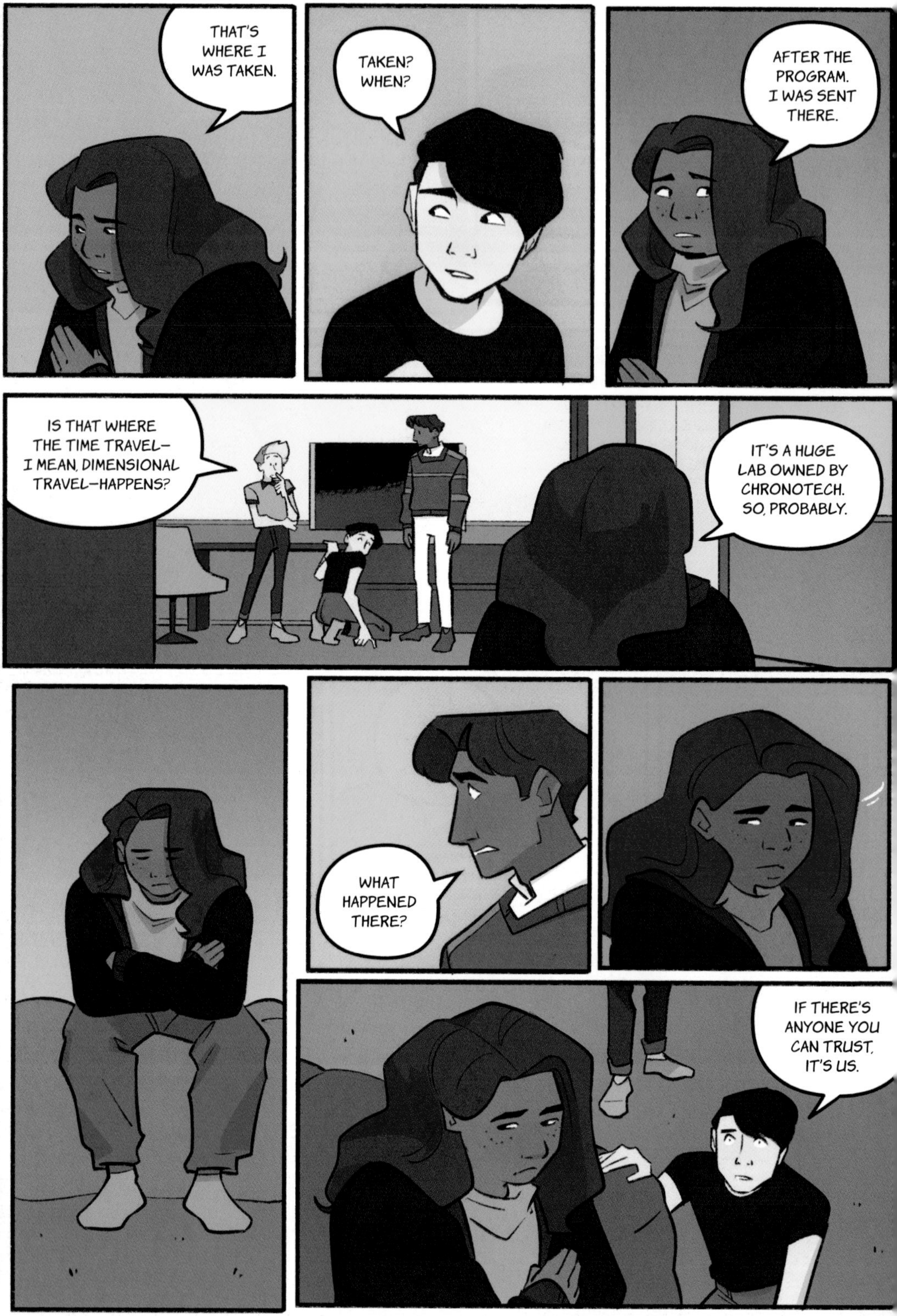
THAT'S WHERE I WAS TAKEN.
TAKEN? WHEN?
AFTER THE PROGRAM. I WAS SENT THERE.
IS THAT WHERE THE TIME TRAVEL— I MEAN, DIMENSIONAL TRAVEL—HAPPENS?
IT'S A HUGE LAB OWNED BY CHRONOTECH. SO, PROBABLY.
WHAT HAPPENED THERE?
IF THERE'S ANYONE YOU CAN TRUST, IT'S US.

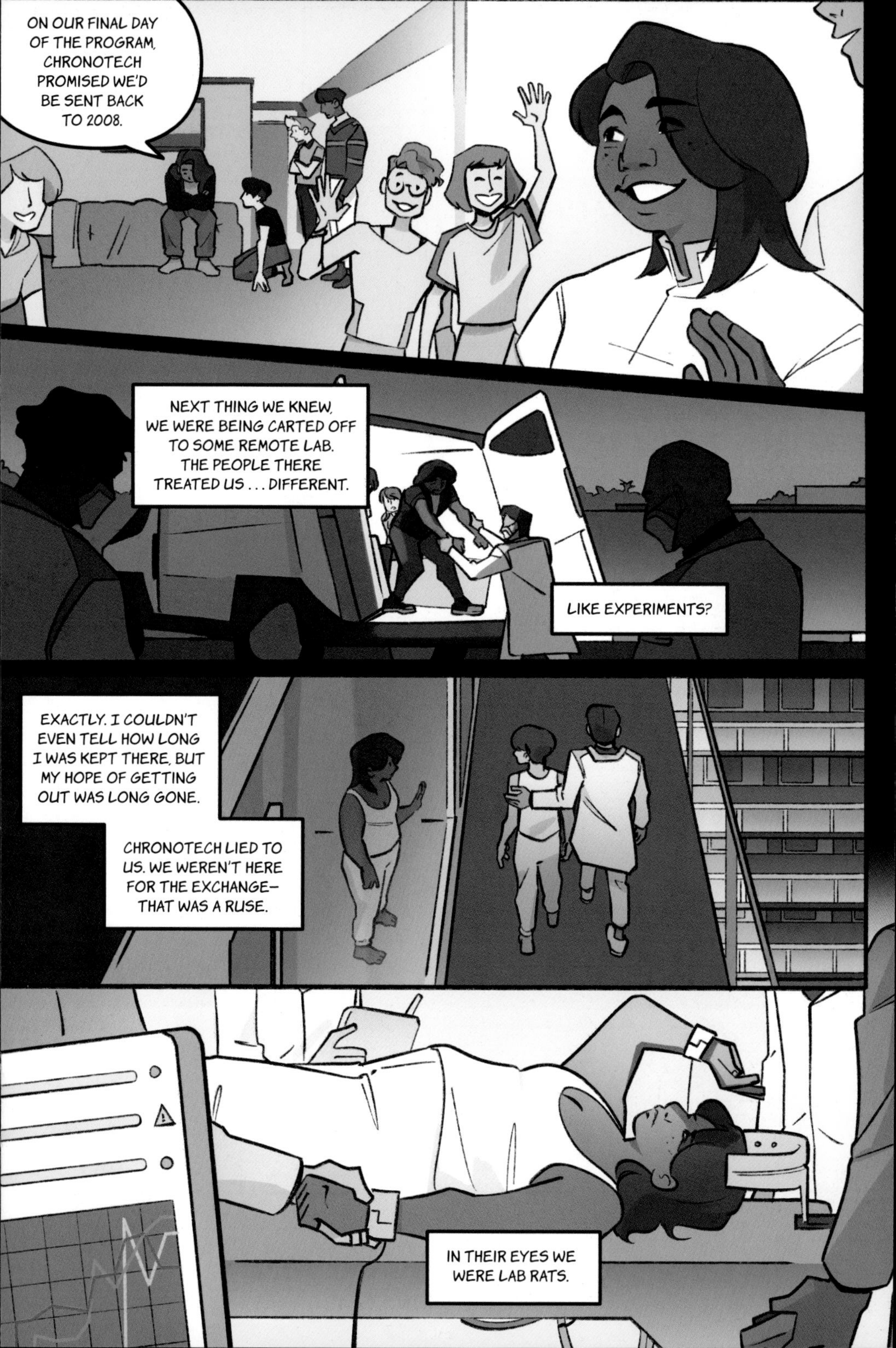
ON OUR FINAL DAY OF THE PROGRAM, CHRONOTECH PROMISED WE'D BE SENT BACK TO 2008.
NEXT THING WE KNEW, WE WERE BEING CARTED OFF TO SOME REMOTE LAB. THE PEOPLE THERE TREATED US . . . DIFFERENT.
LIKE EXPERIMENTS?
EXACTLY. I COULDN'T EVEN TELL HOW LONG I WAS KEPT THERE, BUT MY HOPE OF GETTING OUT WAS LONG GONE.
CHRONOTECH LIED TO US. WE WEREN'T HERE FOR THE EXCHANGE—THAT WAS A RUSE.
IN THEIR EYES WE WERE LAB RATS.

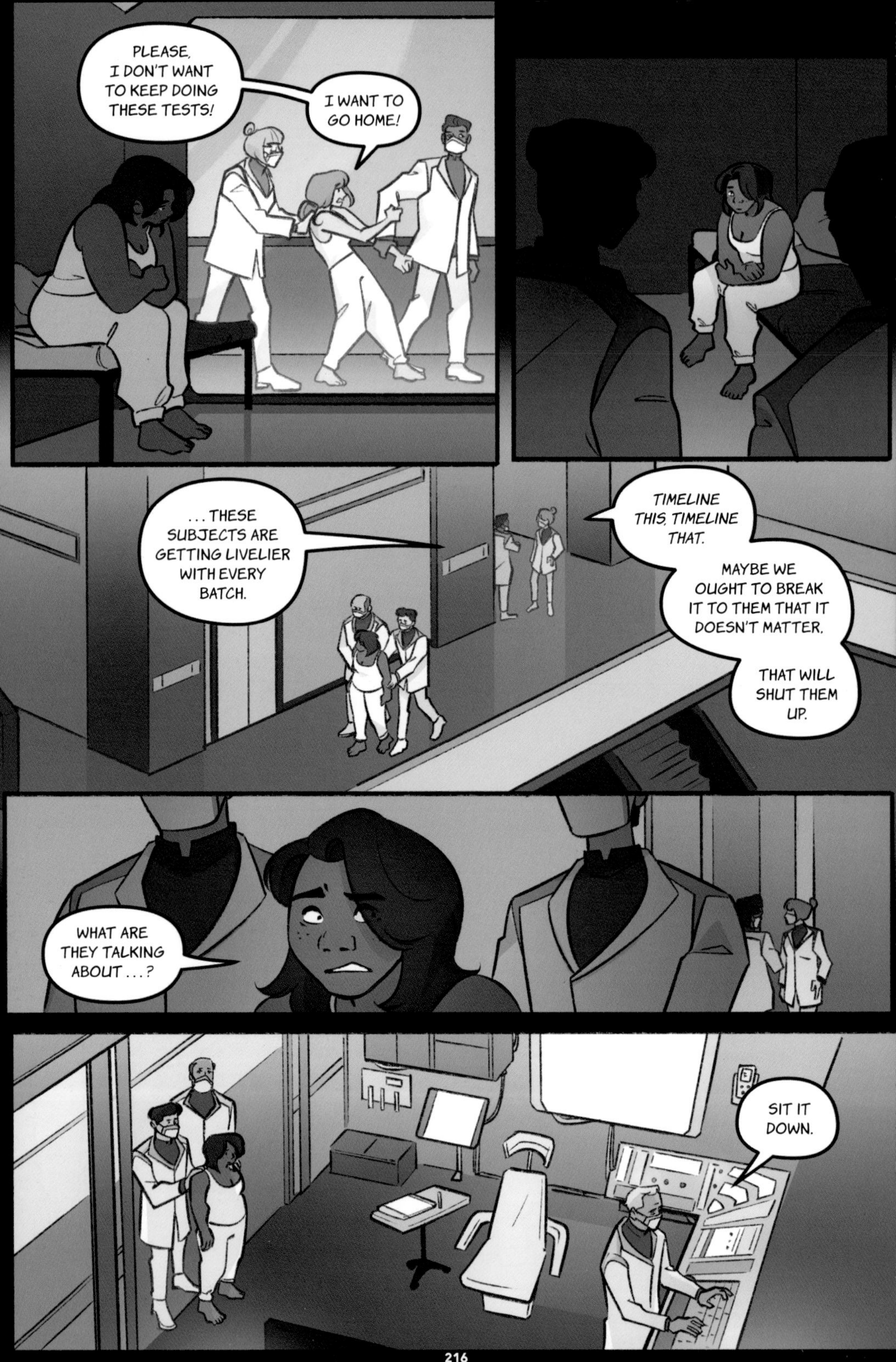
PLEASE, I DON'T WANT TO KEEP DOING THESE TESTS!
I WANT TO GO HOME!
. . . THESE SUBJECTS ARE GETTING LIVELIER WITH EVERY BATCH.
TIMELINE THIS, TIMELINE THAT.
MAYBE WE OUGHT TO BREAK IT TO THEM THAT IT DOESN'T MATTER.
THAT WILL SHUT THEM UP.
WHAT ARE THEY TALKING ABOUT . . . ?
SIT IT DOWN.

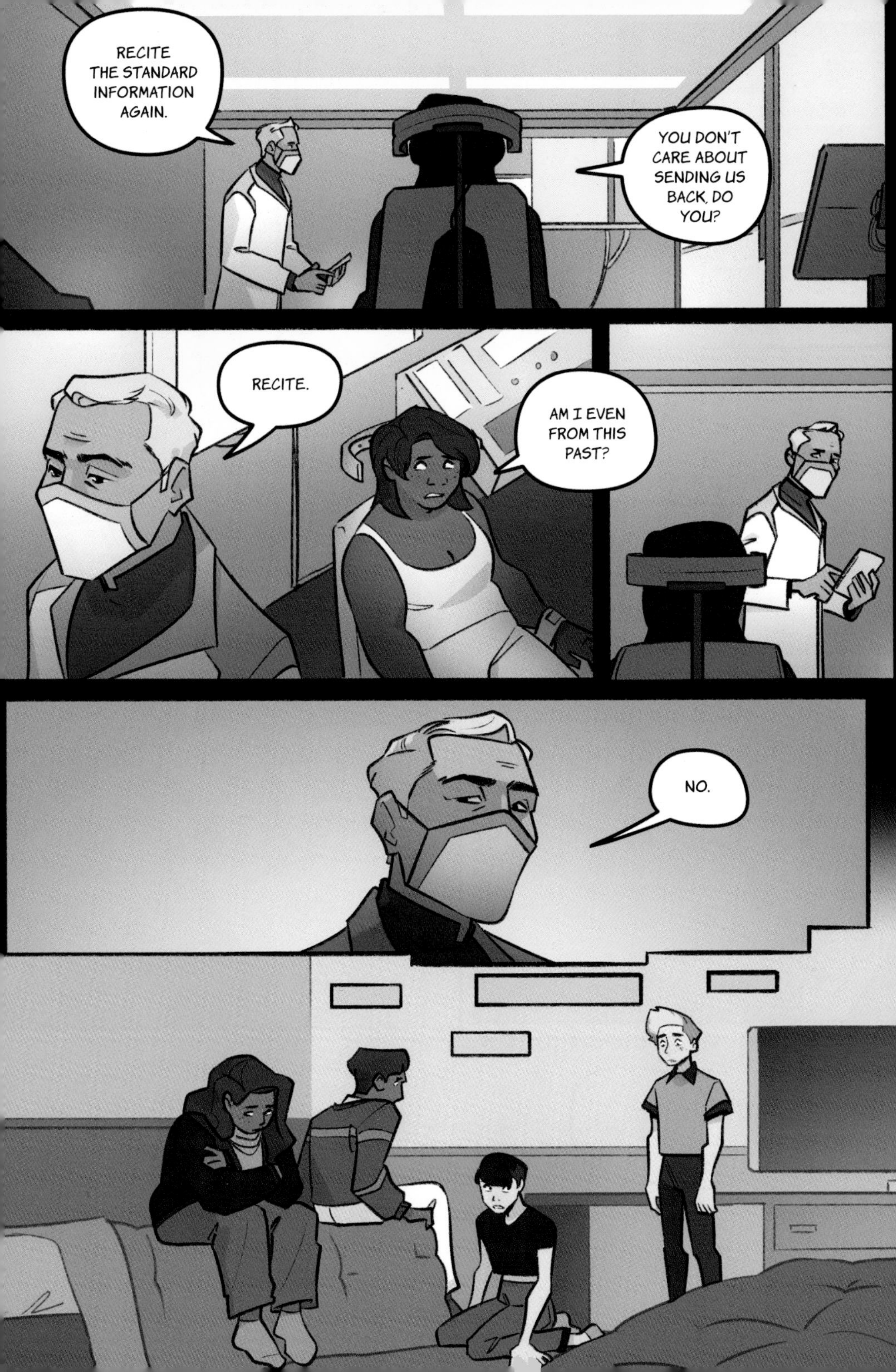
RECITE THE STANDARD INFORMATION AGAIN.
YOU DON'T CARE ABOUT SENDING US BACK, DO YOU?
RECITE.
AM I EVEN FROM THIS PAST?
NO.

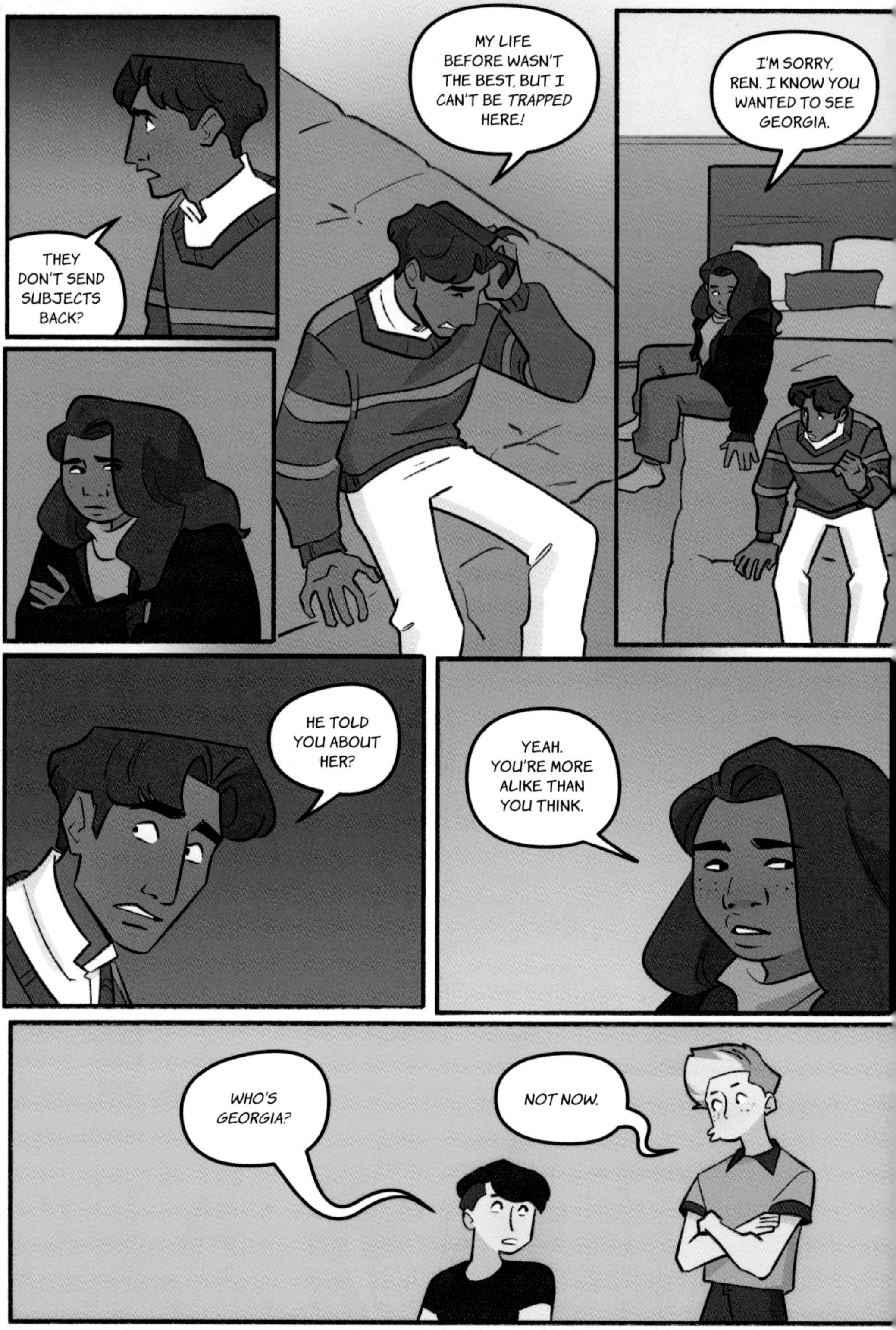

THEY DON'T SEND SUBJECTS BACK?
MY LIFE BEFORE WASN'T THE BEST, BUT I CAN'T BE *TRAPPED* HERE!
I'M SORRY, REN. I KNOW YOU WANTED TO SEE GEORGIA.
HE TOLD YOU ABOUT HER?
YEAH. YOU'RE MORE ALIKE THAN YOU THINK.
WHO'S GEORGIA?
NOT NOW.

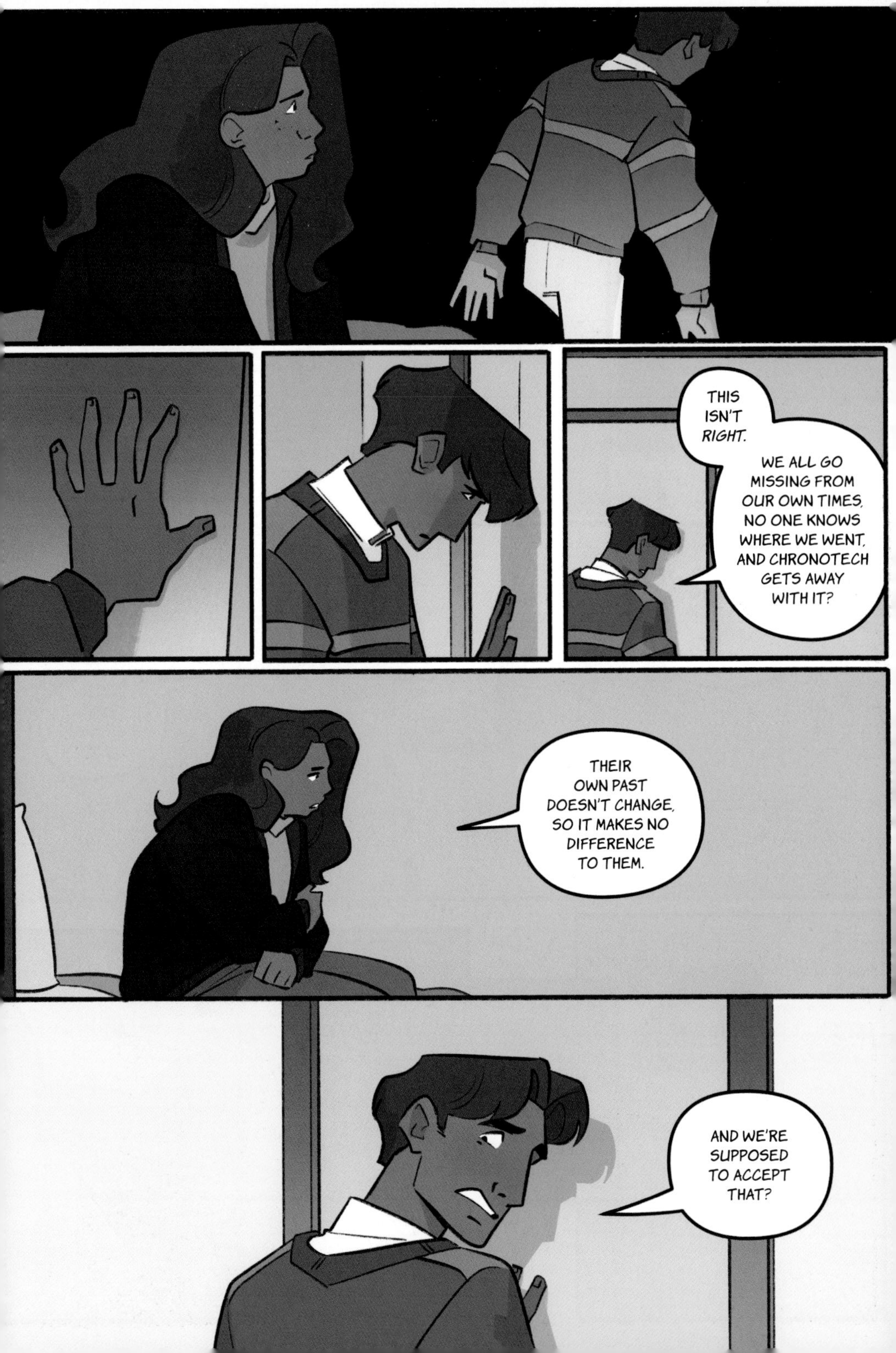
THIS ISN'T *RIGHT.*
WE ALL GO MISSING FROM OUR OWN TIMES, NO ONE KNOWS WHERE WE WENT, AND CHRONOTECH GETS AWAY WITH IT?
THEIR OWN PAST DOESN'T CHANGE, SO IT MAKES NO DIFFERENCE TO THEM.
AND WE'RE SUPPOSED TO ACCEPT THAT?

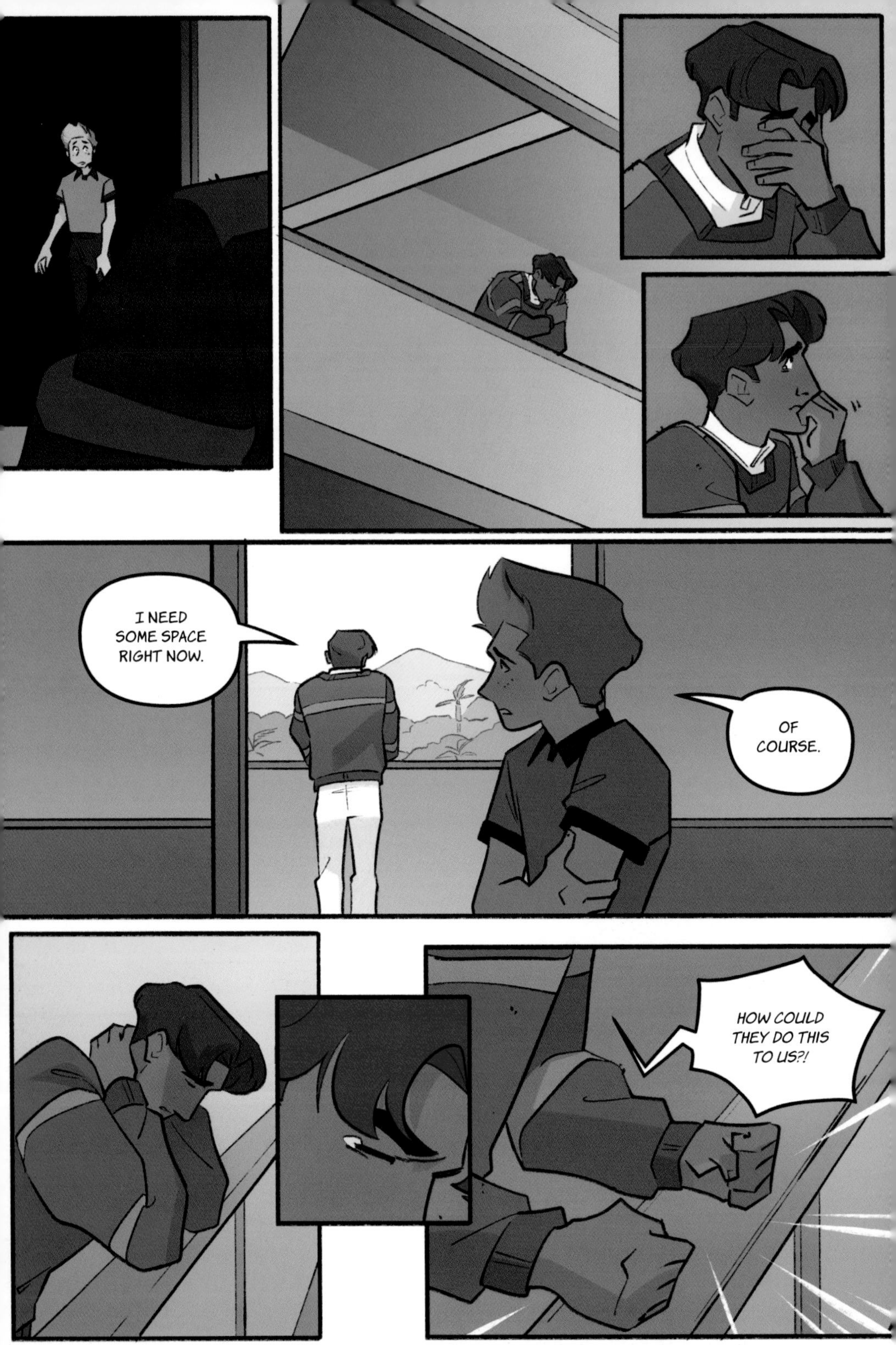
I NEED SOME SPACE RIGHT NOW.
OF COURSE.
HOW COULD THEY DO THIS TO US?!

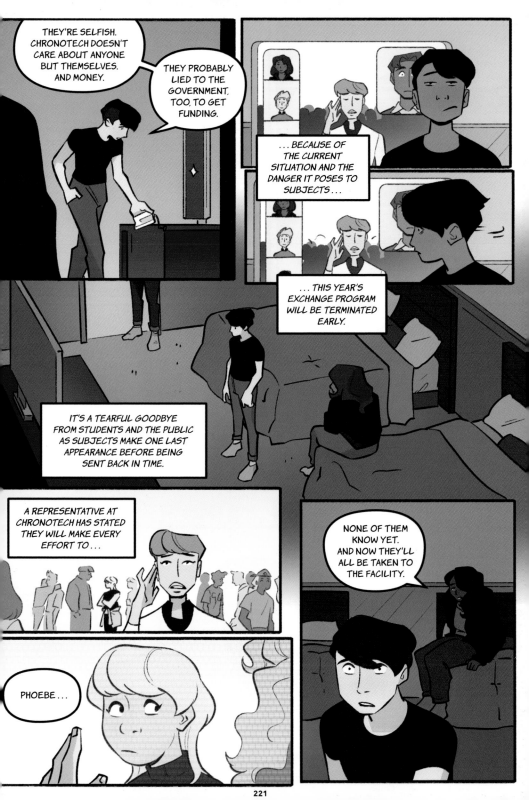

THEY'RE SELFISH. CHRONOTECH DOESN'T CARE ABOUT ANYONE BUT THEMSELVES. AND MONEY.

THEY PROBABLY LIED TO THE GOVERNMENT, TOO, TO GET FUNDING.

...BECAUSE OF THE CURRENT SITUATION AND THE DANGER IT POSES TO SUBJECTS...

...THIS YEAR'S EXCHANGE PROGRAM WILL BE TERMINATED EARLY.

IT'S A TEARFUL GOODBYE FROM STUDENTS AND THE PUBLIC AS SUBJECTS MAKE ONE LAST APPEARANCE BEFORE BEING SENT BACK IN TIME.

A REPRESENTATIVE AT CHRONOTECH HAS STATED THEY WILL MAKE EVERY EFFORT TO...

NONE OF THEM KNOW YET. AND NOW THEY'LL ALL BE TAKEN TO THE FACILITY.

PHOEBE...

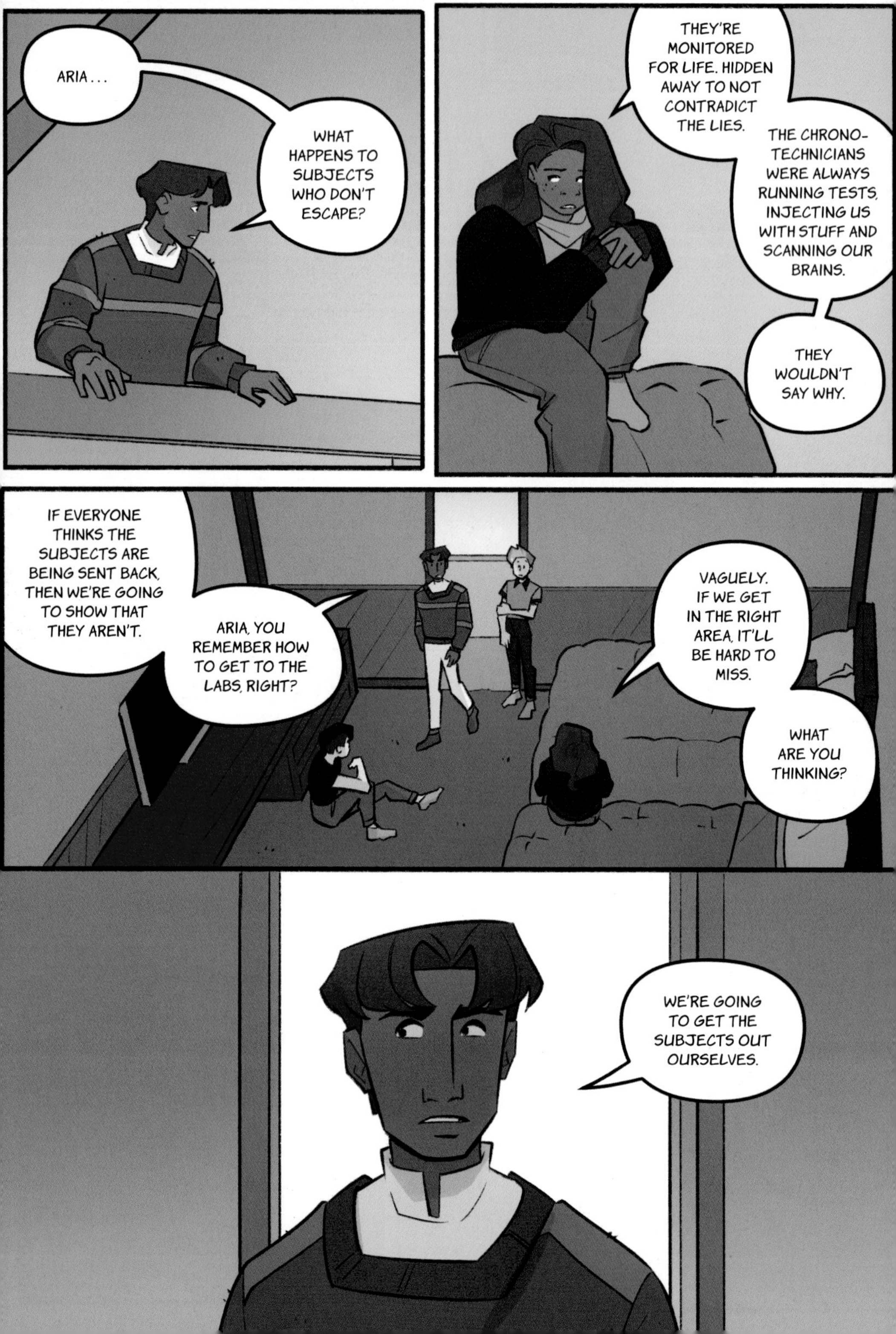
ARIA . . .
WHAT HAPPENS TO SUBJECTS WHO DON'T ESCAPE?
THEY'RE MONITORED FOR LIFE. HIDDEN AWAY TO NOT CONTRADICT THE LIES.
THE CHRONO-TECHNICIANS WERE ALWAYS RUNNING TESTS, INJECTING US WITH STUFF AND SCANNING OUR BRAINS.
THEY WOULDN'T SAY WHY.
IF EVERYONE THINKS THE SUBJECTS ARE BEING SENT BACK, THEN WE'RE GOING TO SHOW THAT THEY AREN'T.
ARIA, YOU REMEMBER HOW TO GET TO THE LABS, RIGHT?
VAGUELY. IF WE GET IN THE RIGHT AREA, IT'LL BE HARD TO MISS.
WHAT ARE YOU THINKING?
WE'RE GOING TO GET THE SUBJECTS OUT OURSELVES.

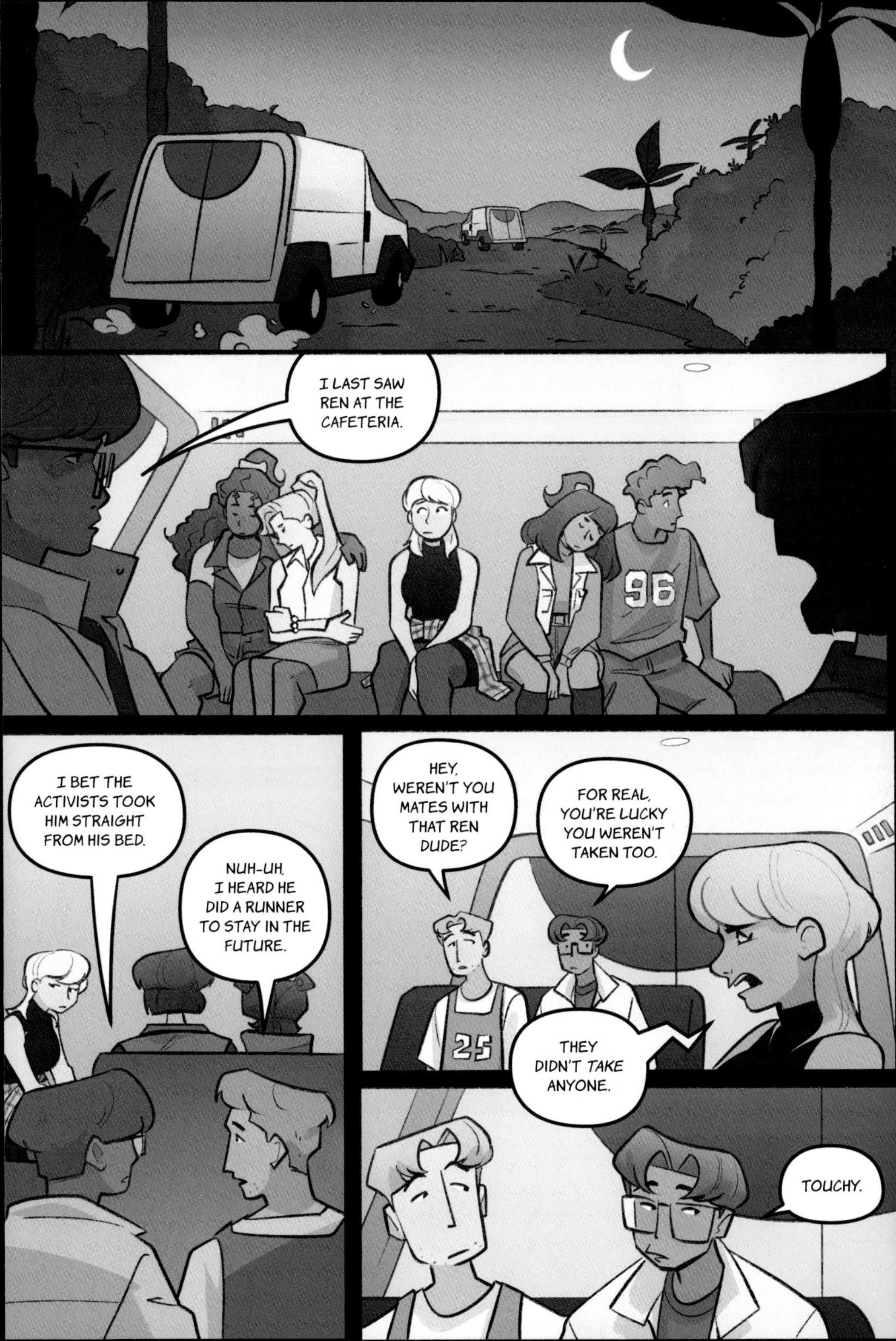
I LAST SAW REN AT THE CAFETERIA.
96
I BET THE ACTIVISTS TOOK HIM STRAIGHT FROM HIS BED.
NUH-UH, I HEARD HE DID A RUNNER TO STAY IN THE FUTURE.
HEY, WEREN'T YOU MATES WITH THAT REN DUDE?
FOR REAL, YOU'RE LUCKY YOU WEREN'T TAKEN TOO.
25
THEY DIDN'T *TAKE* ANYONE.
TOUCHY.

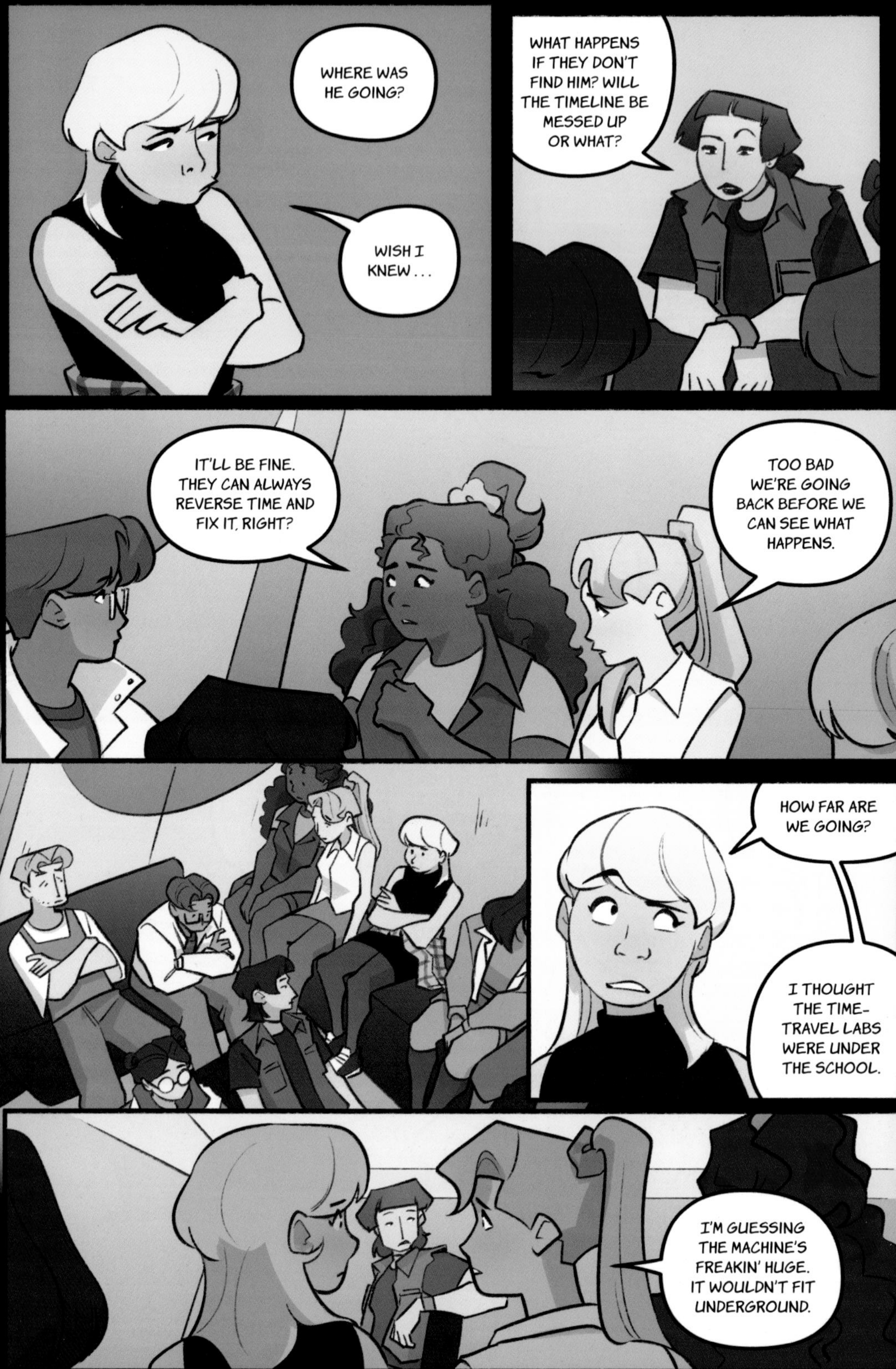
WHERE WAS HE GOING?
WISH I KNEW . . .
WHAT HAPPENS IF THEY DON'T FIND HIM? WILL THE TIMELINE BE MESSED UP OR WHAT?
IT'LL BE FINE. THEY CAN ALWAYS REVERSE TIME AND FIX IT, RIGHT?
TOO BAD WE'RE GOING BACK BEFORE WE CAN SEE WHAT HAPPENS.
HOW FAR ARE WE GOING?
I THOUGHT THE TIME-TRAVEL LABS WERE UNDER THE SCHOOL.
I'M GUESSING THE MACHINE'S FREAKIN' HUGE. IT WOULDN'T FIT UNDERGROUND.

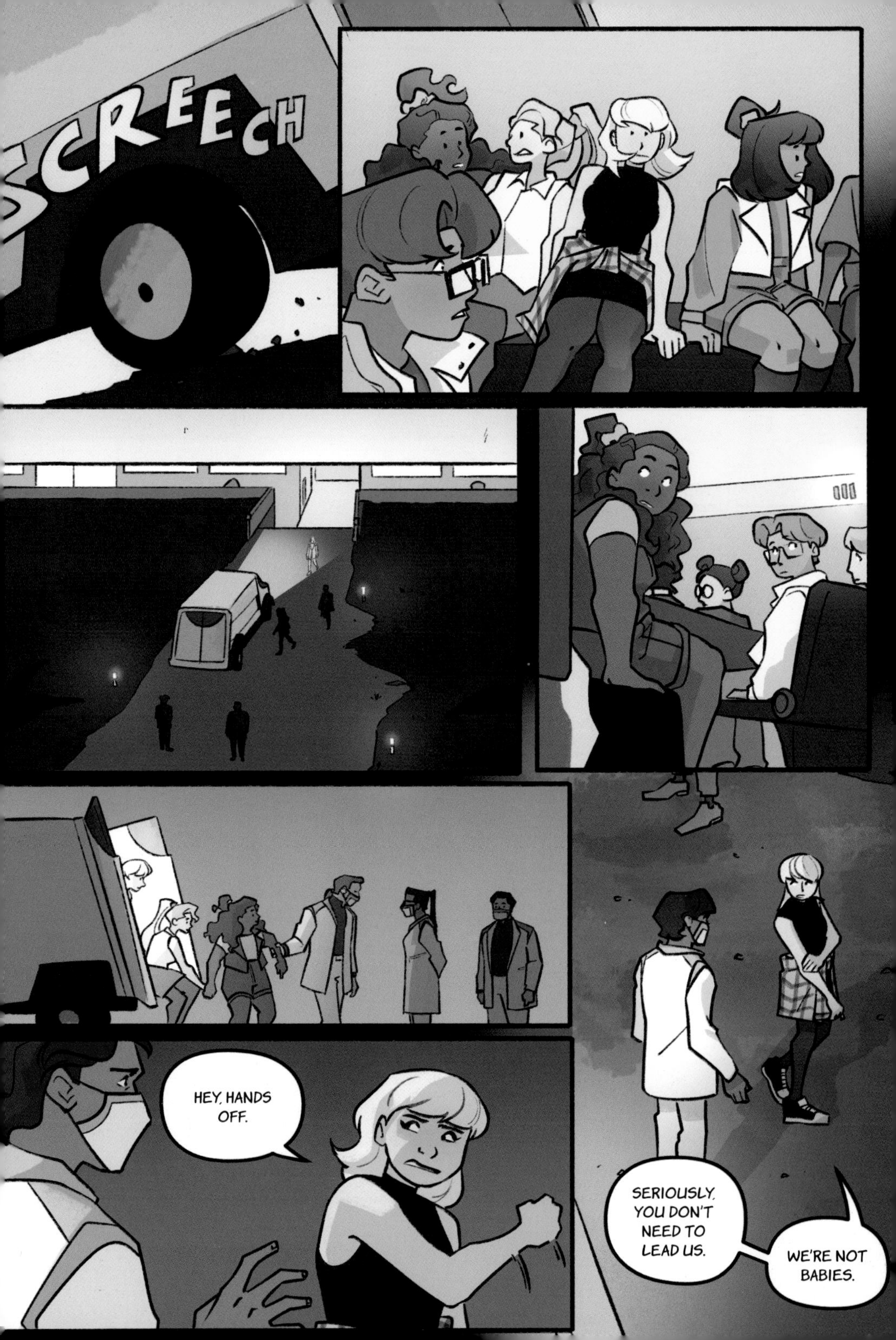
SCREECH
HEY, HANDS OFF.
SERIOUSLY, YOU DON'T NEED TO LEAD US.
WE'RE NOT BABIES.

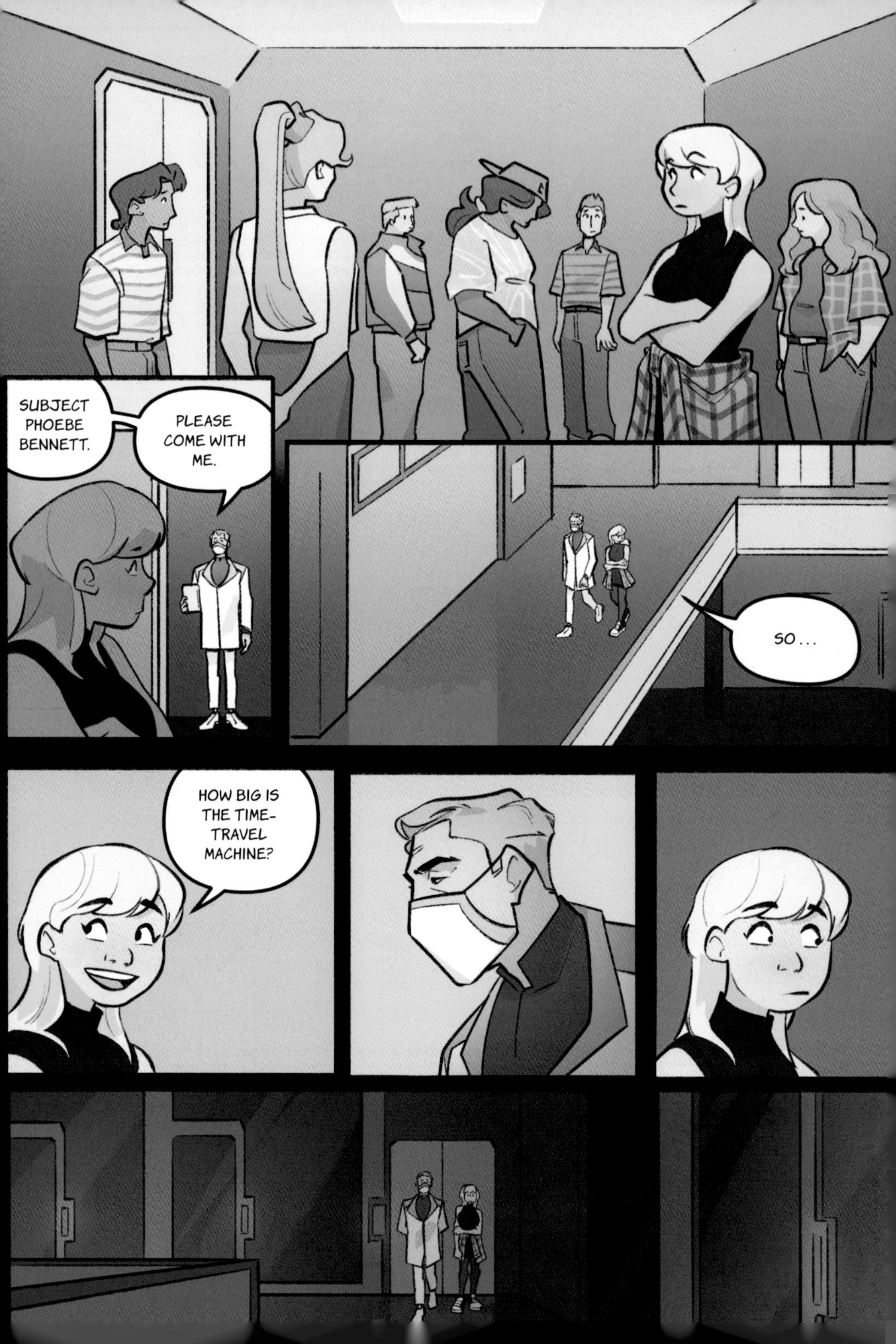
SUBJECT PHOEBE BENNETT.
PLEASE COME WITH ME.
SO . . .
HOW BIG IS THE TIME-TRAVEL MACHINE?

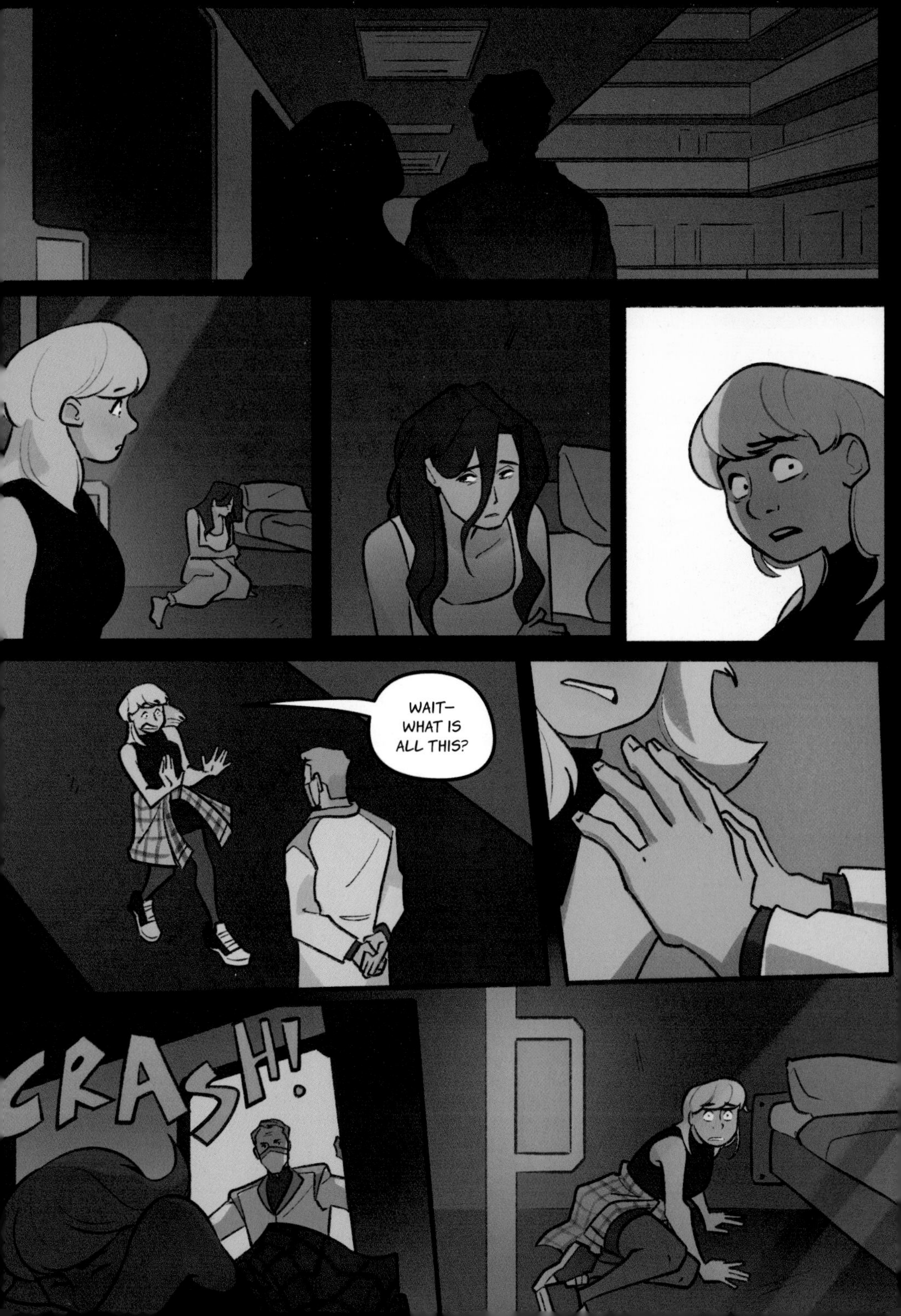
WAIT—
WHAT IS
ALL THIS?
CRASH!

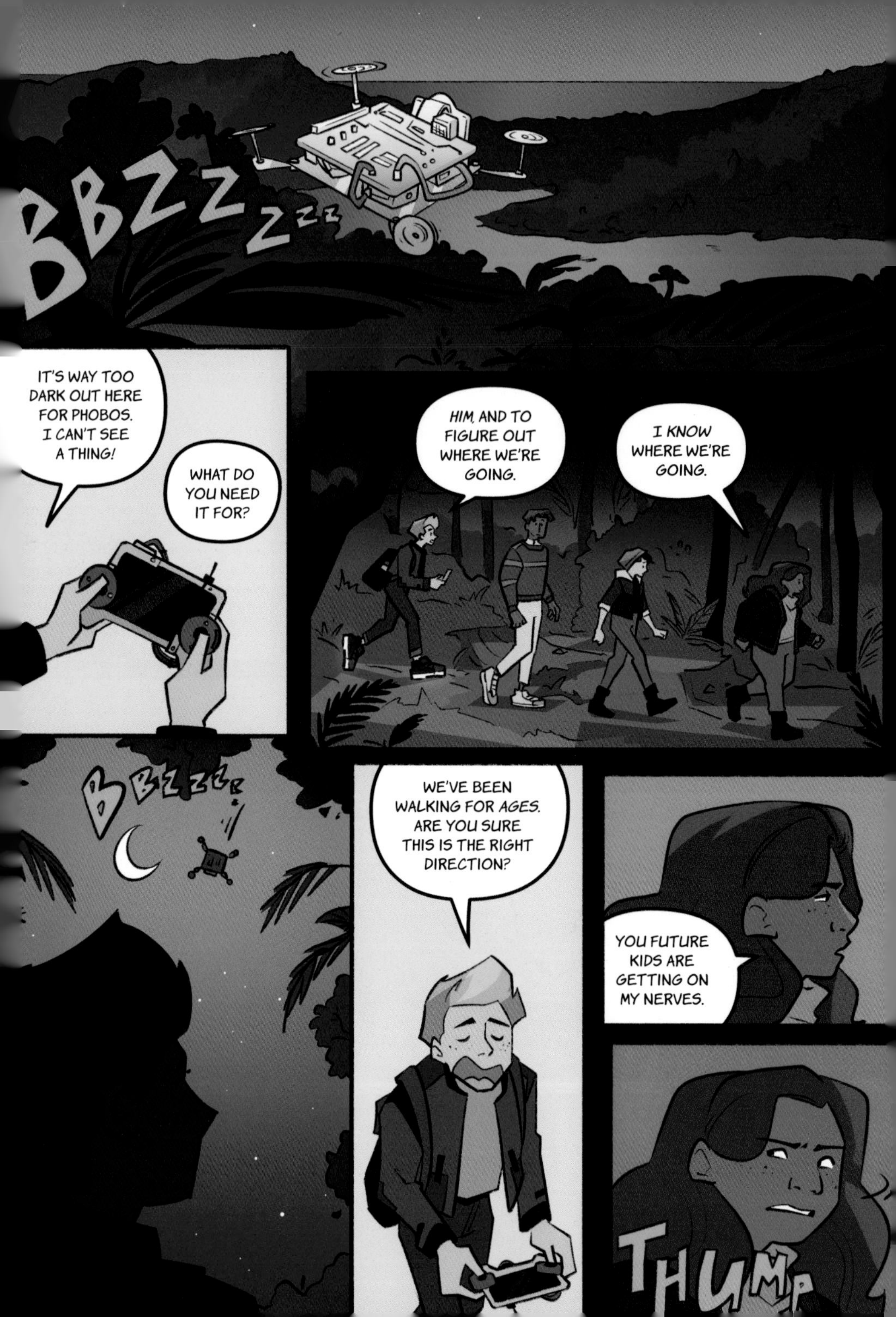
BBZZZ ZZZ
IT'S WAY TOO DARK OUT HERE FOR PHOBOS. I CAN'T SEE A THING!
WHAT DO YOU NEED IT FOR?
HIM, AND TO FIGURE OUT WHERE WE'RE GOING.
I KNOW WHERE WE'RE GOING.
BBZZZR
WE'VE BEEN WALKING FOR *AGES*. ARE YOU SURE THIS IS THE RIGHT DIRECTION?
YOU FUTURE KIDS ARE GETTING ON MY NERVES.
THUMP

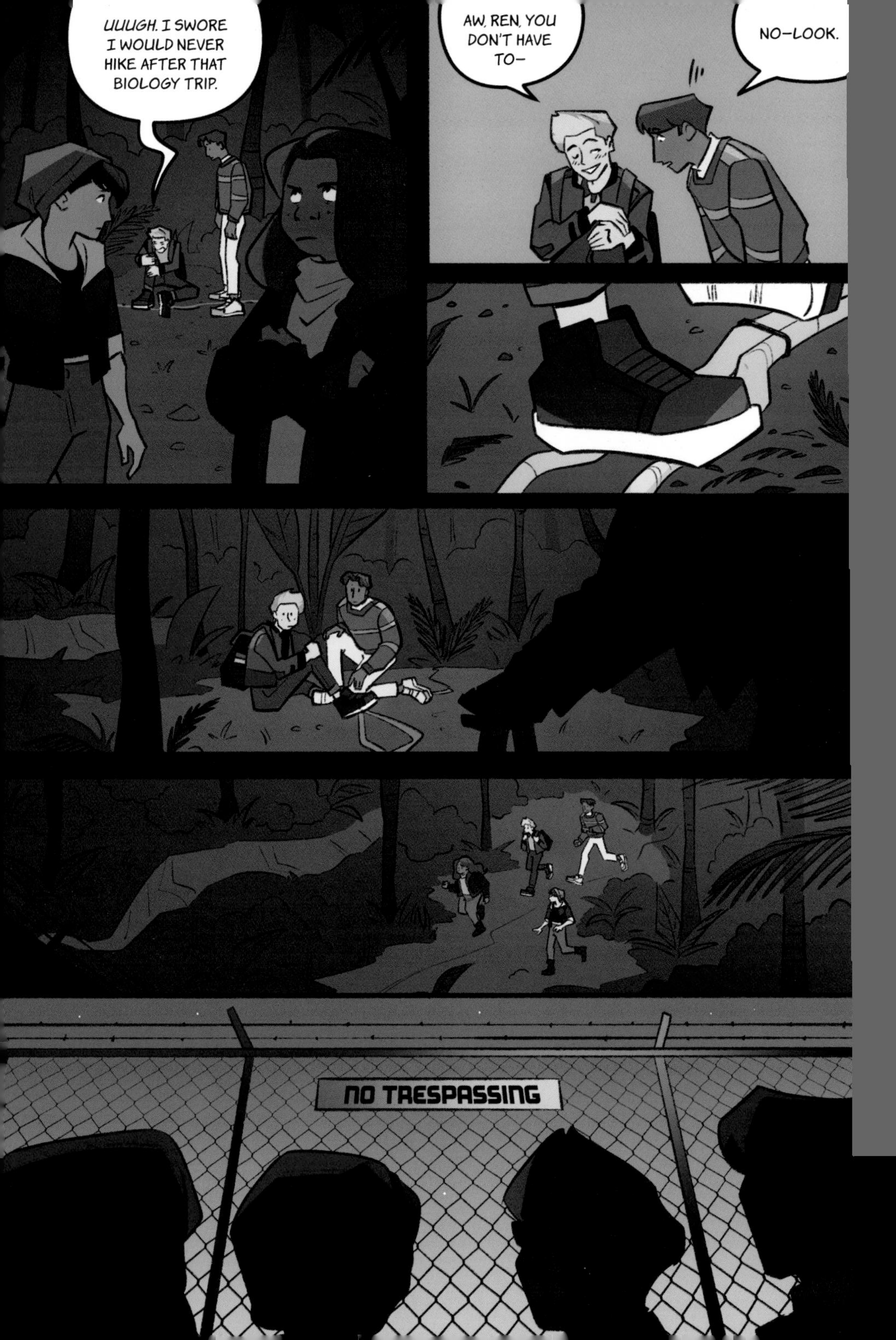
UUUGH. I SWORE I WOULD NEVER HIKE AFTER THAT BIOLOGY TRIP.
AW, REN, YOU DON'T HAVE TO—
NO—LOOK.
NO TRESPASSING

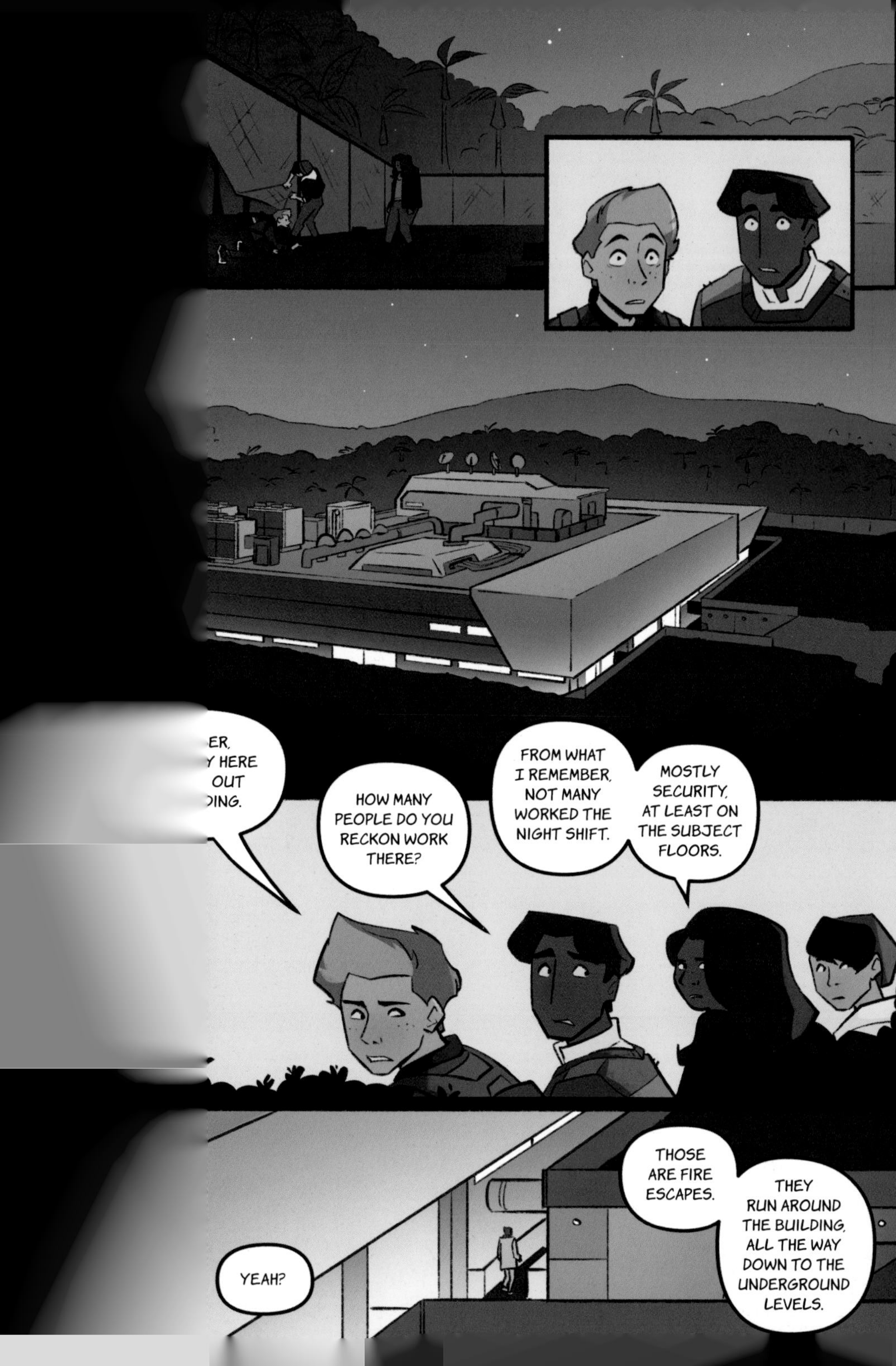
HOW MANY PEOPLE DO YOU RECKON WORK THERE?
FROM WHAT I REMEMBER, NOT MANY WORKED THE NIGHT SHIFT.
MOSTLY SECURITY, AT LEAST ON THE SUBJECT FLOORS.
THOSE ARE FIRE ESCAPES.
YEAH?
THEY RUN AROUND THE BUILDING, ALL THE WAY DOWN TO THE UNDERGROUND LEVELS.

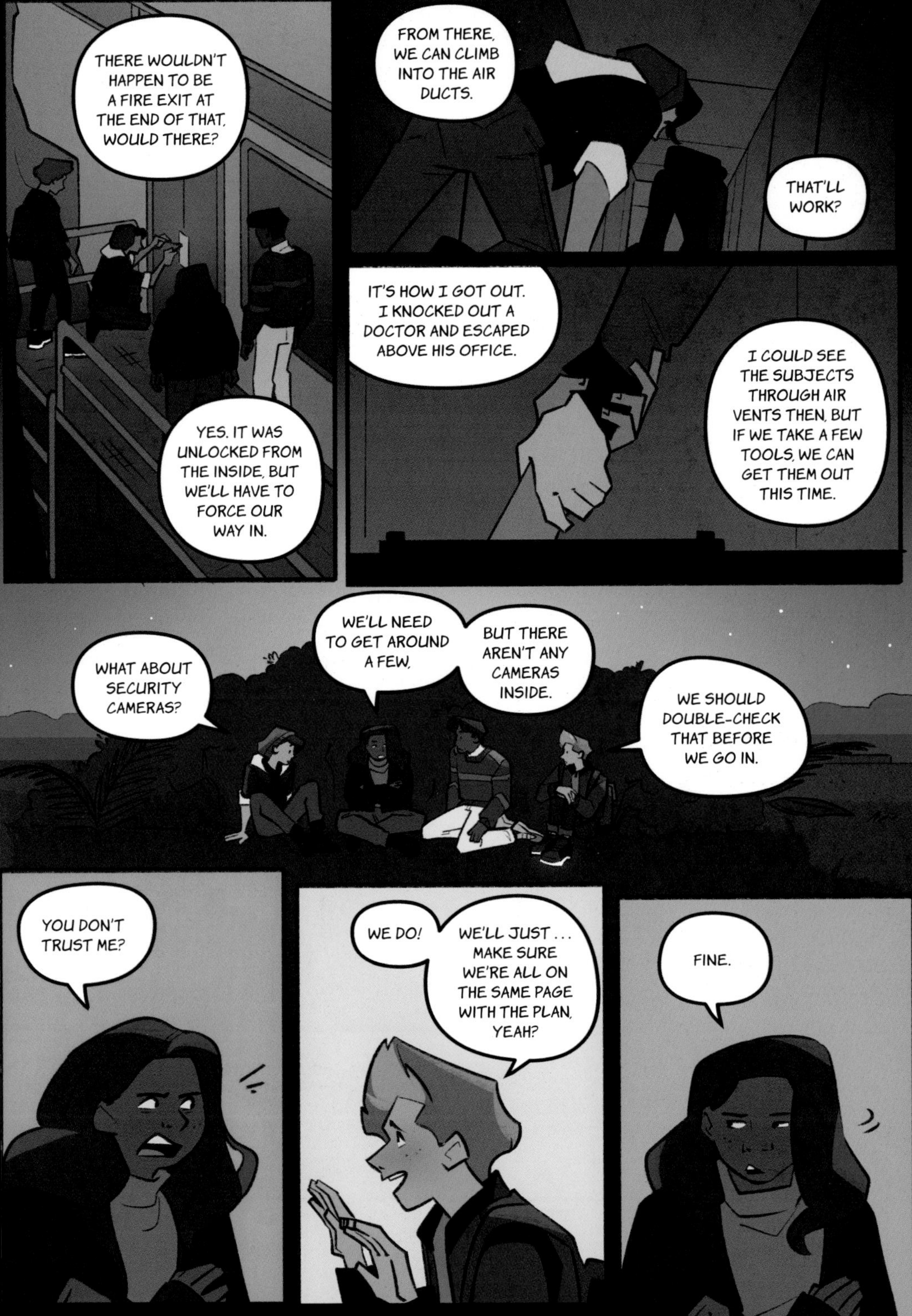
THERE WOULDN'T HAPPEN TO BE A FIRE EXIT AT THE END OF THAT, WOULD THERE?
YES. IT WAS UNLOCKED FROM THE INSIDE, BUT WE'LL HAVE TO FORCE OUR WAY IN.
FROM THERE, WE CAN CLIMB INTO THE AIR DUCTS.
THAT'LL WORK?
IT'S HOW I GOT OUT. I KNOCKED OUT A DOCTOR AND ESCAPED ABOVE HIS OFFICE.
I COULD SEE THE SUBJECTS THROUGH AIR VENTS THEN, BUT IF WE TAKE A FEW TOOLS, WE CAN GET THEM OUT THIS TIME.
WHAT ABOUT SECURITY CAMERAS?
WE'LL NEED TO GET AROUND A FEW,
BUT THERE AREN'T ANY CAMERAS INSIDE.
WE SHOULD DOUBLE-CHECK THAT BEFORE WE GO IN.
YOU DON'T TRUST ME?
WE DO!
WE'LL JUST . . . MAKE SURE WE'RE ALL ON THE SAME PAGE WITH THE PLAN, YEAH?
FINE.

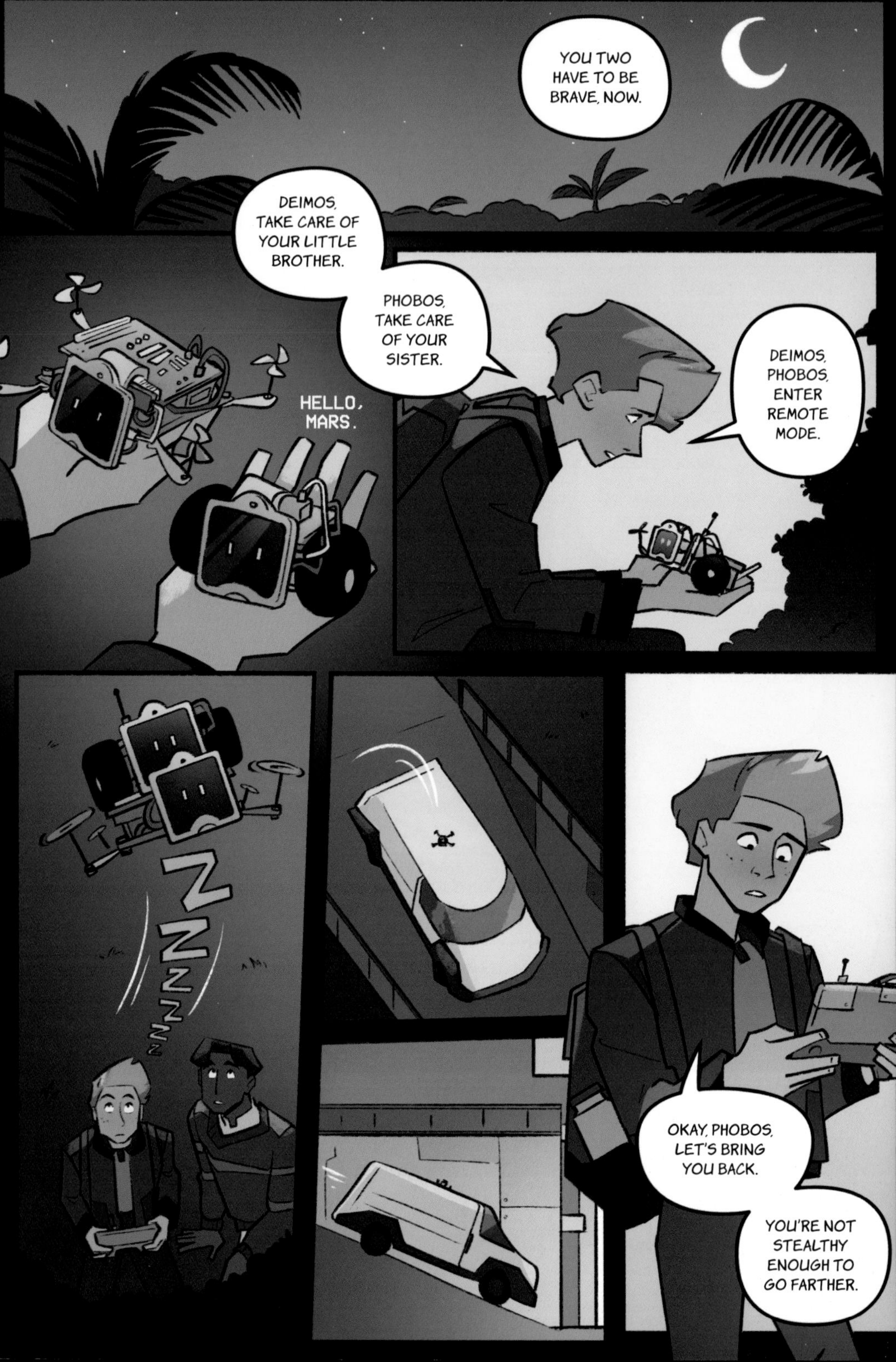
YOU TWO HAVE TO BE BRAVE, NOW.
DEIMOS, TAKE CARE OF YOUR LITTLE BROTHER.
PHOBOS, TAKE CARE OF YOUR SISTER.
HELLO, MARS.
DEIMOS, PHOBOS, ENTER REMOTE MODE.
ZZZZZZ
OKAY, PHOBOS, LET'S BRING YOU BACK.
YOU'RE NOT STEALTHY ENOUGH TO GO FARTHER.

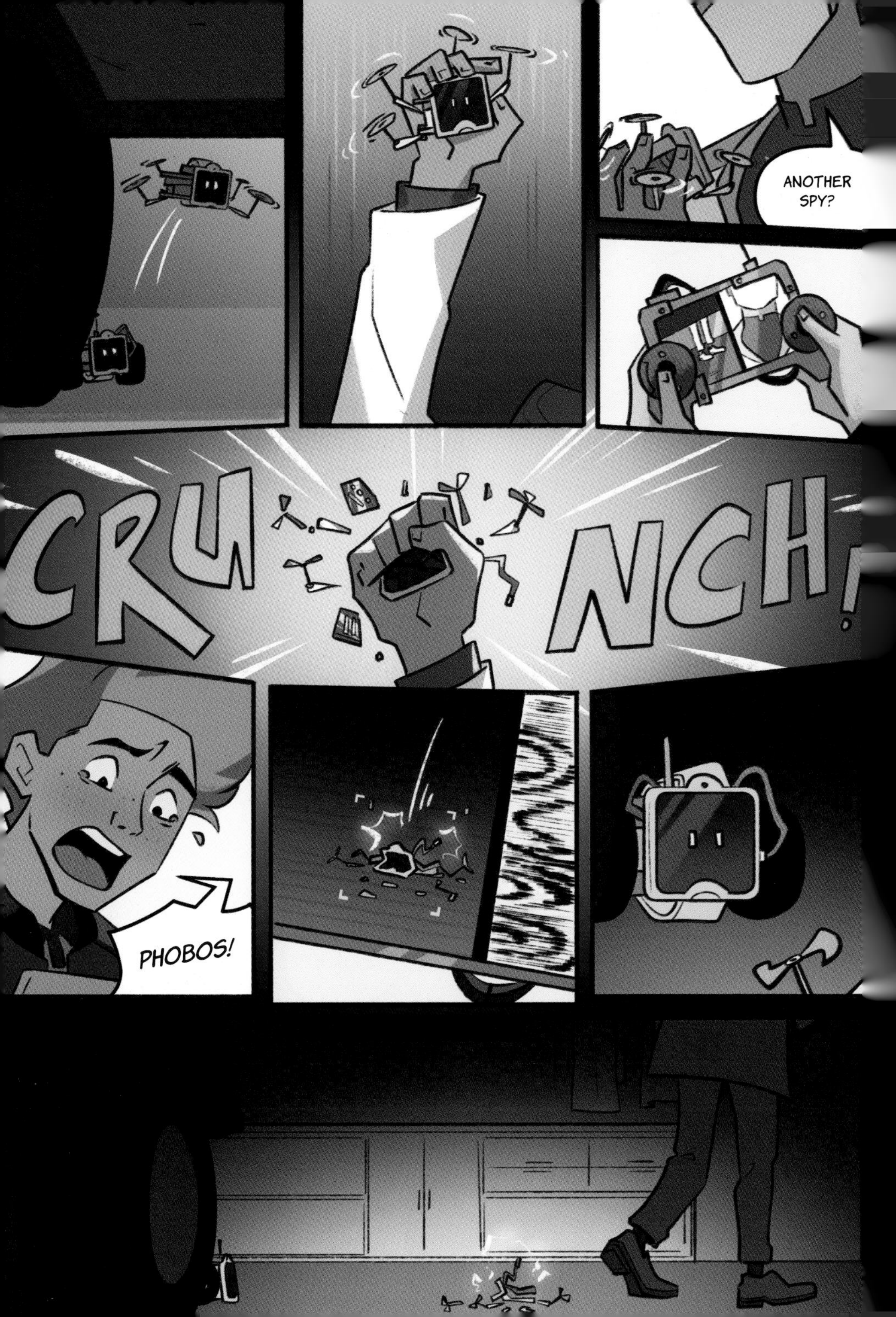
ANOTHER SPY?
CRUNCH!
PHOBOS!

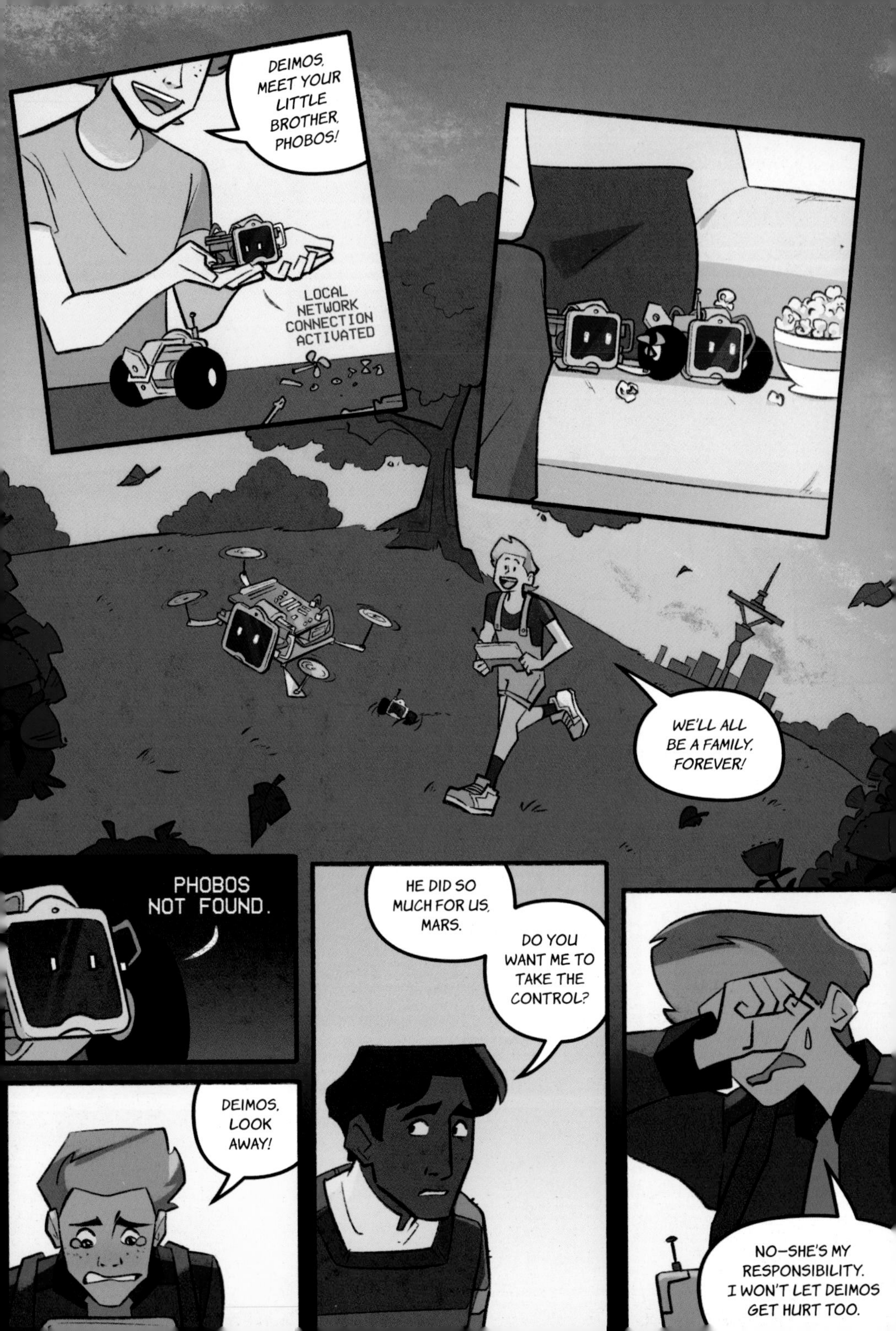
DEIMOS, MEET YOUR LITTLE BROTHER, PHOBOS!
LOCAL NETWORK CONNECTION ACTIVATED
WE'LL ALL BE A FAMILY, FOREVER!
PHOBOS NOT FOUND.
HE DID SO MUCH FOR US, MARS.
DO YOU WANT ME TO TAKE THE CONTROL?
DEIMOS, LOOK AWAY!
NO—SHE'S MY RESPONSIBILITY. I WON'T LET DEIMOS GET HURT TOO.

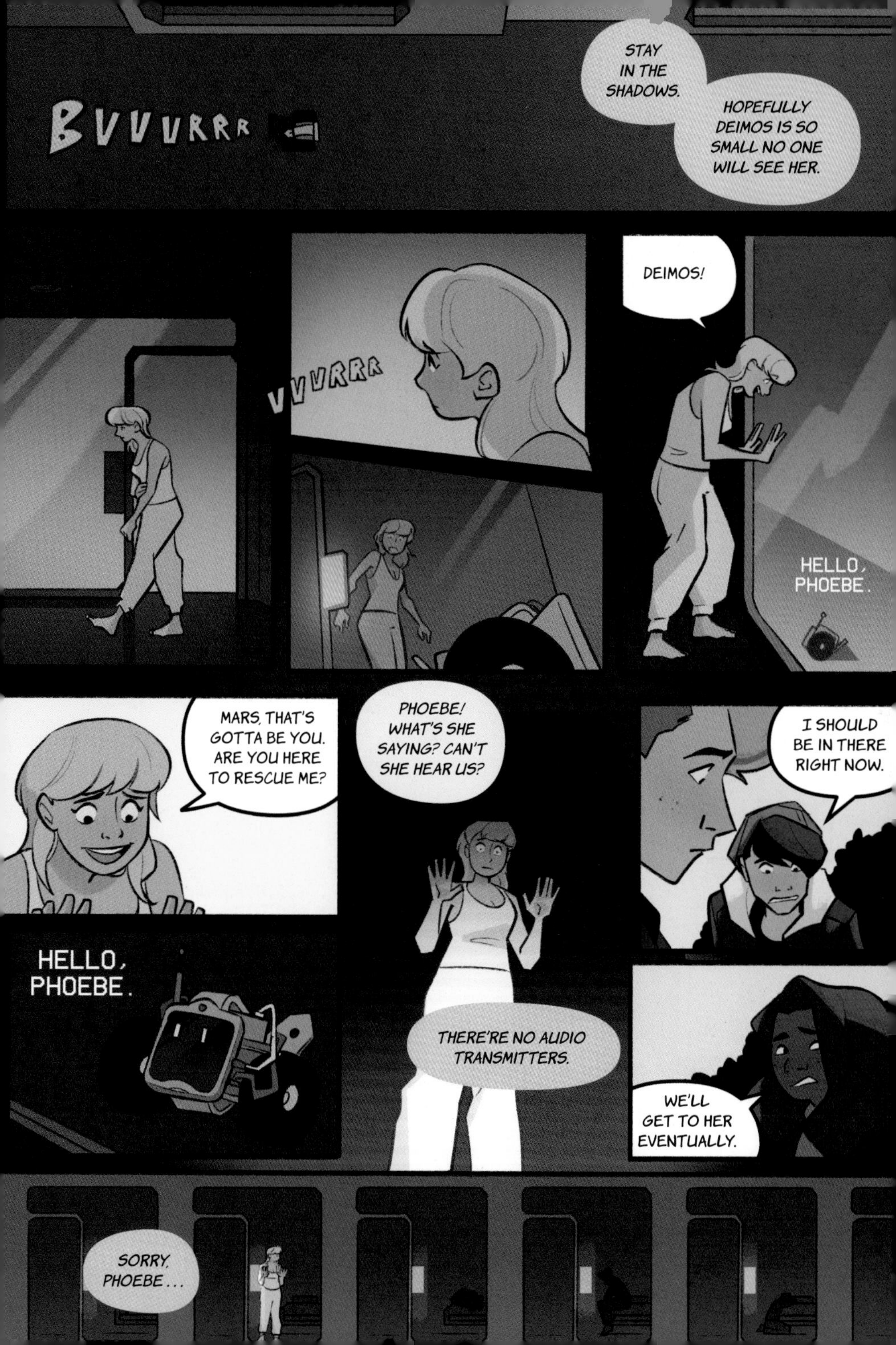
BVVVRRR
STAY IN THE SHADOWS.
HOPEFULLY DEIMOS IS SO SMALL NO ONE WILL SEE HER.
VVVRRR
DEIMOS!
HELLO, PHOEBE.
MARS, THAT'S GOTTA BE YOU. ARE YOU HERE TO RESCUE ME?
HELLO, PHOEBE.
PHOEBE! WHAT'S SHE SAYING? CAN'T SHE HEAR US?
THERE'RE NO AUDIO TRANSMITTERS.
I SHOULD BE IN THERE RIGHT NOW.
WE'LL GET TO HER EVENTUALLY.
SORRY, PHOEBE...

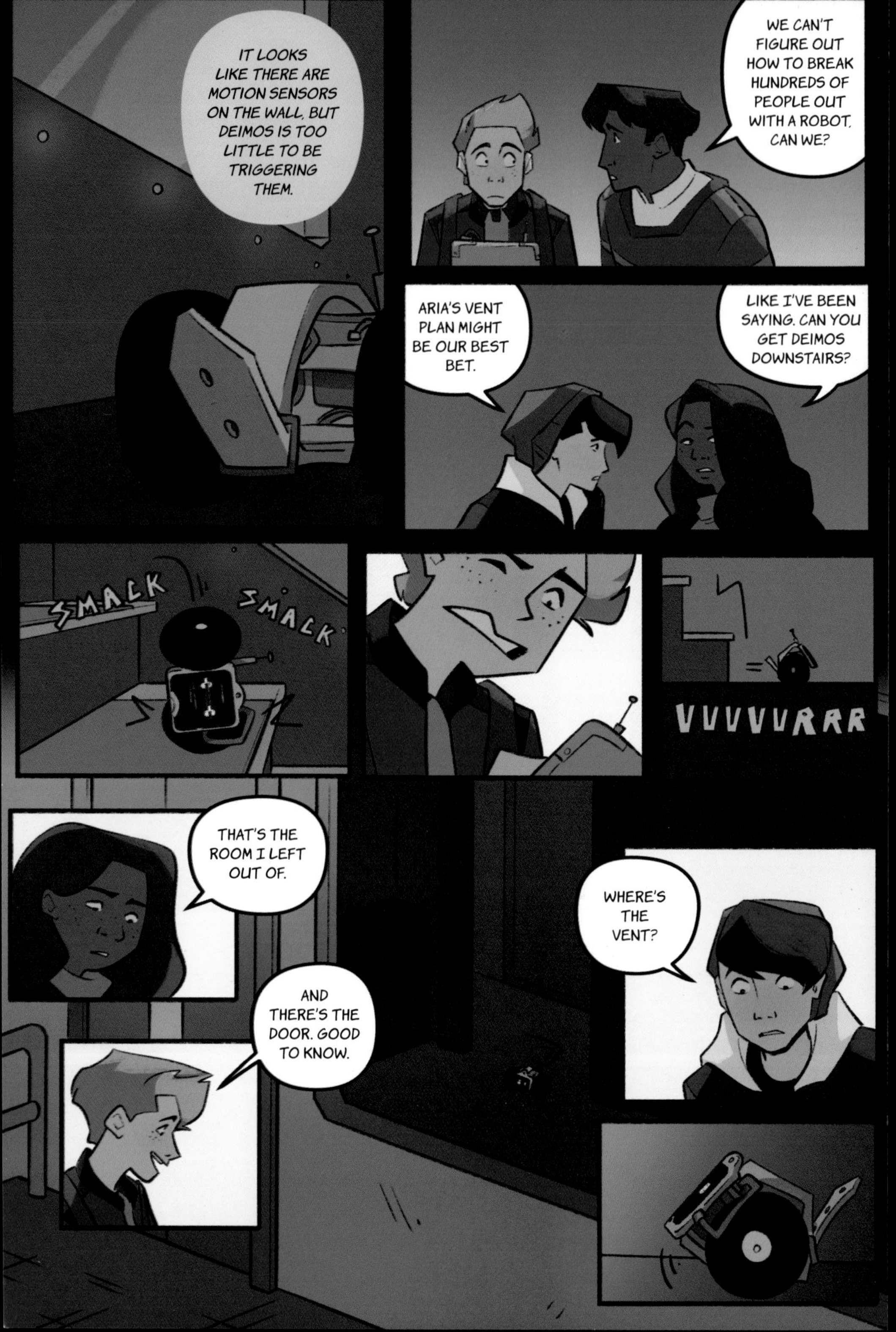
IT LOOKS LIKE THERE ARE MOTION SENSORS ON THE WALL, BUT DEIMOS IS TOO LITTLE TO BE TRIGGERING THEM.
WE CAN'T FIGURE OUT HOW TO BREAK HUNDREDS OF PEOPLE OUT WITH A ROBOT, CAN WE?
ARIA'S VENT PLAN MIGHT BE OUR BEST BET.
LIKE I'VE BEEN SAYING. CAN YOU GET DEIMOS DOWNSTAIRS?
SMACK
SMACK
VVVVVRRR
THAT'S THE ROOM I LEFT OUT OF.
WHERE'S THE VENT?
AND THERE'S THE DOOR. GOOD TO KNOW.

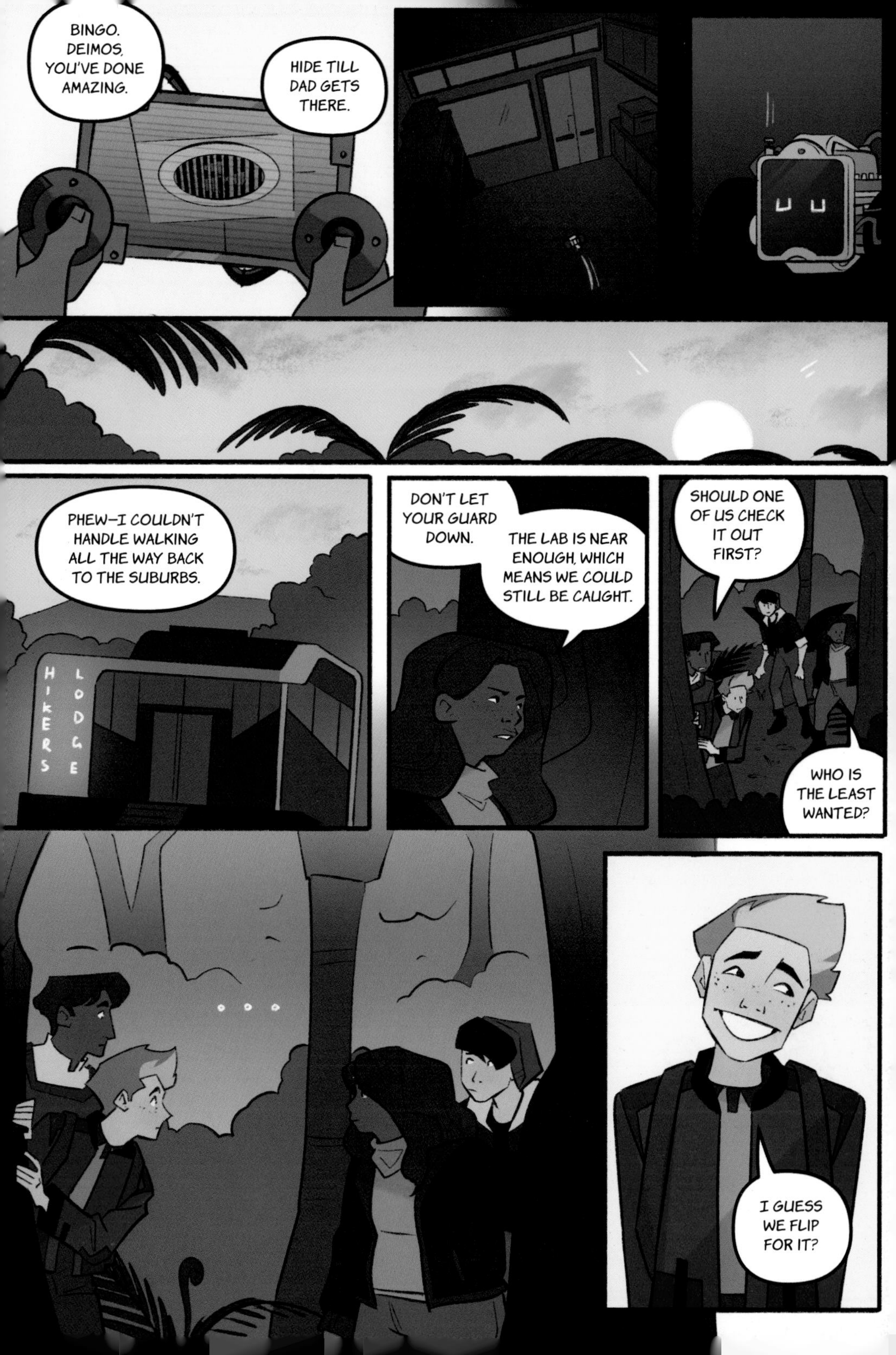
BINGO. DEIMOS, YOU'VE DONE AMAZING.
HIDE TILL DAD GETS THERE.
PHEW—I COULDN'T HANDLE WALKING ALL THE WAY BACK TO THE SUBURBS.
HIKERS LODGE
DON'T LET YOUR GUARD DOWN.
THE LAB IS NEAR ENOUGH, WHICH MEANS WE COULD STILL BE CAUGHT.
SHOULD ONE OF US CHECK IT OUT FIRST?
WHO IS THE LEAST WANTED?
I GUESS WE FLIP FOR IT?

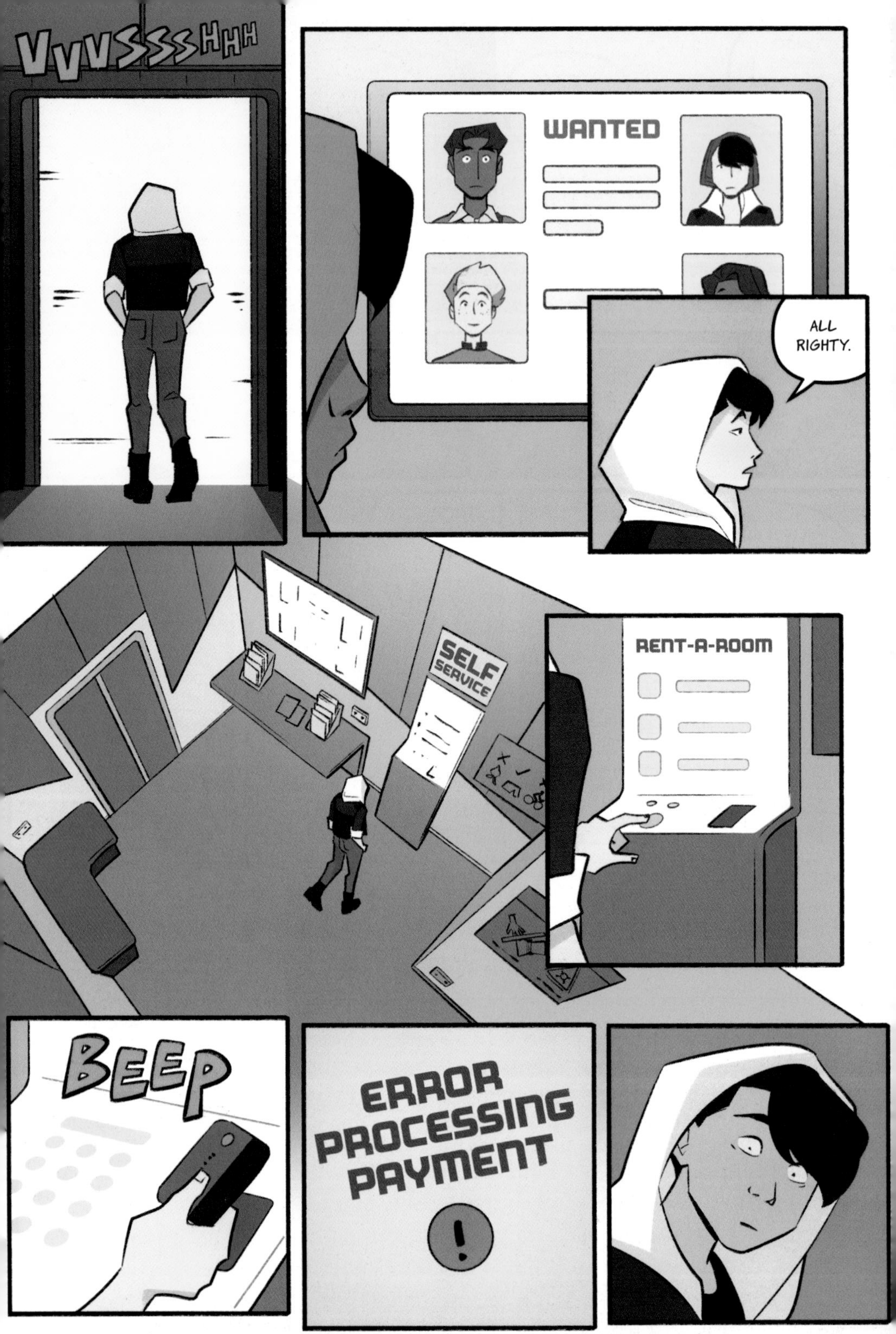
VVVSSSHHH
WANTED
ALL RIGHTY.
SELF SERVICE
RENT-A-ROOM
BEEP
ERROR PROCESSING PAYMENT
!

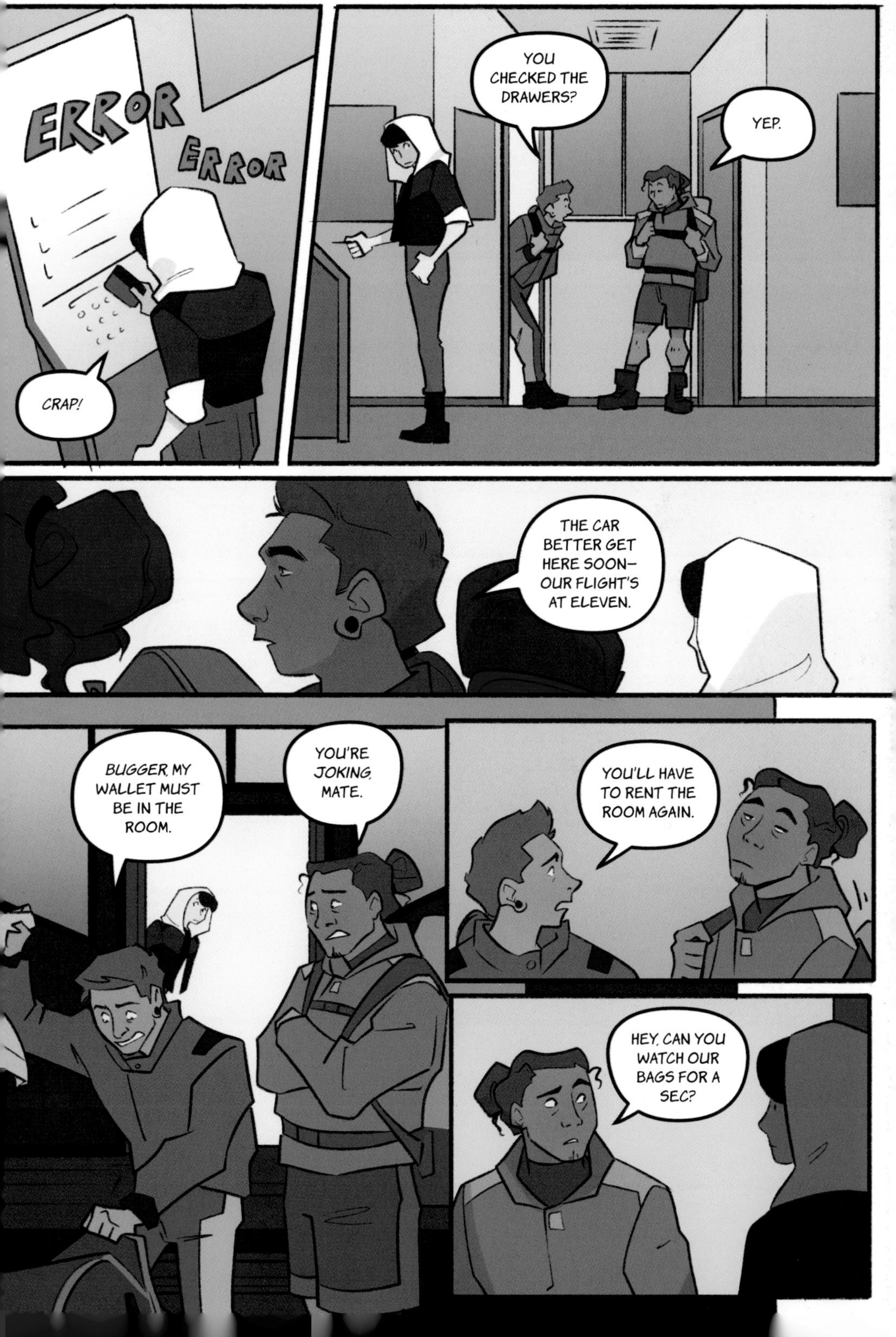
ERROR
ERROR
CRAP!
YOU CHECKED THE DRAWERS?
YEP.
THE CAR BETTER GET HERE SOON—OUR FLIGHT'S AT ELEVEN.
BUGGER, MY WALLET MUST BE IN THE ROOM.
YOU'RE JOKING, MATE.
YOU'LL HAVE TO RENT THE ROOM AGAIN.
HEY, CAN YOU WATCH OUR BAGS FOR A SEC?

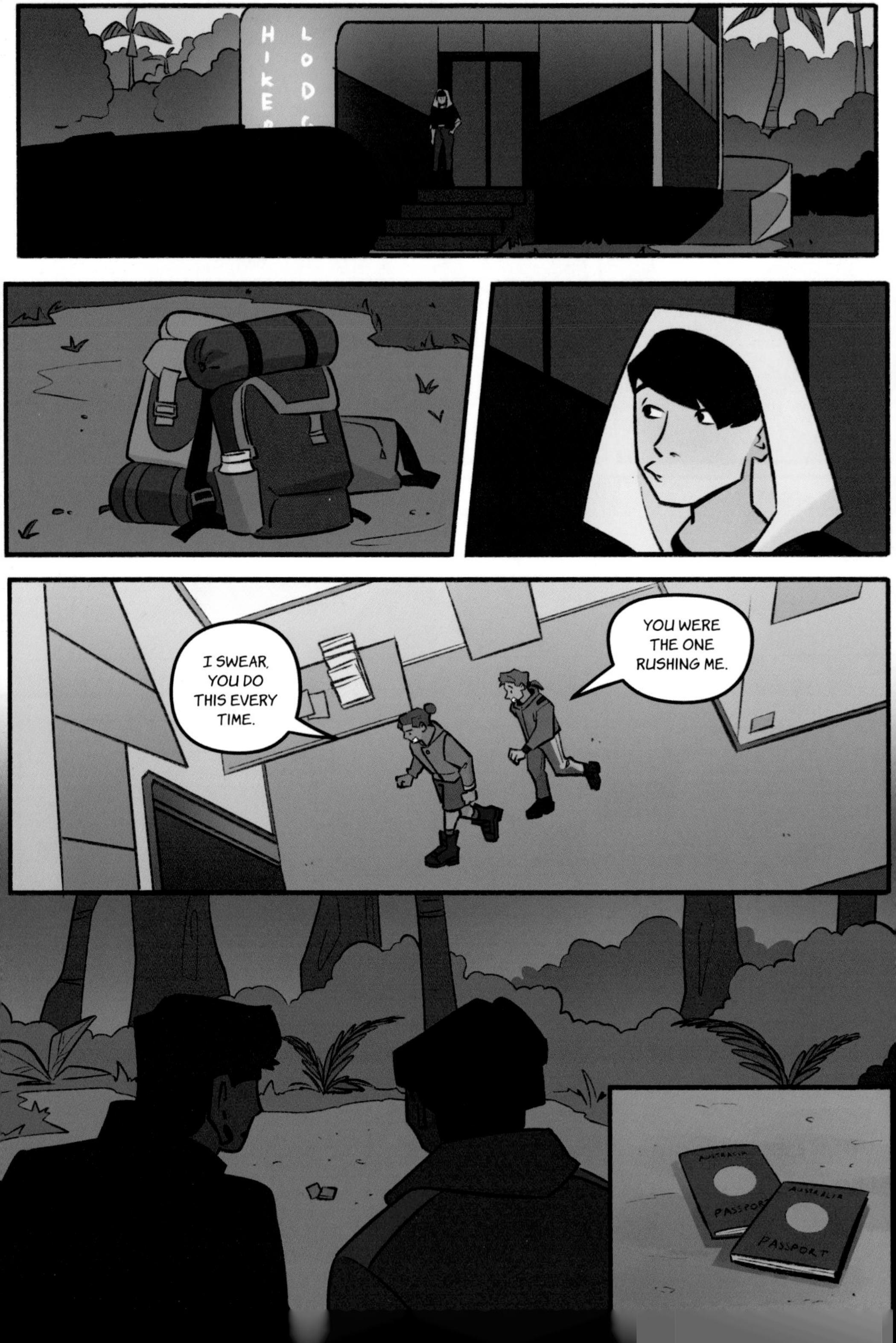

I SWEAR, YOU DO THIS EVERY TIME.
YOU WERE THE ONE RUSHING ME.

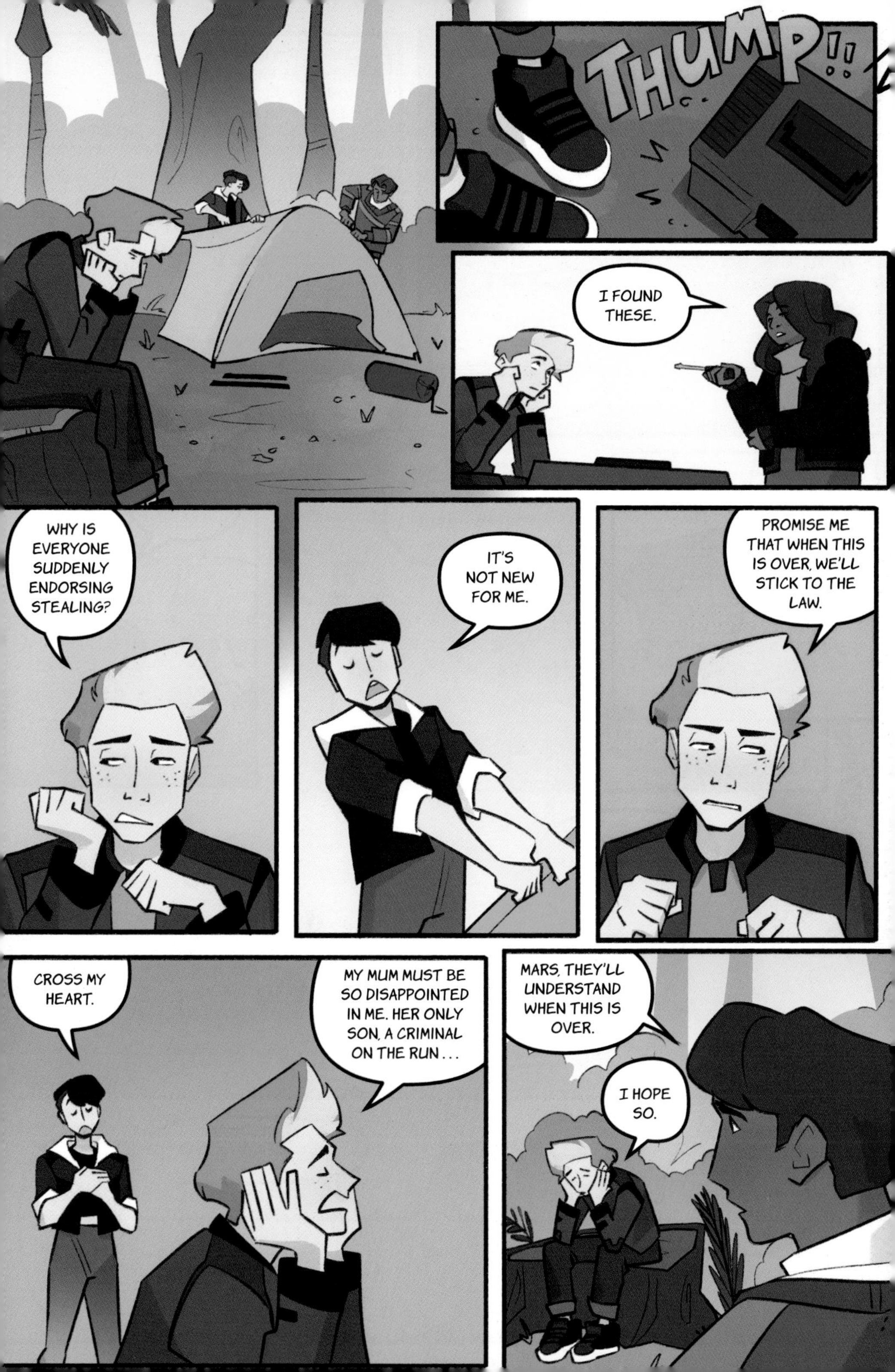
THUMP!!
I FOUND THESE.
WHY IS EVERYONE SUDDENLY ENDORSING STEALING?
IT'S NOT NEW FOR ME.
PROMISE ME THAT WHEN THIS IS OVER, WE'LL STICK TO THE LAW.
CROSS MY HEART.
MY MUM MUST BE SO DISAPPOINTED IN ME. HER ONLY SON, A CRIMINAL ON THE RUN . . .
MARS, THEY'LL UNDERSTAND WHEN THIS IS OVER.
I HOPE SO.

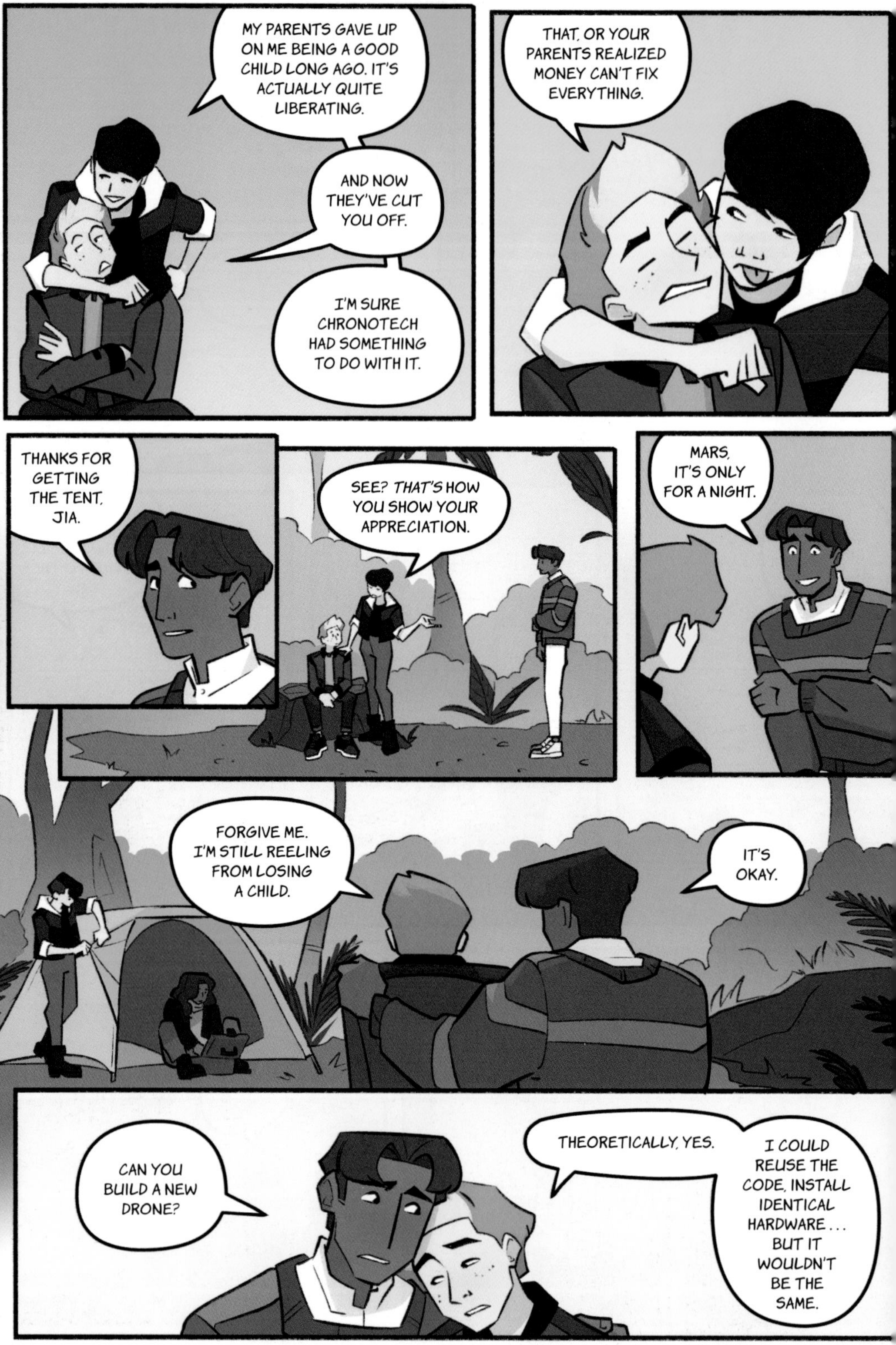
MY PARENTS GAVE UP ON ME BEING A GOOD CHILD LONG AGO. IT'S ACTUALLY QUITE LIBERATING.
AND NOW THEY'VE CUT YOU OFF.
I'M SURE CHRONOTECH HAD SOMETHING TO DO WITH IT.
THAT, OR YOUR PARENTS REALIZED MONEY CAN'T FIX EVERYTHING.
THANKS FOR GETTING THE TENT, JIA.
SEE? THAT'S HOW YOU SHOW YOUR APPRECIATION.
MARS, IT'S ONLY FOR A NIGHT.
FORGIVE ME. I'M STILL REELING FROM LOSING A CHILD.
IT'S OKAY.
CAN YOU BUILD A NEW DRONE?
THEORETICALLY, YES.
I COULD REUSE THE CODE, INSTALL IDENTICAL HARDWARE . . . BUT IT WOULDN'T BE THE SAME.

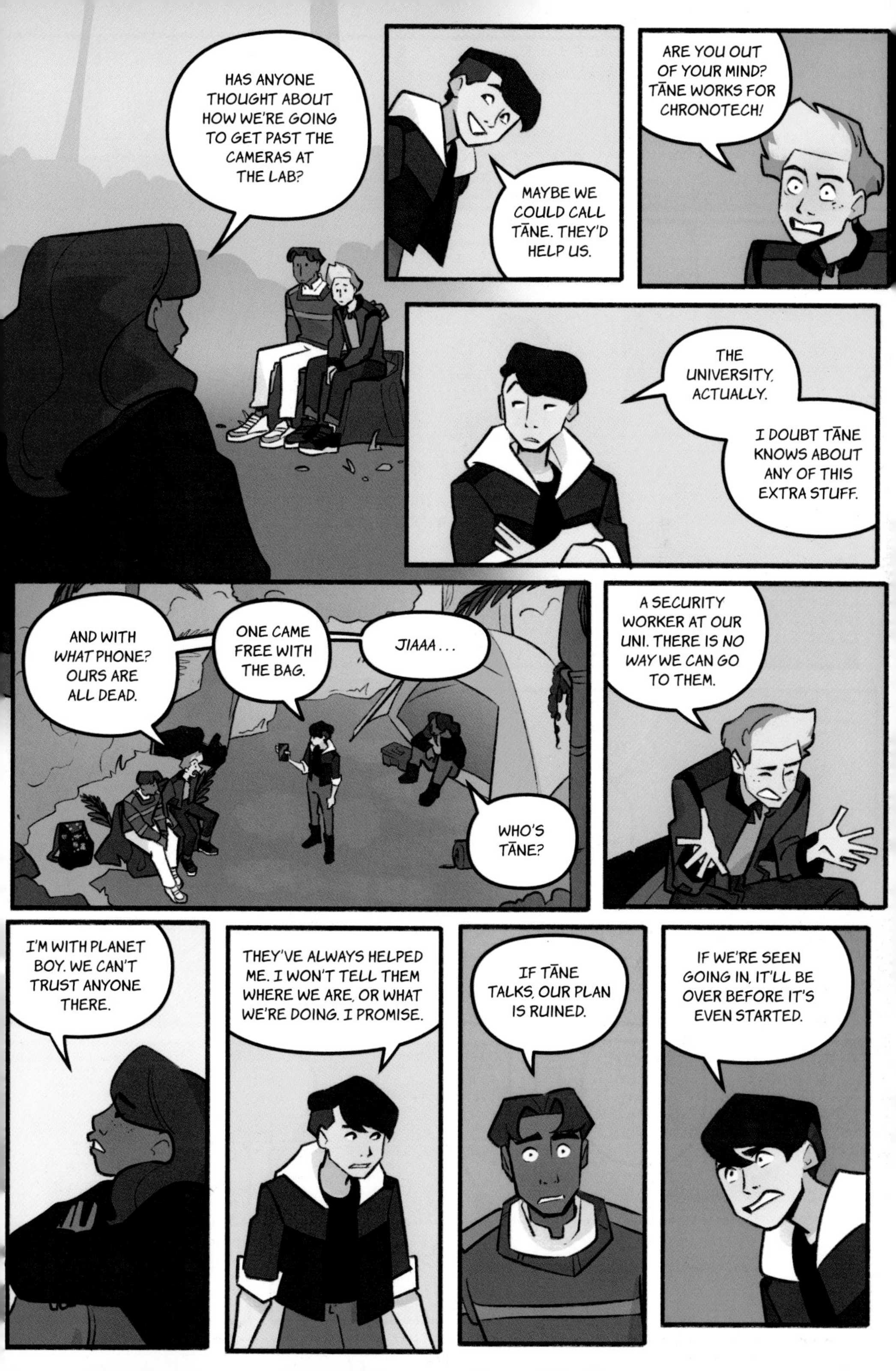
HAS ANYONE THOUGHT ABOUT HOW WE'RE GOING TO GET PAST THE CAMERAS AT THE LAB?
MAYBE WE COULD CALL TĀNE. THEY'D HELP US.
ARE YOU OUT OF YOUR MIND? TĀNE WORKS FOR CHRONOTECH!
THE UNIVERSITY, ACTUALLY.
I DOUBT TĀNE KNOWS ABOUT ANY OF THIS EXTRA STUFF.
AND WITH WHAT PHONE? OURS ARE ALL DEAD.
ONE CAME FREE WITH THE BAG.
JIAAA . . .
WHO'S TĀNE?
A SECURITY WORKER AT OUR UNI. THERE IS NO WAY WE CAN GO TO THEM.
I'M WITH PLANET BOY. WE CAN'T TRUST ANYONE THERE.
THEY'VE ALWAYS HELPED ME. I WON'T TELL THEM WHERE WE ARE, OR WHAT WE'RE DOING. I PROMISE.
IF TĀNE TALKS, OUR PLAN IS RUINED.
IF WE'RE SEEN GOING IN, IT'LL BE OVER BEFORE IT'S EVEN STARTED.

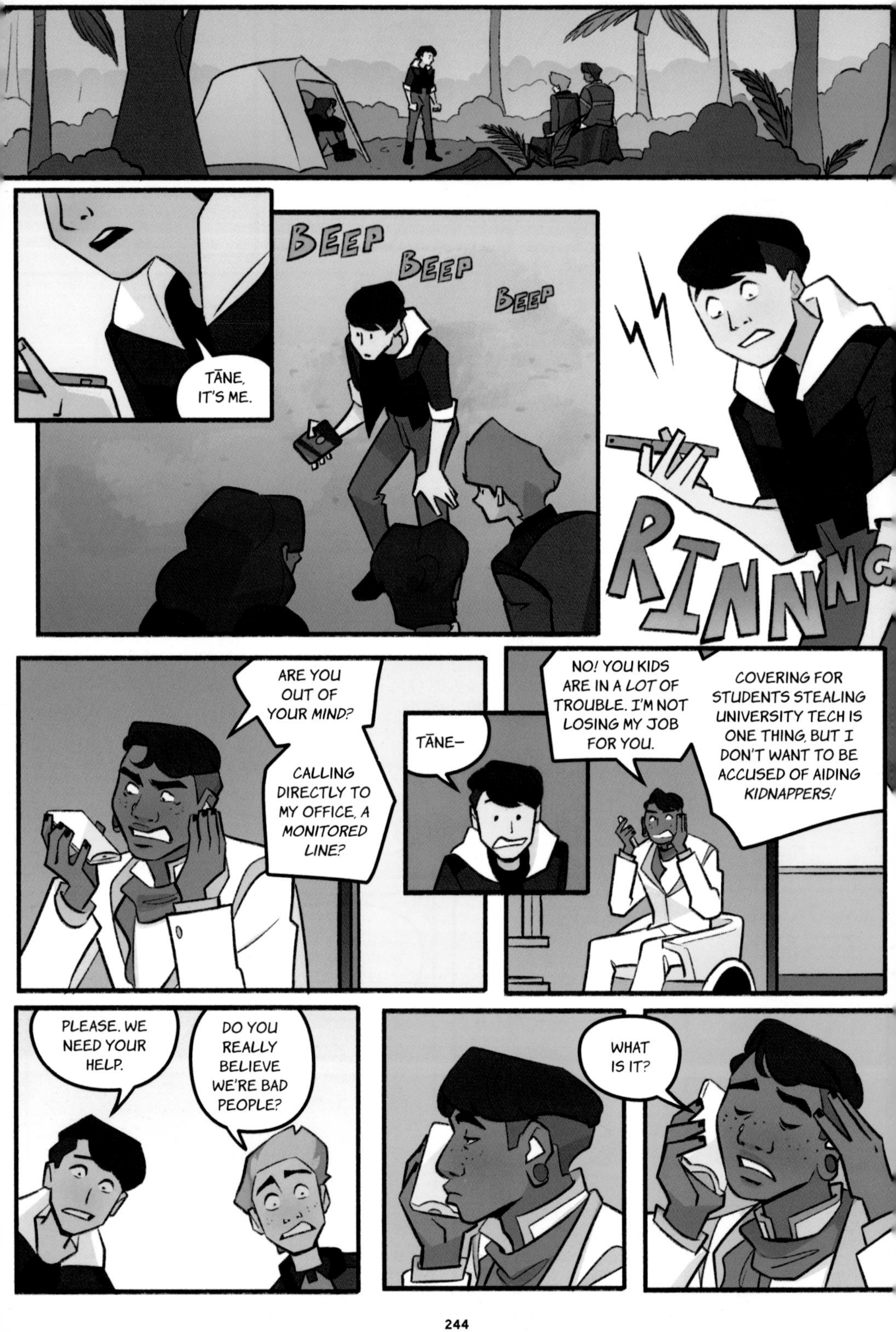
BEEP
BEEP
BEEP
TĀNE, IT'S ME.
RINNNG
ARE YOU OUT OF YOUR MIND?
CALLING DIRECTLY TO MY OFFICE, A MONITORED LINE?
TĀNE–
NO! YOU KIDS ARE IN A *LOT* OF TROUBLE. I'M NOT LOSING MY JOB FOR YOU.
COVERING FOR STUDENTS STEALING UNIVERSITY TECH IS ONE THING, BUT I DON'T WANT TO BE ACCUSED OF AIDING *KIDNAPPERS!*
PLEASE. WE NEED YOUR HELP.
DO YOU REALLY BELIEVE WE'RE BAD PEOPLE?
WHAT IS IT?

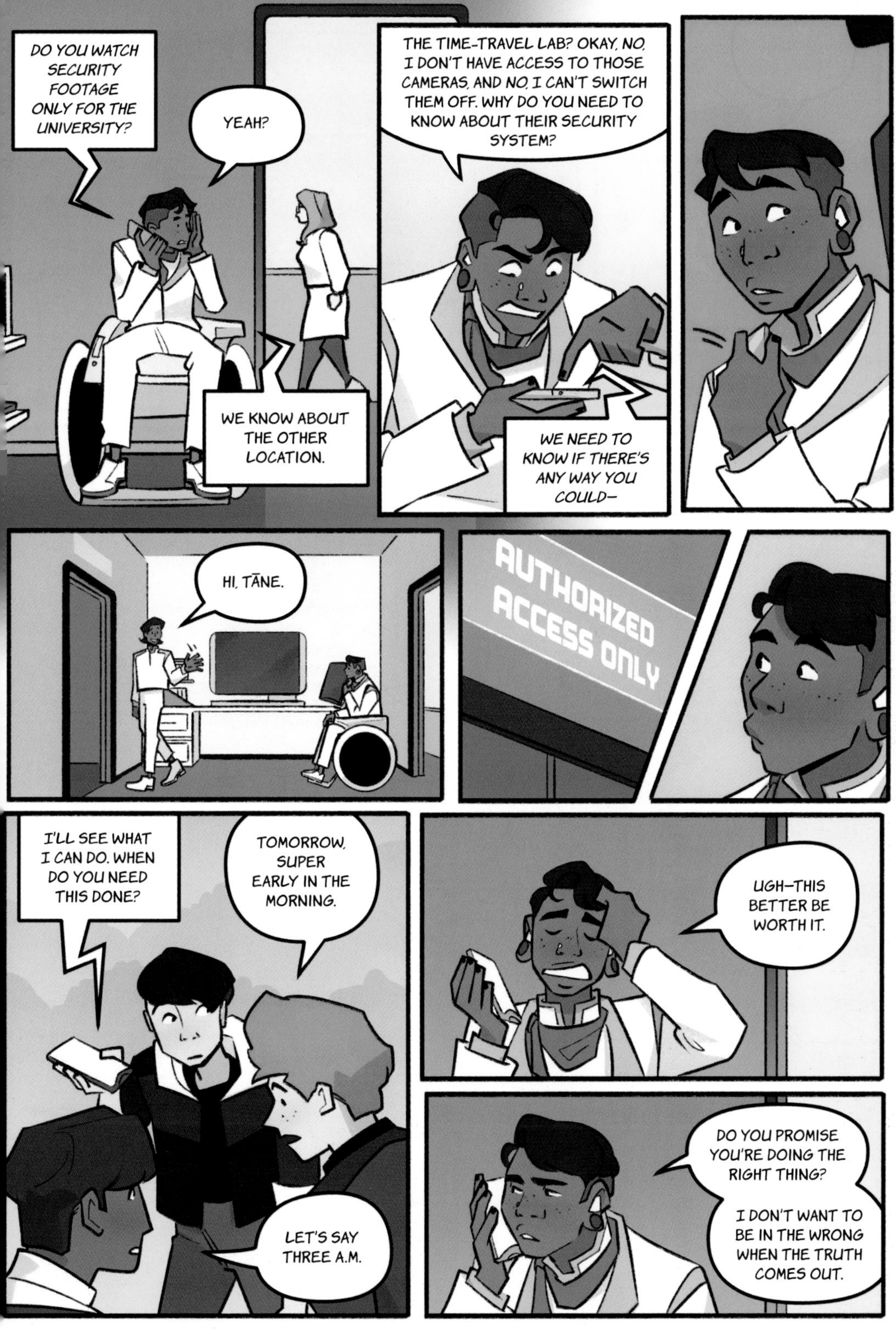
DO YOU WATCH SECURITY FOOTAGE ONLY FOR THE UNIVERSITY?
YEAH?
WE KNOW ABOUT THE OTHER LOCATION.
THE TIME-TRAVEL LAB? OKAY, NO, I DON'T HAVE ACCESS TO THOSE CAMERAS, AND NO, I CAN'T SWITCH THEM OFF. WHY DO YOU NEED TO KNOW ABOUT THEIR SECURITY SYSTEM?
WE NEED TO KNOW IF THERE'S ANY WAY YOU COULD—
HI, TĀNE.
AUTHORIZED ACCESS ONLY
I'LL SEE WHAT I CAN DO. WHEN DO YOU NEED THIS DONE?
TOMORROW, SUPER EARLY IN THE MORNING.
LET'S SAY THREE A.M.
UGH—THIS BETTER BE WORTH IT.
DO YOU PROMISE YOU'RE DOING THE RIGHT THING?
I DON'T WANT TO BE IN THE WRONG WHEN THE TRUTH COMES OUT.

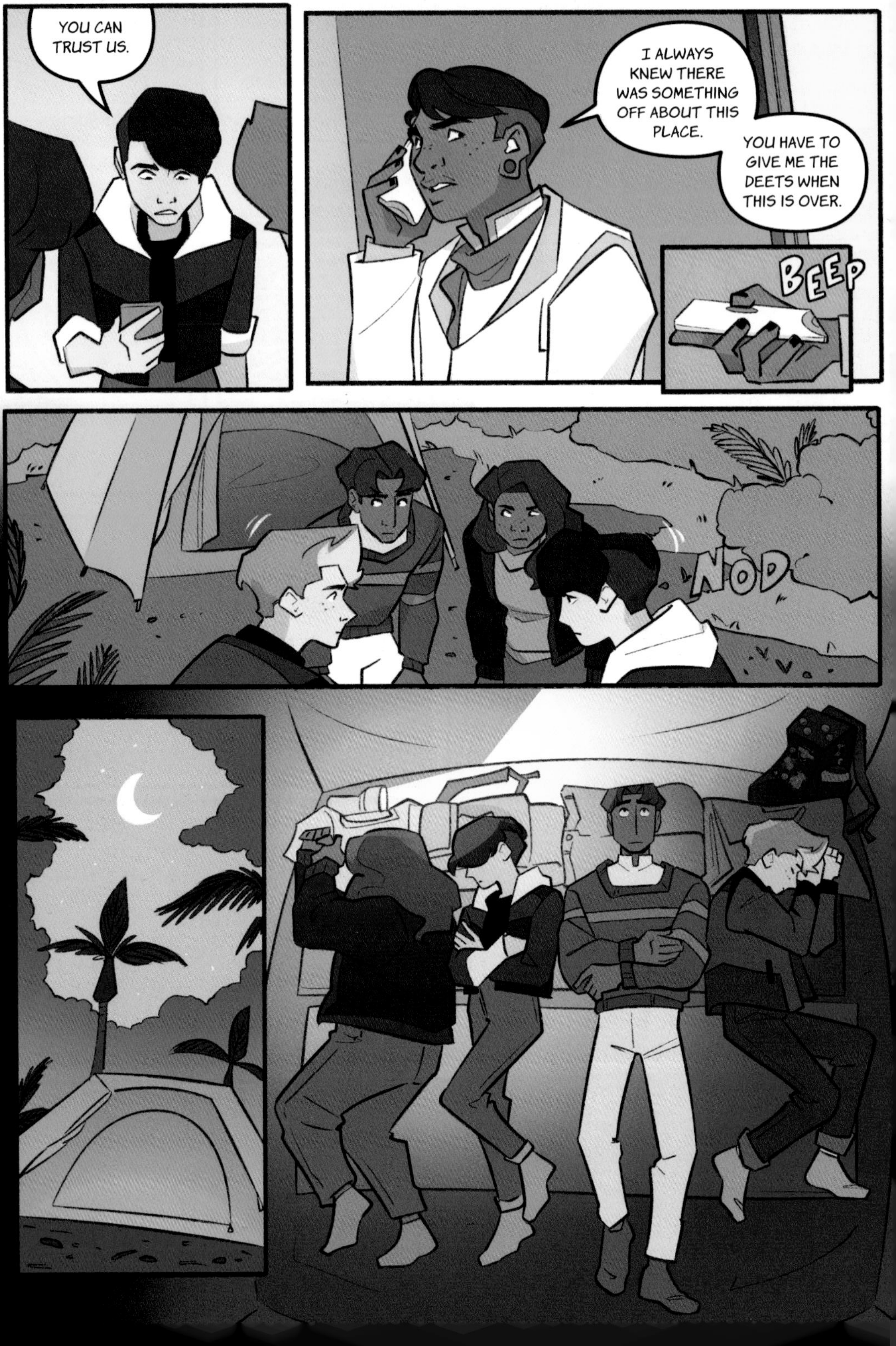
YOU CAN TRUST US.
I ALWAYS KNEW THERE WAS SOMETHING OFF ABOUT THIS PLACE.
YOU HAVE TO GIVE ME THE DEETS WHEN THIS IS OVER.
BEEP
NOD

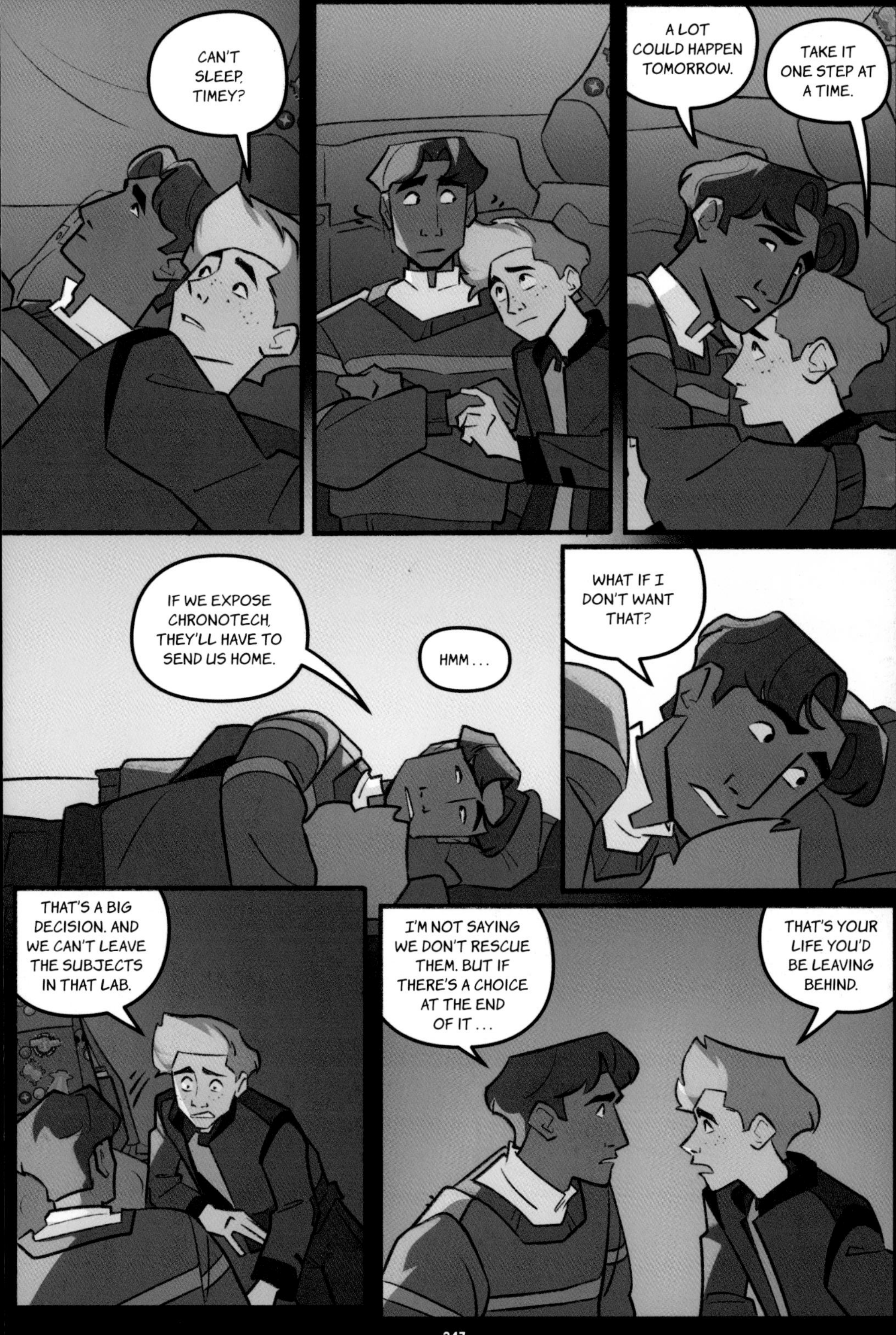
CAN'T SLEEP, TIMEY?
A LOT COULD HAPPEN TOMORROW.
TAKE IT ONE STEP AT A TIME.
IF WE EXPOSE CHRONOTECH, THEY'LL HAVE TO SEND US HOME.
HMM . . .
WHAT IF I DON'T WANT THAT?
THAT'S A BIG DECISION. AND WE CAN'T LEAVE THE SUBJECTS IN THAT LAB.
I'M NOT SAYING WE DON'T RESCUE THEM. BUT IF THERE'S A CHOICE AT THE END OF IT . . .
THAT'S YOUR LIFE YOU'D BE LEAVING BEHIND.

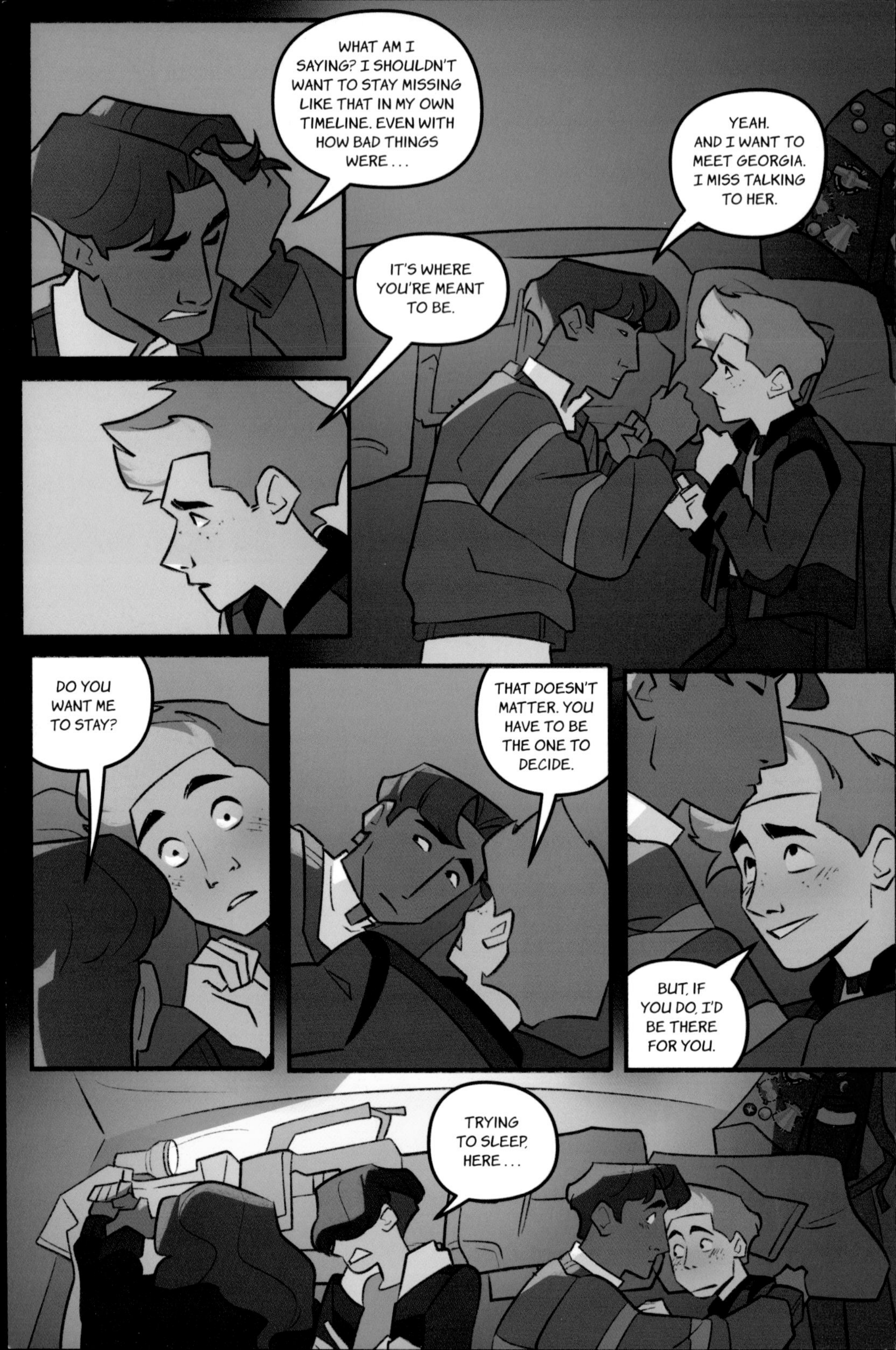
WHAT AM I SAYING? I SHOULDN'T WANT TO STAY MISSING LIKE THAT IN MY OWN TIMELINE. EVEN WITH HOW BAD THINGS WERE . . .
YEAH. AND I WANT TO MEET GEORGIA. I MISS TALKING TO HER.
IT'S WHERE YOU'RE MEANT TO BE.
DO YOU WANT ME TO STAY?
THAT DOESN'T MATTER. YOU HAVE TO BE THE ONE TO DECIDE.
BUT, IF YOU DO, I'D BE THERE FOR YOU.
TRYING TO SLEEP, HERE . . .

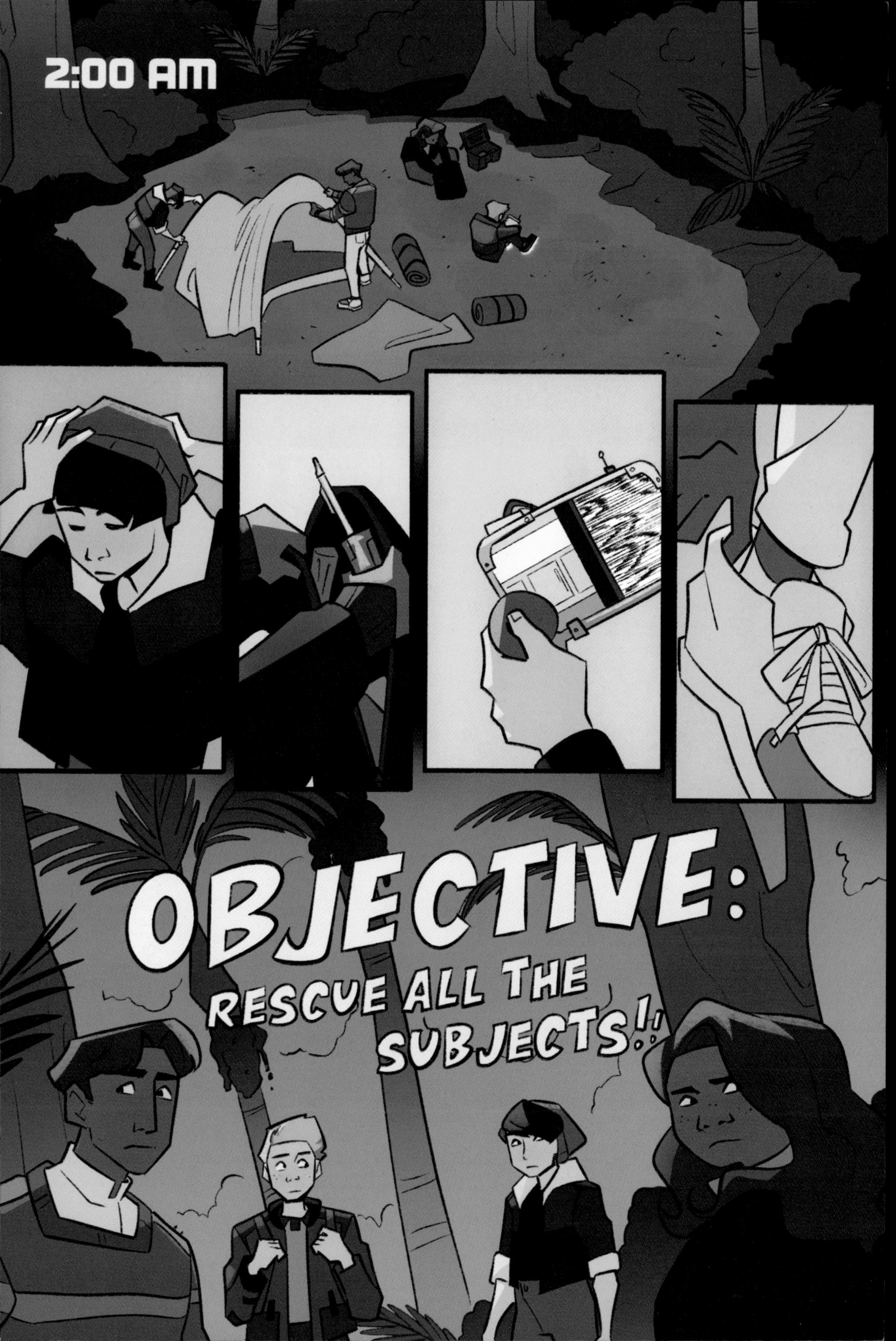
2:00 AM
OBJECTIVE:
RESCUE ALL THE SUBJECTS!!

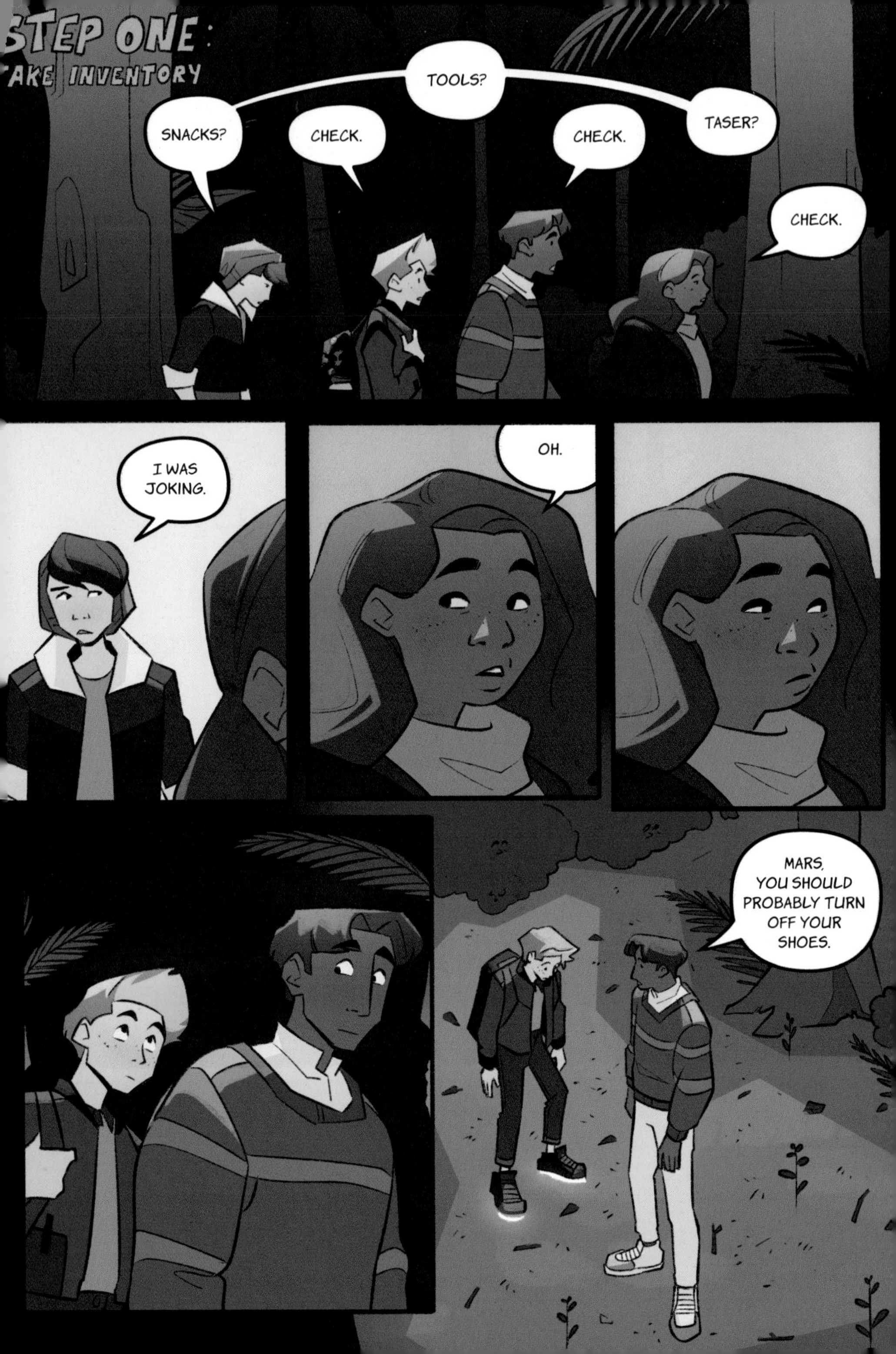
STEP ONE:
TAKE INVENTORY
SNACKS?
CHECK.
TOOLS?
CHECK.
TASER?
CHECK.
I WAS JOKING.
OH.
MARS, YOU SHOULD PROBABLY TURN OFF YOUR SHOES.

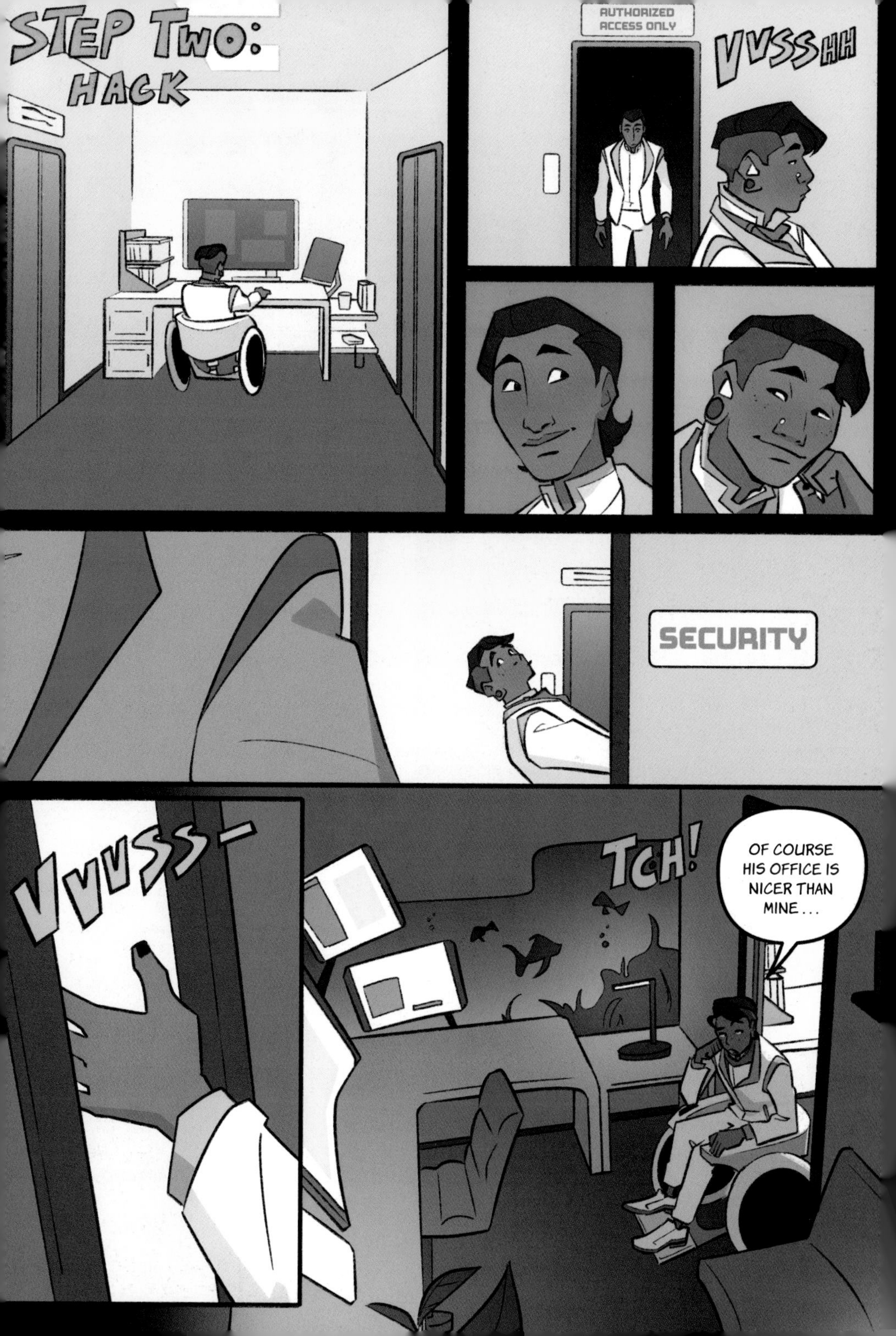
STEP TWO:
HACK
AUTHORIZED
ACCESS ONLY
VVSSHH
SECURITY
VVVSS—
TCH!
OF COURSE HIS OFFICE IS NICER THAN MINE . . .

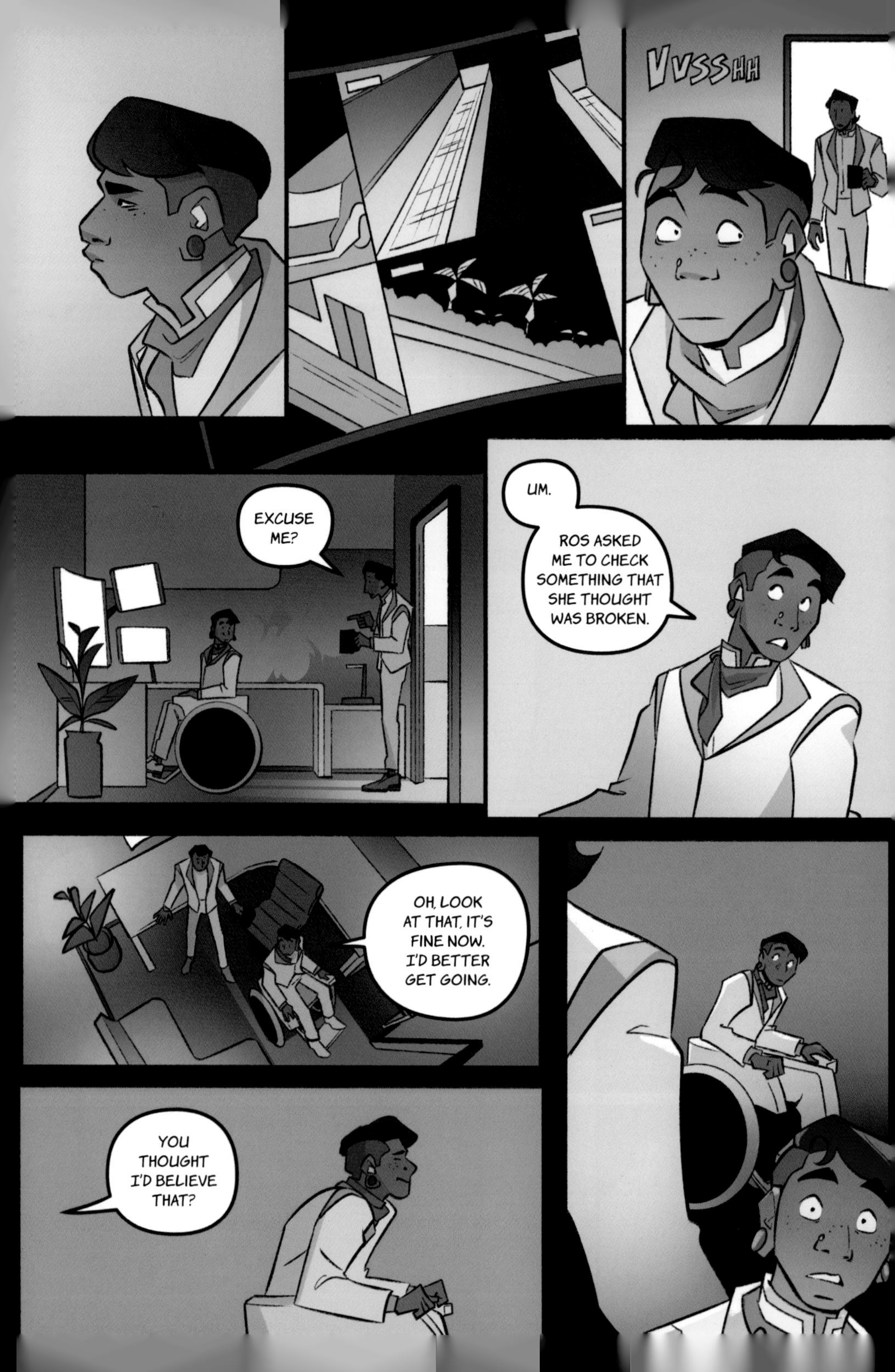
VVSSHH
EXCUSE ME?
UM.
ROS ASKED ME TO CHECK SOMETHING THAT SHE THOUGHT WAS BROKEN.
OH, LOOK AT THAT, IT'S FINE NOW. I'D BETTER GET GOING.
YOU THOUGHT I'D BELIEVE THAT?

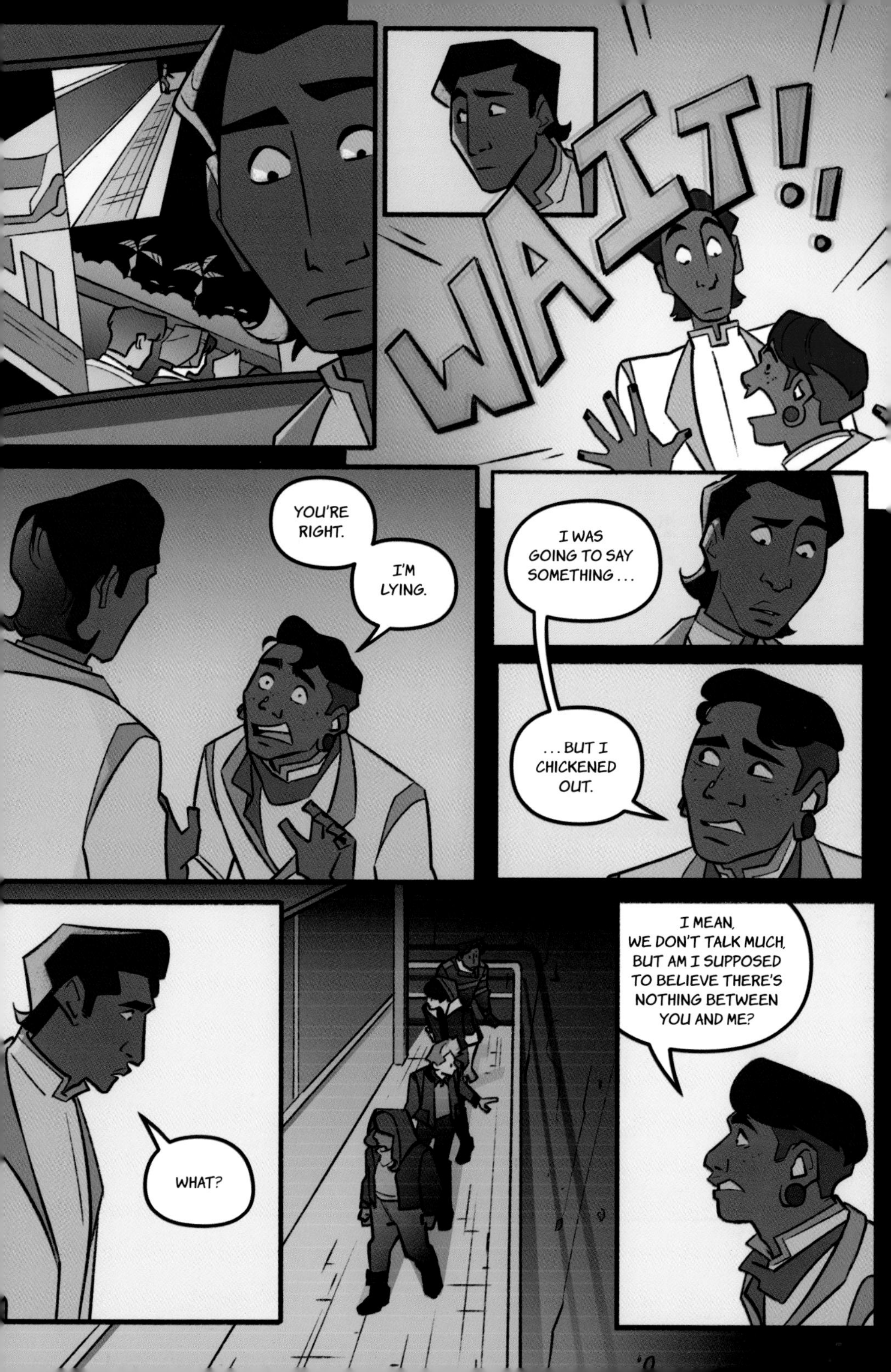
WAIT!!
YOU'RE RIGHT.
I'M LYING.
I WAS GOING TO SAY SOMETHING . . .
. . . BUT I CHICKENED OUT.
WHAT?
I MEAN, WE DON'T TALK MUCH, BUT AM I SUPPOSED TO BELIEVE THERE'S NOTHING BETWEEN YOU AND ME?

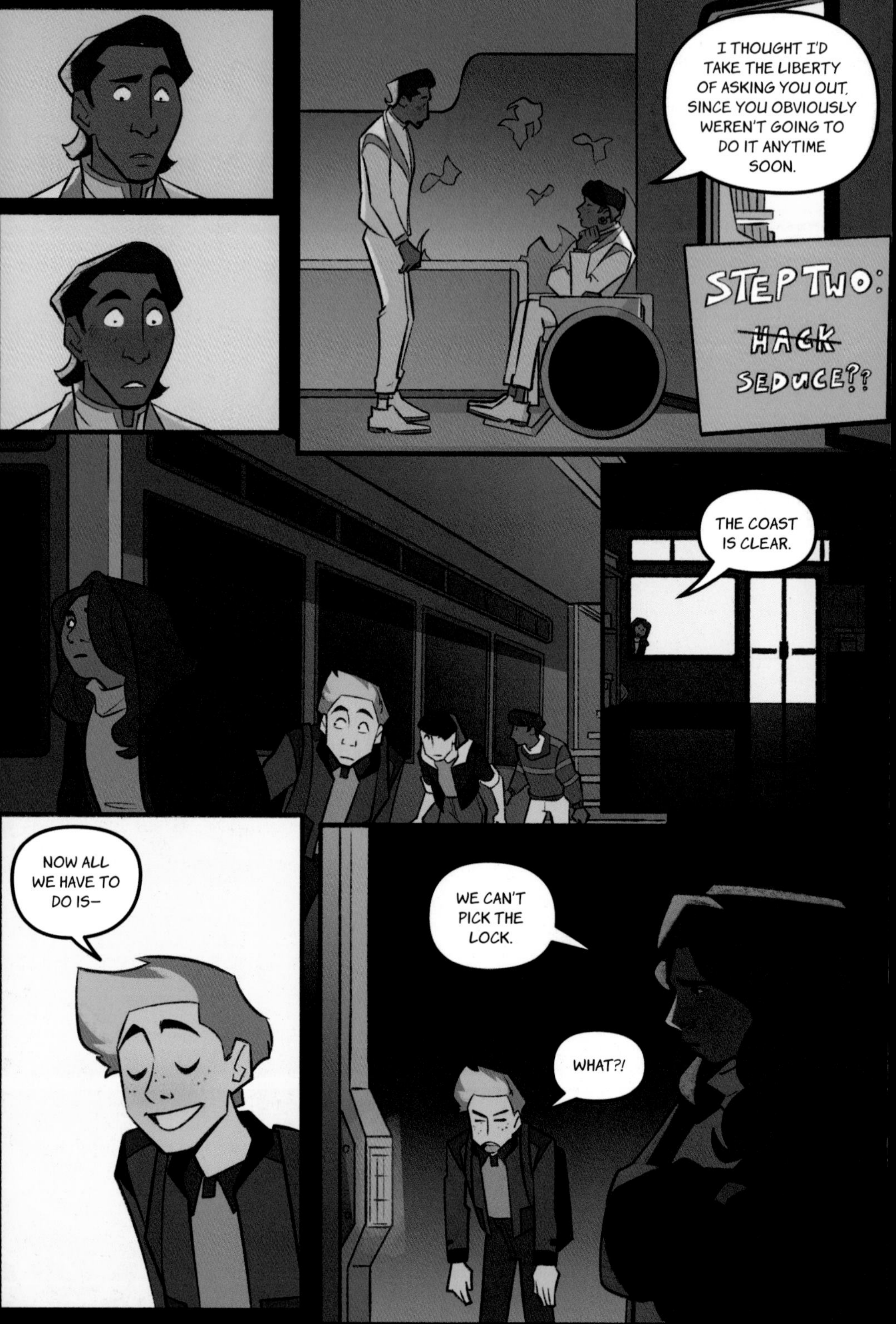
I THOUGHT I'D TAKE THE LIBERTY OF ASKING YOU OUT, SINCE YOU OBVIOUSLY WEREN'T GOING TO DO IT ANYTIME SOON.
STEP TWO:
HACK
SEDUCE??
THE COAST IS CLEAR.
NOW ALL WE HAVE TO DO IS—
WE CAN'T PICK THE LOCK.
WHAT?!

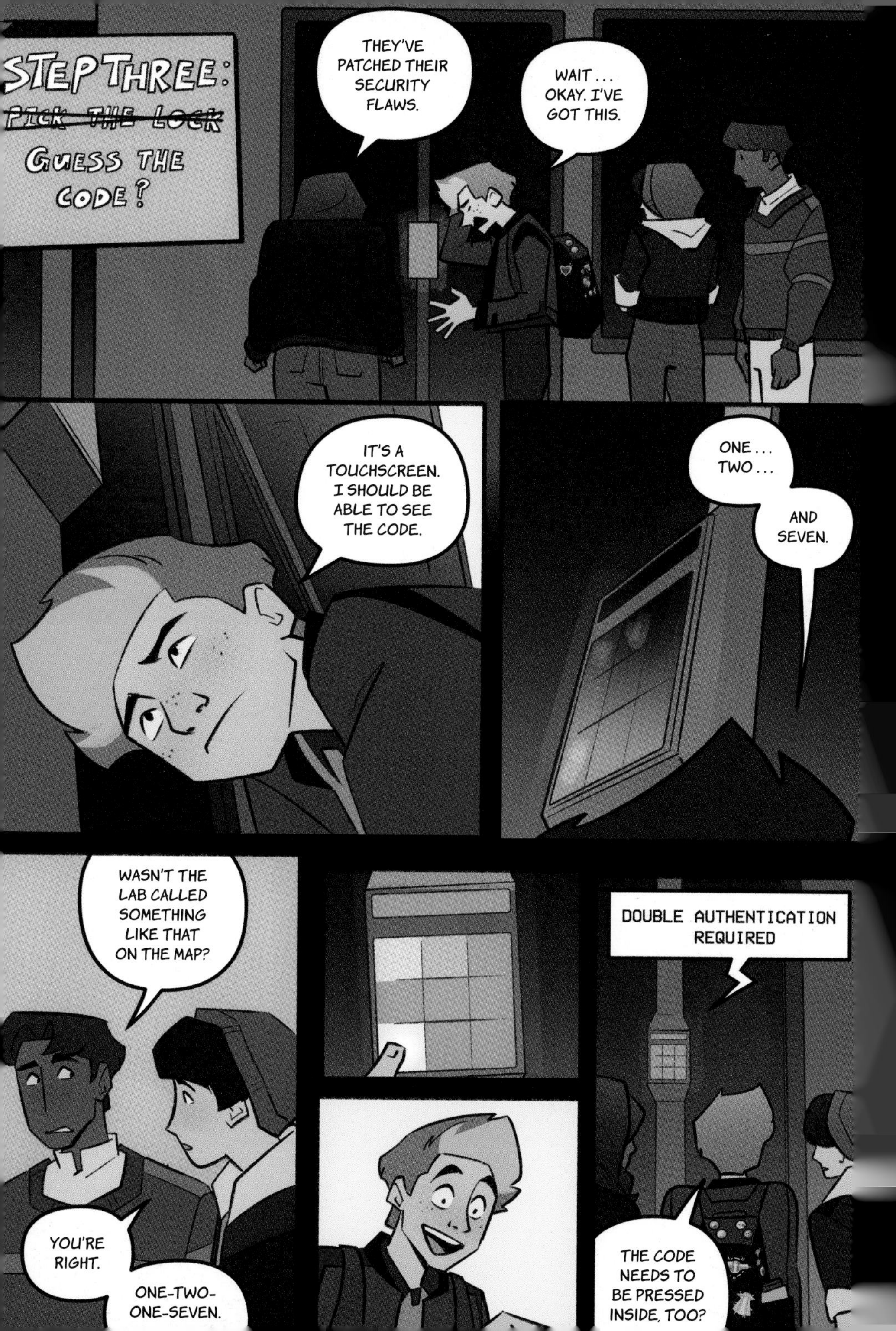
STEP THREE:
PICK THE LOCK
GUESS THE CODE?
THEY'VE PATCHED THEIR SECURITY FLAWS.
WAIT . . . OKAY. I'VE GOT THIS.
IT'S A TOUCHSCREEN. I SHOULD BE ABLE TO SEE THE CODE.
ONE . . . TWO . . .
AND SEVEN.
WASN'T THE LAB CALLED SOMETHING LIKE THAT ON THE MAP?
YOU'RE RIGHT.
ONE-TWO-ONE-SEVEN.
DOUBLE AUTHENTICATION REQUIRED
THE CODE NEEDS TO BE PRESSED INSIDE, TOO?

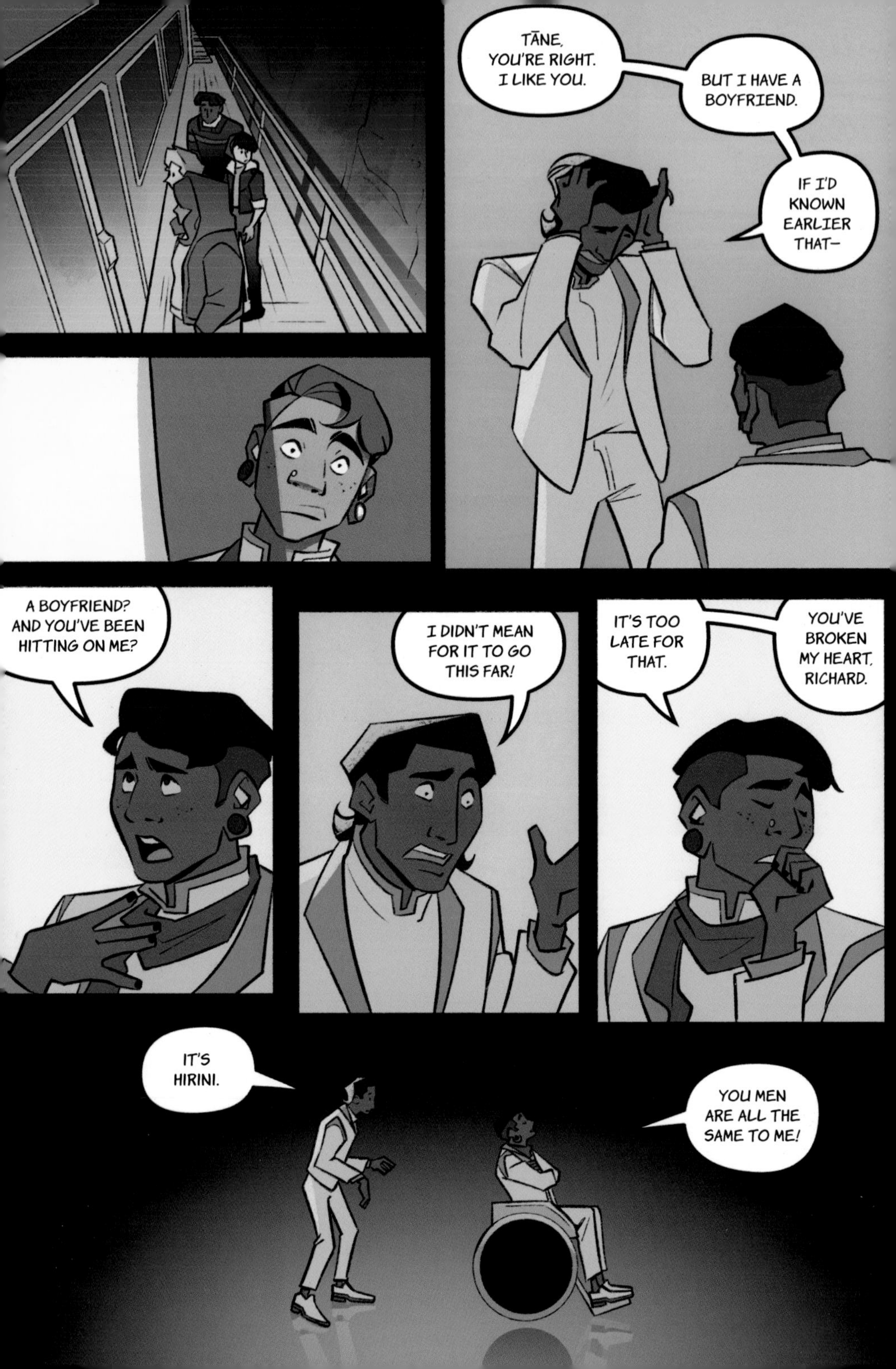

TĀNE, YOU'RE RIGHT. I LIKE YOU.
BUT I HAVE A BOYFRIEND.
IF I'D KNOWN EARLIER THAT—
A BOYFRIEND? AND YOU'VE BEEN HITTING ON ME?
I DIDN'T MEAN FOR IT TO GO THIS FAR!
IT'S TOO LATE FOR THAT.
YOU'VE BROKEN MY HEART, RICHARD.
IT'S HIRINI.
YOU MEN ARE ALL THE SAME TO ME!

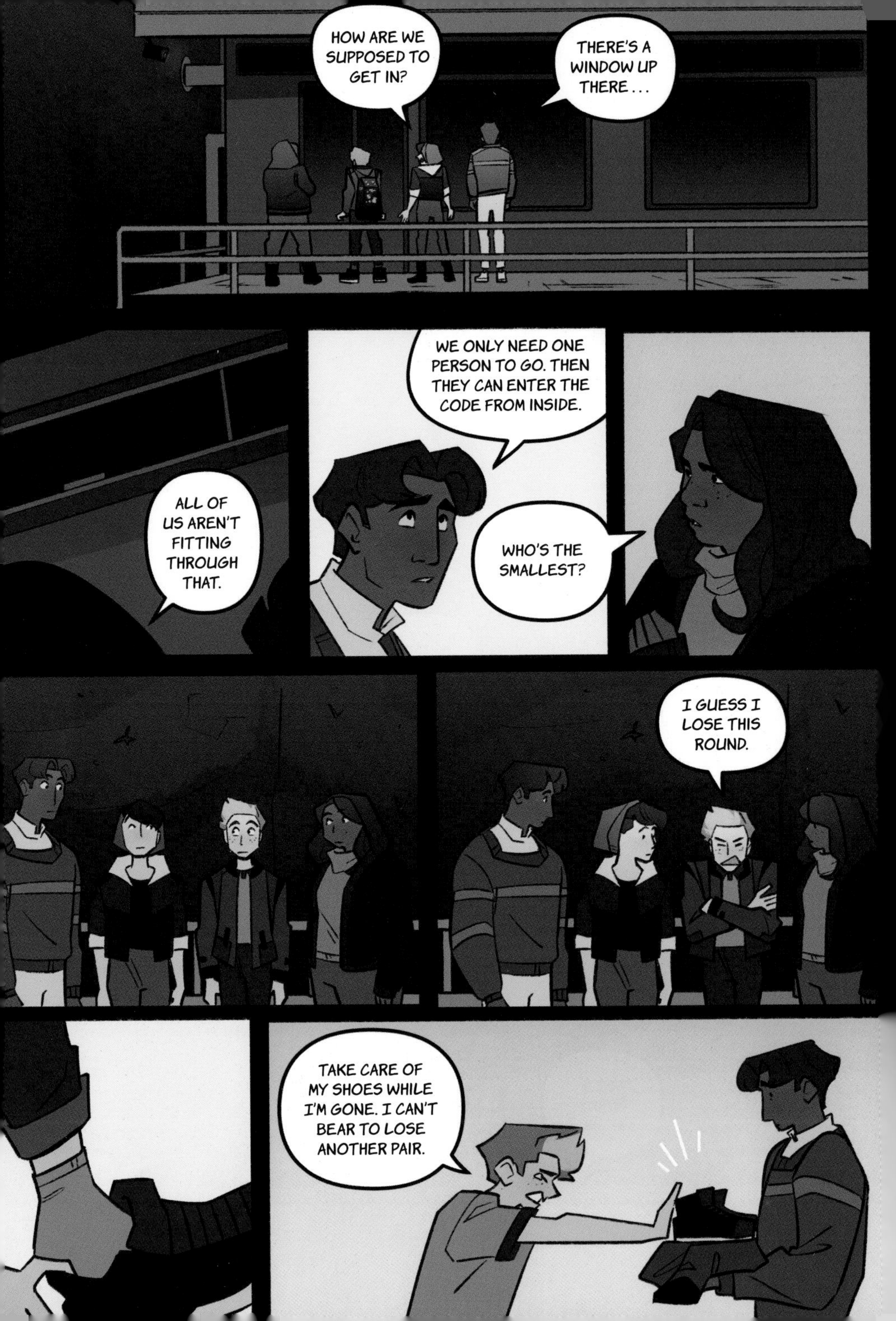
HOW ARE WE SUPPOSED TO GET IN?
THERE'S A WINDOW UP THERE . . .
ALL OF US AREN'T FITTING THROUGH THAT.
WE ONLY NEED ONE PERSON TO GO. THEN THEY CAN ENTER THE CODE FROM INSIDE.
WHO'S THE SMALLEST?
I GUESS I LOSE THIS ROUND.
TAKE CARE OF MY SHOES WHILE I'M GONE. I CAN'T BEAR TO LOSE ANOTHER PAIR.

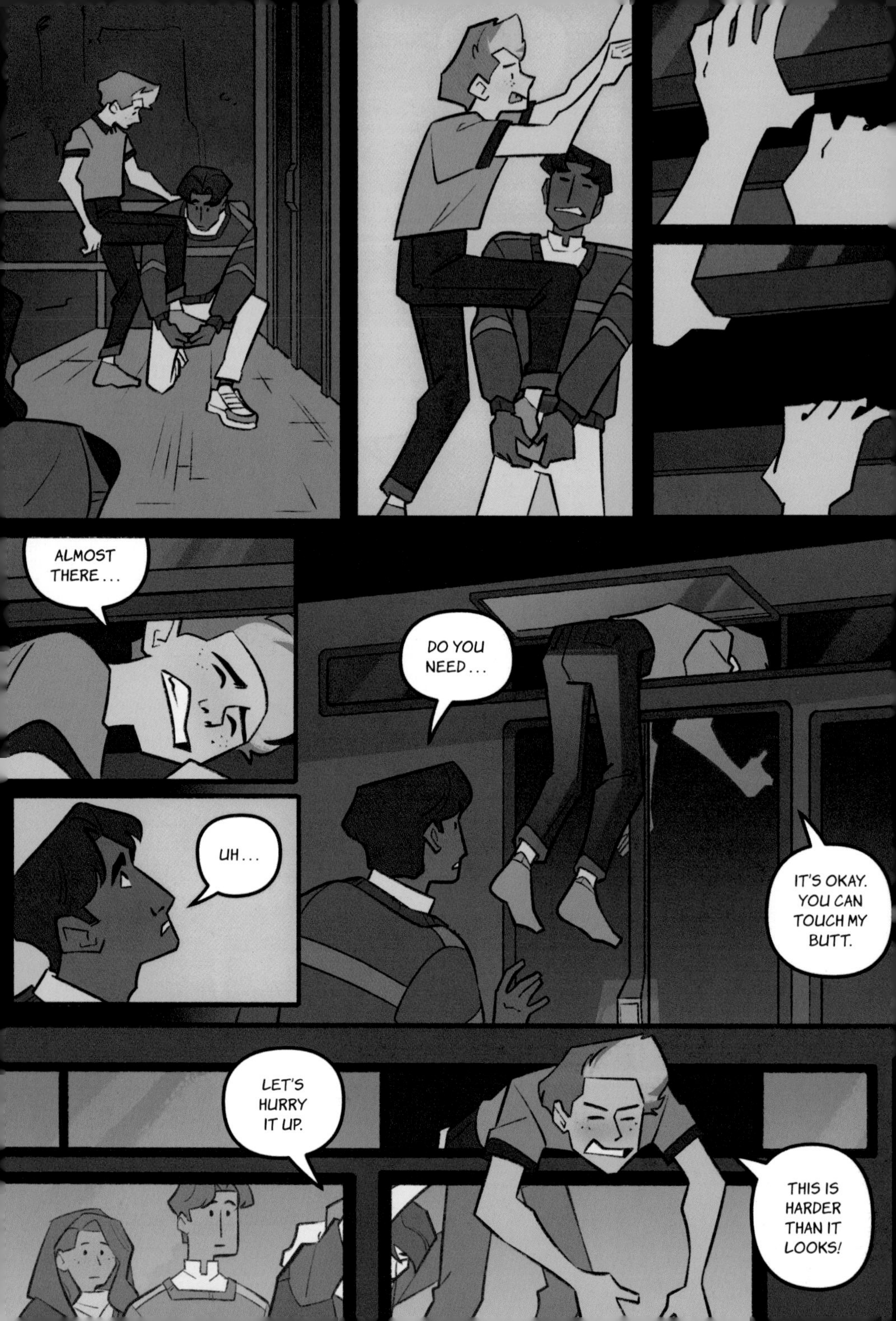
ALMOST THERE . . .
DO YOU NEED . . .
UH . . .
IT'S OKAY. YOU CAN TOUCH MY BUTT.
LET'S HURRY IT UP.
THIS IS HARDER THAN IT LOOKS!

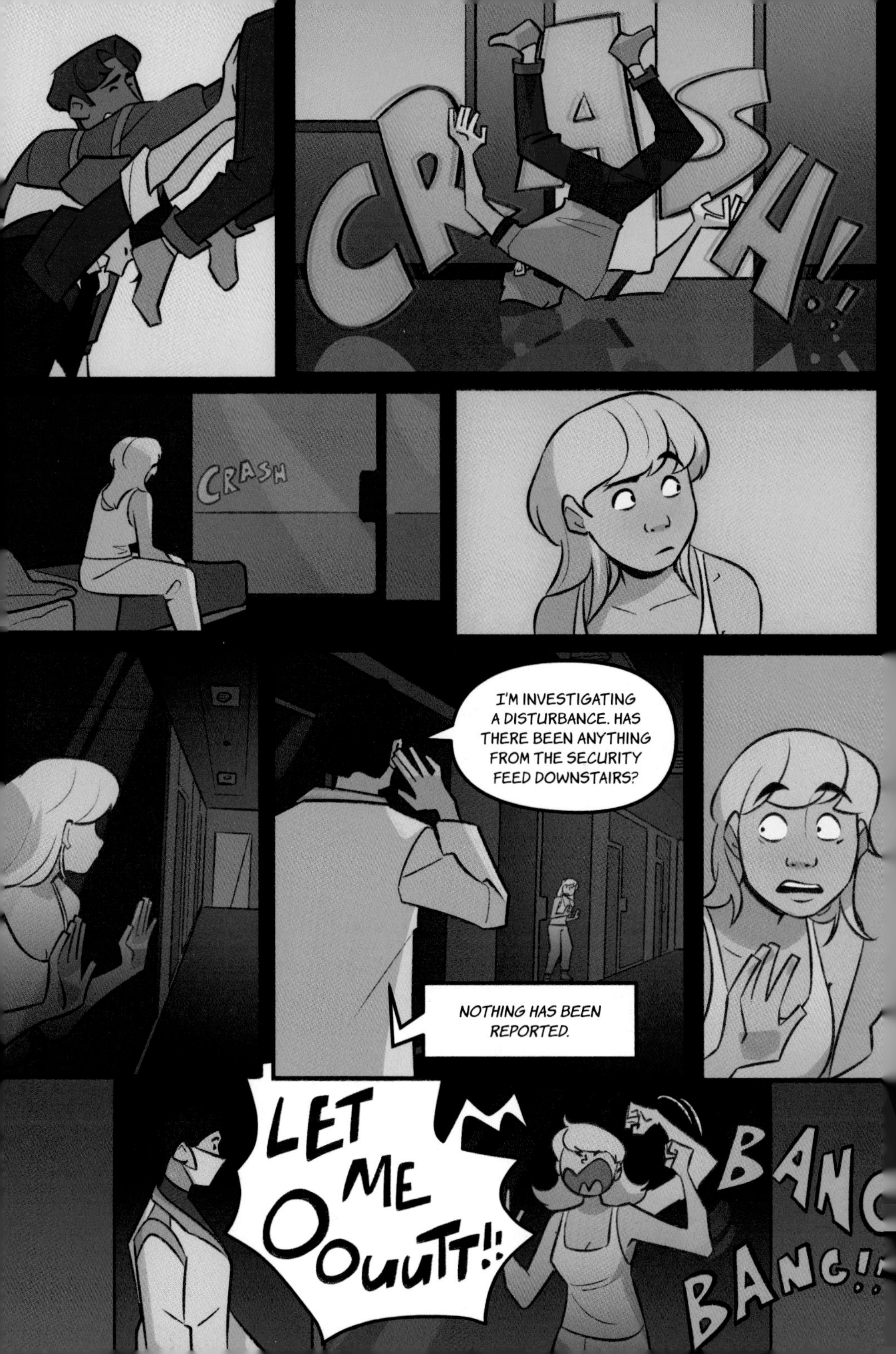
CRASH!!
CRASH
I'M INVESTIGATING A DISTURBANCE. HAS THERE BEEN ANYTHING FROM THE SECURITY FEED DOWNSTAIRS?
NOTHING HAS BEEN REPORTED.
LET ME OOUUTT!!
BANG
BANG!!

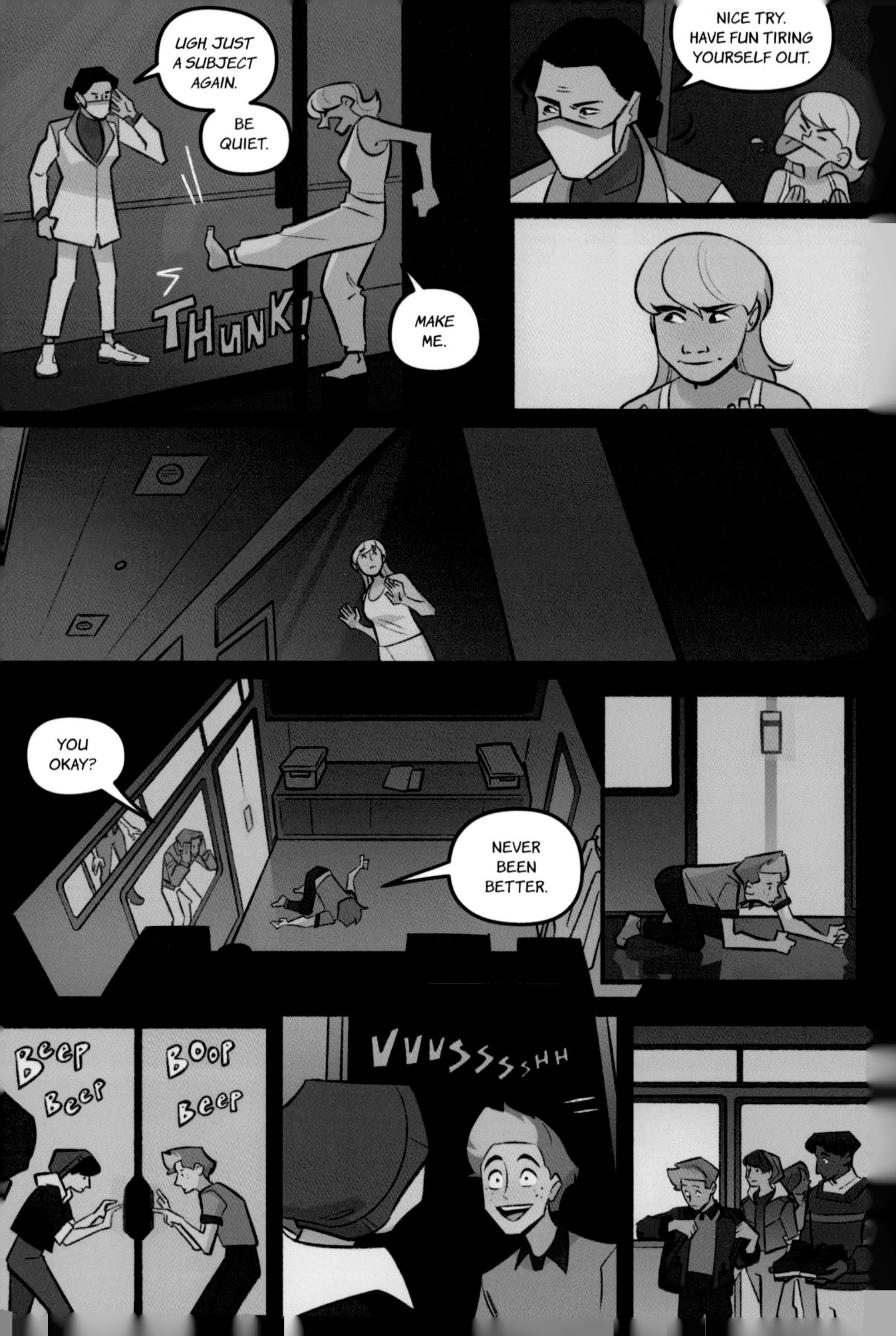
UGH, JUST A SUBJECT AGAIN.
BE QUIET.
THUNK!
MAKE ME.
NICE TRY. HAVE FUN TIRING YOURSELF OUT.
YOU OKAY?
NEVER BEEN BETTER.
Beep Beep
Boop Beep
VUUSSSSHH

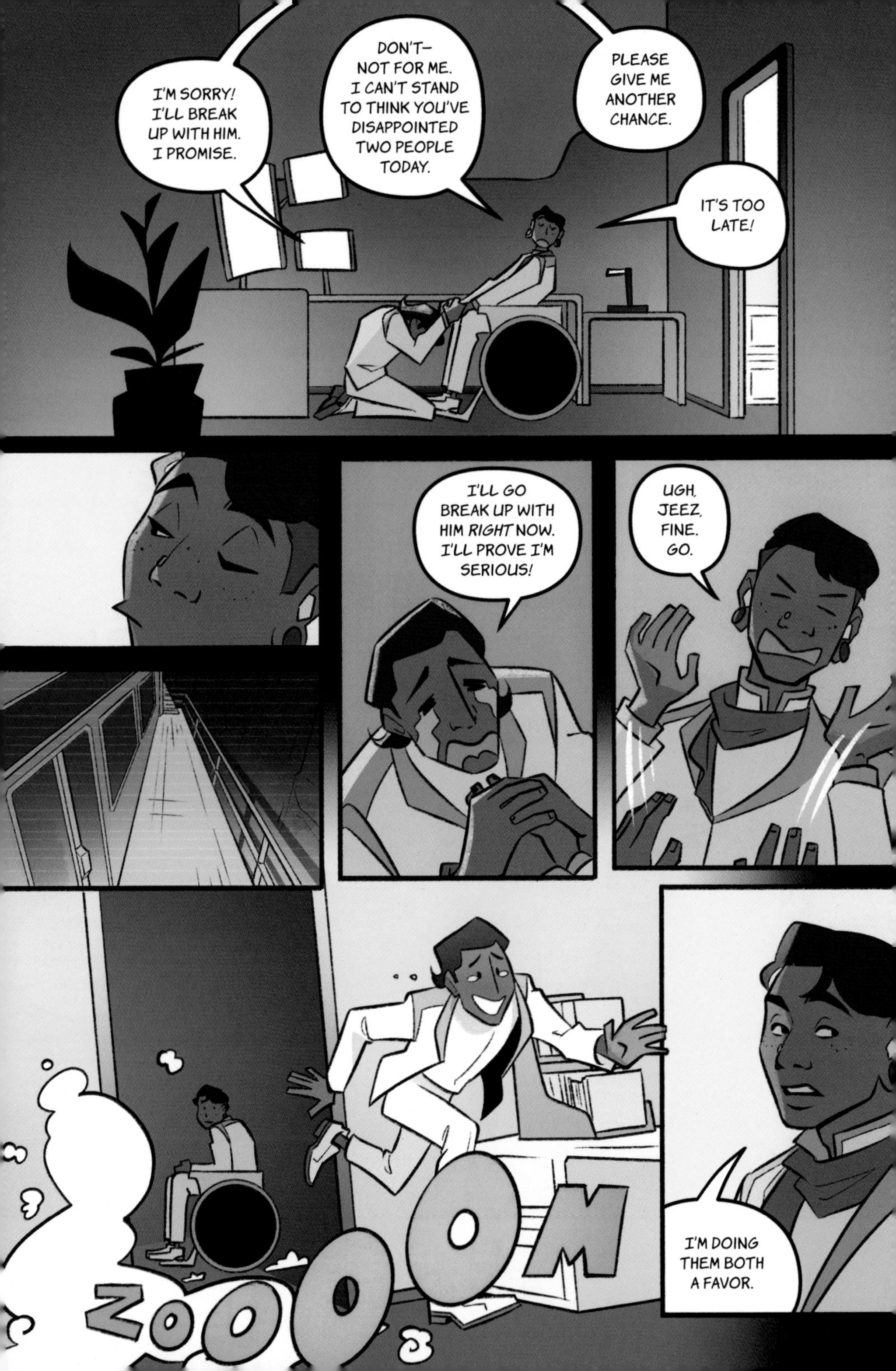
I'M SORRY! I'LL BREAK UP WITH HIM. I PROMISE.
DON'T— NOT FOR ME. I CAN'T STAND TO THINK YOU'VE DISAPPOINTED TWO PEOPLE TODAY.
PLEASE GIVE ME ANOTHER CHANCE.
IT'S TOO LATE!
I'LL GO BREAK UP WITH HIM *RIGHT* NOW. I'LL PROVE I'M SERIOUS!
UGH, JEEZ, FINE. GO.
ZOOOOM
I'M DOING THEM BOTH A FAVOR.

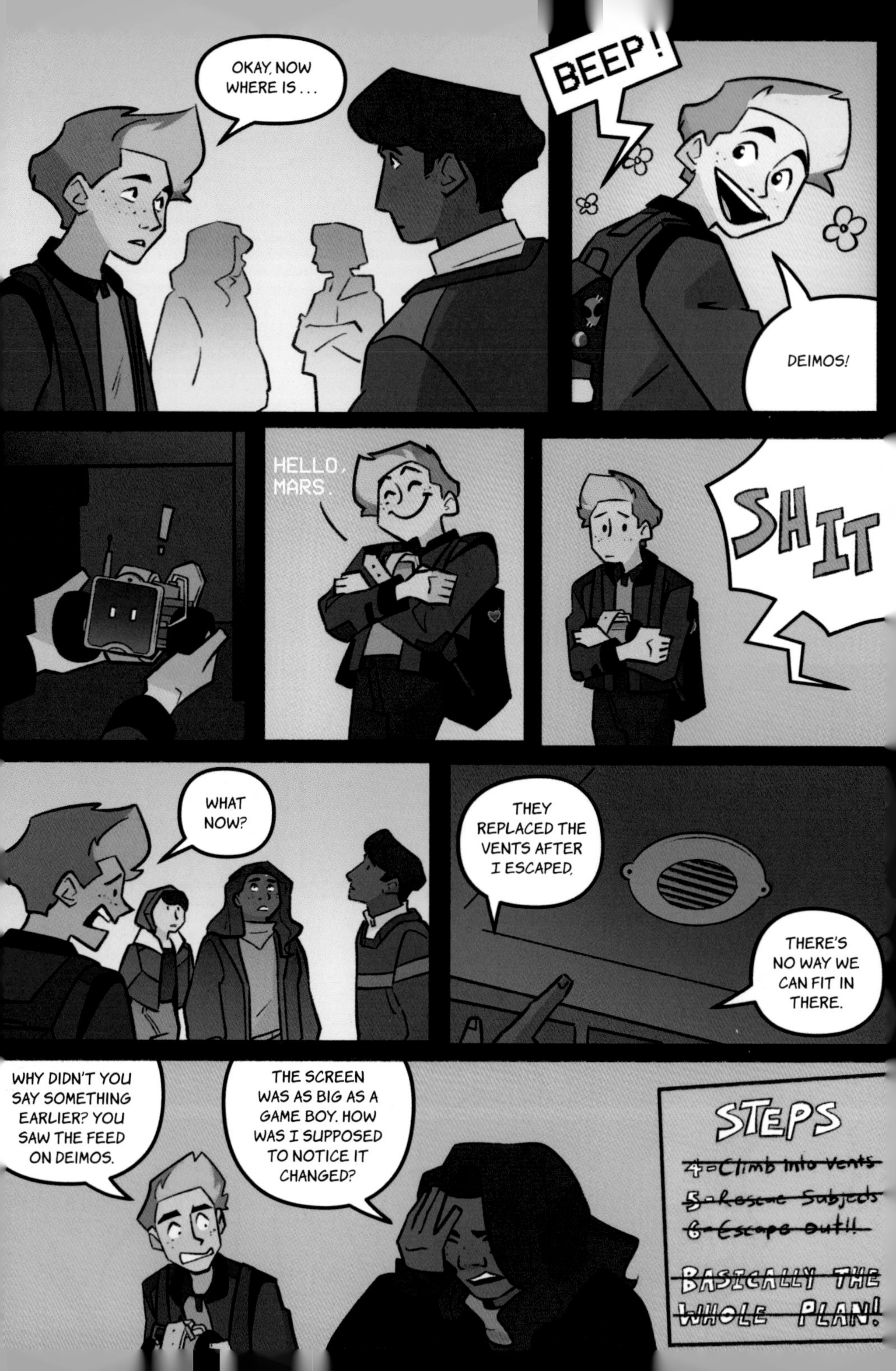
OKAY, NOW WHERE IS . . .
BEEP!
DEIMOS!
!
HELLO, MARS.
SHIT
WHAT NOW?
THEY REPLACED THE VENTS AFTER I ESCAPED.
THERE'S NO WAY WE CAN FIT IN THERE.
WHY DIDN'T YOU SAY SOMETHING EARLIER? YOU SAW THE FEED ON DEIMOS.
THE SCREEN WAS AS BIG AS A GAME BOY. HOW WAS I SUPPOSED TO NOTICE IT CHANGED?
STEPS
4-Climb into vents
5-Rescue Subjects
6-Escape out!!
BASICALLY THE WHOLE PLAN!

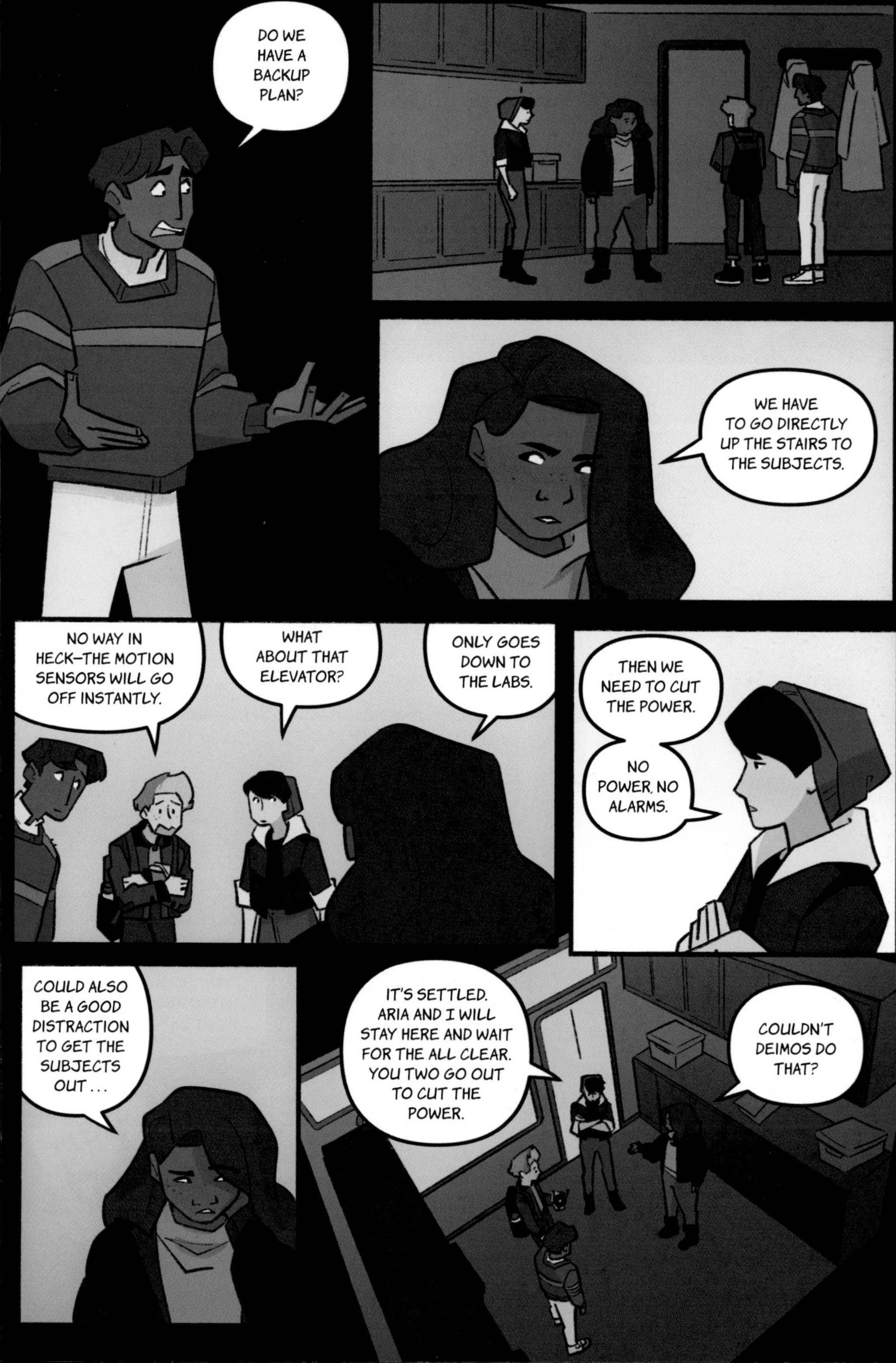
DO WE HAVE A BACKUP PLAN?
WE HAVE TO GO DIRECTLY UP THE STAIRS TO THE SUBJECTS.
NO WAY IN HECK—THE MOTION SENSORS WILL GO OFF INSTANTLY.
WHAT ABOUT THAT ELEVATOR?
ONLY GOES DOWN TO THE LABS.
THEN WE NEED TO CUT THE POWER.
NO POWER, NO ALARMS.
COULD ALSO BE A GOOD DISTRACTION TO GET THE SUBJECTS OUT . . .
COULDN'T DEIMOS DO THAT?
IT'S SETTLED. ARIA AND I WILL STAY HERE AND WAIT FOR THE ALL CLEAR. YOU TWO GO OUT TO CUT THE POWER.

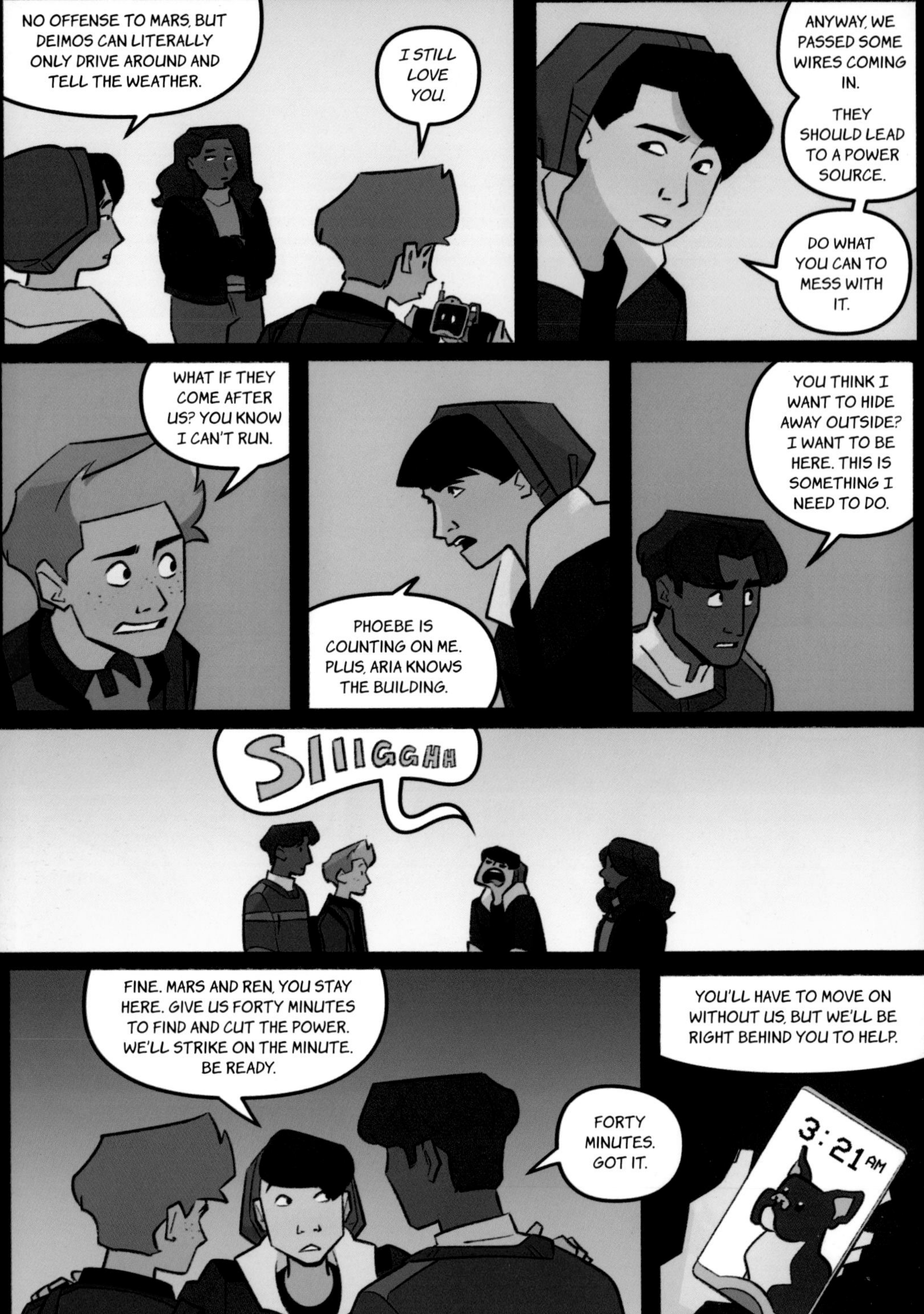
NO OFFENSE TO MARS, BUT DEIMOS CAN LITERALLY ONLY DRIVE AROUND AND TELL THE WEATHER.
I STILL LOVE YOU.
ANYWAY, WE PASSED SOME WIRES COMING IN.
THEY SHOULD LEAD TO A POWER SOURCE.
DO WHAT YOU CAN TO MESS WITH IT.
WHAT IF THEY COME AFTER US? YOU KNOW I CAN'T RUN.
PHOEBE IS COUNTING ON ME. PLUS, ARIA KNOWS THE BUILDING.
YOU THINK I WANT TO HIDE AWAY OUTSIDE? I WANT TO BE HERE. THIS IS SOMETHING I NEED TO DO.
SIIIGGHH
FINE. MARS AND REN, YOU STAY HERE. GIVE US FORTY MINUTES TO FIND AND CUT THE POWER. WE'LL STRIKE ON THE MINUTE. BE READY.
FORTY MINUTES. GOT IT.
YOU'LL HAVE TO MOVE ON WITHOUT US, BUT WE'LL BE RIGHT BEHIND YOU TO HELP.
3:21 AM

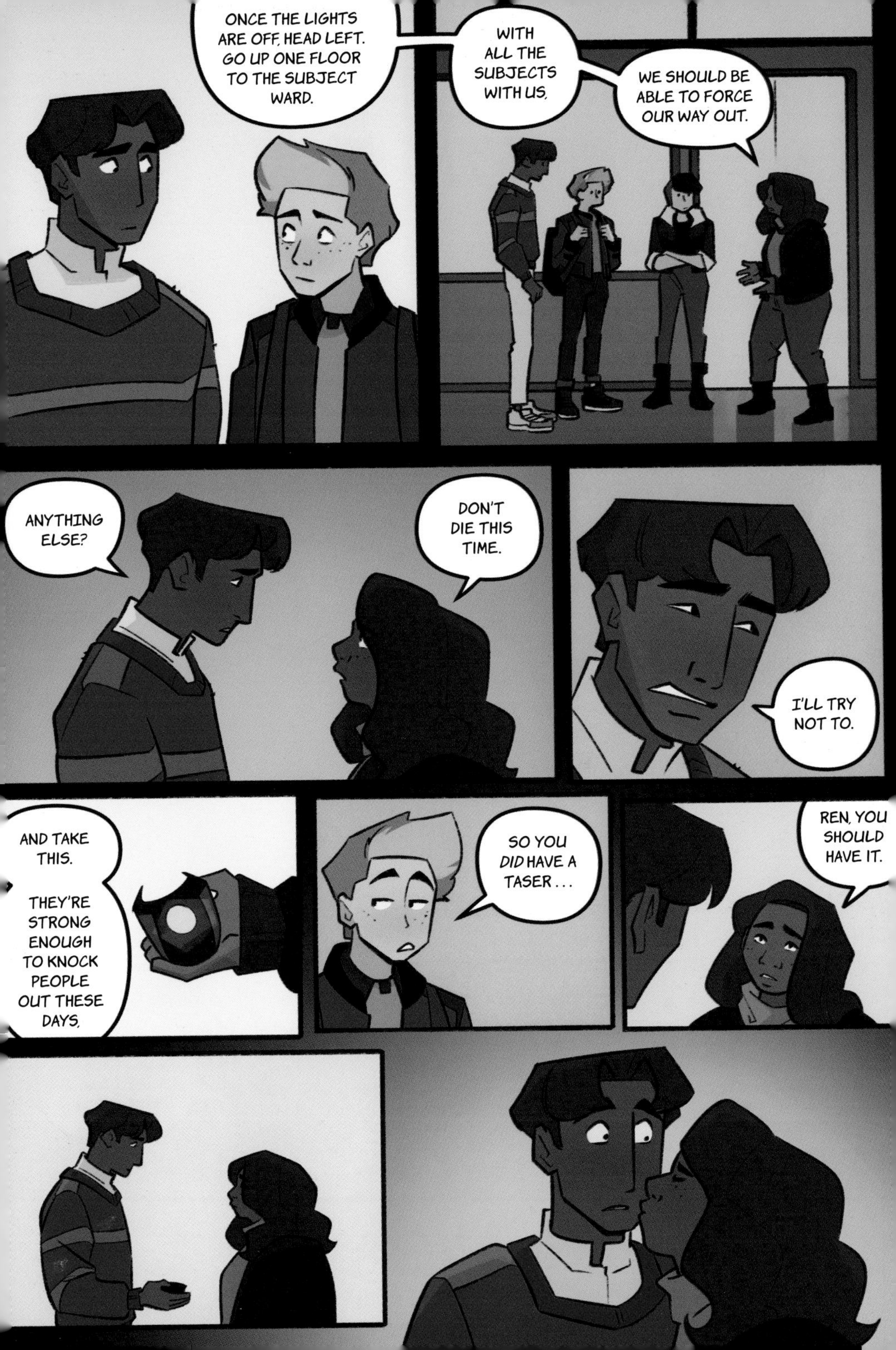
ONCE THE LIGHTS ARE OFF, HEAD LEFT. GO UP ONE FLOOR TO THE SUBJECT WARD.
WITH ALL THE SUBJECTS WITH US,
WE SHOULD BE ABLE TO FORCE OUR WAY OUT.
ANYTHING ELSE?
DON'T DIE THIS TIME.
I'LL TRY NOT TO.
AND TAKE THIS.
THEY'RE STRONG ENOUGH TO KNOCK PEOPLE OUT THESE DAYS.
SO YOU *DID* HAVE A TASER . . .
REN, YOU SHOULD HAVE IT.

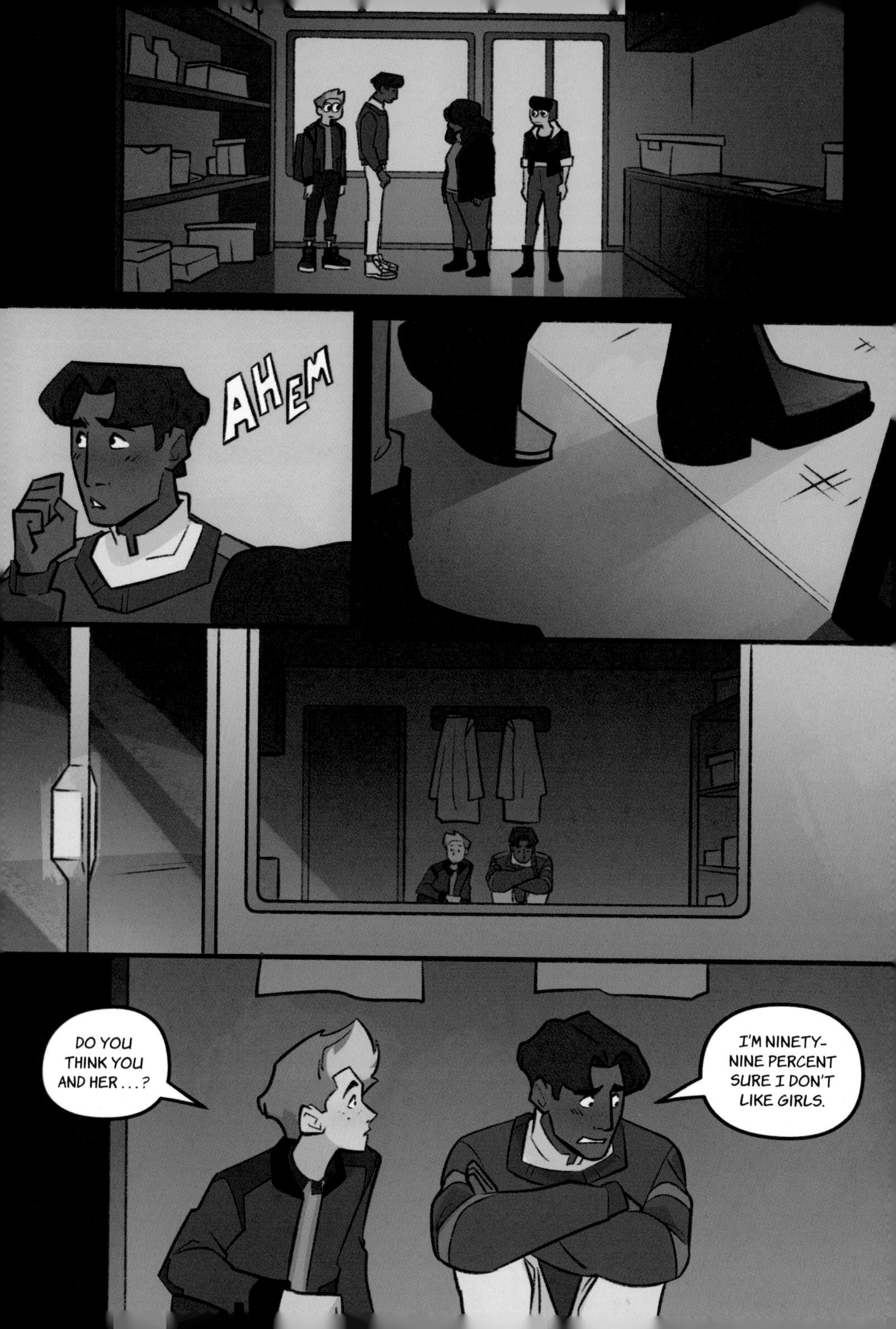
AHEM
DO YOU THINK YOU AND HER . . . ?
I'M NINETY-NINE PERCENT SURE I DON'T LIKE GIRLS.

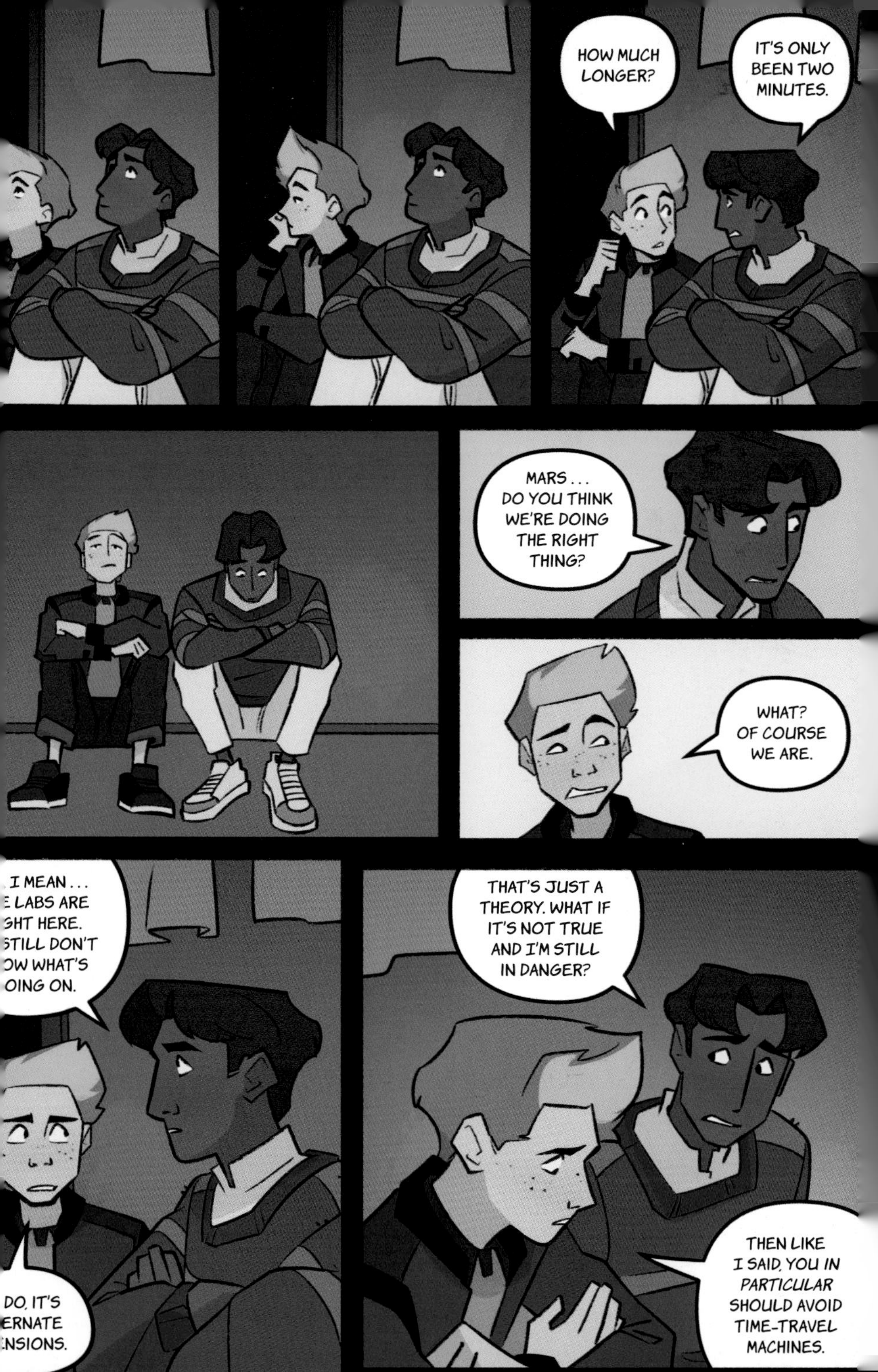
HOW MUCH LONGER?
IT'S ONLY BEEN TWO MINUTES.
MARS . . . DO YOU THINK WE'RE DOING THE RIGHT THING?
WHAT? OF COURSE WE ARE.
I MEAN . . . E LABS ARE GHT HERE. STILL DON'T OW WHAT'S OING ON.
DO, IT'S ERNATE ENSIONS.
THAT'S JUST A THEORY. WHAT IF IT'S NOT TRUE AND I'M STILL IN DANGER?
THEN LIKE I SAID, YOU IN PARTICULAR SHOULD AVOID TIME-TRAVEL MACHINES.

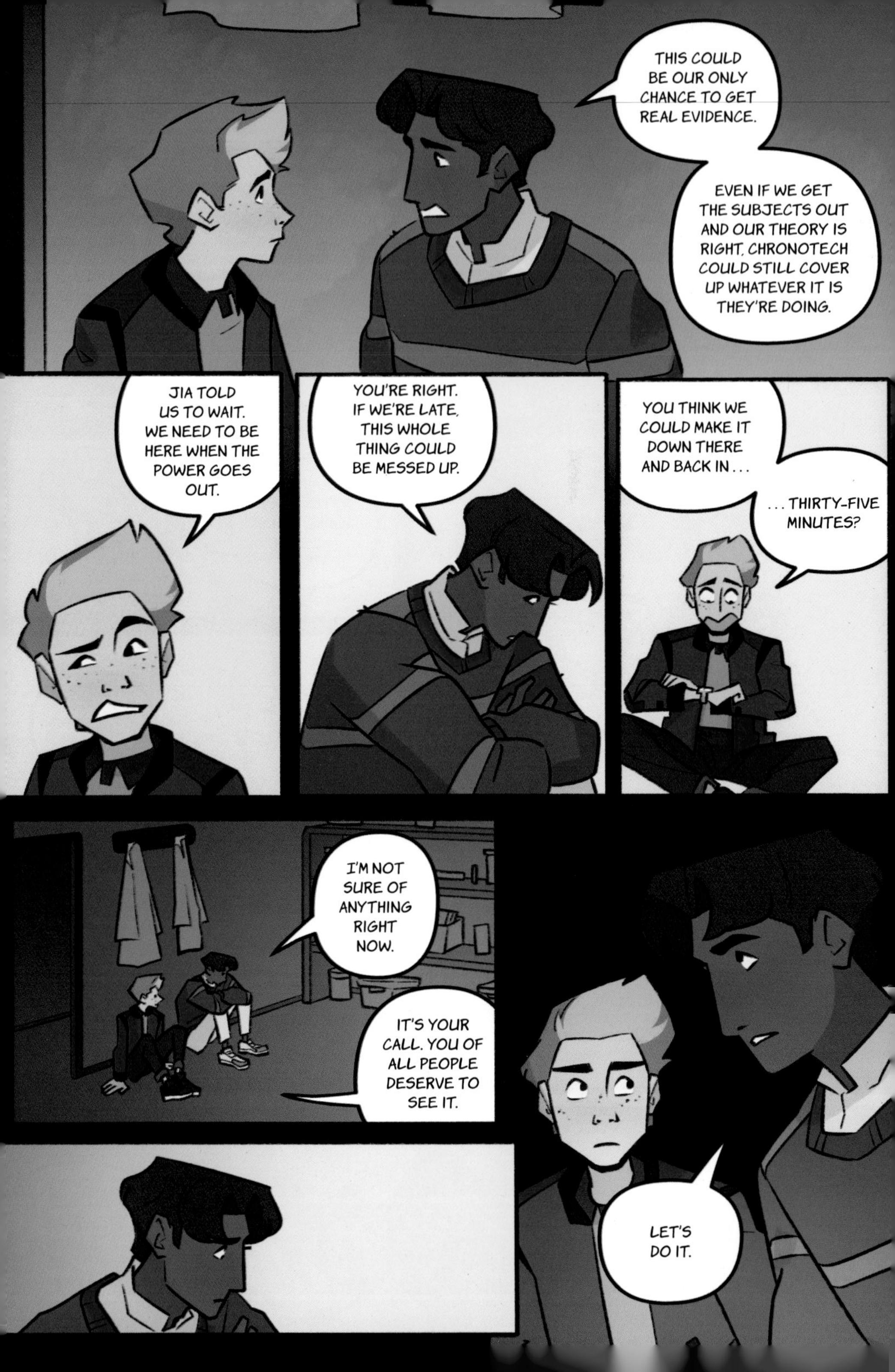
THIS COULD BE OUR ONLY CHANCE TO GET REAL EVIDENCE.
EVEN IF WE GET THE SUBJECTS OUT AND OUR THEORY IS RIGHT, CHRONOTECH COULD STILL COVER UP WHATEVER IT IS THEY'RE DOING.
JIA TOLD US TO WAIT. WE NEED TO BE HERE WHEN THE POWER GOES OUT.
YOU'RE RIGHT. IF WE'RE LATE, THIS WHOLE THING COULD BE MESSED UP.
YOU THINK WE COULD MAKE IT DOWN THERE AND BACK IN . . .
. . . THIRTY-FIVE MINUTES?
I'M NOT SURE OF ANYTHING RIGHT NOW.
IT'S YOUR CALL. YOU OF ALL PEOPLE DESERVE TO SEE IT.
LET'S DO IT.

CHAPTER
FIVE

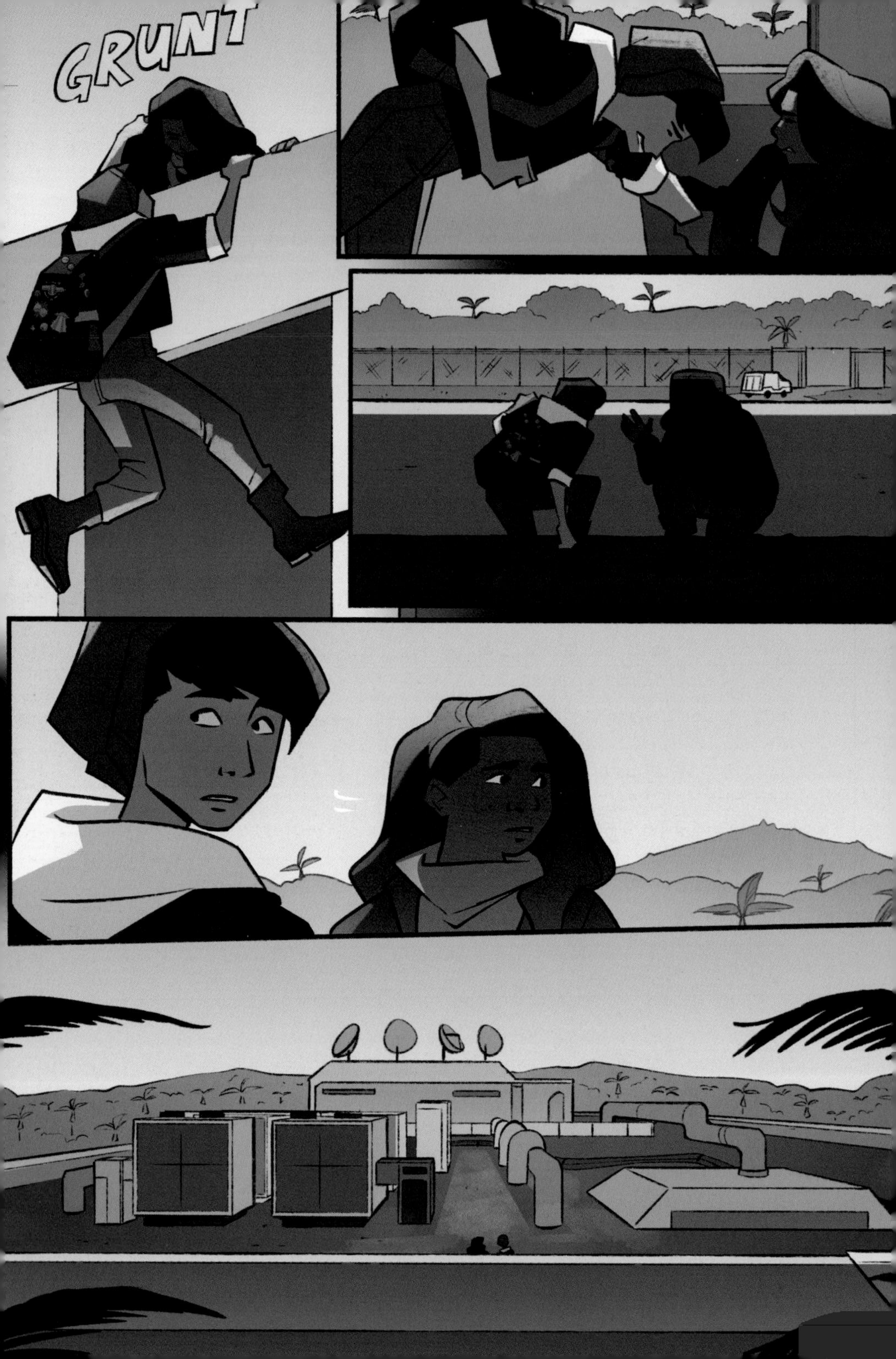
GRUNT

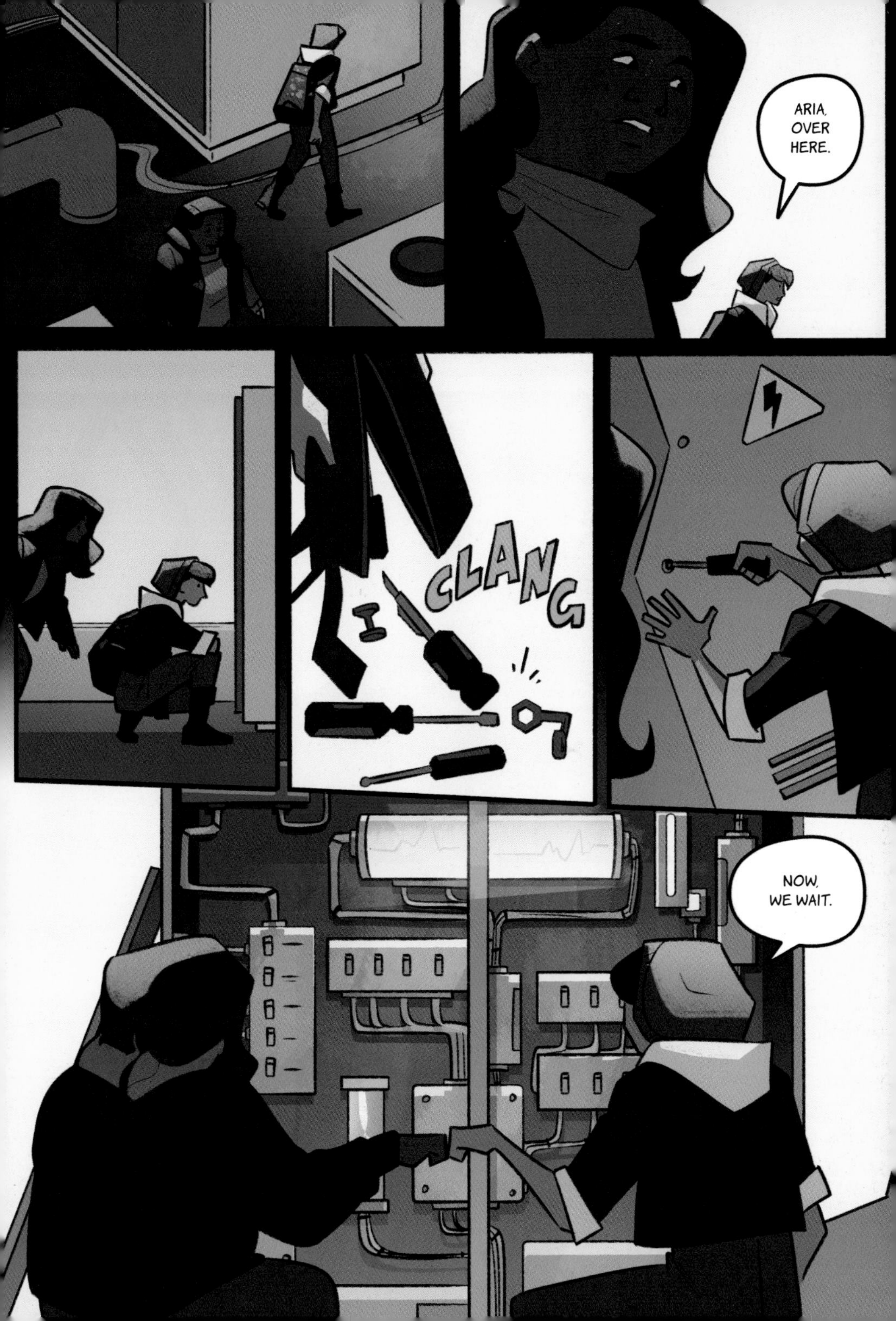

ARIA, OVER HERE.
CLANG
NOW, WE WAIT.

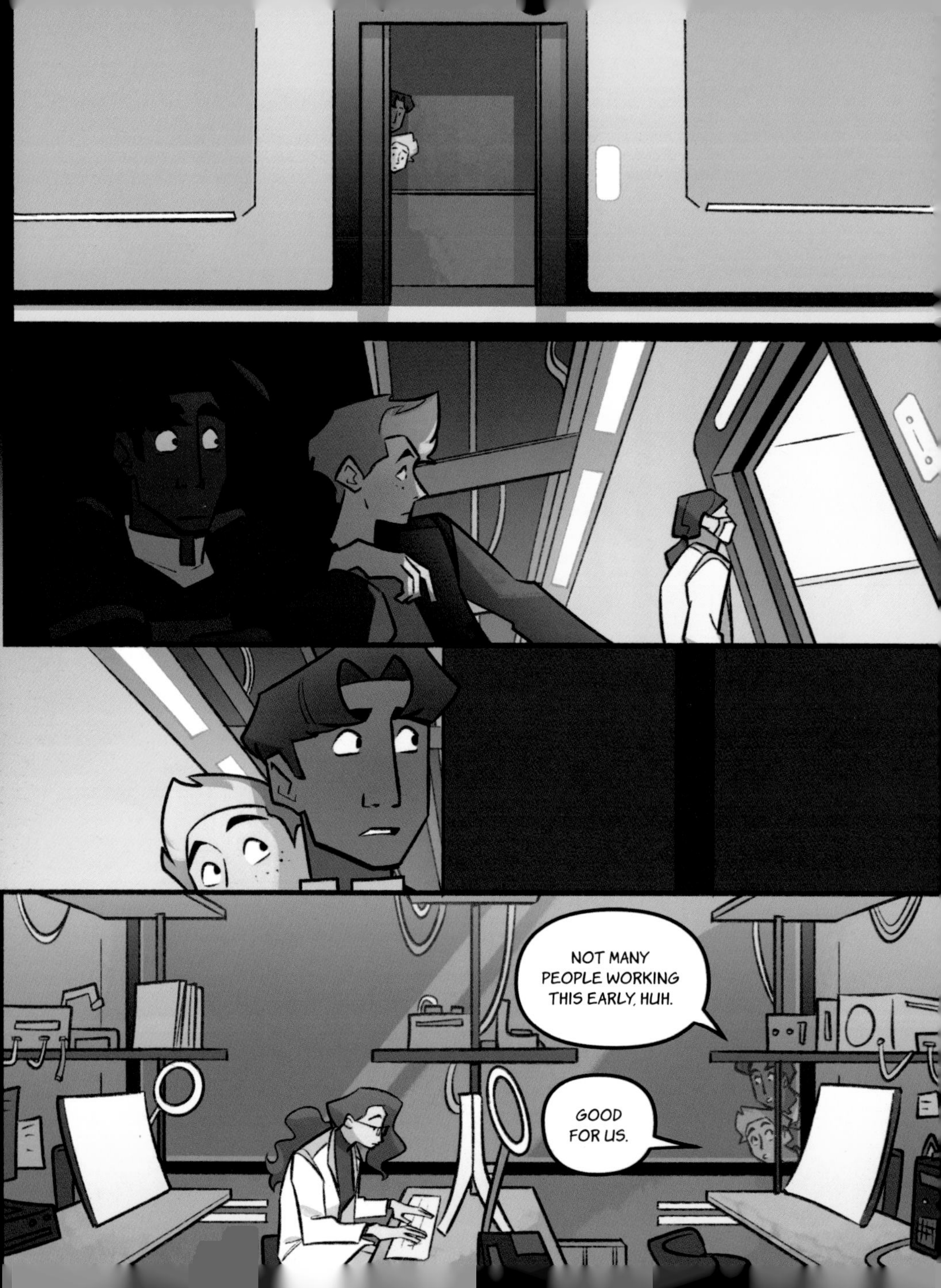
NOT MANY PEOPLE WORKING THIS EARLY, HUH.
GOOD FOR US.

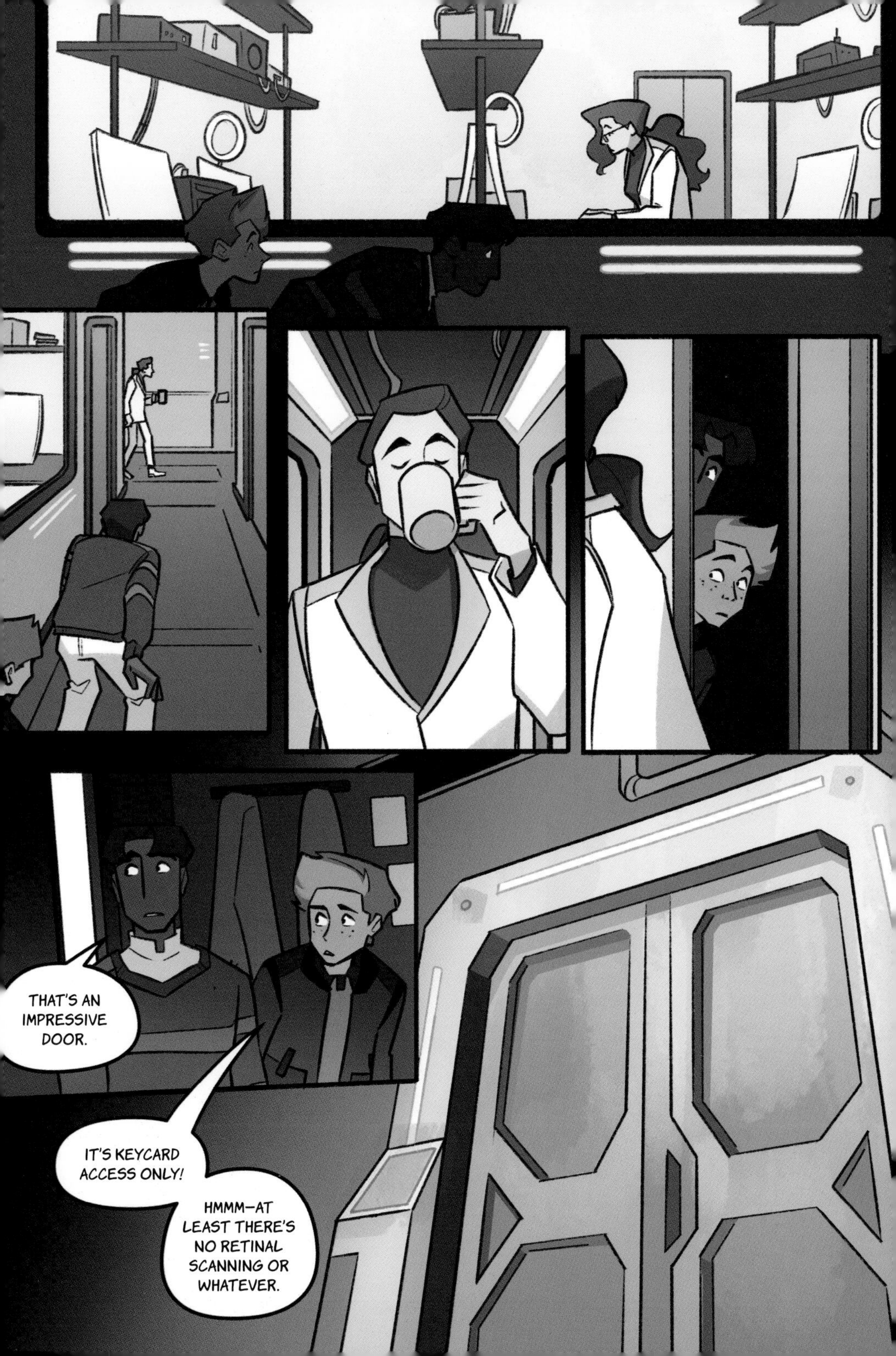
THAT'S AN IMPRESSIVE DOOR.
IT'S KEYCARD ACCESS ONLY!
HMMM—AT LEAST THERE'S NO RETINAL SCANNING OR WHATEVER.

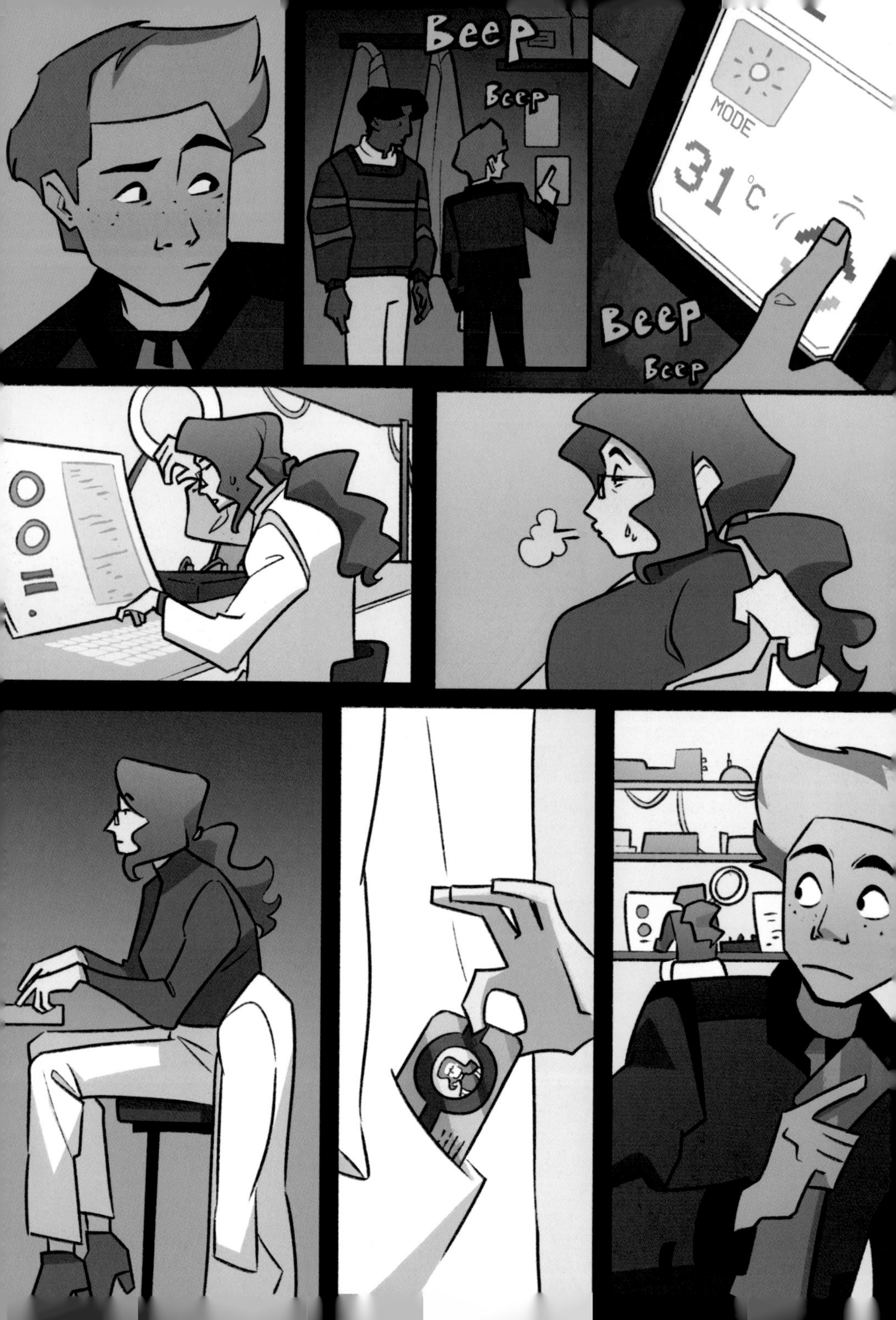
Beep
Beep
MODE
31°C
Beep
Beep

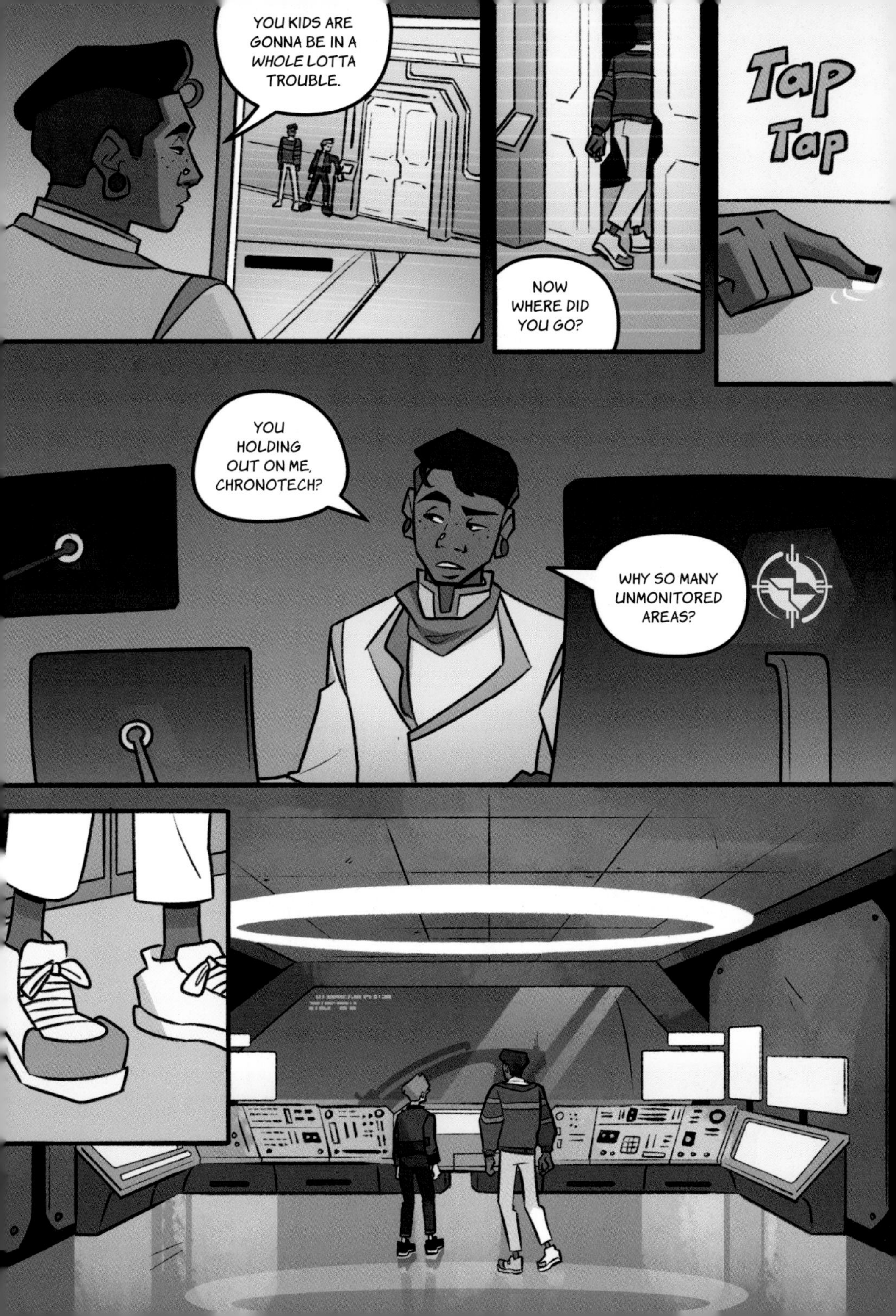
YOU KIDS ARE GONNA BE IN A *WHOLE* LOTTA TROUBLE.
NOW WHERE DID YOU GO?
Tap Tap
YOU HOLDING OUT ON ME, CHRONOTECH?
WHY SO MANY UNMONITORED AREAS?

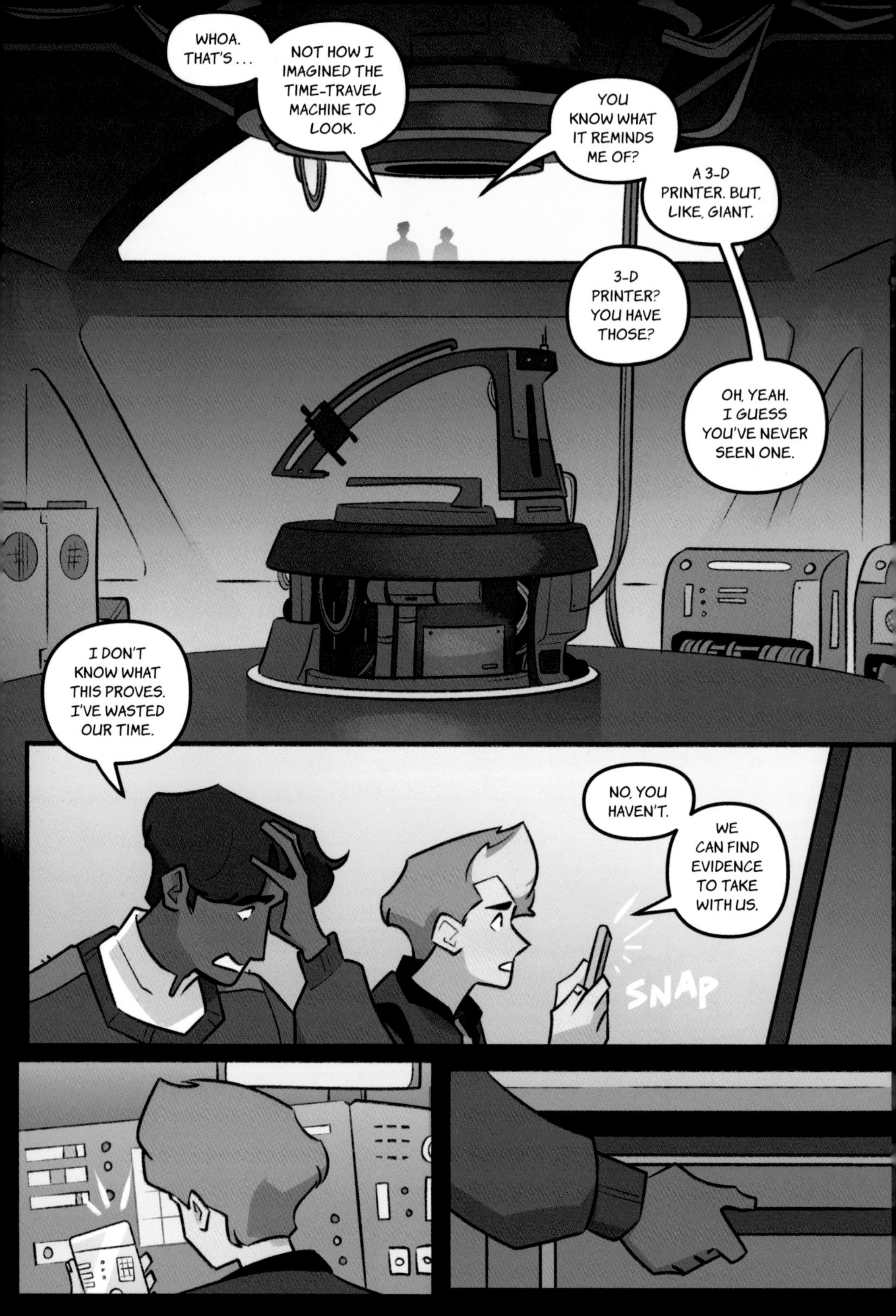
WHOA. THAT'S . . .
NOT HOW I IMAGINED THE TIME-TRAVEL MACHINE TO LOOK.
YOU KNOW WHAT IT REMINDS ME OF?
A 3-D PRINTER. BUT, LIKE, GIANT.
3-D PRINTER? YOU HAVE THOSE?
OH, YEAH. I GUESS YOU'VE NEVER SEEN ONE.
I DON'T KNOW WHAT THIS PROVES. I'VE WASTED OUR TIME.
NO, YOU HAVEN'T.
WE CAN FIND EVIDENCE TO TAKE WITH US.
SNAP

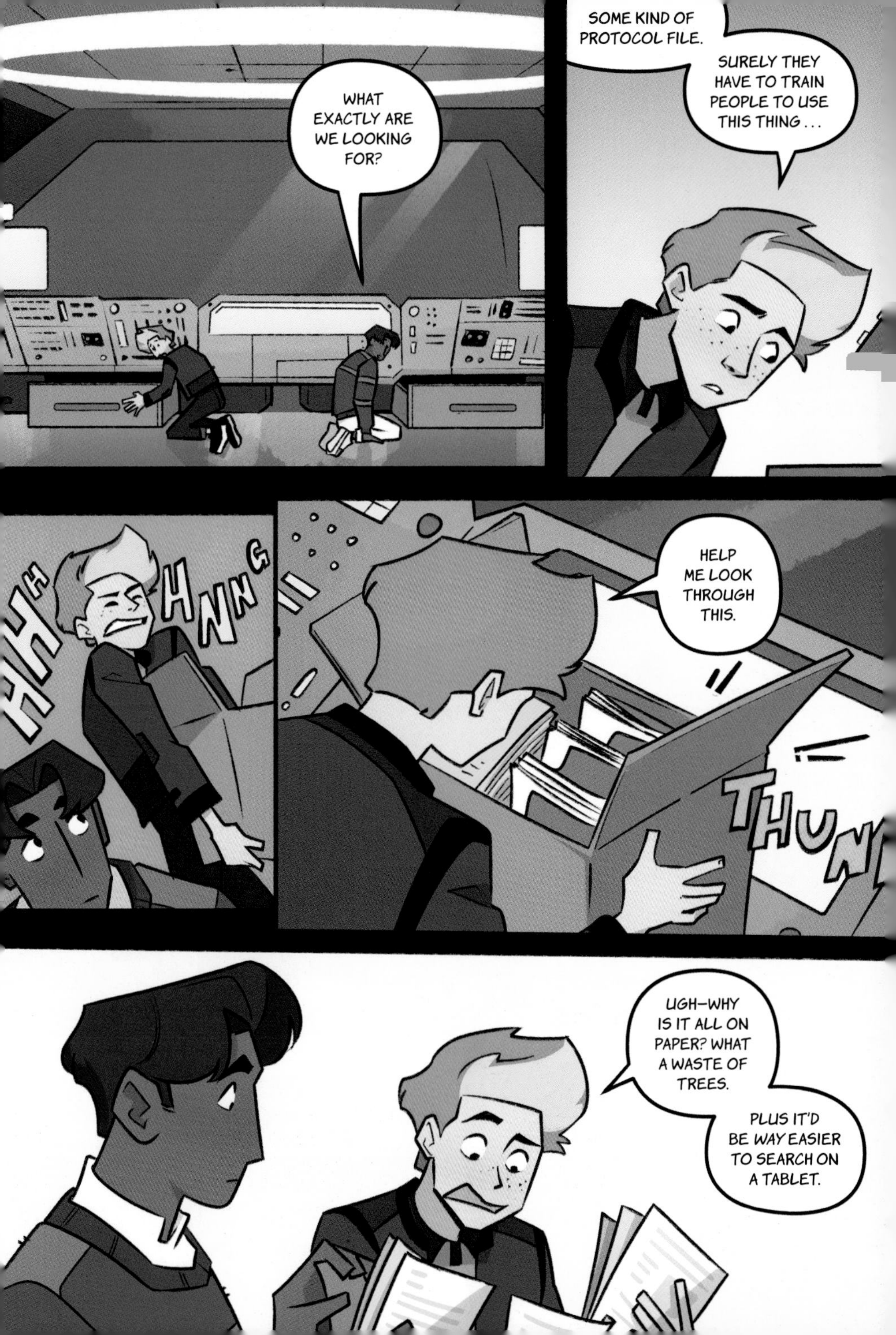
WHAT EXACTLY ARE WE LOOKING FOR?
SOME KIND OF PROTOCOL FILE.
SURELY THEY HAVE TO TRAIN PEOPLE TO USE THIS THING . . .
HHHHNNG
HELP ME LOOK THROUGH THIS.
THUN
UGH—WHY IS IT ALL ON PAPER? WHAT A WASTE OF TREES.
PLUS IT'D BE WAY EASIER TO SEARCH ON A TABLET.

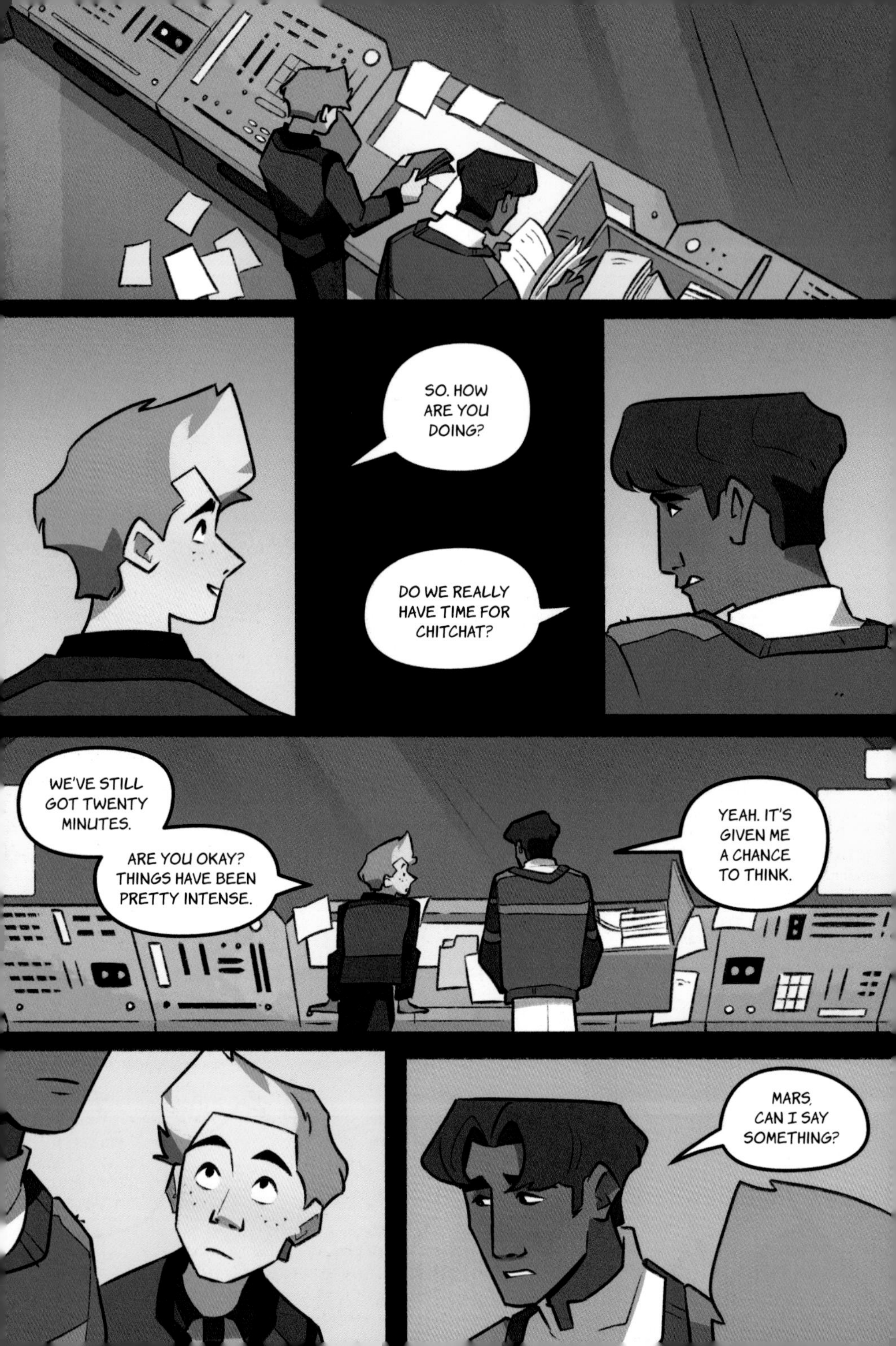
SO. HOW ARE YOU DOING?
DO WE REALLY HAVE TIME FOR CHITCHAT?
WE'VE STILL GOT TWENTY MINUTES.
ARE YOU OKAY? THINGS HAVE BEEN PRETTY INTENSE.
YEAH. IT'S GIVEN ME A CHANCE TO THINK.
MARS, CAN I SAY SOMETHING?

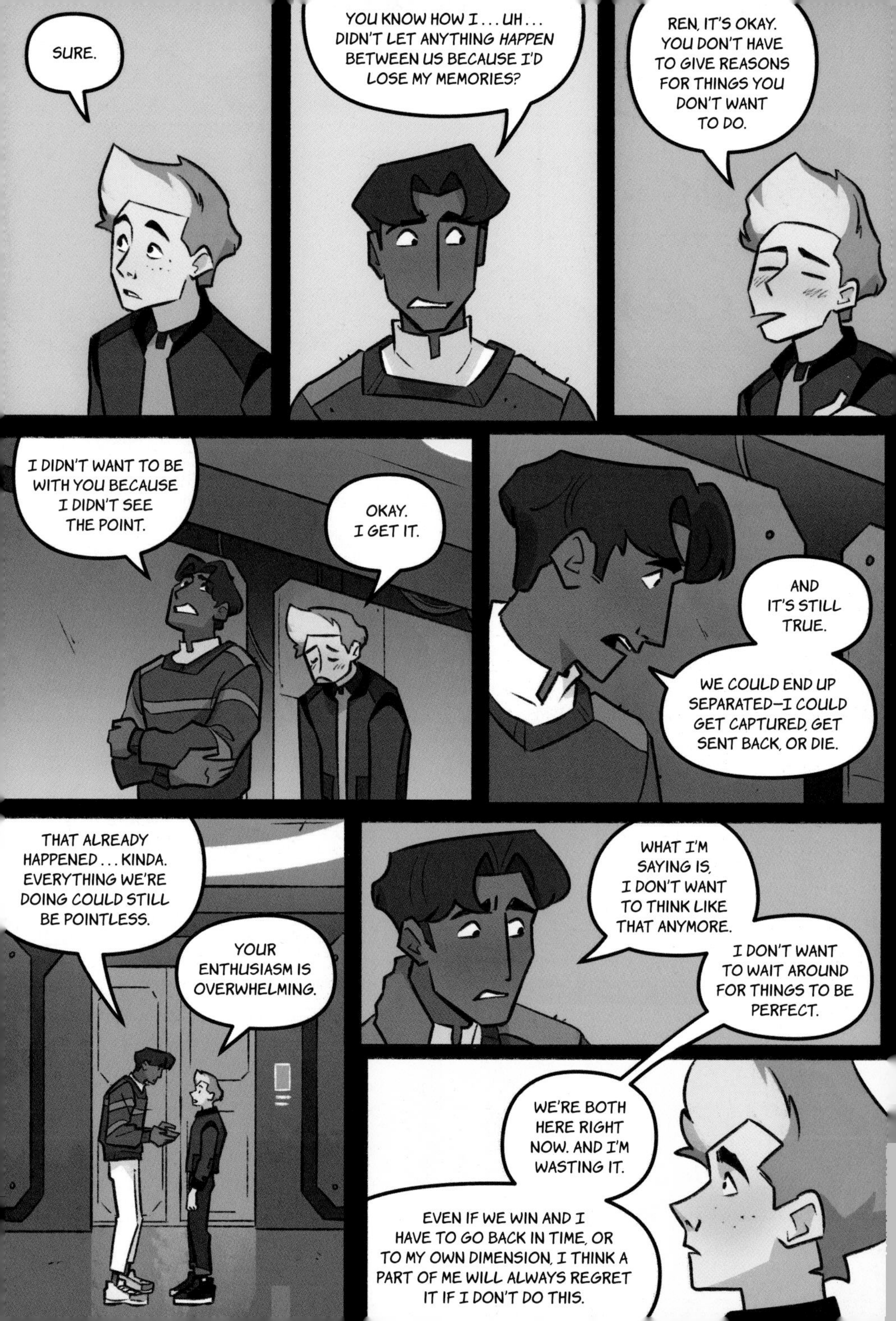
SURE.
YOU KNOW HOW I . . . UH . . . DIDN'T LET ANYTHING *HAPPEN* BETWEEN US BECAUSE I'D LOSE MY MEMORIES?
REN, IT'S OKAY. YOU DON'T HAVE TO GIVE REASONS FOR THINGS YOU DON'T WANT TO DO.
I DIDN'T WANT TO BE WITH YOU BECAUSE I DIDN'T SEE THE POINT.
OKAY. I GET IT.
AND IT'S STILL TRUE.
WE COULD END UP SEPARATED—I COULD GET CAPTURED, GET SENT BACK, OR DIE.
THAT ALREADY HAPPENED . . . KINDA. EVERYTHING WE'RE DOING COULD STILL BE POINTLESS.
YOUR ENTHUSIASM IS OVERWHELMING.
WHAT I'M SAYING IS, I DON'T WANT TO THINK LIKE THAT ANYMORE.
I DON'T WANT TO WAIT AROUND FOR THINGS TO BE PERFECT.
WE'RE BOTH HERE RIGHT NOW. AND I'M WASTING IT.
EVEN IF WE WIN AND I HAVE TO GO BACK IN TIME, OR TO MY OWN DIMENSION, I THINK A PART OF ME WILL ALWAYS REGRET IT IF I DON'T DO THIS.

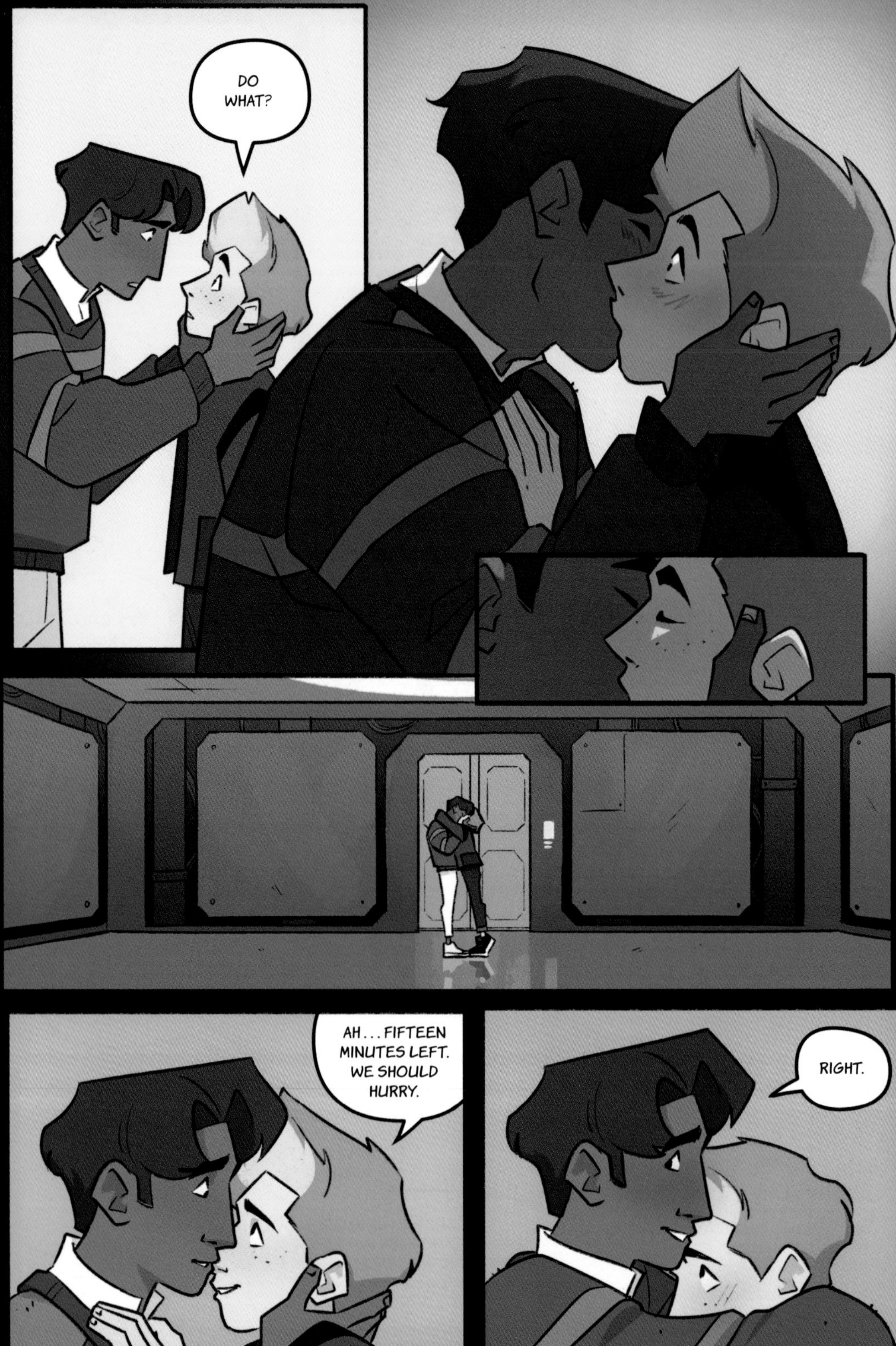
DO WHAT?
AH . . . FIFTEEN MINUTES LEFT. WE SHOULD HURRY.
RIGHT.

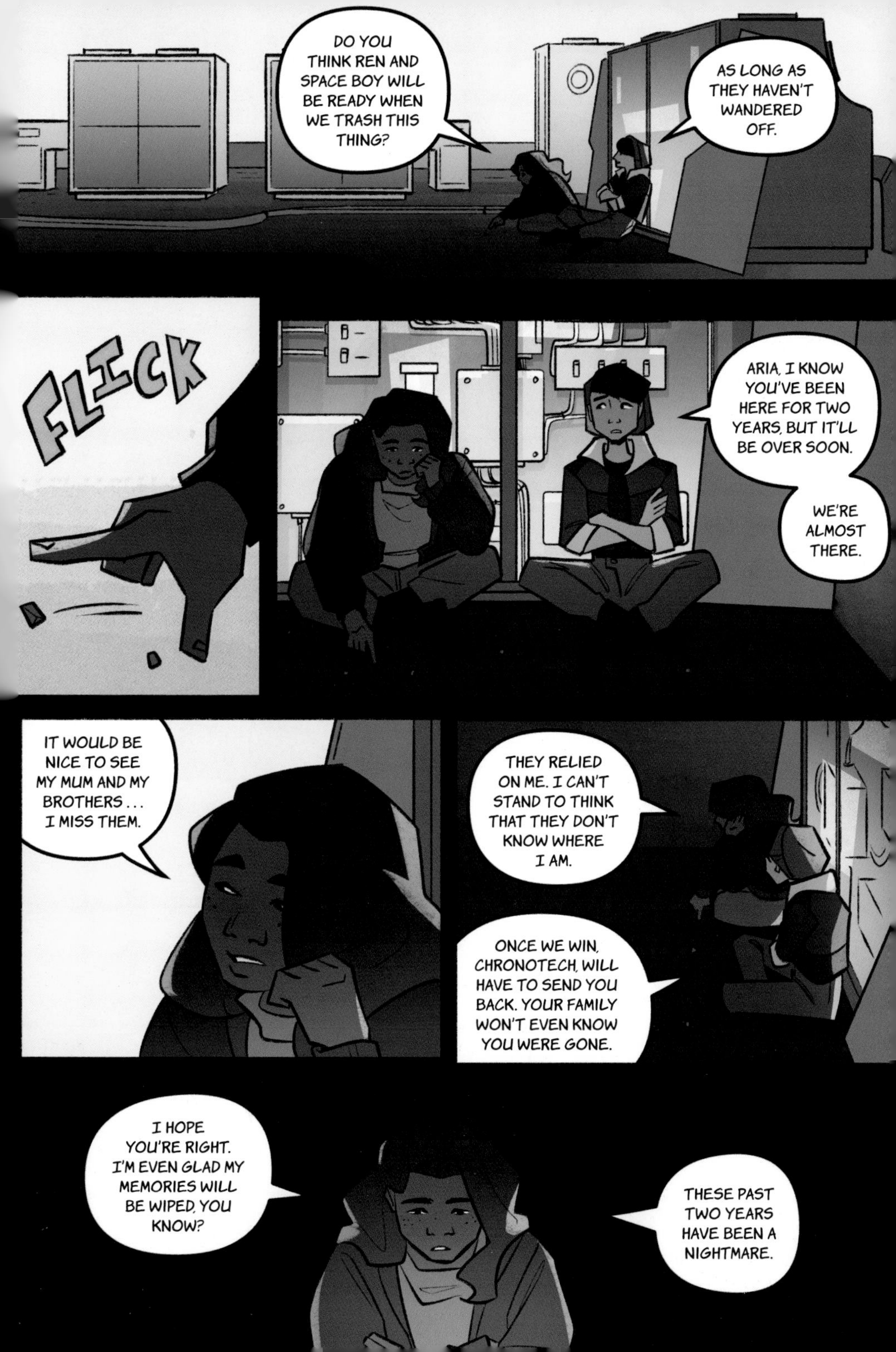
DO YOU THINK REN AND SPACE BOY WILL BE READY WHEN WE TRASH THIS THING?
AS LONG AS THEY HAVEN'T WANDERED OFF.
FLICK
ARIA, I KNOW YOU'VE BEEN HERE FOR TWO YEARS, BUT IT'LL BE OVER SOON.
WE'RE ALMOST THERE.
IT WOULD BE NICE TO SEE MY MUM AND MY BROTHERS . . . I MISS THEM.
THEY RELIED ON ME. I CAN'T STAND TO THINK THAT THEY DON'T KNOW WHERE I AM.
ONCE WE WIN, CHRONOTECH, WILL HAVE TO SEND YOU BACK. YOUR FAMILY WON'T EVEN KNOW YOU WERE GONE.
I HOPE YOU'RE RIGHT. I'M EVEN GLAD MY MEMORIES WILL BE WIPED, YOU KNOW?
THESE PAST TWO YEARS HAVE BEEN A NIGHTMARE.

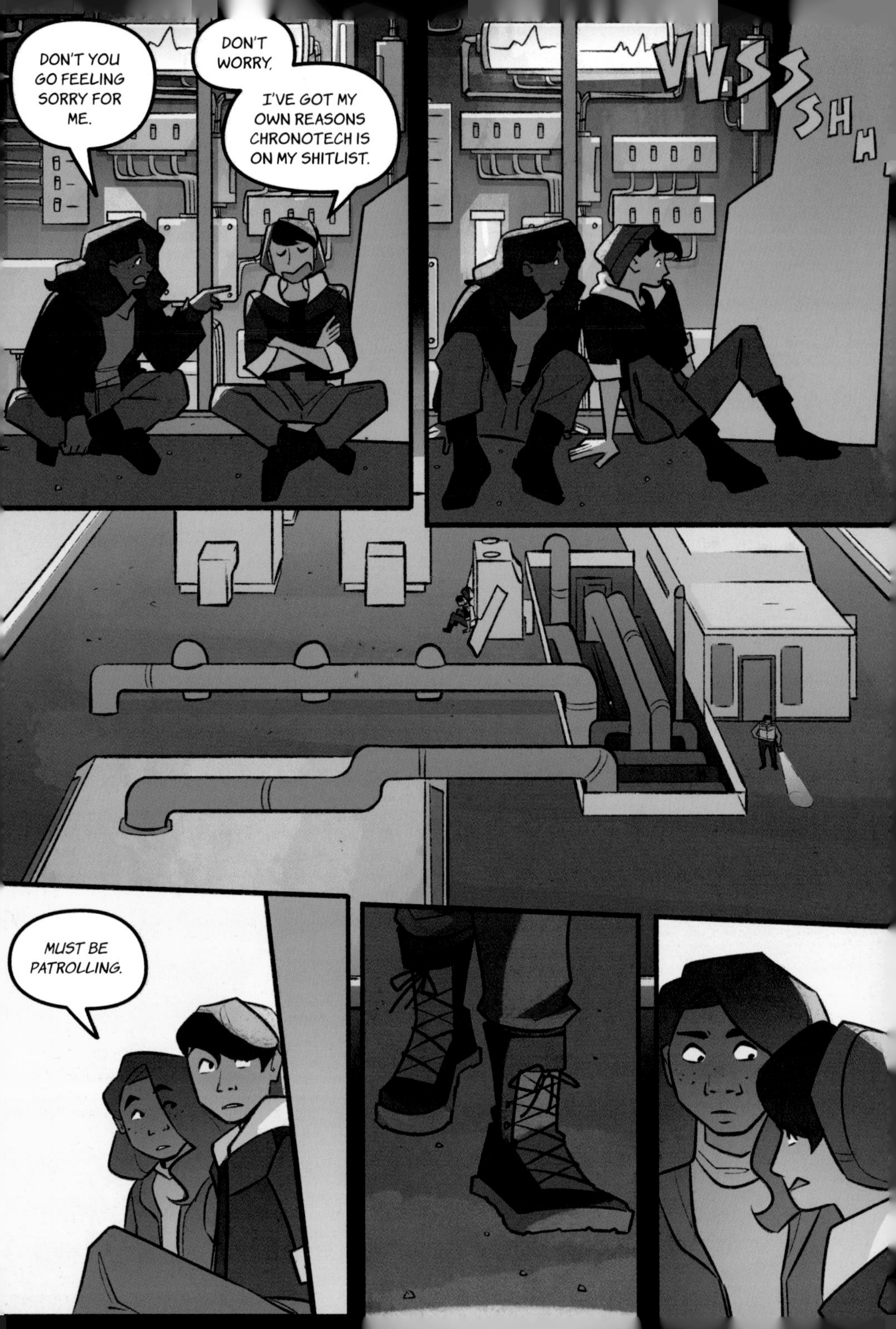
DON'T YOU GO FEELING SORRY FOR ME.
DON'T WORRY.
I'VE GOT MY OWN REASONS CHRONOTECH IS ON MY SHITLIST.
VVSSSHH
MUST BE PATROLLING.

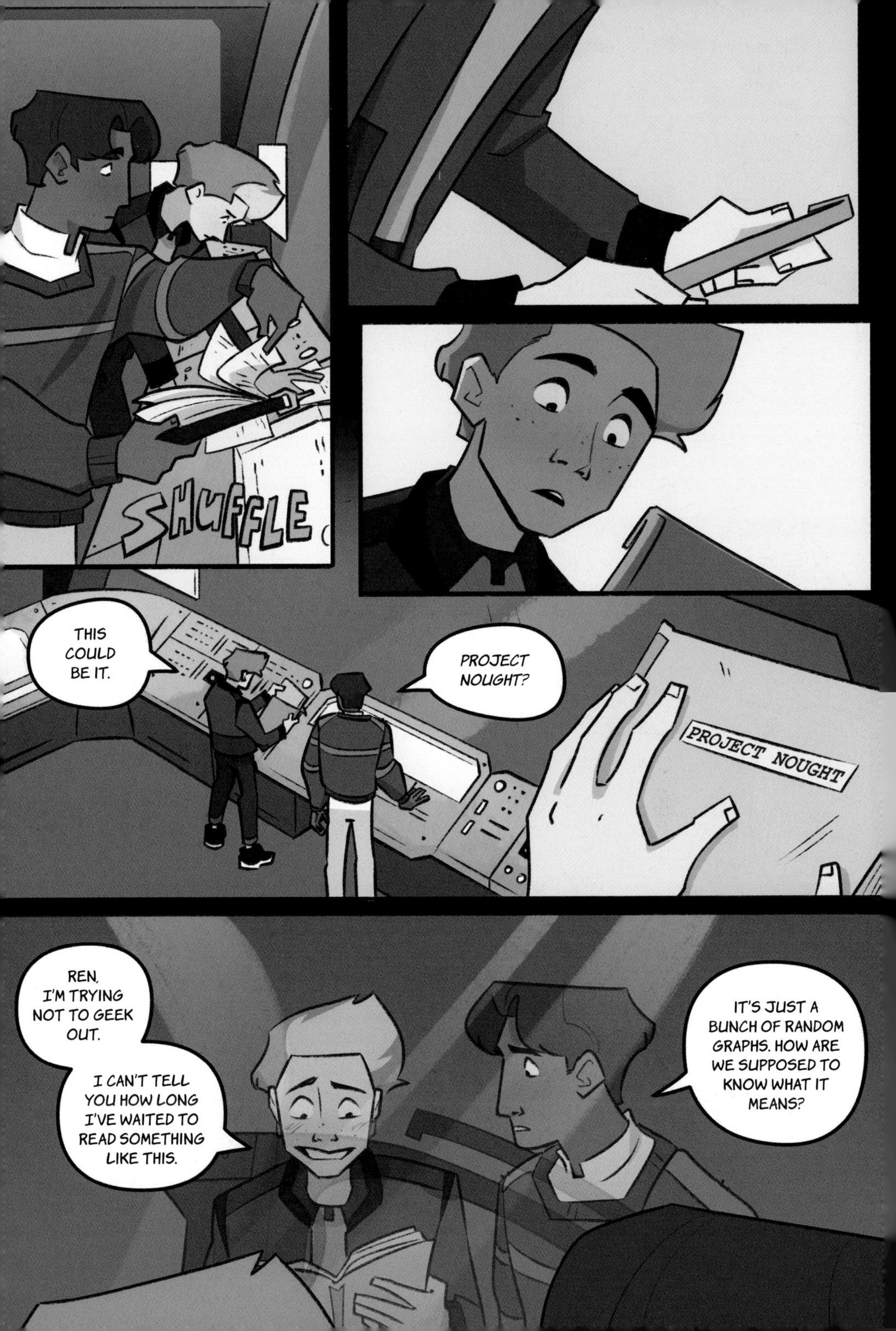
SHUFFLE
THIS COULD BE IT.
PROJECT NOUGHT?
PROJECT NOUGHT
REN, I'M TRYING NOT TO GEEK OUT.
I CAN'T TELL YOU HOW LONG I'VE WAITED TO READ SOMETHING LIKE THIS.
IT'S JUST A BUNCH OF RANDOM GRAPHS. HOW ARE WE SUPPOSED TO KNOW WHAT IT MEANS?

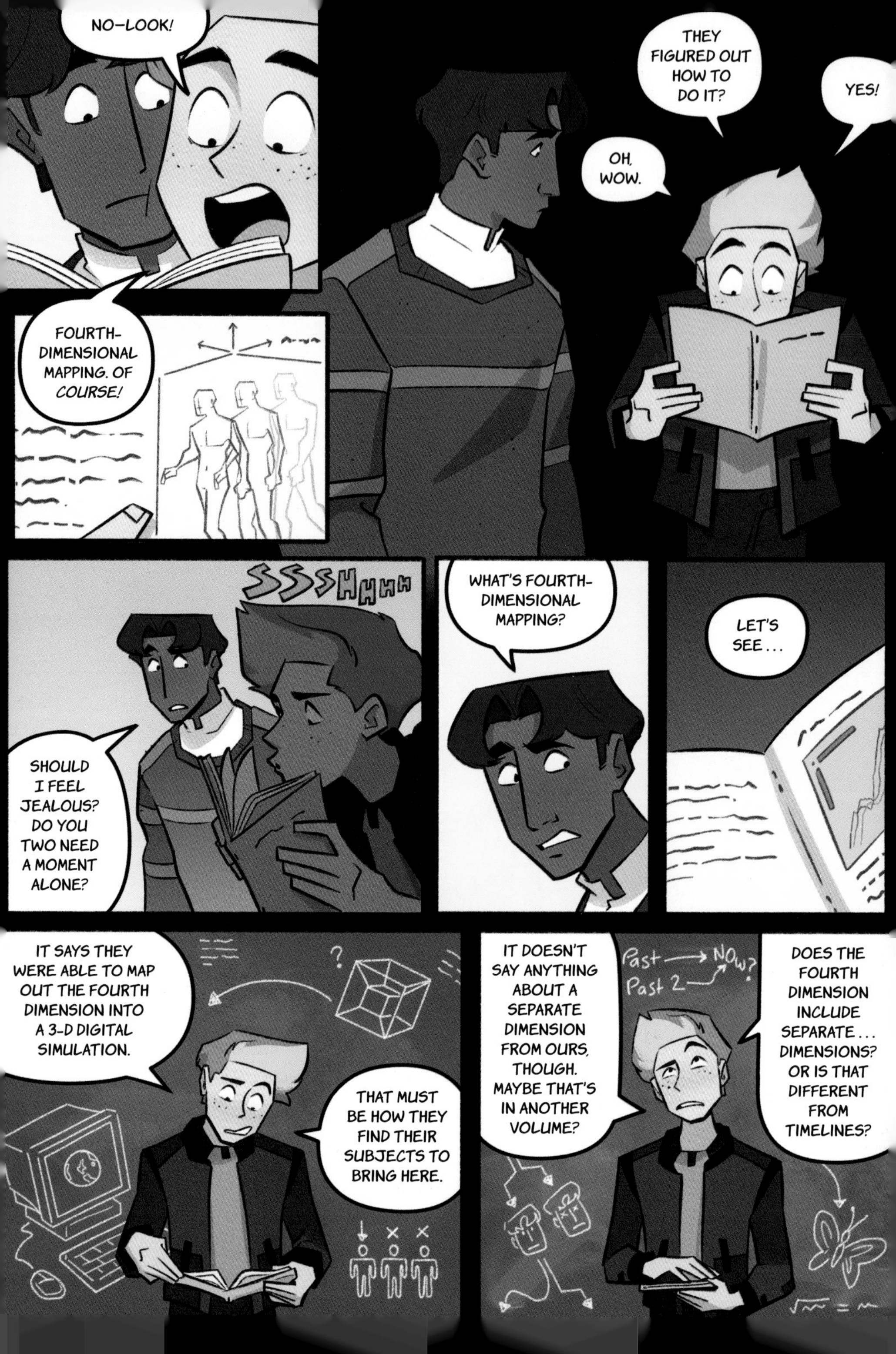
NO—LOOK!
THEY FIGURED OUT HOW TO DO IT?
YES!
OH, WOW.
FOURTH-DIMENSIONAL MAPPING. OF COURSE!
SSSHHHH
SHOULD I FEEL JEALOUS? DO YOU TWO NEED A MOMENT ALONE?
WHAT'S FOURTH-DIMENSIONAL MAPPING?
LET'S SEE . . .
IT SAYS THEY WERE ABLE TO MAP OUT THE FOURTH DIMENSION INTO A 3-D DIGITAL SIMULATION.
THAT MUST BE HOW THEY FIND THEIR SUBJECTS TO BRING HERE.
IT DOESN'T SAY ANYTHING ABOUT A SEPARATE DIMENSION FROM OURS, THOUGH. MAYBE THAT'S IN ANOTHER VOLUME?
Past → Now?
Past 2
DOES THE FOURTH DIMENSION INCLUDE SEPARATE . . . DIMENSIONS? OR IS THAT DIFFERENT FROM TIMELINES?

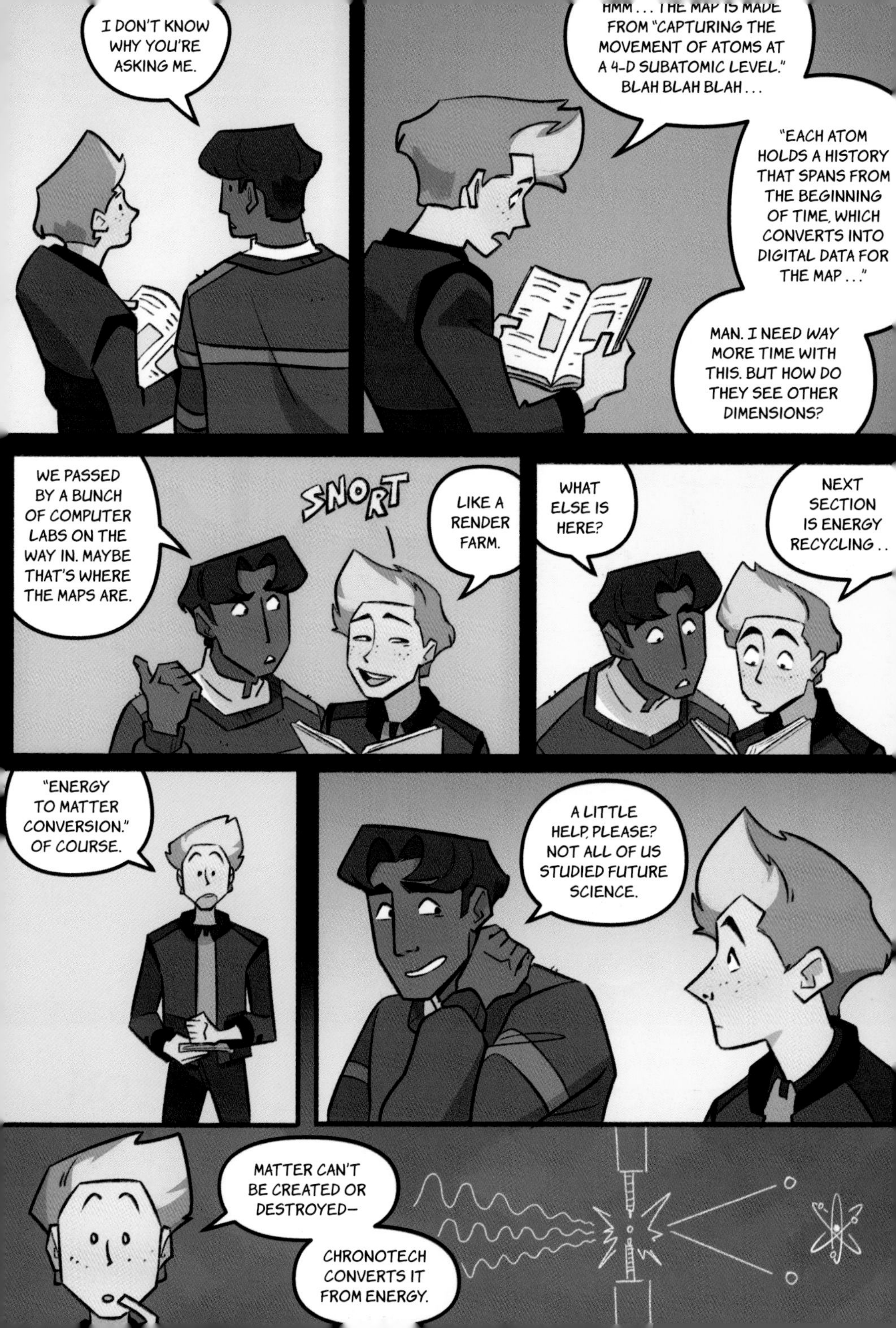
I DON'T KNOW WHY YOU'RE ASKING ME.
HMM . . . THE MAP IS MADE FROM "CAPTURING THE MOVEMENT OF ATOMS AT A 4-D SUBATOMIC LEVEL." BLAH BLAH BLAH . . .
"EACH ATOM HOLDS A HISTORY THAT SPANS FROM THE BEGINNING OF TIME, WHICH CONVERTS INTO DIGITAL DATA FOR THE MAP . . ."
MAN. I NEED WAY MORE TIME WITH THIS. BUT HOW DO THEY SEE OTHER DIMENSIONS?
WE PASSED BY A BUNCH OF COMPUTER LABS ON THE WAY IN. MAYBE THAT'S WHERE THE MAPS ARE.
SNORT
LIKE A RENDER FARM.
WHAT ELSE IS HERE?
NEXT SECTION IS ENERGY RECYCLING . .
"ENERGY TO MATTER CONVERSION." OF COURSE.
A LITTLE HELP, PLEASE? NOT ALL OF US STUDIED FUTURE SCIENCE.
MATTER CAN'T BE CREATED OR DESTROYED—
CHRONOTECH CONVERTS IT FROM ENERGY.

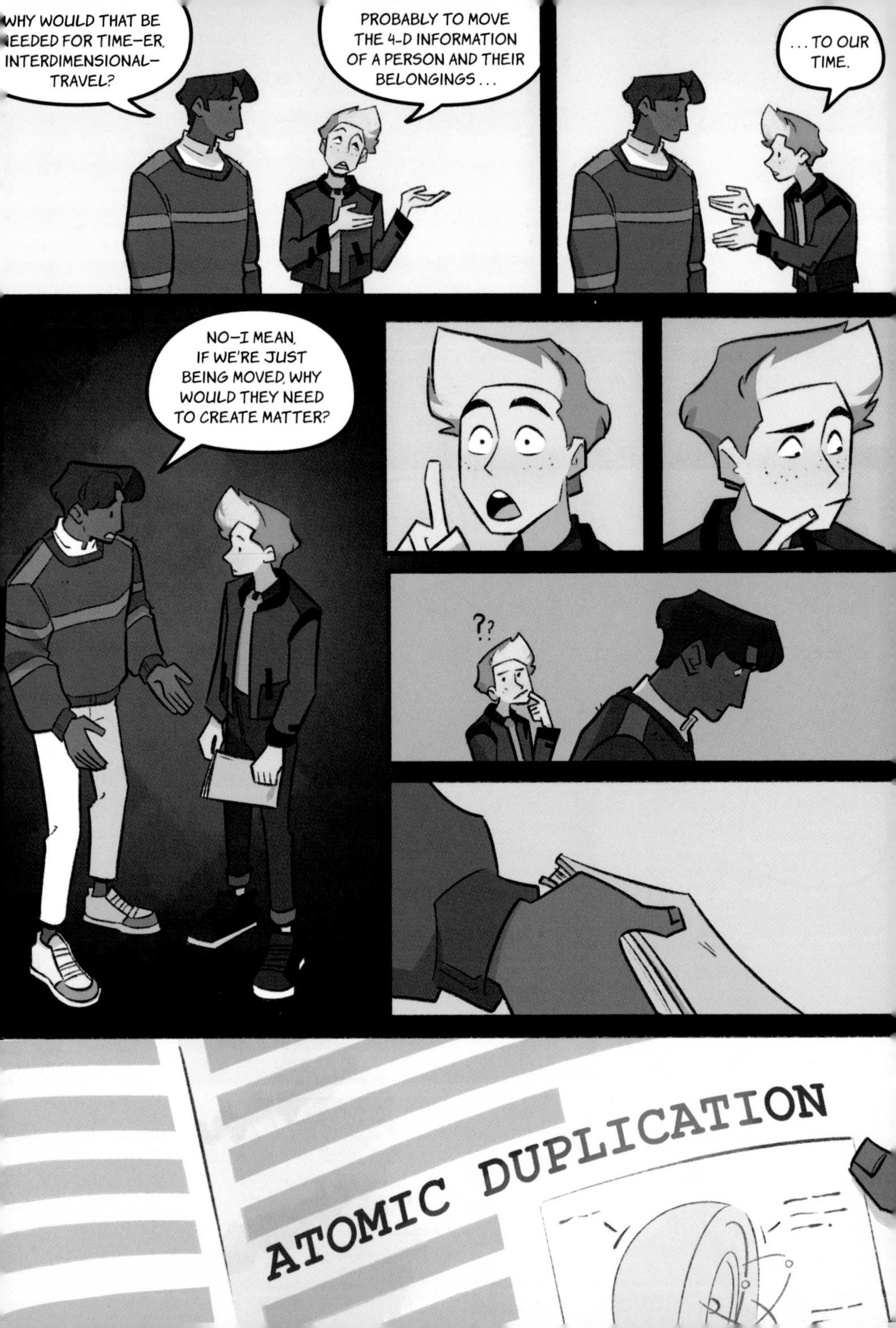
WHY WOULD THAT BE NEEDED FOR TIME—ER, INTERDIMENSIONAL—TRAVEL?
PROBABLY TO MOVE THE 4-D INFORMATION OF A PERSON AND THEIR BELONGINGS . . .
. . . TO OUR TIME.
NO—I MEAN, IF WE'RE JUST BEING MOVED, WHY WOULD THEY NEED TO CREATE MATTER?
??
ATOMIC DUPLICATION

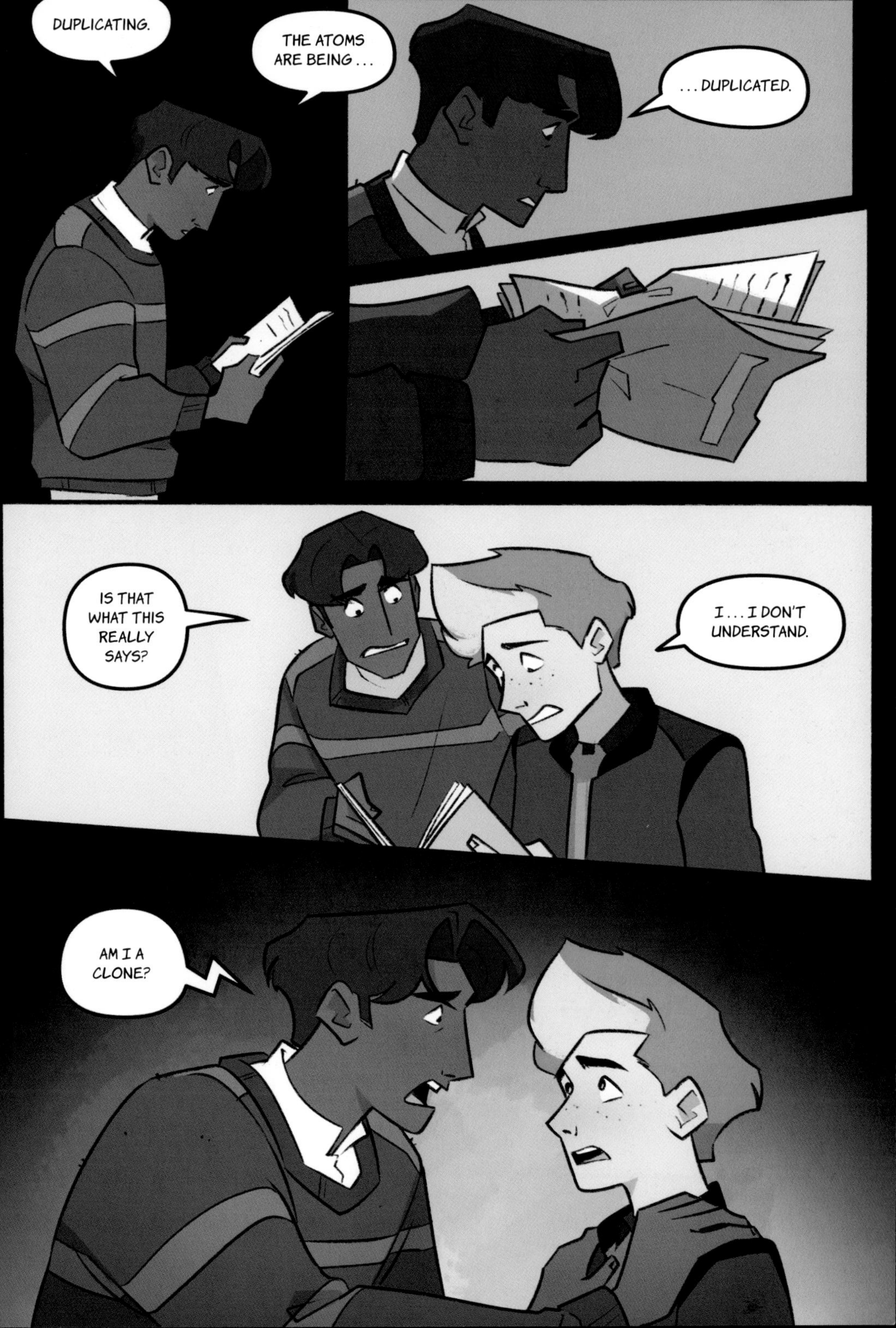
DUPLICATING.
THE ATOMS ARE BEING . . .
. . . DUPLICATED.
IS THAT WHAT THIS REALLY SAYS?
I . . . I DON'T UNDERSTAND.
AM I A CLONE?

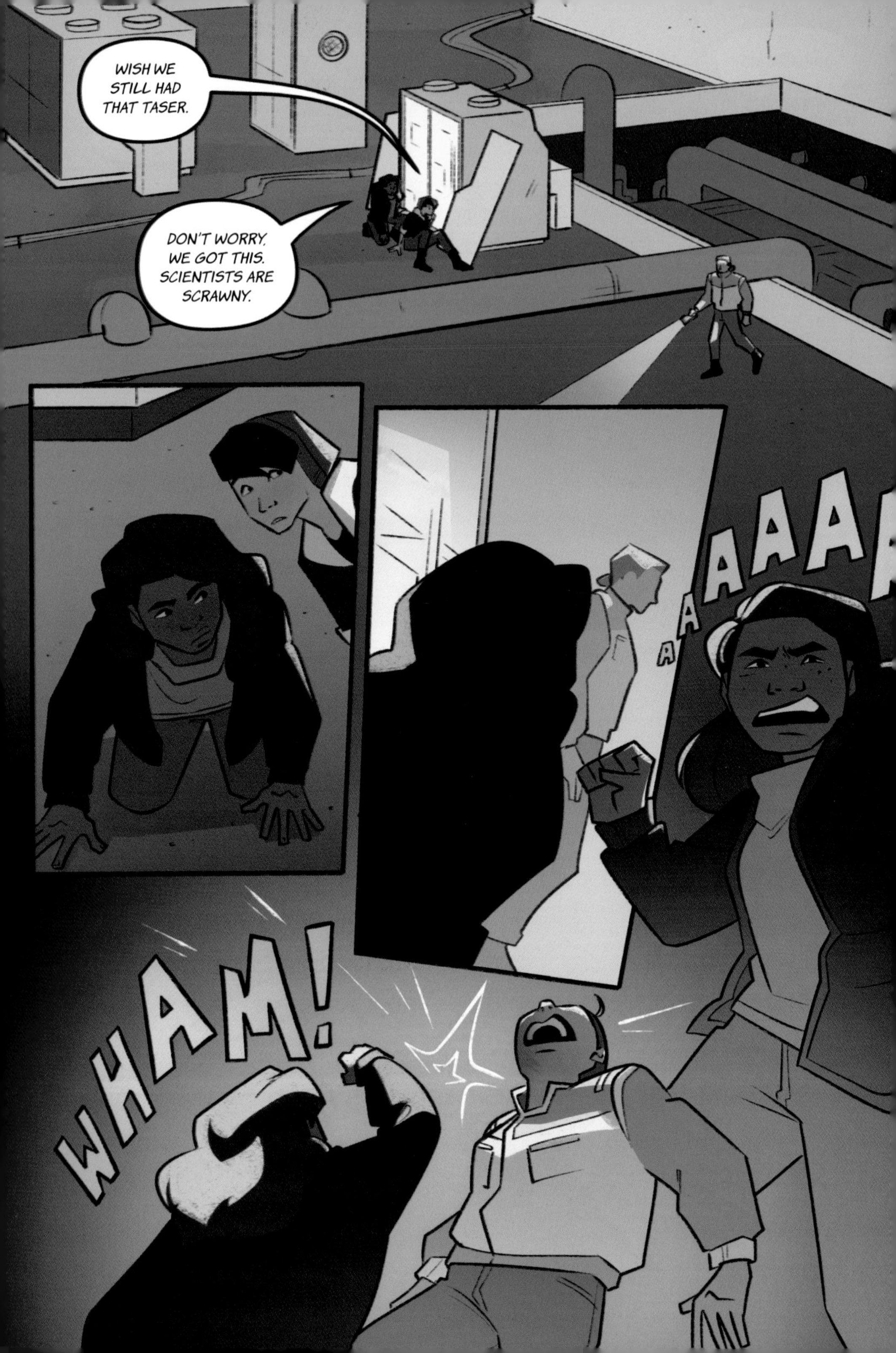
WISH WE STILL HAD THAT TASER.
DON'T WORRY. WE GOT THIS. SCIENTISTS ARE SCRAWNY.
AAAAAA
WHAM!

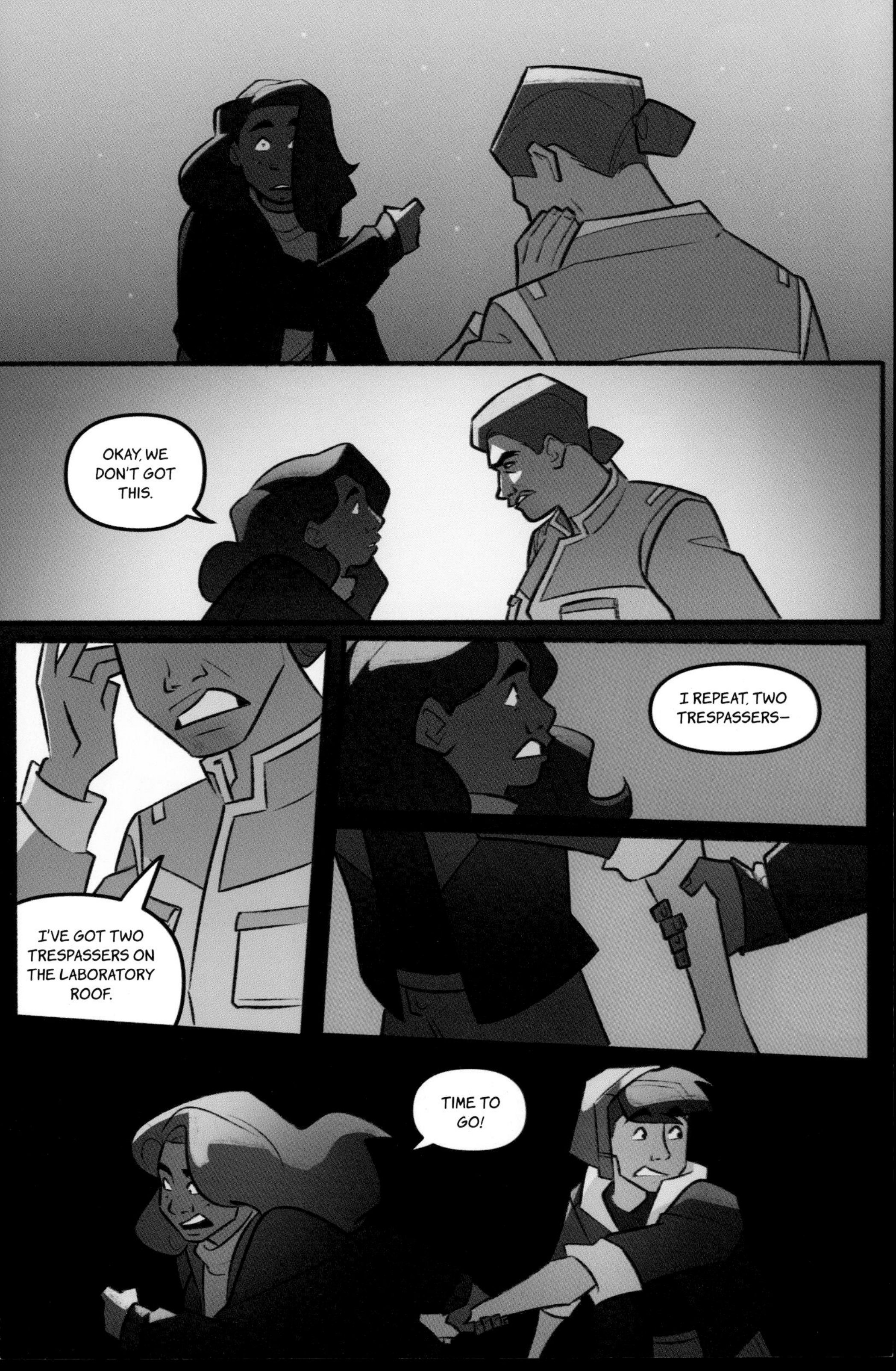
OKAY, WE DON'T GOT THIS.
I REPEAT, TWO TRESPASSERS—
I'VE GOT TWO TRESPASSERS ON THE LABORATORY ROOF.
TIME TO GO!

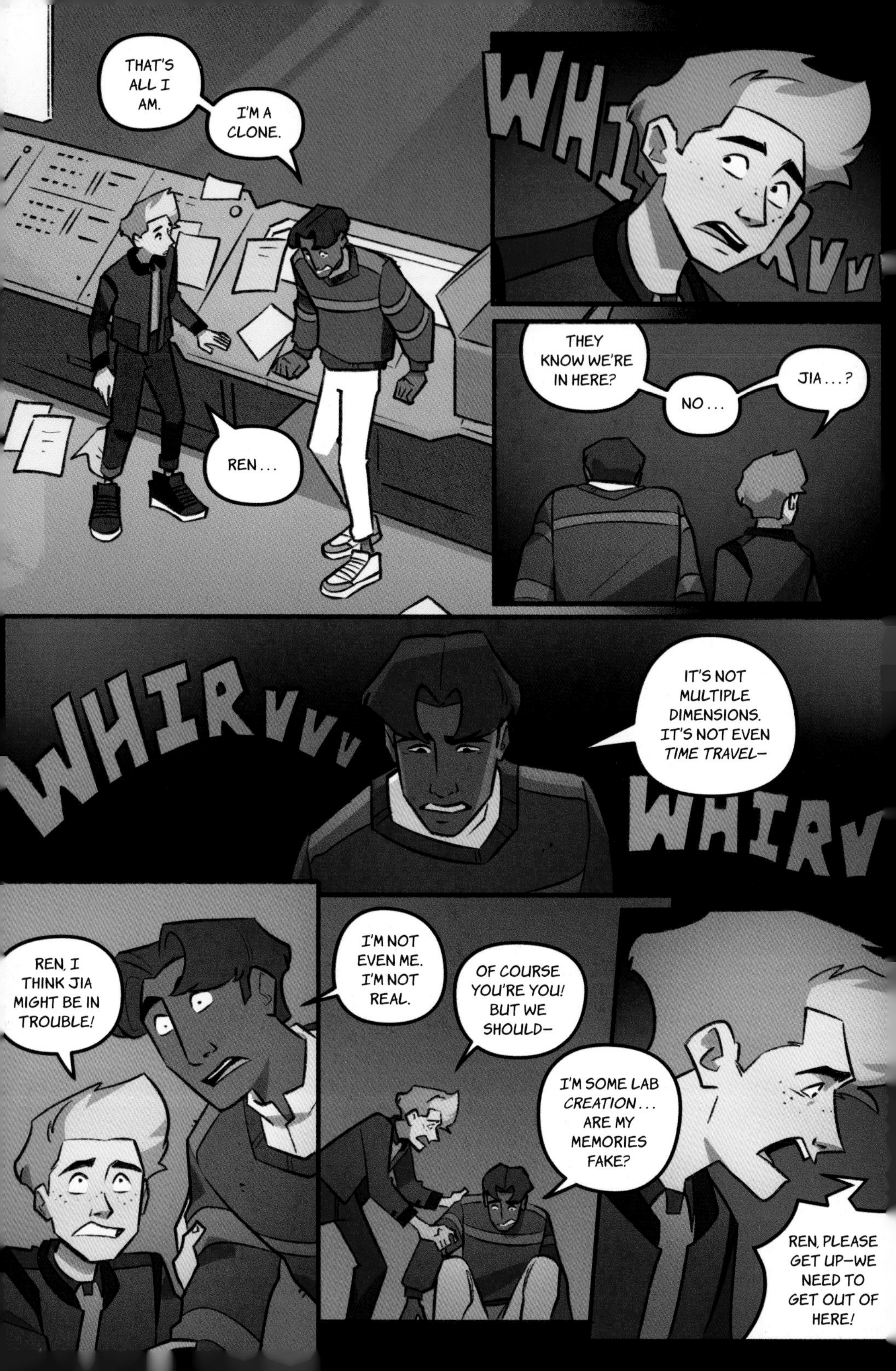
THAT'S ALL I AM.
I'M A CLONE.
RENN . . .
WHIRVV
THEY KNOW WE'RE IN HERE?
NO . . .
JIA . . .?
WHIRVVV
IT'S NOT MULTIPLE DIMENSIONS. IT'S NOT EVEN *TIME TRAVEL*—
WHIRV
REN, I THINK JIA MIGHT BE IN TROUBLE!
I'M NOT EVEN ME. I'M NOT REAL.
OF COURSE YOU'RE YOU! BUT WE SHOULD—
I'M SOME LAB *CREATION* . . . ARE MY MEMORIES FAKE?
REN, PLEASE GET UP—WE NEED TO GET OUT OF HERE!

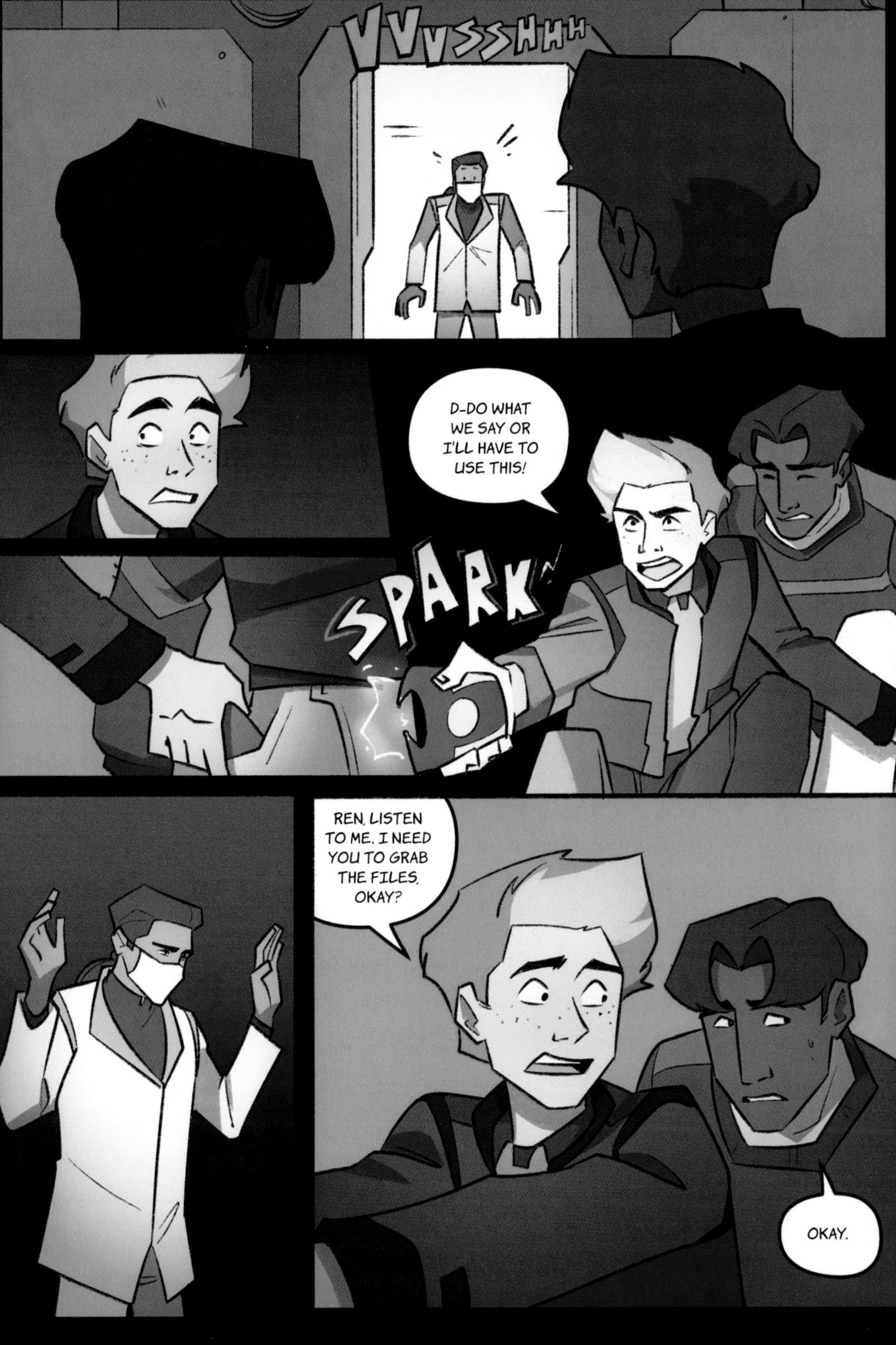
VVVSSHHH
D-DO WHAT WE SAY OR I'LL HAVE TO USE THIS!
SPARK
REN, LISTEN TO ME. I NEED YOU TO GRAB THE FILES, OKAY?
OKAY.

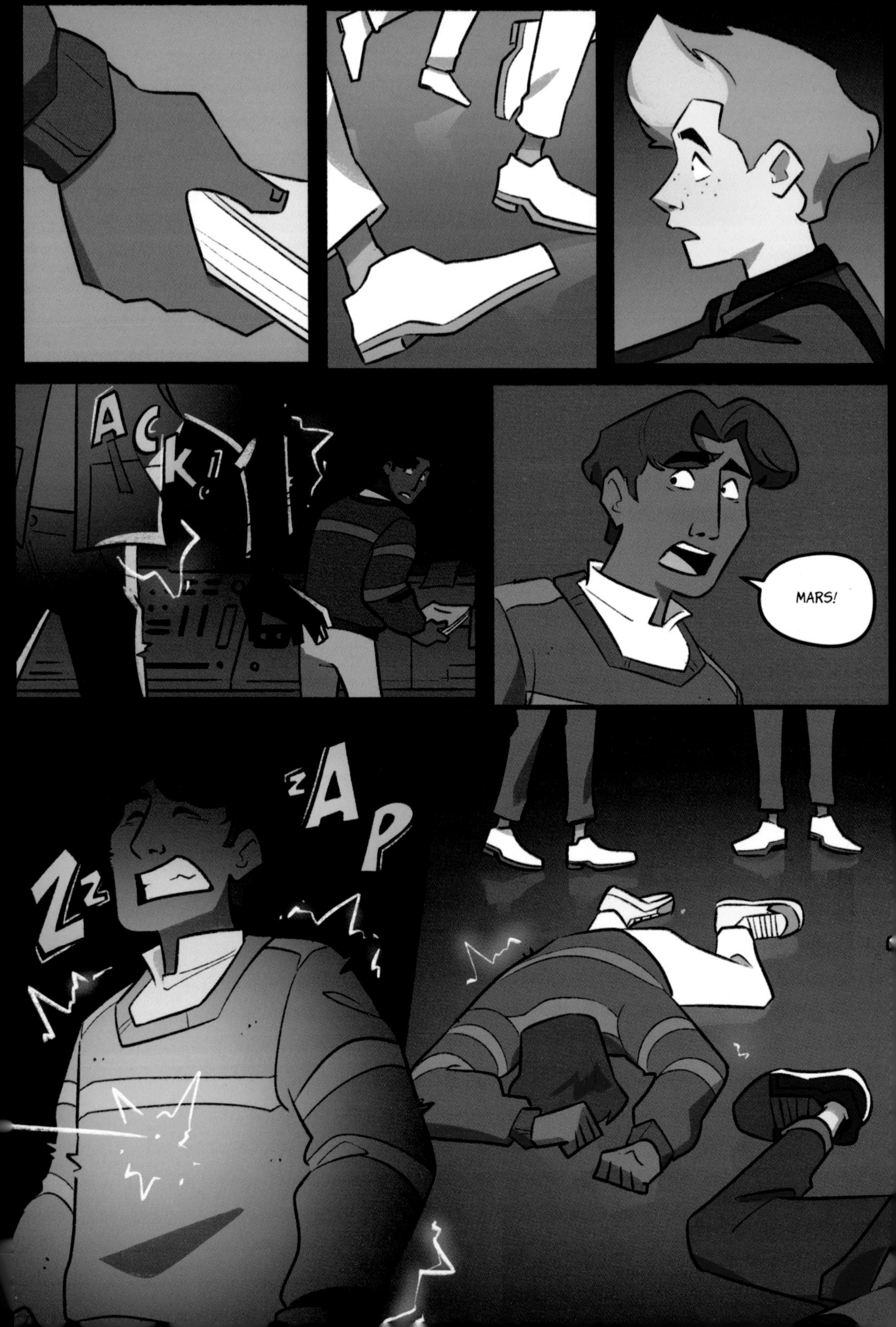
ACK!
MARS!
ZZAP
ZZ

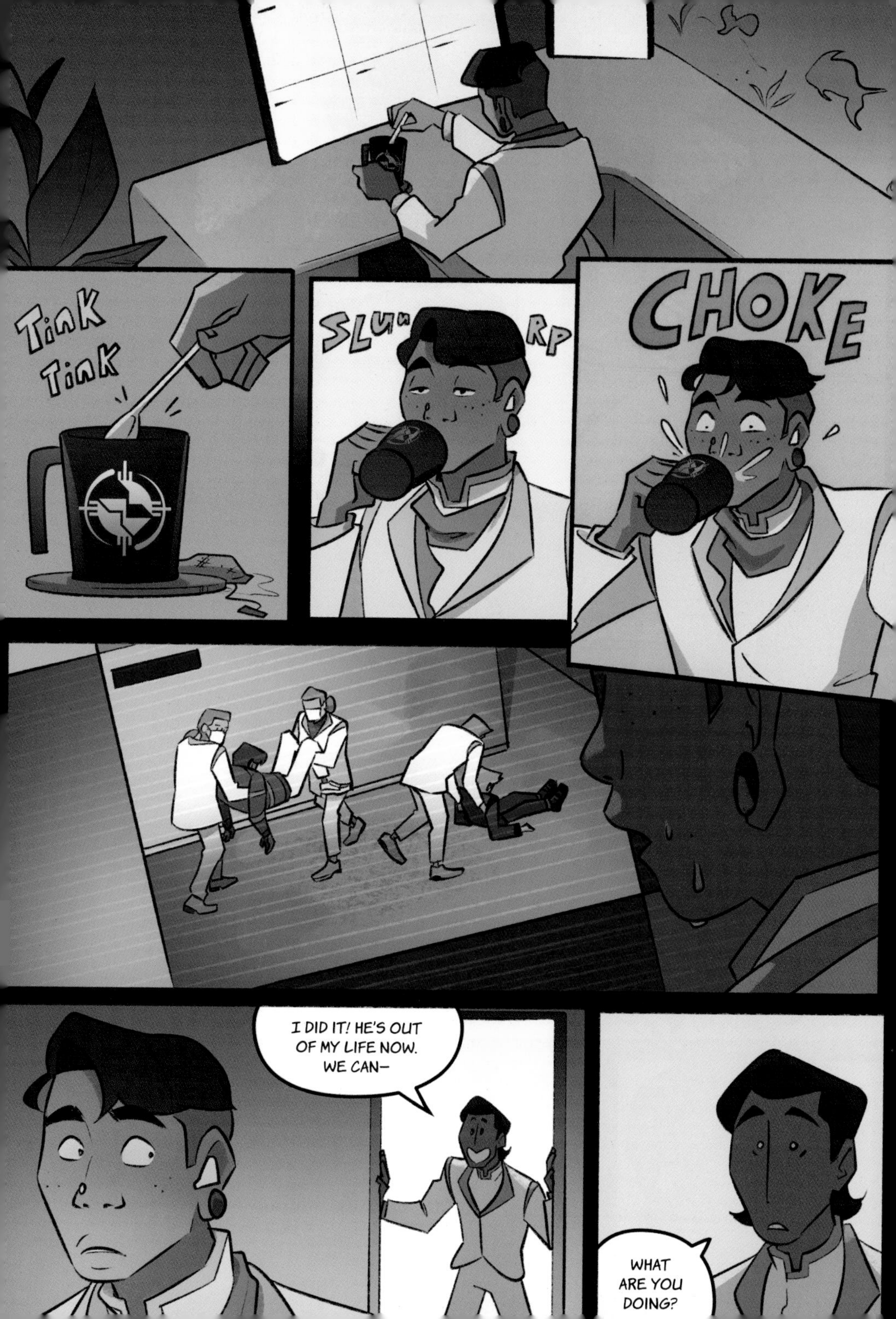
TINK
TINK
SLUuRP
CHOKE
I DID IT! HE'S OUT OF MY LIFE NOW. WE CAN–
WHAT ARE YOU DOING?

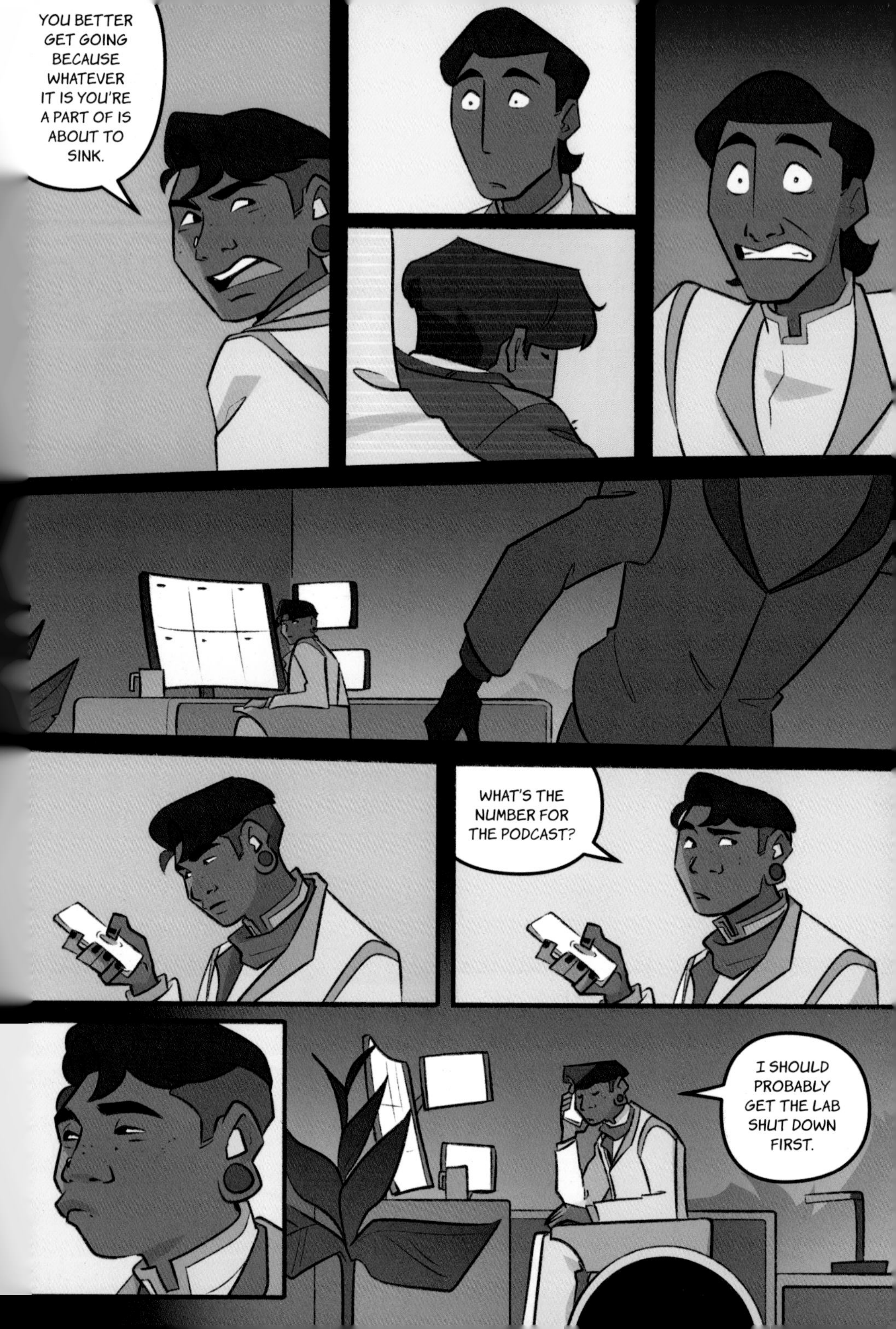
YOU BETTER GET GOING BECAUSE WHATEVER IT IS YOU'RE A PART OF IS ABOUT TO SINK.
WHAT'S THE NUMBER FOR THE PODCAST?
I SHOULD PROBABLY GET THE LAB SHUT DOWN FIRST.

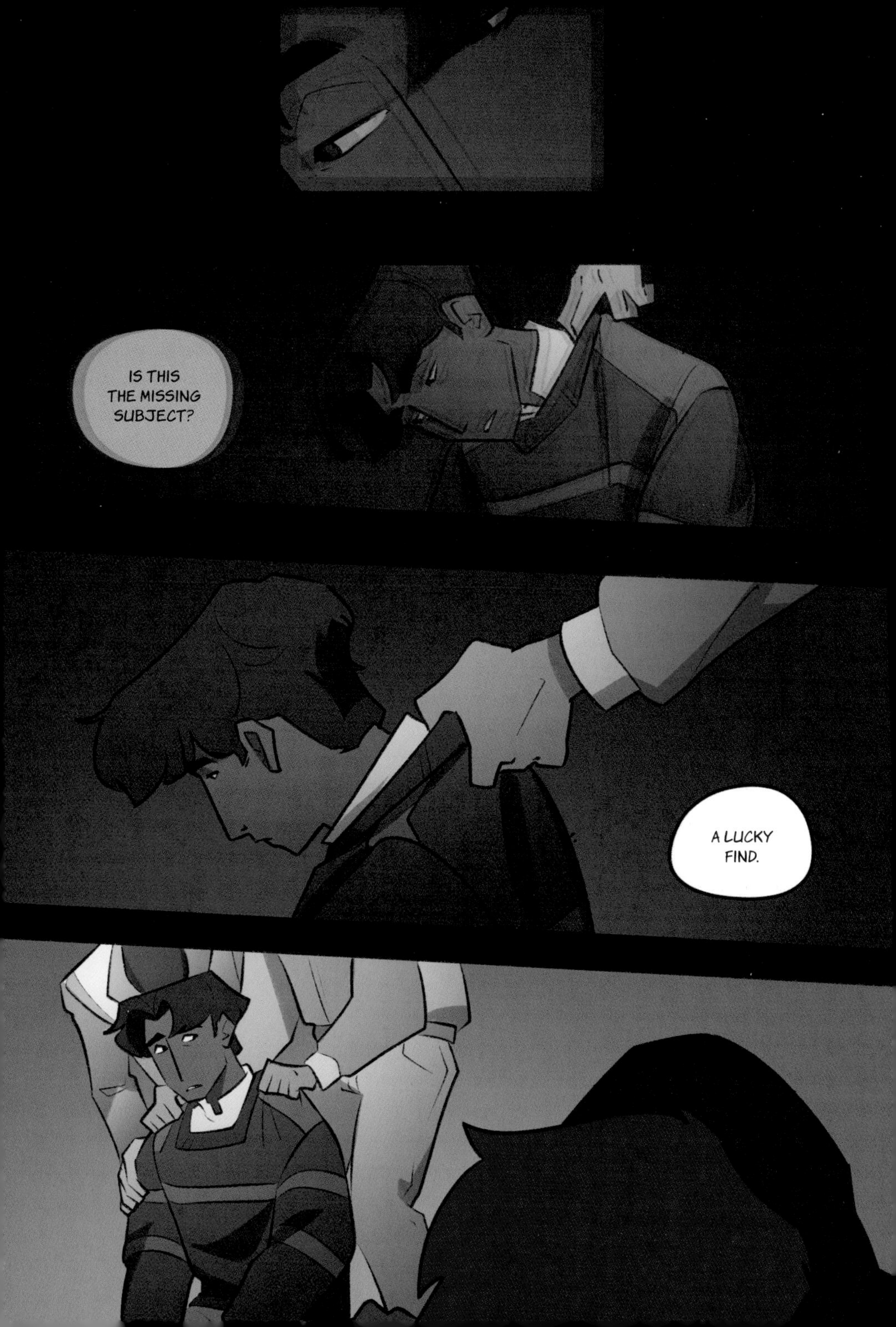
IS THIS THE MISSING SUBJECT?
A LUCKY FIND.

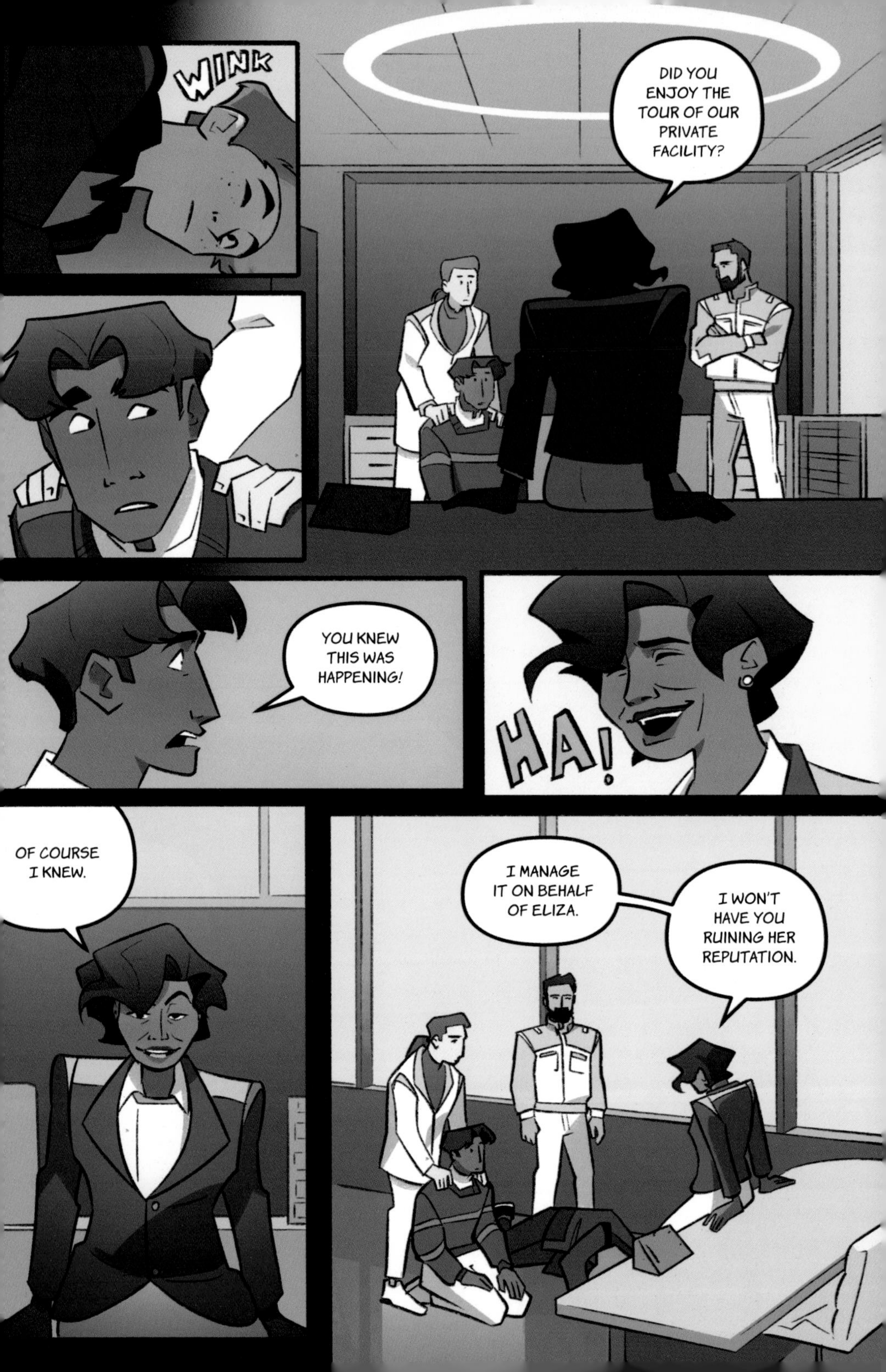
WINK
DID YOU ENJOY THE TOUR OF OUR PRIVATE FACILITY?
YOU KNEW THIS WAS HAPPENING!
HA!
OF COURSE I KNEW.
I MANAGE IT ON BEHALF OF ELIZA.
I WON'T HAVE YOU RUINING HER REPUTATION.

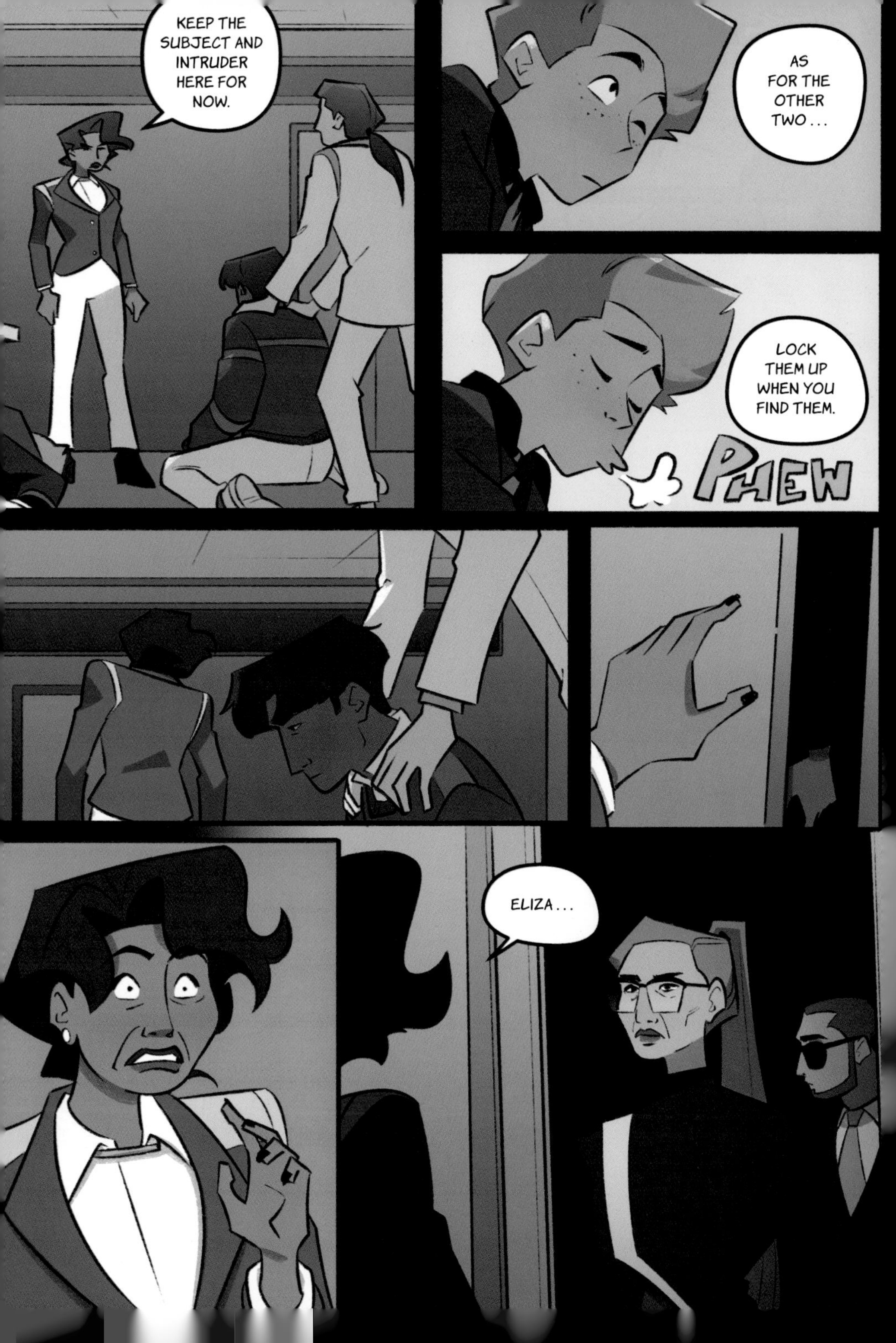
KEEP THE SUBJECT AND INTRUDER HERE FOR NOW.
AS FOR THE OTHER TWO . . .
LOCK THEM UP WHEN YOU FIND THEM.
PHEW
ELIZA . . .

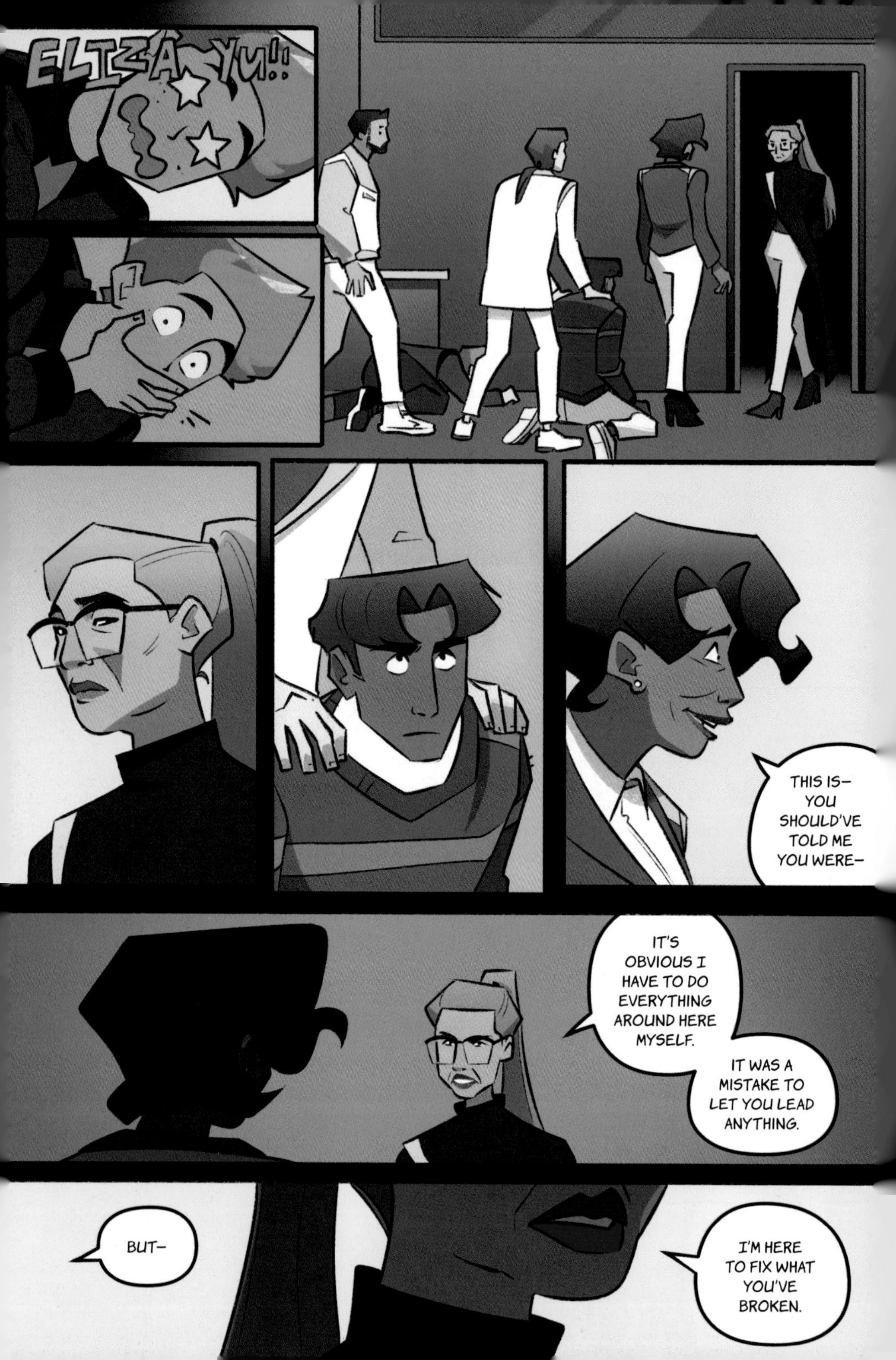
ELIZA YU!!
THIS IS— YOU SHOULD'VE TOLD ME YOU WERE—
IT'S OBVIOUS I HAVE TO DO EVERYTHING AROUND HERE MYSELF.
IT WAS A MISTAKE TO LET YOU LEAD ANYTHING.
BUT—
I'M HERE TO FIX WHAT YOU'VE BROKEN.

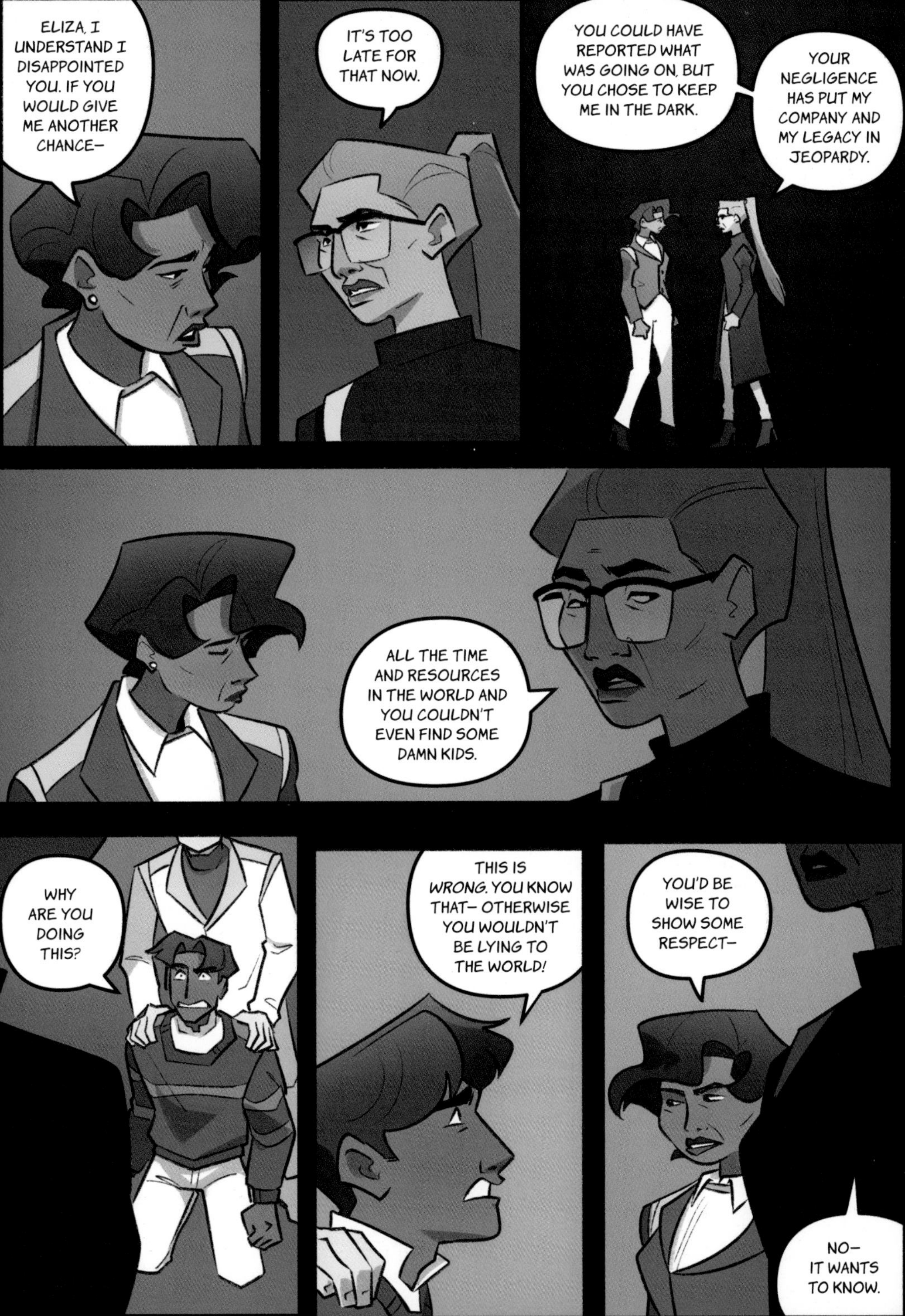
ELIZA, I UNDERSTAND I DISAPPOINTED YOU. IF YOU WOULD GIVE ME ANOTHER CHANCE–
IT'S TOO LATE FOR THAT NOW.
YOU COULD HAVE REPORTED WHAT WAS GOING ON, BUT YOU CHOSE TO KEEP ME IN THE DARK.
YOUR NEGLIGENCE HAS PUT MY COMPANY AND MY LEGACY IN JEOPARDY.
ALL THE TIME AND RESOURCES IN THE WORLD AND YOU COULDN'T EVEN FIND SOME DAMN KIDS.
WHY ARE YOU DOING THIS?
THIS IS *WRONG*. YOU KNOW THAT– OTHERWISE YOU WOULDN'T BE LYING TO THE WORLD!
YOU'D BE WISE TO SHOW SOME RESPECT–
NO– IT WANTS TO KNOW.

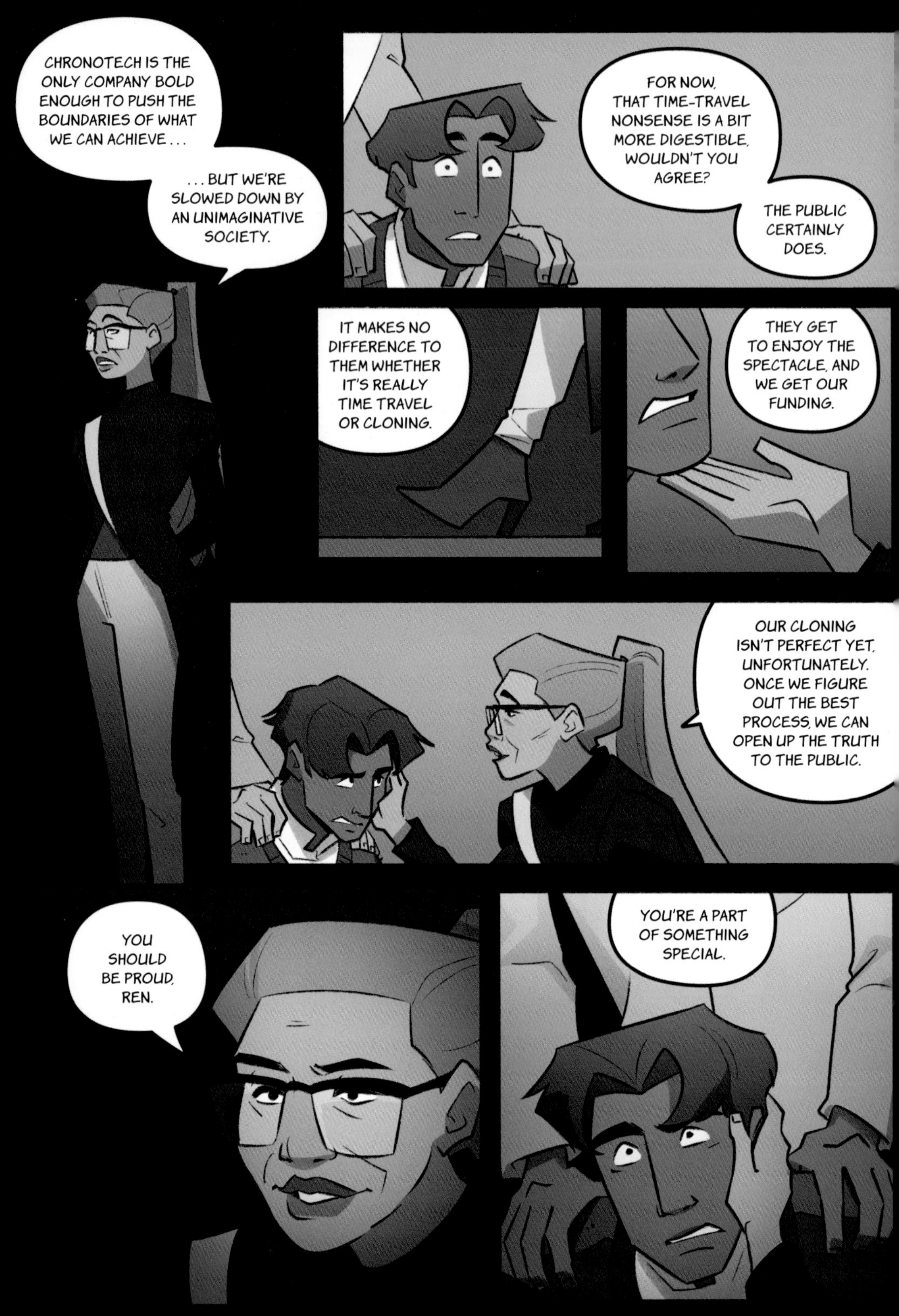
CHRONOTECH IS THE ONLY COMPANY BOLD ENOUGH TO PUSH THE BOUNDARIES OF WHAT WE CAN ACHIEVE . . .
. . . BUT WE'RE SLOWED DOWN BY AN UNIMAGINATIVE SOCIETY.
FOR NOW, THAT TIME-TRAVEL NONSENSE IS A BIT MORE DIGESTIBLE, WOULDN'T YOU AGREE?
THE PUBLIC CERTAINLY DOES.
IT MAKES NO DIFFERENCE TO THEM WHETHER IT'S REALLY TIME TRAVEL OR CLONING.
THEY GET TO ENJOY THE SPECTACLE, AND WE GET OUR FUNDING.
OUR CLONING ISN'T PERFECT YET, UNFORTUNATELY. ONCE WE FIGURE OUT THE BEST PROCESS, WE CAN OPEN UP THE TRUTH TO THE PUBLIC.
YOU SHOULD BE PROUD, REN.
YOU'RE A PART OF SOMETHING SPECIAL.

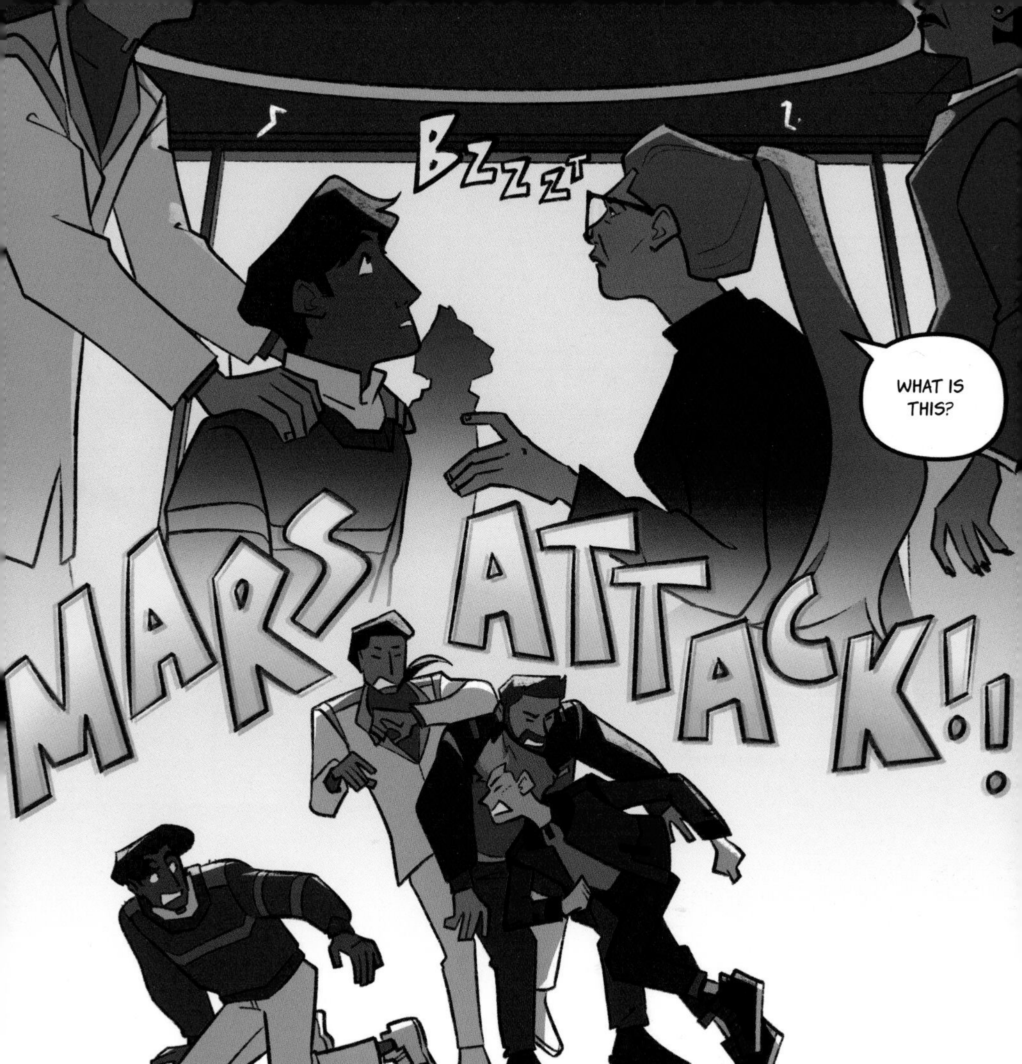
BZZZZT
WHAT IS THIS?
MARS ATTACK!!
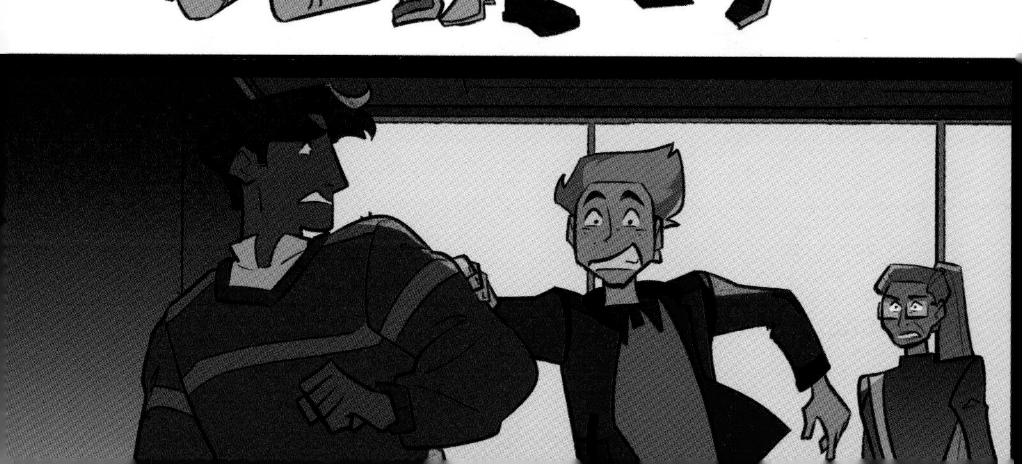

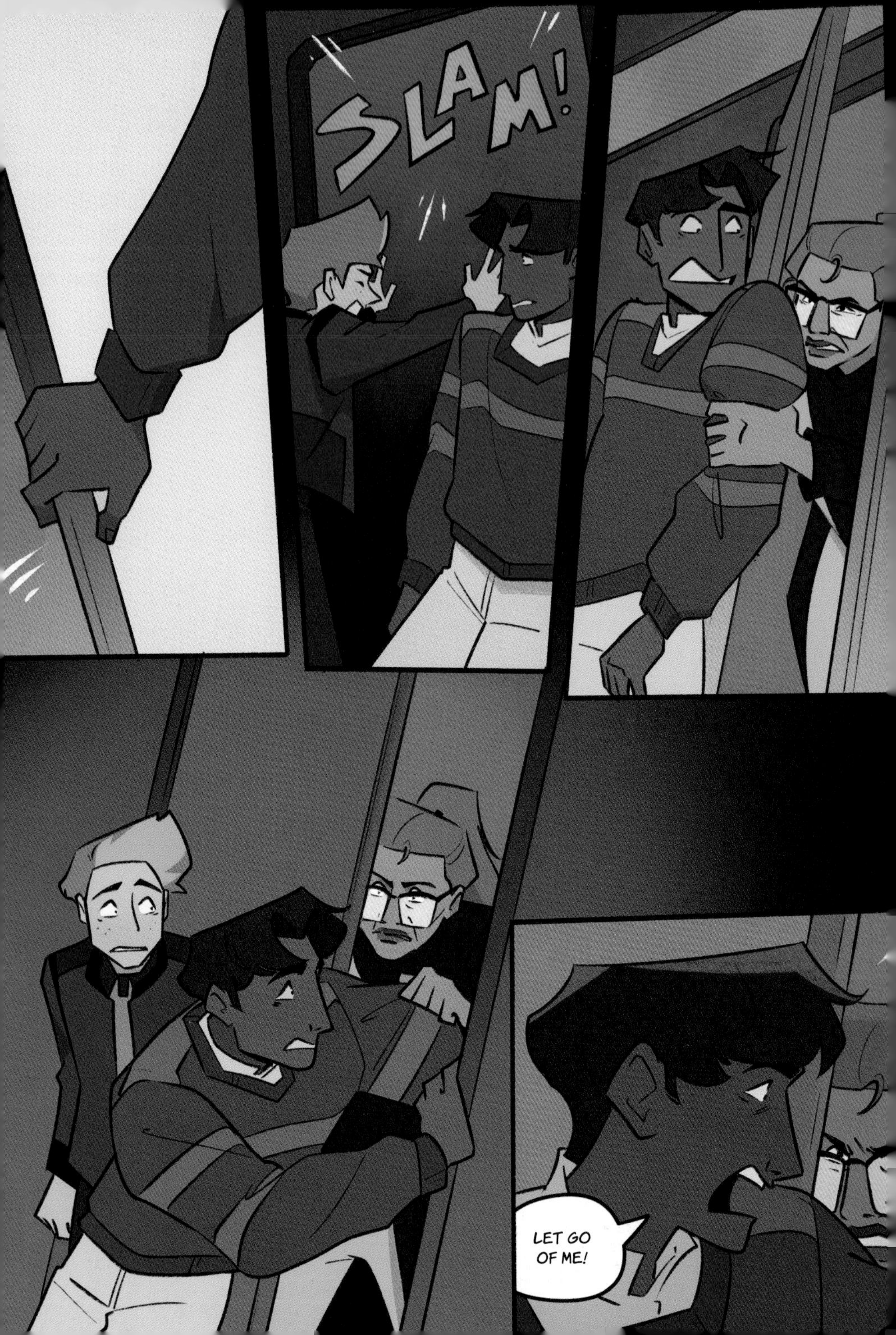
SLAM!
LET GO OF ME!

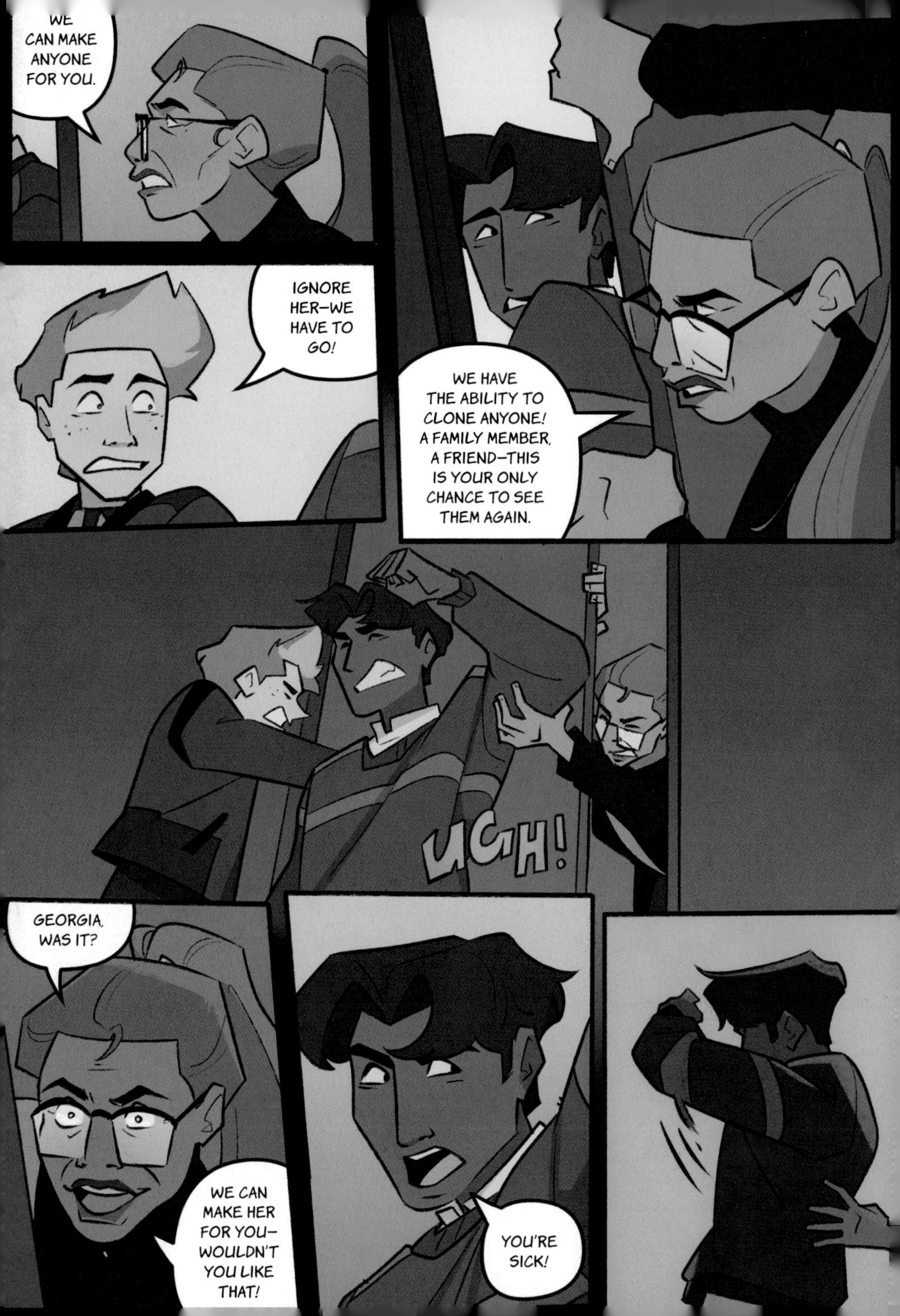
WE CAN MAKE ANYONE FOR YOU.
IGNORE HER—WE HAVE TO GO!
WE HAVE THE ABILITY TO CLONE ANYONE! A FAMILY MEMBER, A FRIEND—THIS IS YOUR ONLY CHANCE TO SEE THEM AGAIN.
UGH!
GEORGIA, WAS IT?
WE CAN MAKE HER FOR YOU—WOULDN'T YOU LIKE THAT!
YOU'RE SICK!

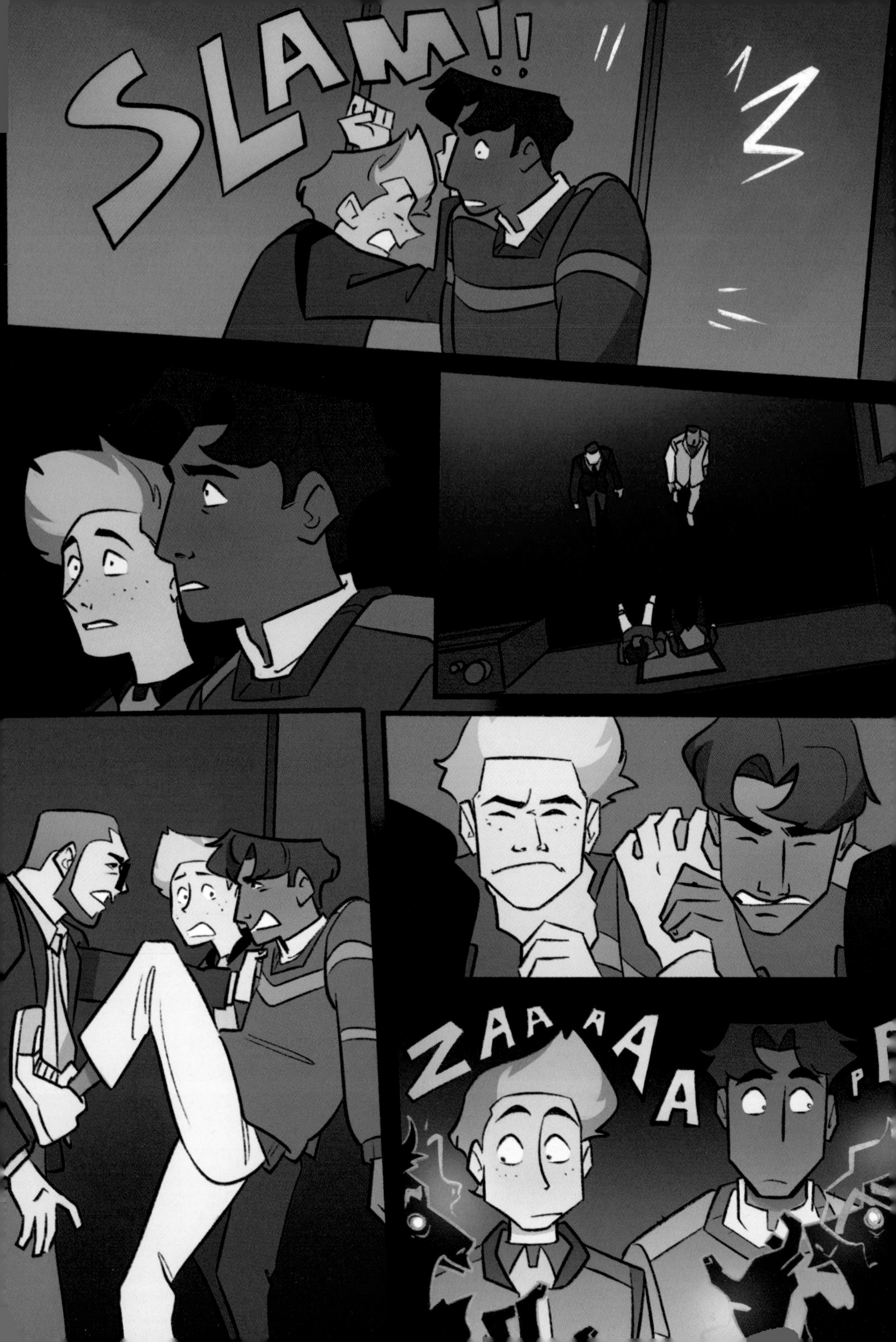
SLAM!!
ZAAAAAAP

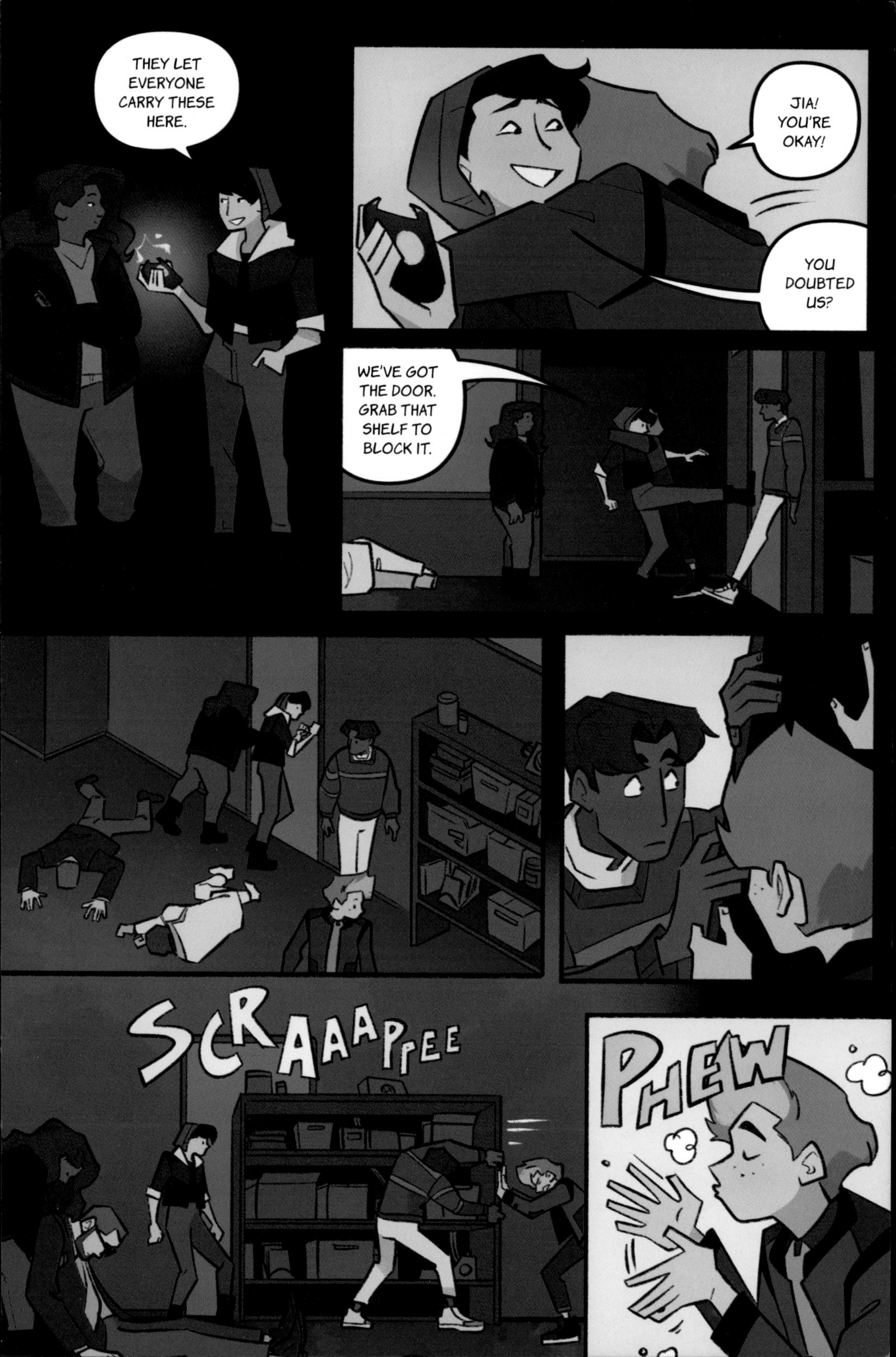
THEY LET EVERYONE CARRY THESE HERE.
JIA! YOU'RE OKAY!
YOU DOUBTED US?
WE'VE GOT THE DOOR. GRAB THAT SHELF TO BLOCK IT.
SCRAAAPPEE
PHEW

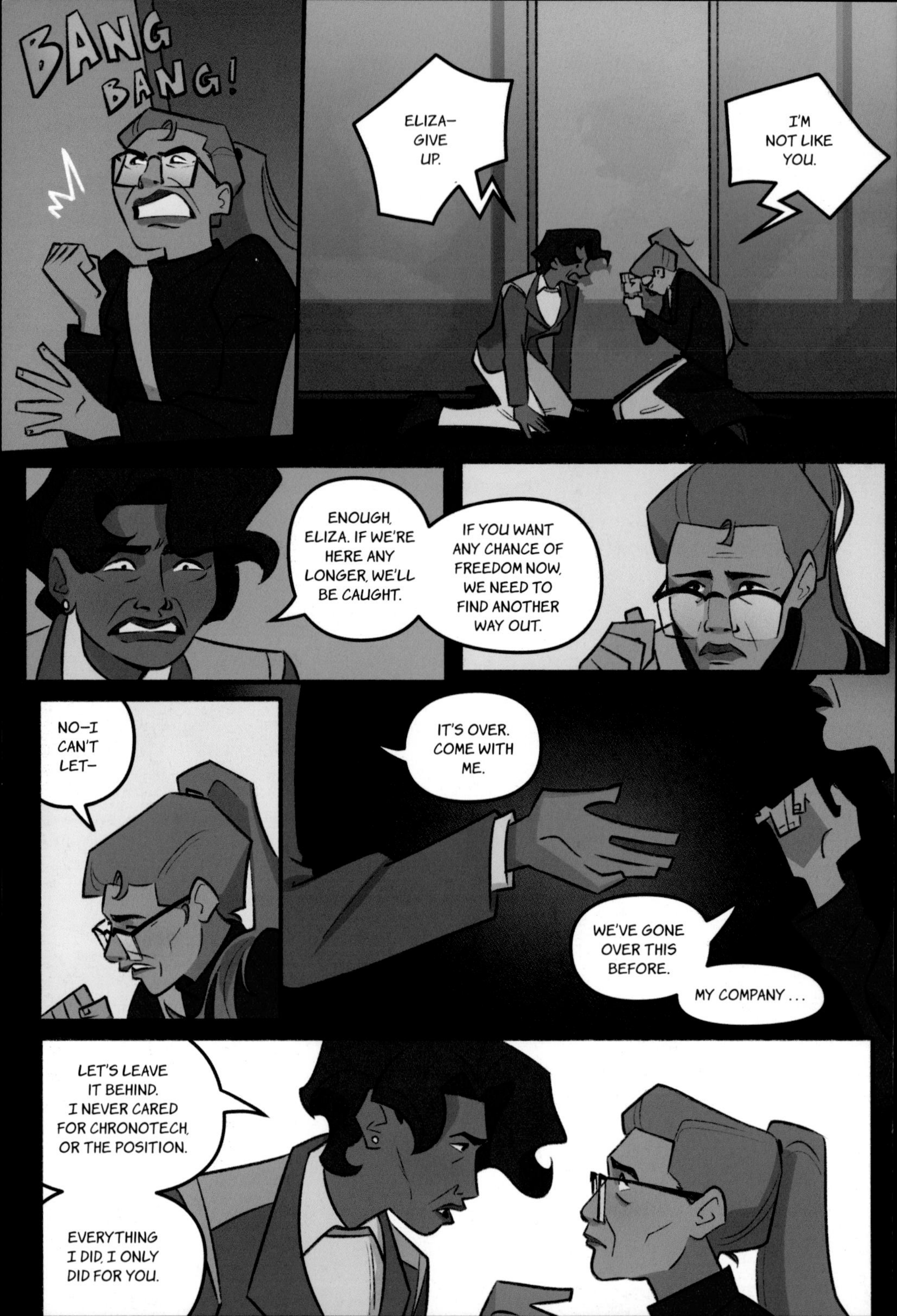
BANG BANG!
ELIZA— GIVE UP.
I'M NOT LIKE YOU.
ENOUGH, ELIZA. IF WE'RE HERE ANY LONGER, WE'LL BE CAUGHT.
IF YOU WANT ANY CHANCE OF FREEDOM NOW, WE NEED TO FIND ANOTHER WAY OUT.
NO—I CAN'T LET—
IT'S OVER. COME WITH ME.
WE'VE GONE OVER THIS BEFORE.
MY COMPANY . . .
LET'S LEAVE IT BEHIND. I NEVER CARED FOR CHRONOTECH, OR THE POSITION.
EVERYTHING I DID, I ONLY DID FOR YOU.

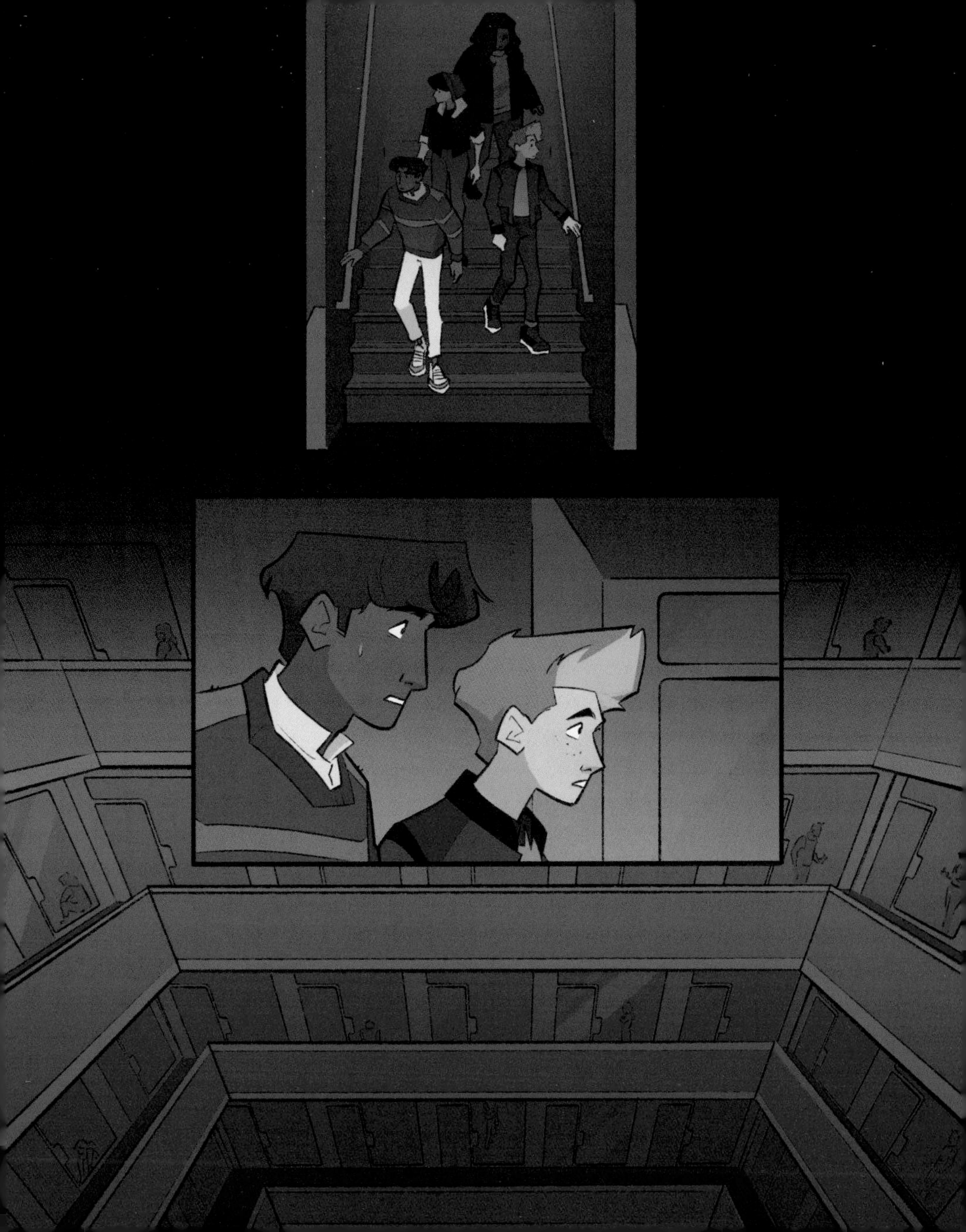

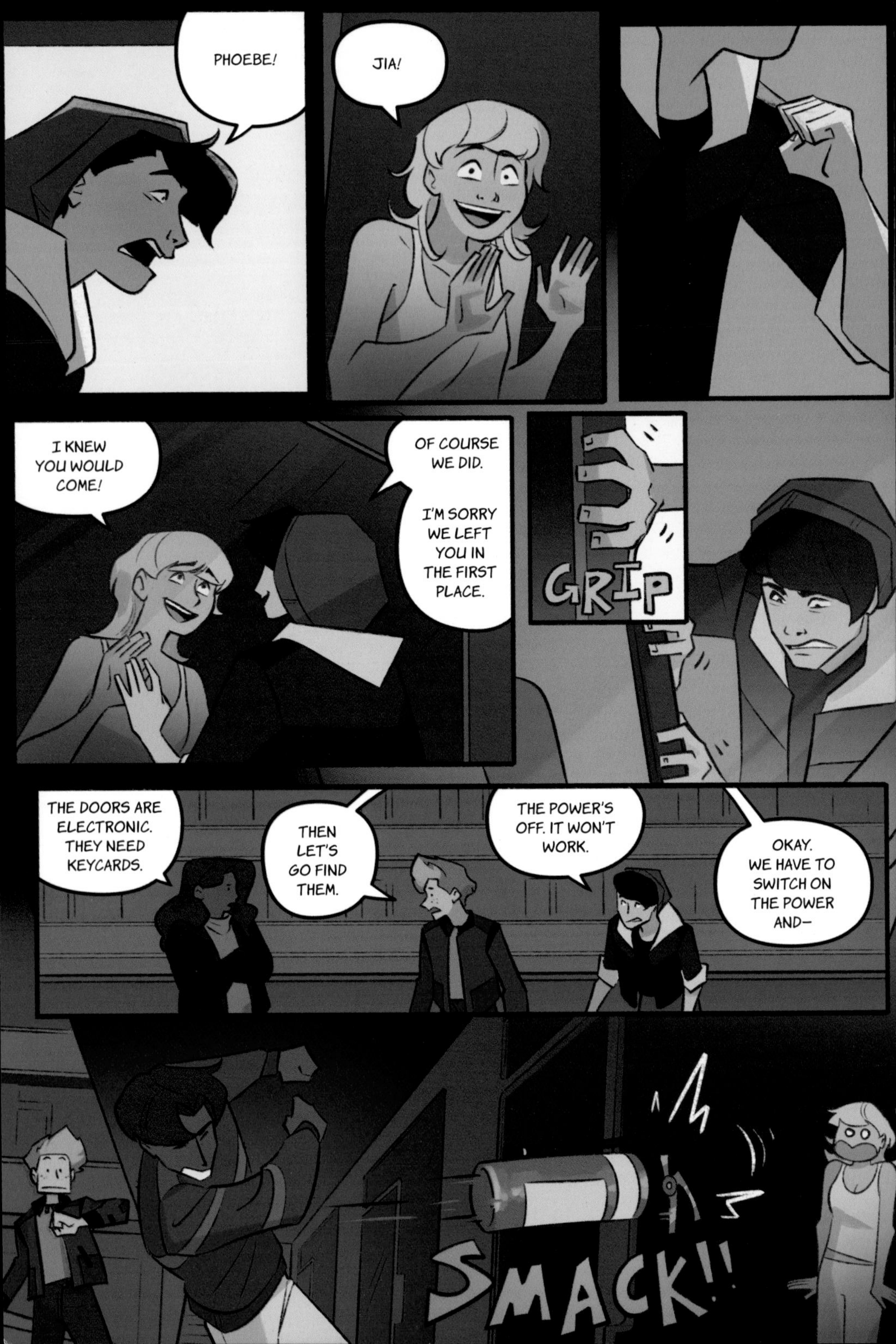
PHOEBE!
JIA!
I KNEW YOU WOULD COME!
OF COURSE WE DID.
I'M SORRY WE LEFT YOU IN THE FIRST PLACE.
GRIP
THE DOORS ARE ELECTRONIC. THEY NEED KEYCARDS.
THEN LET'S GO FIND THEM.
THE POWER'S OFF. IT WON'T WORK.
OKAY. WE HAVE TO SWITCH ON THE POWER AND—
SMACK!!

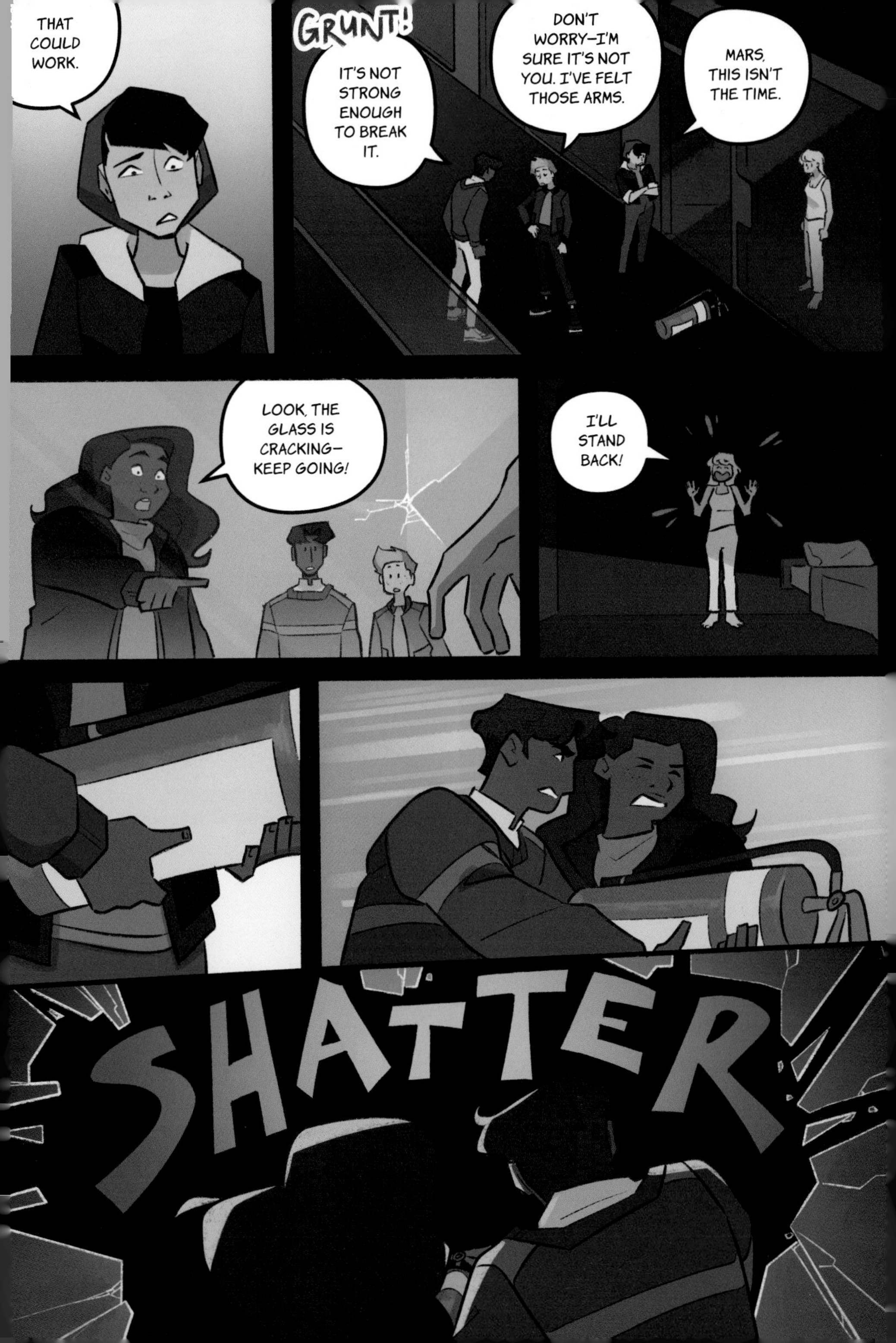
THAT COULD WORK.
GRUNT!
IT'S NOT STRONG ENOUGH TO BREAK IT.
DON'T WORRY—I'M SURE IT'S NOT YOU. I'VE FELT THOSE ARMS.
MARS, THIS ISN'T THE TIME.
LOOK, THE GLASS IS CRACKING— KEEP GOING!
I'LL STAND BACK!
SHATTER

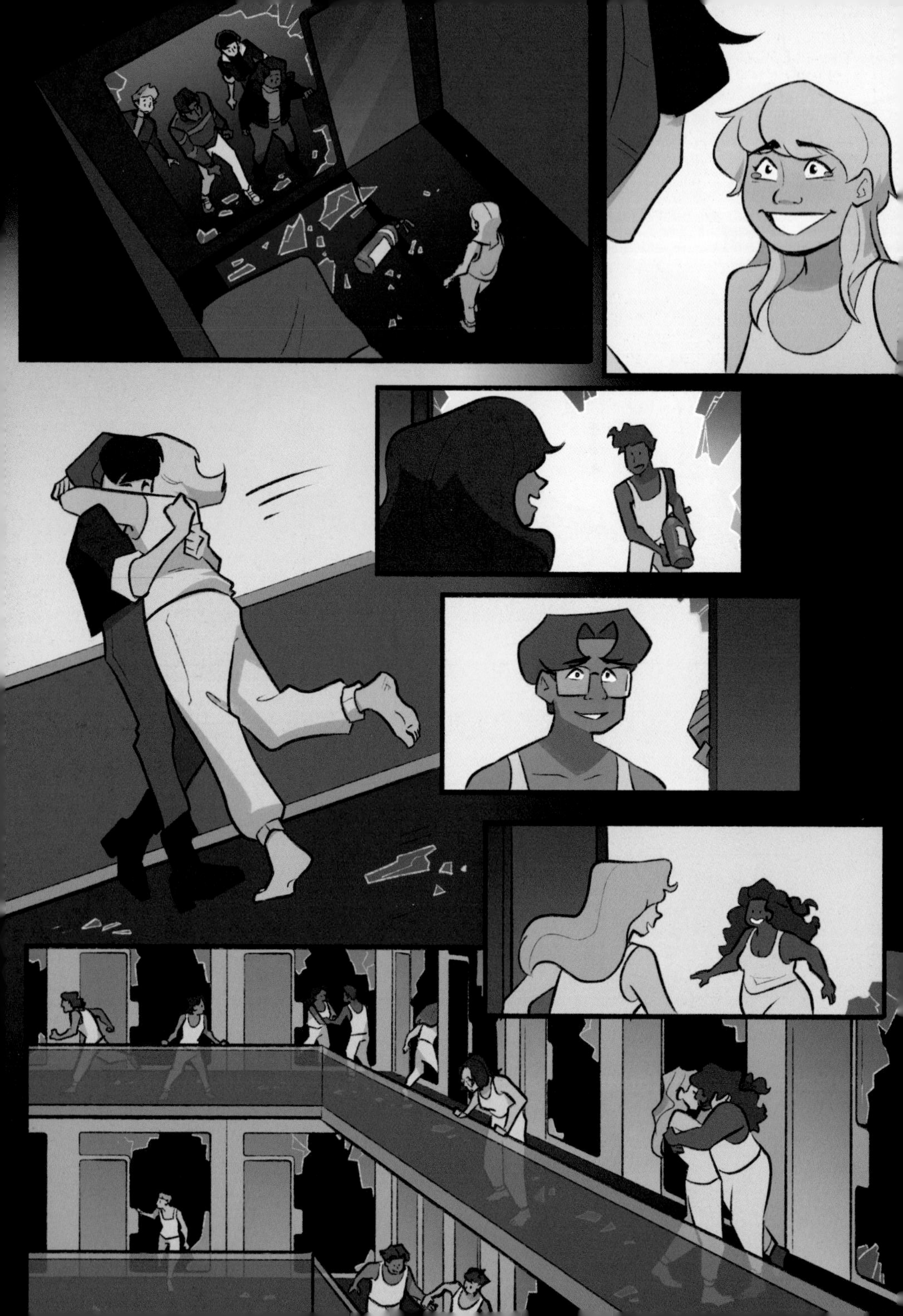

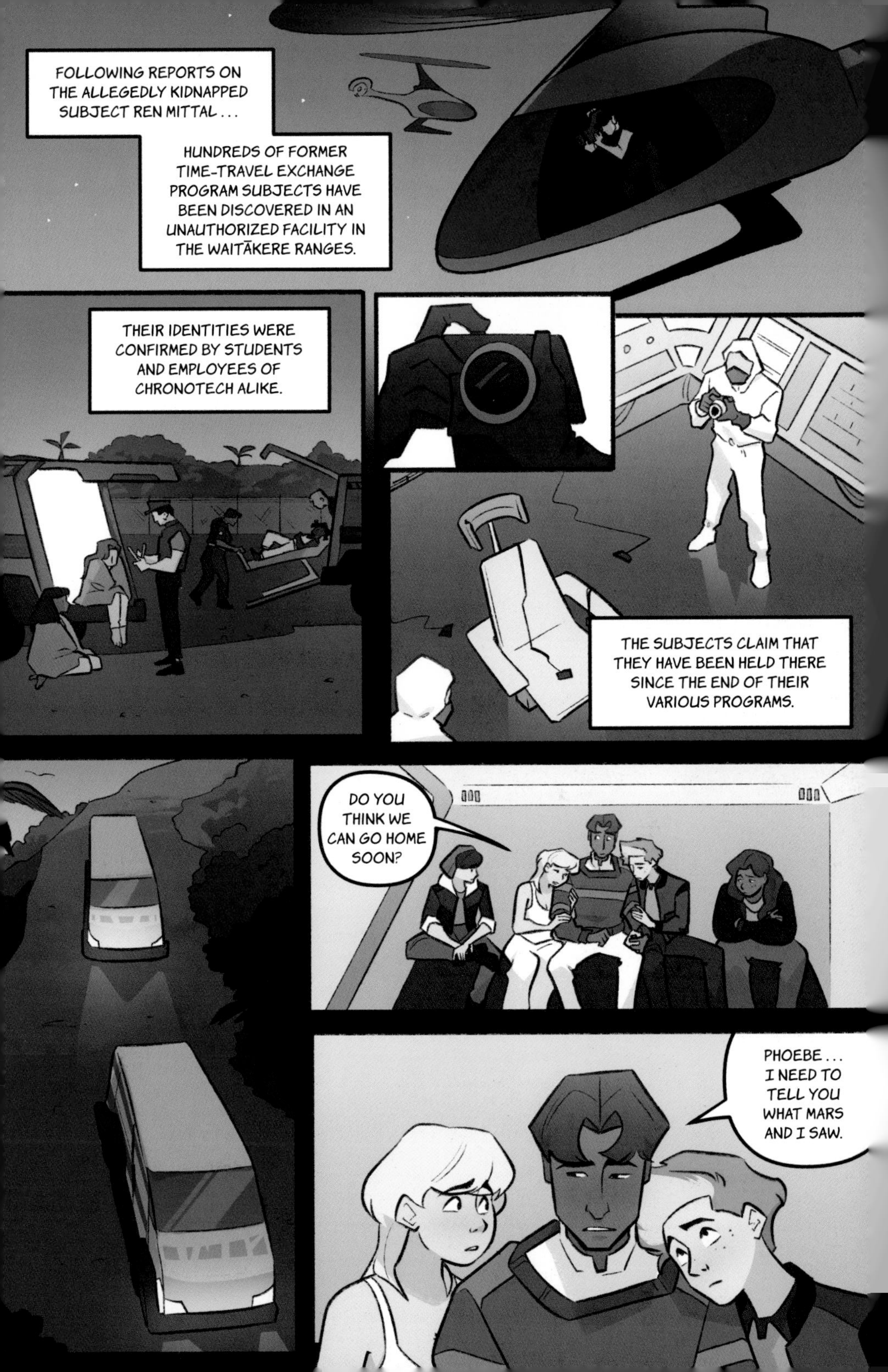
FOLLOWING REPORTS ON THE ALLEGEDLY KIDNAPPED SUBJECT REN MITTAL . . .
HUNDREDS OF FORMER TIME-TRAVEL EXCHANGE PROGRAM SUBJECTS HAVE BEEN DISCOVERED IN AN UNAUTHORIZED FACILITY IN THE WAITĀKERE RANGES.
THEIR IDENTITIES WERE CONFIRMED BY STUDENTS AND EMPLOYEES OF CHRONOTECH ALIKE.
THE SUBJECTS CLAIM THAT THEY HAVE BEEN HELD THERE SINCE THE END OF THEIR VARIOUS PROGRAMS.
DO YOU THINK WE CAN GO HOME SOON?
PHOEBE . . . I NEED TO TELL YOU WHAT MARS AND I SAW.

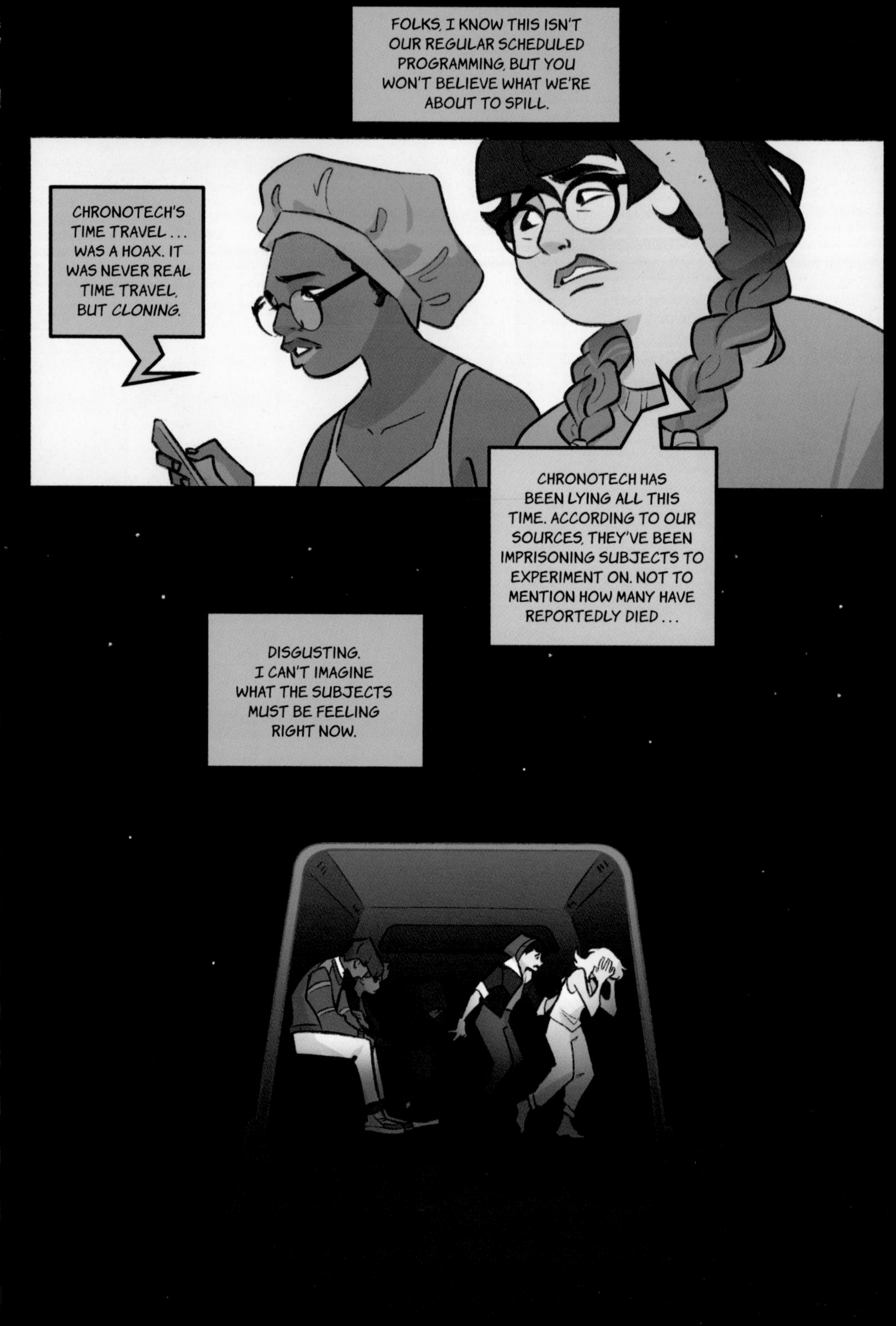
FOLKS, I KNOW THIS ISN'T OUR REGULAR SCHEDULED PROGRAMMING, BUT YOU WON'T BELIEVE WHAT WE'RE ABOUT TO SPILL.
CHRONOTECH'S TIME TRAVEL . . . WAS A HOAX. IT WAS NEVER REAL TIME TRAVEL, BUT *CLONING.*
CHRONOTECH HAS BEEN LYING ALL THIS TIME. ACCORDING TO OUR SOURCES, THEY'VE BEEN IMPRISONING SUBJECTS TO EXPERIMENT ON. NOT TO MENTION HOW MANY HAVE REPORTEDLY DIED . . .
DISGUSTING. I CAN'T IMAGINE WHAT THE SUBJECTS MUST BE FEELING RIGHT NOW.

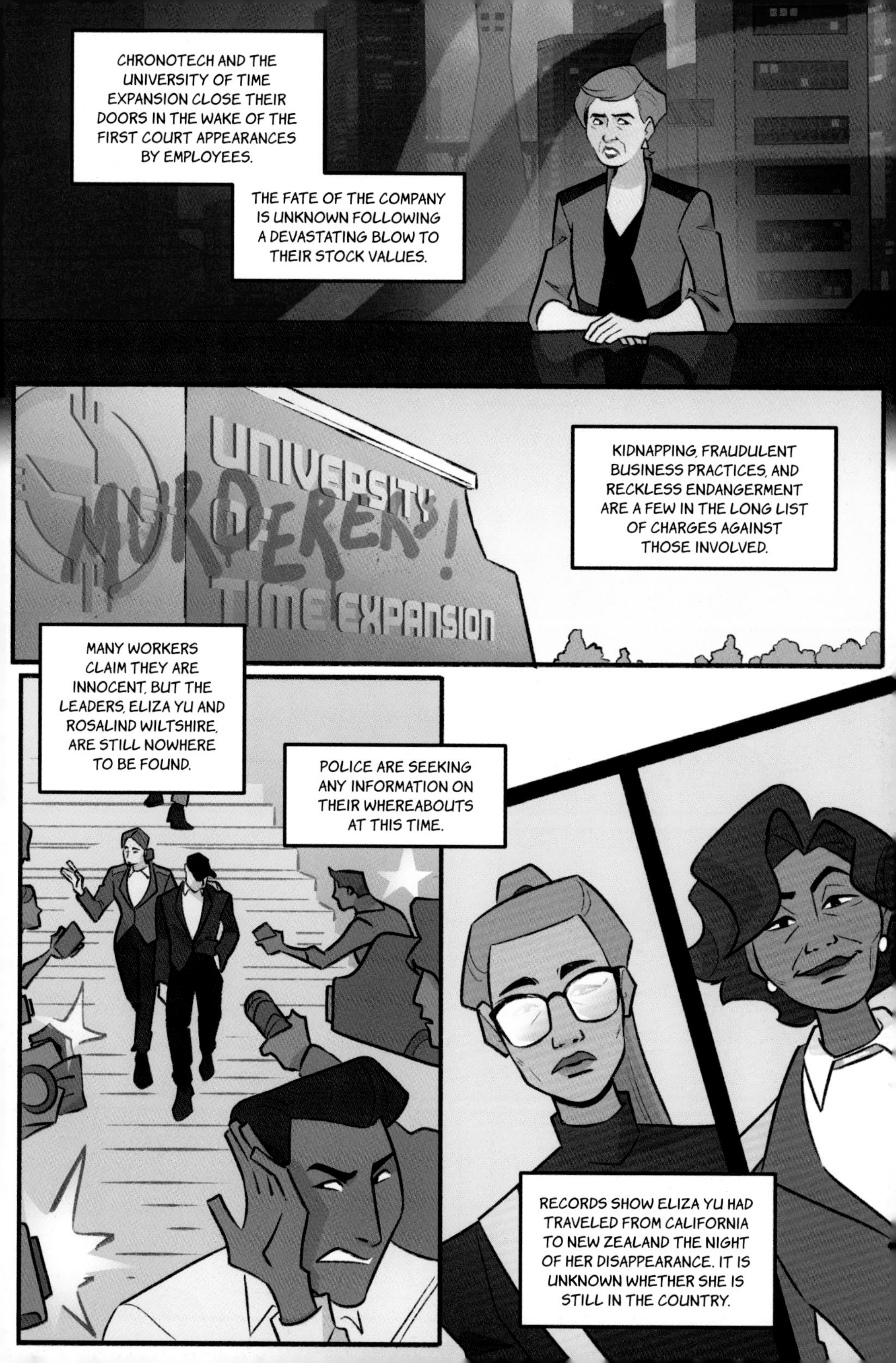
CHRONOTECH AND THE UNIVERSITY OF TIME EXPANSION CLOSE THEIR DOORS IN THE WAKE OF THE FIRST COURT APPEARANCES BY EMPLOYEES.
THE FATE OF THE COMPANY IS UNKNOWN FOLLOWING A DEVASTATING BLOW TO THEIR STOCK VALUES.
UNIVERSITY OF TIME EXPANSION
MURDERERS!
KIDNAPPING, FRAUDULENT BUSINESS PRACTICES, AND RECKLESS ENDANGERMENT ARE A FEW IN THE LONG LIST OF CHARGES AGAINST THOSE INVOLVED.
MANY WORKERS CLAIM THEY ARE INNOCENT, BUT THE LEADERS, ELIZA YU AND ROSALIND WILTSHIRE, ARE STILL NOWHERE TO BE FOUND.
POLICE ARE SEEKING ANY INFORMATION ON THEIR WHEREABOUTS AT THIS TIME.
RECORDS SHOW ELIZA YU HAD TRAVELED FROM CALIFORNIA TO NEW ZEALAND THE NIGHT OF HER DISAPPEARANCE. IT IS UNKNOWN WHETHER SHE IS STILL IN THE COUNTRY.

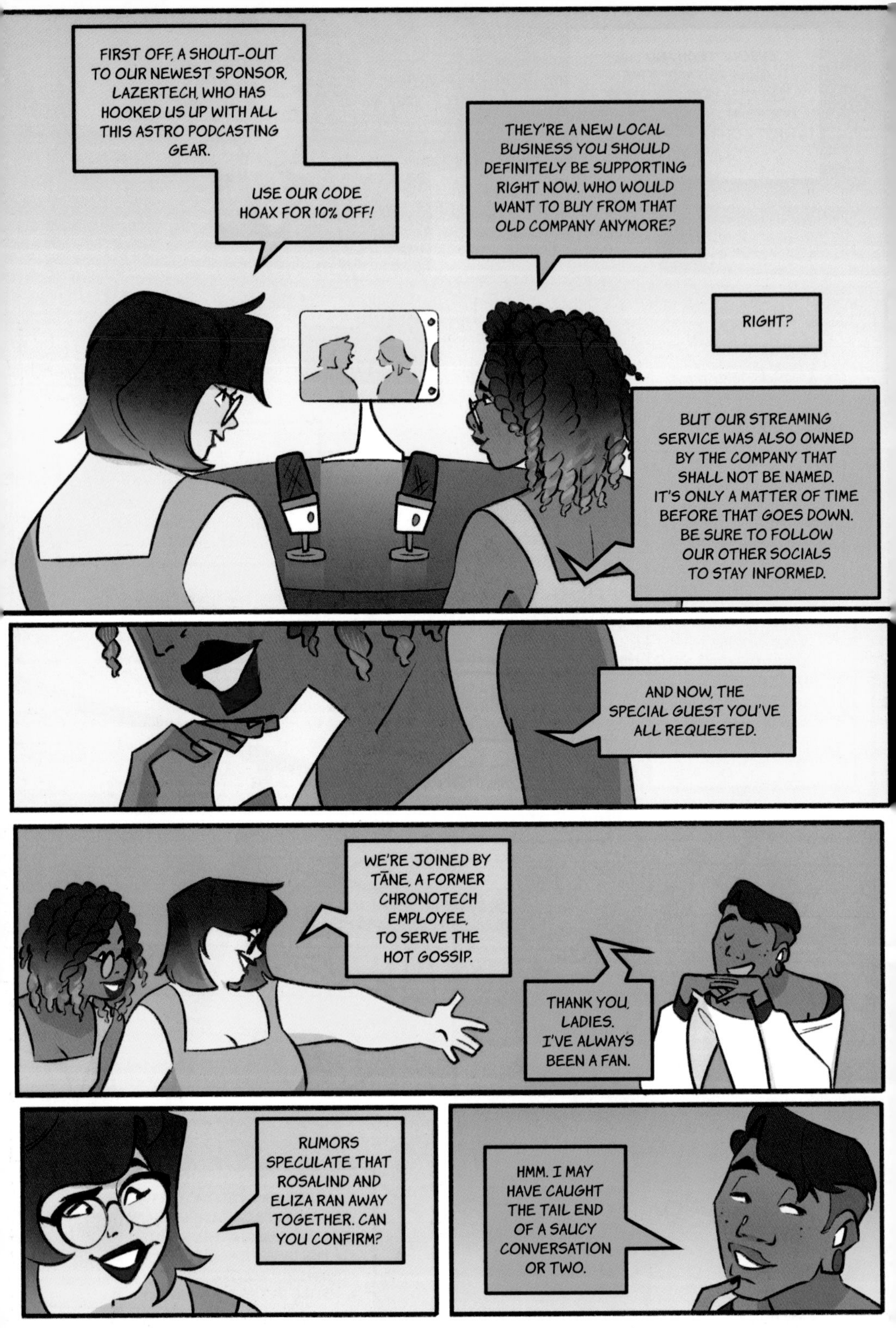
FIRST OFF, A SHOUT-OUT TO OUR NEWEST SPONSOR, LAZERTECH, WHO HAS HOOKED US UP WITH ALL THIS ASTRO PODCASTING GEAR.
USE OUR CODE HOAX FOR 10% OFF!
THEY'RE A NEW LOCAL BUSINESS YOU SHOULD DEFINITELY BE SUPPORTING RIGHT NOW. WHO WOULD WANT TO BUY FROM THAT OLD COMPANY ANYMORE?
RIGHT?
BUT OUR STREAMING SERVICE WAS ALSO OWNED BY THE COMPANY THAT SHALL NOT BE NAMED. IT'S ONLY A MATTER OF TIME BEFORE THAT GOES DOWN. BE SURE TO FOLLOW OUR OTHER SOCIALS TO STAY INFORMED.
AND NOW, THE SPECIAL GUEST YOU'VE ALL REQUESTED.
WE'RE JOINED BY TĀNE, A FORMER CHRONOTECH EMPLOYEE, TO SERVE THE HOT GOSSIP.
THANK YOU, LADIES. I'VE ALWAYS BEEN A FAN.
RUMORS SPECULATE THAT ROSALIND AND ELIZA RAN AWAY TOGETHER. CAN YOU CONFIRM?
HMM. I MAY HAVE CAUGHT THE TAIL END OF A SAUCY CONVERSATION OR TWO.

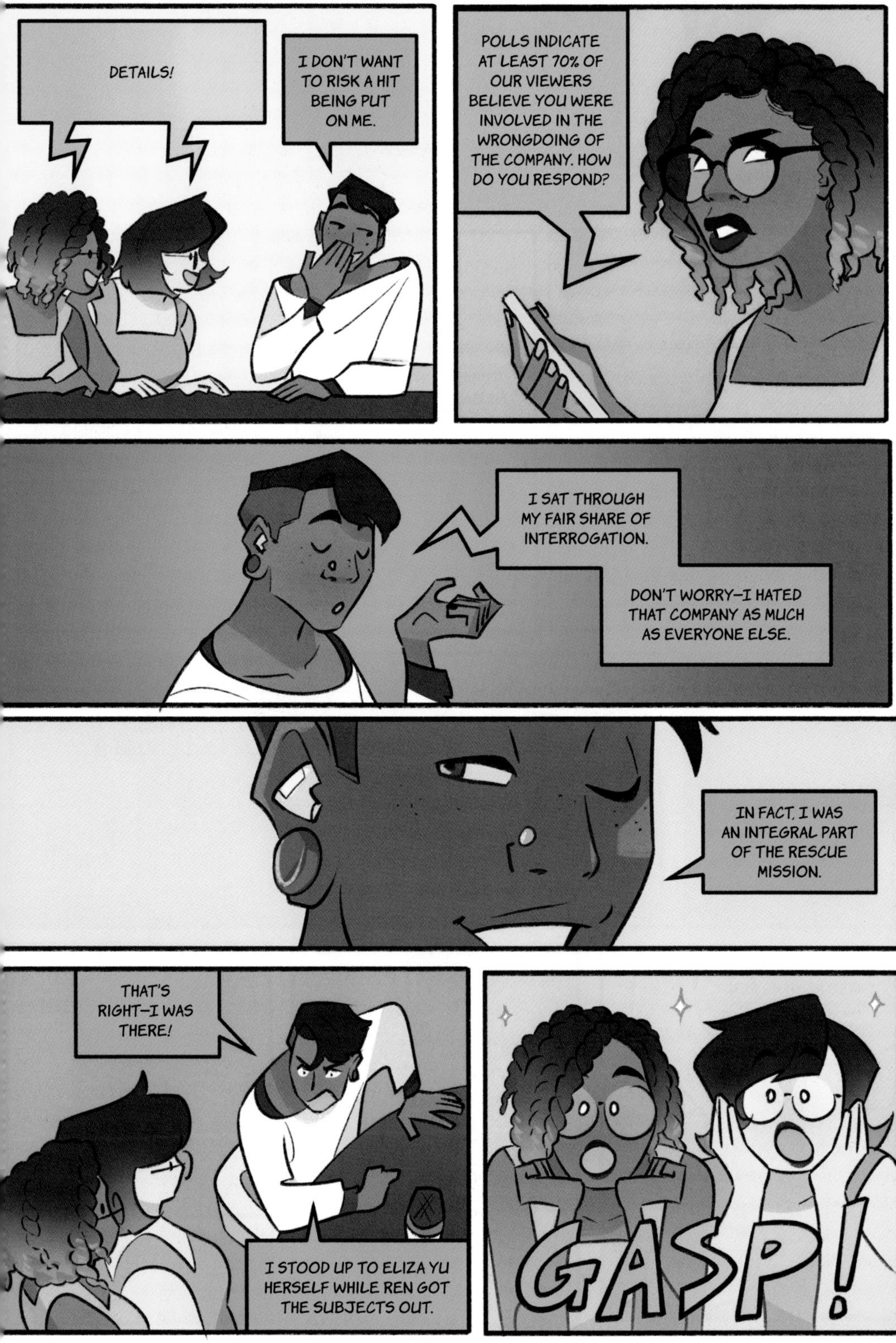
DETAILS!
I DON'T WANT TO RISK A HIT BEING PUT ON ME.
POLLS INDICATE AT LEAST 70% OF OUR VIEWERS BELIEVE YOU WERE INVOLVED IN THE WRONGDOING OF THE COMPANY. HOW DO YOU RESPOND?
I SAT THROUGH MY FAIR SHARE OF INTERROGATION.
DON'T WORRY—I HATED THAT COMPANY AS MUCH AS EVERYONE ELSE.
IN FACT, I WAS AN INTEGRAL PART OF THE RESCUE MISSION.
THAT'S RIGHT—I WAS THERE!
I STOOD UP TO ELIZA YU HERSELF WHILE REN GOT THE SUBJECTS OUT.
GASP!

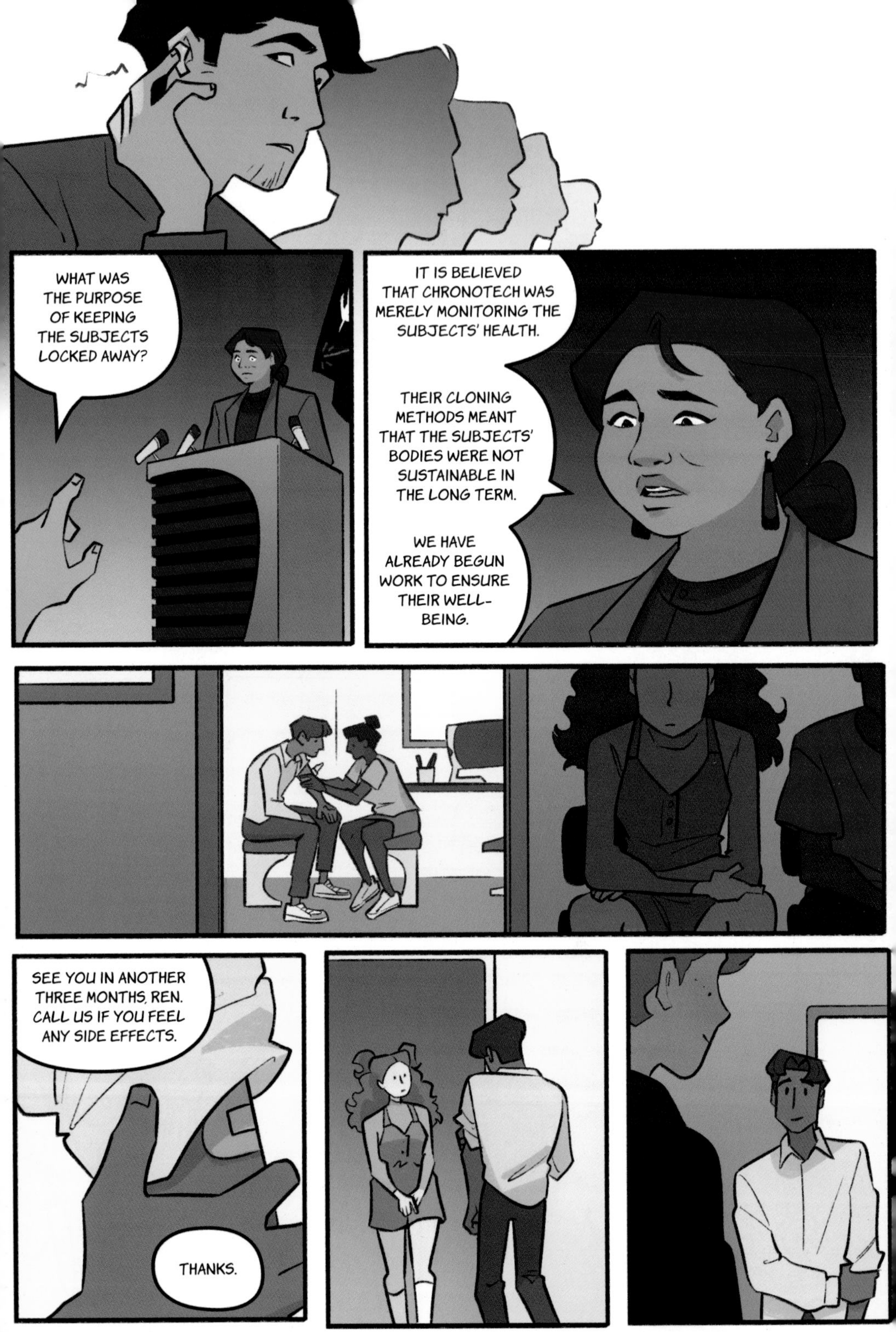
WHAT WAS THE PURPOSE OF KEEPING THE SUBJECTS LOCKED AWAY?
IT IS BELIEVED THAT CHRONOTECH WAS MERELY MONITORING THE SUBJECTS' HEALTH.
THEIR CLONING METHODS MEANT THAT THE SUBJECTS' BODIES WERE NOT SUSTAINABLE IN THE LONG TERM.
WE HAVE ALREADY BEGUN WORK TO ENSURE THEIR WELL-BEING.
SEE YOU IN ANOTHER THREE MONTHS, REN. CALL US IF YOU FEEL ANY SIDE EFFECTS.
THANKS.

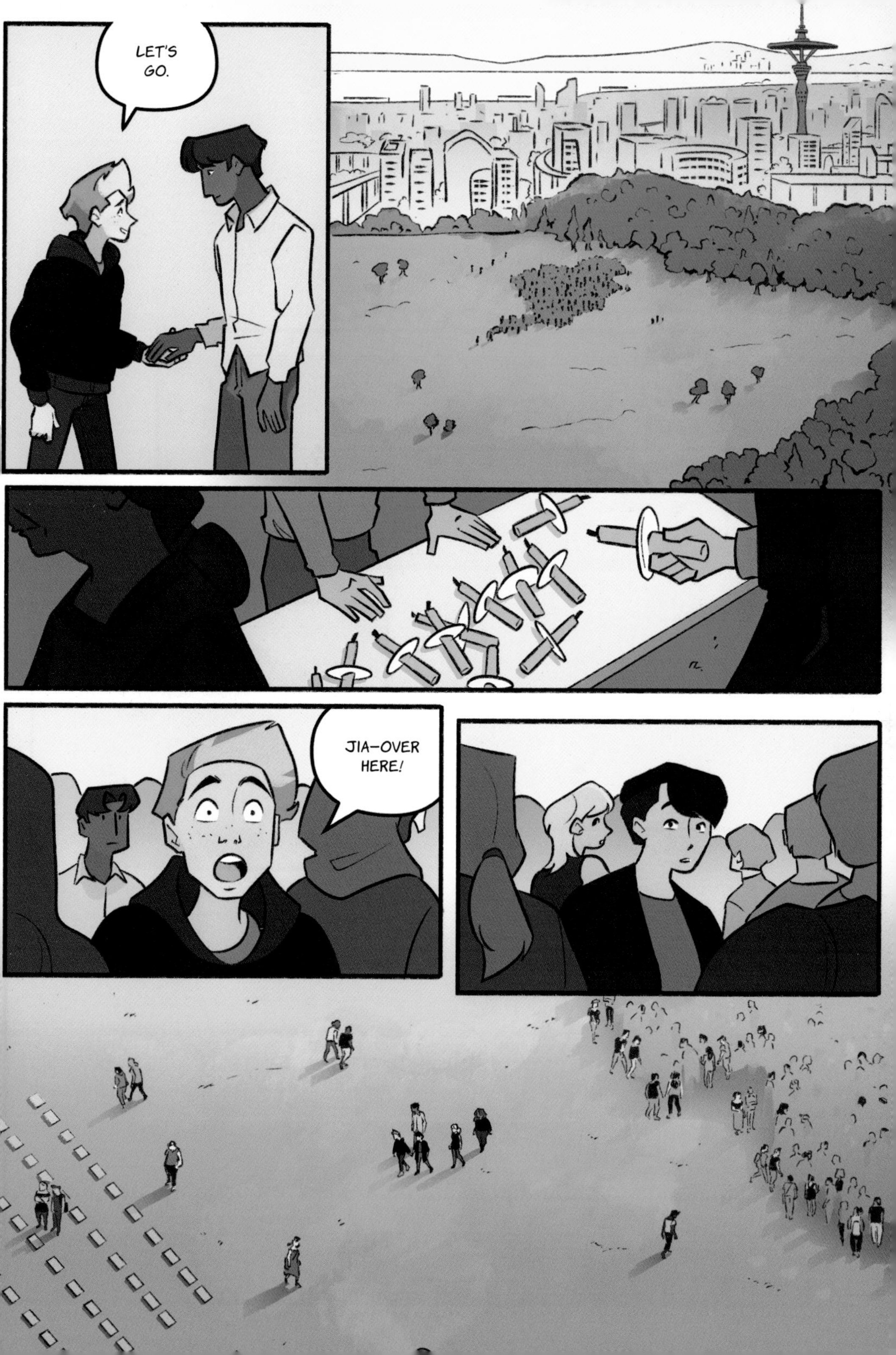
LET'S GO.
JIA—OVER HERE!

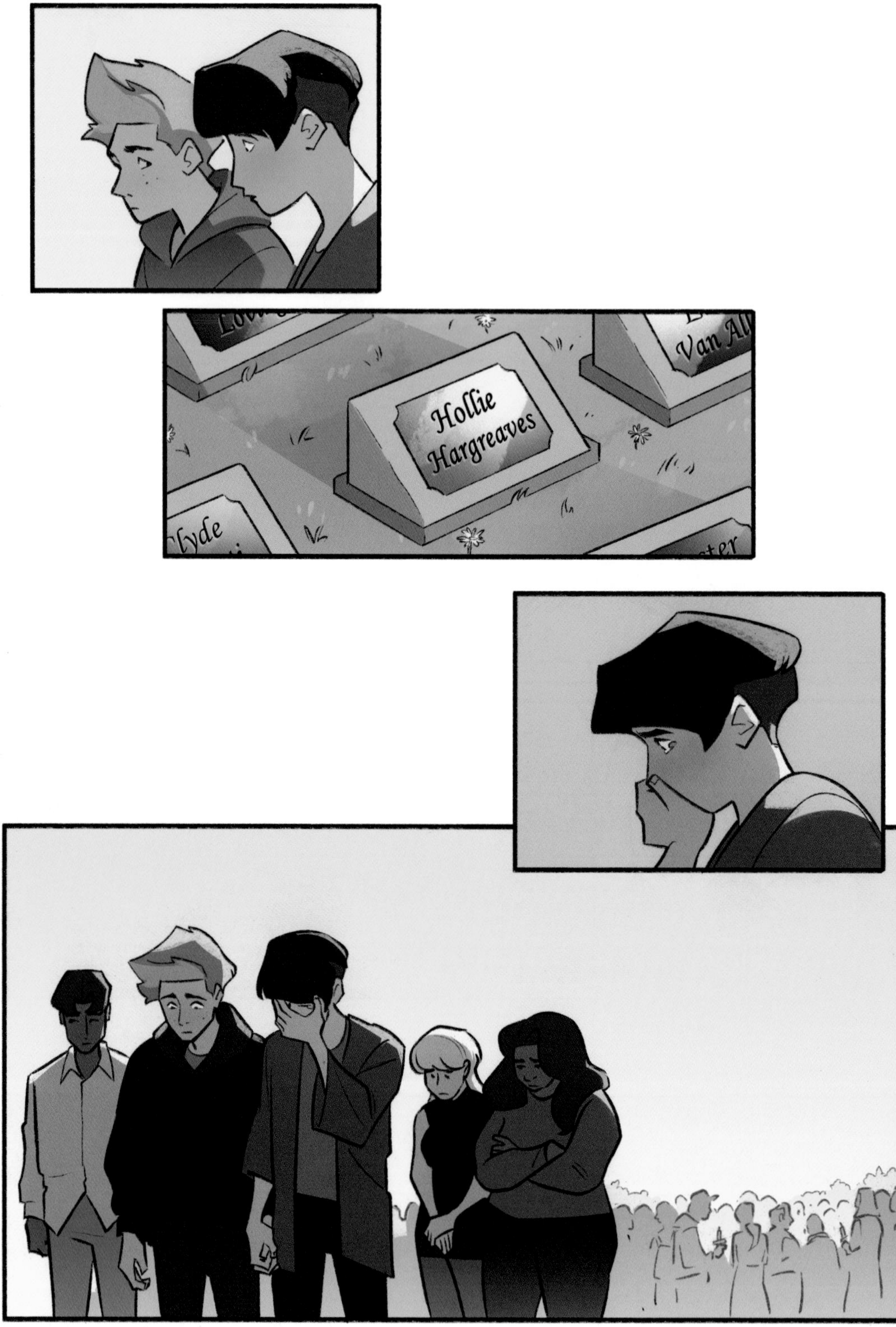
Hollie
Hargreaves
Clyde

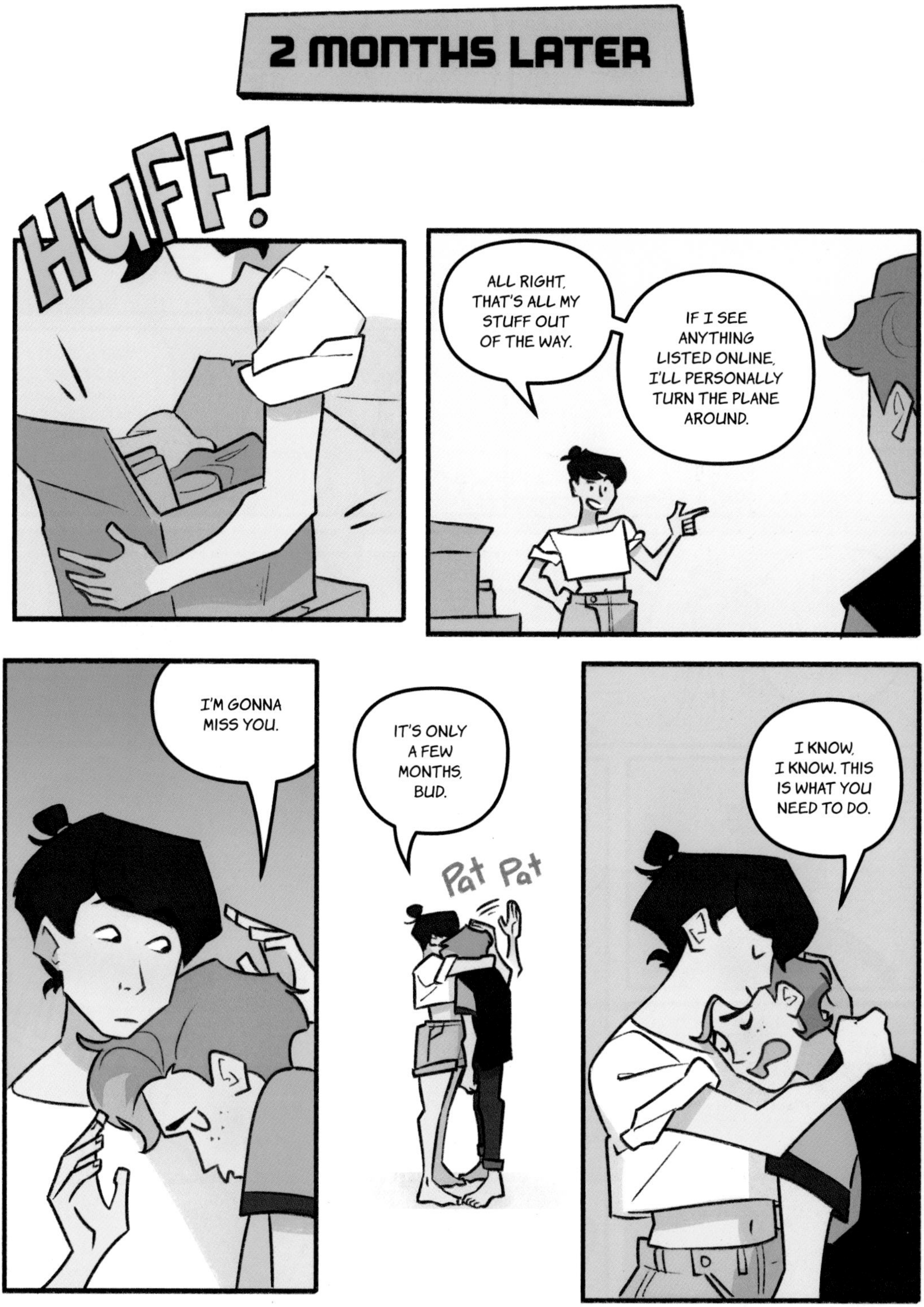
2 MONTHS LATER
HUFF!
ALL RIGHT, THAT'S ALL MY STUFF OUT OF THE WAY.
IF I SEE ANYTHING LISTED ONLINE, I'LL PERSONALLY TURN THE PLANE AROUND.
I'M GONNA MISS YOU.
IT'S ONLY A FEW MONTHS, BUD.
Pat Pat
I KNOW, I KNOW. THIS IS WHAT YOU NEED TO DO.

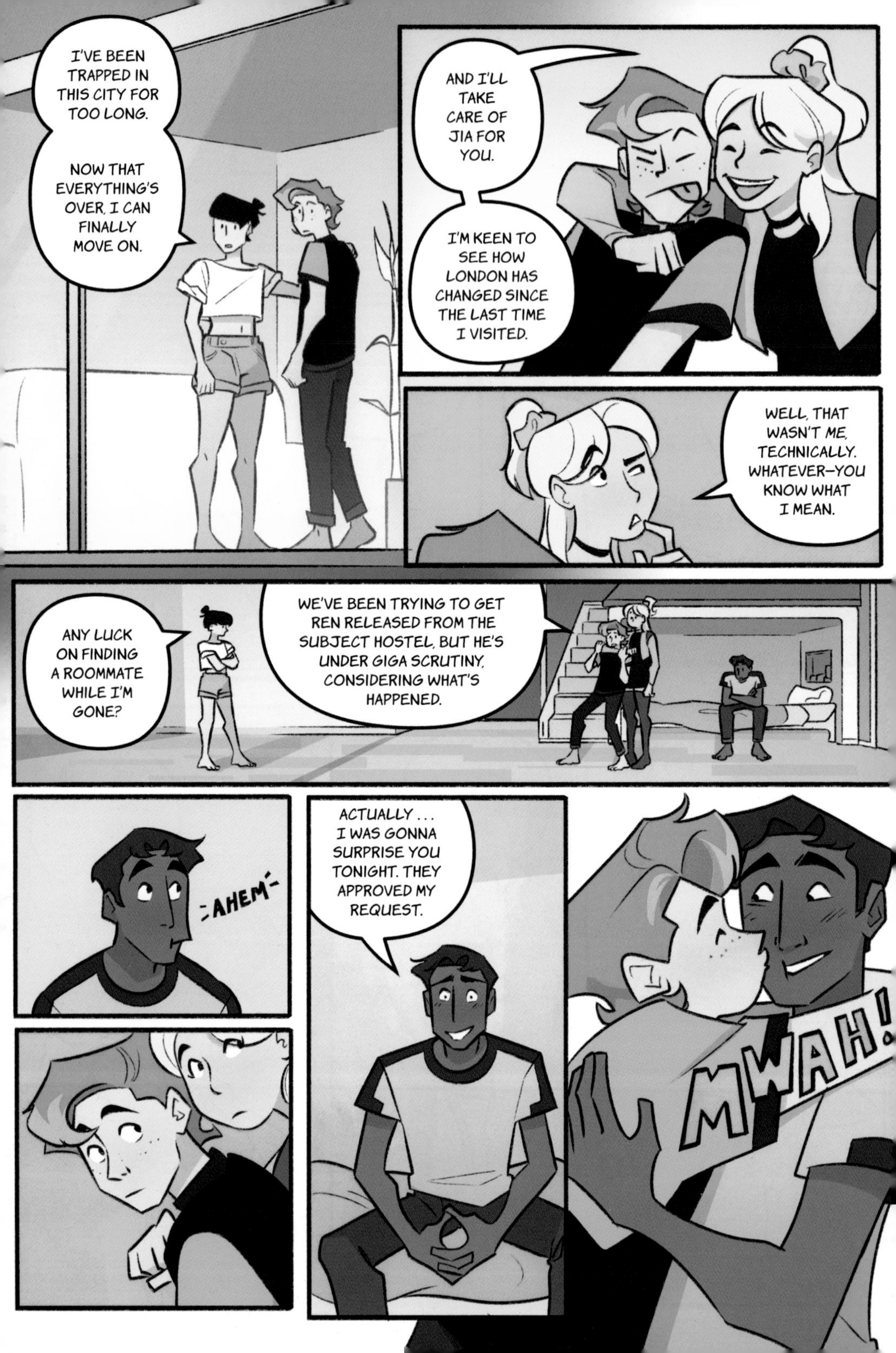
I'VE BEEN TRAPPED IN THIS CITY FOR TOO LONG.
NOW THAT EVERYTHING'S OVER, I CAN FINALLY MOVE ON.
AND I'LL TAKE CARE OF JIA FOR YOU.
I'M KEEN TO SEE HOW LONDON HAS CHANGED SINCE THE LAST TIME I VISITED.
WELL, THAT WASN'T ME, TECHNICALLY. WHATEVER—YOU KNOW WHAT I MEAN.
ANY LUCK ON FINDING A ROOMMATE WHILE I'M GONE?
WE'VE BEEN TRYING TO GET REN RELEASED FROM THE SUBJECT HOSTEL, BUT HE'S UNDER GIGA SCRUTINY, CONSIDERING WHAT'S HAPPENED.
AHEM
ACTUALLY . . . I WAS GONNA SURPRISE YOU TONIGHT. THEY APPROVED MY REQUEST.
MWAH!

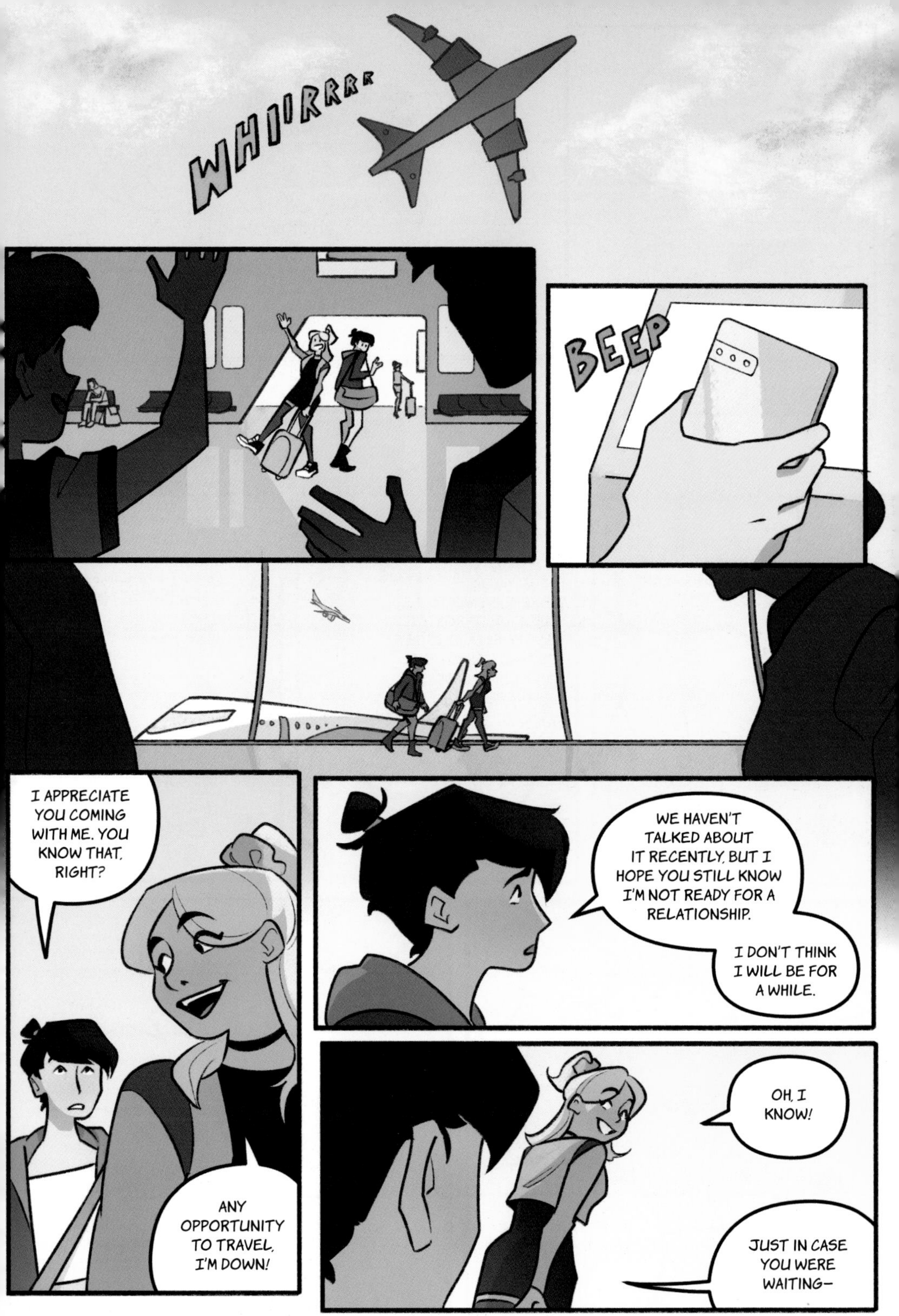
WHIIRRRR
BEEP
I APPRECIATE YOU COMING WITH ME. YOU KNOW THAT, RIGHT?
ANY OPPORTUNITY TO TRAVEL, I'M DOWN!
WE HAVEN'T TALKED ABOUT IT RECENTLY, BUT I HOPE YOU STILL KNOW I'M NOT READY FOR A RELATIONSHIP.
I DON'T THINK I WILL BE FOR A WHILE.
OH, I KNOW!
JUST IN CASE YOU WERE WAITING—

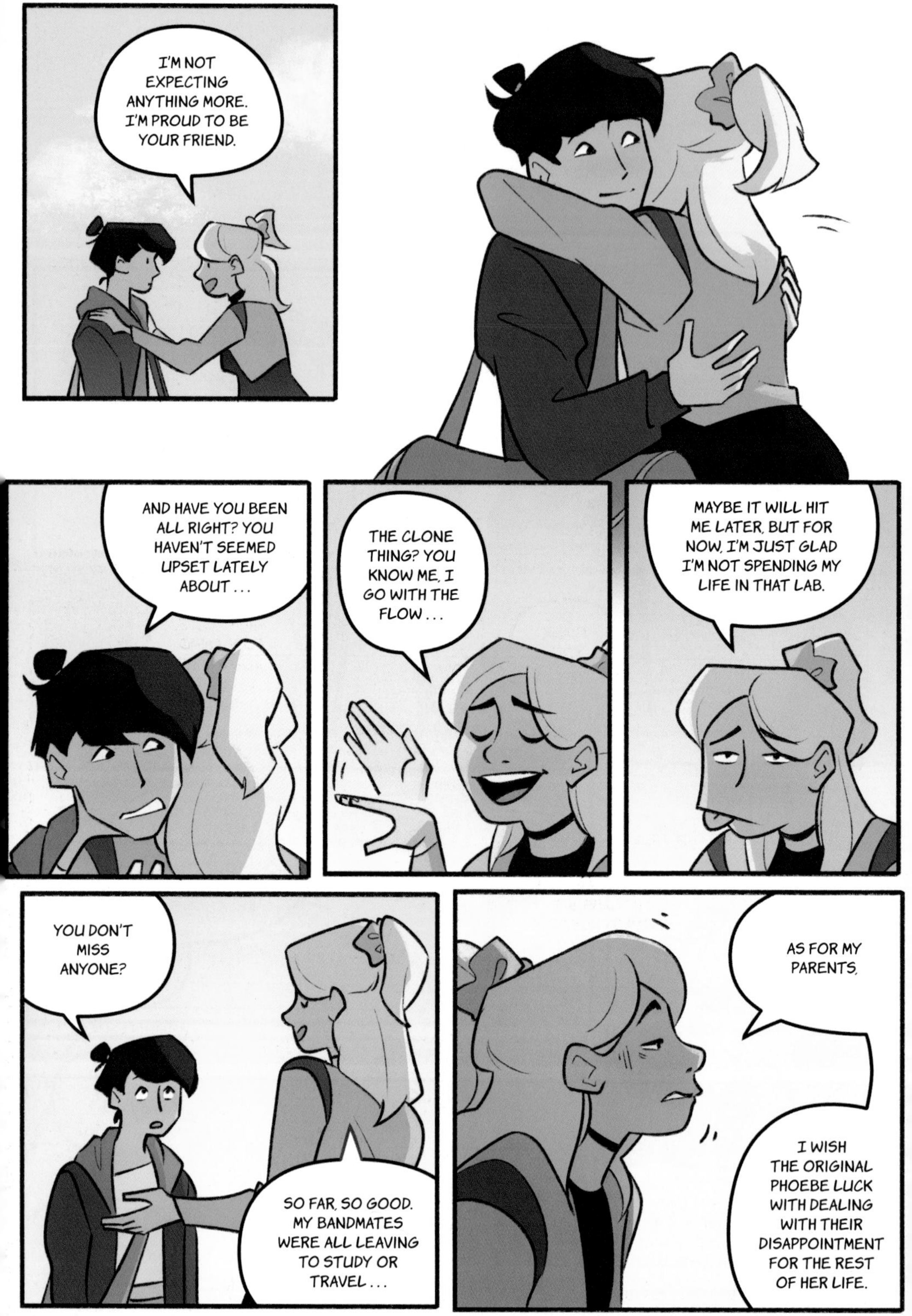
I'M NOT EXPECTING ANYTHING MORE. I'M PROUD TO BE YOUR FRIEND.
AND HAVE YOU BEEN ALL RIGHT? YOU HAVEN'T SEEMED UPSET LATELY ABOUT . . .
THE CLONE THING? YOU KNOW ME, I GO WITH THE FLOW . . .
MAYBE IT WILL HIT ME LATER, BUT FOR NOW, I'M JUST GLAD I'M NOT SPENDING MY LIFE IN THAT LAB.
YOU DON'T MISS ANYONE?
SO FAR, SO GOOD. MY BANDMATES WERE ALL LEAVING TO STUDY OR TRAVEL . . .
AS FOR MY PARENTS,
I WISH THE ORIGINAL PHOEBE LUCK WITH DEALING WITH THEIR DISAPPOINTMENT FOR THE REST OF HER LIFE.

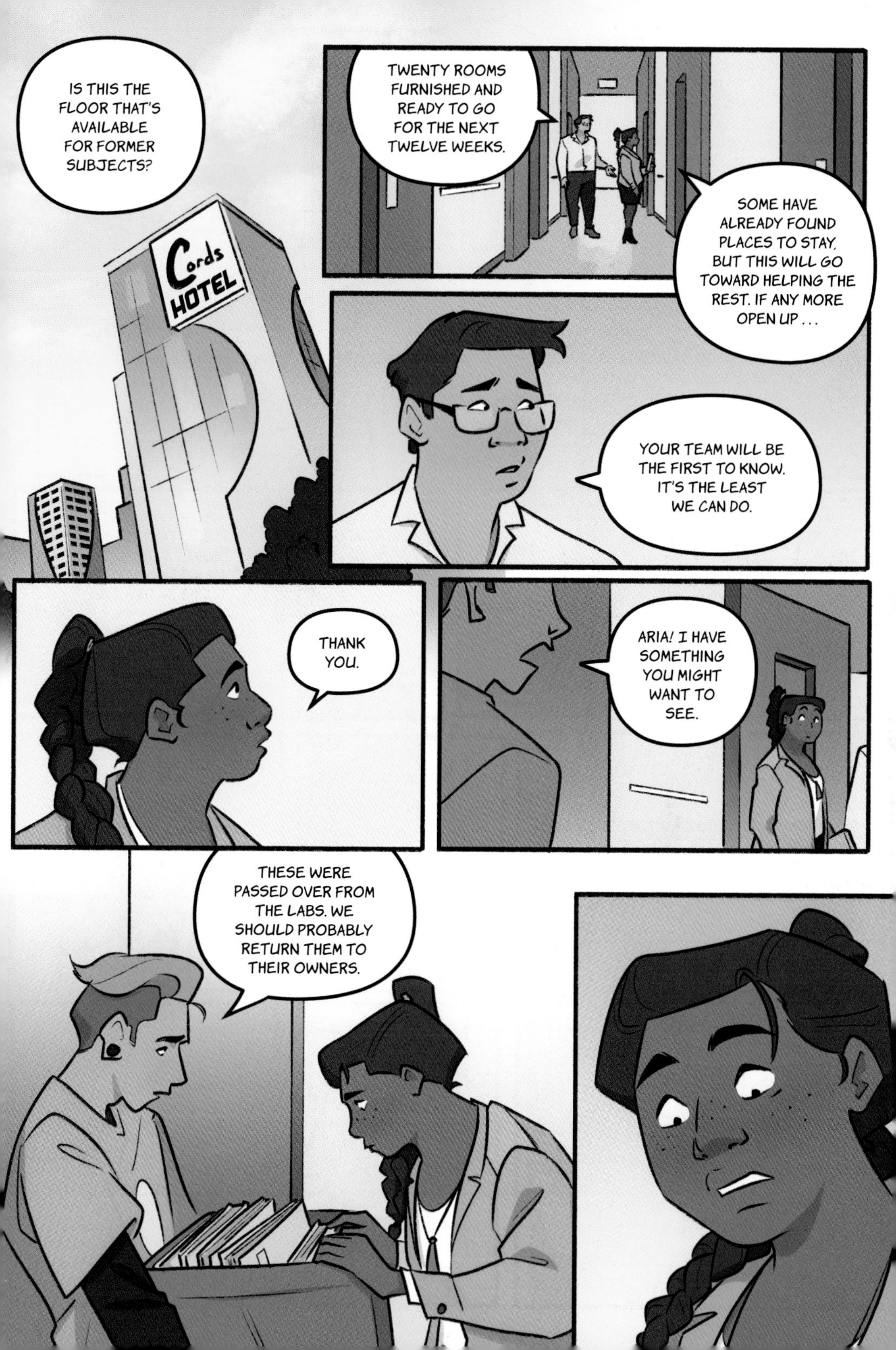
IS THIS THE FLOOR THAT'S AVAILABLE FOR FORMER SUBJECTS?
TWENTY ROOMS FURNISHED AND READY TO GO FOR THE NEXT TWELVE WEEKS.
Cords HOTEL
SOME HAVE ALREADY FOUND PLACES TO STAY, BUT THIS WILL GO TOWARD HELPING THE REST. IF ANY MORE OPEN UP . . .
YOUR TEAM WILL BE THE FIRST TO KNOW. IT'S THE LEAST WE CAN DO.
THANK YOU.
ARIA! I HAVE SOMETHING YOU MIGHT WANT TO SEE.
THESE WERE PASSED OVER FROM THE LABS. WE SHOULD PROBABLY RETURN THEM TO THEIR OWNERS.

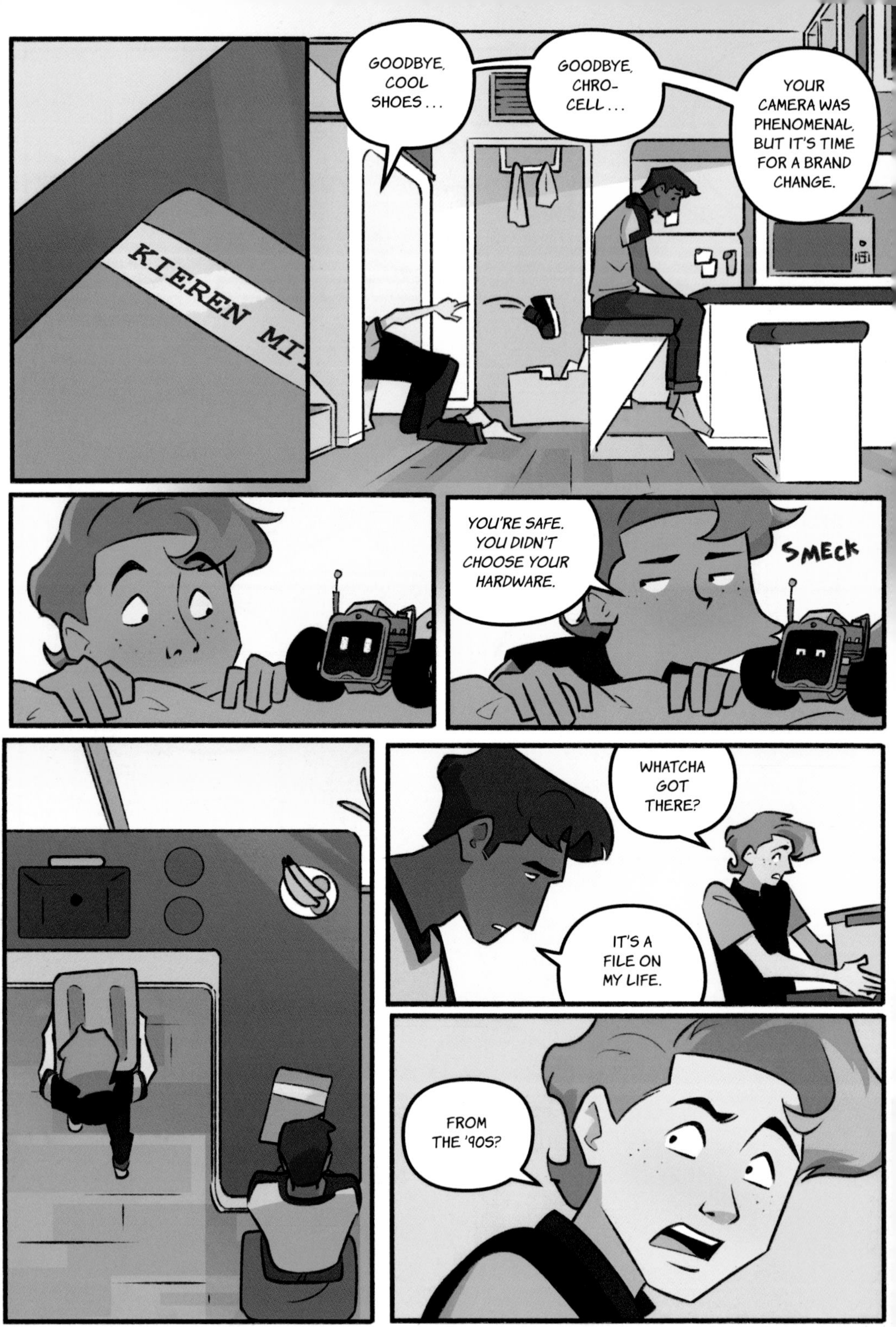
KIEREN MI
GOODBYE, COOL SHOES . . .
GOODBYE, CHRO-CELL . . .
YOUR CAMERA WAS PHENOMENAL, BUT IT'S TIME FOR A BRAND CHANGE.
YOU'RE SAFE. YOU DIDN'T CHOOSE YOUR HARDWARE.
SMECK
WHATCHA GOT THERE?
IT'S A FILE ON MY LIFE.
FROM THE '90S?

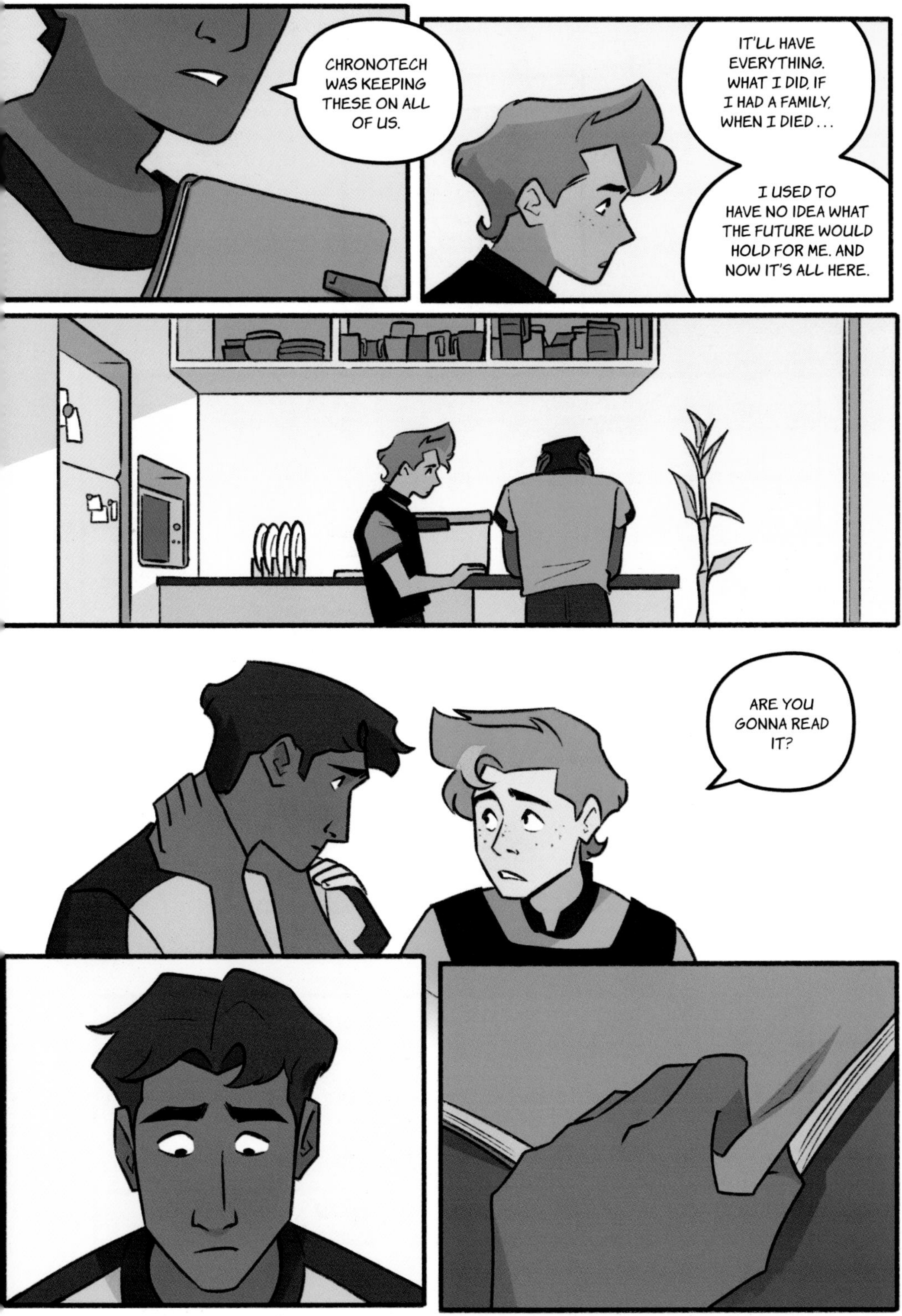
CHRONOTECH WAS KEEPING THESE ON ALL OF US.
IT'LL HAVE EVERYTHING. WHAT I DID, IF I HAD A FAMILY, WHEN I DIED . . .
I USED TO HAVE NO IDEA WHAT THE FUTURE WOULD HOLD FOR ME. AND NOW IT'S ALL HERE.
ARE YOU GONNA READ IT?

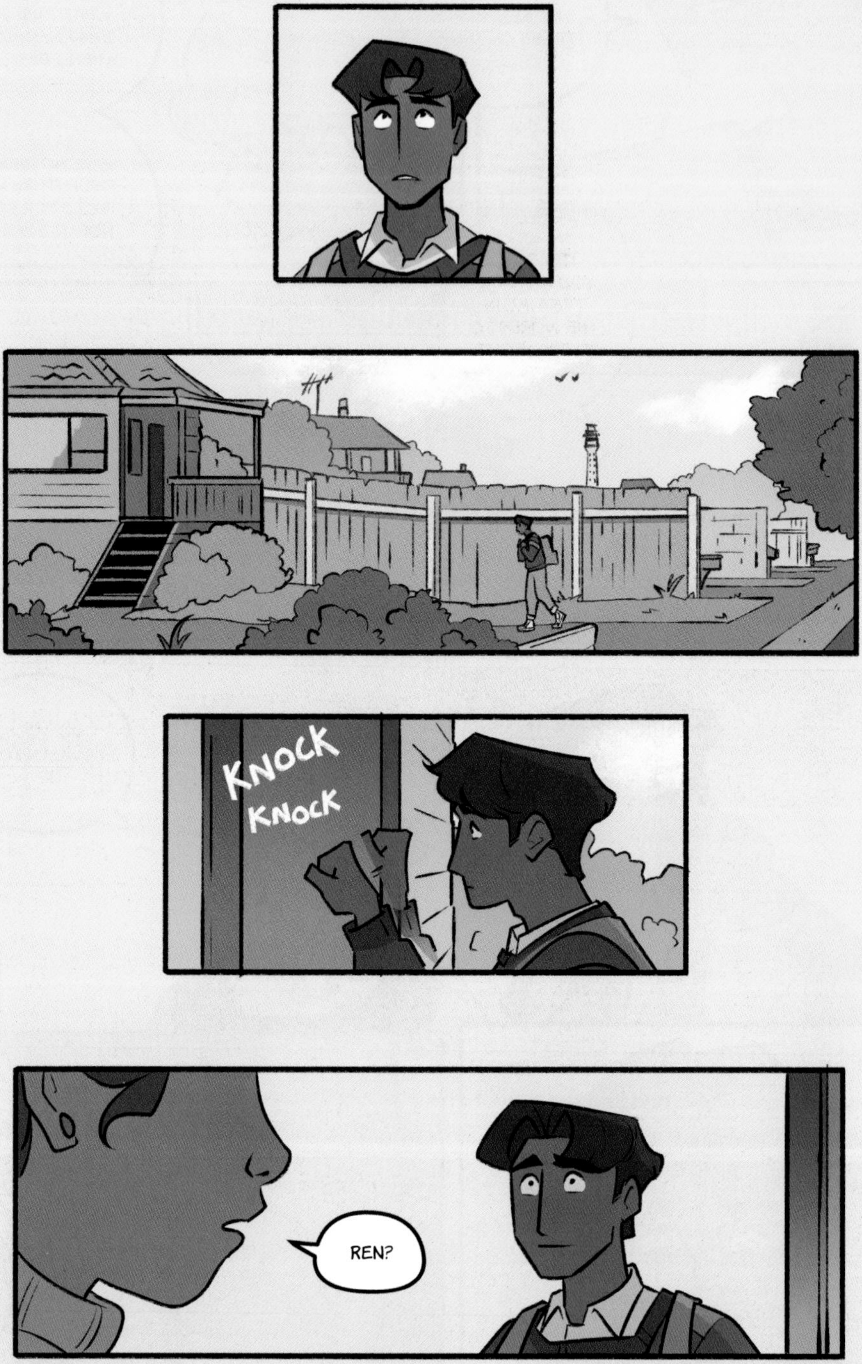
KNOCK
KNOCK
REN?

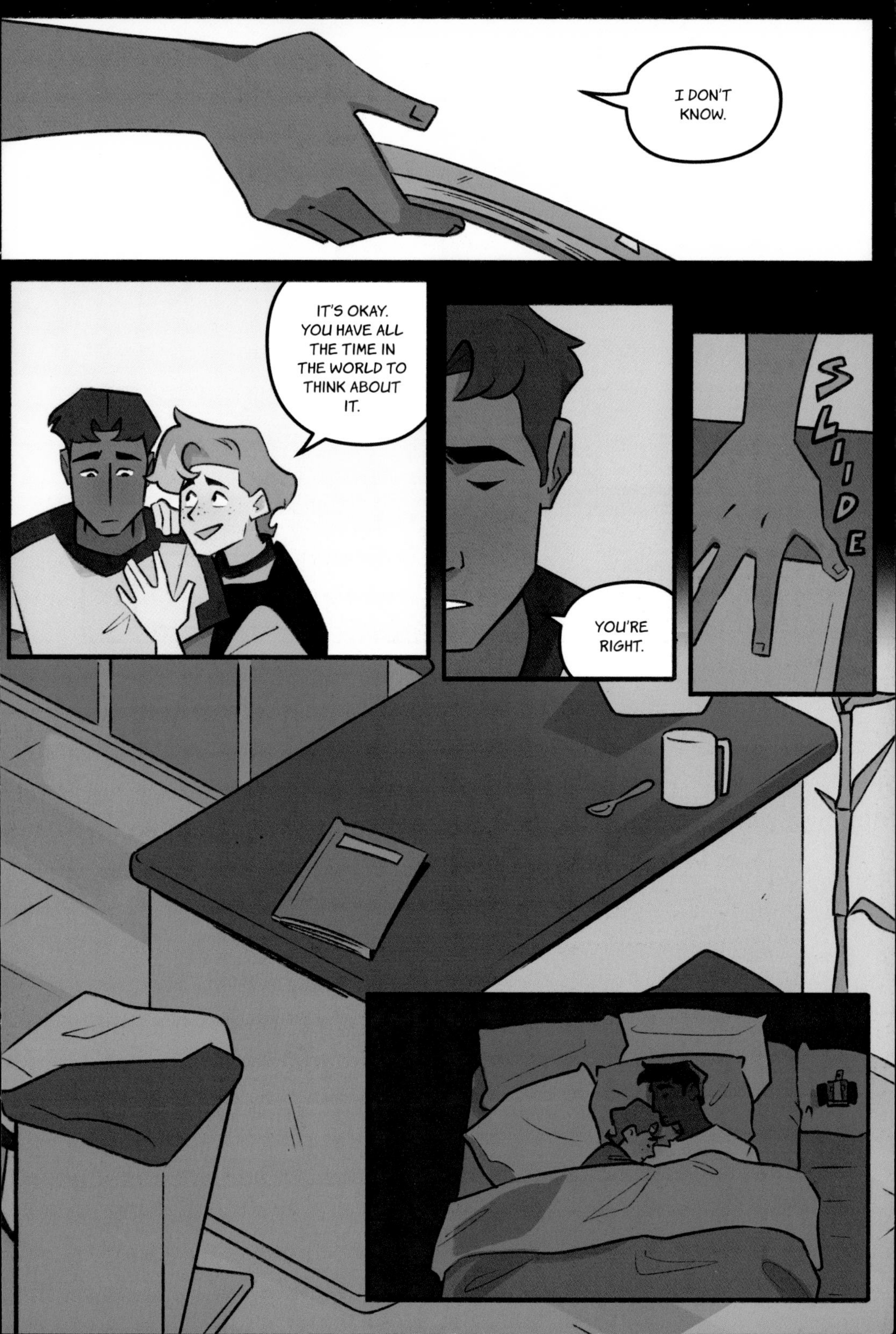
I DON'T KNOW.
IT'S OKAY. YOU HAVE ALL THE TIME IN THE WORLD TO THINK ABOUT IT.
YOU'RE RIGHT.
SLIIDE

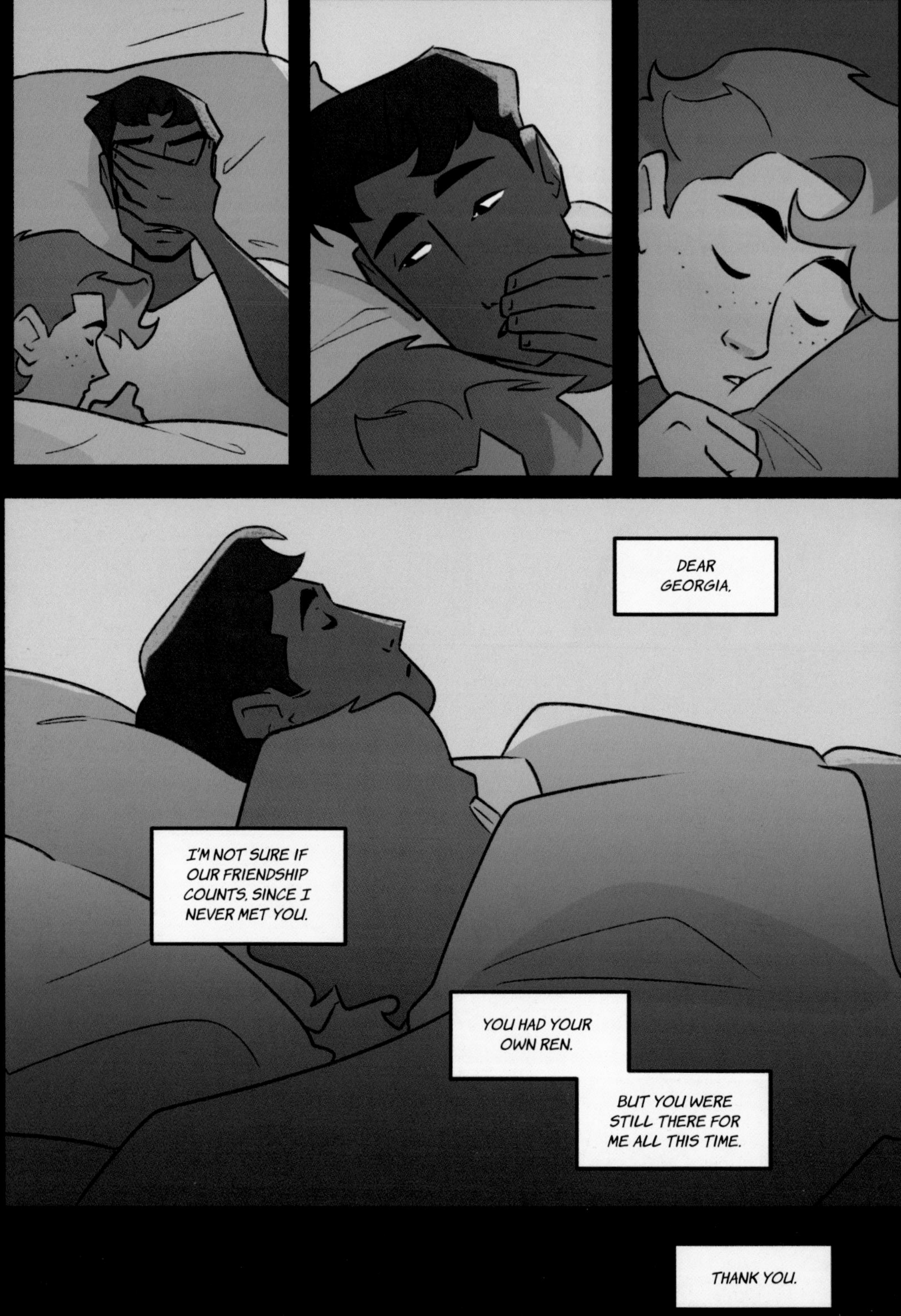
DEAR GEORGIA,
I'M NOT SURE IF OUR FRIENDSHIP COUNTS, SINCE I NEVER MET YOU.
YOU HAD YOUR OWN REN.
BUT YOU WERE STILL THERE FOR ME ALL THIS TIME.
THANK YOU.

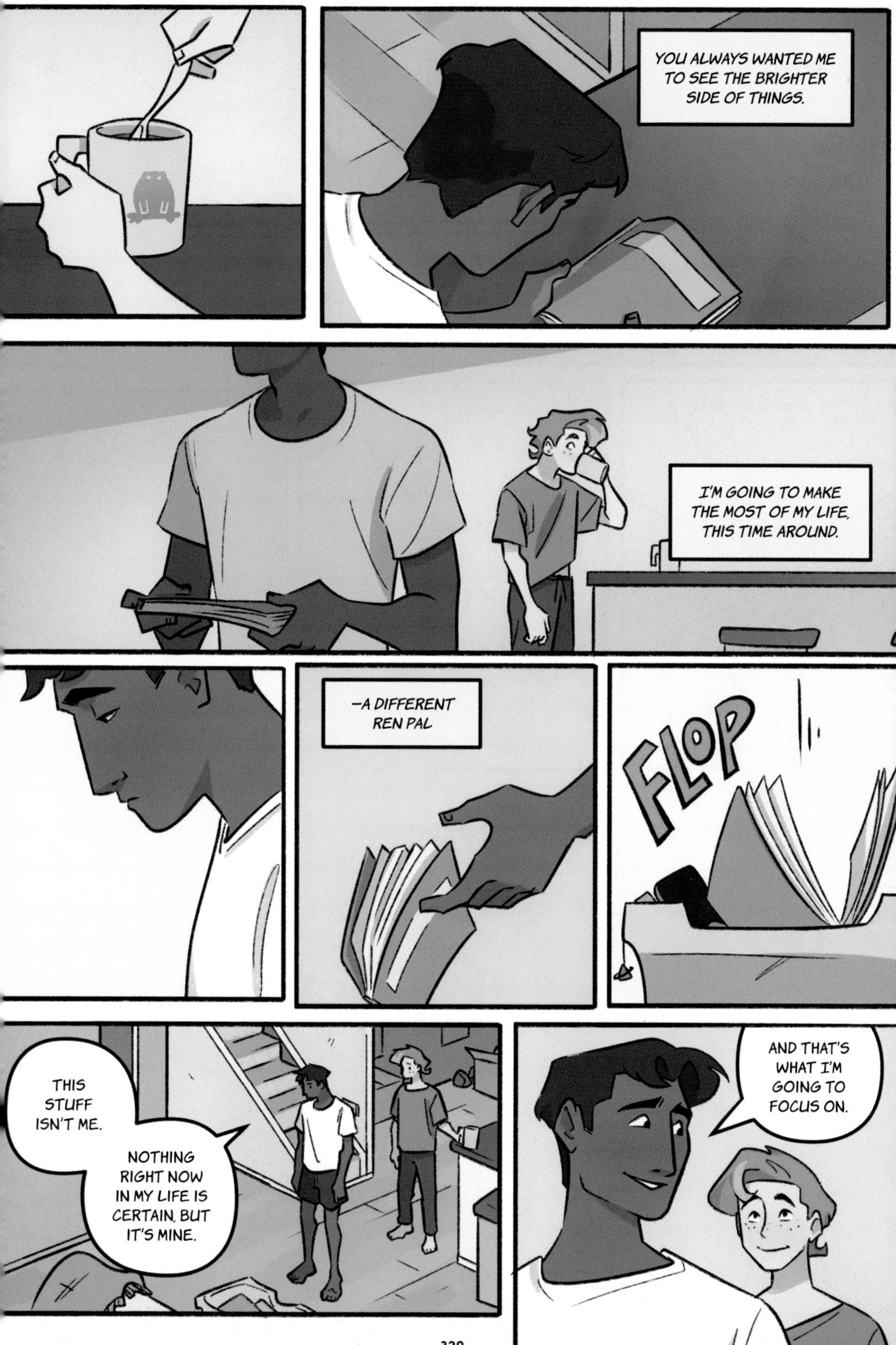
YOU ALWAYS WANTED ME TO SEE THE BRIGHTER SIDE OF THINGS.
I'M GOING TO MAKE THE MOST OF MY LIFE, THIS TIME AROUND.
—A DIFFERENT REN PAL
FLOP
THIS STUFF ISN'T ME.
NOTHING RIGHT NOW IN MY LIFE IS CERTAIN, BUT IT'S MINE.
AND THAT'S WHAT I'M GOING TO FOCUS ON.

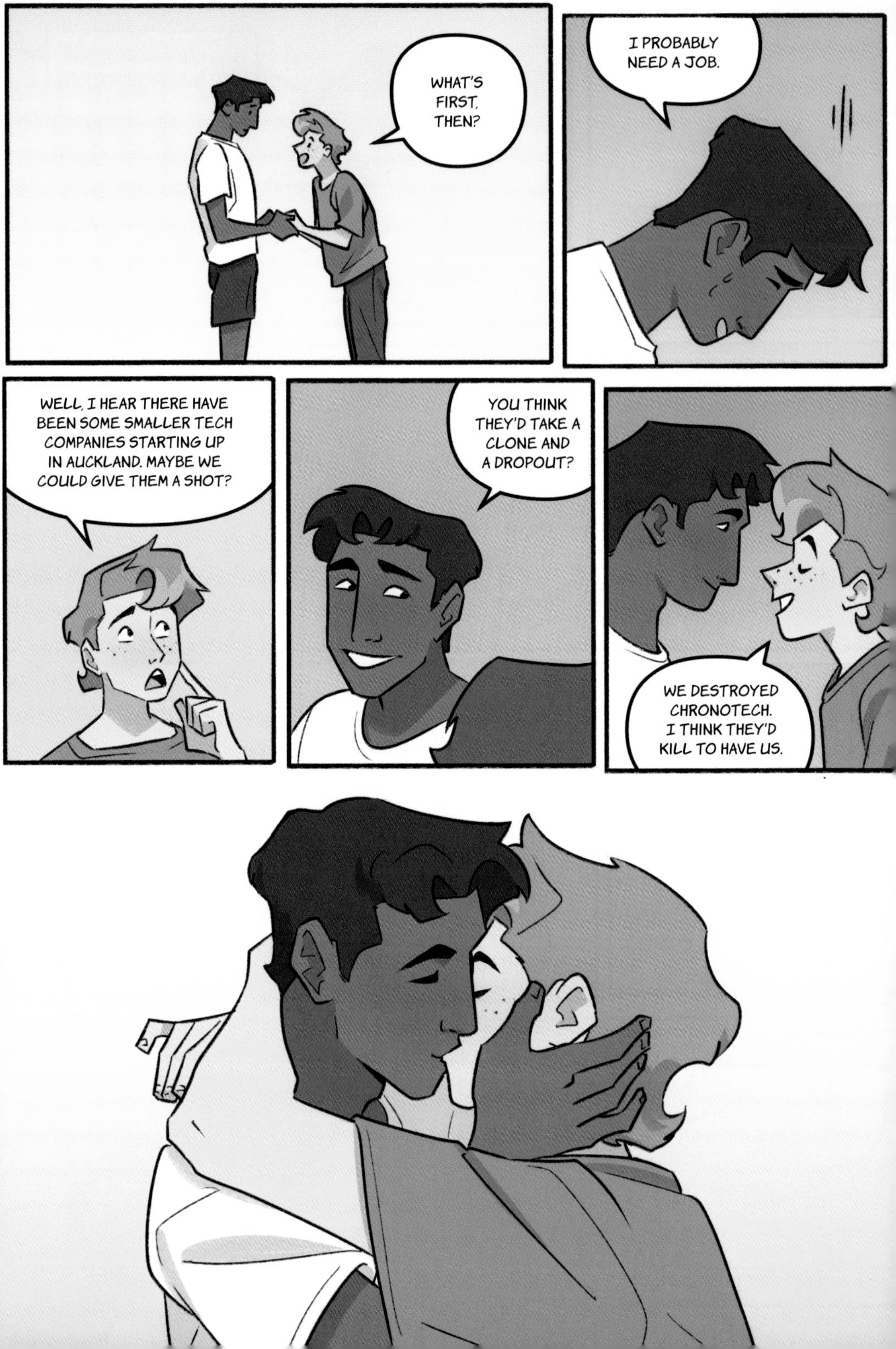
WHAT'S FIRST, THEN?
I PROBABLY NEED A JOB.
WELL, I HEAR THERE HAVE BEEN SOME SMALLER TECH COMPANIES STARTING UP IN AUCKLAND. MAYBE WE COULD GIVE THEM A SHOT?
YOU THINK THEY'D TAKE A CLONE AND A DROPOUT?
WE DESTROYED CHRONOTECH. I THINK THEY'D KILL TO HAVE US.

ACKNOWLEDGMENTS

When I stepped into the world of publishing, I had no clue what a massive project this would turn out to be, or what roadblocks would be thrown my way. Without my publishing team, friends, family, and employers, I would not have been able to cross the finish line.

My biggest thanks would have to go to Del Hahn. You enthusiastically offered to join the team as my flatting artist and carried this book to the end. Without you, I don't know where *Project Nought* (or my hands) would be.

To the Mukpuddy family—thank you for being so patient and supportive as my life was thrown upside down. I could not have asked for kinder or cooler coworkers.

I want to thank the original readers of my webcomics. Since 2015, you've shared so much support and love for my characters. I, unfortunately, had to leave the internet to work on this book, but you stuck with me anyway—even when all I had to share was an occasional snapshot of a silly little character with a silly expression.

I want to thank my agent, Jess, for reaching out to me in the first place. Without you, I don't think I would have ended up down this career path. Here's to many more pitches in the future!

To the entire publishing team, you work your butts off every day to put amazing books out into the world. I'm honored to be the creator of one of them! Thank you so much for lending your incredible talents to *Project Nought* and helping shape it into the best book it could have been.

And lastly, I want to thank Gabrielle, who excitedly listened while I pitched the idea for this story in a random art class in 2013. I hope you like how it turned out!